THE SILVER CORD

a novel

by
Johnson Edwards

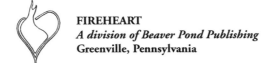

FIREHEART
A division of Beaver Pond Publishing
Greenville, Pennsylvania

Grateful acknowledgement is made to the following in regards to excerpts reprinted from previously published material:

Warner Bros. Records Inc., excerpts from "Sharp Dressed Man," ZZ Top / ELIMINATOR, written by Gibbons/Hill/Beard, ©1983 Warner Bros. Records Inc., ©1983 Hamstein Music Co., BMI. EMI-USA, excerpts from "Bad to the Bone," GEORGE THOROGOOD LIVE, words and music by George Thorogood, ©1986 EMI-USA, a division of Capitol Records, Inc. AOL Time Warner, excerpts from "Ten Minutes in Hell," TIME magazine, October 28, 1991, pp. 31-33, ©1991 Time Inc., Magazines, AOL Time Warner, New York, NY 10110. W.W. Norton & Company, excerpts (various) from THE ELEGANT UNIVERSE by Brian R. Greene, W.W. Norton & Company, New York, NY 10110, ©1999 Brian R. Greene. Pantheon Books, excerpts (various) from A USER'S GUIDE TO THE BRAIN by John J. Ratey, M.D., Pantheon Books, a division of Random House Inc., New York, NY.

Library of Congress Cataloging-in-Publication Data

Edwards, Johnson, 1946-
  The silver cord : a novel / Johnson Edwards.-- 1st ed.
    p. cm.
  ISBN 1-881399-24-9
  1. Physician and patient--Fiction. 2. Coma--Patients--Fiction. 3. Houston (Tex.)--Fiction. I. Title.

PS3605.D887S55 2003
813'.6--dc22

2003063112

FIREHEART
A division of Beaver Pond Publishing
P.O. Box 224
Greenville, Pennsylvania 16125

Then man goes to his eternal home and mourners go about the streets. Remember him—before the silver cord is severed ... and the dust returns to the ground.

— Ecclesiastes 11: 5-7 NIV

The most beautiful thing we can experience is the mysterial.

— Albert Einstein

THE SILVER CORD

CHAPTER ONE

MEADOWHURST, TEXAS
TUESDAY, NOVEMBER 2, 1999

A blue Mustang exits the Burger King drive-thru and heads south on Jackson Road. Delicious aromas circulate through the car, stirring the appetites of the two occupants: a twenty-something woman and her preschool daughter. "Didjuh get *ever*'thing?" the little girl asks from the back seat. "*My* Whopper Junior ... and a *reg*ular Whopper for you, and Daddy one with cheese?"

"That's right, honey," the mother assures amid a laugh.

The preschooler responds with a song: "I love you, you love me ... we're as happy as can be." She learned it, of course, from Barney the purple dinosaur.

The commercialized sprawl gives way to forest, towering conifers on both sides. The sun, big and pink and low, peeks now and then through the trees. The coolish scent of pine joins the Burger King aromas. Happy smells, happy vibes—the mother sighs with contentment as she considers how much their life has prospered since they moved here last year. A flashing light ahead signals the entrance to Sturbridge Systems Inc., one of the many fast-growing high-tech companies in the greater Houston area.

"Mommy, I'm thirsty," the little girl announces. "Can I have a drink of my Coke? Huh, Mommy? I need my Coke *now.*"

"Okay ... but just a sip." Wrestling one-handed, she inserts a straw into her daughter's drink, but as she lifts it from the bag, the lid pops off spilling Coke all over. Giving a motherly sigh, she fishes for a napk—"Dear God!" she gasps, realizing she's in the wrong lane bearing down on a UPS truck, as it pulls out of Sturbridge Systems. She swerves back but overshoots onto the shoulder. The Mustang, skidding out of control, hurtles a culvert, careens down the embankment, and crashes into the trees.

* * *

16 YEARS EARLIER

SPINDLE, TEXAS
TUESDAY, MAY 17, 1983

"Okay, guys, great practice!" Coach Harris barks. "Be here Friday, same time. Our first game is *next* week. We're the Yankees. We're the best!" Harris, a retired Marine, addresses his little-leaguers as though preparing for the World Series.

1

THE SILVER CORD

While most of the kids pile into the back of the coach's pickup or scramble into various cars, Bryan Howard, the team's star shortstop, takes his customary lap around the outfield before heading for his bicycle. The bubbly post-practice chatter gives way to the hum and rip of vehicles departing—then silence. He's the last to leave. Even the other bike-riders have gone. Slowing to a jog, he circles around behind the bleachers—that's where he parks his Huffy. As he catches his breath and prepares to mount, he realizes he doesn't have his baseball glove. Hustling back to the bench, he checks underneath it. His heart skips: NO GLOVE!

Gosh, what the heck is going on? he frets to himself. *I left it under the bench. I did ... I know I did?* He searches the infield, the outfield, under the bleachers, the bench areas again, even the trash barrels—nothing. A lumpy ache burns in his throat. This is no *ordinary* glove; it's a birthday present from his dad, a brand-new Rawlings, a George Brett autographed special.

Swinging reluctantly onto his bicycle, he scans the field one last time, then he pedals north on Farm Road 115. Tears streak his choirboy face, but he doesn't break: he hates to sob openly. Wiping his eyes, he coasts downhill for a bit then commences a hard climb. Heat waves squiggle up from the asphalt, giving off a strong petroleum odor. His head bobbing side to side, he pumps furiously, trying to escape his sense of loss. He pants, his heart pounds, perspiration dampens his T-shirt. It's nearly six o'clock, yet it's still sweltering out. Halting atop the hill, he gulps the steamy air. He removes his Yankee cap and runs his hand over his sweaty crewcut. A breeze cools his brow but brings with it an awful stench. Just ahead lies a dead, half-crushed armadillo. "That's me!" Bryan exclaims. "I'm dead meat. Least, I sure as heck feel like it." A squadron of flies work on the roadkill, while two dragonflies hover like helicopters above it. *What am I gonna tell Daddy?* he goes on, his words going silent. *I just got that glove. Maybe someone took it by accident? No, no ... that's impossible. They took it on purpose. They stole it. Somebody like Jeff Burton; he doesn't like me ... ever since I beat him out for shortstop.* The green dragonflies come closer, as if to taunt him. He swishes them away with his cap— "Get outta here, dang it!"

Resuming his trek, he descends into a shady hollow. He spins across Butler Creek—the creekbed smells of willow and moss and mud—then he pumps up another steep, sun-baked slope. At the crest he turns east on Longley Road, and soon reaches the farm. Clacking across the cattleguard, he pedals up the S-shaped driveway. Buster, his faithful collie, comes running and wagging and barking, yet the sight of his house makes him anxious rather than glad, especially as he spots his father, Henry Howard, sitting on the porch steps. Bryan dismounts well down the gravel driveway and walks his bike, to give him a little more time to think of a manly way of sharing the bad news.

2

THE SILVER CORD

Wallace Howard (Bryan's grandfather) built the family home in 1946; it's a large, white, two-story house with a gray roof and wraparound porch. Wallace grew up in Sulphur Springs but upon his return from WWII settled in Spindle with his new bride. The farm did well in those days but hasn't turned much of a profit since the '60s. The Howards still grow corn and soybeans and keep a few livestock, but Henry makes his living from his job at Homestead Feed & Seed, and Virginia (Bryan's mom) works part-time at Sampson's Poultry. Gramps died last November. Bryan misses him dearly, and especially today. His granddad knew all his secrets and took his side when he got in trouble, and Wallace Howard had a creative way of making bad situations seem less bad—like losing a brand-new forty-dollar George Brett glove.

"Daddy, my glove is gone!" he blurts, after parking his Huffy. "Somebody musta stolen it? And I gotta good idea who it is." His voice quivers, rising an octave; he sounds anything but manly. Fresh tears well up; he sniffles. His dad, a rugged, broad-shouldered man with firm jaw and tender eyes, nods but doesn't reply. He sips his Budweiser rather, then he pushes back his John Deere cap, allowing a few perspiry locks of brown hair to fall onto his forehead. All is quiet save for the drone of the air conditioner in the window. Bryan, looking down, paws at a weedy tuft with his rubber-cleated shoe. The years have ravaged the concrete walkway in front of the house, and the cracks sport grass and dandelions and tiny anthills.

"Now, Bryan, don't jump to conclusions," the elder Howard finally responds, after placing the beer on the step beside him. "Coach Harris probably has it ... in one of the equipment bags?" His country drawl conveys little displeasure. The boy, sensing relief, looks up, and sure enough, his dad's sun-red face shows only fatherly concern, his hazel-brown eyes speaking more than his tongue, as usual. Hauling himself up from the porch steps, Henry places a large calloused hand on his son's shoulder then gives him a quick one-arm hug. "Now stop that sniffling and get to your chores. After supper we'll call around and see if we can locate it." Bryan smells his dad's sweaty, masculine odor, a potent whiff that makes the hug extra reassuring.

* * *

Four hours later, Bryan lies in bed. The phone calls after supper produced no clues, even from Jeff Burton's mom; she said her son knows nothing about the missing glove; and Coach Harris wasn't home; he's in Marlow tonight playing slow-pitch softball. But Bryan feels better anyhow. The fact that his parents didn't get upset with *him* has taken the edge off the whole ordeal. It wasn't his fault, yet they've come down on him unfairly before, like back in March when he got yelled at and grounded after coming home soaked from Crockett Lake. He was fishing with Spanky Arnold and Mr. Arnold, when he slipped

3

on a rock and tumbled into the water. It was an accident, but his parents were already in a lousy mood, over Libby getting loose and running down Longley Road; Libby is their prized Guernsey milk cow.

The key thing with parents is catching them in a good mood, Bryan remarks drowsily to himself, as he turns onto his side. *But mine usually are—in fact, I have the best mom and dad around.* The hum of the window fan lulls him, lulls him (there's an air conditioner, in the other window, but he prefers the fan at night, except when the heat gets brutal in the summertime). Falling asleep, he begins to experience one of his *floating* dreams.

Hovering near the ceiling, he looks down at Buster sprawled on the rug at the foot of the bed. But the most incredible sight is his own body snoozing under the sheet. *What a joke?* he giggles to himself. *This can't be happening? There I am down there, and here I am up here? It's like a dream, but it's not a dream.*

Feeling giddily happy, he ascends through the ceiling, the attic, the roof, until he's above the house. The night is warm, and the moon is out, but lightning flashes in the distance, and he hears the rumble of thunder amid the chorus of crickets. He glides down to the living-room window where he spies on his parents, as they watch the conclusion of *Remington Steele*, or at least his mom does—his dad has conked out on the sofa. Virginia Howard, her ash-blond hair fluffed about a heart-shaped face, sits across the room with Snowball the cat curled on her lap. Virginia (or Ginny, as most people call her) is almost thirty-four, but Bryan still considers her the prettiest mom in all of Texas, especially her dazzling, ocean-green eyes, which are the same color as his.

Leaving the window, he focuses on the barnyard. He ascends until he's above it (he navigates by concentrating intently on his desired destination). He circles the barn, the silo, the chicken house, the other outbuildings. "Hey, Millie, look at me!" he cries to his horse, as he swoops like a hawk over the fenced lot, but the mare shows no sign of hearing him. Bryan sails east, the smell of manure giving way to the sweet fragrances of honeysuckle and milkweed and alfalfa. He skims the moonlit fields then passes over a grove of pine trees, arriving finally at a grassy hill topped by a huge oak tree. He hovers above it. Gramps often brought him to this mighty oak during their many walks and talks. Just down the hill among the willows and cottonwoods is Ruby Pond, its rippled water sparkling with moonbeams. The frogs peep and croak, and he hears now and then a bassy-voiced bullfrog. Butler Creek flows northward across this side of the farm, and Gramps dammed it to make a three-acre pond. Later when his wife died (she was only 38), he named it after her.

Boiling clouds gobble up the moon, the night turning black and haunting. The lightning seems closer, the thunder louder, the wind stronger. What would happen if he were struck by lightning? Is it possible? What about his physical body sleeping back at the house? Should he go back? Danger, trepidation—but then a surge of exhilaration trumps the anxiety. Flying at fifty feet, he zooms to the road then west to 115, then south, retracing the route to the little-league field, but he doesn't stop there. He outraces a pickup then a car. Blue lightning forks the sky, turning night into day. He jets like Superman over his school, the Diary Queen, the high school, the courthouse square, the railroad tracks, finally slowing above a residential area in the southeast part of Spindle. As he drifts over a streetlight, he hears a dog barking amid the collective hum of a hundred air conditioners.

Thunder resounds overhead, cracking, ripping, rumbling. *I better get home,* he cautions himself, but then he realizes he's on the right street, Morgan Street. He can see the Burtons' house in fact. Descending into the backyard, he hovers outside the window of Jeff's room. Chuckling, he looks in on his teammate. *I feel like a peeping tom, but I gotta check out my suspicions.*

Jeff, not yet in bed, tosses a ball, pitching it up, catching it in a baseball glove, again, and again. "That *is* my glove!" Bryan reacts, as the wind buffets the house, thrashes the trees. He can tell that it's a new Rawlings; he can even make out the George Brett signature. "I was right about Jeff; he's a *gosh*dang thief."

CRAAAACK! Deafening thunder! Bryan wakes up, in his bed.

CHAPTER TWO

EIGHT YEARS LATER

SPINDLE, TEXAS
WEDNESDAY, MAY 8, 1991 — 9:57 AM

Blond ponytail, tomboy stride, an angel in faded jeans. "Hey, Mandy, wait up!" Bryan Howard calls out, as he spots his sweetheart between classes. He hurries through the bustling, book-toting throng and joins her beyond the lockers.

"Hi, babe," she greets, her dollface mouth curving into a smile. "Why're you so out of breath?" She rolls her big blue eyes up to him, inquiringly.

"Oh, I just ran out to my truck. I hafta brief Mr. Denham, and all my floppies and reference texts are in here." He pats a knapsack, slung loosely over his shoulder. "I do the dogwork at home ... on my Macintosh. Denham says this project will help prepare me for Baylor pre-med. You know, the simulations I'm doing on organic bonding and disassociation as it relates to the behavior of sub-atomic particles that may affect—"

"Cut it out. I'm having enough trouble with Chemistry 301."

"Well, you *asked*," he banters back; they both laugh. "So how'bout O'Henry's at lunch? We need a break from the caf."

She nods cutely, tossing her bangs and ponytail. "Sounds good. I'll meet yuh at the corner."

"Pretty lady, you're the *great*est," he chortles, throwing her a kiss, as she hurries on to English Lit. He watches spellbound till she disappears into the classroom at the end of the hall. *Amanda Fay Stevens, you ARE the greatest,* he affirms to himself. Unlike the many double-named kids in this rural Texas town (Betty Sue, John Charles, Anna Lea), the "Fay" part never stuck. No one calls her "Amanda Fay" except her mother, when exasperated.

Bryan has had a few puppy-loves, like Dixie Lynn Starr back in junior high, but *nothing* like Mandy. He met her the summer after ninth grade, at a Baptist teen-ministry cookout; she had just moved to Spindle. They roasted marshmallows together, and he held the stick over the campfire, his arms being longer. His heart fluttered, and his knees got weak, and after that they talked and kidded around at school, and at church, but he didn't ask her out until last November when Wendy Lewis (Mandy's best friend) assured him that he would *not* be turned down.

He suddenly realizes he's the only student left in the hall. He skidaddles up the stairs, taking several at a time, second floor, third floor, reaching the bio-lab just as the bell rings.

THE SILVER CORD

* * *

O'Henry's Grill is only a block from the high school, and the kids go there for burgers and fries—the burgers have an old-fashioned pickle-and-onion kick that won't let go. The popular lunch-hour escape is on Jefferson Street, which runs into Main Street (Hwy. 29). Spindle (pop. 3,256) clusters about the juncture of Highway 29 and FR 115. There's a town square with a courthouse, the usual Texas layout, even a few covered sidewalks. Some of the downtown merchants eke out enough business to stay solvent (Byer's Drug Store for example), but many of the antiquated storefronts are boarded up, along with the old Kansas City Southern depot. KCS freights still lumber through, their horns blaring, but Spindle hasn't seen a passenger train since 1962. Most of the local retailing takes place at Linden Court, the new shopping center out by the abandoned warehouse (cotton).

The town dates back to 1851 when it first appeared on the map as Butler Grove, a stagecoach inn and general store. After the railroad arrived, it grew into a modest farming and ranching center—then came the oil boom of 1905, and hence the name "Spindle" (adopted in 1906 when the population skyrocketed briefly to 7100). Some stripper wells are still pumping, but the boom is just a memory in the minds of the oldest old-timers. The large ranchers continue to make money, but farming has dwindled over the years, as cotton gave way to corn and soybeans and watermelons, and fewer acres tilled. The Howards no longer grow *any* cash crops except hay, and they got rid of all the livestock and chickens, except for Millie the horse. A few Herefords and Black Angus still graze their west-side pastures, but these cattle belong to local ranchers, who lease the acreage.

Charbroiled aromas greet Bryan and Mandy as they enter O'Henry's amid the usual noon-hour hubbub. Despite the crowd their favorite spot is open, the last booth by the window. He takes off his baseball hat (his blue Spindle Tiger uniform cap) and places it atop the old jukebox-selector thing—it no longer works. After ordering, he heads around the corner to the men's room where an ammoniac stink assaults him, despite the deodorant pellet in the urinal. He relieves himself then washes his hands. Before leaving the mirror he leans close and fingers a red blemish on his chin: *That's all I need, a dadgum zit.*

But one pimple can scarcely diminish his striking good looks. Early manhood has firmed and squared his choirboy charm, but the cuteness still comes through in his ruddy blush, the dimpled laugh, the eager green eyes; his eyes retain that innocent, little-boy gleam. Yet the strong nose, chiseled jaw-line, and whiskery shadows (he shaves now) leave no doubt to his manliness, not to mention the tanned complexion and darkening hair—it's nearly brown. He favors his mom and dad at the same time, a perfect blend, except the eyes: they definitely come from

7

his mother.

The door opens behind Bryan. "Reckon y'heard about my truck?" Spanky Arnold says, as he steps over to the urinal.

"Yeah, I heard you rolled it Sunday, out by the lake—and y'got banged up pretty good?"

Spanky, a short, wiry, freckled junior with a buzz cut and a huge sunburned nose, replies over his shoulder as he pees: "Awh, it's nuthin' for chrissake, just a sprained neck and bruised ribs. A good excuse to skip school." Waggling his burr head (his hair's dirty blond, but it's too short to show much color), he laughs raucously, a rooster cackle. "The *god*dam road was wet, the one comin' back from Buzzard's Roost ... but I've made that curve at fifty many times." He snorts and wags. "It's gonna cost twelve hun'erd to get the fuckin' thang back on the road, and I got no collision. I reckon I can negotiate a deal with my dad—if I beg like a goddam *dawg*." Most everyone around here speaks with a Texas drawl, but with Spanky it's especially pronounced. "So, slugger, y'ready to kick ass on Saturday?" he asks, shifting the subject. "The playoff game? I reckon it's payback time for those goddam lucky bastards. I hope I get in for a couple of innin's. I'd like to deck a few— I hate Sulphur Springs for chrissake."

Bryan takes out his comb. "Well first, Spanker, we hafta get by Gilmore ... and that black kid who throws ninety-five plus."

"Awh c'mon ... we own that nigger. Last time we got ten runs 'fore they took 'im out."

Bryan's conscience recoils. The word "nigger" bothers him, especially when they have three Negroes on their own squad. Yet he's used to it from Spanky—*and* others; the N-word is inbred among the local rednecks. (Spindle has been officially integrated for years, yet most of the blacks continue to live south of the tracks and west of Caddo Street, in a poor, run-down quadrant, still referred to by many as niggertown or colored town.)

"And y'went deep twice," Spanky elaborates, shaking the last piss out of his pecker. "Hell, I even got a hit. I just hope Coach doesn't bench me for chrissake. He treated me like a *fuck*in' invalid when I dropped by the gym this mornin'." He jabs the handle, flushing the urinal. "But that Gilmore coon's got nuthin' but a fast ball. No guessin'. It may as well be on a *god*dam tee."

Bryan chuckles, as he works on his hair; it's just long enough to comb. "But we can't get *over*confident. We gotta play *one* game at a time." He expects a reaction, and *gets* it.

"You sound like Coach Simms for chrissake. But it figures, y'bein' an honor student an' all, and gettin' scouted by the *god*dam Astros." Spanky moves to the sink, as Bryan steps back. He's a head taller than the fiery little relief pitcher—who, in addition to fast driving, has a reputation for cutthroat poker and mouthing off, both of which get him into trouble; he's wound tighter than a Balata golf ball: spirit and

8

body. Yet Bryan sees a childlike warmth under the cussing and bravado. They've been friends since kindergarten (Bryan is one of the few who knows his real name: Curtis Wayne Arnold), but they're not as chummy as they once were. Spanky had to repeat fifth grade, falling a year behind. "And now you're goin' to goddam Baylor on a scholarship," he fusses on, "and to top it off, y'plucked the ripest plum in the whole junior class." He cackles. "She's out there waitin' for yuh. But you're so *straight*-laced—damn, I betcha haven't even gotten into her panties?"

"C'mon, Spank," Bryan admonishes good-naturedly, heading for the door. "That's enough. You talk like it's a dirty joke."

"Sorry, slugger. I didn't mean to get crude for chrissake."

Bryan gives a little salute as he exits but no response, except to himself: *I reckon I'm the only virgin on the team. Spanky may have a gutter mouth, but he's sure got me pegged. Still, it's right and godly to wait. We have our whole life ahead of us.* Nonetheless, the word "panties" lingers in his mind, deliciously so.

He slides back into the booth—the food has just arrived: two cheeseburgers and a shake for him, a hamburger plus a Dr. Pepper for her, and fries for both. Mandy gives him a smirky welcome. "What took yuh so long, babe? I thought maybe you *fell* in?" She titters, smacking her lips, then grabs the ketchup.

"Oh, I ran into Spanky," he explains, blushing and dimpling as if she knows what he was just thinking about. "And we got to talking about baseball. We hafta beat Gilmore tomorrow to tie Sulphur Springs. If we do, we play off on Saturday for the title."

"I hope yuh go all the way," she declares, her voice clogged with fries. She pops open the chilled can of Dr. Pepper, inserts the straw, then sips—a glass of ice came with the soda, but she likes it straight. "I can't stand those Hornet prima donnas."

"Gosh, pretty lady ... you sound just like Spanky. Well, not ex*act*ly like him, but—"

"Y'mean I don't *cuss* like him? Well, mister, you've never seen me get *real* mad yet." She giggles, then grins widely, showing her teeth. Her canines crowd the incisors causing a bit of overlap; it's hardly noticeable, yet she's self-conscious about it. But Bryan *adores* her teeth, her lips, her tongue, especially when she grins and laughs, and her eyes dance, and her cheeks go pink; it melts him. He feels like leaping over the table and devouring her, but takes some fries and a gulp of milkshake instead. "Y'shoulda heard me the last time I got ticked at Mama," she goes on, "and I've called my little sister a few names I can't repeat in public."

"No way," he teases, feigning disbelief. He attacks his first burger, then swigs more shake.

"Go ask Gretchen," she quips. "No, on second thought, yuh *better* not." More giggles. "But back to Sulphur Springs ... they need a good licking. Their girls' team kills us in softball, and they're haughty and *stuck* up ... and they're lean and mean, and tall as all heck, like a bunch of dadgum *am*azons. Same thing in basketball." She downs a couple of french fries, after dunking them in ketchup. "And that witchy-faced southpaw ... she struck me out three times last game. I was so mad I felt like charging out there and tackling her—course, that woulda caused a brawl."

Bryan snickers, thickly. "That's for *sure*. And the way you gals scratch and pull hair, it woulda been a *hum*dinger."

"Now don't get *ma*cho on me," Mandy kids, as she prepares to dig into her hamburger. (He loves how she talks, the bouncy emphasis here, the inflection there, the sensual undertones; she has a slight huskiness in her voice, which gets more pronounced, almost sultry, when they make out.)

"I'm not," he retreats, dimpling into a grin. "I was there that day. She's got awesome speed ... like *im*possible."

Mandy sucks hard on her straw, drawing in a big shot of Dr. Pepper. Her gusto turns him on: he likes it that she goes for old-fashioned Dr. Pepper, when most girls drink only diet soda. She complains about putting on weight (particularly on her backside), but she can't stand the taste of artificial sweeteners. Bryan kids her whenever she fusses about her butt, yet he sees her body as ripe and sumptuous, sexy beyond words, *especially* her buttocks. Nonetheless, he takes it as a given that she's a virgin. Although hotly curious about her carnal side, he dares not ask about it. She did have a boyfriend before, a guy at the church named Derrick. At least, she hung around with him a lot during the teen-ministry activities, but Bryan doubts anything happened, since Derrick moved away before he was old enough to drive.

For a while they eat in silence. He finishes his first cheeseburger, half his shake, and most of his fries, then he can't help but watch Mandy, as she dines, her attention on her food. Her yellow-gold hair flows in opposite directions from a side-to-side part, most of it converging back into a ponytail, but she has bangs in the front, which adorn like a valance her sweet oval face. The bangs are feathery and mussed, and she has freckles on her nose, which is cutely knobbed at the end—all of which gives her that adorable, puppyish, country-gal look. She drinks some soda pop, without looking up. Her fingernails, though neatly trimmed and girlishly tapered, are not long or red or gaudy.

He's glad she's a jock, and a tomboy, who's not all groomed and proper and covered with cosmetics; she rarely wears makeup, save for lip gloss and a touch of eyeliner. And yet, the golden lustre of her hair, a rich, heavenly hue like ripening wheat at sunrise, surpasses that of any blond covergirl. He swigs his shake, nearly draining the cup. In addition to her Levi's, she wears a red and blue madras shirt. She dresses conservatively compared to most of her peers—she doesn't show a lot of skin except at the lake. Yet you rarely catch her in a dress, aside from church, and she often wears pants or jeans there as well. Her high, soft, Scandinavian cheeks are naturally fair, yet they pulse pinkly warm, partly from the sun, partly from exuberance—and because of *him*, he knows full well. He likes how her ponytail tumbles to the side, caressing her neck and shirt collar; the collar is canted open showing a slice of tan shoulder, her wondrous tan shoulder. Mandy looks up, discovering his rapt attention. Their eyes lock; time stops. Bryan feels dizzy, as though falling into her big blue gaze: blue, blue, azure blue. The sensation is warm and soft yet magnetic and all-encompassing, like when you're a kid on a summer day, and you spin around then drop into the grass and look up at the sky. It's like the beginning of one of his floating dreams (he still has them, one or two per year), yet this is even more mind-blowing, for he's sharing this feeling with her. The moment is erotic to be sure, yet the intimacy goes beyond sex, beyond the flesh, beyond word or thought even. Their love has a power that's "unspeakable and full of glory." Too much—leaning over the table, they kiss, their lips meeting briefly but tenderly. "I love you, pretty lady," he whispers.

Yet romance turns quickly to laughter: "Hey, you big jock ... y'just gave me your chocolate-shake mustache."

"Well, precious, like I say: everything I got is *yours* too."

She dabs her mouth with a napkin. More laughing—then shy titters, as the waitress comes with the check. As they finish up, the conversation shifts to school concerns: Bryan's Biophysics briefing, Mandy's history test, and so forth. They both excel, yet she has to work harder for A's and B's than he for straight A's (except for English). And her career goals are less ambitious: she plans to be a teacher.

As they get up to go, Bryan says, "You wanna grab an ice cream after practice, at the DQ?"

Her face clouds, not a dark cloud but noticeable, especially compared to the radiance of a few minutes ago. "I can't. I hafta scoot right home on the jock bus, like right after softball. I told Mama I'd go to service with her tonight, since I overslept on Sunday. Y'know how she *gets* if I skip church too much."

"I reckon I should go more myself, and not just on Sunday. But for *some* reason I like going to the Dairy Queen better."

They laugh, her countenance brightening, then she says, "Well, babe, I have an idea. Why don't yuh *start* tonight? Come by and get me, and I'll ride with you. That'll work better anyhow, since Mama has to go early for staff meeting. I doubt she'll mind, even though it *is* a school night."

* * *

Mandy warms up at first base, tossing ground balls to shortstop Wendy Lewis (also a junior). Mandy, at five-six, could use more height as a first baseman, but she has good hands, a good stretch, and she's agile around the bag. To add realism to this pre-practice routine, she starts at the edge of the outfield grass then hustles to the base to take the throw. She's strong-boned and solidly built, yet she's not hard and muscled up like some female jocks. And her nubile curves leave no doubt that she's *all* woman. Even the loose practice garb cannot conceal her modest bust, prim waist, and rounded hips. Her ponytail, cutely suspended out the back of her cap, swings about, bouncing on her neck.

After fielding twenty grounders, Wendy joins her blond buddy for some running. The air is verdantly sweet, from the freshly mowed outfield grass. "So, kiddo, tell me the latest about you 'n Bryan," she pants, as they catch their breath, hands on knees, out by the right-field fence.

"Nothing new to tell," Mandy says, giving a sheepish giggle. "Not really." She leans back against the low chain-link fence, which is just right to support her elbows. The wee shortstop comes over as well, though the fence is too high for *her* elbows.

Wendy, a brown-eyed, pimpled brunette with an odd bulbous nose and dental braces, is barely five-one, yet she's fleet of foot and quick as a feline, and she has a strong arm. Her hippish shape is womanly enough—guys no doubt check out her caboose—but her looks are B-minus, and she talks weird, because of the braces. Yet her face does have an elfin appeal, if you ignore the pimples. She could pass for fourteen, but she's actually seventeen. Her eyes vary from brown to hazel, depending on the light.

Mandy fidgets her mouth, pursing, smacking, then she bites the upper lip, then she crinkles her nose (she's practiced this cute, rabbitlike habit from a small girl, despite her mom's efforts to make her stop). Above them the vast Texas sky looms hazy blue and vague; it's hot out but not oppressive, and there's just enough breeze to feel good after the running. The other players are arriving, most pairing off to play catch near the dugouts.

Wendy gestures, palms up; she gives a wide grin, showing her braces. "I take it then that the *big* secret is still in the bag? Your mother, I mean—you didn't tell *her*?"

Mandy blushes, her cheeks heating. "No way. She's the *last* person I could tell. You're the only one who knows, Wen."

"Well, I think it's awesome, like *wick*ed cool. I've done a lot, but I've never been en*gaged*. And you're *younger* than me?"

"Tell me about it," Mandy quips, then she leans closer to her friend, her words becoming hushed. "But it's gonna be a *secret* till I graduate next year, then we'll announce everything ... with the idea of getting married in June of '94."

"Gosh, kiddo," Wendy hisses through her braces. "That's *three* years from now?"

THE SILVER CORD

"I know. I'll be old, like *twenty* almost, but Mama will *freak* if we schedule it any sooner. She'll probably freak anyhow. You know how she frets. She even gets on my case about going st—"

A whistle interrupts: Coach Perkins is on the field. Mandy and Wendy hustle in to join their teammates.

* * *

"God is not *mocked*!" Pastor Ron Brooks exclaims, hewing the air with his hand. "For whatever a man soweth, in Galatians 6:7, that shall he also *reap*!" He paces in front of his pulpit, wielding a wireless microphone. A portly, fortyish, balding preacher with heavy jowls and a stentorian voice, he's been at Pleasant Hill Baptist for four years, and the flock has grown steadily since his arrival. The tan-brick edifice (nestled among the pines on the high ground west of Crockett Lake) has grown as well, with a new educational wing and an enlarged sanctuary, which still smells of Sheetrock and joint gunk, and new paneling and carpet.

Bryan and Mandy, in a pew near the back of the forty-plus midweek turnout, sit with Helen Stevens (Mandy's mom) and Gretchen (Mandy's sister, actually half-sister). The eight-year-old usually goes to junior church, but she begged to sit next to Mandy and Bryan tonight, and her mom relented. Helen works part-time as church secretary (besides her assistant-manager job at Kroger's), and she never misses a service. Bryan's parents are also members at Pleasant Hill, longtime members in fact, but the Howards are strictly Sunday-morning Christians.

"Let's refocus on our text in Colossians," the pastor directs, having retreated to the lectern. "If ye, then, be risen with Christ, seek those *things* which are above.... Set your *affection* on things above, not on things on the earth." His voice is calmer, yet the mood remains solemn, his eyes stern. He often uses humor to make a point, but not tonight. "This exhortation from Paul is for all of us, but it speaks *especially* to teenagers, and I'm glad to see so many of you here on a Wednesday. God has a special concern for young people—that's why we conduct a full-scale youth ministry here at Pleasant Hill, with Pastor Ted Clemens ... a ministry which is *cru*cial as we move into school vacation."

Pastor Ron resumes his pacing. "Yes, Lucifer will use all his devices and ploys to lead you astray, but I pray you'll make this summer *count* for God." He goes on to warn about movies and beer and rock music and dancing, then laziness and disrespect for parents, then TV and VCRs and church attendance. Then ka-BOOM!—the heavy artillery: "But Satan's greatest snare is the *FLESH*! More young lives are ruined by fornication than any other sin! This's why God warns us to *FLEE* youthful lusts in Second Timothy! Lust leads to parking and petting and...."

13

THE SILVER CORD

* * *

"I've never touched hard liquor or cigarettes," Bryan relates an hour later, as he talks with Mandy in the pickup; they're parked in the Stevens driveway behind Helen's Escort. "And it's been a long time since I even had a beer—but for me it's more because of baseball, to stay in top condition. I'm sure God isn't thrilled about those habits, but it seems overdone, the way preachers put it down. At least, that's what my grandfather used to say, and he smoked cigars, yet he had the kindest heart I ever—well, I've toldjuh before, and my dad drinks beer, and he skips church some, but I don't think of him as being *luke*warm ... or ungodly."

"It's mainly a jock thing for me too," she replies. "That's why I never got into cruising and partying and drinking, or doing weed, like half the girls at school. Course, Mama would freak if I even had one swallow of beer—if she found out."

After the service they went to the Dairy Queen. Her mom gave the okay, as Mandy promised to be home by nine-thirty, and she is. They live on Colby Drive in the northeast part of town; it's a two-story rent-house with a big front porch. The porchlight has a yellow bulb, the bug kind, and it gives a tawny cast to things, like the hood of the truck, and Bryan's slacks, and Mandy's blouse, even her face and bangs, especially her bangs. But her jumper looks dark gray, as does Bryan's shirt. The truck looks weirdly pink, muddy pink instead of blue. The '79 Chevy once belonged to Gramps, and it has that country-pickup smell: grease, grime, gasoline, horse feed and hay, even a hint of cigar.

Bryan toys with the Stevie Nicks cassette, as it protrudes from the tape-player (the *Rock a Little* album which includes "Talk to Me," their favorite). They listened to it going to church but not on the way home, not after Pastor Ron's hard-hitting sermon—which they're finally discussing. "But being close to Jesus is more than an *out*ward show," Mandy elaborates, speaking toward the house. "My stepfather harps on everybody about receiving Christ, yet he's a two-faced alcoholic. I reckon he can't help it ... and he's not a *bad* guy. I mean, he treats me okay. But the booze makes him totally irresponsible. That's why we moved back here from Arkansas." She fiddles with the Bible on her lap, then the latch of her purse; she has her saddle-bag purse instead of the little gray one. "Now my *real* dad hardly ever went to church. Mama says he was a dreamer and a good-hearted guy, but he could never humble himself and get right. But I like his letters; he told the truth ... like he didn't BS around. She let me read a few, the ones from Vietnam; he flew those Huey helicopters." Mandy, shaking her head, gives a husky little chuckle. "It's amazing ... Mama was just fifteen when she met him; he was twenty-one. And she was barely seventeen when they got married—she was pregnant. She's so godly and careful now. It's hard to believe she was *doing* it when she was

14

sixteen, but *I'm* the proof." She chuckles again but quickly sobers; she rubs her thumb on her lower lip, her eyes widening into a wistful gaze. "We lived in Marlow when Daddy died. He crashed his cropduster into the trees down on Route 115. It was a biplane. I was three years old. It's like a lost dream in my head ... but I do remember how he'd come in and kiss me goodnight, and he read to me on his lap sometimes; he had big hands, and his cheeks were scratchy, but he smelled good ... like Old Spice." She shifts sideways, her back against the door. "You know the story, babe. And you saw his picture, the one by my bed. He was super good-looking, like James Dean, but he was blond like me. And his name was James too, or Jimmy, but most people called him Buzzy."

A little nightbreeze blows in the window, bringing with it the fragrance of honeysuckle which obscures for a moment the farm-truck smell. Bryan grabs the top of the steering wheel, with both hands; he grips tightly then releases, working the tension out. "Your dad sounds like a character. It's too bad what happened."

"Yeh ... and when I get rebellious or feisty, Mama shakes her head and says, You're *just* like your daddy." Mandy titters, her mood lifting. "I wonder how it would be if he hadn't crashed. I reckon I'd be Amanda Miller instead of getting my adopted name, from Charlie. Course, my dad and mom might not've stayed together, but I think he woulda balanced her out. She's so into God now. I mean, it's good to seek God, but she's almost fanatical." Mandy tosses her head, making her ponytail dance; it's fluffy soft; she washed her hair before Bryan picked her up. "I don't mind church I reckon, but somehow I don't think we're getting the *whole* story. How can anyone ... even Pastor Ron, know *exactly* how God feels about stuff, or *exactly* how to interpret the Bible? He knows way more than us, but still? And when you dig deep, it gets dadgum confusing. So I stay with the simple stuff like ... Jesus loves me, this I know, 'cause the Bible tells me so." Giving an open-hand gesture, she smirks cutely.

"But whaddabout tonight?" Bryan asks, now getting to the core of the matter. "He really came down on kids making uh—well, yuh know what he said?"

"It bothers me some, but I've heard it a jillion times, and he doesn't harp on it like *some* ministers. He mainly talks about the loving side of God, so when he lets loose with a heavy 'get right' message, we hafta mix it in with the good stuff he preaches."

Bryan dimples. "Well, pretty lady, that was a *lot* easier to do before I paired off with you."

"No kidding," Mandy agrees, her eyes sparking. "I reckon it's good we can't go out on school nights, *except to church.*"

* * *

Sometime later, after a fervent session of cooing and necking—they've never gone below the neck—Mandy hurries inside. She hustles up the stairs, heads for her room. "D'yuh *know* what time it is, young lady?" comes a hushed voice from the bathroom. Before Mandy can reply, her mom emerges, wearing a terrycloth robe—and a frown. "It's ten-thirty I have yuh to know." Pixie-faced with gray-hazel eyes and a short bob of brown hair, she looks young enough to be Mandy's sister, yet they don't favor each other except for the mouth; Helen has the same cupid lips, yet her overall prettiness is rather plain by comparison.

"Is it *that* late?" Mandy replies innocently, despite the fever between her legs, and dampness—her panties always get wet when she and Bryan kiss a lot.

"It most *cer*tainly is," Helen affirms, hands on hips. "In fact, it's past ten-thirty. And it's a *school* night for goodness sake."

Mandy opens her bedroom door but doesn't go in. "But, Ma, we've been here since nine-thirty ... least in the driveway." She's glad her room is at the shadowy end of the hall away from the bathroom, so her mom can't see her flushed, chafed face, though it's hardly a mystery what she was doing out there in his truck.

"I know ... and that's better than being somewhere else, but still—" Helen pauses, her face relaxing into that concerned-mother look; she moves closer. Her voice softens as well, "Oh, Amanda Fay, you're growing up so fast, yet you're still so young and naive." Mandy looks down. "I'm happy for you ... but afraid for you as well. I can't blame yuh for being attached to Bryan; he's probably the brightest and best-looking young man in the senior class, but looks can be deceiving, as *I* well know, and our emotions can get us into *big* trouble. That's something I learned the *hard* way." She sighs. "Now as far as I can tell, he's a good Christian boy, from a good Christian home, and I was delighted he came to service tonight. But, honey, you're *only* sixteen."

"I'll be *seven*teen in July," Mandy reacts, mildly. "And Bryan is gonna be eighteen next week. And it's not like I don't know the facts of life. We're not gonna do anything foolish or stupid."

"I'm glad to hear you say that, hon, but hormones can defeat even the *best* intentions, as Pastor Ron said tonight. I just pray that you two will heed the word of God, and take it easy, which means less necking in the truck." She gives her daughter a quick peck on the side of the head. "Now you get to bed ... and be quiet about it; Gretchen just fell asleep a little while ago."

CHAPTER THREE

SPINDLE, TEXAS - OILER PARK
SATURDAY, MAY 11, 1991 — 1:46 PM

The Spindle Tigers and Sulphur Springs Hornets bring identical 24-6 records into this one-game playoff. The winner takes the Tawakoni Conference title, thus advancing to the East Texas Regionals. (Spindle did get by Gilmore on Thursday, as Spanky predicted, though it took a four-run ninth to do it.) The sports-media types (the few who cover baseball) rate Sulphur Springs the favorite, because of their powerhouse, defending-champ status. Spindle hasn't won the conference since '85. But the Tigers do have Bryan Howard's bat: 16 home runs plus a .398 BA.

Unlike high-school football, which is big in Texas (with huge crowds, bands, cheerleaders, and hoopla), baseball attracts mostly parents and girlfriends. But today's game is hardly typical, and there are some three hundred fans in the bleachers of this old 1950s ballpark, which was once the home of the Spindle Oilers, a hot semipro team that toured all over until disbanding in 1978. It's two miles west of downtown, just off Highway 29.

Sunny, mid 80s, perfect for baseball: Mandy Stevens, seated behind the Tiger dugout with Wendy Lewis and Henry and Ginny Howard, digs a pair of sunglasses out of her gray, envelope-style purse. The stands still have a distinct pine-lumber aroma, despite the decades of rain and sun, which have turned them grayer than elephant skin. They're parked on beach towels—Ginny brought several—to protect their backsides from the rough, splintery planks. Bryan is on the field taking infield practice. Goosebumps ripple up Mandy's arms, as she watches him field a grounder, throw to first, take the catcher's peg. He's good, really good; it's no wonder the Astros are scouting him. She normally works at her waitress job until three, but she managed to get off early, since the game starts at two, and Wendy gave her a ride to the ballpark (Mandy has a license but rarely gets her mother's car). Before leaving the diner, she ditched her work uniform in favor of Levi's and a knit shirt, plus her softball cap. Bryan, taking a toss from Hector, makes the double-play pivot. He covers so much ground yet seems to glide along without effort—he moves on a baseball diamond as a fish moves in water. Mandy has seen him play many times, but she's still amazed at his graceful, fluid moves. He looks sleek and beautiful in his white, blue-trimmed uniform (#12); he's elegant and stunning, and un*speak*ably sexy.

At six-two, one-ninety, he's big for a high-school second baseman, yet his physique is streamlined and proportioned, like that of a buck deer. (He's built like a wide receiver, a position he played his sophomore

17

year, but he gave up the gridiron when he realized he had pro-baseball potential.) Coach Simms had him at shortstop last season, but this year the Tigers have Hector Perez, a 15-year-old Latino phenom, at short, so Bryan (the team captain) moved to second base. As Mandy looks on, she thinks how lucky she is, and baseball is only *part* of the story: Bryan is *her* man, and they have a big, wonderful future ahead of them.

* * *

After eight innings the underdog Tigers hold a slim 1-0 lead. Roy Collins has shut down the mighty Hornets (nine K's, one scratch hit), while José Castro (a wily, junk-throwing Chicano lefty) has done almost as well for Sulphur Springs. But in the ninth, Collins walks the leadoff man. Bryan moves in to double-play depth. *O God,* he prays, *help us get outta this inning.* Coach Simms paces in the dugout. He has Spanky Arnold heating in the bullpen. The next hitter takes a strike, then another, as the lanky Spindle hurler paints the outside corner. "Attah boy, big Roy!" Bryan chatters, popping his fist into his glove. "Hey, Roy baby! Hey now, ba-ba-ba-baby!" Roy comes inside, to move the batter back, but the fastball soars wildly, plunking him in the shoulder.

Two men on, no outs: Coach Simms strides to the mound. Bryan joins them. Leroy Simms, a beefy, ex-minor leaguer with pouchy eyes and grotesque nose (broken years ago by a bad-hop grounder), has run the Tiger program since '82. Though soft-spoken, he has a dark, penetrating glare that can turn you to putty. He asks Collins if he's got anything left. Roy, looking down, kicks the mound: "I'm okay, Coach. No problem." Simms trots back to the dugout. Bryan pats Roy on the shoulder, tells him to keep the ball down—in hopes of getting a DP grounder.

Maybe we shoulda let Spanker close this thing? Bryan frets to himself, as he lifts a closed fist toward the outfield, signaling no outs. Despite the "I'm okay" assertion, he fears that Roy is leaking oil, losing his stuff. *Coach must think that Spanky's still hurting from his pickup wreck?*

Bryan's stomach turns, as the Hornets' all-state shortstop, Brady Wilson, saunters to the plate. A tall left-handed hitter with a Ted Williams swing, he jacks the first pitch out of the park, a mammoth shot, but FOUL. Bryan sighs. Yet after a called strike, Roy hangs a curve, and Wilson is *all over it,* smashing a rope to right center. One run scores, but Bryan, taking the peg from the center fielder, fires a strike to Calvin (Calvin Brower, the Tiger catcher) gunning down the second runner. Bang, bang: it happens so fast that Wilson, on his way to third, must retreat to 2B.

One out, tie game, go-ahead run at second: Coach Simms brings in Spanky Arnold. "Y'gotta work around this guy," Simms instructs, referring to Hank Musgrave, the Hornet catcher, who waits his turn at bat. "First base is open, so give him junk, and keep it *off* the plate. This kid's damn dangerous ... but he tends to hit bleeders when he goes after a bad pitch." The coach scowls for emphasis, his slate-colored eyes fixed and potent. His big veiny nose looms crookedly above Spanky who stares right back, his own snout just as big and red, though not yet broken (and the redness is from the sun rather than middle age).

Bryan remains at the mound, while the wiry reliever takes his warm-up tosses. "Shitfire, Muskrat's no sweat," Spanky declares cockily (he refers to this most-familiar foe as "Muskrat," a put-down moniker). "He's a goddam punch-'n-judy hitter. Swings like he's swattin' flies for chrissake."

But Bryan has a sinking, this-one's-getting-away-from-us feeling as he returns to his position, especially since Musgrave, a feisty, Pete Rose–type hitter, beat him out for the conference batting title, posting a .408 average. He's built like Rose as well, like a fire hydrant. *Maybe we should walk him?* Bryan second-guesses to himself, as he holds up one finger to the outfield: one out. *Nawh, José is next, and he's a helluva hitter for a pitcher.*

Spanky starts with a curve in the dirt. *Yes!* Bryan exults to himself, as Musgrave chases, misses: strike one. But the Hornet senior is seasoned, and cunning. He's played Spindle enough to know Coach Simms's tactics. He backs out of the box, stares at the mound, flexing his stout, sun-browned arms—his biceps seem ready to burst out of the blue-gray pullover jersey. He lays off the next pitch, another deuce low and outside, then swings and misses at the third, swatting weakly at a change-up that's *way* off the plate—he couldn't have hit it with a lawn rake. One and two: he's down in the count. *Uh-oh,* Bryan realizes at second base. *Musgrave's doing a psyche job on Spanker.*

Coach Simms seems to realize the same, as he hops out of the dugout, but Bryan has already gone to the mound, along with Calvin from behind the plate, so the coach retreats, not wanting to be charged with an official visit. "This guy's playing games with you, Spank," Bryan counsels. "Don't take the bait."

"But I can *blow* my heater right by this tight-assed Muskrat," Spanky boasts, as he steps back and picks up the rosin bag.

"That's exactly what he wants," Bryan rebuts. "First base is open. Y'gotta give him deuces and junk ... like Coach said ... but don't *hang* anything—and, Cal, you forget number one."

"I'm just puttin' y'all on," Spanky cackles, wagging his head. "I know what we hafta do for chrissake." The home plate umpire breaks up the meeting.

Spanky, back on the rubber, looks in to get the sign. He takes his stretch, checks the runner, then steps off, going back to the rosin bag. Bryan sees what's coming but is compelled to stay put. It's bigger than him, like fate or destiny. The crowd is hushed. He finds his sweetheart in the bleachers behind the dugout: Mandy, dear Mandy. He quickly returns his attention to Spanky and the waiting Musgrave, but she remains big on the screen of his mind, giving him a sense that *all* is well, no matter what happens today. "C'mon Spanker, Spank, Spank!" he chatters, as he awaits the inevitable; he spits into his glove, bangs it with his fist. "Hey now! Hey ... now, now, now! C'mon Spanker!" He retreats a few feet, onto the edge of the outfield grass.

The wiry reliever stares in. Musgrave crouches, cocking his bat. Ignoring Calvin's sign, Spanky comes with number one, his best heater, but it's grooved, like down the pipe, and the Muskrat smacks a line drive toward center field. Time expands, or so it seems. Bryan, whipping to his right, leaps into the air. Ball, ball, a slowly spinning orb: he sees the seams, the scuffs; he sees it sail over his outstretched— no, at the last millisecond he gets up to it, snaring it in the web of his glove. He then trots over to the bag doubling Brady Wilson—inning over. Tie game: 1-1.

* * *

Bryan heads to the plate to lead off the home half of the ninth, an ironic twist which torques to the point of pain the palpable, gut-wrenching disappointment among the Sulphur Springs faithful, but Mandy, eagerly hopeful for more heroics, sees it as fitting and just. The Tiger captain digs in, awaiting the first pitch from Steve Vaughn, the lean, icy-cool Hornet closer, who has replaced Castro. Vaughn's a good-looking lad, but his steely-eyed, whisker-dark gameface (he always pitches with a two-day beard) makes his ninety-plus fastball all the more intimidating. It's no surprise that the righty reliever finished the regular season with an ERA of 0.32, a Tawakoni Conference record.

Bryan lays off a wayward heater, hits a long foul, then swings over a splitter: strike two. He jerks away, as a vicious brushback just misses the bill of his batting helmet: ball two. Murmurs of indignation ripple through the crowd. Vaughn retreats behind the mound; he fiddles with his belt then his hat.

Mandy stands up. "Wait on him now!" she exhorts, her voice hoarse from cheering. "He's coming with goofy stuff!" Wendy stands as well, and Bryan's parents—all the Tiger fans rise to their feet, buzzing with anticipation. Bryan steps out; he smacks the dirt from his cleats with the barrel of his bat then takes one practice swing, a slow deliberate swing. Then he digs back in. "Just make contact, babe!" Mandy shouts—and he does.

Vaughn spins a slow curve, and Bryan drills it down the left-field line, and by the time the umpire signals it fair, he's around first, flying toward second. The ball takes one hop into the foul pole then bounces crazily back into fair territory, zigzagging away from the left fielder. "GO, BABE! GO!" Mandy shrieks. "GO! GO! This could be an inside-the-parker!"

Bryan tears around second, heads for third, losing his batting helmet. Simms, coaching at third, windmills his arm, waving him on. The left fielder chases down the ball, fires it to Brady Wilson, the shortstop, who lets go with a bullet toward the plate. Bryan hurtles toward home, arriving just as the ball does—*CARUNNK!* The ball caroms toward the mound, as he slides across the plate amid a cloud of dust. Musgrave (the catcher) tumbles on top of him. The ump signals safe: TIGERS WIN! The local fans cheer berserkly, as the Spindle players rush onto the field, hugging each other, and jumping and shouting—piling into a happy heap.

But Mandy suspects that something is wrong, terribly wrong. A dreadful numbness shudders up out of her stomach taking her breath. She couldn't tell if the ball hit Bryan or the catcher's shin guard, but she heard the strange, blunt sound, and she hasn't seen her babe emerge from the celebrating pile of Tigers. Her fears are quickly confirmed, as jubilation gives way to a collective *GASP!*

The umpire and coaches disperse the players, and Mandy sees what she never wanted to see: Bryan's crumpled body, sprawled like a rag doll just beyond home plate. "The ball hit him in the head!" a fan hollers from the first-base side. "I saw it!"

* * *

The sky is deep blue and cloudless. Bryan feels himself ascending, floating, yet there's no pain, no fright, only a profound sense of well-being. *What the heck is going on?* he wonders, as he hovers halfway between home plate and the pitcher's mound. *I just scored the winning run? I think? But what am I doing up here, and why is everyone gathered around?* "HEY, what's going on!" he shouts. *They can't hear me, or see me? It's like I'm having an OBE, one of my out-of-body experiences ... but why now?*

* * *

"O God, please!" a stunned and horrified Mandy Stevens cries out, having hurried as close as she can to her fallen sweetheart. "Please, *dear God*, let him be all right." Her knees wobble, she feels nauseous, she takes Ginny Howard's hand.

"Let's move back!" Coach Simms commands, addressing the throng. "Give the doctor room!" The physician, a burly, middle-aged Sulphur Springs fan (presumed from his Hornet cap and casual attire: knit shirt over Bermudas), seems to be checking Bryan's neck. The Tiger coach pushes the air with his hands, to emphasize the move-back order. "Please, folks! Give us room! We have an ambulance on the way."

Mandy, retreating a few steps, cries softly without sobbing; a searing ache burns her throat. Removing the sunglasses, she wipes her eyes. She's still close enough to see the bloody left side of Bryan's head, as the doctor attends to him, but the bleeding is not profuse; it's not gushing at least. His upper body is limply twisted, his face toward the back-stop. "I can't find a pulse," the mustached MD rasps—his voice is rough and croaky.

* * *

That's Dr. Wilson, Brady Wilson's dad, Bryan realizes, as he floats toward the pitcher's mound. (George Wilson, a primary-care MD, runs a family practice in Sulphur Springs—Bryan even went to him once, with the mumps in third grade.) *And there's Spanky and Wendy Lewis, and Mom and Dad, and my precious Mandy. But who is Doc Wilson working on? It's one of our guys: he's wearing a Spindle uniform, but his face is turned away. I wish I could get closer, but I'm drifting the other way. I don't have any control, and I'm getting higher in the air.*

* * *

Doc Wilson looks up through wire-rimmed glasses. "Help me turn him over," he tells Coach Simms. "I have to check the carotid." Simms seems hesitant. "It's okay, Coach; there's no spinal injury—but *let's* get with it. There's no time to lose!"

They gently roll and straighten Bryan's body, giving Mandy a better look at his injury: the whole temple area appears to be crushed in— she can see bone amid the bloody tissue; his left eye is partially open. His complexion is ashen, his lips purple. She seeks solace in Ginny's arms. Henry consoles them both.

"Damn, there's no pulse *at all*," Wilson declares, "not even in the neck."

"I don't think he's breathing either," Simms adds.

"You got that right, Coach. He's in cardiac arrest. We've got to start CPR. Can you compress his thorax, while I do mouth-to-mouth?"

"Let's do it, Doc; I know CPR."

Ginny whispers a tearful plea: "Lord, please save my son, my baby." She continues to pray until interrupted by a warbling wail. Louder, closer, louder: the boxy ambulance wheels through the center-field gate, followed by a police cruiser. At home plate Dr. Wilson breathes directly into Bryan's mouth, while Coach Simms applies synchronized pressure to the chest. The orange-and-white emergency vehicle lurches to a halt along the third-base line.

* * *

Bryan hovers above the mound, but he's higher now, about the height of the light poles. *There's Mark Adams and Mr. Post,* he remarks to himself. *They're the same ambulance guys who came to school last month, to Denham's EMS practicum. Our player must be in super-bad shape, if they're here—but who is it?*

THE SILVER CORD

* * *

Coach Simms hops out of the way, as the uniformed paramedics, equipment in hand, rush to the fallen Tiger. "Forget it!" Doc Wilson directs, as Mark Adams, the stocky, younger EMT, whips out a blood-pressure cuff. "This kid's got *no* pressure, *no* pulse. It's a code blue. Y'gotta shock him ... and quick, dammit!"

Wilson, scrambling to his feet, grabs a cellphone, from the Hornet coach. The just-arrived police officer (Gene Riley, whom Mandy waits on at the diner) has taken over crowd control. (The medics also frequent the diner.) Senior EMT, Johnny Post, slim, poker-faced, and fortyish, scissors off Bryan's jersey, while Mark whips out the defibrillator unit plus a bunch of wires. The aura of death fills the air, so pervasively Mandy can smell it, a clammy stench, or maybe it's just her own dread.

"CLEAR!" Johnny barks, as he applies the defib paddles. Bryan's body heaves upward. "Anything, Mark?"

"Nothing yet ... still straight-lining."

* * *

That's MY number, Bryan realizes, as he notes the "12" on the jersey, which lies in three pieces on the grass behind home plate. *That's ME they're working on.* But this truth doesn't disturb his sense of well-being. It grows stronger in fact: blissful delight. He hears music, country music, and then he's moving, taking off, a tremendous skyward surge. The ballpark shrinks below him then disappears, as he rockets through a black tube, hurtling toward a circle of light; it grows brighter, and larger, and brighter.

* * *

Mandy, having slipped her sunglasses back on, stares in a bleary-eyed daze at the ongoing nightmare, her heart surrendering to despair, her mind moving toward an unbearable yet seemingly inescapable conclusion: they've *lost* him.

Johnny Post, exhibiting the precise, detached manner of a seasoned paramedic, fills a long-needled syringe with some kind of drug—he moves quickly yet without haste. "Okay, I'm going in with the epinephrine. Then we'll bang him at max voltage." He forces the long needle into Bryan's chest cavity, then he retrieves the defib paddles. "Now, Mark, give me 360."

"Roger on that, John—we're all set."

"CLEAR!" A powerful bolt lifts Bryan, higher than before.

"We got him," Mark Adams declares, as the heart monitor begins to beep. "I've got a pulse."

"And respiration," Post adds, impassively. "He's breathing."

"Folks, he's alive!" proclaims Dr. Wilson, giving a high-sign with the cellphone.

Cheers and applause. Mandy, her hopes rebounding, hurries toward

23

THE SILVER CORD

Bryan, along with his parents—but the senior medic halts them: "No, no, please; we hafta get an i.v. going, and the respirator, plus we gotta get him secured on a stretcher."

"It's best for now," Doc Wilson affirms, coming quickly over to Mandy and the Howards. "He's still unconscious; he can't hear us— but I *do* have some positive transportation news."

* * *

The rhythmic popping of rotor blades, some ten minutes later, signals the approach of a helicopter. Dr. Wilson, using his local connections and influence, was able to divert the Dallas-based medevac chopper from a mock highway-disaster drill in Velma, east of Sulphur Springs on I-30. Virginia Howard, her eyes red and puffy, gazes back over the stands toward the oncoming *whop-whop* sound. She has said little since her desperate prayers during the resuscitation of her son. She did ask Dr. Wilson if she and Henry could accompany Bryan on the flight, but the doctor explained that medevac flight-rules prohibit non-medical personnel, but that he as an MD should be able to go along. The crowd has grown, as curious townspeople and kids on bikes and barking dogs have joined the throng inside the baseball park, but the cops (two more squad cars have arrived, one local, one from the state police) have kept the onlookers well back.

It's a miracle to get a copter so fast, as if God sent it himself. But Mandy is also thankful for Doc Wilson; he strikes her as warm and genuine, despite his gruff manner. Nevertheless, she's more anxious than ever, as the triumph of getting Bryan's heart going has given way to a much bigger battle.

"Please level with us, Doctor," Henry Howard asked earlier, while they waited for the aircraft. "What are my boy's chances?"

"Any prognosis is premature," Dr. Wilson replied, speaking hoarsely under his gray walrus mustache—his voice grates like he has gravel in his throat. "I'm no specialist of course, but he *was* breathing on his own before they inserted the respirator tube, and his vital signs *have* stabilized. Still, we must be prepared for the worst, especially since his heart was stopped for more than two minutes, and there's possible bleeding inside the cranium." The doctor cradled his thick-fingered hands, as if holding a skull. "But then again, this might be no more than—" He paused, as his son Brady came over. The slender, craggy-faced lad, much taller, looking nothing like his dad, offered his regrets about the whole situation, since he's the one who made the fateful relay-throw to home plate, but Henry and Ginny put him at ease, declaring that it was a just a terrible accident beyond anyone's control.

Also while they waited, Mark Adams allowed Mandy a moment near the stretcher (actually a low gurney) where her dear babe lay blanketed and strapped, tubes in his nose, in his mouth, an i.v. attached

24

to his hand, a turbanlike bandage about his head. "I love you forever, Bryan Howard," she whispered amid pangs of longing and awe. Blowing a kiss, she placed it on his cheek.

After circling the field, the black-and-brown whirlybird, its engine shrieking, lands behind the pitcher's mound. The rotorwash scours the infield, creating a dust cloud; the tempest buffets Mandy, peppering her dark glasses with sandlike particles. The jetlike wail gives way to the *swish-swish* of slowing blades. Adams and Post transfer Bryan to a pair of white-helmeted aeromedics, who quickly load him aboard. Dr. Wilson boards as well.

The rotor whirls, *womp ... womp*, then faster, a throbbing *whop-whop-whop!* More shrieking and blowing of dirt: the blade quickly accelerates, easing the chopper into the air. Banking toward the outfield, it pitches its nose slightly downward, as if nodding good-bye, then it begins its westward climb toward the sun, toward Dallas. The large black cross plus the bold printed words FLIGHT OF LIFE leave a chilling impression. The *whop-whop* sound quickly diminishes. Only the exhaust fumes remain: they smell like kerosene. Bryan Howard is airborne (again).

CHAPTER FOUR

DALLAS PRESBYTERIAN HOSPITAL
MAY 11, 1991 — SATURDAY EVENING

It's past seven p.m. when Henry Howard swings his white '86 LaSabre into the hospital parking lot. His wife rides beside him, Mandy in the back seat, their hastily packed bags in the trunk, their hopes in the hands of God—and the doctors at Dallas Presbyterian. Located in the northeast part of "Old Dallas," DPH maintains one of the best trauma centers in the country. A sprawling complex with manicured lawns, beautiful magnolias, plus stately oaks and pines, the place seems more like a college than a hospital, not to speak of the ongoing construction.

Henry had the Buick humming all the way, but they were delayed getting out of Spindle, as Mandy had to rush home—she promised her mom she'd be back no later than Sunday night—and the Howards had to stop at the farm. Wendy Lewis saved them precious minutes by driving Mandy to Colby Drive then out to the farm. Wendy was prepared to skip work (at Byer's Drug Store) so she could drive her friend all the way to Big D, but the Howards insisted that Mandy ride with them.

During the 130-mile trip, Ginny reminisced about her son: the happy milestones, as when he first rode Millie by himself; the tragedies, as when Buster was killed in '84 (the collie got hit on Longley Road); and heart-revealing secrets only a mother would know, as when he came to her in tears, after killing a robin with his BB gun (he never shot birds again). Mandy confided that she and Bryan were in love and planned to get married someday, though she didn't divulge the details.

But there were also silent, unbearable stretches during which Mandy pleaded with God, lashed out at God, her tortured thoughts reeling like ants in insecticide. How could it be? It's not fair? Not now? Then came pangs of guilt, guilt for loving Bryan *too* much, as if this tragedy was *her* fault, as if *she* had allowed this love to grow and grow till it was bigger than anything, bigger than all other pursuits and duties, bigger than *God*, and God had to—but then she felt even guiltier for *feel*ing guilty. In any case, her life, her world, her happiness lay close to death, three days short of his 18th birthday (if not already gone). Too much: she escaped to happier times. She recalled the spontaneous "neat" feeling, the heart rush, when they met at that teen-ministry cookout; she was only fourteen, but when he gave that first dimpled grin while they roasted marshmallows, she knew they'd be together—in due season. She relived their first kiss, in the hayloft last fall, as he beckoned with his eyes, those ocean-green eyes. She recalled the windy afternoon they played hide-in-seek after church, chasing each other in the pine grove, and the February romp in the snow, the two inches that fell on Valentine's Day, and the happy times at O'Henry's, the DQ, and watching movies with the VCR, and listening to tunes in the pickup, like Stevie Nicks and "Talk to Me"—it played in her head as they crossed Lake Ray Hubbard sending fresh tears from her swollen eyes.

Henry, giving a tired-driver sigh, gets out of the car and stretches, then drawls something about the sky and the zilch chance of rain. He said little on the way aside from an occasional "Yeah," or "I reckon so," or "We just don't know." After a quick check of her bangs, Mandy exits as well, purse and jacket in hand. The breeze is warm, but she may need the windbreaker inside, because of the air conditioning. She's still in the clothes she wore to the game: pale-blue polo plus jeans. The trees look orange in the setting sun, a gorgeous fiery hue, and the blue-purple shadows stretch forever. How can the sunset be so pretty, the air so sweet, on such a horrifying day? It bothers her that she's even thinking of the weather and the trees and her gosh-dang jacket. Nonetheless, as they trek to the main entrance, she exchanges small-talk with the Howards about these and other mundane matters, not *daring* to speculate on the momentous news awaiting them. The back-and-forth chatter strikes Mandy as weirdly festive and holiday-like, a farcical evasion. Ditto for their happy, leisure-day attire. The Howards, as with her, are still in their baseball-watching duds (Ginny in culottes under a sleeve-less blouse; Henry in khakis plus a knit shirt).

Up close, the boxy, concrete-and-glass hospital looms cold and monstrous, as the many wings and towers and annexes dwarf the original red-brick edifice. This grotesque and jumbled bigness makes Mandy feel tiny and powerless, quickening her sense of dread, as does the antiseptic smell that assaults them inside, an odor akin to Windex and rubbing alcohol. You still enter through the old hospital, though it's now little more than a vestibule. "We just got here from Spindle," Henry informs a chubby, snub-nosed receptionist, one of several seated around a circular kiosk in the main lobby. "My son, Bryan Howard, was injured in a baseball game and flown here by helicopter. Dr. Wilson is—"

"That's fine, sir," the sow-faced woman interrupts. "I *just* need his birth date."

"May 14, 1973," he informs her, giving a brusque sigh.

The receptionist clicks a few keys on her computer; her fat doughboy hands have no knuckles. "Yes, Bryan Wallace Howard: he was admitted to the Trauma Center at 5:31 p.m."

"So what's the latest on his condition?"

"I'm sorry, sir ... but *I* don't have that information."

Henry sighs again. "Well, where can we find Dr. Wilson?"

"You mean Dr. Nadler? There's no Dr. Wilson on this report?"

THE SILVER CORD

She forces a grin, the smile just as pudgy as her fingers. "But before you look for anyone, I must fill in the gaps on the admission file." She whips off a series of curt questions: about Bryan, about insurance (BC/BS), about the family. Henry answers them just as curtly, his face grimacing with impatience. He seems ready to lose his temper, rare for him, but then his attention shifts, as Coach Simms comes across the lobby.

"Bryan's in surgery, on the fifth floor of Ferguson Wing," the coach explains to the anxious trio, who've hurried around the kiosk to meet him. "Doc Wilson said he survived the flight, but things are touch-and-go. He told me to have y'all wait for him in the Trauma Center ICU; it's in the same wing, the third floor—I was just up there."

"Show us the way, Leroy," Henry replies, giving him a double handshake. Virginia, fighting fresh tears, nods her assent and thanks the coach for being here, but they don't move just yet, since she's searching for something in her shoulder bag.

Simms elaborates: "The doc said he was stable going into surgery, his vital signs ... but he was still unconscious—that's all I know." He sucks a deep breath, his nostril wings flaring like gills. The coach's big, mangled nose looks redder than usual, as if he's been blowing it, as if he's been dealing with his own emotions.

The news on Bryan, though better than the worst, offers little relief to Mandy. She needs to hear that he's okay, *totally* okay, just a bad bump on the head. She yearns to be with him back home, back on the farm, back where God is good, and life is happy. She doesn't want him here in this alien, awful hospital, with its many signs and doorways and lost plodding faces, and fast-moving, official types who carry clipboards and wear plastic badges, not to mention the tubby receptionist with the pissy attitude. Mandy feels like going back and screaming at the rude bitch. Her eyes burn, her throat aches: she needs to weep some more, like Ginny—no, she needs to break down and have a *good* sobbing, shrieking fit. If she were at home, she'd be in her room bawling her head off, but not here. She tenaciously maintains her composure; she can't make a spectacle in such a public place.

After Ginny finds the Kleenex packet she's looking for, they follow Coach Simms across the atrium-style lobby to a wide, ornately banistered stairwell; the interior has been modernized, but the marble stairs retain an early 20th-century look, with fluted balusters and a bronze statuette atop the newel post: a seminude, goddesslike figure holding a torch. "We could take the elevator," the coach remarks, as they climb the well-worn treads, "but it's quicker this way." Simms has changed into street clothes but still wears his ripple-soled coach's shoes. Reaching the third floor, they jog left, then right, then left. The hospital smell grows stronger, like iodine, like old-fashioned Mercurochrome. They cut through a ward, passing by the patient rooms: 315, 317, 320, 325. Mandy *hates* this place. Finally, they go through a large gray door, which says: Ferguson Wing - TC / ICU.

Their sneakers squeaking on the polished floor, they hasten down a bright, beige-walled corridor to the visitor's lounge, a large, low-ceilinged room with institutional seating (blue-vinyl upholstery, wooden arms) plus tables strewn with magazines. It's suddenly quieter, because of the carpet underfoot, brown carpet. A half-dozen Spindle players huddle in one corner along with a few parents. Spanky (still in uniform) is here, and Roy Collins, and Calvin Brower, and Jacki Simms, the coach's wife (a pretty, redheaded gym-teacher). The players hang back shyly, but the adults come over. Jacki hugs Ginny, and Henry, and Mandy.

"Are the Howards here as yet?" comes a kind voice from behind. "Bryan Howard's parents?"

"That's us," Henry replies, as a tidy, prim-faced woman joins them, a fliptop clipboard in her hand.

"I'm Jane Caldwell, your family-support hostess. We have private suites inside, if you'd like to wait there?" She nods toward the ICU entrance. Dark-haired, wearing glasses, and dressed in a snappy pale-olive suit, the lady looks like a real-estate broker, like Ms. Creighton from Century 21 who eats at the diner; they dress the same anyhow. And her manner conveys consideration and professional competence, a welcome change from the fat bitch back in the lobby.

"Yes, that would be helpful," Ginny tells the hostess between sniffles—she dabs her eyes with a tissue.

"Okay, please come with me then, and I'll get you situated." Her skirt swishing, Ms. Caldwell escorts the threesome through the double doors. Her low-heel pumps click on the floor tiles, as they leave the carpeted lounge. "We have three ICUs here at DPH, but this one is uniquely designed for trauma patients."

A long, wide foyer leads to the nurses' station and patient cubicles, but the hostess hangs a right through a door that says IMMEDIATE FAMILY ONLY; she takes them down a narrow hotel-like hallway past several occupied rooms. The last room, Suite E, is empty; she ushers them inside. "It's not actually a suite," Ms. Caldwell acknowledges amid a chuckle, "unless you count the coffee nook and the restroom." She gestures toward the bathroom door in the far corner—it sports a unisex symbol. "But this *is* a large room, and 'suite' sounds more inviting." More chuckles. "And I might add ... we're the only hospital I know of that provides private space for the immediate relatives of ICU patients. Sometimes, two or more families have to share a suite, but we're not very crowded this evening, so make yourself—"

"Oh, forgive me," Henry drawls, interrupting her. "I'm Henry, and this's my wife, Virginia." He gives a bashful grin, gesturing with his callused, farm-roughened hands. "And this's Amanda Stevens, my son's girlfriend, or *Mandy* as we call her."

"Well, I'm just *Jane*," the hostess quips, as they shake hands all around. "And, Mandy, I'm putting you down as a *bona*-fide family member." She makes a few notations on her clipboard.

Mandy slips on her jacket; it's chilly in here, but she likes the laid-back mood of the room, with the sofas and easy chairs, and the lilac wallpaper, and the plush magenta carpeting. The soft lighting (table lamps and gold-curtained windows) reinforces the homey feel. The unisex restroom plus the no-smoking signs, slapped tackily on the walls, make it clear that this is *no* living room, as does the formica-topped, caf-style table at one end, yet it's far more cozy than the visitor's lounge, not to mention the floral scent, from a vase of bluebonnets, *real* flowers.

Closing the clipboard, Jane sobers. "I want you to know that I'm truly sorry about Bryan, and I do hope for a good outcome."

"Did *you* see him?" Mandy asks naively, shifting her weight nervously from one foot to the other.

"No, honey," Jane replies. "He's been with the trauma team since his arrival." She gives Mandy a consoling pat on the arm. "But I'm sure Dr. Nadler will brief you folks ... when he can."

Jane makes Mandy feel better—she's been to big hospitals before, like the one in Longview when Grandpa Sullivan (her mom's dad) had his heart attack, but there was no hostess or anything. Still, she'd rather have Bryan healthy and *out* of here.

"What about Dr. Wilson?" Ginny asks, no longer dabbing tears. "He said he'd meet us here?"

Jane flips up the metal cover on her clipboard. "Hmmm," she says, "I just have Dr. Nadler, Bryan's neurosurgeon, on the printout. Is Dr. Wilson your PCP at home? your family doctor?"

"Not *ex*actly," Henry explains, "not recently anyhow ... but we *do* know him, and he was at the game when Bryan got hurt. He also arranged for the helicopter—we *thank* God for him."

"Well, I'll try to locate your Dr. Wilson ... and tell him that you're here." She turns to leave but halts in the doorway. "If you need to turn down the AC, the unit's under the windows. Now the coffee's on us, and you're welcome to keep your sandwiches and snacks in the fridge, and there's ice too. There's more ice at the end of the hall plus vending machines. But the main cafeteria is downstairs, one floor below the lobby ... and my office is right here, on the other side of the foyer, if you need me."

* * *

Same suite, ten minutes later. "Let's all have a seat," Dr. Wilson says, after brief hellos; he gestures toward the gray-formica table. He's dressed as before minus the Hornet hat. Pangs of dread set Mandy's heart to pounding. If he had *good* news, he would've said so right out? Feeling feverish, she sheds her jacket. "First of all," Wilson declares once everyone is seated, "I can assure you that Bryan is in *ex*cellent hands." He adjusts his glasses then finger-sweeps his bald head, as if smoothing invisible hair. "I'm not on staff here of course, but the DPH trauma team is the best ... way out of *my* league." Despite the positive start, his tone conveys wariness, as do his squinty, wire-rimmed eyes. "Dr. Joe Nadler, the surgeon in charge, will brief you in detail as soon as he gets out of the OR, but I'll tell you as much as I know. And I'll also give you my private number, plus my cellphone, since I must return to Sulphur Springs as soon as Brady gets here with my car. I have two critical patients at Memorial."

Clearing his throat, a harsh, growly "harrumph," he spreads his hammy paws on the table. "As we all know, Bryan suffered a horrendous blow to the head causing cardiac arrest. I was in the boxseats on the first-base side, so I saw the ball hit him—I had a good angle. Yet as I rushed to your son, I assumed ... at worst ... that we had to deal with a brief concussion-induced loss of consciousness, as when a boxer is KO'ed—it happens routinely in high-school sports. But what I discovered at home plate was *hard*ly routine." Shaking his head, he gives a breathy *whew* under his walrus mustache. "The medical term is TBI, or traumatic brain injury. He was clinically dead until the paramedics brought him back; that was the *first* miracle. And we got him here in forty minutes; that's miracle number two. We covered the ninety air-miles from Spindle in record time, according to the flight crew. Now Bryan retains the capacity to breathe on his own. At least, he could when they changed the ventilator upon his arrival, so he's *not* brain-dead—that's miracle number three. But I'm afraid we're going to need at least a couple more."

Removing his glasses, he massages his eyes, the bridge of his nose, as though trying to figure out a less painful way of saying what he has to say. Finally, he gives a resigned snort, slips the spectacles on, and begins to elaborate: "First off, there's the intracranial hemorrhaging, which—"

"The what?" Mandy asks, shifting to face the bad news.

"Forgive me, young lady," he responds, giving her a nod. "I'm getting into Dr. Nadler's territory." His squinty violet eyes (a shade darker than the wallpaper) brim with direful sympathy behind the gold-rimmed glasses, or so it seems to Mandy. She feels suddenly detached, unhinged, as if the whole cosmos is collapsing around her, leaving only darkness and despair—along with Doc Wilson's ruddy, pouchy, mustached face. "What I mean," he expands, "is that we have bleeding inside the skull. The radiologist showed me Bryan's CAT-scans, or CTs, which are like super-duper X-rays. They indicate considerable displacement of cerebral tissue, from swelling pressure, and this can cause brain-stem trauma—that's the lower, vital-function part that sits atop the spinal column. It could even result in brain-death ... if the bleeding is not halted. That's why they're operating on him." The doctor, leaning back, wraps his loglike arms about his chest. "But there's potentially another problem ... frontal-lobe damage which may have occurred during cardiac arrest, when his brain was oxygen starved, and such damage is often irreversible. Now he may have gotten some oxygen, while your coach and I were giving him CPR, but it's hard to be sure."

"So he may never regain consciousness?" Henry inquires. "Even if they *stop* the bleeding and swelling?"

"I'm afraid so. At least, we have to face this possibility."

Mandy, still focused on Doc Wilson, is not surprised by his reply, yet having good intuition scarcely softens the impact, especially as Ginny begins to whimper across the table. The lump in Mandy's throat burns, as if she's choking on a hot coal. Tears blur her tunnel-like gaze. The country MD leans forward, taking her hand. "It's quite all right, my dear," he consoles. "Let it out, each of you. I know you folks love the boy, and this ordeal has torn you up. But I didn't mean to imply that our situation is hopeless. God has brought him this far, so let's...." Mandy doesn't hear the rest, as she dashes sobbing into the bathroom.

* * *

DALLAS PRESBYTERIAN HOSPITAL
SATURDAY, MAY 11, 1991 — 8:15 PM

The AC is off, and the TV, leaving only the sporadic moan of the minifridge to keep Mandy company. She sits alone in Suite E, her poplin windbreaker wadded in her lap. Henry and Ginny have gone down to the cafeteria with Dr. Wilson. But Mandy feels too distressed to be around a lot of people, and she has no appetite anyhow. Right after they left, she turned the TV on, just long enough to learn that the medical tests on President Bush turned out A-OK, that last week's jogging scare did no cardiac damage whatsoever. For him to be well, when Bryan is dying, adds to her hurt, to her sense of injustice.

So he may never regain consciousness? I'm afraid so. She hears this dire exchange again and again. Although Dr. Wilson only said it was a possibility, she has leaped beyond the ifs and what ifs. Her babe will *nev*er laugh again, or hold her hand, or give that dimpled grin, or yearn for her with his beautiful green eyes. There'll be no wedding in three years, no honeymoon, no sex, no babies, no growing old together. It's *over*. She wrestles *against* reason, a tortuous grappling, for logic leaves room for hope, and hope is unbearable, for it only gets dashed. She prefers finality, acceptance of the inevitable. Her grief has gone dry and prickly, her tears giving way to bleary eyes and hoarse snuffles, the lump in her throat disintegrating into fiery stickleburrs. She actually felt better while sobbing, especially when Ginny came into the bathroom and they cried in each other's arms.

Before they went down to the caf, the doctor called the fifth floor and was told that Bryan wouldn't be out of surgery until nine o'clock, at the earliest—then Dr. Nadler would brief the family. But Mandy foresees this briefing as a formality, an official confirmation of the worst-case scenario. To add to her woe, she questions and blames herself again, as she recalls what they heard at church Wednesday night: *Set your affections on things above....* She grips the windbreaker, so tightly her fingers hurt. *Maybe I want him TOO much, and God has to—no, no! God would never punish us for loving? But why the hell is this happening? I sure don't see how it's working for good. O dear Jesus, where the heck are you? This's a super-shitty day, the worst of my life. Forgive my language, but where are YOU?*

The hot pricking in her throat demands relief. Grabbing some change from her purse, she goes down the hall (to the left) then around the corner to the vending machines where an elderly woman scans the floor. "Excuse me, dear," the white-haired lady says, "but I was trying to get a Coke, and I dropped one of my quarters." Her bright blue eyes seem too pretty and lively to be socketed in such a hideously wrinkled face. "I have more in my bag here, but—"

"Let me help," Mandy interrupts reflexively. Looking down, she searches the cubbyhole vending area.

"There it is, child," the lady rasps, her voice just as withered as her face, "over by the ice bin." She points with her cane.

Mandy retrieves the coin and gives it to the old woman, who proceeds to get her can of Coke. Her veiny, clawlike hands and wizened forearms look more chickenlike than human. "My sister Lucille is eighty-four," she mutters, turning toward the window where the twilight has turned the trees black, the sky ivory above a pink horizon, "and I'm seventy-nine. It's sad ... it is ... to face all this." The long-necked lamps in the parking lot have come on, giving the cars a weird amberlike cast. "Forgive me, child, I'm talking to myself, but Lucy fell and broke her hip, then she got a blood infection after they operated, to pin it. I doubt she'll ever come home." Before the high-schooler can think of anything to say—she's hardly in a consoling mood—the oldster drops the Coke into her huge satchel-like handbag and totters off, leaning on the rubber-tipped walking stick, which makes a *thunking* sound on the linoleum. Wearing a plaid-flannel shirt with the sleeves rolled up, plus corduroys and sneakers, she seems oddly attired for such an old lady, though the black handbag surely fits. The *thunking* goes soft as she reaches the carpeted part of the hallway and disappears around the corner.

Mandy, moving mechanically, deposits her own coins in the adjacent machine. She pushes the Dr. Pepper button, grabs the can, pulls the tab, and takes a swig. The fizzy-sweet liquid soothes her throat but nothing else. The daggers of pain continue to rip and tear. *Bryan's not coming home either,* she tells herself. *It's no accident—that old lady talking to herself. God wants him in Heaven. I gotta let go.* She gazes wide-eyed at the black-flecked linoleum floor, which is so polished it seems rippled under the fluorescent lights, like Ruby Pond on a breezy day. But she'll never go to the pond again, or the big oak, not with Bryan anyway. The harsh fluorescence seems inert and cold. She closes her eyes, escaping the light, but not the sickly sweetness; the vending area smells stinky sweet, from spilled soda pop and such. *Oh, dear Jesus, why can't I wake up from this nightmare?*

* * *

DPH - FAMILY SUITE E
SATURDAY, MAY 11, 1991 — 11:24 PM

"*C'mon*, Andy!" Barney Fife fusses, his voice cracking above the canned laughter—an old *Andy Griffith Show* plays at low volume on the TV. The room is dark save for the flickering television and one lamp. Henry dozes in a club chair, while Ginny naps on the sofa across from Mandy, who's drowsily stretched out herself but awake. Tossing off the hospital-issue blanket (Jane brought several a good while ago), the ponytailed lass stretches to her feet, digs some things out of her roll bag, and pads sneakerless to the restroom. Henry got their overnight bags from the Buick, detouring to the parking lot on his way back from the cafeteria.

Mandy, after peeing and brushing her teeth, and adjusting her bangs, decides to make fresh coffee. Back to the bathroom: she fills the glass pot with water, to the six-cup level. She doesn't drink coffee much, but it'll make the doughnuts taste better, the ones Ginny brought up from the caf. She also brought Mandy a ham sandwich plus an apple; both remain uneaten save for a few mouselike nibbles. But the teenager feels a bit better now—no, "better" is not the word. She feels numb, as though her heart died *with* Bryan: she's resigned to his demise. He died during surgery. It *has* to be. That's why it's taking so long. They were supposed to see Dr. Nadler at nine, then ten-thirty, and now eleven-thirty, which is unlikely, since it's only a few minutes away.

Returning to her couch, she slips on her sneakers. Dr. Wilson departed the hospital about nine-thirty, as did Coach Simms plus most of the Spindle crowd. Mandy didn't go out to the lounge, but the Howards did, long enough to tell everyone that there'd be no news until very late, and it could be tomorrow. Only Spanky and Roy Collins stayed. They dropped by the suite an hour ago, still in their uniforms; they didn't hang around because of the family-member rule, but Spanky made his feelings quite clear: "I ain't gonna leave till I know one way or the other for chrissake. I know I cain't see 'im or anythang ... but still, I gotta know."

The coffeemaker gurgles and sighs, and pops its lid. Henry goes on dozing, but Ginny sits up. "You made fresh coffee?" she remarks between yawns, the blanket still on her lap.

"That's right, Mom Howard," the teenager replies. "It's almost ready." She found herself calling Ginny "Mom Howard" when they were crying together in the bathroom four hours ago, and she plans to call her that from now on, even without Bryan.

"I reckon I should get Henry up," Ginny says, fingerfluffing her hair. "It's eleven-thirty." She nudges her husband—he snorts and stretches—then she grabs her handbag and heads into the bathroom. She, as with Mandy, seems resigned, yet they've not talked much since the crying session, though Ginny did lead the three of them in prayer, after the Howards got back from supper.

Five minutes later, as they have their coffee and doughnuts, a rap comes at the door then a bright burst of hallway light along with Jane Caldwell's voice: "Dr. Nadler is ready to see you. I'll escort you up."

Mandy and Ginny are slow to react, but Henry's moving, turning on lights, grabbing his shoes. "Can we see Bryan?" he drawls, not wasting any time, or words.

"I don't know," the spiffy-prim hostess replies. "But Dr. Nadler will tell you about all that ... I'm sure."

Yeah, he's gonna tell us, Mandy mocks, but only to herself. *He's gonna tell us we can have a last look before they cart him away.* Acid pessimism—because hope is unbearable.

Jane escorts them back through the visitor's lounge to the elevator—they nod at Spanky and Roy across the room, but there's no conversation. Reaching the fifth floor, she ushers them into a small, modern, but sparsely furnished office; it's beige and gray (like the elevator, like the hallways, like the whole goshdang hospital, save for the family suites). There's a desk and a phone and a blinking computer, plus several stacking chairs. A white marker-board covers one wall, the kind you draw on with wipe-off markers, and on the other wall is one of those panels that light up to look at X-rays. "I'll tell Dr. Nadler that you're here," Jane says, as she leaves. "I'll be going off shift in a few minutes, but I hope to see you folks tomorrow afternoon."

O God, let's get this over with, Mandy laments silently. *It's SO weird. I mean, Bryan always talked about being a brain doctor, and now I'm sitting here waiting for a brain doctor ... who's gonna say it's over, and—*the door interrupts: Dr. Nadler.

"I'm Dr. Joe Nadler," the neurosurgeon announces upon entering. He greets the trio then plunks down at the desk. A tall, dark-complected physician, with handsomely chiseled features and black wavy hair, he looks to be in his late forties, maybe fifty. He's still wearing the blue-green OR duds, minus the cap. Slipping on his glasses, he opens the folder he brought with him. "I'm sorry I couldn't see you sooner, but the surgery took longer than we expected, and I wanted to make sure that Bryan had stabilized in recovery. They're now taking him down to the ICU, on the third floor where you've been waiting. He's unconscious, but you'll be able to see him in an hour or so ... after they get him hooked up and calibrated."

THE SILVER CORD

He's NOT dead, Mandy reacts to herself, her thoughts racing. *He didn't DIE in surgery. We can see him in the ICU. But, but....* She quickly retreats into resigned pessimism, so that whatever else this doctor reports, it can only be positive, or neutral—it will not devastate. Nadler's guarded tone and sober expression tell her that he, as with Dr. Wilson, is not the bearer of triumphant tidings. He hasn't smiled except when shaking their hands, and even that seemed restrained.

"I'm sure you're anxious to hear our prognosis," he goes on, his baritone voice just as chiseled as his face, "and I wish I could tell you with assurance that Bryan will survive, and fully recover. I cannot. He remains in very critical condition. It can go *either* way. Nonetheless, we're in better shape than when he came off the medevac copter. The surgery went well—we stopped the intracranial hemorrhaging, and that should reverse the herniation as the swelling goes down. And we reshaped the fractured cranial wall. And I think we got in quick enough, so the brain stem was not damaged. At least, it's still functioning, as of now. We'll be doing more scans tomorrow, to confirm all this: both CT and MRI." He sighs, slowly wagging his head. "But even if those scans are good, we still have the anoxia concerns. Please forgive all this medical jargon. I'll try to simplify as we go along, and do feel free to ask questions." Though his timbre is precise and professionally detached, his gestures and body language convey sensitivity, and he has gentle eyes, hazel-colored like Henry.

"As you know," Nadler goes on, "Bryan has suffered a severe TBI, and I must say it's hard to believe a baseball caused such damage. The tomography suggests a blow from a hammer rather than a ball." Getting up, he steps over to the marker-board where he draws a human skull with a blue marker. "I'll show you the X-rays in a moment, but first I want to give you a quick anatomy class. He draws various shapes inside the skull. "Now strictly speaking, our brain, as with all mammals, consists of a hindbrain, a midbrain, and a forebrain. But since our cerebrum fills the upper two-thirds of the cranial cavity, I like to refer to the human brain as having two divisions, upper and lower. But regardless of how we divide it, this big half-circle up here *is* the cerebrum." He points with the marker. "It's actually two cerebral hemispheres, and this's what we usually think of when we think of the brain: the fissured gray matter, which is also called the cerebral cortex. Now the cerebrum is critically vital, since it controls voluntary movement and intellectual functions such as speech and abstract thought, and it works closely with the limbic system to integrate sensory perceptions, making us aware. You might say, it gives *content* to our consciousness." He pauses to study his diagram. "I don't think I'm going to draw the limbic system, or get into its different components, except to say that it's also part of the forebrain, though much smaller— the thalamus, for example, is about the size of a lima bean. The limbic system is like a master traffic-control complex that regulates emotional response, as well as the integration and transfer of sensory information. It adds *feeling* to our consciousness. The cerebral hemispheres, especially the right one, also participate in the creation and transformation of emotional impulses."

Much of this shoots over Mandy's head, but she does recall some from Denham's tenth-grade Biology. "The lower brain is equally vital, actually more so," Dr. Nadler elaborates. "Down here toward the lower back of the head is the cerebellum, which fine tunes our muscular coordination among other things, while just inside it lies the brain stem"—he points at a thumby-looking thing—"which is perhaps the most important of all. It consists of the midbrain, the pons, and the medulla." He draws three little blobs inside the thumby thing. "We call it the brain stem, since it's like a posthead on which the forebrain rests, and it carries impulses from the spinal cord to the rest of the brain and vice-versa, but it also regulates respiration and blood pressure, and oversees the autonomic nervous system, and perhaps most crucially, it maintains the ascending reticular activating sys—"

"You lost me," Ginny interrupts, as Mandy was about to.

"Forgive me," the surgeon replies. "Simply put, we can look at the brain stem as giving us the *capacity* for consciousness. It's the closest we get, biologically, to the notion of soul. And the loss of stem function leads to brain death, or coma dépassé, which is irreversible. We can keep a brain-dead body alive with our modern life-support systems, but they're not *really* alive."

"But you said that *his* stem is okay?" Henry inquires.

"That's right, sir," the surgeon affirms. "Your son, though we have him on a respirator, does have the capacity to breathe on his own, and his pupils do respond to light—this tells us that his stem function is adequate, and the EEG confirms it. Respiratory paralysis, or apnea, is the crucial sign of stem failure, and so far we haven't had to deal with it, except during the concussion-induced cardiac arrest back at the baseball field. But his brain-stem function came back strong when he was resuscitated. And that's why we rushed him into surgery; we had to maintain this function in the face of the intracranial bleeding, as I'm getting ready to explain." He gestures with the blue marker. "Now the effects of anoxia on the *upper* brain, that's another problem—but no, Mr. Howard, your son is *not* brain-dead."

Mandy, though glad to have him affirm this so emphatically, has yet to hear anything to counter the hope-dashing words from Dr. Wilson nearly five hours ago when he said Bryan may never regain consciousness, even if he's *not* brain-dead. In any case, she remains safely resigned to losing him, if not to death, to permanent sleep, which would be *worse* than death.

The surgeon takes an X-ray from his folder, steps to the light board, clips the print in place, and clicks on the light. Mandy and the Howards shift around so they can see. "Here's where the ball struck Bryan," he explains, now using a telescopic pointer. "You can see the craterlike fracture above the cheekbone, plus the radiating cracks. But it's inside the skull where the real problem occurred. The ball impacted at just the right angle to splinter the interior cranial wall here, and a piece of this fractured bone lacerated a blood vessel here; it's a bit hard to see on this print. The damage to the temporal lobe itself is minimal, as we confirmed during surgery, but the lacerated vessel led to profuse bleeding inside the supratentorial compartment of his skull, the main, upper part here, and the pressure has caused the brain tissue to herniate downward through the tentorial opening"—he points at a conelike projection—"between the cerebral hemispheres and the cerebellum. This's why we had to operate at once, because the hernia threatened the brain stem. If we hadn't stopped the bleeding, the pressure cone of herniated tissue would have crushed the stem causing irreversible damage—and therefore brain death. We have, however, dodged that bullet for now. With the bleeding halted, the herniated tissue should retreat."

"But Dr. Wilson said he may not wake up anyway?" Mandy offers, going right for the jugular of her nightlong despair. "Even if he's *not* brain dead?"

"That's correct, Mandy," he replies, "and we have to talk about that." She gives a half grin, acknowledging his attention, then she purses and fidgets her mouth like she does. His eyes are more friendly than his doctor-voice, and to have him call her by name makes her feel very included—he actually remembered it from when they shook hands. He seems all at once to be an ordinary "Dr. Joe"—no longer Dr. Nadler, the chief surgeon. Hopeful vibes tug on her heart, but she fights them off.

The doctor sits down and takes a legal pad from the folder. The cursive scrawl on the yellow paper looks hastily penned. "The intracranial bleeding was something we could deal with, but if there's anoxia damage to the cerebral hemispheres, there's not much we can do. As is often the case in brain trauma, we face *more* than one enemy. This's what Dr. Wilson was talking about—the oxygen deprivation. Circulatory arrest lasting more than two minutes can cause widespread and irreversible damage to the cerebral cortex while sparing the brain stem, which is more resistant to anoxia. So it *is* possible for a person, who's not brain-dead, to remain unconscious for months, years, or decades even, until they die of other causes." Ginny snuffles and dabs her eyes, but Mandy, having braced herself for this, sits stony-faced.

Dr. Nadler, removing his glasses, exhales resignedly and leans back in the desk chair. He looks again at Mandy, the same kindly way, then at the Howards. Finally, he continues—he speaks slowly and deliberately. "And this remains our biggest concern ... until we see *some* evidence of frontal-lobe activity. Now since Bryan was in cardiac arrest for almost three minutes, one might well conclude that he's in a

THE SILVER CORD

persistent vegetative state with little chance of waking up, but I think it's premature to make any such judgment. I'd prefer to say it could go *either* way. We do know, from Dr. Wilson, that CPR was administered, so that's another factor. Right now, we can only wait, and hope, and pray, and—"

A *beeping* pager interrupts. After checking the device on his belt, Nadler makes a quick phone call during which he mainly listens—he says "yes" a few times, and "I understand" and before hanging up, he asks, "Are you *sure,* Doctor?"

He's getting good news on Bryan, Mandy intuits, a wellspring breaking loose in her bosom.

Nadler quickly confirms, "This is *in*deed remarkable; it looks like we have the frontal-lobe evidence we were hoping for."

"What? What evidence?" Ginny asks eagerly.

The surgeon smiles broadly for the first time. "That was Dr. Browning," he explains. "She was supervising Bryan's transfer down to the ICU, and she says that when they wheeled him into the elevator, he mumbled and grabbed at the mouthpiece, then gripped the side bar of the gurney. He quickly lapsed back into unconsciousness ... but this episode *is* encouraging."

* * *

DALLAS PRESBYTERIAN HOSPITAL
SUNDAY, MAY 12, 1991 — 1:01 AM

Their mood guardedly optimistic, Mandy and the Howards exit Suite E and head for the intensive care unit. Henry has already checked with the ICU shift chief, and she said to come back at one a.m. He also updated Spanky and Roy in the lounge, telling them about Bryan's brief return to consciousness.

Dr. Nadler remains cautious. "Bryan is not out of the woods yet," he counseled an hour ago, in his closing remarks up on the fifth floor. "Dr. Browning's news is certainly positive, since it tells us that enough higher intellectual function has survived the anoxia for him to regain consciousness, but we won't know the extent of his cerebral capacity until he becomes fully awake. He could be mentally impaired, or paralyzed, or have his vision affected, not just from the anoxia, but from any number of things related to his injury. And we still need some good CTs to confirm that the herniation threat is passed. And even if he recovers completely, we're looking at months of therapy." The surgeon, however, could go only so far with disclaimers. "Don't get me wrong. I'm very heartened by this development, and it *is* rather amazing—and whatever happens from here on, I'd have to say that it was Dr. Wilson's quick action, the CPR at the baseball field, that made the difference."

As they squeak along through the polished ICU foyer, Mandy dares

39

to hope, as intuition persuades her that Bryan's unique and wonderful spirit is very much alive—if he tried to talk and pulled at the air tube. That's *just* like him; that's exactly what he would do. And even if he has neural impairment or never walks again, she'll gladly spend the rest of her life caring for him. *Thank you, dear Jesus,* she prays silently. *I just pray he'll wake up again, and soon. Please—don't let anything terrible happen now.*

She and Ginny hang back, as Henry checks in at the nurses' station, a humming, high-tech command post packed with monitors and keyboards and electronic readouts, and printers and phones and recording graphs, and all sorts of buttons and switches and blinking lights—it looks like something out of *Star Wars,* as does the entire ICU. The patient cubicles (the glass-faced rooms) surround the oval-shaped control center. Mandy scans an airport-like TV-monitor suspended from the ceiling. There are twelve slots on the screen, giving the room numbers and patient names. She quickly finds the pertinent info: #3; Bryan Howard; AP: Dr. Nadler; ICU-RN: J. Johnson.

"I understand y'all had a very worrisome time of it tonight," Nurse Johnson says, after exiting the oval and introducing herself. A busty, robust, middle-aged woman, with graying hair and a commanding presence, she speaks with a thick, very Southern drawl—more Mississippi than Dallas.

"That's for sure," Virginia affirms, "but we feel better now."

"With good reason," the nurse declares, a grin overtaking her stout country-gal face. "Dr. Browning briefed me." She escorts them to cubicle #3. "Okay, I'm gonna take y'all in, but only for a couple minutes. He's unconscious now, so he won't hear yuh."

The cubicle doesn't have a regular door, but glass partitions that open and closes on runners, like giant patio doors. As they enter the beeping, hissing, softly lit setting, Mandy goes straight to the head of the bed, Ginny to the opposite side, while Henry hangs back, advancing only a few feet into the room, which is equipped with all kinds of electronic gear (much the same as the stuff at the nurses' station) plus a sibilating respirator and i.v. poles sporting clear-plastic pouches and tubes, and there's a catheter apparatus collecting urine and various wires and electrodes attached to his body. "Bryan Howard ... I love you *so* much," Mandy whispers, leaning close. "I thank God for you."

Ginny, placing her hand on his, also expresses her love.

Henry steps to the foot of the bed. Patting Bryan's leg through the blanket, he says, "Son, we're pulling for you."

Bryan's face, wrapped like a mummy from the top of his nose upward, is almost unrecognizable. A large bluish tube runs from a big plastic thing in his mouth, while a tiny set of clear tubes go up his nose, and it's all secured to his face with tape. Yet he seems peaceful and comfortable under the white blanket.

"Okay, folks," Nurse Johnson announces, as she comes back in.

"Time's up. Y'all can come back in the mornin'." She gives a friendly chuckle. "In fact, I'll still be here I reckon, since I'm workin' a double. I don't normally work mid-shift, but I'm glad I did tonight, so I could get my new patient all set up myself."

After they exit the cubicle, Henry asks the RN a question, "Why's he still on that machine? It must be uncomfortable, if he was pulling at the tubes? I thought his breathing was okay?"

"It is, Mr. Howard, as far as we can tell ... but the respirator is part of Dr. Nadler's standard post-surgery routine—it's just a precaution. I'm sure we'll have him off it soon."

* * *

DPH - FAMILY SUITE E
MAY 12, 1991 — SUNDAY DAYBREAK

Mandy wakes up to a sweet fragrance, not the bluebonnets but old-fashioned, oversweet perfume. Opening her eyes, she finds, to her surprise, an elderly lady knitting on the sofa across the room, the same lady she saw at the Coke machine. "Forgive me, child," the oldster says, smiling at Mandy. "I didn't mean to startle you, but the other rooms are locked until eight, except Suite A, which is rather crowded. Since you were all alone in here, I didn't think you'd mind, and this lamp was already on."

"No problem," Mandy replies groggily, her voice thick from sleep. Rubbing her eyes, she manages a yawny grin then sits up on the couch and stretches.

"And do allow me to apologize," the white-haired lady goes on, "for being so rude last evening, when you were so kind and helpful. I was so disturbed about Lucille I didn't even introduce myself. But we can fix that now. My name is Nora Davis." She extends her bony, veiny, shriveled hand—it's sort of yellowish and dappled with old-age spots, purplish dime-sized spots.

Mandy steps over and shakes it—it feels just as chickenlike as it looks. "I'm Amanda Stevens, but they call me Mandy." Going to the window, she opens the curtain. The hospital grounds look fuzzy gray, as does the cityscape beyond. "D'yuh know what time it is? It's just getting light." (She has a Timex at home, but the band makes her wrist itch).

"Sure, dear; it's 5:35. I got here at five, mind you. My grandson Ricky dropped me off; he handles baggage at the airport and has to be there at six, so I had to come here very early today. Lucy was doing a mite better when I left last night, but she's heavily sedated now, so I can't see her for several hours. This sweater I'm knitting is for Sherry, my great-granddaughter, Ricky's youngest. I have fourteen great-grandchildren and...."

Mandy scarcely hears, her thoughts turning to Bryan: *O God, I*

41

wonder if anything happened to him during the night. And Mom Howard and Henry won't be here until nine. Pangs of hunger tell her she needs to eat, but breakfast can wait.

Grabbing her purse and overnight bag, she hustles into the bathroom where the mirror greets her. "Good gosh, I'm a mess," she declares hushedly, as she pushes down her jeans and panties, plunking down on the toilet. After peeing, she returns to the mirror. She needs a shower, but there is no shower. She settles for a cat-scrub plus an extra dose of deodorant and perfume. Her sleep-mused hair is the worst. *I need my hat to cover this haystack* (her softball cap is in the Howard's Buick). *My bangs are all clumpy, and my ponytail is yucky and limp. And my eyes are puffy.* She considers changing her underwear and socks but decides not to, but she does trade her blue polo for a clean pink one.

After seeing Bryan at one a.m., Ginny Howard suggested they check in at the Holiday Inn—it's a few miles back toward the interstate. But Mandy insisted on staying here. After some discussion Henry and Ginny agreed, so this's how Mandy ended up sleeping alone in Suite E. (Before the Howards left, they and Mandy said good-bye to Spanky and Roy in the visitor's lounge, as the two players finally headed back to Spindle.)

Exiting the bathroom, Mandy slips on her jacket, gives Nora Davis a nod, then heads straight to the ICU. She looks for Nurse Johnson but doesn't see her among the personnel manning the high-tech command post, all of whom seem occupied with their monitoring duties. Mandy, on impulse, bypasses the nurses' station altogether, heading boldly around toward Bryan's cubicle. She sees him through the glass—he looks much the same.

"Pardon me, miss!" comes a military-like voice, stopping Amanda in her tracks. "Where d'you think you're going? Please report over here at once!"

"Uh, uh—well?" Mandy responds abashedly, as she connects the stern voice to an equally stern face. Her cheeks warming, she reports to the oval kiosk as ordered—to a tall, beady-eyed nurse, whose scowl is so pronounced that her eyebrows seem impaled into the bridge of her beaky nose. She has the face of an irate hawk. The name tag says: Hixson.

"So, young lady," Nurse Hixson interrogates, "why are you here alone, at *this* hour?"

"Well uh ... I came to see Bryan Howard," Mandy explains sheepishly, her blush growing hotter. "He's in number three, and I uh ... I was looking for Nurse Johnson?"

"Nurse Johnson is on break—your name please?"

"Amanda Stevens."

"Are you family, immediate family?"

"Well, no ... but yeah, sort of? Jane said I was. I mean, Ms.

Caldwell. But uh ... I'm not uh...." With this fumbling answer, Mandy realizes she has *blown* it.

"And how *old* are you?"

"I'm seventeen, no sixteen actually." Her every word seems to make matters worse. The nurse slips on her glasses, enlarging her beady eyes. "I'll make a note of your request, but *I* can't allow you in."

"But can'tcha at least tell me if he's okay?"

"I'm *sorry*, miss. You're not authorized to even be in here."

"But I *am* family. I'm *clo*ser than family." Her eyes filling, Mandy hurries out of the ICU.

* * *

DPH - FAMILY SUITE E
SUNDAY, MAY 12, 1991 — 6:03 AM

While Nora Davis continues to knit, Mandy surfs the TV: The Weather Channel, Headline News, C-Span, the History Channel, a few Sunday-morning preachers. She said hello upon her return to Suite E, but little else. She made a quick visit to the bathroom where she fought off the tears; she's not going to *weep* over that ICU witch, not after what she's been through, and Bryan and everyone. Nevertheless, she needs to talk, to ventilate: at first she felt guilty and embarrassed for breaking the ICU rules and causing a scene, but it's now hurt and indignation that fire her emotions, a sense of being wronged. It's not fair, being turned away like that. On her way back from the ICU, she stopped at the hostess office in the foyer, in hopes of finding a sympathetic ear, but the door was locked.

"Forgive me for prying, dear," Ms. Davis remarks, "but you seem a mite restless, the way you're switching the television?"

Killing the TV, Mandy joins Ms. Davis, taking a seat on the edge of the sofa. She talks about Bryan, the whole ordeal. The old lady's presence distracts her initially, the bony, desiccated figure, the snowy hair, the shriveled face, the wattled neck—the perfumed ruins of womanhood. But Ms. Davis soon captures the teenager with her eyes— blue, vibrant, warmly responsive eyes, which comfort Mandy, freeing her to get it all out. She speaks with her hands as well as her mouth, and before finishing, she's up pacing like Pastor Ron. She even acts out the injury scenario, as if she's Brady Wilson. She takes an imaginary throw from the outfield then pegs the pretend-ball toward home plate. Finally, she sprawls limply on the carpet, becoming Bryan.

"Now *that's* quite a story," Ms. Davis rasps, gesturing with one of her knitting tools, "much more thrilling than being *old* and on the sidelines." Her eyes narrow, as if recalling a time when she was Mandy's age. "For me and Lucy, it's more or less normal to be dying, but I reckon—" Stopping midsentence, she stuffs her knitting into her

43

big handbag then removes her glasses. "Why don't we go down and have some breakfast, hon? You must be starving? And I'll share my story—well, not all of it, or we'll never get back." She gives a croaky laugh.

* * *

"My daddy helped build this hospital, mind you," the old woman declares as they dig into their eggs and sausage and toast, a basic breakfast for both, though Mandy has homefries too. "He was a bricklayer, and he brought me over to look at it a few times; I was seven that year." She talks and talks, covering everything, personal and public, that has happened in North Texas since 1915, or so it seems to Mandy. Then toward the end of the meal, she says, "My, my, child ... you *were* starving."

"Yep, I can put it away when I'm hungry," the high-schooler laughs, her mouth half full.

As they depart the chilly cafeteria—the AC's going full blast despite the early hour—a warm wave of drowsiness grips Mandy; the few hours of couch-sleep were hardly enough; she rubs her eyes, shakes her head. She has to walk slowly to accommodate Ms. Davis's tottering, cane-assisted pace, but she can't help but like this gruff-voiced great-grandmother, and having someone to talk to until the Howards arrive has occupied her anxious mind. Reaching the Ferguson Wing elevator, they hum back up to ICU visitor's lounge where the doors open on a pitiful scene: a doctor (looks like a doctor) is talking with a distraught woman, while two weeping girls, little girls, cling to her waist. The lounge is otherwise empty. Mandy's pulse quickens, chasing her sleepiness, arousing her fears.

"That was Mrs. Lafayette out there," Ms. Davis tells Mandy, once they're back in the family suite. "Her husband must've died this morning. I've seen her here a few times this week, and I talked with her yesterday, when I was in Suite A. She *said* he'd taken a turn for the worse. He was in a car crash up on I-35, and was doing okay until Thursday when he developed pneumonia."

"It's truly sad," Mandy replies. "Those kids lost their daddy." She sighs, her thoughts going silent: *That could've been me last night, getting the final news on Bryan. Why does God allow it to happen? Yet we all hafta die sometime? But why? I know what the Bible says, but it still seems cruel? Why does—and I still don't know the latest on Bryan. And Dr. Nadler said last night that he wasn't out of the woods.* Her confidence shaken, she can't sit still while waiting for the Howards. After a quick visit to the john, she grabs her jacket and tells Ms. Davis she's going for a walk.

* * *

Mandy strolls behind the Ferguson Wing. A wide sidewalk circles the main complex, and she's halfway around. The sunny morning smells of dew and dandelions. It's just cool enough for her windbreaker, maybe 60°, yet there's no wind to break. The birds seem happy and content as they salute what promises to be another pleasant, late-spring day. But Mandy grows more *dis*contented with every step. "I can't stand this, dang it!" she exclaims in a hushed but angry voice. She purses her lips then sucks the upper one. "I'm going back. No old biddy of a nurse is gonna keep me from seeing my Bryan." She marches the other way, her arms pumping, her ponytail bouncing.

But a familiar voice stops her before she gets far: "Hello there, young lady. How's our ballplayer?" She whips around: it's Dr. Nadler getting out of a sporty-looking car. He's wearing casual weekend clothes, plus a grin for Mandy.

"Dr. Joe," she blurts, using his first name—her defiant state of mind has emboldened her. "Gosh, am I glad to see you. I've been here *all* night, and they won't let me see Bryan, or even let me know how he's doing, and I couldn't find Nurse Johnson, and his mom and dad are at the Holiday Inn."

"Hey, let's go see him together," Nadler says, giving her a pat on the shoulder. "That's why I'm here so early ... to see him, and a couple of other patients." She follows him up a flagstone walkway leading to a restricted entrance. "Actually, I hope to get away to the golf course," the doctor confesses, as he unlocks the door and ushers her inside; he laughs. "That is ... if everything's okay, and I assume it is, since no one tried to contact me."

Mandy, her sense of assurance soaring, can scarcely contain herself, as she follows Dr. Nadler through various hallways and doors then up a narrow stairway. Christ *him*self has appeared to save her, or so it seems. In any case, this wonderful surgeon has taken on godlike status. He escorts her into the ICU, using a private door just a few paces from the nurses' station. Mandy struts by the beady-eyed Nurse Hixson. The nurse, glancing up, gives a surprised grimace, as the vindicated teenager laser-beams her with a try-and-stop-me-now look.

Proceeding to cubicle #3, they meet Nurse Johnson coming out. She gives Mandy a quick but warm greeting, then she says, "Doctor, I reckon this boy's tryin' to wake up again."

Dr. Nadler, telling Mandy to wait outside, goes in with the nurse. The teenager paces excitedly, expectantly. Another guy, a younger guy in hospital duds, soon enters the room. A doctor? A technician? Finally, after five minutes that seem like fifty, Dr. Nadler emerges, while Nurse Johnson and the younger fellow continue to hover around Bryan.

"I must say, Mandy," the surgeon declares, "that boyfriend of yours is showing a lot of spunk." Nadler nods toward the cubicle. "He's lapsed back now, but these stirrings do encourage me. And yet, we mustn't leap to conclusions. His prognosis remains uncertain, though we *do* know he can move his arms, and his lung function is excellent.

That's why I've asked Dan—he's an inhalation therapist—to take Bryan off the respirator, and Nurse Johnson is removing some of the bandaging, so his eyes are no longer covered."

"So uh ... is he gonna wake up for good?" Mandy asks.

"There's no way to know ... but like I say, these episodes *are* positive signs. His cerebral function has apparently survived, or much of it, and the swelling pressure has been alleviated. The normal breathing and strong vitals tell us this, even without seeing good CTs, though he's still scheduled for a series later today. But still, I've known comatose patients who moved and thrashed off and on for years, yet *never* fully revived. I'm hoping for more in his case, but we must *not* jump to conclusions."

"So can I go in now?"

"Yes, by all means. You're welcome to stay with him until his parents arrive. But there's no visitor's chair, let me get you something to sit on." Nadler retrieves, from cubicle #2 (which is unoccupied) a fancy wheelchair. "Here," he chuckles. "This's better than a LA-Z-BOY. It not only reclines, but it also rolls."

* * *

8:25 a.m. Mandy, relaxing back, holds Bryan's hand, having positioned the super-duper wheelchair close to the bed—she holds his right hand, since the left one has the i.v. attached to it. Dr. Nadler's cautious assessment has dampened her enthusiasm, not to mention her lack of sleep, but being close to her dear babe helps her to hope, and cope. Plus, she feels secure in here. Nadler left instructions with Nurse Johnson, *and* Nurse Hixson, that Mandy was to be treated as priority family, that she had special permission to stay with Bryan until the Howards arrived. She even has a pillow now, provided by Nurse Johnson. There's enough high-tech gear in here to launch a space shuttle, or so it seems. There's a window too, but the view—glass, brick, and concrete plus a peek-a-boo slice of sky—is less than spectacular. No biggie: she's quite content to gaze at Bryan. She caresses his hand; she whispers loving words between silent prayers.

Staring at her sweetheart and loving him and loving him, in this awful ICU where people die daily, gives her an ineffable sense of oneness, as though her soul has merged with his, a realm to which only shared calamity could deliver her. This soul-oneness confirms, as much as anything, that her babe is very much alive, and very much the same. The hissing sound has ceased, since the ventilator is off, but the heart thing is still active, and the steady beeping is almost hypnotic.

Now it comes back, the warm sleepy feeling she had right after breakfast. Seconds turn into minutes. She drifts off then awakens with a start, as Nurse Johnson taps her on the arm—no, it's NOT THE NURSE! Mandy bolts out of the chair. It was Bryan who touched her arm? It had to be?

THE SILVER CORD

She kisses him on the cheek then takes his hand. "Oh, dear babe," she urges, "if you hear me, squeeze my fingers. It's me, Mandy." Bryan's thumb twitches then closes, along with his fingers. "Yes!" Mandy exclaims, feeling his grasp. "It's okay, babe. You're okay now."

He grimaces, trying to talk: "Mmm ... umm ... Mand ... dy?" His eyes blink open and quickly focus, on her—those *won*derful green eyes. He grimaces again, but this time it turns into a little grin, just enough to show his dimples. "We won the game, right? I got in under the tag?"

"Oh yes!" she exults, weeping happily, as she grasps his hand with both of hers. "We won. We won. Thank *God*, we won!"

THE SILVER CORD

CHAPTER FIVE

THE HOWARD FARM
SATURDAY, JUNE 1, 1991 — MIDAFTERNOON

Bryan Howard grooms Millie in the barn, her tail swishing, her back rippling in response to the comb. As he smoothes out her mane, she whinnies, tossing her head. The chestnut mare seems glad to have him home, and Bryan feels *more* than glad to be back in this old barn with its beams and lofts and cobwebby corners, not to mention the very unhospital-like aromas of hay and horseflesh and manure, all of which reminds him of his grandfather. He halfway expects to turn around and find Gramps standing there in his muddy overalls and tattered Texaco cap, a stubby cigar in his mouth. He swears for a moment he can smell one of those cheap stogies. His granddad seems even more real because of what Bryan experienced at the ballpark the day he got hurt, a secret he's shared with no one. But he plans to share it this very afternoon, which leads to the *biggest* reason for his gladness of heart: Mandy is due anytime now.

After fourteen days at Dallas Presbyterian, Bryan returned home in time to make up his finals and graduate with his class (ranking third with a 3.92 GPA). He's very much recovered, remarkably so, with no apparent disability except for blurred vision in his left eye, which seems better each day. And he looks as good as ever, as long as he's wearing his Tiger cap: it hides everything except the reddish scar tissue at his left temple. Without the hat he still looks like a skinhead rowdy, especially with the zipperlike surgical seams. But his hair *is* growing— it's about the length of a short crewcut, which is better than the shaved, cue-ball dome he saw in the mirror after they removed the bandages. He also has a terrycloth headband, the kind tennis players wear, for when he can't wear the baseball cap, like at graduation last night. He can't ride Millie as yet, nor can he play summer baseball or do his usual hot-season work around the farm such as haying and tree-cutting. He has to take it easy for the next two months, and the best thing about that is: Amanda Fay Stevens. They'll have *much* time together, now that summer vacation has arrived. The hectic pace *this* week, the last week of school, has allowed them only a few minutes here and there since he got home Monday evening. And last night everything was stiff and formal and rushed, including the "Class of 91" graduation ball. Mandy looked stunning in her turquoise gown, her hair feathered out, but she had to be at work at six this morning, so they only made a cameo appearance at the dance. They rarely go to parties anyway, much preferring the more-relaxed times when they can be themselves, like today.

He hears her now, the crunch and pop of tires on gravel—it gives him butterflies. *This's gonna be WAY better than any graduation hoopla,* he exults to himself. He steps around Millie to confirm. Yes, he can see the green Escort through the open barn door. Mandy gets out. She's still in her waitress uniform, a blue-denim skirt with crossed suspenders over a white shirt, but minus the checked apron that says Goddard's on it. She saunters up the walkway headed for the front door. Bryan loves how she moves, her slouchy, loose, jock-tomboy gait, her head bobbing with each pace—she's not rigid and falsely postured, like some of the junior and senior gals, who've turned into prima donnas, as they try to act collegiate and socially proper.

Chuckling boyishly, he hides just inside the barn door. "Hey, Bryan, Mandy's here!" Virginia Howard hollers a minute later, from the kitchen. He spies his sweetheart through a crack in the plank siding, as she thumps down the back-porch steps and jogs out to find him. She has ditched the new Reeboks in favor of her old bum-around sneakers, with no socks, and her softball cap is turned around, the bill canted cutely back over her ponytail, a sure sign she's in a frisky, buoyant, summerlike mood.

As she enters the barn, he jumps out and grabs her amid girlish shrieks of delight. He kisses her. She squirms and giggles, but quickly gets into it, kissing him back so fervently that his legs quiver. Then she breaks free, her hat flying one way, she the other. She playfully eludes him, until he catches her near the loft ladder. "Boy howdy, you big jock," she pants, as he holds onto her. "Y'sure don't waste any time kissing hello, d'yuh?"

"Well whaddabout you, pretty lady?" he flirts, as he pulls her closer, wrapping his arms about her. "That hello you gave *me* set off shivers and shakes all the way down to my toes." He laughs then tickles her— she squeals happily, twisting free.

"And you're not supposed to be running and chasing, mister," she chortles. "I'm gonna tell Dr. Joe."

Ten minutes later, they're ambling hand-in-hand along a weedy, two-rut tractor trail which skirts the hayfields. It's a breezy, gorgeous, upper-70s afternoon, with lots of fair-weather cumulus, quite comfortable compared to yesterday when the temp soared to 97°. A storm rumbled through early this morning chasing the hazy heat and humidity, and it has left in its wake a spectacular blue sky, a pure, vivid, liquid blue, stunning even in winter, and most rare during the warm half of the year. The green, fast-growing alfalfa gives the air that rich, June-on-the-farm fragrance. The familiar smell of the hayfields, as with the barn, reassures Bryan, reminding him that he's *indeed* home; he's not still at the hospital imagining this Saturday stroll with his precious Mandy. He unbuttons his shirt, an old plaid thing, letting the breeze in. He likewise wears raggedy jeans plus his old running shoes, which are now gray and timeworn, the left one tongueless.

"So, pretty lady, how'd it go at the diner today?" he inquires.

"All right, I reckon. The fishing crowd showed up early, like seven o'clock; that storm musta chased 'em off the lake. Plus, we had a few smart-ass truckers—that's nothing new. But most of the regular customers are friendly and easy to deal with. And Uncle Billy and Aunt Marge are tolerable. At least, I can think of worse bosses to work for ... but it's not hard to tell that Mama and Marge are sisters. My tip totals are better ... now that I'm going in at six a.m—my summer routine. But these nine-hour Saturdays are a real grind, especially since I'll be working Monday and Wednesday too." She titters. "And I smell like *gosh*dang grease. I coulda gone by the house and taken a shower and put on some jeans, but that can be risky, since Mama has a habit of reclaiming her car anytime it's in the driveway." She titters again, a snorty laugh half through her nose. "I did throw my old sneakers into the car 'fore I left this morning, but this skirt's no good for hiking. The bugs'll be after me for sure."

They're headed for Bryan's "special" place, the big oak tree which commands the knobby high ground on the eastern, more wooded side of the property. The two-hundred-acre farm is by no means large, as Texas farms go, but neither is it small, though to call it a "farm" is more habit than fact, since hay is their only crop, besides the family vegetable garden back near the house.

"You said once that Millie's the same age as me?" Mandy remarks, switching the subject. Bryan finished grooming the mare before they left the barn. "That means she's nearly seventeen?"

"Not quite. We got her when I was five—she was three then, so she'll be sixteen in October. But she *is* getting up there."

"How long do horses live?"

"Twenty-five years I reckon, give or take, but there's a 33-year-old stallion down on the Palmer farm, a retired show-horse named Old Buck. Gramps took me to see him perform at the rodeo when I was little ... at the coliseum up in Sulphur Springs."

"So Millie's not *su*per old?" Mandy asks—her tone suggests that death concerns, perhaps lingering from the whole hospital ordeal, are pecking away at her cheerful frame of mind.

"Nawh, she'll be around for a good while yet," he replies, then he abruptly shifts: "Guess who came by this morning?"

"Can I have a hint?"

"Well, it was really two people, and they're related, and it has to do with my injury."

"Related? Uh, uh—I don't have the slightest idea. I give up."

He dimples and snorts. "Goshdang ... you'd never make it on *Jeopardy*—remember Dr. Wilson? George Wilson?"

"Sure ... I could never forget him. But you said *two* people? You tricked me." She laughs and gives him a playful bump with her shoulder. "So don't talk about making it on *Jeopardy*, you big jock, until you learn how to ask the ques—"

"But it *was* two people. Brady came too—his son."

The conversation ceases while they help each other through a barbed-wire fence. By crossing here, they can take a shortcut through a grove of pine trees. Bryan goes first then holds the strands open for Mandy. He can't help but notice her glossy-ripe, honey-colored thighs, as she bunches her skirt to keep it from getting caught on the rusty barbs. *O God, this summer's gonna be a test,* he declares to himself, as a hot tingling commences between his legs. She makes that nibbling, fidgety move with her mouth, like she does, then gives him a flirtatious side-glance—as if she knows his thoughts. Love, heat, brimming eros— it's scary yet thrilling, like *noth*ing else.

"So Doc Wilson was *act*ually here today?" Mandy says, as they follow a footpath into the woods, hand-in-hand as before.

"Yeah, they were nearby anyway, looking at some land, so they came by to check on me. We kept it light ... mainly ... but I did thank him, and they wished me good luck at Baylor."

"I like Dr. Joe the best. He got me back into see yuh, after that witchy nurse kicked me out—y'know, I toldjuh about it. But I also like Dr. Wilson, and I did meet Brady ... at the ballpark."

Bryan makes a throaty *hummmph* sound. "It sure was ironic, Brady knocking me out and his dad saving my life."

"You got that right," Mandy agrees, her tone sobering. "It's a *mir*acle he was there, like an angel from Heaven. He knew what to do, and he did it quick—oh, babe, I hate to think about it."

He doesn't reply, lest he stir up more painful memories. They're going uphill now, not steeply, but steadily. There's no sound save for the wind sighing through the conifers, and even that is softened, soaked up by the carpet of old needles. Unlike the thick, dark woods down in the hollow, down along Butler Creek, this pine grove is relatively open, with lots of sun making it through. The splotches of sunshine grapple with the shadows, advancing, ebbing, doing a little waltz, keeping time with the swaying branches above. *Maybe I should tell her my secret now,* Bryan says to himself, *so she won't think of that day as totally horrible?* But he elects to wait, since they're coming out of the pines into a hillside meadow. It's only a little farther, maybe a hundred yards; he can see the giant, solitary oak ahead, standing like a leafy monument at the top of the hill.

As they continue up the path, which meanders back and forth, Mandy snickers all of a sudden. "What's so funny," he inquires—he's relieved to hear her laugh.

"Oh, I was just thinking about Dr. Wilson."

"What about him?"

"He reminds me of Gus Witherspoon."

"Who?"

"Y'know, babe, that funny guy on *Our House*, on TV, the old

51

lovable grouch. I don't think it's on anymore, but we used to wa— Wilfred Brimley; that's his real name. And Doc Wilson acts grumpy and bothered too, but he's really sweet—like Gus."

"Yeah, pretty lady, come to think of it, he *does* look like Wilfred Brimley, especially the mustache. They even have the same rough way of talking. I never watched *Our House* much, but I've seen him in a few movies ... but Brady doesn't look anything like that. It's amazing—he's lanky and graceful, while his dad is built like a tree stump. Brady must take after his mother's side of the family?"

"Or maybe the *milk*man?" Mandy quips. This sets off a fit of hilarity, forcing them to stop and catch their breath.

"That joke's *way* out of date," Bryan kids her. "Even Gramps used to tell it." The laughing gives way to quietness.

Their emotions limbered, they can't help but melt into each other's arms. After a few rounds of kissing and smooching and necking, during which they both lose their caps, Mandy clings to him tightly, burying her head into his shoulder. "Oh, babe," she coos softly, "I'm *so* thankful to have you back." Bryan caresses her head, but doesn't say anything. "During the worst part," she goes on, "I figured we'd never take any more walks like this. And we had just made our wonderful plans, right here on this hill." She shifts her face more to the side, so she can press even tighter to his bosom. "I thought maybe the Lord was chastising me for loving you too much, and being so excited about our future together, and keeping it a secret from my mom, and for setting my affections on this life too much."

"No, no, precious," he assures. "Even if I hadn't come out of it, that wouldn't have been the reason. God would never—at least, not the Jesus I look to." He pats her gently on the back.

"I know, I know. I can see now how my head was messed up. I've never liked to think of God as a mean judge who allows bad things ... to punish us, even if some preachers say it. But when Doc Wilson said you might die, or never wake up, I jumped to the worst, most horrible conclusions. I convinced myself that God wanted you up in Heaven, and I had to let go. It was the most *terrible* feeling I ever had. But I was wrong ... *so* wrong."

A gust of wind swirls down around them, as if the Lord is confirming these convictions. Holding her tight, Bryan realizes more than ever that she's the linchpin holding his world together, a pin more vital than the air he breathes. He kisses her head, her golden hair— then all at once she gives a whoop of delight and runs ahead of him up the path.

"I *love* coming here!" she exults girlishly. She throws her arms into the air, as though signaling a touchdown. He watches in lovestruck wonder. Her spontaneity thrills him, awes him. After going a little farther, she stops and does a quick little be-bop routine, shuffling on one foot, then the other, then she dashes back to him. "C'mon, mister, we don't have all day."

Grabbing her hat, and him, she leads the way, and they soon reach the crest of the hill, where the mammoth, many-limbed oak awaits them like an old friend. A million leaves rustle in the breeze, flashing their lighter-toned undersides then going dark green again. A few of the enormous limbs hang low making the tree fun and easy to climb. The wind-tossed crown seems more wide than tall, yet the upper branches stretch over sixty feet into the air. Bryan and Mandy assume their favorite position at the foot of the tree. He sits betwixt two roots with his back against the massive, four-foot trunk. His knees spread, he holds her from behind, as she leans back into him, her cap on her lap, her legs stretched out amid the grass and twigs and leaves, last year's leaves, now brown and matted and damply rotting. Dabs of windblown sunshine jitterbug around them and on them. The shaggy oak shades the top of the hill like a circus tent, but it's a tent with holes in it. Facing east, toward Ruby Pond, they don't talk for a spell, a blissful interlude.

The clouds resemble tattered gobs of cotton as they drift over the distant fields and woods and hollows. This old tree marks the highest point on the farm, and they can see half of Hollis County and part of Crockett Lake. The hill is actually the nose of a ridgeline that pokes onto the Howard property from the north, and it's not that high; they've only climbed a hundred feet since leaving the barnyard. But in Texas you don't have to be high up to see a *long* way, especially with the downslope in front of them (down to Ruby Pond), and the view is all the more enchanting and vast today, without the haze. The rolling landscape has that verdant, flourishing, yellow-green look which comes after a good rain—but not for long: summer will soon scorch this scene, paling the green hues while burning in browns and tans (Bryan recalls a year, maybe two, when it was cloudy and wet all summer, and the hay rotted in the fields, and everything smelled of mildew, but such seasons are rare). The heat really cranks up in July and August, yet for now the pond laps at the spillway, and the meadowgrass is thick and lush and dusted with wildflowers. Milkweed and daisies nod in the breeze above the dandelions and chickweed and wild clover—yellow, white, pinkish blooms, all of which exude zesty fragrances, not to speak of the heavy-sweet aroma of the oak itself. Down by the small lake, the cottonwoods and willows look equally lush, as does the crescent of junglelike growth on the other side of the water.

"My grandfather loved this old tree," Bryan says, breaking the silence—he's ready to share his secret, but he'd rather ease into it, and Gramps is a good lead-in. "He came up here to think and get away from it all. And he brought me with him a lotta times, like I toldjuh. We'd fish for bass and bluegill in the pond, then come up here afterward. This oak is almost holy to me."

"I know, babe," she replies, speaking away, toward the puffy clouds. She twirls her softball cap on her finger. "I could tell this spot was special to you, even that first time you brought me up here last December. I wish I'd met your grandfather. He sounds like a character, like eccentric but *good*."

"He was, believe me, and he was more like a best friend than a relative. I'm named after him, my middle name, but that's not the reason. He watched over me a lot, especially after my mom started working at Sampson's. I tagged along, while he took care of the farm. I'd ride on the back of his tractor, or on his lap so I could help steer. He even let me drive it by myself, once I got big enough to reach the footpedals; we still use that tractor, the old International parked by the woodshed. And I always hung close to him during the haying and the corn harvest. Those were *big* jobs that required everybody, like Dad and Billy Ray Campbell, and Mom too. And when the watermelons got ripe, these big trucks came to haul them away. I even helped some, but I was little then, and the watermelons were heavy as all heck." Bryan chuckles. "But for the routine chores it was just Gramps and me. He taught me how to milk Libby, our dairy cow, and we fed the chickens and the steers, and Millie and Sadie; we had two mares for a while, and we kept about ten Herefords. I helped him clean out the stalls and the chicken house—those chores *stank* like you wouldn't believe, especially since I was small and *right* down in it." Bryan gives a quick laugh. "But I liked helping him, and we fixed fences and cleared brush and split firewood and hauled hay, plus a hundred other things. And he had a special pet name for me. He called me 'Buddy.' But just him—no one else ever did."

Mandy tosses the blue-and-white hat onto the grass, which is weedy and thin near the tree because of the roots. Picking up a twig, she runs it over Bryan's knee, which pokes nakedly through a rip in his jeans. "It makes sense that you bonded with Gramps ... since y'don't have any brothers or sisters."

"That did throw us together a lot," he agrees—the twig feels good on his leg, and quite sensual, because *she's* doing it. "Many days when I got home from school, it was just me and him and Buster, my dog. I'd get off the school bus, and Gramps would be there waiting for me, like next to the mail box. Sometimes, he'd have a can of worms and two cane poles, and we'd hoof it right to the pond. He looked a bit like my dad, but he wasn't so broad in the shoulders, and he was shorter by a couple inches. Dad and I are built much the same, but Gramps was slimmer, like lean but strong, and his face had that creased, leathery look that farmers get from the wind and sun. He loved baseball, and he helped me learn the game, the old-fashioned way. He gave me hours of batting practice. Gosh, I'd knock balls everywhere, but he didn't mind. We'd just go pick 'em up, and he'd start pitching again." Bryan gives a nostalgic sigh. "One day, we were headed back to the house after fishing, and storm clouds were rolling in, and it turned *pitch* black. Thunder and lightning boomed all around. But Gramps held my hand tight, then he looked me in the eye, and said, 'It's okay.' That was all I needed to hear."

Mandy shifts a trifle. He loves the warm give of her midriff as he embraces her from behind. "Yet even if I wasn't an only child," he goes on, "I think we woulda been tight. The things he said rang true to me. He loved working this land, and if farming was still viable, I reckon I might stay right here and do what he did." Bryan sighs again, this time resignedly. "But all the family farms are going under. Dad tried to carry on after Gramps died, but it was too much, and he didn't dare give up his day job at the feed store. So we got rid of all the chickens and livestock, except Millie, and we cut *way* back on the farming. We don't grow any cash crops now, aside from hay, but even that's a lot of work, especially with that ancient baler ... and then there's the general upkeep of the property. Of course, that's how I've made most of my money, working around here for my dad."

"Didn't you work at the feed store too?"

"Yeah, from time to time, especially when they had big shipments coming in. But they've practically eliminated their day-labor budget." Bryan stretches then resumes his cozy hold on Mandy. "I'm not sure what Dad's gonna do, now that I'm going off to college. Even if he gives up the hay, the routine work around here is a big job. I reckon he'll be hiring Billy Ray a lot more. But Gramps saw it coming. Even when I was seven, and we were still producing corn and watermelons and soybeans, he said these farms would lose out, because the huge corporations were taking over agriculture. He would shake his head and get a faraway look in his eyes. He had kind gray eyes, but they had a sad yearning in them, because of his impossible dreams. 'No man can serve two masters,' he'd say. 'You can't love your fellow man and buy him off at the same time.' He quoted Jesus a lot, not in a religious way, but in a simple, common sense sort of way, and he'd change the words to fit our times. It bothered him to see how big money was exploiting the little guy, and taking his land and heritage. I learned so much from Gramps, things you'd never learn in school, or even at church. I felt closer to him than to anyone, even my parents— at least, until I met you, pretty lady." Bryan laughs and chucks the side of her chin. "But I'm not sure everyone liked him as much as I did."

"Whaddeyuh mean?"

"Well, he was sort of a loner, ever since Grandma Ruby died. She died of breast cancer before I was born. And Mom says he was never the same afterward. But I like how he was. Gramps wasn't a recluse or anything—he did go to church with us, and he got along with Dad and Mom for the most part, and he had a few friends, like Red Bakerliss who came over to play dominoes, but he *never* kissed up to people to gain their favor. And he—"

"That's how my daddy was," Mandy interjects. "My *real* dad.

Mama says he was stiff-necked. Y'know, I toldjuh. And when she's on my case, she says I take after him."

"I'll agree to *that*," Bryan chortles. She laughs as well, giving him a playful slap on the thigh, then she returns to his knee, drawing little circles with the twig. "But Gramps didn't worry about what people thought about him. He wore old-fashioned overalls, and he usually had gray stubble on his chin, except on Sunday—he shaved on Sunday—and most days he smelled like cigars and barnyard manure, from his boots. And he said what was on his mind, and that makes a person less than popular with the snooty, go-getter crowd."

"No *kid*ding," Mandy agrees. "It's like that at school, and at church." She sweeps an insect off her calf, perhaps a chigger or a sand flea. The crawly bugs have discovered that she's wearing a skirt. But the wind keeps the gnats and mosquitoes away.

"My dad is sorta like Gramps," Bryan elaborates. "He doesn't kowtow to people either, but Dad's more diplomatic. In fact, he doesn't talk at all, while Gramps boldly declared his opinions, not that he blurted everything to everybody, but when it was *time* to speak out, he didn't hold back. I'm more like Dad I reckon. It's like I've learned to bite my tongue, to keep things cool ... but I wish I was more like Gramps—at least, I wish I wasn't so self-conscious about what people think."

"It's harder when you're young. We hafta deal with our peers every day, and we're always competing and getting graded and judged, like when I'm around the uppity girls at school, the stuck-up types—they make me bashful about expressing myself."

"I do the same with the guys on the team, except Spanky—and we don't talk as much as we once did."

"That's why I like Wendy. I trust her ... and she doesn't bow down to peer pressure."

"I reckon Gramps faced the same bullshit in his younger days, but by the time I came along, he showed no sign of being bashful about his convictions—*that's* for sure." Bryan gives a nasal titter. "He despised phoniness and waffling more than *any*thing. That's why he loved animals. He'd say, 'Now, Buddy, our animal friends never put on false airs like humans do. Even the snakes and weasels are *way* ahead of us when it comes to being genuine.' He said we'd be a lot better off if we behaved more like animals."

"I sure haven't heard any adult say *that*," Mandy quips—she scrawls on Bryan's thigh, as if signing her autograph with the twig. "Not at my house anyhow."

More laughing. "I guess Gramps *did* raise a few eyebrows."

"So why'd he call you 'Buddy'?"

"I never knew. He just did ... and it made me feel special."

Tossing the twig, she lifts her knees; her skirt falls back, exposing her thighs. Bryan, spellbound, gathers her flesh with his eyes, as when they slipped through the barbed wire. He'd *love* to reach bet*ween* these wondrous legs, to fondle her, to check out that secret passage that makes her a girl, a female, a woman. Yet wanting is one thing, doing is another. He's never touched her down there, save in his solitary fantasies, and she quickly relieves the tension, as she pushes the denim skirt up then leans forward, hugging her uplifted knees. "Oh yeah," she purrs, as he massages her back and shoulders, an okay, non-petting way of touching.

"I like what your grandfather said about animals," she offers a minute later. The back-rub has turned her voice cozy and thick, the husky, lazy, sensual tones coming to the surface. "And it's true: like Toby, our tomcat—he never pretends to be something that he isn't. If he's hungry, he'll bug me and Gretchen ... until one of us gets up and gives him some Friskies." Bryan gives her a little love-pat, ending the massage. She leans back and he wraps his arms about her waist, as before. "I mean ... Toby never tries to win brownie points by pretending to be contented if he isn't, like people do—it's like we're expected to paste on a happy smile every morning no matter what, and some people are *really* good at it, like Charlie my stepdad, or the church gang Mama hangs out with."

"Yeah, I like Toby," Bryan replies, chuckling, "the way he struts around, and demands royal treatment. He *cer*tainly has no problem with self-esteem." More laughing, both of them. "But Snowball, our old female cat, is the same. When she wants out, she mews and scratches and carries on, and refuses to take no for an answer, yet when she wants a lap to curl up on, she comes for it just as boldly. And that's what Gramps was getting at. We used to talk about it right here at this tree, about how the four-legged creatures are not *less* than us; their *pers*onalities are just as alive and sensitive as ours, yet they don't lie and spin and hype, like humans do. Gramps said you can always read a person's heart by the way they treat pets and livestock and wildlife. And that's why he never killed for sport. He wasn't against eating meat or anything, but he saw it as a sacred thing, the taking of animals for food; y'know, like the Indians did. When we went fishing, he always told me: if you catch anything, you have to eat it or *let* it go. And he said the same thing about hunting, though I never saw him shoot anything except tin cans down at the watermelon patch. He taught me to shoot his .22 Marlin, and we popped off bottles and cans, but I never shot an animal. I did kill a robin once, with my BB gun when I was in second grade. It was a bad, bad feeling, the *worst*, to see that poor bird lying there lifeless, all because of me, and I did it just for fun—but *nev*er again."

Mandy gives him a peck on the cheek. "That's a sad story, but sweet too. I heard it before ... from Mom Howard."

"Yeah, I told her right away, but not Gramps. I was ashamed to tell him about that robin ... though I did eventually. And when I did, I couldn't help but cry. But he just took me on his knee and said it was all part of growing up ... that God uses hard lessons to teach us about love. He always told me the truth ... but he never put me down." Bryan gazes into the distance, the clouds going blurry. "Then one day, I came home, and Gramps wasn't there by the mail box. And there were strange cars at the house. It was November, and the wind was raw, and he was gone—that quick, from a stroke." Bryan pauses to collect himself.

After the tender moment has sunk in, he proceeds: "Now Gramps accepted most Christian beliefs, especially the words of Jesus, but he didn't care much for the way churches operate or the way they pushed for money, or the way they come up with certain interpretations, especially the one about animals not having souls, so they can't go to Heaven. That was *one* thing that got him going, and he'd declare, even as we left the church, that his animal friends were more godly and innocent and loving and honest than any preacher or pewsitter, and if *they* aren't allowed into Glory, then he'd rather go where *they* go."

They share a laugh, then Mandy says, "You're more like your grandfather than you realize, Bryan Howard—but I'm *glad* you are." She gives him another peck, on the chin. "And you always talk about him when we come up here to this tree. But I must admit, I've never heard you talk about him *this* much."

"Well, I think I saw him recently."

"You what?" she asks incredulously, as she shifts around to face him. "You mean like a ghost?"

"Sorta, but not like we usually think of ghosts." He pauses to garner his thoughts. She scoots around and plops down in the grass to his left, sitting Indian-style, her legs crossed under her skirt. "Remember, Mandy, how I toldjuh that I've had floating dreams? Like paranormal trips?"

"Yeah, you told me in the hayloft, back in March. You said you float out of your body and travel around ... but you weren't sure if they were regular dreams or what ... and in one of them you went to your friend's house, and he had your baseball glove—he stole it at practice. That was the most way-out part."

"It *is* way out. In fact, it sounds downright *loony*. That's why I waited a long time before I mentioned it to you. It's happened about fifteen times, or maybe twenty, since I was four; that was the first time—I was sick with a fever. The first few times, I just floated around inside the house, but then I learned how to go outside, like passing through the walls or roof, which was scary at first but way more exciting. You're the only one I've ever told except for Gramps ... and my mom and dad, but with them I mostly emphasized the 'dream' aspect of it."

"But they *could* be regular dreams ... didn't you say?"

"Yeah, but I said it mainly so you wouldn't take off running."

They both laugh. "Truth is, I feel pretty dadgum sure that I do come out of my body somehow. At least, it's very different than a regular dream, like *way* more real." Removing his baseball cap, he lightly fingers the scar at his hairline—it itches a trifle. "I've done a lot of reading on soul-travel, and hardly anyone takes it seriously except psychics and mystics, and druggies. The few authentic researchers who've dared to investigate it have lost their credibility among their peers. You sure won't hear about it in Denham's classes or at college, and it doesn't fit into most people's beliefs, especially here in the Bible Belt. So I've always had to wrestle with this, from Sunday school on." He replaces the cap. "I believe strongly in Jesus. I mean ... his integrity and the way he describes God as loving and all, but my out-of-body experiences, or OBEs as I call them, have forced me to keep an open mind, especially when it comes to doctrines dealing with the nature of reality, and the same goes for my classes at school. Now I can't rule out the regular-dream explanation—doubts come and go ... but like I say, I feel pretty *dadgum* sure."

"Like when you caught your friend with you missing glove?"

"That *was* awesome. I was ten, and I flew to Jeff Burton's house on Morgan Street, and I saw him tossing a ball and catching it with *my* glove. Some friend he was. I suspected him all along, and the OBE confirmed it. But even that doesn't prove my OBEs are real."

"Why not? And how does this relate to your grandfather?"

"Forgive me, I *am* dragging this out. I just needed to give yuh some background before I get to the Gramps thing. But anyway, the Jeff Burton OBE didn't prove itself beyond doubt, because the next time we had little-league practice, I found the glove in the ball bag. It coulda been in with the balls all along, or maybe Jeff put it there, since he always rode to practice with Coach Harris. I confronted Jeff, and he got mad as hell ... like ready to fight. He said he knew nothing about it, yet after that he always looked at me funny, like a cocky grin, like he'd pulled something over on me. But he never liked me anyhow, so it's hard to be sure. Then he moved to Tyler the next winter, so I never saw him after fifth grade." Bryan sighs. "In any case, I'm still pretty darn sure about my OBEs ... especially *now* ... after what happened at the ballpark that day I got hit in the head."

"Whaddeyuh mean, babe?" she asks, her blue eyes growing large. She gestures inquiringly, an eager pulling of the air.

Bryan adjusts the bill of his baseball cap. He replies upward, as if addressing the oak leaves—he speaks slowly and deliberately, his timbre a trifle lower than usual: "Well, something amazing happened to me when I slid into home with the winning run. I haven't told anyone, but I hafta tell *you*. I was gonna share it with you the day you and Mom brought my birthday cake to the hospital, but then I decided it would be better if I waited until we were up here at the oak tree." He gives a murmur, then sucks a long breath. "Now this's even *more* far out ... like twilight zone." He returns his attention to Mandy, to check her reaction.

"So *tell* me," she urges, all agog with wonder.

"It's hard to believe, but when I slid into home, it's like time jumped ahead, and the next thing I knew ... I was floating toward the pitcher's mound." He shimmies his hand to indicate. "It was like an OBE ... except I had no control." He speaks a bit faster, resuming his normal pace, and pitch. "I can usually go this way or that by concentrating, but this time I couldn't. I saw Doc Wilson working on some Spindle player, but I never imagined it was me, because I was feeling no pain at all. In fact, I was feeling downright blissful. And I saw you and Wendy Lewis standing with my parents, and—"

"*Ho*ly shit!" Mandy exclaims—she uncrosses her legs then goes up on her knees. "Pardon my language, but this blows me away— *wow!* I'm uh, I uh ... I mean don't stop. Tell me the rest." She flails her hands and arms, as if fanning away gnats.

"Well, I hovered near the mound, then I saw the #12 on the uniform. That's when I realized it was *me*, lying there. And that launched me like a rocket." He thrusts his arm into the air. "I went higher and higher, like headed for orbit, then all of a sudden I was zooming through a dark tunnel towards a light, and the blissful feeling got bigger and stronger, till it was beyond anything on earth. It was like awesome and mind-blowing, the love and acceptance coming from the light, which was somehow personal, like God or Christ, and this God-light spoke to me, not out loud but inside me, so I knew everything was good and perfect."

Mandy hops to her feet. "Go on, babe. I can't sit still."

"As I approached the end of the tunnel, I was suddenly three years old again, and Mom was playing with me behind the house, and making me laugh; it was a hot summer day, and she'd chase me, and I'd run through the lawn sprinkler. And then I was in first grade feeling homesick, then I was romping with Buster, and riding Millie bareback, and helping Gramps on the farm. Then came high school and baseball, and you, pretty lady ... like everything, right up to that climactic slide at home plate, and none of it seemed rushed, and yet it couldn't have taken more than a few seconds. Then I flew out of the tunnel into another dimension where the 'being of light' surrounded me like a super-bright cloud, like fog, and the sense of love and joy was so strong I coulda stayed there forever, no problem." He spreads his hands expansively. "Then different colors began to flash within the fog, blue, green, then red like crimson, then it parted, the cloud ... and I glided over green fields and—"

"It's like yuh went to Heaven," Mandy declares. "The *real* Heaven. This's so weird—it's enough to make me think *I'm* dreaming." She picks up her softball cap and wades into the deeper meadowgrass, just far enough to get out of the shade into the sunshine. "Wow ... like

THE SILVER CORD

super wow! We always talk about Christ and Heaven, my whole life, but when it actually happens, it uh, it uh—well, I gotta let this sink in." She sweeps the air with her cap, as though signaling God that she needs help in digesting all this. "I'm sorry, babe. I cut you off, right in the good part."

"No biggie," Bryan replies amid a laugh. "This's not exactly *rou*tine news." He speaks louder, projecting his voice. "But like I was saying, I glided over green pastures and wooded hills. The green color was super vivid and awesome, like rich and deep and breathtaking. *All* the colors were—it was like my eyes were a thousand times more sensitive." He pauses, as Mandy, facing away, cants her hips, slouching from one leg to the other. Her sense of wonder seems to be turning into bewilderment. She puts on the cap, she takes it off, she wags her ponytail. Her sunbathed hair gleams like spun glass.

Pangs of concern—he can't finish this from a distance. Springing to his feet, he hustles to his sweetheart; he hugs her from behind. "Everything was magnificent," he continues, now speaking hushedly, "and wondrous and beautiful. Yet the landscape was somehow familiar, and I soon realized why ... as I approached this very hill we're on right now. I saw the pine grove and the meadow, and the oak tree. Then all at once I was hovering, no longer moving, and I was low near the ground, like five feet above the grass near the foot of the hill ... back where the footpath first comes out of the pine grove. So the oak was above me in the distance, and I saw someone standing under it, a *lone* silhouette against the sky. I knew immediately it was Gramps, though I never got close enough to see his face. The moment I saw him, everything started receding, like a video playing in reverse. Yet I heard him speaking to me; he said, 'Buddy, it's not your time yet, but I *love* you, and I'll be here waiting for you.' It's not like he shouted or anything, or even that I heard anything, but it was inside me again, tender word-thoughts. Then I was suddenly sucked back through the tunnel, and the next thing I saw was the elevator at the hospital; I was in an elevator, and I tried to get loose from the tubes and all."

Giving no reply, Mandy turns around inside his embrace, nestling close. He caresses her head. The sun feels good, and the breeze, as it ripples through the high grass. A black-and-yellow butterfly, riding the updrafts and eddies, flits from one blossom to another, while down the hill a pair of cawing crows chase each over the pond. *O Lord,* he prays silently, as he gazes skyward, *help her handle this.* Above the cumulus, jet trails now crisscross the wild blue yonder, but the azure hue remains just as dazzling.

"You mean, the whole time we were crying and praying and watching them *shock* you with electricity," she responds at last, "you were up there behind us, just *float*ing around and feeling blissful?" She laughs, relieving him—his prayer is answered.

"Yeah, I reckon so—but I was *try*ing to get your attention."

"Well, you big jock, you," she sports, her tone now frolicsome. "I should *tick*le you for that." Amid a burst of giggles she goes after his naked ribs, taking advantage of the unbuttoned shirt. He tries to escape, but she tackles him. "I'm gonna getcha good!" she gushes giddily, as they roll and wrestle in the grass. She finally clambers up onto him, straddling his waist as he lies laughing on his back. Giving her goofy little-girl grin, she beams and blushes, her teeth showing unabashedly (when happy, she has an adorable, blushing, starry-eyed way of smiling that's unbound and childlike). She resumes the attack, working both sides of his rippled, rock-hard stomach. He tries to tickle her back, but he's laughing too hard to gain the upper hand, so he resigns, allowing her to pin his arms to the ground. "I *like* your hair short," she chortles a moment later. He lost his hat while they were rolling around. "It's cute and fuzzy, like you're a little kid again."

"Well, being cute and *fuzz*y is hardly a fashion statement," he quips, dimpling, "unless you're a cartoon character. Especially when you have surgical scars, like Frankenstein."

"No way, babe. I can hardly see 'em anymore, except by your ear. And that just adds character to your good looks."

"C'mon, pretty lady ... you're crazy, and y'know it."

"Yeah, crazy over *you*."

They laugh some more, then she stills. She fidgets her lips like she does: pursing, folding, biting the upper one. She's busy admiring his brawny abs, or so it seems (he's lost *some* muscle tone since the injury but not much). She looks so eager and fetching, her cupid mouth, her big blue eyes, her disheveled bangs, her freckled nose, her baby-soft cheeks. Venturing inside his open shirt, she massages his chest and shoulders. Her touch entrances him, numbing his head while charging his flesh. She adjusts her straddling position, as he lifts one knee to make room for his growing erection. He aches to kiss her, but holds back, allowing the want to grow, and grow. He studies the girlish fuzz on her forearm, faint blond hairs which look even blonder against her tan, then his eyes scurry upward over her white shirt sleeve, up her wonderfully nubile shoulder and neck to the side of her face, to the silky sun-bleached down in front of her ear, a feathery tuft, a softly innocent lock like you'd see on a wee lass. But she's hardly wee— she's *sixteen*, nearly seventeen, and she's got it all, the full female package, X-rated, darkly adult, and yet she retains that ruddy, prepubescent glow, a dynamic contrast that gives unspeakable potency to her sex-appeal, especially as her panty crotch presses hotly upon his belt buckle—she's wearing a *skirt*. And she has to feel him, his trapped boner, as it works up his raised right leg. She's sitting on it, her left butt-cheek. He's never seen her naked, but he pictures her as ginger-brown inside her undies. His knees shake; his dick throbs. He'll have NO self-control when they kiss, and he knows they *have* to kiss, and soon. But first, she captures him with her eyes—blue, blue, and calling. He feels that dizzy vertigo high that comes when they gaze at each other, as if he's on a mountain cliff looking down.

"Oh, Bryan honey," Mandy coos finally. "I love you *so* much. Even more after today. God, I can't believe you're real. We're so lucky. I'm so lucky." Her blue gaze is going trancy.

"I love you too, pretty lady," he declares, as she leans down and gives him a teasing smooch on the cheek. She quickly shifts to his mouth, kissing him aggressively. He pulls her to him, as they roll onto their sides. He devours her lips, her tongue, her neck, then he covers her cheeks with a barrage of tender pecks. She finds his mouth again, kissing, probing, twisting, until his soul seems ready to burst, not to mention his Levi's. Swirling into a vortex of desire, he burns to pull off her shirt, to fondle her breasts, to lift that denim skirt and find her wetness, to touch her, to thrill her, to satisfy—to *know* her completely. Sweet torture. Can't wait. No *way* can they make it three years. To hell with the consequences!

She probes with her tongue, darting, pushing, going deep—then she abruptly ends the kiss, her willpower exceeding his by a wide margin. Hugging him tightly, she nuzzles between his neck and shoulder. He strokes her hair, respecting her decision. It *is* best and *wise* to wait. Plus he has no protection. He's considered keeping a rubber in his wallet (like Spanky, like half the guys on the team), but has so far rejected the idea, lest it remove another obstacle, not to speak of the fact that he's a naive "awh shucks" country boy when it comes to prophylactics. (The high schools back East may distribute condoms, even demonstrate their use, but this is not the rule in Texas, especially in rural, Baptist farm country.) Bryan has only examined a couple, out of curiosity—at Spanky's house two years ago.

Cozy embrace: he can still taste her lip gloss. His nuts *ache* fiercely, as they always do after heated kissing. Blue balls: he'll deal with it tonight. He used to feel guilty about self-gratification, but not so much anymore, despite the 'perversion' label most pastors put on it. Healthy or sinful, the need is *un*deniable, and he doubts that it's ungodly anyhow. If it is, then Hollis County harbors a hard-jerking horde of country-boy perverts. Bryan doesn't discuss it, but it's not hard to gather (from Spanky, from the team bus, from all the lewd guy-talk since junior high) that every lad older than thirteen has tossed in the towel in this fight, even the apple-polishers at church. But what about the young ladies? Ever since Bryan learned about orgasm, he's been hotly intrigued about girls getting off, and after seven months with Mandy his carnal curiosity approaches torment. But no *way* is he going to bring up such a taboo subject. He's always pictured females as less horny, yet when he and Mandy neck, she seems just as turned on as he. But maybe unsated desire doesn't affect her the same? Perhaps girls can table their lust, and let it go. Perhaps they don't have to masturbate later like a guy—or ever? Not according to Spanky: he says that chicks are even *more* crazy for climax. But you hear all kinds of scuttlebutt, a million different spins when it comes to girls and sex. Bryan made A's in all his biology-related classes, and he aspires to be a doctor, but these are things a lifelong virgin cannot learn in the classroom. And save for Spanky's *Playboy* collection plus a few X-rated videos, he's never seen a sexually mature woman in the raw—he did see his mom when he was a little kid, but that doesn't count.

As they lie in the grass, the ticking seconds spin a cocoon of contentment about them, the coziness of their embrace more than compensating for the lack of consummation. He can hear her breathing, in then out then in. Her hair smells of shampoo, and he *can* detect the diner, a faint hint of deep-fry grease, but nothing to warrant the concerns she expressed earlier. He senses perfume on her neck, but there's also a deeper scent, an earthy, lanolin-like aroma that is unique to Mandy herself. It's not from perfume or soap or antiperspirant, or anything she puts on. It's her tag, her flesh, and he can't get enough of it. The odor is similar to the mink-oil lotion he uses on his baseball glove, just a bit more salty. Most people relegate scent recognition to bloodhounds and would see Bryan as weird for saying he discerns such a thing, but he notices *every*thing about her, even this singular aroma which clings to her clothes and hangs in her locker at school and lurks in her bedroom at home. It gets on him when they neck, and he hates to wash it off.

* * *

"So, babe, what's the latest on your scholarship?" Mandy asks thirty minutes later, as they trek back up the slope toward the giant oak. After their kissing and cuddling session, they went down to the pond, where they lounged a while on the bank. They also skipped a few rocks, or tried—the flat stones didn't bounce very well on the wind-rippled surface.

"Dr. Nadler is sending a report to Waco," Bryan replies, his arm happily about her waist. "He says I can play college ball, as long as my tests in July are okay. That's when I get the green light to resume my normal life. And he foresees no problem."

"What about the Houston Astros? D'yuh hafta tell them?"

"Nawh, that's all in the future. They did a scouting thing on me, but nothing more. Y'gotta be a hundred-plus, pure-aspirin pitcher to sign right outta high school, but if I do big things at Baylor, then I may get a chance." He gives a snorty laugh. "I'm not sure about the rules concerning contracts and college and all. But to tellyuh the truth, I'm not so psyched about it as I was."

"Yeah, I guess having all this incredible stuff happen puts a different light on things?"

"I'll say. It reminds me of what's important, and it makes me more excited about my pre-med program. But I still look forward to baseball

THE SILVER CORD

... and that's how I'll be paying for college."

Reaching the oak, they head for a low-hanging limb on the south side of the tree. There are a number of low arms coming out of the trunk, but this one is the lowest and strangest. Where it forks out of the trunk the thick limb is above their heads, but as it goes out, there's a huge egg-shaped deformity the size of a beer belly, perhaps a healed fracture from long ago. The limb elbows down from this deformity then levels off about four feet above the ground before swinging up again. Mandy leans back against it, while Bryan mounts it and sits bestride it, as if in a saddle, his long legs dangling, not quite reaching the ground. He checks his watch. "It's five-thirty," he says. "If we're gonna eat with my parents, we'll hafta go back pretty soon."

"Sounds like a plan," she chirps in reply, as a leafy splotch of sunshine highlights her face and bangs. It shifts and wiggles with the wind then changes shape; it renders her adorable, almost angelic, yet her expression strikes him as rather devilish. She works her mouth and wrinkles her nose, doing her cute rabbity routine, then she gives a husky little titter.

"What's so funny?" he asks.

"I was just picturing your first class at Baylor ... like you getting up and announcing that you come out of your body at night and fly all around, and just this year you went to Heaven and saw God ... and your grandfather too." This sets off a fit of guffaws and giggling: Bryan laughs so hard he almost falls off the limb, while Mandy turns so red her freckles look white.

"Not hardly," he pants, wiping tears of mirth from his eyes. "I reckon I'll wait until my *second* day to tell 'em that." More laughter, as he gives her a playful love-tap on the shoulder.

"So I'm the only one you're gonna tell?" she asks, after sobering. She folds her arms, hugging herself.

"For now anyway. I do plan to tell my parents when the time's right ... like I said. But it's not something you can talk about much. Maybe when I get into more advanced pre-med, like my junior and senior year, I can incorporate my OBEs into my research ... without creating too big of a stir?" He blows a silent whistle into a cupped hand. "After all, it's my paranormal trips that got me interested in being a doctor in the first place ... and this near-death thing whets my curiosity all the more—and *how*." He gestures toward the limbs and leaves above them. "Why me? It's such a mystery. Why'd God choose *me* to have such powers? It's like he's preparing me for something? I can't say for sure what his intentions are, but it sure seems *more* than coincidental. But I gotta be cool about it, or they'll come with a strait jacket."

"It's too bad," Mandy replies. "It seems like everyone would be glad to hear that death is not the end of us. It's like y'can confirm what we hear in Sunday school and church—the hope."

"No kidding. It's the *ultimate* question ... and it's *way* bigger than church. I mean, I have a *yearn*ing about it. It's big and deep, and I can't get past it. But we *all* have a yearning to live forever. Kids our age put death out of their minds, because they see it as far away, as something that just happens to old people, but it's still the *ult*imate question, the most crucial thing ... and it can happen at *any* age, like with me." Bryan sighs; he rotates his hat back on his head. "And it's not just a fear-of-death thing, though that's a biggie to be sure, but it's like we have this *forever* feeling in us ... no matter what religion we're brought up in, whether it's Baptist or Catholic or Mormon ... or Muslim or Hindu ... or whatever. We all ache for more, for going on and on, even the atheists I wager—but especially *me*. God gave me an awesome preview, and it seemed *gosh*dang real, as real as anything. Yet I wanna know more; I wanna be *sure*. It's like an obsession now, like a calling ... like a *quest*."

Her blue eyes gazing without focusing, Mandy ponders a moment, a tight-lipped Mona Lisa expression on her face. "Gosh, babe, I can't think of a *better* thing to seek after."

"I know ... but I still hafta be careful. I mean, people have brainlock when it comes to death and the soul and the afterlife, especially when more souls are supposed to go to Hell than Heaven. Most folks shy away from anything that deviates the least bit from their lifelong religious concepts, especially when it comes to astral phenom—"

"Astral?"

"That's just a pop-culture term for the paranormal or the metaphysical. And most pastors say it's Satanic deception ... and Baptists can be the worst." He sighs. "Even when there's new evidence, they don't wanna look at it ... or the *old* evidence, like Paul being caught up to Heaven in 2nd Corinthians Twelve: 'I knew a man in Christ above fourteen years ago (whether in the body, I cannot tell; or whether *out* of the body)—such a one caught up to the third Heaven.' I mean—"

"Goshdang, you big jock; you know the Bible better than my mother."

"Not *hard*ly," Bryan snickers. "I just memorize the parts that ring my bell. ... but anyway, most preachers claim that the Devil uses the illusion of astral phenomena to lead us astray."

"The Devil's devices: I hear *that* all the time ... from Mama. It's like—" Mandy stops midsentence. She thumbs her lower lip, as if pondering. After a long moment she shifts the subject: "So how long does medical school take?"

"It's three years, I think ... after four years of undergraduate work. But if I get a shot at pro ball, then it'll take longer for me, since I'll only be going during the off-season."

"That sounds exciting, and we'll be married then—which is even *more* exciting." She gives him a flirty side-glance. "So when you finish, you'll be like Dr. Joe?"

"Could be, if I go all the way, and become a neurosurgeon. But right now I'm looking more at the research side of it ... after what happened to me, my quest and all. It's like I wanna delve into the mind and discover the bounds of consciousness, and how it all relates to the soul." He blows a silent whistle. "But most doctors don't even *bel*ieve in the soul. Yet *I* know from experience that our mind transcends the physical ... if I'm not deluded anyway." He laughs. "In any case, I'd like to dig as deep as I can. And dig and dig ... till I find the silver cord."

"The what?"

"The silver cord ... the cord that connects the soul to the body, the sense of self to the brain. I'm not talking about the dictionary, but the Bible. The dictionary defines it as the human umbilical cord, or it can symbolize the emotional bond between a mother and her child. In fact, there's an old theater-play called the *Silver Cord* which brings out this mother-child sense of the word—but I'm talking about the *ultimate* umbilical cord, like in the Book of Ecclesiastes where King Solomon describes the sorrow and pain of growing old, and the 'loosing of the silver cord' when we die."

"Gosh, babe, I reckon you really *are* into this."

Indeed he is—Bryan's on a roll. Still seated on the limb, he gestures with his hat. "All through history you find thinkers and priests and psuedoscientists speculating about the 'seat of the soul,' but there's never been much rational inquiry, even today, because of the wall between the secular and the sacred. Doctors and scientists still don't like to include the soul in their reality, or God, or the astral realm. They stay strictly with the physical, while the Church continues its allegiance, blind allegiance for the most part, to *very* strict doctrines concerning the soul, what it can and cannot do. So it's hard to get people to be reasonable about this subject. Only a few researchers have investigated near-death experiences in a scientific way, like Dr. Raymond Moody and Dr. Elizabeth Kübler-Ross. I've read their books, and they talk about patients who had experiences similar to my own, but they don't get so much into the neurology of the whole thing ... like I wanna do."

Mandy doesn't reply. A frown is working to gain control of her countenance. "What's wrong, precious?" he asks.

She scratches her knee. "Oh nothing. My legs are just itchy ... from grass burns and chigger bites."

He suspects there's more, but he doesn't press.

"Oh, babe honey," she laments a bit later, confirming his suspicion. "I wish I could skip my senior year and come to Baylor with you. This has been such a super-neat day, and now I'm thinking about you going away, and it's a real *down*er."

"It won't be *that* bad," he consoles. He also dreads the idea of being apart, but he'd like to salvage the moment. "And before you know it, pretty lady, you *will* be down there with me. And we'll be officially engaged—it won't be a secret then."

"What if I don't get *ac*cepted at Baylor? And what if I can't afford it? That whole scholarship thing seems farfetched now. I'm too *short* to play for the Lady Bears. I saw 'em on TV, and they're *all* tall, like giants. And I haven't heard a dadgum thing since Coach Ames talked with me at the finals in Tyler, and that was back in March. She probably crossed me off the list?"

"Whaddeyuh talking about? Five-six is *plenty* tall. Y'don't see giant girls at *point* guard. And I doubt she's seen anyone who can hit from outside like you do. Besides, with your transcript and SAT scores, you'll have no sweat getting *some* kind of scholarship. And once you're in Waco, then time's gonna pass fast, and before we know it, we'll be married. '94 seems far away, but it's not really. It's all gonna work out, just like we planned. And even this year, we'll be together a whole bunch, like on special weekends and holidays."

"I sure hope so," she replies, stepping away from him, away from the low-hanging limb. "But there's another thing too."

"What's that?"

"It's *Mama*—she bugs me. Like yesterday evening before you came by to get me, for the graduation and everything. I'd been asking her all week if I could have the car today, since I knew she didn't hafta work. She hemmed and hawed and complained, then last night she finally said yes." Mandy gives a huffy murmur then stomps her foot. "But early this morning, like ten till six, she was already downstairs having coffee while I was rushing to get ready for work ... and she snapped at me and said, 'Now, Amanda, I don't wantcha to think you're getting my car every time I'm off work. After all, it's *only* ten blocks to the diner. And don't get it into your head that you're gonna spend all your free time this summer with Bryan. Once a week is *enough* for you two to be together ... or twice.' "

Before she gets the last sentence out, Bryan's down from the tree. He hugs her from behind, as she elaborates, her voice wavering, "I didn't say anything earlier, because I was all excited to see you, and I didn't wanna spoil our first real day together since you got home— and it's been *so* good, the best time ever. But I uh ... I uh...." She doesn't finish the thought; she shifts around rather, and they hold each other.

"It's okay, precious," he offers, lifting her chin. Her blue eyes glisten with tears, but none spill out. She manages a little smile. "Let's just enjoy the rest of *this* day."

A sudden gust whirls about them. The leaves rustle and swish, as the huge crown sways this way and that, the limbs popping and creaking. The old tree is speaking, *more* than speaking—it's dancing, and singing a melody. And the music it makes with its partner, the wind, is good and comforting. Bryan feels a warm rush, as if the wind is blowing inside him, and he's sure she feels it too. "This oak is a hundred years old," he tells her, as he glances up at the swishing canopy. "It was here in 1918 when Gramps was born, and it's *still* here, even after he's gone."

"No, babe ... he's not gone. He's somehow part of this old tree. I feel it in the wind ... like he's here with us right now."

THE SILVER CORD

CHAPTER SIX

THE HOWARD FARM
SATURDAY, JUNE 29, 1991 — 8:10 AM

The old AC mutters and clunks, the compressor kicking in, then it continues its steady whir, though louder. Bryan lies snug in his bed. Hugging his pillow, he imagines Mandy with him. Her hair is fragrant, her breathing slow and measured—it's that real. A warm upwelling floods his bosom. His traumatic brush with death, and the freed-up schedule resulting from it, has taken their love to new heights: spirit, soul, and—well, not in body as yet, despite their almost-daily togetherness (Helen Stevens hasn't followed through on her threat to restrict Mandy's time with him). The joy is so wondrous it seems unbearable at times, as does the longing and frustration. His flesh cries for completion, for liberty, for untied wings to join his soaring affections. He's pulled, like an overstretched rubber band, twixt earth and paradise. Nonetheless, this month ranks as the happiest of his life— by far.

Hauling himself out of bed finally (eight is late) he pads to the bathroom. He pictures Mandy at work—she's been there since six. They're going to the lake this afternoon, but it would sure be neat to see her sooner. Before he reaches the toilet, he's made his decision. After emptying his bladder, he brushes his teeth, then slaps cold water in his face.

"Bryan!" Virginia Howard yells up.

"Yeah, Mom?" he responds, grabbing a towel.

"If yuh want some breakfast, y'better get down here."

Tossing the towel aside, he leans out of the bathroom, so he can answer in a normal tone, speaking over the stairwell banister, "Thanks ... but y'don't hafta fix anything for me. I'm gonna grab a bite at Goddard's before I do my walking." He can't run as yet or exert vigorously, so to keep in so-so shape, he takes long, easy-going walks, a few miles a day. He hikes around the farm, or treks up and down Longley Road, or Misty Hollow.

After donning his cutoffs and beach sandals, plus a baseball underjersey and his Tiger cap, Bryan splashes some Brute onto his face grabs his workout bag (which contains his sneakers plus socks, etc.) and hurries out to the pickup, giving his mom a kiss on the way. A half minute later, he's spinning west on Longley Road, a dust plume in hot pursuit. *Maybe I shoulda shaved?* he says to himself, fingering his chin. *Nawh, I'll shower and shave after I get back. We won't be necking at the diner.* He gives a chuckling laugh. He actually likes his beard when it's grown out a day or two—it gives his manly jaw-line a manly shadow—but for Mandy's sake he usually shaves before they get together.

The dingy-bright sunshine has just begun to pop the daily flotilla of cumulus, little puffs of cloud barely discernible in the haze, one here, one there, a few over the hills in the distance. The sultry-sweet aroma of grass and cow manure, sweet to Bryan anyway, blows in his open window. The rush of air, though quite warm, is still more refreshing than hot.

The athletic department at Baylor, based upon Dr. Nadler's report, has preserved his place among the baseball freshmen, as long as the July CTs are A-OK. And Bryan is confident they will be, since he feels great—even the blurred vision in his left eye has cleared up. He feels like a slacker in fact, compared to past summers when he worked long hours on the farm, in addition to playing American Legion ball. But considering what he's doing with his time—Mandy, Mandy, and more Mandy—he's quite glad to bum it for a while. And being idle has hardly hurt his finances. During the past three years, he's earned $8,000 working for his dad and the feed store. He's spent some on incidentals, and he used $2,000 last September to buy his computer (the Macintosh plus accessories), but he has over four thou left. This, coupled with the money his grandfather left him, gives him about nine thou in his account. And his parents gave him five hundred as a birthday-graduation present. Besides, he and Mandy are hardly extravagant. The DQ, the diner, and O'Henry's are inexpensive places to eat, and Mandy also treats on occasion. Bryan's not wealthy by any means, but for a country boy in Hollis County, he's in darn good shape, certainly compared to the wild-spending, poker-playing Spanky Arnold, who's *always* in debt.

Reaching FR 115, Bryan turns left toward Spindle. Now on a paved road, he rolls the window up then pushes the pickup up to 60 mph. The '79 Chevy purrs along like a much younger truck, and in a way it is. Wallace Howard bought it new, and he just had it a few years when he died. Henry drove the truck some, but he mostly kept it covered in the barn, until Bryan got his driver's license. So in spite of its age, it has only 37,000 miles on it.

As he crosses Butler Creek, a boyish glee takes his emotions. Clicking the radio on, he punches the middle button, *Country Rock 104* (FM 104 out of Sulphur Springs), and gets a hot Texas tune: *ZZ Top* and "Sharp Dressed Man."

> Clean shirt, new shoes ...
> Silk suit, black tie ...
> They come runnin'
> as fast as they can,
> 'cause every girl is crazy
> 'bout a sharp dressed man.

THE SILVER CORD

The rocking guitar chugs along with the hard-driving V-6 under the hood. It quickens Bryan; it thrills him; it kicks him in the butt. His excitement revs up and up, and *up,* until it seems the Chevy engine is pumping inside his bosom, the pistons. He bangs his thigh keeping time to the rhythm. Mandy, Mandy: he's going to see her soon, her blushing grin, her jockish moves, her laughing eyes. And when those big blue eyes go from laughing to gazing, it gets him so high. "O Jesus, I can't wait," he cries.

Next thing he knows, he's at the diner. The parking lot is almost full, typical for Saturday morning. He just drove through the heart of Spindle, past the Dairy Queen, the stadium, the practice fields, past Courthouse Square, left on Main (Hwy. 29), then past the Texaco station and the old train depot, all the familiar places, but he was too Mandy-drunk to notice. Removing his aviator shades, he lifts his hat and checks his head in the rearview mirror. His hair now hides the evidence of his surgery, and the scar-tissue is fading, becoming flesh-colored, but it's hard to break this self-conscious habit. Satisfied he looks okay, he sniffs his underarms to make sure the Ban roll-on is working—it is. He notices a blue thread dangling from the sleeve of his shirt; he pulls it off. The beige underjersey once had three-quarter-length sleeves, designed to extend out from *under* a baseball uniform, but he cuts his off at the biceps, and they tatter and fray.

Exiting the truck, he pats his back pocket to make sure he has his wallet. Steamy morning, glaring sun: heat waves wiggle up from the black, stinky, recently rolled asphalt. Uncle Billy just had the lot repaved. In the old days this eatery was a flat-roofed, shoebox affair, the usual "diner" look. The stainless-steel front is still there, with its entrance vestibule and train-style windows, but the place has been remodeled and enlarged a few times over the decades, making the modern version more square than oblong, with the back half sporting a pitched roof and vinyl siding.

Located on the east side of town, across from the long-gone railroad yard and not far from the grain elevator, Goddard's is famous for its breakfast specials, which attract the truckers and fishermen, plus many locals. Highway 29 runs east-west through Spindle, but if you look at a map, it actually runs southwest from Interstate 30, then jogs west through Spindle, then it swings south toward Mineola and I-45. So many truckers come down 29 as a shortcut, and most of them know about Goddard's. Same goes for the fishermen, who come here for breakfast and bragging after their early-morning outings on Crockett Lake, which is only twenty minutes away. At 15,000 acres the lake is sizable, though not huge by Texas standards. Nonetheless, some of the biggest bass in the region inhabit its waters, and serious fishermen come from all over, hoping to land a trophy lunker.

Before Mandy's Uncle Billy (William Goddard) bought the diner in '77, it was called Courtney's Kitchen, and before that the Whistle

Stop. Forty years ago, back when the KCS switching yard was humming, the crews would come over here to eat. They called the yard Linden Junction, since several rail lines converged on Spindle, and one of them ran southeast to Linden Refinery near the biggest oil field. But only the KCS main line survives plus one weed-choked sidetrack near the grain elevator. Linden Court, the new shopping plaza, occupies some of the old railroad property (hence its name), but most of the area lies vacant, just weeds and ballast and gopher holes plus some half-buried ties left behind. The abandoned cotton warehouse is still over there, and Homestead Feed & Seed where Henry works. The feed store hugs the KCS main, in the shadow of the towering elevator, which has been empty as long as Bryan remembers. The feed business was once tied closely to local grain storage, and to the railroad, but now it's strictly retail, like an Agway, and everything arrives by truck. Yet in the office, pictures adorn the walls showing the rail yard in its heyday, the countless tracks, the hoppers, the boxcars, the tank cars, the diesels, even a few steam locomotives.

Whoosh. Pulling open the door, then the second one, Bryan steps inside the diner, into the clatter and clink of dishes and utensils along with the collective buzz of table-jabber. The refrigerated air smells of coffee and bacon and pastry. He scans for his sweetheart, but she's evidently in the dining room, or the kitchen. Going left, he follows a well-trod path in the black-mottled linoleum. He plops into a tiny booth not far from the end of the counter. The formica-topped table wobbles a bit, while ugly strips of duct tape, like giant Band-Aids, keep the blue-vinyl upholstery from spilling its guts, yet he likes this booth. It's off by itself (in a recessed nook), and the glare is tolerable. Ceiling-mounted florescent tubes, naked tubes, illuminate this old "diner" part of the restaurant, as opposed to the mellow, lounge-like lighting in the big dining room around the corner, which could pass for a dowdy version of Denny's. He looks over the menu, yet he always orders the same thing: eggs, bacon, hash browns, toast, orange juice, a cup of decaf. He often gets pancakes too, but he'll forgo the extra calories this morning, since he's not as yet allowed to burn them full blast. His breakfast order is so predictable that Mandy calls it the "Bryan Howard special."

Billy and Marge keep the place tidy and presentable despite the tacky hodgepodge decor (*decor* is hardly the word). The various renovations over the years have never been reconciled, but these hungry folks don't give a damn about decor—they're here to enjoy the *best* breakfast-cooking in these parts: eggs and bacon, eggs and sausage, eggs and ham, pancakes, waffles, french toast, steak and eggs, hash-browns, homefries, grits, cantaloupe, honeydew melons, hot cereal, cold cereal; plus toast and muffins and doughnuts and cinnamon rolls. The lunch and supper items are also quite tasty, just not so notable. Bryan has always liked the diner, especially this old, original part, going all the way back to when Gramps used to bring him here—but now he has a much *big*ger reason. "Hey, good-lookin', how'bout some coffee?" he barks playfully, as he spots his sweetheart behind the counter. She's facing the kitchen slot, reaching for an order.

"Be right with you, *sir*," she says, feigning a businesslike response, as if he's just another Saturday-morning customer, but her voice cracks on "sir," giving herself away, as does the wink and blush when she scoots by seconds later, taking several plates to a foursome of fishermen in the large booth near the front door. At least, they're dressed like they came from the lake: coveralls, sweat shirts, camouflaged hats— the long sleeves and no shorts are the tip-off: the bass anglers have to cover up, even in hot weather, to protect against mosquitoes. One of the guys looks vaguely familiar, the portly one who's doing the talking. She makes two more trips to their booth, her ponytail bouncing and swinging. Happy helium makes Bryan giddy, or so it seems, the buoyant Mandy vibes in his head, in his bosom.

"Good *morn*ing, Mr. Howard. What can I get for you?" she asks playfully a minute later, as she places a steaming cup of coffee, his usual black decaf, on the table. She gives a coy smirk.

Bryan says nothing. He just dimples and gathers his dear Mandy with his eyes. She looks so neat and adorable in her Goddard's outfit, the checked apron, the denim skirt, the white shirt. The summer sun has bleached her bangs and pinked her face, leaving cute spots of peeling on her nose and cheeks. Her smirk grows into a grin, which draws him up to her big blue eyes which send a dizzy chill up and down his spine. Too much—he toys with the order book in the pocket of her apron.

Slipping into the booth, the other side, she leans across the table, propping her hand under her chin. "Now, let me ask you once again, *sir*," she flirts hushedly, her voice going husky like it does. "What d'yuh *want* for breakfast?"

"I'll tellyuh, but first you need to come a little closer." She does, and he pops a quick smooch on her lips. "You look *aw*ful nice, pretty lady," he whispers, as he senses a stirring inside his shorts—but the romantic interlude ends abruptly, as boisterous laughter and hollering erupts by the door. "What's all the *ruckus* about?" Bryan asks, as she exits the little booth.

"Oh, that's just Big Wes Allen, and three guys from New York. Big Wes lives up in Oklahoma, but he's down here a lot. Aunt Marge says he's a fishing guide ... and rich guys pay him big bucks. They were out on the lake before sunrise, and they claim they caught a buncha big bass, one a seven-pounder. But they *always* brag to the waitresses, all the fishing crowd. If they caught as many as they claim, the lake would be *emp*ty by now."

They both laugh, then Bryan says, "So, pretty lady, you all set to go to lake yourself?"

"I can't wait. It's gonna be *tot*ally hot by afternoon. I got a few things to do at home, so come get me there ... around four."

He tickles her ribs. "I'm gonna *get*cha all right."

She squirms away. "You behave, mister, or I won't get your breakfast ... your *Bryan* Howard special."

"Yeah, then I'll come get it myself and kiss you good, and make a *big* scene." He tries to tickle her again, but she dodges away, doing a frisky little shuffle back behind the counter.

* * *

SPINDLE, TEXAS - COLBY DRIVE
SATURDAY, JUNE 29, 1991 — 4:02 PM

Bryan parks in front of Mandy's house. After quickly checking himself—he's now showered and shaved—he adjusts his Tiger cap and gets out of the truck. He's still wearing sandals and cutoffs, but he's replaced the baseball underjersey with a fresh white T-shirt—and he has his swimsuit on underneath. The breeze fans his face, a tepid little wind that offers little relief from the sweltering heat. "Hello there, Gretchen," he announces, as he strides up the walkway. She and her playmate are seated in the porch swing.

"Hi, Bryan; this's my friend Molly Ann," Gretchen replies in that chirpy, tell-all manner of eight-year-olds. "She gets to spend the afternoon over *here* ... while her mother's working. Then I'm gonna sleep over at *her* house tonight." Gretchen hops out of the swing; her friend follows, tentatively. They're both in shorts and knit shirts; Molly is taller, almost a head taller.

As Bryan comes up the steps, Gretchen mounts the porch railing and maneuvers precariously toward him, her arms extended as if walking a tightrope. A short, freckled lass with moppy red hair and lots of leftover baby fat, she looks much like Charlie, her dad. She only favors Mandy in the eyes; she has blue eyes like her older half-sister—and it's rather *obvious* she has the same tomboy genes. Reaching the corner post, she hooks her arm around it and grins proudly, showing her rabbity front teeth. "Molly's *al*ready nine," she proclaims, "but I won't be nine till No*vem*ber. Mama said we can play outside, as long as we don't leave the yard, but we *haf*ta stay in the shade, and if we get overheated, we *haf*ta go inside and play video games in the living room. It's like *really* cool in there, 'cause the AC's on high."

"Glad to meetcha, Molly Ann," Bryan says, shaking the taller girl's hand. She blushes, smiling reservedly. A slim brunette with pigtails, she has a pretty, fine-featured face, but her prematurely long legs make her look skinnier than she is.

"Bryan got hurt playing baseball," Gretchen declares, now directing her words to Molly. "You *know*, I toldjuh. But he's okay now, and he's going to college ... and he goes out with *my* big sister—

hold on, and I'll get her." Vaulting off the railing, she whips open the front door and yells: "*Man*dy! Bryan's here!"

Mandy doesn't appear right away, so Bryan plunks down in the old wooden swing. Gretchen, scooting in beside him, launches into another tell-all tale about Toby their cat, how he brought a half-eaten mouse onto the back porch this morning, and on and on. Molly, leaning against the porch railing, rolls her eyes, as if to assure Bryan that *she* has outgrown such juvenile babble.

* * *

"Sorry I took so long," Mandy says ten minutes later, as she and Bryan depart in the pickup. Her tone is sober, her cheeks flushed, and it's not like her to be late.

"Anything the matter, precious?" he asks.

"Oh, I just got *into* it with Mama." Without elaborating, she fishes her sunglasses out of her purse, slips them on, and looks the other way, out her window—silence.

His heart pangs, but he doesn't push, except in his thoughts: *What's THIS all about? I mean, she was so frisky and happy this morning?* After going three blocks east on Colby, he jogs north on Henley Avenue. The backstrap of her green bikini shows through her T-shirt, and her shorts dig a bit into her thigh—she's wearing pink-denim shorts, which are rolled up to make them shorter. Her softball cap lies crumpled on the seat beside her, next to her purse. He wishes she'd say something, *any*thing. He adjusts his hat and sunglasses; he clears his throat.

Reaching Butler Road, they go east. A quick glance tells him she's still facing away, the wind lifting her bangs. The silence in the cab has become a low roar, as the saunalike afternoon blows by the open windows, fanning and buffeting. On days like this he wishes the old Chevy had air conditioning, yet the hot weather is scarcely his main concern.

"Oh, babe, forgive me," she blurts, as they pass Sampson Road (which cuts south to Sampson's Poultry Farm). Removing her sunglasses and sliding over to him, she gives him a peck on the cheek. "It's not *your* fault. It's Mama; she's *all* in a dither about Charlie. He claims he's a changed man, and he wants her to come back. He's going to some Bible college up in the Ozarks. He says the *Lord* has delivered him from alcohol." Mandy gives a scornful snort.

"So what'd your mom say to Charlie?" Bryan asks, as he puts his arm around his sweetheart. This Charlie-matter could sure complicate things, yet he's relieved that she's *talking* about it.

"Mama didn't give him an answer, not yet. But she did invite him down ... to discuss it. That's what gets me mad ... 'cause I know how he smooth-talks her. He's gonna try to persuade her to move back to Arkansas. She says she has *no* intention of moving, but it's only fair to hear him out. I told her I wasn't going *any*where, no matter what. No way am I changing schools for my senior year, no *F*-ing way. Charlie's such a—well, it's not that I hate him or anything. But I wish he'd get off this 'God delivered me' bullshit. He's been saying that ever since he and Mama broke up."

"Yeah, like the hotshots at church, who get up and give testimonies all the time. 'Don't trust *any*body who testifies at church'—that's what Gramps always said." They share a good laugh. The mood in the truck has lifted, to Bryan's delight.

"I get along with Charlie okay," she goes on, now gesturing for emphasis, "but I also know how he operates. Mama lets her feelings get in the way—she should listen to *me*. And to top it off she says, A*man*da, I wantcha home by eight. Y'been going out *way* too much since summer vacation started." Mandy blows out a sputtering gust of disdain which seems more feigned than serious. "Course, she's the *mother*, so when we get into it, she always uses her authority to get in the final word."

"Well, pretty lady," he responds, giving her a quick one-arm squeeze, "I'm sure we'll be back by eight, and the whole thing with Charlie will probably blow over." Bryan chuckles hushedly. "But if *all* else fails, you can live at our house your senior year. My mom and dad would love to have yuh."

Mandy blushes. "Yeah, until they *really* got to know me."

"You can even have my room," he adds, as he hangs a left on Hwy. 29.

She replaces her dark glasses, which make her look kittenish yet alluring. "Now that would be a neat deal, sleeping in *your* bed, but I'd rather sleep there *tonight*, while you're still in it."

She tickles him. He gets her back, grabbing her naked flesh just above the knee. She scoots giggling to the other side of the cab. Frisky thighs, denim-clad crotch. *O Jesus,* he sighs silently, his thoughts returning to the normal frustrations. *Do I ever wish she was gonna be in my bed tonight.* His eyes are back on the road, but he can't get her legs out of his mind, especially the dents of creamy-tan flesh where the rolled denim digs in.

The bluish waters of Crockett Lake look most appealing, as Bryan eases the truck down a little incline into the dusty parking area at South Beach. He can smell the lake as well, that mossy, algal, not-quite-fishy odor. He usually drives around to the dam, on the northeast side, where the water is deepest, and there's a tower you can jump from, but he can't do vigorous swimming anyway, so South Beach will do just fine, especially since it's the closest to Spindle, and despite the heat the crowd is rather sparse for a Saturday. It's almost July, so going to the lake has become a ho-hum thing, unlike those first hot weekends each spring.

After parking under a pine at the back of the lot, Bryan gets out, stretches, then strips to his bathing suit. The black, well-worn, boxer-style trunks fit him snugly, but they're a little loose at the waist, since the elastic is failing. After tossing his clothes onto the seat, he saunters around to the other side of the truck where he can't help but notice the extra-*fine* lines on his woman, as she eases out of her shirt and shorts. Her leggy, high-schooler bod has that well-toned, girl-jock look, and yet she's not tight-muscled or sinewy like some of the butchy gals who excel in sports. Her flesh is cushiony firm and feminine rather, rendering her curves softly pliant. She's solid yet succulent, like a well-conditioned cheerleader, with just enough midriff to hide her bellybutton in a cute, shadowy dimple. As she bends to pick up her shorts, her tits jostle whitely inside the triangular slings of her bikini bra, giving him a glimpse almost to the nipple, while her upper thighs and groin, ivory-fair above the tan-line, peep out seductively from under the skimpy swimsuit bottom, as does the jiggly fat of her butt cheeks, until she adjusts the bikini, stretching it down a trifle. It's skimpy but still covers most of her backside, unlike those thong things that many gals wear.

Slipping on her sunglasses, she gives him a little smirk, partly bashful, partly proud, then she hoists her canvas beach-bag out of the back of the truck, a gray satchel-like thing. Mandy in shorts is tough enough, but to peek at her most-secret, most-female areas where the sun never shines, and his hand never ventures, makes him woozy and weak-kneed—his dick tingles. He *loves* her in this green bikini, if only—O Jesus God! He can't get enough, yet he dares not stare, lest he spot something that'll bring greater torture, like the pouty folds of her pussy pushing against the stretch-fabric, or a curly virgin hair escaping under the crotch-elastic. He feels almost relieved when she says, "Turn around, babe, and I'll rub some sunscreen on yuh." Her hand feels good on his back, too good. *O Lord,* he confesses in his thoughts. *I'll never make it through this summer.* The familiar odor of sun-block lotion wafts up about them, that unmistakable cocoa-butter aroma that goes with summer and sand and water, and towels and beach blankets, and bathers in various states of near-nudity.

"I don't know if I should take yuh down there," he kids, as she does his neck and shoulders. "The way those sick puppies stare and gaze around."

"What are you *talk*ing about, Bryan Howard?" Mandy asks, playing dumb. But the sensual undertones in her voice, together with a coquettish laugh, betray her pretense.

"They might knock me off and steal you away—I'm just joshing you, pretty lady, but I'm sure they'll be giving you the eye. Course, you can't help it that you're so *darn* good-lookin'."

"Well, whaddabout you, mister? Girls look too, y'know?" She grins then gives him a quick, but very sensual kiss. "And I want yuh *all* to myself." She tosses her ponytail flirtatiously. The warm tingling inside his bathing suit has grown into a throb.

THE SILVER CORD

They're soon down by the water spreading their big towels on the hot sand (sand trucked in years ago). They've escaped to the north end, avoiding the congestion near the pier. The sun is torridly bright despite the haze and ranks of cumulus overhead; a shadow blows over them, cast by one of the puffy clouds, but it's anemic and quickly gone, drifting on. The southeasterly breeze feels stronger as it blows in off the water pushing the little lake waves up onto the shore; the wavelets are only a few inches high, but they make a steady *lap-lap* sound as they break and recede.

Kicking her sneakers off, Mandy plunks down on her knees. Bryan loves how her ponytail bobs when she moves, and how her summer-bleached bangs jitterbug around above her dark glasses and freckled nose. She rummages in the beach satchel. The sun highlights the silky lock in front of her ear as it merges upward into the golden stream of back-pulled hair. The sunshine also brings out her freckles, even the fainter ones on her cheeks, not to mention the rosy spots of peeling. As she rummages, she puckers her nose and works the mouth cutely like she does. Her little-girl exuberance spices up her teen-gal sexuality, adding that innocent yet earthy allure that enabled young Dolores Haze to cast her spell upon Humbert the professor. Mandy's too old to be a Nabokov nymphet, but she could surely pass for Lolita when she's wearing those *sun*glasses—O God.

As if ready to settle for a spell, she pulls a thermos out of the satchel then a big bag of pretzels and Gretchen's video-pinball game. Finally, she fishes out her softball hat, but doesn't put it on, which should've tipped Bryan off, along with the smirk on her lips—"Bet I can beatcha to the water," she gushes, shedding the sunglasses. She gives him a playful push then dashes the other way toward the lake, her arms churning, her ponytail bouncing, her bare feet spewing sand. He sprints after her, running faster than he's supposed to. Yet she still splashes into the water ahead of him. He wades out chest-deep; the water chills him. He wiggles and kicks then waves his arms under the surface, then he dunks his head a couple times to get used to it. Ordinarily, he's a chicken when it comes to entering the water, even Crockett Lake, which is hardly cold in the summer. He dislikes the initial shock, so he normally eases in slowly—but not today.

"I beatcha good, didn't I?" Mandy teases—she's a few yards behind him now. "I won the race, and I didn't even hafta run my *fast*est." She sputters and laughs then gives her goofy grin.

"Yeah right. Y'come on out here, and we'll *see* who won."

"Only if yuh promise not to get my hair wet. I'm not sure I wanna get it wet today."

"No deal; I'm not making any promises—except I'm gonna tickle you *good*."

"Well, in that case, mister, I'm staying right here. It's up to my boobs—that's deep enough."

She laughs, but he cuts her short with a shout: "Look out, Mandy! There's a *huge* water bug right behind you!"

"No way. You *stop* it!" She whirls around and slaps the water.

His ruse working, he quietly submerges, swims underwater, and attacks her from behind. Grabbing her around the waist, he hoists her up out of the water. "BUG! BUG!" he yells. "I'm a *monster* bug!" She shrieks and thrashes, but he holds onto her, and they both crash backward into the water, under the water.

"You big jock, you," she scolds playfully, as she finally escapes. "Y'got my hair totally *soaked*."

"Lo siento mucho, mi bonita senorita," he laughingly apologizes (he learned just enough Spanish in school to whip out a few witty phrases now and then).

"Plus, Dr. Joe said y'weren't supposed to *lift* anything?"

"It's okay in the lake; you're lighter in the water, y'know?"

She replies by sticking out her tongue, poking it sassily at him, then she pushes her bangs back and proceeds into deeper water, doing a sidestroke. She's soon cavorting like a seal, twisting, rolling, swimming on her back, then dogpaddling in a circle, then treading in place. Snuffling and snorting and spitting lake-water, she bobs about five yards from him. A reflective wobble, from the little waves, shimmers ghostlike on her face. With her hair plastered down and her freckles glistening among the water droplets, she looks eleven at most. Bryan can hardly believe she's the same sexy-thighed honey who's been turning him on since they left her house. Her eyes spark mirthfully, and he can see just enough of her mouth to make out a mischievous grin. His feelings lurch in a paternal direction: he longs to protect her, to provide for her, to comfort her *for*ever, and *ever*.

He ventures out until the water is up to his neck but decides not to swim out to her. The lake bottom is no longer firm and sandy, but gooey like mud; he grips it with his toes.

Now where'd she go? he wonders a moment later. He just took his eyes off her a few seconds, and now he can't find her. He scans in all directions, his fatherly feelings rushing toward fear—but *not* for long. "AAAAAH!" he screams, as a powerful tug jerks his swimsuit halfway down his thighs. He fights to pull them up but loses his balance, as Mandy, an excellent underwater swimmer, holds onto them tenaciously. He falls forward, flailing in the water, which only makes it easier for her to jerk them over his knees, then all the way off. By the time he regains his balance, she's racing toward the shore, swimming then wading. He pursues, to no avail. Reaching waist-deep water, he has to go down on his knees, lest he create a scene.

"TA-DAH!" she taunts triumphantly—she slaps the water with the pilfered trunks. "Look what I got, big boy. You got anything to put inside these? How'bout standing up, and showing me whatcha got ... and *every*one!"

THE SILVER CORD

Giggling hysterically, she twirls her dark trophy over her head, as she continues to backtrack toward the beach. Bryan shuffles forward on his knees. "C'mon, Mandy," he implores. "Give 'em back! This's *too* much. It's not fair."

"Whaddeyuh mean, not fair? I'm just getting yuh back. You're the *one* who snuck up on me and got my hair all wet."

* * *

The sinking sun hovers hazy-orange above Tiger Stadium across from the Dairy Queen—the SHS football field sits well back from the road (FR 115), with parking lots and practice fields all around it. Football reigns in these parts, and on Friday nights in the fall there'll be three thousand fans, and buses and marching bands, and police directing traffic, but on this sultry, next-to-last day of June the mammoth bleachers loom silent and green and vacant.

Seeking privacy, Bryan and Mandy pull around behind the DQ where the evening shadows are well established; they park facing Bixby, the side street. He hops out and soon returns with a foot-long chilidog for each, plus fries and drinks; they both smell like the beach, like sunscreen, but they quickly focus on the tasty aromas of their DQ supper. Young Mr. Howard finally got his bathing trunks back, after much pleading and cajoling, and he was able to get them on without creating a scene. Afterward, they sunbathed on the beach towels until the sun got low.

Despite the eight p.m. curfew (she has to go right home after they finish eating), Bryan feels happily laid back. No doubt he'll still need his post-Mandy release when he hits the sack later, but today's erotic charge comes more from looking than necking. They kissed some while lying on the beach, but they couldn't get hotly into it with the other bathers around—which is probably a good thing, considering how naked they were.

The DQ is not overly crowded as yet, but it'll be packed after dark; it's one of the main "drags," and the local teens come here in droves to gaze and gab and hang out, especially on hot summer nights, while others just cruise through to see who's here. Sipping his chocolate shake, Bryan watches his sweetheart eat. She still looks adorably childlike, much like when she was bobbing in the water, maybe not eleven, but fourteenish anyway, especially with chili on her mouth and her sun-dried bangs jutting in every direction. On the way here, she worked on her hair, combing it and rebanding her ponytail, but it still looks rather wild.

"That sure hit the spot, babe," she declares a while later, speaking around her straw, as she sucks up the last of her Coke float. "Next time, it's my treat."

"Glad to oblige you, my dear," he responds in a humorous, theatrical fashion, his dimples showing, "whether it's my money or *yours.*" He gives her a playful jab on the shoulder. As he does, a big red pickup skids to a halt beside them.

It's Spanky Arnold and Roy Collins. *VAH-ROOOHM! VAH-ROOOHM!* Spanky guns his souped-up Ford to announce his arrival then jumps out and struts around to Bryan's window, while Roy peers shyly in on Mandy's side. Spanky wears his T-shirt Fonzie-style, the sleeves rolled. "Where the *hell* you two been hangin' out?" he drawls, sticking his red, buzz-cut head halfway into the truck. He reeks of Aqua-Velva, and he's so sunburned that freckles are showing on his scalp. "I don't thank I've seen y'all since graduation for chrissake. But you're lookin' good, slugger—so what's the doc sayin'?" Spanky's huge, sun-blistered nose looks like it's been roasted over a fire, and it's got some kind of ointment on it that resembles axle grease.

"Everything's okay so far," Bryan answers. "But I'll know more next month, after my t—"

"You're not lookin' too bad yourself, Mandy," Spanky cuts in. "If I was Bryan, I sure wouldn't be too keen on leavin' yuh here in *god*dam Spindle, not with all these horny hayseeds *sniffin'* around—don't mind me, I'm just *run*nin' off at the mouth. But I reckon I'd pack yuh off to Baylor with me, even if I hadta hide yuh in a goddam laundry bag to getcha in the dorm."

Spanky cackles; they all laugh. "Sounds *good* to me," she quips in reply, blushing at the attention.

"So, Roy, tell us more about the regionals?" Bryan offers, to acknowledge Roy's presence and to shift the spotlight away from Mandy. "I didn't get much chance to talk with you guys that last week of school. Coach Simms just said that we got shellacked."

"That we did," Roy responds, giving a polite smile and a nod of his cowboy hat. "Those Mineola guys hit everything I served up, but we still made a game of it, until the last two innings."

"Hell, if we'd had your bat, Bryan, we woulda killed 'em," Spanky declares—twenty seconds is about the limit when it comes to keeping his mouth shut. "And we still coulda pulled it out ... if I hadn't hung that fuckin' deuce in the eighth innin'. Pardon my dirty mouth, Mandy—but that was the fattest *god*dam pitch I've thrown since little league."

"Yeh ... if I hadn't got hurt," Bryan says, shifting Mandy-ward to give Spanky more head-room. "But then again it's hard to say. You guys still had a great team, *with*out me. Who knows? You and Roy might lead them all the way to the state title next year, and not even notice that I'm gone."

"Shit *fire* and save matches," Spanky grouses. "We'll be lucky to have a winnin' season at all next year. What the fuck ... we're also losin' Calvin and Gary Bob, *and* Clyde Jensen. I won't miss Clyde none—he's a lazy goddam showoff ... but he *can* hit the long ball." Stepping back, Spanky coughs and hacks and spits, then leans in again.

Bryan pushes his hat back. "I always hoped we'd go all the way be*fore* I graduated. Yet we still had some good times, and we *did* win the Class C Legion Tournament last summer—I'm gonna miss Legion ball this year; I hear y'got a new coach?"

"Yeah," Roy says. "Coach Sollars is moving to Denton. He's gonna be the assistant running-back coach at North Texas State. He's a football guy. He just ran the Legion team, because Coach Simms is gone each summer. But he's still an A-plus baseball c—"

"You goddam *right*," Spanky cuts in. "That's why I quit the team Thursday night. We got wiped, and that asshole new coach, Henderson, didn't even give me a look. I spent the whole *fuck*in' game on the bench. The team's already O-and-four for chrissake, and that fat fart doesn't know shit about pitchin'. He's a hillbilly hack from Linden, but he thanks he's goddam Tony La*Russa*." Spanky snorts indignantly, then steps back to spit again.

After a little more back-and-forth on baseball, Bryan changes the subject: "So, Spanker, your truck's running okay? That bodywork came out great; I can't even tell you even wrecked it."

"Yeah, it's all fixed up I reckon. I just hafta pay my old man back. I still owe him five hun'erd, and I had it won last night, the whole fuckin' thang—least for a while, didn't I, Roy?"

"You sure did," Roy affirms, giving an awh-shucks smile, "for all of three minutes, till yuh put the whole wad into the next pot and lost it to Cal."

Spanky cackles and wags his head. "And all I *had* was a pair of deuces for chrissake. And everyone folded but goddam Calvin Brower, and he *al*most did. He almost threw in trip kings."

"Maybe *I* should get into one of your all-night poker games," Mandy teases. "I do pretty good when I play with my sister and Wendy Lewis."

"You can sit at my goddam table any time," Spanky quips, "but only if we play five-card strip. And if you're in the game, honey, we're talkin' *high* stakes." With that, Bryan starts the pickup amid another round of cackles and chortles. The banter is getting a bit spicy; besides, it's almost eight o'clock. Yet Mandy hardly seems in a hurry; she's still blushing and grinning broadly, showing all her teeth, which she rarely does except with Bryan.

After they exchange good-bye salutes, Bryan backs up and prepares to pull out onto Bixby, but before he can, Spanky hustles after him. "I'm glad you're okay, slugger," he confides hushedly, soberly, his blue eyes earnest and warm. He pats Bryan on the shoulder. "Now we gotta get together and shoot the shit, at least *once* before you go off to goddam Baylor."

THE SILVER CORD

SPINDLE, TEXAS - COLBY DRIVE
SATURDAY, JUNE 29, 1991 — 8:13 PM

This thing is still damp, Mandy remarks to herself, as she rolls her bikini bottom down her legs. *But I at least kept my suit on today, which is MORE than I can say for Bryan.* She giggles, as she harks back to her beach-frolic triumph. She feels a chilly pricking sensation, as her butt cheeks goose-pimple from being in the clammy swimsuit; the bedroom is coolish with the AC going. Leaving the skimpy figure-eight of green fabric on the rug, she grabs, from her chest of drawers, a faded bra plus a pair of hip-hugger panties, pale-yellow. But before she can put them on, the mirror beckons, the full-length glass on her closet door. *The lake really messed up my hair,* she notices immediately, *but I don't feel like taking that scrungee off, so I can fool with it.* She focuses on her nude figure instead. *My ass is getting bigger.* She twists one way then the other, checking out her white, goose-bumpy bottom; it looks especially pale compared to her tan legs and back. *It's not huge or anything. I just need to jog more.*

Bryan is downstairs, having decided to hang around, since her mother isn't here. It was a bummer coming home at eight, but now they have some extra time, and that has buoyed Mandy's mood. When they got here, she found a note from her mom saying she had to go to the church and fax some stuff to Pastor Ron, who's at a conference in Dallas. The note also reminded Mandy that Gretchen was sleeping over at Molly Ann's house.

My thighs are a bit flabby at the top, the maidenly high-schooler observes, as she continues to study herself in the mirror, *but it's hardly noticeable. And they don't puff out or anything, like Mama's legs do. And even her thighs aren't bad. In fact, she looks pretty good for thirty-five. She sure looks better than a lot of the ladies at the lake today—with their legs all bubbly and rippled from celluloid. No way is that gonna happen to me.*

She assumes a sexy pose, her shoulders canted one way, her hips the other, her hands gesturing provocatively, as if modeling for *Playboy.* Giving a mischievous titter, she assumes another pose and another. *I bet I could get accepted as a skin-model ... but I'd hafta get rid of these tan lines. My butt and crotch are ghostly white, and my tits too—they look like scoops of vanilla ice cream. I reckon I need to sunbathe naked in the backyard. Now Mama would love that, and the neighbors.* More titters, then comes an erotic rush, as she imagines Bryan walking in on her. She twirls about then prisses back and forth as if dancing for him; she nods her head sassily, swinging her ponytail, which is clumpy and lank after being in the lake. It turns her on when he gazes at her body, like today. For that matter, it turns her own that *lots* of guys like to look at her, though Bryan is the *only* one she seriously fantasizes about, at least since December when they started making out in earnest.

As she continues her dance, in slow motion, it dawns on her that it's been a while since she got off. A delicious shiver wiggles up her spine as she recalls the last time: she was in the tub, her thoughts shuttling between Bryan's beautiful green eyes and his big, ruddy, awesome cock, which she's never seen. The fantasy got her so hot that when she finally let go and climaxed, she sobbed and almost passed out. Too much: she forces the bathtub rapture out of her mind and quickly gets dressed.

The longer she goes without doing it, the bigger the orgasm when she does give in, so she fights the temptation until she's horny to the limit. Before Bryan came into her life, she could go a *long* time, a month or so, but now ten days is hard, even with *her* strong will. Sometimes she feels guilty about it, depending on whether her religious or rebellious side is in control—lately it's been the latter (the more time she spends with Bryan, the more free-spirited she becomes). It's a given that guys masturbate (she figures he does—he must?), but young ladies getting off? Now that's a super-taboo thing. No one knows about her orgasmic escapades, not even Wendy. At church they call it a sin—maybe it is? maybe it isn't? In any case, it's Mandy's *favorite* sin, ever since she learned how at thirteen. Maybe some Christian girls can live without it, but not *her*, and they couldn't either, if they were kissing Bryan Howard almost every day.

O Jesus, she declares to herself, as she visits the bathroom before going downstairs. *I need to get married, the sooner the better, or at least to live together with Bryan. I wish he WOULD sneak me into his dorm at Waco ... like Spanky said.*

* * *

Look at that jet," Bryan remarks a little while later, as he and Mandy lounge lazily in her porch swing—he points at a shiny, high-flying speck. "It's neat how the sun has gone down, but it's still shining on that plane. It looks like it's on fire."

"It seems like it's barely moving," she adds, cuddling close to her man. "And the white trail behind it looks super bright, like florescent paint. It's really pretty, with the pink sky under it."

He pushes now and then with his sandal, just enough to keep them swaying gently. The old chain-supported swing cries rustily, but the rhythmic squeaking is actually soothing, as it joins the crickets and a cooing dove to create an evening melody, together with the low hum of the air conditioner around the corner of the house. It's still hot and muggy, but without the sun blazing down, the heat is quite tolerable. The streetlight has yet to come on, but it's getting darker by the minute, giving them added privacy. The mosquitoes are out, yet they've only had to swat a couple. The homes on Colby are going gray, losing their color, and the lawns and the street, and the parked cars, but not the sky. Bryan likes summer sunsets, how they turn fuzzy pink in the haze, as though God airbrushed the horizon with ruddy paint, darker below, lighter above. And Mandy makes this one *extra* special.

The breeze has diminished, and the puffy clouds are shrinking and going wispy, as they do at dusk, except for one towering cumulus to the south—an isolated buildup that didn't quite push high enough to become a thundershower. The sultry air, though no longer suffocating, still smells more like afternoon than night: sun-baked roofs, hot pavement. But Bryan is focused on more intimate fragrances, those of his sweetheart: her lake-washed hair, her sunscreened skin, a hint of perfume or deodorant (faint but fresh). He aches to kiss her, and he senses the same want in her, but the necking is always better when they resist until they can't stand it. And it turns him on the most when she makes the first move. They still have an hour till her mom gets here (the note said nine-thirty), and this's all bonus time anyhow.

"I wonder if *I* could go that high," Bryan muses aloud, as he continues to follow the jetliner, "like up where that plane is?" He dimples, but the idea excites him.

"Whaddeyuh mean, babe?"

"Y'know... in one of my floating dreams ... an OBE."

"That would be *tot*ally neat, chasing a jet. I wonder if *you'd* leave a contrail."

"Get outta here," he banters, as they both laugh heartily.

"So, has it happened lately?" she asks, after they settle a bit. "You haven't said much about it since that day at the oak tree?"

"No, nothing at all. It's a big mystery, the whole thing. And like I toldjuh, they don't happen very often. And it's usually after some big change, like some emotional thing, like when Gramps died or when I lost my glove that time." He gives a quick chuckle. "Or after I first met *you* at that weenie-roast."

"So *I* was a big change, huh?" she flirts.

"I'll say ... though it took a while before I acted on it."

"Yeah, like *two* years!" They share a frolicsome laugh, then she snuggles close again.

She has on bike shorts now plus her madras shirt. While she was upstairs changing, Bryan visited the downstairs toilet then waited in the living room, where he played with Toby—all the time wishing he was up in Mandy's room helping her change. He couldn't help but picture her pussy hair, springy like wood moss, as it came out of that green bikini. Just knowing she was naked up there made his head spin, his conscience numb. "So where d'yuh think it's going—that jet?" she asks, shifting back to the plane.

"Maybe Chicago? It's headed north? Or it could be going all the way to Europe, on one of those great-circle routes?"

"I wish *we* were on it, babe," she sighs, "flying to Paris for our honeymoon, or even to Italy, like in that movie *Room with a View* we saw on your VCR—that was a super-good story."

"Maybe we will, if the summer of '94 *ever* gets here. But by then I reckon we'll be ready to honeymoon *any*where, even at the Super Eight in Sulphur Springs."

"You got that right, mister," she purrs emphatically, her breath fanning his ear and neck.

Desire quickens Bryan, as an insistent calling expands behind his fly. *O Lord,* he cries in his thoughts. *She sounds SO ready, and I'd love to oblige her. Damn ... I have a SUPER EIGHT I'd love to give her right now—hotel or not.* He can't help but laugh.

"What's so *funny*?" she asks smirkily, shifting a bit, resting her head on the back of the swing.

"I'm not telling," he teases. "Not a *chance*."

Mandy gives him a playful jab then kicks her sneakers off. She crosses her legs seductively, left over right, then right over left. The gray spandex shorts don't show as much skin as the pink-denim pair she wore to the lake, but the thigh-hugging fabric captures her shape *all* the more. Pink shorts, green bikini, gray shorts: after four-plus hours, he's stoned on her legs, but he's surely not complaining. Even her ankles turn him on, and her feet (many good-looking gals have thick, out-of-proportion ankles and big knobby feet, so they look goofy with their shoes off, but not Mandy: she's gracefully tapered ... right down to her toes). He's almost glad they're *not* going out tonight—if they were, she'd be in jeans.

She slides away, turning sideways, lifting her bare feet into the swing. Her blue eyes sparking, she kicks off his baseball hat then toes him in the ribs. He gets her back, grabbing the underside of her knee, one of her most ticklish spots. Giggling and wiggling, she escapes his grasp, retracting her leg. She hugs her upraised knees, hiding in feigned shyness her puppylike face.

After a long moment she reappears, a smirk on her mouth: "So d'yuh think I'm getting fat, babe?"

"No way, precious."

"But look how much I can grab," she counters, as she squeezes the flank of her right hip.

"C'mon, that's nuthin'. Besides, yuh need a little heft on your backside. It makes you look like a *real* woman—way more'n those skinny-assed models who look like greyhounds. You're *just* right, pretty lady." He dimples, his face warming. "And you're a *total* knockout in that bikini of yours."

She giggles then squints at him. "Yeah, I saw yuh looking."

"And I'm sure I wasn't the *on*ly one." Her coquettish squint, cutely held, melts the remnants of his conscience, the cautious sectors of his mind puddling like silly putty. The fever in his crotch grows more insistent. He blows out a silent whistle; he adjusts the bill of his c— no, he just fingers the air, forgetting that his hat lies on the porch beside the swing, where it fell when she kicked it off. Dropping the hand to his mouth, he fakes a cough. "I think you're manipulating me," he flirts.

"Whaddeyuh mean?"

"Y'bitch about your butt, just so I'll tell you how sexy it is."

"No, I don't."

"Yes, yuh do."

"Get outta here," she titters. "You think you know *every*thing, don'tcha?" But her laugh and blush—she's now redder than the sunset—give her away.

"It's okay, pretty lady. You can get me going on *this* subject anytime you want."

"Well, my ass *is* getting bigger, and it's your fault, mister ... the way you're feeding me chilidogs and taking up *all* my time. I haven't done any running this *whole* month hardly. I don't *dare* get on the scale. I reckon I've gained five pounds since school got out." Mandy, smirkily averting her eyes, looks down into the intimate space between her shirt and uplifted knees.

The sporting gives way to quietness, save for the crickets and the AC, and the brassy wail of a distant train. The streetlamp has come on, but it's still light out, enough for Bryan to inspect, with his eyes, the blondish razor-stubble on Mandy's shins, tiny, pore-seated whiskers stippling the glossy tan. He finds this sight most beguiling, as it testifies to her sexual potency, while bringing to mind (again) that thicker, darker swatch of hair, the ultimate, unseen (by him) evidence of her womanhood, which is now nestled and flattened inside her fresh panties. *She probably shaves it, the sides?* he tells himself, his thoughts hot with carnal wonder. *Spanky says all the girls do, at least in the summer.* Bryan pictures Mandy as brownish down there, not real dark, yet not blond either, but more of a ginger brown like her eyebrows (Spanky calls it the eyebrow rule: a girl's pubic hair matches her eyebrows not the hair on her head).

She glances up, giving him a quick roll of her big blue eyes, as if she knows she's naked in his thoughts. The attraction between them builds and builds, until it seems that fire is ready to break out. "Well, pretty lady," he teases, "yuh ready to call it a night? Your mama's gonna be here soon."

Mandy, scooting quickly over, kisses him long and hard. "Does *that* answer your question, mister?" Her words are husky and short of breath. They go at it again, and again. Then she whispers, "Oh, *babe*, I don't wanna stop. Let's get outta here."

THE SILVER CORD

* * *

THE WATERMELON PATCH
SATURDAY, JUNE 29 — 9:23 PM

Bryan, his knees trembling, his balls aching, fumbles with the buttons on Mandy's shirt. The muggy night drifts in around them, the smell of weeds and earth and daisies mingling with the warm, intimate aromas of serious necking: perfume, perspiration, and sunscreen—she still smells like the beach, like cocoa butter. They've said little since parking here, but they've kissed so much, that his mouth is numb. Now he's moving down, going where he's never gone. *Oh, babe, I don't wanna stop*—that's what she said back on her porch. He's not sure what she meant, but so far she's not stopping. She's helping in fact. Giggling at his left-handed struggle with her buttons, she undoes them herself, then reaches around and unhooks her bra. After she's cuddled back to him, he moves *inside* the unbuttoned shirt, his pulse skittering excitedly at the realization that she's invited him. Working around the loose cups, he fondles her breasts—they're softly full and warm, perfect handfuls of mammary flesh, and they retain their high, youthful perch, even without the bra. He quickly homes in on her nipples, one then the other. She mews lustfully. He feels them budding, firming—*O God.*

Mandy, her eyes closed, her face dreamy in the moonlight, twitches her cupid lips then curves them into a blissful half-grin. He can't help but kiss that grin. She responds, nibbling, sucking, seducing with her tongue—while her hand fondles his thigh, then the crotch of his cutoffs. "You're *so* hard," she pants, "and it's even *bigger* than I thought. I can feel it through your shorts."

Her touch thrills yet tortures, setting off deliriums of Mandy madness. He can't think; he doesn't *need* to think. He proceeds instinctively downward from her breasts, slipping his hand inside her bike shorts. After all the years of ignorance and fantasy and guy-talk concerning girls and sex and the female anatomy, he's suddenly drowning in firsthand knowledge. He probes her belly dimple then caresses her tummy, the pillowy heat of her midriff drawing his fingertips onward—to the last line of defense, a low-cut pair of undies. "Oh, precious, I love you so," he whispers, as he plays teasingly with the pantywaist, running his finger back and forth under the elastic. She utters a throaty moan, a little growl, then her tongue advances, swabbing his mouth.

O Jesus, he cries to himself, as she parts her knees, sliding her haunches forward on the seat. Taking advantage of the better angle, he finger-combs her bush, a thick but narrow strip of pubic moss, springy to the touch, and curly. He feels the whiskers on the side. *She DOES shave it. O God, she's hot and—*

"No, no, time out," Mandy gasps before he can venture over the edge of her mound. She grabs his hand, which he instantly removes.

"Oh, babe, we can't." Sitting up, she scoots away from him, just enough to give a little space between them.

He retreats the other way until he's pressed hard against the driver-side door. He feels awkward and embarrassed, his ego deflating as fast as his hard-on. She rehooks her bra and rebuttons her shirt. Scary thoughts threaten him: this petting episode might corrupt their fairy-tale love, even cause them to break up. And it's not just a Baptist, flee-youthful-lust thing but also a fear of change. If you're on a mountain peak, you can only go *down*.

The rising moon peers oblong over the tree-line, giving everything a silvery cast. There's no sound save for the crickets, and the frogs croaking at Ruby Pond. They're parked on the east side of the Howard farm, in an overgrown field: the "watermelon patch." Gramps grew the big green melons here, hence the name. To get here, you have to negotiate a weedy, two-rut trail that runs north from Longley Road—it snakes through the pines and scrub oaks east of Butler Creek, east of the pond. When Bryan was a young lad, there was a wooden gate you had to open to get into this field, but it now lies to the side, having long since rotted off its hinges. This's the first time he's brought Mandy here, though he's told her about it. It's the most private place they can escape to in a vehicle, and not just any vehicle. The Johnson grass and shrubs flailed the truck as they chugged up the boonie road, not to speak of the pine branches.

Mandy, leaning forward, fiddles with her hair. She removes that elastic, rubber-band thing then finger-fluffs her ponytail.

"I'm sorry, pretty lady," Bryan offers meekly. "I mean—"

"Now you stop it, Bryan Howard," she scolds in her blunt down-to-earth manner. "You don't owe me any darn apology." She gives a perky little chuckle, letting him know she's not mad or anything. "What we just did was natural and normal—and fun. And it was *bound* to happen, with us being together all the time. I'm not even sure why I stopped, or *how* I did. Goshdang, you big jock, you sure know how to get me hot." She rolls her moonlit eyes. "But I reckon I have a fire alarm in my brain ... from my mom, all her warnings about purity and getting pregnant." Mandy pops that elastic thing back around her ponytail.

"Well, it *would* be a tough situation if you got pregnant. And I don't carry protection, but maybe it's good that I don't?"

"I'm not so *sure* about that," she replies, tossing her newly fixed ponytail. She gives a wee grin then sits back.

He moves closer and takes her hand. "But really, Mandy, I want our first time to be right and perfect. I want you as my wife. I want to make *real* love to you."

She softens, her countenance going tender. "Oh, dear Bryan," she replies, tears glistening. "You're so serious and good. But I *am* your wife, at least in my heart." She hugs him. "And this doesn't change *any*thing; our plans are still the same, no matter *what.*" She holds him tighter. "I am now and forever yours." Her emphatic bull's-eye declaration relieves his big fear, and she's not finished. "I just wish we could run off and get hitched tonight. Then we'd never have to stop, or feel *weird* about doing it."

He strokes her back and shoulder. "Oh, precious Mandy," he whispers. "You're my love, my life, my whole universe. I can't even fathom what it would be like without you."

"You're *my* universe as well," she coos, giving him a smooch on the cheek. "When I'm apart from you, I only look forward to seeing you again. But when we kiss and neck, it drives me *crazy*—I guess you noticed. It's like ... I'm outta control."

"Well, pretty lady, I was hardly a champion of self-restraint while ago. I'd hafta say this going-crazy problem is pretty much a mutual thing." He laughs. "But we'll survive this somehow."

"Yeah, if we both wear chastity belts," she quips, as she slides the other way to get some talking room. "But seriously, babe, it's a miracle we've gone this long. We've paced ourselves rather well if you ask me. Most kids would be screwing their brains out after seven months, even the goody-goodies at the church, like Sandy and Gary Bob: I know they're doing it." Mandy's on a roll; she paddlewheels her hands—they look ghostly in the moonlight. "And at school, it's even more—well, almost all the girls brag about their sexual adventures, and half of 'em are on the pill. I don't say anything, except to Wendy, but I hear 'em telling their naughty secrets—at lunch, on the bus, in the hall."

Bryan has never heard her talk so candidly about sex. Until tonight they've always just flirted about it, using innuendo and code words. And he's always pictured girls (despite Spanky's stories) as less horny, and much less prurient, than guys, especially Christian girls. "So, pretty lady, is tonight the farthest you ever went with a guy?" he asks, taking bold opportunity while the subject is still hotly in play.

She gives him a playful slap to the knee. "Just whaddeyuh think?" she giggles, as she retreats to her window. "Y'got pretty *dad*gum close, mister. Another couple inches and your fingers woulda been wet I tellyuh." Her countenance goes dreamy again, as if wishing she hadn't stopped him. Her moonlit features seem cutely out of focus, a smeary buzzed look befitting the risqué direction of the conversation.

His dick comes up again, a chugging tumescence. "Well, what about that guy at the church you used to hang with before I got up the nerve to call yuh, the one who always liked to pray out loud at the teen-ministry meetings?"

She knits her brow, feigning mental effort. "Oh, uh ... you mean Derrick? Yeah, we were friends, but he moved to Florida."

"I know, but did you guys uh ... well—"

"Did he *fond*le my tits? Is that what you're asking? Well, I'm not *tell*ing." Mandy blushes, her cheeks flushing—they look more gray than red in the lunar light. "But I reckon y'were jealous, weren't yuh? Well, it serves you *right,* for not calling me sooner." She *rat-ah-tats* her fingernails on the roof of the pick-up. He figures she's putting him on about the tit-fondling—but either way his revived boner presses his fly. "Nawh, Derrick was *tot*ally geek," she confirms, tittering. "He was funny and all, but he seemed more like a little brother. He was my age, but he acted younger. We never even kissed—oh, maybe once or twice."

"I reckoned as much."

She pokes a sassy tongue at Bryan. "You think you're so smart, but y'don't know *all* my secrets." She fidgets her mouth then crinkles her nose, doing her rabbity thing. "So what about you, mister? How many girls have *you* kissed and fondled?"

"Not one," he chortles (it's true he never fondled any, but he did make out with Dixie Lynn Starr). "I never even *looked* at another girl, except you, pretty lady."

"Yeah right ... like I'm *really* gonna believe that."

Bryan laughs but lets her have the last gibe, as their sporting gives way to quietness—except for the crickets and frogs, and Mandy's fingers going *rat-ah-tat-tat* on the roof again. His hard-on dwindles, but not the ache in his balls.

The lengthy interlude, two minutes maybe, cools their emotions, but not the subject. "It is rather amazing," she says matter-of-factly, as she brings her right hand back into the truck.

"What is?" he asks, fiddling with the keys in the ignition—he figures it's almost time to go.

"That we've gone all these months without doing anything below the neck—until tonight. Take Wendy: she went all the way in ninth grade, with Clyde Jensen, in the back of his father's Oldsmobile. And the next summer she did it with her cousin while he was visiting from California. And all this year she was boffing Jerry, until they broke up, even after they broke up. Yet I don't see her as a slut or anything. And the girls on the softball team: a lot of 'em are doing it with their boyfriends—or girlfriends when it comes to the lesbians, like Thelma Jo." Giving a coy chuckle, Mandy stretches toward the windshield, toward the moon. "But I reckon it's good we didn't go any farther tonight, since I'm most likely ovulating—it's been two weeks since I got my last period." She clears her throat then gives a spunky little snort. "But it's just a matter of time; it's gonna happen, and I'm not gonna feel one darn bit guilty about it, no matter what I hear at church." She gives a dismissive wave of the hand. "Oh, I suppose it *is* sinful in a way, according to the letter of the Bible ... and all the pastors hafta preach against it, but it's like a natural thing, so I can't see God getting all lathered over it, like Mama does. She talks about lust and premarital sex like it's worse than murder."

"But what we have is *way* bigger than lust," he replies. "We want sex because of love?"

Mandy gives him a saucy side-glance. "Well, love keeps us together *after*ward. But I also want sex for *sex*—because it's fun and wild, and it *feels* good, like *nothing* else." She titters sassily. "So lust is a key thing, and a good thing ... 'cause it makes us crave it; it makes sex awesome and mind-blowing. Otherwise, mating would be a bore ... like homework."

"Gosh, you're as bad as Spanky," Bryan kids her, as he starts the truck, willfully fighting off a need to kiss her again. "You're *wilder* than I thought."

"Very true—but, mister, you haven't see *any*thing yet."

* * *

This whole night has been like a wet dream, Mandy declares to herself, as Bryan drives her home. She cuddles next to him, her head on his shoulder. They ride in cozy silence, save for the rattling of the pickup. They're headed south on Misty Hollow Road, a bumpy, winding ribbon of gravel and clay that will get them to Butler Road—it's a shortcut to her house, shorter than going west to 115. *I reckon it's good we stopped, but he sure has the equipment to take me all the way—and HOW.* Her own genitals are still tingling with the after-currents of her arousal. He took her well up the mountain, as her wet panties attest, but her hormones are back in the barn, at least enough to keep her hands off him. It's after ten o'clock, so she expects a big-time lecture from her mom—but she's content to pay that price, considering.

This back road, occasionally impassable during spring rains, is otherwise tolerable, though tough on the shocks. But Mandy is scarcely thinking about the bumpy ride: *It felt so big, his dick—it was like a bat handle in his pants. I wish I could see it in the raw.* She fantasizes about Bryan's cock, but she's never seen it, hard or soft, even at the lake today when his bathing suit was off—the water was too murky. For that matter, she's never seen any post-pubescent penis, not in real life. She did watch an X-rated movie once, during a basketball trip when she was a sophomore. They were playing in a tournament in Longview, and they stayed at the Ramada Inn. One of the seniors rented a triple-X video and they all crowded into one room to watch it. Though Mandy was quite captivated by the loose women and the hunky guys with boners, she felt guilty for being there—so she slipped out before it was over, returning to her own room. Yet the sex-movie added authentic phallic content to her sexual fantasies from then on.

Bryan slows the truck, as they trundle over a narrow bridge. Mandy lifts her head to see where they are. It's only five minutes more to her house. Moths and June bugs swirl like snowflakes in the high-beamed headlights. Replacing her head on his shoulder, she closes her eyes. She wishes they were going the other way, toward the Super Eight in

THE SILVER CORD

Sulphur Springs.

* * *

Bryan motors west (northwest actually) on Colby, then Bixby, having just left Mandy at her house. He walked her to the porch but didn't go in. The Escort was in the driveway, so he figures she got a less-than-positive welcome. Nonetheless, he can't help but feel good about what happened at the watermelon patch.

O Lord, she likes sex just as much as me, he declares to himself, as he turns right on FR 115 and accelerates northbound (the less-bumpy way home) *and when she gets going about it, she talks like a horny guy. Whew, it's enough to make me weak. I never knew girls—well, I guess Spanker was right after all.* He blows out a silent whistle. *I reckon I should put a couple of rubbers in my wallet.* He chuckles under his breath.

And contrary to society's loose-and-naughty label (Christian society in particular) for gals who boldly embrace their sex drive and the erotic pleasure it gives, his respect for Mandy has not diminished, but has skyrocketed rather, along with his love and need for her. He sees her wanton, naughty-girl appetites as good, good, nothing but *good*—and he's excited about her honesty and openness, the spunky, candid way she talks about sex and lust.

As the pickup hums by the moonlit little-league fields, he whips on the radio—it's still on *Country Rock 104*—where he finds Kenny Rogers and Dolly Parton doing "Islands in the Stream." He feels pumped and proud, even more so than this morning, when he was listening to *ZZ Top* on his way to the diner. This day has come full circle, and he'll never forget it.

THE SILVER CORD

CHAPTER SEVEN

SPINDLE, TEXAS - COLBY DRIVE
SUNDAY, JUNE 30, 1991 — 9:15 AM

"I know, *Mama,*" Mandy reacts, as she slurps her Rice Krispies. "But we *already* had this fight ... last night when I got home."

Helen Stevens, clad in her blue terrycloth robe, is at the sink doing dishes. "Yeah, when you got home *two hours* late."

"I *am* seventeen, y'know? Almost anyway? Whoever heard of someone my age having to be home on Saturday night ... in the summertime no less. It's *tot*ally weird."

"That's not the point, young lady ... as I've said ten times."

"Goshdang it; you treat me like I'm younger than Gretchen."

"In a way you are—at least, she was responsible enough to get up for the Sunday-school bus this morning, even at Molly Ann's house. Vicki called and said Gretch and Molly both went on the bus, and it was Gretchen's idea. She's only in grade school, but she's already persuading her friends to get closer to the Lord. That's more than I can say for you, Amanda. And if you're so old and grown up and all, how come you're not up here doing these dishes? They've been here since *yes*terday?"

"Well, I'm gonna do *these* ... when I'm done."

Helen sighs. "You used to ride the bus every week ... but you haven't gone to your Sunday-morning teen class since Easter."

"Whoop-whoop, whoopee-do," Mandy sasses, as she takes a bite of her toast.

Helen whips around and glares at her daughter. "You better *watch* it," she warns, her pixie-face bunched about the bridge of her nose, her hazel eyes narrowed. "You're not too old to get slapped, y'know?" She employs her disturbed-mother voice, which is higher in volume but more so in pitch.

"Just 'cause I skipped teen-ministry Sunday school?"

Helen returns to her dishes, and her normal timbre: "No, because of your smart-aleck, *know*-it-all attitude."

Mandy spills some milk, from her cereal spoon; it splatters on her bare thigh; she wipes it with the paper towel she's using as a napkin. She still has on the baby-doll nightie she wears to bed in the summer. "Well, Mama, there's one thing I *do* know. None of my friends hafta stay home on Saturday night. It's not fair—I should be able to stay out till midnight, like them."

"Normally true ... but *this* time I wanted you home by eight, and yet you de*fied* me; that's the reason I got upset."

"But we *were* here at eight," Mandy declares, her mouth full of toast, "just like I toldjuh last night."

"I know, I know. I saw your bikini on the floor in your room when I got home—but I'd like to know the *rest* of the story."

"The rest?"

"That's what I said, Amanda Fay. I'd like to know *why* you took it upon yourself, to just take off again with Bryan?"

Last night Mandy managed to escape to her room without telling a blatant lie, but now she's forced: "No, it's not like that. We uh ... we sat on the porch for a while, then we decided to go back to the DQ, that's all." She gives her mom a head nod, a nonchalant gesture. "So what's the big deal? It's not like we eloped or anything?" She suffers a pang of guilt, for the lie—she hates to lie—especially as she considers where she and Bryan *actually* went and what they *actually* did, not to mention her erotic dream and the ensuing fit of self-gratification.

"I have my doubts," Helen declares.

"So whaddeyuh have doubts about?" Mandy asks, painting herself into a corner that will surely require more equivocating. She dabbles in her cereal, having lost her appetite. Helen, now finished with the dishes, is busy clearing the counter, so she doesn't answer right away.

I wish I was grown up and out of here, Mandy murmurs to herself. *Then I'd never have to lie about me and Bryan. We'll be legally married and going on our honeymoon, to some exciting, faraway place, like on that plane we saw at sunset.* For that matter, she'd like to be anywhere right now instead of sitting guiltily in this all-too-familiar kitchen with its yellow '60s-era appliances, and yellow formica, and yellow curtains—yellow everything. She's seated in her usual spot at the table, her back to the laundry-room door. The cottage curtains are actually more khaki than yellow, but she's still tired of seeing them every day, with their prim pleats and ruffles and perfectly adjusted tiebacks. The sash of her mother's robe is tied just as perfectly, in a precise, squared-off bow, and save for a darkish spit curl dangling on her forehead, her hair looks flawless, even after sleeping on it.

She's so darn neat and proper and careful, Mandy goes on in her thoughts, as she sweeps her own hair back—it's not in a ponytail, so it's hanging all over like a windblown haystack. *I almost expect her to sprout a beak, so she can preen herself. I can't imagine her parking with a guy or petting, much less having a sweaty, mind-blowing orgasm, yet she must've with Charlie. And she had to park with my real dad, if they were doing it when she was sixteen. But she's a godly MOTHER now. I love her, but if I tell her the truth, I'll be grounded for a YEAR..*

After wiping off the counters and letting the water drain out of the basin, Helen dries her hands on a kitchen towel—as she does, she answers her daughter, finally: "I have my doubts that you two were at the Dairy Queen after you left here."

"But, *Ma,* we were," Mandy lies emphatically. The half-eaten toast on her plate looks suddenly disgusting, as do the soggy Rice Krispies. Her stomach churns. "Since you weren't home, we just figured we'd go back for an ice cream. It's no big deal ... really."

"I'll bet," Helen snorts. "The way your face was all raw and red, you musta been eating some *pow*erful ice cream. All I can say is ... you two better *not* be doing anything below the neck."

"We're not, Mama. We're not. How many *times* do I hafta say it?" The sick churning in Mandy's gut swirls downward, like the dishwater in the sink. She feels suddenly confused and alone, a far cry from the bold, Devil-be-damned aplomb she displayed in the pickup last night. Her eyes fill, her throat tightens. Now it comes, the urge to confess, to repent, to tell *every*thing, but she fights it off, biting her tongue. Bryan flashes into her mind, his kisses, his eyes, his roving fingers, his bat-handle boner. She wishes she had no sex drive—it sullies her dreams; it forces her to lie; it makes her crazy and loose in the head.

Helen, as if sensing Mandy's dismay, comes over and places her arm around her daughter. "Oh, Amanda," she consoles, her tone now gentle. "I don't mean to harp, but I worry—well, y'know what I mean. I don't wantcha to get your emotions all hyped and twisted and outta whack ... like I did. You're so young. You're not even out of high school." She pauses, taking a slow breath—she smells like coffee. "I know you're very attached to Bryan ... and I'm sure that things have been super intense for you ... with him getting hurt, and you two being together most every day since. I haven't put my foot down about it ... because I've prayed, and God has given me peace, even though I don't always show it, like last night." She laughs. "But we're gonna get through this ... with the Lord's help."

"I know, Mama," Mandy replies, as she gets up from the table. "I've been praying too." (This is not a lie.) She gives her mother a hug. Her throat hurts, but she holds back the tears.

"Oh my," Helen declares. "It's almost nine-thirty. I've got to get a move on it if I'm gonna get to the church on time—I hafta be there at least thirty minutes before service."

She exits the kitchen, but Mandy stops her, "Oh, Mama?"

"Yes, dear?"

"I think I'll ride with you this week, instead of Bryan. I just hafta call him, so he won't come by to pick me up."

* * *

SPINDLE, TEXAS - COLBY DRIVE
SUNDAY JUNE 30, 1991 — 12:35 PM

Why are God's rules so impossible? Mandy sighs to herself, as she slips out of the lavender shirtdress she wore to church. *Maybe we should just see each other twice a week, like during the school year?* She stares at the telephone on the night table beside her bed. *Maybe I should call him right now? No, I'll wait. O dear Jesus, I don't know what to do, but last night was way out of bounds. We can't be—it's still three years. We hafta cool it.*

Tossing the dress onto her unmade bed, she grabs a pair of Levi's plus a polo. Her maidenly body, sporting only bra and panties, looks just as sexy and photogenic as last evening, yet she pays scant attention to the mirror as she pads about her room. *Pastor Ted can't preach like Pastor Ron, but there's no escaping what he said. Walk in the Spirit, and ye shall not fulfill the lust of the flesh. I wish Bryan had been there. I wonder what happened to him.* After pulling on the jeans and shirt, Mandy fluffs her hair but doesn't band it back into the usual ponytail; she feathered it out for church and decides to leave it that way. *I love Bryan, but he needs to hear the Word as much as me, especially when he's had all those strange dreams. Maybe he really did come out of his body, but it might be some kind of deception? Mama would freak if I told her, just like she freaks over sexual stuff.*

Plunking down on her bed, she slips into her bum-around sneakers. *We can't be touching each other. I don't wanna hurt Bryan, but I can't be lying to Mama every day, and yet it doesn't seem—goshdang it all! It's HARD to walk in the Spirit. I don't know what to do.* Mandy gives a little snuffle, as she notes the green bikini, still on the rug where she left it last night. (A huge oval rug, the braided kind, covers most of the hardwood floor.) *This room is a disgusting mess, and the dust is thick enough on my desk to write my name, and Toby's hair is all over.*

Bouncing to her feet, she scoops up the swimsuit, her bike shorts, her madras shirt, her pink-denim shorts, her shorty night-gown, plus assorted socks and underwear; she also gathers the pile of clothes from the bean-bag chair in the corner, including her waitress uniform from yesterday. To the hallway: she dumps the armload of clothes near the head of the stairs. After rehanging her Sunday dress in the closet, she strips the dirty sheets from her bed and piles them in the hall as well. Then she grabs clean stuff from the linen closet and hustles back into her room.

"My, this *is* quite a change," Helen declares, looking in on her daughter. "And on a Sunday afternoon no less."

"Good a time as any," Mandy replies, as she makes up the bed. She does her lip-puckering, nibbling routine then gives a quick little grin, but it feels like a grimace.

"It'll just be us for lunch, since Gretchen's going to the lake with Molly Ann. Then I hafta go to Kroger's this afternoon—they're debugging our new computer system; a special team is here from Dallas. But I reckon I can make some sloppy joes?"

"Sounds good. That'll give me just enough time to vack and dust in here ... after I get a load going in the washing machine."

* * *

Two hours later: Bryan Howard, wearing new Levi's and a button-down shirt, squeaks to a halt in front of the Stevens house. He'd rather be in shorts and such, but the dressy attire (dressy for a summer afternoon in Spindle) goes better with his less-than-relaxed state of mind. Getting out, he adjusts his Tiger cap then strides up the walk. Overhead, the sun peers fuzzily through a deck of cirrus, which has muted the shadows, cutting the heat back some ten degrees from yesterday. The high, rainless clouds, together with the haze and lack of wind, give the afternoon a dingy, sterile, gray-callous air—a most apt setting. The triumphant confidence that buoyed him as he left here last night seems a distant memory. He's been wrestling with negative vibes, ranging from simple unease to near-panic, since he woke up this morning, and especially after she called: "I'm riding with Mama, so you don't hafta pick me up for church."

Before he gets to the front door, Mandy comes out. He gives a little grin, painfully forced. "So, pretty lady, d'yuh wanna go for an ice cream," he asks—more to confirm his fears than with any hope of actually going to the DQ. His mood, poised to go down, does so instantly, as her blank countenance and listless body-English telegraph her reply.

"I can't go *any*where today," she says, stepping away from him toward the swing, beyond the swing. "I hafta fold laundry." Her detached tone hurts as much as what she's saying. "Plus, I told Mama I'd mow the backyard and weed her flower beds while she's at Kroger's." Still facing away, Mandy drums her fingers on the corner post of the porch. "By the way, we missed you at church this morning? Pastor Ted preached the message."

Bryan moves closer but stays on his side of the swing. "You can't even get away for an hour?" No answer. "Whaddeyuh mean you hafta fold *laun*dry? I never heard such a thing. Y'just don't wanna go— right?" No response. Her mum remoteness hits him much harder than yesterday on the way to the beach, for this silence has nothing to do with her stepfather, and everything to do with the watermelon patch— at least, that's how he reads it. "C'*mon*, Mandy, tell me the truth." She shifts her weight from one sneaker to the other, but says nothing.

O Jesus, it's over for us, he cries in his thoughts. *I knew it. I knew it.* He leaps beyond logic to arrive at such a dire verdict, yet on this grayish afternoon there's little chance of seeing things objectively, not when the prospect of losing her rips and claws at his sanity. *It hasn't even been twenty-four hours since we were sitting in this swing, laughing and teasing and flirting. And now she's gone. Yet she looks so beautiful with her hair fluffed out—and adorable and huggable and kissable. O Lord, I lost it in the truck last night. I shoulda kept my hands to myself.*

Anguish grips his bosom. "Damn it, Amanda!" he barks, his hurt igniting. "What's wrong with you? Why won't you *say* anything?" He kicks the swing; it sways crazily.

"I already did," she replies, finally—still facing away.

"Yeah, a bunch of *crap* about laundry and church."

She pops the porch railing with the palm of her hand. "You don't hafta get so *huffy* with me."

"Well, I can't help being huf—"

"And it's *im*portant what happens at church," she interrupts, giving a snort of exasperation. "It sure wouldn't hurt you, mister, if you paid a little more *attention* to what the Lord has to say. Or have yuh decided to leave God *out* of your life now?"

"That's not fair, Mandy—and why don'tcha turn around, so I can see you?"

"You *can* see me."

"Yeah, your *back*. This's crazy. What's wrong with you?"

"*Me*? Nothing's wrong with me. *You*'re the one who's pissed off. *You're* the one who skipped service today, and *you're* the one who started unbuttoning my shirt. And now you're pushing and prying and digging ... but y'don't know what I go through. You're a *guy*. You have no *F*-ing idea what it's like to be a girl. And your parents always give you *every*thing you want. You never had to live in a rent-house with a *single* mom. So just *stop* it." She stomps her foot for emphasis.

"I uh ... I uh," he stutters, his eyes filling, his words crumbling amid a ragged thickness in his throat. Silence overtakes the porch, save for the drone of the AC and the parched whirring of grasshoppers. He pulls a handkerchief from the back pocket of his jeans, not something he routinely carries, but this day is *hard*ly routine. He dabs his eyes, trying to regain his composure, and he does after a minute, at least enough to say, "Oh, pretty lady, we need to *talk*." His quaking voice leaves no doubt that these words are straight from the heart.

"I know, babe." Though still speaking the other way, off the end of the porch, her voice has lost its combative edge.

Bryan exhales, his hopes quickening—they've made it past the critical point. But alas, the sound of a car pulling up snatches his attention before either of them can say another word. It's Wendy Lewis in her beat-up Subaru.

* * *

I like Wendy, but her timing sucks, Bryan laments, as he turns off Butler onto Misty Hollow. The sky has brightened, the clouds thinning. But sunshine makes *this* road darker, because of the trees—at least this stretch near the bridge. When Wendy arrived, all cheery and chirpy, her braces gleaming, he realized his cause was lost. So he quickly departed, telling Mandy he'd call her later.

The air, though warm, has that mossy, mucky, dry-creekbed smell. After rattling across the one-way bridge, Bryan swings left, then right before attacking a long, gradual hill. There's gravelly peastone on this upslope (unlike most of Misty Hollow), but it's still bumpy—the rippled undersurface peeks through here and there like so many washboards.

THE SILVER CORD

This century-old byway (once a cattle trail) meanders northward in the shallow valley defined by Misty Creek and Butler Creek (in contrast to Longley Road, a straight section-line road that gets more maintenance). He feels better after the emotional exchange on Mandy's porch; they did, after all, get past the fighting part to the let's-work-it-out part—no, that's a lie: he feels worse, lousy, sucky; they'd be hugging and kissing right now if Wendy hadn't appeared on the scene.

Reaching Longley, he hangs a left toward his house, but no way can he go home now. He should rush back to Mandy—maybe Wendy's already gone? No, it could make things worse. Killing the impulse, he takes a right, rumbling down onto the two-rut trail which runs to the watermelon patch. But unlike last night he goes only a hundred yards, just far enough to hide among the pines. Bumping to a halt near Butler Creek, he kills the engine. No breeze, not even a whisper—most rare for a summer day, or any day in Texas. The trees seem strangely silent, as if listening: *Damn ... this whole situation sucks. I can't figure it. Mandy was so bold and free last night: "What we just did was natural and normal—and fun. Goshdang, you big jock, you sure know how to get me hot." But today she snaps at me about unbuttoning her shirt— and yet SHE's the one who unbuttoned it?*

In his right mind he'd surely see this spat with Mandy, their first real tiff, as inevitable, but he's *way* too involved to realize the obvious. Shifting his long legs, he slumps back against his door. *Dear God, I know I haven't been as devout as I should be. And I know I'm supposed to set my affections on things above, and I'm supposed to flee youthful lusts, but when it comes to Mandy, I can't HELP myself. I love her more than anything, including you, God ... to be honest.* He lifts his hands, a resigned gesture. *I'd like to think that loving her and loving you is the same ... with NO downside or shame, like in my near-death experience where the love was glorious and free and inclusive and unlimited. But church is different. When I'm at church, I tend to feel guilty, like my Mandy-love is a sin, or at best a weakness. And the same goes for my OBEs—they just don't fit. Goshdang it all! Maybe I'm a deluded, lust-crazed sinner? I don't know. Yes, I do. It can't be sin. It can't. But how can I be sure?* Bryan removes his cap, placing it on the dashboard. Wringing his hands, he gives a dejected murmur. *This whole month was like—well, everything was going SO good, super good, even last night, especially last night. But then—oh shit, I can't figure it.* He buries his face in his hands. He feels again the thickness in his throat, the need to cry. Colors dance in his darkened mind, red, green, blue, purple, as if the northern lights are flashing in his palms. *Why do we hafta condemn our biggest, most wonderful feelings and dreams in order to be godly?*

Scooting to the other side of the truck, he throws open the passenger-side door. Sitting sideways on the end of the seat, he watches a gray squirrel, as it scurries about under the nearest pine tree. The lump in his gullet dissolves but not his need for answers. *Where does love end and lust begin? A hug-thought is godly and pure, while a sex-thought is dirty and obscene—until we say vows and get paperwork. Yet when I was zooming through that tunnel on the way to see Gramps, and to get my glimpse of Heaven, I didn't hafta suppress anything. But to be godly down here, you hafta pretend that you're someone that you're not. I do have youthful lust for Mandy. In fact, I have wild, burning, raging, stormy, unSPEAKABLE lust for her! There's no MAYBE about it. I do want her. I do! I do! And yet, this's WAY bigger than sex. It's all part of an awesome and beautiful dream.* He shakes his head, giving a weary little snuffle. *It's so dadgum confusing, the whole human sex thing—like why do we go through puberty at thirteen if we're supposed to wait until we're twenty or twenty-five before we start fucking? Excuse my language, God ... but can yuh ANSWER that for me?*

God doesn't reply. At least, young Mr. Howard doesn't discern any audible answer coming down. He hears only the crickets and grasshoppers plus the occasional chattering of the squirrel, who's now high up in the tree. Bryan knows full well, as with any lifelong Baptist, that you look inside for the counsel of God—the Lord speaks through a "still small voice." But on this trying day he needs more; he needs loud, clear answers: PLAIN ENGLISH. Giving a sigh, he slaps his knee. He wishes Gramps was here. He'd surely understand what he's going through. Gramps *must* know he's in love with Mandy, however it is that departed souls get knowledge about earthly things. To communicate with a dead person, they teach at church, you must pray to God, and he (the Holy Spirit), or one of his angels, like Gabriel, will pass it on—if it's God's will to do so. This teaching strikes Bryan as contrived and convoluted, especially when he was able to read his granddad's thoughts directly during his NDE. But today's gloomy confusion casts doubt on that even. He can't be sure he actually went out of his body on that day at Oiler Park. Maybe it was all a dream? Plus his OBEs? Maybe his whole life is dadgum dream? No, no—he has to claim some things as being *real*.

He could talk with his mom; he does confide in her, though never about sex. His dad, as a man, would identify more, but they seldom talk about *any* kind of personal stuff, and the mood is always awkward when they try. Bryan could go look for Spanky, or Roy, or Billy Ray Campbell, *someone* to hear his story. They might be at the bowling alley, and he could grab a couple of beers in the lounge to soothe his mind, or he could go down to Benny's Billiard Hall on Caddo Street; that's where Billy Ray hangs out. (Both places are lax about checking IDs, especially with jocks.) *C'mon, get with it,* he admonishes himself amid pangs of self-disgust. *You haven't touched beer since you started going out with Mandy. And that pool room is the seediest place in town.*

THE SILVER CORD

He goes on wrestling till his mind seems ready to blow a fuse. Finally, he exits the truck to take a leak, pissing near the tree the squirrel scurried up. An underground rock pokes up grayly among the pine roots like the back of a sea turtle. The stream of urine splatters on the sandstone turning it black. He hasn't resolved anything, but the foggy exhaustion in his brain feels almost like relief, like how you feel when you finish a three-mile run. *I'll go to the house and rest, and grab a bite to eat. Then I'll call her.*

* * *

As Bryan heads home, Mandy and Wendy talk in the kitchen on Colby Drive. "So you're actually gonna get your braces off?" Mandy replies, as she fiddles with the coffeemaker—it looks like a Mr. Coffee, but it's really a cheapo imitation from K-mart (most everything in the house came from K-mart or Wal-Mart).

"Yeah, in two weeks," Wendy affirms—she's already seated at the kitchen table. Just off work, she's still spiffed up: skirt and blouse plus her Byer's Drug name tag. "Dr. Nickles says my teeth are ready; he's my orthodontist." But as of now, she still has her braces, along with that sibilating undertone in her voice, sort of a wet but gritty hiss, as though she has buckshot in her mouth.

"Dr. Nickles ... he's in Sulphur Springs, right?"

"Yeah, most of the local girls go to him. Course, they're all younger than me. I didn't get my braces until I was fifteen. I feel wicked weird when I go there, like I'm back in junior high."

The coffeemaker gurgles and coughs, filling the room with the aroma of fresh brew. Mandy, her arms folded, leans back against the counter. She acts relaxed, but her emotions churn and ache. She doesn't give a goshdarn about braces or which girls are going to Dr. Nickles. She needs to talk seriously: about her and Bryan. But cautionary pangs in her conscience are making her hesitant, and Wendy is also avoiding the subject. No doubt she knows that something *intense* was taking place when she arrived thirty minutes ago. The two girls did chat and joke around on the porch before coming inside, and yet the topics out there were even less personal: the drug store, the diner, softball, basketball, money, cars, and so forth. "I shoulda got braces myself," Mandy responds finally, "the way my teeth overlap."

"Ah, that overlap of yours is *noth*ing. Your teeth are wicked nice. You saw mine before. I could whistle between my front teeth." They both giggle. "But now I've had wires and metal in my mouth for two years. It's dis*gust*ing."

"Not to me, Wen. I think your braces are cute."

Wendy gives a sour, closed-eye grimace, as if she just chewed the skin of a lemon. "Cute, cute: I'm wicked tired of being *cute*. Cute is okay for puppies and hamsters, and teenyboppers, but I'm seventeen, kiddo." Giving a hissy laugh, she sweeps her hair back. Her moppy, mouse-brown locks are normally mussed from being under her softball cap, but today her hair is nicely groomed, in a breezy, blow-dried, go-to-work 'do.

"But you *are* cute," Mandy persists teasingly—she continues to act nonchalant. "And I like your hair; it's *tot*ally cool."

"Well, Mrs. Byer gets wicked pissed if we come in with bad hair. It's one of her pet peeves."

After pouring coffee into a mug for Wendy, Mandy searches for something sweet to munch on. "Well, you outdid yourself, Wen, like A-plus-plus."

Wendy blushes, as she doctors her coffee. "Thanks, kiddo—I like your hair too; you should wear it fluffed out more often."

Finding a package of oatmeal cookies, Mandy opens it and puts some on a plate. "I can deal with it on Sunday, but wearing bangs plus a ponytail is way easier ... not as easy as pulling it *all* back, but I hate that blah, bare-foreheaded, super-jock look—it makes yuh look like a guy." Wendy titters but doesn't reply, as she's busy dunking one of the cookies. Mandy pops open a can of Dr. Pepper. "I'm not much into coffee. I get my caffeine this way." She gestures with the can then plunks down across from Wendy, who's already dunking a second cookie.

"I got hooked on coffee in seventh grade," Wendy says, her voice clogged. "That's the same year I tried cigarettes, but I didn't get hooked on them, thank goodness."

O God, I can't stand this small-talk, Mandy declares to herself, as she nibbles a cookie. It's hard to get started when it comes to sharing super-personal stuff, even with her best chum, especially today when she feels bad about lying to her mother, not to speak of Pastor Ted's sermon. Not only did he come down hard on the lusts of the flesh, but he also warned about the "wicked" influence of worldly friends ("wicked" in the evil sense, as opposed to the slangy superlative Wendy employs). Mandy could never think of Wendy as being evil, no way, never, never, but there's no denying that she's worldly. And yet, it's her worldliness ironically that makes her fun to be with—and *extra* valuable as a confidant. Despite the fact they're only months apart in age and Mandy outshines her friend when it comes to looks, Wendy is much more experienced when it comes to guys and romance—and sex *for sure.*

The bottled-up ache inside Mandy corkscrews downward, twisting hotly in her stomach. Nevertheless, after a quick sip of Dr. Pepper, she maintains the relaxed facade. "So your braces will be long gone when school starts again?"

"That's right, kiddo. And it's gonna be wicked weird going back with nothing but teeth in my mouth. No one's gonna recognize me." She laughs, as does Mandy. "Now if I could just get rid of these *damn* zits."

"Your complexion looks pretty clear to me," Mandy replies, exaggerating a trifle to encourage her.

"Get outta here. I *do* look in the mirror, y'know?"

But Mandy's assessment is not entirely out of line. Wendy's pimples *have* decreased in number, making her elfin face more appealing, even with the braces and odd, puggish nose. And her hairdo helps a lot, the way it's parted slightly off-center, and styled into soft wings that tickle the brow and accent her brown eyes, making them more lively and alluring. She looks most chic and ladylike as she sits there sipping coffee, a far cry from the sweaty, dusty, hard-charging Wendy on the softball field.

I wonder if Bryan went home, Mandy grapples silently, while Wendy elaborates about her pimples, then her extra pounds: how they show more on her short frame. *Maybe I should call him? I was so mean to him when he was here.* Her throat tightens. She stares at the cookie in her hand, her eyes welling. But then the tender vibes give way to pricks of guilt. How can she talk with worldly Wendy about romance and lust and sex and heartache, and then go back to church tonight? (She promised her mom she'd go to evening service.) The clashing emotions bring her closer to tears, but she clenches her jaw against them—she can't get all weepy now, not without telling Wendy what's going on.

Thunk!—a noise. Mandy's heart jumps, as if her mom has arrived, knowing all. But it's just Toby popping in through the cat door. The gray-and-white tom struts right over to Wendy; he greets her warmly, rubbing against her bare legs, his back arched, his tail high, then he jumps up onto her lap. He loves attention, especially from one of his favorite visitors, and he gets plenty of it, as Wendy strokes his back and head. His purr is louder than the AC in the living room, and it has the same rumbling under-tone. Having Toby come in is a relief to Mandy, since it gives her a chance to regain her composure. He hops onto the table, a bold move he'd never get away with if Mandy's mom was here. After sniffing and rejecting the platter of cookies, he pads over and gives Mandy a nuzzle.

"So, kiddo, you're really getting your own wheels?" Wendy says a minute later, after the tomcat has tired of the limelight and disappeared into the living room.

"That's right," Mandy affirms, the tightness in her throat having eased. "After my birthday. That's when I get my dad's money. It's three weeks from now, July the 20th."

"You're getting money from your dad, your *real* dad? I thought he died when you were little?"

"He did. But right after I was born, he put $1800 in a special trust for me, in a mutual-fund thing. It was set up so I couldn't touch it till I was seventeen." Mandy swigs her pop. She doesn't mind this digression, since it's lifting her mood all the more. She always feels bolder and more self-possessed when thinking about her real daddy. "I guess my father planned on adding to it, but he died in the plane crash, like I toldjuh. And yet the money has grown anyway, to almost four thou. And I have $1600 of my own from working at the diner—which took some doing."

"So what kinda car are yuh getting?"

"I got my eye on a red Firebird over on the Currier lot." Mandy drinks more Dr. Pepper then gestures with the can. "It's an '84, but it's loaded, and it's in *super* condition, so they're asking six thou. I think I can get it for $5500. If not, I can borrow the rest from Mama."

"Does she like the idea? The car thing?"

"No, not really. She says that money was intended for college, but she agrees that it's *mine* to use as I choose. Besides, I'm hoping to get a scholarship, like I toldjuh." Hopping up, Mandy grabs the coffeepot and freshens Wendy's cup.

"Thanks, kiddo. You do that with *real* style, the wrist move and all—you must be a waitress or something?"

"Yeah, the wrist-turn," Mandy quips. "That's the key, Wen. That's how I get my tips." Titters, from both.

"So where *is* your mom ... and Gretchen?" Wendy asks, as Mandy sits back down.

"Mama had to go to Kroger's. And Gretchen is still over at Molly Ann's house. You know, Molly Ann Heimberg—Alfred Heimberg's little sister?"

"Yeah, I know who she is," Wendy replies, after sipping her new coffee. "She's gorgeous for a little kid, especially being kin to Alfred. He's skinny and bug-eyed, and he's got that wicked case of acne. I never had zits that bad, even last year. Plus, he wears those thick glasses. But he's probably gonna graduate number *one* in our class ... if you don't beat him out, kiddo."

"No way," Mandy snorts. "I only hafta get ten more credits, give or take, to graduate, so I'm not about to bust my butt trying to be number one. Besides, he's well ahead of me, along with a few others. I do okay in English and history and such, but he aced Algebra II, and this year I hafta take physics from Denham. Guys do better in math and science—it's true—and those courses carry more weight, just like with Bryan. He finished third in his class, mainly because of math and science."

They both go quiet at the mention of Bryan's name. Bingo: the time has arrived. "So what the *hell* is going on with you and Bryan?" Wendy asks, gesturing with her mug. "He sure didn't look *happy* when he trotted by me on the way to his truck."

Mandy munches a piece of cookie, washing it down with the last swig of her Dr. Pepper. But before she can get into the story, Wendy says, "I bet you guys went all the way, or got damn close, and now you're fighting about it?"

THE SILVER CORD

Mandy laughs sheepishly, her face warming. She does her fidgety nose-mouth routine, pursing, puckering, smacking, biting her lip. "Goshdang, Wen, how'd yuh guess it so quick?"

Wendy grins, just enough to show her braces. "Well, I *am* past puberty y'know, and I haven't been living under a rock this whole year. You guys have been going together since Christmas, so what else could it be, except sex, sex, and *sex*? To do it, or not to do it—that *is* the question." Brief titters. "And sometimes you don't even have time to ask it, much less answer it, like my first time, with Clyde, and I was barely fifteen." Wendy giggles harder, then sips. "So uh ... are we talking *al*most, or *all* the way?"

"Almost," Mandy replies, her blush deepening, though she's most glad to be into the subject.

"When?"

"Last night."

"Where?"

"In his truck, in the woods up by his house—it was a neat place, like a field in the woods and the moon was super bright."

"Ah ... so when I arrived a while ago, you guys were still reacting and backpedaling and feeling guilty and finding fault?"

"You can say *that* again."

"No wonder Bryan gave me that drop-dead look."

After many more questions and answers, Wendy knows most everything, the love thing, the passion thing, the petting thing, the confusion thing, the mother thing, the God thing, the guilt thing, even Bryan's near-death thing back in May, every*thing*—except how Mandy deals with her unsated desires.

After a visit to the tiny hallway bathroom (around the corner opposite the stairs), Wendy reseats herself and drinks the last of her coffee. Mandy lounges back in her chair and toys with the empty Dr. Pepper can. She gives a knowing smirk.

Wendy begins, her voice softening, as much as it can considering the braces: "Well, kiddo, you know I don't go to church, except on Easter to Wesley Methodist, and sometimes on Christmas. We used to go more, before my dad left, but my mom works on Sunday, since she got her job in Mineola, at the Holiday Inn. It's a good job, running the desk—I toldjuh before. Now I still believe in God and Christ and all, or at least, I hope with all my heart that there is a loving God up there. But I'm not into it like you, Mandy, and I sure don't know the Bible the way you do. Now don't get me wrong. I don't fault you for going to church—it's the way y'were brought up, and I know you're serious about it. But I feel closer to God outside of church, like when I'm walking in a field with Butchy my dog, or in the woods, or going to the lake, or watching a movie that makes me cry, or even when we're all hot and sweaty in the late innings of a softball game, and the adrenaline is flowing. I can't explain it, but those are the times I feel most stirred and alive, and of course when I'm excited about a guy, which is the *most* alive I can get."

"Now we're cutting to the chase," Mandy interjects.

Wendy titters then sobers again. "I mean it, kiddo. To me, love and passion and sex, and pillow talk, like all of it—that's the biggest piece of God we get in this life. Now Jerry can be a total prick, especially since he started hanging with the stoners and greasers and punk nerds, but still, those special times with him, like last fall, were wicked good, like totally the best. We really got to know each other— I mean, the *nak*ed truth." They both laugh. "But not just our bodies, we also got into each other's head. I told him my true feelings. I burped and farted in front of him. We were wicked honest, like just being ourselves, like real love without acting—and I see *that* as God ... my God anyhow. But then other gods got in the way, like pot. He started pushing me to smoke weed with him all the time. I did a few times, but things were never quite the same." There are two cookies left on the plate. Wendy breaks a piece off one, pops it into her mouth. "Now I'm not saying that you and Bryan should get into it like Jerry and me. You guys hafta decide whether y'wanna wait or what. But it's the love that counts, not the damn paperwork." Wendy gives a jaunty toss of her head, along with a little hand-salute. "And it's not something to feel guilty about or to reject yourself over ... and if Jesus himself appeared right now in this kitchen, he wouldn't come down on you about last night. I mean, d'yuh think he's *shocked* that you two got totally hot with each other? Gosh damn, kiddo, it's God who created the sex drive, and the lust that fuels it. And he made love too ... *all* kinds of it. God *is* love, remember? So your love for Bryan is godly, godly, *nothing* but godly. At least, that's how I see it. And when it comes to his soul-travel experiences, especially the near-death thing, I say don't rule it out. We can't reject stuff ... just because it seems weird ... or doesn't fit with accepted tradition. So *there*."

Mandy, her heart overflowing, starts to reply, but Wendy isn't done: "It's a dead-end street to get all in a dither about trying to live up to the Bible or God's will, or your mother's hopes." She pauses, her brown eyes filling. "How you feel in your heart—that *is* God's will. It has to be, because it's *you*, and you're a good and wonderful person, Amanda Stevens. I see more God in your pretty blue eyes, than I *ever* saw in any church. And I'm wicked glad that you're my best friend."

The next thing Mandy knows, they're up hugging each other, while choking back tears.

* * *

Same day, 4:18 p.m. Bryan, seated at his Macintosh, moves a lab-report folder to a floppy disk, a folder he won't need at Baylor. It's hard, with his dreams in jeopardy, to get psyched about moving old homework files to free up memory. He's tempted to pick up the phone but resists, sticking with his game plan (he decided on the way home to call Mandy at five). With a few more mouse clicks he fills up the floppy. After ejecting it from the drive, he gets up and opens the curtains on the window behind his computer, a large bay window offering a panoramic view of the hilly northeast quadrant of the Howard property. His heart pangs, as he gazes at the giant oak tree in the distance, its sun-washed crown looming majestically above the pine grove. *This whole month was so good,* he sighs, *but now June is over, and things are different—ever since last night.* He stares at the tree until it goes blurry, then he dutifully returns to his work.

The makeshift desk matches the knotty-pine wall-paneling. His father fashioned the desktop by laying planks between the oblique walls which bracket the bay window, giving him a work surface some five feet long and three feet deep, with file cabinets underneath. When the place was built in 1946, this room had the same post-war decor as the rest of the house, but Gramps and Ruby refinished it a few years later (it was their bedroom), adding the paneling plus log pilasters and ceiling beams, to give it a more rustic, Western mood. Ruby died in 1962, but Gramps continued to occupy this room until his own death twenty years later. For five years or so the room remained empty, until Bryan moved in—it was August of '87, right before he started ninth grade. He had outgrown the smaller bedroom down the hall.

He moves a dozen more homework folders, clicking and dragging and copying and trashing, until he can't stand it any more. Too much: he has to call her. Swiveling his desk-chair to the right, he reaches for the phone, but it rings before he can pick it up. His heart leaps: "Hello?"

"Oh, babe, I'm sorry," Mandy gushes, her voice as sincere and sweet as it ever gets.

"I'm sorry too," he tells her, as relief rushes from his head to his bosom, where it becomes a warm, healing balm.

"I was so hateful to you on the porch. I had no right."

"It's okay, pretty lady. This was bound to happen—our first real argument."

"I suppose ... but I hate the feeling."

"Me too. This whole day's been a bummer—until *now.*"

Mandy laughs huskily, filling Bryan with happy electricity. Then she says, "So y'wanna go running with me tomorrow, after I get off work? I gotta get back into my routine."

"I can't run yet," he teases.

"Cut the crap, you big jock," she chortles. "*I'll* be doing the running, while you drive behind me in your pickup. We can do that two-mile stretch on Misty Hollow Road."

"Hmmm ... let me check my calendar. Well, whaddeyuh know? You're in luck, Miss Stevens. I *do* have a couple of free hours tomorrow afternoon."

"Get outta here. Y'don't have a dang thing on your schedule, and it's the least you can do."

"How's that?"

"Well, it's *your* fault my butt's so big," she quips. "Taking all my time and feeding me ice cream and chilidogs. So I reckon you oughta help me work out."

"Okay, I'll do it, as long as we can go to the DQ afterward."

This sets off a fit of giggling. "Goshdang, you big jock, I'll have to run all the way to Sulphur Springs to come out ahead."

They tease and flirt a bit longer, then he says good-bye, but she doesn't hang up. He waits, realizing she has something serious to add: "Bryan, I love you more than ever ... but we hafta cool it, don'tcha think?"

"Oh, I agree ... I do. I can't take another weekend like this."

THE SILVER CORD

CHAPTER EIGHT

THE HOWARD FARM
FRIDAY, JULY 26, 1991 — 9:40 AM

After tucking the shirttail of his baseball underjersey into his cutoffs, Bryan Howard hurriedly makes his bed. As he does, he spots a pair of dirty socks underneath it. He tosses them into the laundry basket he keeps in his closet. *That oughta do it,* he tells himself. *I've cleaned and straightened enough.*

His room still smells faintly of Gramps' cigars, despite his mom's many scrubbings—and the carpet on the floor; before Bryan moved in here four years ago, his parents had wall-to-wall carpeting put in (short-piled, cocoa brown). The carpet exuded a strong acrylic "new" smell, obscuring the cigar odor, but it slowly came back as the carpet lost its newness. He's glad it did. He loves the rustic, masculine bigness of the room, and the cigar smell adds to the mood; it all reminds him of Gramps. But the room also speaks of Bryan's boyhood and adolescence. There's the gun rack he made in junior-high shop class, and the Reggie Jackson bat rack with its bantam-sized bats and gloves (souvenirs of his little-league days), and the shelves of trophies and awards, and his Daisy BB gun on the gun rack, along with the Marlin .22 and a Zebco fishing rod, plus his pennants and pictures on the wall. He feels secure in this room, in this house, on this farm, but he knows he can't stay here. This realization is exhilarating and adventurous, yet scary and worrisome, especially when it comes to Mandy; he can't take her with him, not yet.

He cranks the AC up a notch then parts the venetian blinds above and peers out (looking south). "She should be here *any*time now," he whispers expectantly, his words lost amid the clunky groaning of the ancient air conditioner (the window-mounted Fedders still cools well enough, though it's older than he is). He checks the driveway, then looks east on Longley Road: nothing yet. Mandy usually takes Misty Hollow, so she should be coming from that direction. The hazy, glaring sky seems little changed from yesterday when the temp hit 104°. Brownish hues tint the meadows and hollows beyond Longley Road, giving the late-July landscape its usual sepia-sage cast, as if he's looking through smoked glass. It has only rained once this month, a cloudburst ten days ago, like three inches in thirty minutes; the gullies and creeks rushed with water, but the next day they were dry again. Hollis County bakes all summer, sometimes dry heat, sometimes muggy heat. A southeast wind brings up steamy Galveston air, whereas a southwest wind blows torrid and desertlike. The arid West Texas regime has prevailed lately.

Stepping away from the window, Bryan checks his surgical scars in the picture-frame mirror which hangs next to his dresser. He has to look diligently to find them in his back-to-normal hair. He returned to Dallas Presbyterian on Monday for the follow-up CT-scans and MRIs plus other tests, and everything came out okay—he got the results yesterday, along with a letter from Dr. Nadler, which gives Bryan the green light to participate without restriction in the Baylor baseball program.

So it's official: young Mr. Howard *is* going to Waco—in five weeks. He's psyched, happy and anxious, all of it, yet it's also a bummer to think that he and Mandy will soon be living a hundred and sixty miles apart. When he's with her, he's happy, high on love, living in the moment, but when they're apart, the questions haunt him. What's going to happen the rest of the summer? Will they be able to control themselves, as they have since the tiff on her porch? Do they really *want* to control themselves, or should they do it, at least once, to bond completely before he leaves? Or will crossing the line, even into petting again, jeopardize their whole relationship, considering they won't be married for three more years? If Mandy preached at him over fondling, what will she do if they actually have intercourse? Or maybe if they visit that heavenly pinnacle, they'll be addicted.? They won't be able to quench the fire once it's roaring—bliss! bliss! oh rapture and glory! How can they part in September? It's impossible!

So they have to wait? They must? But three years? No way; they can't? Even seeing her three times per week (part of their cooling-things-down agreement) hasn't reduced his raging desire, and she's now seventeen and riper and more flirtatious than ever. And she's just as lust-crazed as he—she has to be? They haven't talked about it since the watermelon patch, but she *has* to be. They can't wait? They have to consummate or break up?

But with Christ all things are possible—He'll give them the strength to wait three years? But what's going to happen when he's in Waco, and she's still here in high school? Will she look at other guys ("I sure wouldn't leave yuh here in goddam Spindle ... not with all these horny hayseeds *sniffin'* around"—Spanky was bullshitting and showing off, and Bryan trusts Mandy even more than he trusts himself, but it still bothers him)? And what about him? Will he be attracted to the Baylor babes—no way? But then again, he's bound to notice the good-looking chicks roaming the campus? And yet, it'll just be for a year: Mandy will be in Waco the following September ... if she gets her scholarship?

Questions, questions, so many questions—but they've receded for now to the back of his mind. She'll be here *shortly*: that's *all* that matters. Their last few times together have been *especially* awesome and lively, like Wednesday when she got her dad's money, and they went to Currier's to pick up her car, the '84 Firebird. She took him for a joyride, all the way to Sulphur Springs. The sporty coupe is hot and spirited, and so is Mandy when she drives it—her untamed, carefree side took charge, rocking and rolling and flirting the whole way there and back.

Returning to the window, his heart turns over, as he spots his sweetheart, but she's approaching from the west—she came on 115 instead. She zooms up the driveway in her shiny red Pontiac, the dust churning behind her. After a gravelly, skidding halt, she hops out. Tan legs, smirky mouth, pink shorts: she hustles up the walk then disappears onto the porch underneath him. *She's pumped,* he declares to himself, as he pads barefoot out of his room to the head of the stairs. *And I love her in those short, pink-denim things. O God, help me.* He sucks air, a calming breath. *I should go down and let her in. No, there's Mom; she's got the door.* He retreats a few steps, so he can't be seen.

"Hi, Mom Howard," Mandy chirps, after Ginny opens the door. "So where's Bryan?"

"Oh, he's up in his room," Ginny replies, after letting Mandy in. "He's working at his computer I think. You can go on up."

"Gosh, it feels good in here—I love my car, but the AC's not working right. They're gonna fix it next week."

"It does look like another scorcher outside. I reckon we need rain, but then again the dry weather is good for haying, and we have a lot of cutting and baling to do the next few weeks."

Bryan hurries to his desk, to his Macintosh, a show of cool indifference (another teasing routine). "Hey, Bryan!" Mandy hollers, as she charges up the oak stairs. He chuckles, as he pictures her skipping every other step, like she does, and vaulting over the landing. He puts on a poker face, as if absorbed in some project. She bombs into the room. "Guess what? Good news."

He tries to hold his sober pose but has no chance, for she's quickly in the chair with him, sitting on his lap, her naked thighs so luscious and agonizingly desirable that he dares not dwell on their tanned and supple fullness (she wears shorts more often now, and not just to the lake). Blushing and smirking, she whips off her softball cap and places it on his head, bill backwards; she gives him a smooch on the cheek, then on the lips.

"So, pretty lady, what was all that hollering about?" he asks, after a brief round of kissing—he dimples. "The good news?"

She tosses her bangs. "I got my *scholar*ship—I just got the letter from Baylor. They sent it yesterday ... to the school. Coach Perkins called me this morning, right before I left my house. I just picked it up on the way up here."

"Well uh? Whadda? Who ... uh?"

"Control yourself," she laughs. "I'll read it to yuh."

Hopping up, Mandy pulls a folded envelope from her rear pocket. After getting the letter out, she crinkles her nose and purses her smirky mouth, the rabbity routine. Finally, she reads: "TO: Amanda F. Stevens, blah, blah, blahty-blah. REF: Women's athletic scholarship (Freshman class, '92), blah, blah, blah. Dear Miss Stevens: We are pleased to announce that your selection for a girl's basketball scholarship, as we discussed when we visited your home in February, has tentatively been approved by the blah, blah. It will cover tuition, room and board, plus books and incidentals, as outlined in the blah, blah. Formal notification will be forthcoming after the November deadline, in accordance with NCAA blah, blah, blahty-blah, but Coach Ames has listed you, so you may consider this to be firm, as soon as you return the preliminary acceptance paperwork, which you should receive next week, blah, blah. Congratulations, and best wishes for your senior year at SHS. Sincerely, Brenda M. Fitzgerald, Assistant Director of Admissions, The University of Baylor at Waco."

"So you're *in* for September of '92?" Bryan responds.

"Yep, babe—looks like we're actually gonna be together."

"Yahoo!" he yelps, catapulting out of his chair. He picks her up and swings her around. She shrieks and giggles. Her softball cap, still propped backwards on his head, slips sideways then topples onto the floor. After a few more dizzying spins filled with laughter and yelling, he seats her on his desk, to the right of his computer amid the floppy disks and papers and books and whatnot; he gives her a huge hug.

"What's going on!" Virginia Howard calls from downstairs.

Bryan pads to the door and sticks his head out. "We're just celebrating, Mom. Mandy got her scholarship ... for fall of '92."

"That's really good to hear," Ginny replies. "We've had a lotta good news this week." He starts to close the door, but his mom has more. "I'm going to work at eleven, hon. But if you two are gonna be here, I have cold cuts in the fridge. Or you can have that leftover meat loaf from last night."

"Thanks, Mom, but we're leaving too. We're going running, and then to the lake. So we'll grab a bite at the DQ probably." He laughs. "I reckon this's my last week to laze around, since we're gonna be haying on Monday."

"That's right," Ginny affirms. "So don't forget Billy Ray. Y'gotta call him. He's working this week at the old Palmer farm, but he knows y'need him on Monday. Y'just hafta tell him what time. And Dad says you should check out the baler."

"I will, Mom. I'll take care of it."

With that, Bryan closes his bedroom door and returns his attention to Mandy—she's still sitting on his desk, a cocky little grin on her mouth. "I must say, pretty lady, this scholarship thing is really A-plus. I figured you'd get something, but this'll cover the whole enchilada." He dimples and gives her a little love-jab to the shoulder. "And I never heard of anyone getting picked before they start their senior year."

She playfully pokes his tummy through the baseball under-jersey. "Hey, you big, good looking, stud of a cowboy jock," she declares, reeling off the mouthful without missing a syllable. "You ain't looking at no small-town Texas nobody. I reckon they do wait until November for most girls, but I've led our conference in scoring the last two years, plus I got a 3.56 grade point to boot, and 1380 on my SATs. So I reckon they made an exception for *me*." She throws her head back proudly, her ponytail spilling onto her back. She gives him a sassy squint.

He wraps his arms about her. "You spunky devil, you."

"And this year's gonna be a real breeze," she brags on.

"How's that?"

"Well, I just hafta get by Denham's class, plus English comp, and trig from Mrs. Ritchie."

"And?" Bryan asks, stepping back a bit.

"And nothing. Nada, zippo. That's all I need to graduate. I'll be taking a few electives, like word processing, and maybe American Poets, but I already got most of my required stuff out of the way. I took extra credits each year."

"Damn, you really *are* a hot ticket." Flashing a big smile, he goes after her ribs. She squeals but tickles him back. He breaks free then does a jig around the room. He wiggles and shakes and jitterbugs berserkly.

Mandy giggles and snorts. "You really are crazy, you big jock. I may hafta build a cage for you."

Bryan bobs and weaves like a boxer; he punches the air. Finally, he goes limp and flops backward onto his bed. Rolling onto his side, he gazes at his sweetheart, while she checks out the goodie bowl. Behind the Macintosh he keeps a dish full of gum and mints and Life-Savers, and red-hot balls. She helps herself to a piece of Juicy Fruit then kicks off her sneakers. She makes herself right at home, as though his room and his things are hers too. He likes it that she does this, since it makes it seem like they're already married and sharing everything. She no longer looks proud, but adorable and girlish rather, as she smacks her gum and dangles her bare feet, no socks. Her bangs are soft and feathery, freshly shampooed. She beams and blushes, her sun-freckles showing, her eyes sparking.

He drinks her in, yet his thirst remains unquenchable. Even his glimpse of Heaven cannot trump the glory he sees in her sweetly endearing smile, in her big, blue, unfathomable eyes, in her frisky gestures and body talk, in her irresistible woman-child sexuality, and it can't be Heaven anyway, unless *she*'s there with him. He loves her more than anything, whether real or imagined, whether in this life or the next, or in any life anywhere. She's the sun, the moon, the anchor—she's the magic princess who daily quickens his dreams, bringing the fairy tale back to life, again and again. And he knows as surely as his name is Bryan Howard, that he'd wither to nothing without her. This knowing, this love, this truth, supersedes all, and cannot be revoked or changed or repented of—it's more relentless than gravity. He loved her at first sight, second sight, and *every* sight since. He feels faint with feeling, so much so that he has to close his eyes.

* * *

Several minutes later, Bryan's eyes are still closed, and Mandy wonders if he's gonna take a nap or what. But then he suddenly rolls off the bed onto his feet. "Guess what, pretty lady?"

"What?" she replies, between smacks of her gum.

"I have a letter to show you as well."

"So show me."

He doesn't reply; he seems suddenly puzzled. "It's from Dr. Nadler, but I can't find it. Y'know, the scan results I toldjuh about on the phone." He shuffles through the clutter on his desk, the books and papers and floppy disks. "Doggone, Mandy, this's crazy. I was just looking at it before you got here."

Dropping to his hands and knees, Bryan searches under the desk. Mandy shifts a bit to give him more room. As she does, she catches sight of an envelope protruding from underneath *her*—it says Dallas something. Moving a trifle more, she verifies that it says Dallas Presbyterian Hospital. Her very own butt is covering up the missing medical report. "Well, looks like it's lost, babe," she kids, sensing a great opportunity for some fun. She adjusts her position until the entire letter is hidden. "I reckon you'll just hafta call 'em ... and have 'em send yuh another copy."

Coming up, Bryan gives a resigned murmur then plunks into the desk-chair. Swiveling left of her dangling feet, he extends his legs under the makeshift desk. "I know, I know; it's no big deal, but it's just bothersome to lose something like that." Developing the situation, she runs her toes up under his practice jersey, onto his stomach and chest. He gives a forced grimace. "C'mon, pretty lady, don't be messing with me. I need to find that letter."

Spreading her knees, she straddles him playfully, her bare feet working on his thighs, like a cowboy spurs a horse. "Oh, babe, we can find it later. Right now, I need yuh to hold me and kiss me. C'mon, mister, I'm really *hot* for you." Laughing in spite of himself, he rolls the chair closer. She knows he can't resist her sporting, especially when she's wearing shorts. Leaving the chair, he goes for her lips, but she eludes him, leaning back on her hands. Then like a hungry octopus she locks her legs around him. She kneads his back with her heels. More laughter and giggles.

Embracing her with one arm, he takes a step back, and she's up off the desk, her legs still wrapped about him. As he lifts her, she grabs the letter. "Abracadabra!" she gushes, as she thrusts it into his face.

"What the heck? You little devil, you." They laugh so hard that Bryan can scarcely hold her. He drops her on the bed, then leans over her, his green eyes full of mirth. "You had that darn letter all the time, didn't yuh?"

"Well, sorta."

"Whaddeyuh mean, sorta?"

"It was under my butt, silly! You sat me down on top of it!"

* * *

SPINDLE, TEXAS - COLBY DRIVE
SUNDAY JULY 28, 1991 — 12:30 PM

"Amanda?"

"Yes, Mama?"

"Are you coming downstairs, honey?"

"Yeah, be right there. I'm putting my tennies on. And I hafta fix my ponytail."

"I made some tuna-fish sandwiches, plus we have the slaw from last night."

"Okay, I'll be down in a jiff."

It woulda been neat to go with Bryan after church, Mandy remarks to herself, as she ties her left sneaker. *But I'll still be there by two-thirty. Plus, it's more fun to take my Firebird—I LOVE that car.* She giggles, as a romantic rush courses through her. Stepping over to the mirror, she bands her hair back with a scrungee then works on her bangs. *I'll say hello to Charlie when he arrives ... but then I'm outta here.* She twists left then right, admiring her new summer duds: beige polo, gray Bermudas. Her mom gave her fifty dollars for her birthday, and she finally spent it yesterday, at Wal-Mart. She also got a primrose polo and a white short-sleeve turtleneck she can wear with her waitress skirt.

A minute later, she trots down the stairs and bounces into the kitchen, a big I-got-wheels smile on her face. The smell of tuna salad greets her, along with her mother's old-fashioned Chanel perfume, the usual Sunday fragrance. Helen Stevens still has on the pale-blue suit she wore to church, minus the jacket.

"Well, you certainly have a *spring* in your step," Helen quips, as she grabs some paper napkins from the package on the counter. "Pastor Ron's message must've *really* inspired you, but I reckon it was more *Bryan Howard* than the Holy Spirit, the way you two were gawking at each other."

"Now, Mama," Mandy kids, "you *know* you're not supposed to be looking around at everybody during church; that's what you always taught me, ever since I was a little girl." She laughs, while Helen rolls her eyes and gives a resigned shake of the head.

Mandy peers out the window over the sink, to verify that her red Pontiac is still parked in the driveway, actually to the left of the driveway, next to the green Escort. (Their rent-house has a garage, but it's packed with furniture and stuff belonging to the landlord.) "So where's Gretch?" she asks her mother, as a blinding sun-reflection flashes off the windshield of the Firebird.

"Oh, she inhaled half a sandwich then took off on her bike for Molly Ann's house. I did get her to drink her milk—after she put in three spoonfuls of Nestle's Quik." Helen gives a motherly chuckle, a clucking henlike utterance. "She's gonna have a weight problem before she gets to junior high."

Whap, whap: Toby bangs in through the cat door. He rubs against Mandy's leg, looking for attention, looking for a snack. She pets him then fills his dry-food bowl with Friskies, then she rummages in the cabinet under the counter and comes out with a bag of Lay's potato chips, sour cream and onion. "I like that shirt, honey," Helen offers, as she sidesteps her daughter, so she can fetch a pitcher of ice tea from the refrigerator. "Beige goes good with *your* hair." More henlike clucking. "Just be glad you got your daddy's blond genes instead of this muddy mop I got on *my* head." Her brunette bob, cut perkily short for the summer, hardly looks like a mop—it's prim and perfect as usual, though the brown hue *is* rather drab. Helen laughs. "Buzzy sure got the best of me when it came to passing on traits to you, Amanda."

Mandy laughs too (she likes her dad's nickname: he got it during his Army-pilot days, because of his free-spirited, low-flying ways), yet she's apprehensive about her mom's good mood: *She's been extra nice all day? Too nice? Maybe she's gonna ask me to do something— no, it's probably Charlie, the fact he's coming to visit, and they're getting along better?*

Mandy plops down in her usual spot at the table (her back to the laundry room) and takes one of the tuna sandwiches, two halves actually, from the platter. Ripping open the potato chips, she grabs a handful, and puts them onto her plate. "You need *this* more than chips," her mom chides good-naturedly, as she gives Mandy a big helping of coleslaw, which is more colorful than the kind served at the diner. Helen's slaw contains, in addition to the whitish strands of cabbage, orange and green shreds: carrots and broccoli. And she also adds raisins to give a fruity touch.

After stuffing her mouth with food, Mandy chugs some ice tea. "So Gretch already took off on her bike?" she says, her voice thick from eating. "I told her I'd give her a ride later? It's almost a mile to the Heimbergs', and it's super hot outside."

Helen sits down across the table. After a quick silent prayer (they usually say grace, but she doesn't make it a ritual thing, unless it's a big meal), she replies to her daughter, "I know, but Gretchen couldn't wait. When I told her she had to be home by four-thirty, she got all flustered and impatient."

"Four-thirty?" Mandy inquires, her sense of apprehension growing. "Why four-thirty?"

"Well, Charlie should be here by then, and I thought we'd *all* go out to eat at O'Henry's before the evening service."

"But, *Mama*, I'm going to Bryan's farm this afternoon?"

"That's fine, honey, as long as you're back early, no later than five anyhow."

Mandy's stomach sinks. "But I'm gonna help him check the hay baler, and he wants me to stay for supper. He says they're gonna cook hamburgers outside—and I thought Charlie was coming earlier, like *two* o'clock?"

"He was," Helen explains, gesturing with a sandwich, "but when I talked to him this morning, he said he couldn't get out of Newbury until noon, because he had to usher at their regular worship service, the one at the Bible-college chapel." She gives a quick nod of her head, an upbeat nod. "I think Charlie means it this time. He sounds so serious and responsible now. I think he's finally mended his ways, with the Lord's help of course."

I figured as much, Mandy interjects huffily, but only to herself. *This's why she's so bubbly and nice today.*

"I still haven't decided anything," Helen goes on, between sips of ice tea. "But I can't just slam the door on his offer. After all, he *is* serious about his college work, and they recently made him a deacon, because he's older, and more seasoned as a believer ... compared to the younger students. And like I say, the Lord has finally given him victory over his alcohol problem. He's b—"

"Yeah, I'll *bet*," Mandy interrupts derisively.

"Y'better *check* your attitude, young lady," Helen snaps, her face contracting into a scowl. Her cheery disposition vanishes as quickly as Toby, who scurries out the cat door, as if he realizes a mother-daughter storm is brewing. "It's about time you learn to *show* some respect. Charlie was a good stepfather to you when you had no father ... and he *still* is. He loves you as much as he loves Gretchen, and you *know* it."

"I realize that, Mama. But still ... I can't forget what we all went through back in Fayetteville, especially *you*. And Charlie's always repenting and getting right with God, like every summer almost." Mandy swats the air above her plate. "It's not that I blame him for backsliding. I reckon he can't help it, but it gets me *tot*ally mad when he comes down here to snow yuh ... with all his smooth talk. It's crazy to even *consider* getting back with him. He'll just mess up your whole life again, and Gretchen's too, and *mine*—just like today. I have plans with Bryan, and now y'want me to change 'em ... just to fit Charlie's schedule, just so we can go out to eat, and pretend that we're a happy fam—"

"So that's it," Helen retorts, tossing her wadded napkin onto her half-eaten lunch. "Your nose is out of joint because you may lose a couple of hours with *Bry*an."

"Well, he's gonna be haying every day, starting tomorrow, and I hafta work extra days at the diner, until Aunt Marge hires a new girl, and I hafta take my car in to have the AC fixed. So after today, we won't be seeing each other near as much."

Giving an indignant snort, Helen bounces up and goes to the sink. "Good!" she exclaims out the window, her back to her daughter. "I'm *glad* you can't see him. You see him *way* too much. You're obsessed, and living in a fantasy. You think it's love, but it's not, at least not the kind that *God* honors. It's just an adolescent e*mot*ional thing." She slaps the counter, so hard the stainless-steel sink rings like a gong. "You're not *old* enough to be in love, Amanda. The heart is deceitful—above all things. That's why true love is a not a *feel*ing. It's a careful decision, a godly and prayerful decision. Bryan may be a sweet Christian lad, but he's hardly mature in the Lord, and he's *cer*tainly not ready for a wife. And you ... you're scarcely more than a child! You're both too young to even *think* about marriage. And if yuh can't get married, y'shouldn't be together all the time. It just energizes your flesh and leads to lust and *forn*ication ... and babies outta wedlock. Love's not a dadgum fairy tale. Y'hafta face reality, Amanda. That's what it *means* to grow up."

Mandy seethes, a volcano on the verge, but she bites her lip against the rage, against the hurt. Folding her arms, she gazes at her mother's back, at her short, prim, sternly taut presence.

"You must consider you ways, young lady," Helen continues, still speaking out the window. "Bryan, Bryan, Bryan ... that's all I hear. You've been with him almost every day this summer. I let things ride after he got hurt, in hopes you'd realize what's important." She gestures plaintively upward over the sink, as though praying, as though the Lord is just outside, hovering above the driveway. "But no, Amanda, you went even more gah-gah over him. I held my tongue, and held it, and held it, even this morning at church—but *now* I'm saying my piece." Helen shakes her up-lifted hands, her neck pulsing pinkly at the nape. "You put Bryan ahead of everything, and everybody—even the Lord. It's too much, and it's unwise; there's no balance; it can only lead to trouble. Besides, he's going off to college." Mandy, her cheeks hot with indignation, shifts her gaze to the refrigerator, to all the papers and whatnot affixed to it with magnets: church schedules and notices, Gretchen's art-class creations (rainbows, mountains, V-shaped birds), yellowed newspaper clippings (articles and pictures depicting Mandy's softball and basketball feats), two recent birthday cards (Mandy's). She tries to tune her mother out, but she can't: "This whole *Bryan*-thing is outta control. It can only hurt yuh, Amanda. If y'weren't so ga-ga, you'd realize, like *me*, that it's wiser to back off, and just be friends. You may have that hot car, and a license to drive it, but that doesn't mean you're *grown* up." Mandy fiddles with her ice-tea glass, running her finger through the condensation, making an "M" in the moisture. "You hafta *grow* up in Christ, and so does Bryan, and you hafta get an education, so you can be responsible and self-sufficient, then when you're twenty-two and out of school, you can marry whomever the Lord leads ... but it's unlikely to be Bryan Howard. High-school romances rarely lead to marriage, and those that do, usually end in divorce. That's why I'm not too keen about your scholarship to Baylor. I doubt it's God's will for you to follow him there."

"How can *you* know God's will for *me*?" Mandy responds, finally. Her words are controlled yet biting. "And *what* gives you the right to judge me and Bryan? Who are *you* to say it won't last?"

"I'm your *mother*—that's who!" Helen exclaims, whirling around. She glares at Mandy, her eyes ablaze: hazel fire. "And I'm responsible for you, before *God*. And I've lived twice as long as you, so I *know* from experience ... and the *word* of God! Flee youthful lusts. Honor thy father and mother." She wags her finger at her daughter. "And I've scrimped and worked myself halfway to death just so we can have a roof over our heads." Giving a sigh of exasperation, Helen pauses, her frown relaxing a bit, and her voice. "It would be nice if life *was* a fairy tale, and all our fantasies came true—but that's not how it is, honey. Things are gonna change. Bryan is going away to college, but you're still in high school. You're still gonna be here. And we love you and need you. I need you, and Gretchen needs you, and Marge and Billy, and Charlie too. You're barely seventeen, Amanda. Romance can wait. Besides, if my prayers are answered, we could all be moving to Arkansas—before the summer's over."

"NO *WAY* IN HELL!" Mandy shrieks, knocking over her ice tea, as she explodes to her feet. "I'm not moving *any*where!" Tawny fingers of spilled tea race across the yellow formica; a few find the edge and drip onto the linoleum. The glass itself rolls off, bouncing on Helen's chair on its way to the floor; it *bongs* and *pings* but doesn't break. "And no way in hell am I gonna split up with Bryan! It's *my* life dammit! Not yours!"

"You watch your language, young lady!"

"No, I'm not watching *anything*! No way in hell! Everybody needs me, needs me. But what about me, Mama? What about my damn needs? D'yuh have any concerns about *my* feelings? I *am* a real person you know?"

"Amanda—"

"No, Mama! Don't 'Amanda' me! I'm sick and tired of being everybody's Cinderella. And let me remind you, I worked my ass off for my Baylor scholarship. And dammit, that's exactly where my butt's gonna be come September '92!" *Ka-WHAP!* Mandy slaps the table sending tremors through the spilled streams of ice tea. "And when it comes to Bryan, there's nothing more to say. I've heard your counsel ... and I reject it, all of it, every *damn* bit of it. I love Bryan ... and someday I'm gonna be his wife." She whaps the table again. "I love him! I do! Don'tcha get it?" She sucks a breath then exhales loudly. "If God is *love*, like the Bible says, then how can it be sinful for me to love Bryan? And how can you be so damn self-righteous, when you were *SCREWING* Daddy at the age of sixteen! Or was it *fif*teen!" Her words scorch the air like tracer bullets, a hot volley designed to hurt.

"Don't you *dare* talk like that in this house!" Helen shouts.

"Well, you were! And *I'm* the proof!"

Helen pulses angrily: red, pink, red. Her frown sharpens, as if she's ready to launch into another tirade, but she doesn't. She looks down rather, her body language loosening, going languid. Mandy waits, her heart pounding. *I went too far,* she declares silently, as pangs of regret join the drumming in her breast.

Helen slumps into her chair, her eyes glistening with tears. "I admit it, honey. I did sleep with your father at a very young age. It was foolhardy, and that's why we never had a normal life as a couple." She picks at her thumbnail. "Our marriage was rocky and unpredictable right up till the day he crashed. We never had a chance to grow up. Yet I've *never* regretted having you, Mandy, not *once*. God took Buzzy, but he gave me you. It's a mystery ... God's plan. But all things *do* work together for good—I hafta hold onto that verse."

Mandy's throat constricts, her eyes filling. "Well, Mama, why can't God can make it work for me and Bryan?"

"He can make *any* situation work for good, but there's always pain when we go against his perfect will, and that's why I'm so concerned, Amanda. I know your emotions are all charged up over Bryan, but that's why the Lord cautions us about the flesh. I mean, you two remind me of puppies in heat. It's normal, but it leads to unwise choices and heartache ... when you mistake it for more. I know all about those feelings, honey, and I don't wantcha to go through what I went through. It really sidetracked me, my schooling ... like I hadta to drop out in eleventh grade."

"But you *did* get a diploma ... finally?"

"Yeh ... when I was twenty, a G.E.D. It's not the same, and I reckon that's partly why I had so much trouble with Charlie later ... and all that anxiety, when I came close to having a breakdown. For whatsoever a man soweth, he shall also reap. I learned the hard way about youthful folly and obedience and love, and I'm just trying to help yuh avoid the same pitfalls. And I don't want to lose you until it's time ... until you're truly ready to go out on your own. And this's why I want us to stay together as a family, even if it means moving back to Ark—"

"Mama, *please*. We're not gonna resolve our differences like this." Turning away, Mandy covers her ears with her hands; she's heard enough of this convoluted Christian pleading. She heads for the hallway, for the stairs, as if ready to escape up to her room, but she doesn't. She halts abruptly in the doorway rather, leaning forward, supporting herself on the jambs, one hand on each.

THE SILVER CORD

"But, Amanda honey, it's still *un*decided; it's not a done deal ... the move. Yet even if we go, it won't be as bad as you think. You can finish high school there ... and you can get a basketball scholarship to the University of Arkansas, or maybe by next year you'll decide to go to Bible school, if the Lord leads."

"Mama, stop it," the high-schooler replies, her indignation returning, though the emotion is now more weary than hot. She speaks toward the living room, toward the humming AC which occupies the window above the walnut dining table.

"Honey, I'm just trying to look at things reasonably. You tend to go with gut reaction ... just like your father did. But I believe it *is* possible to talk out our differences."

Mandy doesn't reply, except to herself: *I'm glad Daddy went with his gut feelings.*

"The Lord is faithful, Amanda. He'll get us through this."

Mandy, bolstered by the thoughts of her dad, pushes off the doorway, rotating back into the kitchen. Her hands on her hips, she looks her mom in the eyes. "Mama, I'm sorry I yelled at you," she declares in a loving but resolute voice. "And I'm sorry I cussed and showed disrespect. You know I love you no matter what, no matter if we disagree. And I love Gretchen too. I mean, I've watched over her ... and baby-sat a jillion times ... while you were at work, and going for counseling, even when I was thirteen and you were in the hospital after your breakdown. Anytime you were gone, I fixed the meals, washed the dishes, did the laundry, emptied the trash, vacked the floors, and mowed the grass. And the past two years, I've waited tables at Uncle Billy's diner."

Mandy hand-sweeps her bangs. "Mama, I've tried my best to make you proud. I don't smoke, or take drugs, or get drunk ... or hang out with the wrong crowd. I make straight A's or close, and it's not *easy*. Many times I've studied past midnight. I excel in sports, and I've been on the Student Council. Mama, take a good look at me. I'm not a 'little girl' any longer. I'm a woman now. And whether it fits your opinions or plans ... I am *tot*ally and completely in love with Bryan Howard." Mandy shoves the air, as though passing an invisible basketball to her mother. "Y'talk about facing *real*ity. Well, the main reality, as I see it, is that I'm seventeen, and I'll soon be leaving to live my *own* life. But that doesn't mean I love you any less. I'm not against you, Mama. I hope you 'n Charlie *do* make it this time. I really do, though I fear he'll let you down again. But either way ... I'm not moving to goshdang Newbury, Arkansas!"

"Forgive me, honey," Helen replies after a long moment, as tears streak her pixie face. "Forgive me for reacting so angrily. It's just my flesh, but the thought of losing you makes me feel empty inside. I know I can't keep yuh, yet it still hurts to think you'll soon be gone ... and I *am* truly grateful for all that you've done to help." Grabbing a fresh paper napkin, she wipes her eyes. "You've kept me going ever since Charlie and I split up."

Mandy, moved with compassion, strides boldly over and takes her mother by the shoulders, as she sits in the chair. Helen averts her eyes, but doesn't react against her daughter's firm grasp, or firm words: "Now, Mama, you don't hafta say *any*thing else. I know yuh love me. Neither one of us is perfect, and we both have *strong* opinions ... so I reckon we're bound to fight, especially when we're together all the time in this house."

"I know, honey," Helen replies between sniffles. "I know."

Slipping around the chair, Mandy hugs her mom from behind. "So, Mama, y'don't hafta feel guilty. And neither do I. It's good to air our differences, even if we can't resolve them right now."

After giving her mom a peck on the cheek, Mandy heads for the back door, but before opening it she turns and says, "If you insist on me being home by five, then I'll be here, but I have a better idea. If I leave for the Howard farm right now, then Bryan and I will have the whole afternoon practically, then I'll bring him to church tonight, and we'll meet y'all there." Mandy titters then gives her goofy little-girl grin. "But either way, we're gonna take *every*one for ice cream afterward. Now, Mama, don'tcha think that's a fair and fun way of settling all this?"

Helen's tears have turned into laughter: "I declare, Amanda, you're so much like your daddy. He always got his way by doing some *fun* thing for everyone. What can I say?"

"Well, y'just told me I have his genes," Mandy chortles, as she opens the door. "I guess you're *right* about that—oh, wait a minute, d'yuh want me to clean up that ice tea before I go?"

"No, I'll do it," Helen replies amid a laugh. "But y'better get outta here before I come to my senses."

* * *

THE HOWARD FARM
SUNDAY JULY 28, 1991 — 2:55 PM

Picking up a small rock, Bryan throws it low and hard onto the calm end of Ruby Pond. It skips twice before digging into the glassy surface. "Pathetic," Mandy teases, as she looks for a perfect stone in the dried muck at the water's edge. "My little sister could get more skips than *that*." She giggles girlishly.

He laughs too, yet he can scarcely keep his mind on skipping rocks, not while she's bending over in front of him. *O God, she looks so good in those darn Bermudas. I wish—no, no way.*

She finally finds a flat, smooth one. "Now lemme show yuh how it's done," she taunts, as she winds up like a pitcher and hurls it sidearm onto the pond. It skips one, two, three, four times, then again and again and again, too many to count. "Ta-DAH!" she whoops triumphantly, pumping her fist and leaping into the air. "That baby skipped ten times. That's a new *re*cord."

"Oh, pretty lady, where d'yuh get the energy to jump and shout? It's a hundred degrees out here." The sun is brutal indeed, but Bryan likewise needs a break from her wiggling buttocks.

Retreating under the willows that guard the southwest corner of the small lake, they plop down on a big grayish rock, one of the many sandstone outcroppings that poke up here and there on this side of the farm. Most are small and flush to the ground, but this huge slab, blockish and oblong like a half-buried refrigerator, is perfect to sit on—at least during the dry season. In March and April you often have to wade to it, but on this late-July afternoon, it's well back from the water, like five yards, far enough for grass and clover and dandelions to grow up around it. Each summer the pond gets smaller, yet it remains large enough and deep enough to support a stable fish population: bass, crappie, and bluegill, along with lesser numbers of bullhead and rock bass.

"This shade's a *lot* better," Bryan says, toying playfully with Mandy's ponytail as it dangles out the back of her ball cap. She sits forward, her elbows on her knees, her chin in her hand, but she doesn't reply. He pats her back affectionately.

A leaf flutters down beside them, settling onto a patch of clover. The overhanging willows have deposited a generous sprinkling of these skinny, knifelike leaves, some green, some turning yellow. The black willow sheds all summer, not just in the autumn, and they exude a pleasant, slightly pungent fragrance, but the wind soon dies, allowing the less-than-agreeable lake odor to drift up to Bryan and Mandy, not a great stink but certainly noticeable. It doesn't come from the pond actually—the water is fine, having the usual algal odor—but from the exposed moss and mire and lakeweed, not to mention the mussels that die and leave their lustrous but foul-smelling shells in the muck. During winter and spring there's no reek at all, but when the water goes down, the rotting fetor comes back, especially on hot afternoons. This is partly why Bryan doesn't swim much in the pond anymore—you need a raft or a pier to swim off. When he was a small lad, he had both. He and Spanky made a raft out of plywood and inner tubes, and they swam for hours on summer days, plus there was a boat dock then, near the west end of the dam—you can still see a couple of the pilings sticking up. Gramps even swam with them a few times; he'd hoot and holler and do cannonballs like he was a kid again. Those were magical years, but now Bryan has grown up and discovered greater wonders—and greater torments.

He loves the feeling, the erotic high he was riding before, but he can only take so much of her frisky cavorting without kissing her, and it's way too early for that. They save the heavy necking until right before they part, so they have a better chance of adhering to the "we gotta cool it" pact they made after things got out of hand last month at the watermelon patch. Loving, lusting, kissing, aching—then going home to get his rocks off *alone*. This oft-repeated routine seems *less* righteous to him, certainly less honest, than going all the way *with* his sweetheart. Flee fornication. He hates that word—it makes sex sound like a capital offense. But what choice do they have? They *must* wait.

"I reckon it's gonna be just as hot tomorrow," he remarks after a bit. "It's a dry heat, but it's still gonna be brutal cutting hay. Y'should play hooky from the diner and come help Billy Ray and me." He snickers. "That'll give your butt a workout."

Mandy offers up a muted little laugh, like two syllables, but she doesn't reply—she hasn't said a word since they sat down here. No bantering, no quips, no teasing comebacks—she seems subdued and preoccupied. *What's going on?* Bryan wonders to himself, as tugs of concern pull down on his own mood. Yet he doesn't press, lest he jump too quickly to a negative conclusion.

The breeze, having picked up again, stirs the willow branches overhead. Supple and slender, they sway gracefully like hula skirts. And the ripples have reappeared on the north and east sides of the pond. Bryan notices a pair of water turtles near the spillway, their black heads bobbing like fishing corks amid the little waves. He and his grandfather fished here so many times, mainly from Gramps' little boat—he had an eight-foot pram he kept down here. Another turtle, its smooth back glistening, suns itself on a fallen tree to the right of the old dock pilings—it's a huge limb actually, from the cottonwood that anchors the middle of the dam. Back during those carefree, boyhood summers, Bryan and Spanky had a rope in that big cottonwood, so they could swing out and drop into the water. There are also snapping turtles in this pond, but their shells are horny and rough. The two turtles bobbing near the spillway could be snappers?

A small beetle crawls up onto Bryan's leg, parking just below the frayed bottom of his cutoff jeans. "That wind feels good," he says, after flicking the bug off. "I hope it blows tomorrow." He makes this comment mainly to raise Mandy, to get her talking, but she still says nothing. All is quiet save for the faint swishing of the willow fronds overhead and the bassy bellowing of a heat-crazed bullfrog on the other side of the pond. The frogs croak at night for the most part, the smaller ones only at night, but you do hear a bullfrog now and then during the day.

Something's wrong, he frets to himself. *She's gone mum like she does.* Removing his Tiger cap, he places it on the rock beside him. He pulls a rag out of the back pocket of his shorts and dabs the sweat off his brow. He kept the flannel work-rag (a piece of ripped shirt) on him after tinkering with the baling machine. He shifts forward a trifle, while Mandy continues to sit as before, her chin in her hand. "What's the matter, precious," he asks, as he strokes her shoulder. She utters a little mewing sound—then falls sobbing into his arms, knocking her hat sideways on her head. He holds her, caresses her, until the sobs give way to sniffles.

"It makes me feel empty and sucky," she laments amid a shuddering breath, her cheeks blotchy, her eyes red. He lets go of her, as she shifts on the rock, facing again toward the water. She wipes her nose with the back of her hand then sheds her ball cap, tossing it on the ground beside the rock.

"What does?" Bryan asks. No reply—she wipes her nose again. He retrieves his rag. "Here, use this. It's not exactly clean, but it's just greasy on one end, and it's better than your hand."

"Thanks," she says, her voice full of hurt and yearning.

"Y'can tell me if you like ... but y'don't hafta."

"It's *Mama*," she snuffles huskily, as if addressing the pond. "It's always Mama."

"You mean the argument y'were talking about before ... back when we were working on the baler?"

"Yeah."

"But I thought it got settled, when yuh told her we'd meet them at church tonight? Y'seemed super upbeat about it?"

"I know, I know. I thought it was all worked out too. In fact, I felt really good about standing up to her. But I reckon I was more affected than I realized. Besides, it's not really settled, this *thing* with Mama. We came to a compromise about tonight, but it's not settled." Mandy dabs her eyes, wipes her nose. "When we first came over here to sit on this rock, I started thinking about you cutting hay ever' day and me working extra hours, and how you're gonna be going away to Waco real soon, and how Mama says that high-school romances never work out—oh, Bryan honey, I don't wanna be a*part* from you." Her eyes fill again.

A consoling rebuttal races to the tip of his tongue, but instead of voicing it, he gives her a one-arm embrace and waits for her to elaborate: "And then Mama got into her dadgum holy preaching: 'You put Bryan ahead of everything—even the Lord. It's too much, and it's unwise; there's no balance; it can only lead to trouble.'" Dropping the rag onto her lap, Mandy gestures with uplifted hands, just as her mom did over the kitchen sink.

"I reckon she was just upset," Bryan offers, finally, "because of the Charlie thing and—"

"And while you're at Baylor," Mandy interrupts, "I'll still be here in dadgum Spindle for a *whole* year, putting up with Mama, and I'll still have school, and I'll still be working at Goddard's and baby-sitting my little sister." She sniffs then shakes her head, resignedly. "I wish I'd taken extra classes last year, and this summer—then I'd be going to Waco with yuh."

"Yeah, but whaddabout your senior year? You're gonna be near the top academically, and all-state in basketball ... and don'tcha wanna graduate with your own class?"

"Nope. No *gosh*dang way. I want my Baylor scholarship, but I don't give a rat's zit for all the other hoopla. I could finish in January, except I need Trig to complete my program, and it's not offered till spring. I shoulda taken no-brainer math, instead of choosing a college-prep curriculum, but it's *too* late now. And Mama's gonna be all over me every time I wanna drive down to see yuh, or when you're home for a visit. This's gonna be the *hard*est year of my life—oh, babe, I wish we could *run* off and elope today, and never come back. I do. I do." Picking up the flannel rag, she twists it back and forth, as though wringing it out.

"I'm not sure eloping is a viable option," he replies, as he pushes off the rock onto his feet. "But I *can* escort you to a better place ... like up the hill."

"Y'see that beautiful land out there?" he says a good bit later, as they stand hand-in-hand near the giant oak tree. He sweeps his free hand toward the hazy, sun-washed panorama, toward the pine grove and the fields beyond, toward the green barn and silo and the roof of his house. "Well, one of these days, it's gonna be ours, or some place like it, a home place where we can raise our kids and grow old together. Isn't that what you want, Mandy?"

She nods but doesn't reply. She still has his grease rag, stuffed like a referee's flag into the back pocket of her Bermudas, but her sniffling has stopped. "It's hard to predict where we'll end up, but we're gonna be to*gether*, just like we've planned all along. I believe God created us for each other—I do. He's gonna make love win. He's way bigger than rules and fear and judging sins."

"But whaddabout the dark side?" Mandy asks. "Like that lady at the hospital who lost her husband, and her kids were crying. Why didn't God keep them together? You got healed, and we've had lots of happy times, but there's no fairy tale for *them*?"

"I know, precious. Death is heartbreaking, like with Gramps ... though I'm pretty darn sure it takes us to a good place. But I have a deep conviction that *our* story is just beginning, that God wants to show us what it means to be 'one flesh.' We *will* face it one day, but that's for the end of the book—right now we're still in chapter one. God didn't heal me for nought. He has a *plan* for us. So even the sucky and painful things have a purpose."

Bryan strokes her cheek. She looks down. "I know we can't run off," she concedes a long moment later. "I know we hafta wait. I just had to get it out, the emotional thing. I've needed to cry about this for weeks, and now I have."

Pulling her to him, he hugs her from behind. She gives a little murmur that turns into a laugh. He laughs too. "I figured you'd feel better, pretty lady, once we got up here to the oak tree."

"Yeah, you big jock, what is it about this tree anyhow? Every time we come here, you talk about high and lofty subjects like you're a dadgum preacher, or some kinda guru?" More titters, as she twirls out of his embrace. Her blue eyes spark with renewed mirth. Turning her hat backwards on her head, she gives him a seductive smooch—he senses they'll soon be necking in earnest. "I may be a hot-blooded, *full*y charged gal," she sports, "but I *know* we can't elope." She giggles huskily. "Goshdang it all, we're nowhere *near* eloping. Damn, we haven't even seen each other with our clothes off." More giggles and guffaws. "But that's what Mama's scared of. It's not you, babe; she likes you. It's *me*. She's afraid I'm gonna run off and get pregnant, because that's what *she* did with my daddy. She just can't *get* it into her head that I have *more* self-control than she did."

"Well, pretty lady, you *sure* have more of it than I got."

"So, that's not *say*ing much," she quips, giving him a playful punch to the ribs.

CHAPTER NINE

THE HOWARD FARM
TUESDAY, AUGUST 6, 1991 — 11:55 AM

Shedding his cowboy hat, Billy Ray goes down on one knee, his good knee, then sticks his head up the chute of the hay baler. "I reckon we got some *god*dam trouble," he drawls. "This thang's a piece ah shit." He wheezes and growls, saying something about the wire spool, but Bryan can't hear him clearly with the tractor going. A PTO (power take-off) hitch, from the tractor, drives the old green baler, which looks almost brown from rust.

"What'd you say?" Bryan asks, pulling off his work gloves, as he steps over for a closer look.

Billy Ray hobbles over to the tractor and kills the engine; he drags his left leg like Chester on *Gunsmoke*. His hat-creased hair looks like greasy lake-moss, while his untanned forehead shines garishly white above his ruddy, leathery, sun-baked face.

"What'd you say about the spool?" Bryan asks again.

Billy Ray grabs his grubby hat from the top of the baler and puts it on, but he still doesn't answer. Instead, he fishes a bag of Beechnut from the pocket of his overalls. Taking three fingers full, he stuffs it into the side of his mouth. He reeks with BO, as Bryan can't help but notice, a squalid stink which goes beyond hot-day sweat—he doesn't bathe often. Finally, after returning the red-and-white Beechnut bag to his pocket, he explains the situation, the chaw of tobacco crowding his hickish twang: "The fuckin' spool ain't feedin' no wire, nary a bit. We done lost the goddam tightenin' bolt. The fucker sheared *right* off." He spits tobacco juice; it splatters on the stubbled ground between the last two bales that emerged successfully. "That there couplin' belt is loose 'round the spool, which means we cain't get no wire into the balin' chamber." Giving a juicy snort, he wipes his hands on his overalls, which are already black with grime.

"Can yuh fix it?" Bryan inquires.

"Yep, I reckon I can get 'er goin' again—long as the fuckin' belt is still intact, and it looks to be."

"So d'yuh need my help?"

Billy Ray spits again. "Nawh, Bryan, ain't nuthin' y'can do. We cain't do a *damn* thang till I get a new tightenin' bolt. I'll hafta run into town and see what they got at Haley's Hardware."

A haggard, hatchet-nosed redneck with a seedy reputation, Billy Ray Campbell has worked part-time for the Howards since he was a teenager (Gramps hired him as a picker the last summer they grew cotton on the farm). He's in his late thirties but could pass for fifty, because of the sun wrinkles and boozy, hound-dog eyes. He became an alcoholic during his hitch in the Army, and that's also where he got his limp. He got wounded in Vietnam: a piece of shrapnel from a booby-trap grenade wrecked his knee. He never drinks on the job, but booze did ruin his marriage, to Theresa Sampson. Most folks look down on Billy Ray, though none can deny his mechanical genius. He works as a hired hand on a half-dozen farms and ranches. He's also an auto mechanic, spending two nights a week at Tom's Texaco on Main Street.

"Well, it's a bummer that it broke right now," Bryan offers, leaning one-handed against the John Deere machine. "Another thirty minutes and we woulda been done with this field." They got an early start this morning, since it was cloudy most of the night, making the dew lighter than usual.

"Ain't that the truth. And we lost two days *last* week waitin' for the goddam welder to fix that conveyor bracket." He fires another shot of tobacco juice then gives a gruff laugh. "Y'should tell your daddy to get one of those new-fangled balers, the roller kind like most folks use these days. Hardly anybody does the goddam stackin' bales anymore."

Taking off his Tiger cap, Bryan wipes his sweaty brow on the back of his arm (steamy Gulf air has replaced the dry heat of last week). "We've considered the round bales, but the square ones are easier—we sell 'em mainly by the pickup load, and we store 'em in the loft, to keep 'em dry. Yet we *could* use a new baler."

"That's for *damn* sure. This here thang's older than you are. Hell, I reckon it's almost as old as me. And that goddam tractor is even older. Course, they made those Internationals to last."

Bryan swats a horsefly off his naked shoulder. "But then again, I'm gonna be away at college now, so Dad may lease these acres next year—or maybe not. It's hard to say. I'm not even sure about the autumn hay, since I won't be around this October."

"Goddammit all. You're actually goin' off to college. Now I *really* feel like an old fart. I'll be forty 'fore long, y'know?" He spits, as they share a laugh, then Billy Ray nods adieu and heads for his pickup, limping through the mowed but unbaled alfalfa. "I'll try to get back this afternoon," he yells, as he gets into the battered Dodge. "But I may hafta go over to the John Deere guy in Marlow ... if I cain't get the right bolt at Haley's."

I doubt I'll see him again today, Bryan tells himself, as he watches the gray pickup trundle up the tractor trail toward the barn. *I reckon he's headed straight for Benny's.*

Billy Ray dropped out of school in tenth grade, yet he's street smart and has strong opinions about the world, opinions he shares while they work: "Politicians are whores. They're all on the take; it's legalized goddam bribery." Or: "I didn't see nary a rich kid in 'Nam. It was just poor whites and niggers gettin' killed and fucked up. That war sucked, and it's still suckin' I tellyuh." Or: "Those holy motherfuckin' Baptists don't care a-tall for me, so I come to church out *here*. This's *my* church, these hayfields and woods." Or: "The sweet-assed country gals 'round here are fuckin' irresistible, but I reckon there's a mean bitch inside each one of 'em, and there's always sumpthin' to bring 'er out. If it's not money, it's jealousy; if it's not jealousy, it's goddam religion; if it's not religion, it's reputation and gossip." Or: "Take Terri—I still love 'er despite all, but her *god*dam daddy messed up her head. They're all too good for me, just 'cuz they own that cocksuckin' chicken farm. Now, Bryan, I know your mama works for the bastard, but it's different when yuh marry into the family ... and that's only because I knocked her up her senior year. They wanted it to look proper and Christian ... but we *did* love each other, and we mightuh still made it, if I hadn't got fucked up in Vietnam." Or: "Old-man Sampson's a damn nigger-lover, not that he really loves 'em mind yuh, he just loves the low wages he can pay 'em. Hell, after Terri kicked me out, he fired my brother Gene. Said he smelled whisky on his breath, which was a *god*dam lie. Gene don't drink nary a bit, least compared to me. Shitfire, he musta wrung ten thousand chicken necks, and he never made more'n six bucks an hour. But the old bastard hired some *nigger* mammy and paid her even less. That's how rich fuckers are. They're all greedy and two-faced, just like the damn politicians."

I should load these bales, Bryan tells himself, as he heads for the other end of the pasture where they left the flatbed truck and the mower (they rent the flatbed). *This humidity is brutal, and those little clouds are worthless. I doubt we coulda worked all afternoon.* His Levi's are clingy and wet, soaked with sweat, but he has to wear long jeans, plus cowboy boots. Your legs get cut and irritated if you work in shorts, not to speak of the chiggers and ticks. But he did remove his T-shirt a good while ago.

Grabbing his Igloo jug from the cab of the truck, he takes several big slugs of ice water then after removing his hat, he lets the rest of the water run onto his head, his face, his neck, his chest, an icy, shocking, but bracingly good sensation. He's also hungry, but quenching his thirst and cooling off ranks ahead of eating. He has a few granola bars in his work bag but decides to save them, since he'll be going to the house soon. His mom's at work, but she said there'd be something in the fridge for him and Billy Ray—now just him. He takes a deep breath, filling his lungs. He loves the spicy-sweet aroma of freshly mowed hay.

After I have some lunch, I'll work at my computer, he says to himself, as he enjoys the cooling effect of the breeze on his water-doused bod. *Then I'll give Mandy a call when she gets off work. Maybe we can get together tonight?* This thought stirs him. *I haven't seen her since Sunday at church. With her extra shifts and me haying every day, it's hard to get our schedules in sync. She might even hafta work tonight?*

THE SILVER CORD

High above the pine grove a buzzard circles slowly in the haze. *It's already August. I'll be leaving for Waco soon.* Tremors of anxiety disturb him, threaten him. *This's gonna be a BIG change. She's gonna be here, while I'm at Baylor. Maybe her mother is right? Maybe—O God, I don't wanna think about it.*

He drives the flatbed over to the broken-down baler, where he positions it amid the thirty or so bales they got done before the machine failed. Getting right to work, Bryan swings the fifty-pound bundles of hay up onto the truck with relative ease, his strength and stamina as good as ever, or close.

What the heck! he exclaims to himself a few minutes later, as a car honks behind him—a red Firebird. His heart bounds: *Mandy! Oh, wow!* She rumbles down the tractor trail then charges right at him, beeping and fishtailing through the unbaled alfalfa. She skids to a halt on the grassy stubble surrounding the flatbed.

"Hello, you good-looking hunk, you," she announces, after rolling down her window. "Let's take a ride. I got a picnic basket full of food and a great place to go. Let's have some *fun* today." She beams, giving her goofy, girlish grin, showing her teeth.

"I thought you had to work till three?" Bryan replies, his mood soaring, his cheeks dimpling.

"Well, you said to play hooky and come help yuh?"

"That was *last* week?"

"Yeah, it took a while for me to escape." She blushes and giggles, scrunching her face. "Nawh, I was only working today as a last-minute favor, so Aunt Marge let me go at eleven." More giggles. "Mama's at Kroger's, and my sister's at the church for VBS, and she's going over to Molly Ann's afterward. So I had to find *some*thing to do." She adjusts her softball cap, allowing more sun on her grinning face; the summer freckles make her look especially puppyish. "Mama has to work late, so I'll hafta baby-sit tonight. But I'm free till five—like really *free!*"

"Well uh, I uh. I just hafta—"

"C'mon, you big handsome half-naked jock. Don't just stand there babbling. Get in. You can finish that hay later."

Grabbing his T-shirt, he hops into the Pontiac, and Mandy peels out toward the tractor trail, spewing dirt and stubble and loose hay. The AC (it's now fixed) hums full blast; it quick-chills his flesh but fires his soul—much like the ice water before.

"You stink, mister," she chortles, as he slips on his still-damp T-shirt, "but I *like* it. You smell like a *real* man."

Gosh damn, Bryan declares to himself, *this's gonna be a real test—but I love it. And she's wearing those tight shorts. O God.*

THE SILVER CORD

* * *

MAGRUDER STATE FOREST
TUESDAY, AUGUST 6, 1991 — 1:35 PM

"Looks like *all* these campsites are empty," Mandy says, as she eases the sporty coupe down the gravel road, which winds left then right. "But let's go to the last one. It's in a thicket down by the stream. That way we'll have *max*imum privacy." The forest looms darkly about them. She removes her sunglasses, placing them on the gearshift console.

"Yeah, the more privacy the better," Bryan chuckles, barely able to control himself. She's been flirting and teasing the whole way here (they're fifty miles north of Spindle). He knows they can't do anything below the neck, but he's riding an awesome Mandy-high, an eager fever. Even if they can't yield fully to this magical energy, the sense of amorous adventure invigorates him, numbing his inhibitions, making his dick tingle. And those pink shorts of hers are forever burned into his brain, the way they dig into her thighs. He's crazy to get his lips on hers. He did kiss her a few times on the way up, but those were just pecks on the side of the mouth, lest she wreck the Firebird.

"It's good we came on a weekday," Mandy adds, giving Bryan a provocative glance, as though excited by his lustful attention. "And I don't think they allow overnight camping at these sites. They hafta go to the west side of the park, the RV's and such."

Killing the AC, she cranks down her window; he opens his as well. The outside air, sultry and pine-scented, wafts in along with the crunch of tires on crushed stone.

"I've been to this forest a number of times," he remarks, forcing himself to look at the large, stately pine trees, "but I never knew about *this* road. How'd yuh find out about it?"

"Oh, Pastor Ted brought us here last summer. I reckon you were playing Legion ball—course, y'were already a *bigshot* jock, so you didn't have much to do with the youth-ministry kids." She gives a husky little snicker and a toss of her head, her ponytail dancing cutely on her neck.

"You talk like I was stuck *up* or something."

"Well, you *were* ... least till I got into your life."

"Get outta here. I'm just a shy country boy."

"Yeah right—but anyway, that's how I found out about this spot. It's super neat, especially the stream. It's icy cold, like from a spring, and there's this big pool among the rocks. And it doesn't have that rotten-egg stink, like over at Sulphur Springs."

She pulls into Campsite #9, the last one. They park near the trail that leads down to the creek. He can see the rocky stream amid the trees plus the big pool. He snickers hissily, sort of a half whistle. "I'm not too keen on *cold* water, pretty lady."

134

"Oh, don't be such a *sissy*."

"Well, I might go in with you—if you're *good* to me."

Reaching around, she stuffs her purse into the lift-top picnic basket. "How can a big hunky jock-stud like you be timid about a little spring-fed creek? I'm the *girl*. I'm the *one* who should be timid." She snorts huffily, playfully. "Besides, we gotta eat before we do any wading—and I hafta give yuh your present."

"My present? Uh ... whaddeyuh mean?" He jabs her teasingly on the shoulder. "Now y'got my curiosity stirred."

She giggles and hops out. "That's my plan, to getcha *stirred*." She sticks out her tongue sassily then gives him a blushing side-glance. "You'll see what I *got* soon enough."

He senses a double meaning in her words. *Maybe today IS the day?* he remarks excitedly to himself, as he gets out. *No, we can't; we can't.* Nonetheless, his knees go wobbly at the thought.

A few minutes later, they plunk down on a beach towel, in a shady, grassy area near the stream. Gray, time-weathered stumps poke up here and there around them, indicating that this spot was carved out of the forest. There's a picnic table back up the hill, but it's prettier down here. Bryan pulls off his boots and socks. "Oh, your feet are *dis*gusting," she kids, as she digs around inside the brown-wicker picnic basket.

"It's not *me* ... but these socks."

"Yeah right. Well, lemme tellyuh, mister, you're *def*initely going into the water, as soon as we eat." They laugh mirthfully, as he pushes the sweaty, grimy socks into the cowboy boots then tosses the boots well to the side, into the grass.

Cocooned by the forest, not only pines but also oaks and willows with lots of smaller trees underneath plus bushes and vines and ferns, this grassy creekside spot seems more intimate than a room with walls, and it's certainly more enchanting. "This place is awesome," Bryan declares, "and there aren't any mosquitoes or anything. And it's not so hot down here by the creek, and I like the pine scent and the gurgling sound, and the water's not one bit swampy-looking."

"I knew you'd like it," she replies, as she gets out the paper plates and plastic forks. She gives him a proud little smirk. "I've been wanting to bring you here a *long* time."

The wilderness looms dark and densely green all around, but a patchwork pattern of sun and shadow gives the campsite itself a lively, vivid, many-hued character, as if they've escaped into a Monet painting: yellows, greens, purples, browns, myriad shades and tones. A tall pine, spared among the stumps, accounts for most of the shadows. And there are wildflowers too: daisies, pink violets, buttercups, tiny white flowers, purple blossoms on a near-by shrub. The stream shimmers in like fashion: azure water, white tumbling rapids, sunny sparkles, clear water, mossy rocks, gray rocks, tan rocks. And the deep part, the pool, looks darkly translucent tending toward blue.

THE SILVER CORD

And yet Mandy, kneeling on the towel amid the dabs and shreds of sunlight, trumps the picturesque setting—by a *wide* margin. In addition to the sexy shorts, she wears a yellow-knit shirt, also sexy as it loosely reveals her perky hillocks. Working in wifely fashion, she arranges their picnic, her ponytail swishing behind her cap. She cants her cupid mouth, a little know-you're-looking-at-me smirk. A hot wind blows through Bryan; he yearns to hold her, to make out in the grass. The longing grows, nearing torment—but then it breaks like a wave leaving in its wake a warm, soothing sensation that spreads through his psyche, as if he's on Percocet. He couldn't call up the concerns he had back at the hayfield, even if he wanted to, and he doesn't.

"So where'd you say Billy Ray went?" she asks a while later. "You mentioned it in the car?"

Gesturing with his second peanut-butter-and-jelly sandwich, Bryan gives a rehash of what happened this morning, the baler breaking down and whatnot. Mandy's picnic menu is simple and easy, but he likes peanut butter and jelly. It was his favorite sandwich as a little kid, and he's never outgrown the sweet and nutty goodness. She also brought apples and Oreo cookies, plus a thermos of lemonade, and there's potato salad from the diner. He grabs an Oreo but never gets it to his mouth, because she gets there first. Going up on her knees, she kisses him. Her lips taste of lemonade and mayonnaise, from the potato salad. "I love you, Bryan Howard," she coos breathily—but then she adds a shot of humor: "Even if yuh do stink like a *locker* room."

Shedding her cap, she kisses him again, and again, her tongue tingling with electricity. Ditto for his penis, now "boner" hard inside his jeans. Finally, they collapse, cuddling in the grass beside the beach towel. He smells her shampoo, her perfume, her knit shirt, which still has that "new" smell. *I knew we'd be kissing sooner than five o'clock,* he chuckles in his thoughts. The sound of a distant, downshifting truck reminds him they're still on this trouble-plagued planet, but when he's holding her like this, he has no room in his mind for fear or doubt. He caresses her hair then her back. *What's this? There's no strap—NO bra?* This discovery makes his boner pang. Lust calls him to fondle those unfettered bunnies, but he fights off the need with a laugh and a quip: "So tell me, pretty lady? Didyuh forget *some*thing when you were getting dressed?" He goes up on his elbow.

"What?" Mandy teases, as she scrambles friskily around the wicker basket to her side of the big white towel.

"You know *what*?" he flirts, returning to the towel himself.

Assuming a cross-ankle sitting position, she abandons her pretense: "Mama would *shoot* me if she knew, but I don't really need a bra. Don'tcha agree, mister?" Sitting up straight, she inhales, lifting her chest inside the knit shirt—to prove it.

"Nawh, I reckon y'don't. I couldn't tell anyway—not by looking." She giggles then gives him a seductive roll of her big blue eyes. He dimples, turning red as well—he feels heat in his face, not to mention the fever between his legs. If their lips meet again, he'll be inside that lemon-colored polo. And her sitting posture makes her shorts dig all the more into her thighs, the rolled denim. He loves the sight but can't bear it, especially when that same wondrous pink fabric hugs her crotch, conveying in bas-relief her most-intimate contours, the pubis mound, the pouty folds, even the furrow between. Too much: he stands and stretches, then pads barefoot up the path, up the hill. "I hafta take a leak," he announces as he veers off into the forest.

"If yuh gotta go, then yuh gotta *go*," she chortles loudly.

He walks gingerly, since he's barefoot. While in the woods, his passion notches back to a tolerable level. Ditto for his dick. And when he returns, he finds her more relaxed as well. "You forgot my present," he says, as he plunks back down.

"No way," she laughs. "I was just waiting for things to calm down." Swinging the picnic basket around, she retrieves the gift, which is wrapped in blue paper and pink ribbon. "Here, babe."

Bryan slips the ribbon off then rips the paper from a flat, white box, which is roughly eight by ten. Mandy looks on with a grin, her eyes eager, happily anxious. Removing the lid, and the folded tissue paper, he finds an elegant leather binder. He takes it out and opens it. "Oh, pretty lady," he exults, as he discovers a beautiful photo-portrait of her. "It's *awe*some. I love it."

While she blushes bashfully, he reads the note, engraved in gold leaf on the opposite side of the binder: "To my beloved Bryan—Whether we're hand-in-hand walking in the fields, or sitting together under our special tree, or even if we're ten thousand miles apart, our hearts shall remain forever joined. Babe, I thank God for you. All my love, Mandy."

His heart overflowing, he studies the picture itself. Wearing a gorgeous sky-blue dress, which brings out her eyes, she lounges on the grass, her legs together but to the side. Her golden ponytail is brushed and full-bodied, and it's highlighted with a matching blue bow. She holds a single white daisy, her expression angelic, as she gazes at the flower. And to make it *extra* special, she's posing under the big oak tree, with Ruby Pond in the background.

"When didyuh—I mean uh.... how'd yuh get this?"

"Wendy took it ... like two weeks ago, back in July. It was that day y'were in Dallas with your mom. Y'know for your tests and all? We took a whole roll, like twenty-four, but this one came out best, so I got it enlarged."

How could I ever doubt her? he asks himself, as he reads the inscription again. *Like I was just doing back at the farm?* His eyes go blurry, his joy giving birth to tears.

* * *

"Yikes, that's cold!" Bryan fusses twenty minutes later, as he pokes his foot into the stream. Retreating, he utters a snorty shuuu-*wee!* The water *is* cold, but he hypes his reaction to get a rise out of Mandy—and he does.

"Awh c'mon, y'big sissy. Lemme check it out." Kicking her sneakers off, she goes in ankle-deep. "It's chilly, but *nothing* to run from." She laughs then makes a face at him, scrunching her features. The playful mood has returned, replacing the sweetly romantic interlude, as she was giving him the picture. "In fact, it feels *great* ... once y'get in." She goes a little deeper. "And it's not slimy at all. Hey, c'mon! Who's supposed to be washing anyway? You're the one with the stinky feet?"

"I *am* washing my feet," he declares, venturing out onto a wide, flat rock which is barely two inches under the surface.

"Maybe I should getcha a life jacket," she quips, as she wades downstream, her blond hair radiant in the sunlight. "Just in case." Entering the deeper, blue-tinted pool, she squats down, clothes and all, until she's neck deep. "Ahh ... this water feels re*fresh*ing. C'mon, don't be such a chicken."

"Now, pretty lady, don't make fun. I got long jeans on. I can't go in as deep as you."

She giggles. "Sure yuh can. I got *my* clothes wet." He kicks the water but stays on the rock. "Okay, if you're not coming in, I'm getting out." She wades back, retracing her steps, splashing him as she passes. Her sopping-wet, semi-translucent polo clings tightly, revealing in sculptured detail her perky-proud, teen-gal breasts and erect nipples—no *way* does she need a bra.

O Jesus, he remarks to himself, as she grabs the beach towel, *she might as well not have a dadgum shirt.* She dabs her limbs with the towel, as water continues to drip from her wet clothes. Her denim shorts look darker, more gray than pink.

"Gosh," she complains good-naturedly. "It's the dang middle of summer, and you're spooked about a little spring water."

"Well, don't be in *such* a rush. I like to take my time."

"So you're going in after all?"

"Yeah, I'm ready. I'm ready to take the plunge."

She hisses and huffs, feigning displeasure. "Fine, Bryan. Just fine. I get dried off as best I can, and *now* yuh finally wanna get in. Well, y'can go in *by* yourself."

"But, pretty lady, it's no *fun* if you don't come in with me."

Shaking her head, she throws the towel down, as if tired of this game, but the mischievous glint in her eyes gives her away. "Okay, you big jock, I'll go in with you—on *one* condition."

He hops from the rock back onto the bank. "What's that?"

She gives him a spunky side-glance, a frisky roll of the eyes.

THE SILVER CORD

"Naked—we gotta strip totally 'jay bird' naked."

"N-n-naked?" he stutters, a whirlwind tangling his thoughts.

"Yep, stitch-less," she affirms, her hands on her hips, a smirk on her lips. "It makes *per*fect sense. I gotta get these wet clothes off, so they can dry, and y'need to get outta yours, so they won't get wet." She compresses her lips folding the smirk, her cheeks flushing. Her blue eyes spark mirthfully. "It's elementary logic. And it's about time we saw each other *any*how."

"But whaddabout uh ... you know?"

"Well, we're not gonna *touch* or anything. This's just for having fun, for skinny-dipping, and like I say, it makes perfect sense. We'll even make a no-kissing rule: we can't smooch while our clothes are off—that'll be for *your* sake, mister ... since *you* don't have self-control like *I* do." She giggles and wiggles, giving a sassy shake of her damp denim-clad butt.

O Lord God! Bryan exclaims to himself, his carnal curiosity raging. *She's totally uncorked, but I love it.* His conscience tries to intervene but has NO chance. He plunks down on the nearest stump—to collect his wits.

* * *

"Hey, you big jock, how yuh doing?" Mandy sports a few minutes later, as she cavorts in the grassy area where they had their picnic; her tits jostle sassily inside the wet shirt. Bryan doesn't reply; he's too captivated. The game plan calls for skinny-dipping, but she seems at present more interested in dancing than stripping. He's crazy to go after her, to undress her himself, but he somehow manages to stay seated on the stump.

Throwing her hands into the air, she prances around the assorted stuff piled to the side: the wicker basket, a plastic bag of picnic refuse, Bryan's present (the photo-portrait), her sneakers, his boots, her softball cap, the crumpled beach towel. Shaking and stomping, she utters a war-hoop of delight then skips back to the grassy center-stage where she executes a coltish whirl halting in front of him, one leg forward, shoulders canted, hands on hips (which tilt opposite her shoulders). As she catches her wind, her wondrous, polo-clad breasts lift then recede. His penis quivers hotly as it swells behind his fly. *O Jesus in Heaven,* he gulps to himself, pushing his Tiger cap back on his head.

She does her rabbity, lip-pursing, nose-crinkling bit then tucks her chin, giving him a wink along with a beguiling school-girl grin that's partly silly, partly shy, yet naughty underneath, a most Lolita-like expression, especially when it's capped cutely by those soft, sunny-blond bangs, which didn't get wet before.

Their eyes connecting, he dimples into a big smile of his own.

"What?" she titters.

He gives an open-handed gesture. "So yuh decided to keep your clothes on, huh?"

"I reckon so, mister," she flirts, reversing her hips, and shoulders. "I doubt y'could handle it ... if I *actually* got naked."

You got that right, he affirms, but only to himself.

She tosses her bangs. "I reckon we better get packed, and get on back." But the bold twinkle in her eyes tells a different story.

Quickly confirming, she utters a husky little growl, then resumes her dance. She bops right then left; she gives him a head fake, a hip turn, then she lifts her polo flashing her bellybutton, a teasing shot. She flashes her tummy a few more times then lifts the shirt higher. He catches a glimpse of white nubile flesh, the undersides of her untanned tits—but it's only a ploy. Keeping the shirt on, she jitterbugs back and forth, her ass swinging, her head bobbing cutely like it does—all her movements exhibit that adorable Mandy character: jockish, slouchy, tomboyish.

She's pretty good at this, he observes silently, as she pivots and spins as if going in for a lay-up on the basketball court—her towel-frizzed ponytail flies up off her neck. *At least as good as those strippers Spanky taped off the Spice Network.*

Mandy reaches for the sky like a ballerina, her cheerleader calves tightening as she goes up on her toes—but she quickly loses her balance. Giggling, she stumbles sideways regaining her footing. She's no ballet dancer, thank God. But she entwines her hands anyhow, awkwardly over her head, a pair of drunk swans in a mating ritual. More giggling, then she gives up on the graceful moves in favor of her foot-stomping Indian jig.

Bryan laughs. This whole thing is torturing him, yet it a good way. He feels woozy good and wobbly, eager for more, and she gives him *more*. Rolling her eyes, she executes a playful about-face then eases the wet shirt over her head. Without turning around, she saunters to her left and drapes it on a big shrub, the one with the purple blossoms. Her naked back is satiny smooth and nicely tanned, save for the ribbon of white left by her bikini top. Still facing the shrub, she gives a saucy wiggle of her pink-denim butt; the pink color is coming back into the shorts, the hot afternoon having dried them a trifle.

It's like a dream, all of this—ever since she came bombing across the hayfield to pick him up. He's never seen her this free, and she's just now getting to the high point. Gyrating her hips more slowly, she unzips then lowers her shorts a few enticing inches, just enough to give him a backside view of her blue pantywaist. She waits; he waits. The birds sing; the creek gurgles.

"C'*mon*, pretty lady," he blurts. "Don't stop *now*."

She laughs, a ragged titter. "I told*juh* y'couldn't handle it."

She wriggles out of the shorts, pushing them down her legs, her hip-hugger undies coming down damply at the same time. Bryan, his heart thumping, marvels at her succulent, vanilla-white ass, with its wide, womanly roundness and soft, squeezable cheeks—they jiggle temptingly, as she hangs the pink shorts on the shrub, next to her shirt. Slanting tan-lines depict the shape of her bikini bottom, her beach exposure, but most of her behind is pale, and it suddenly seems even whiter, as she sidles into a pine-filtered beam of sunshine, a perfect striptease spotlight.

"Well, mister, that's *all* I can take off," she announces, after wringing out her blue underpants and hanging them to dry—she's still facing away from her babe. "I reckon it's time for me to get back into the water, into that *deep* pool."

"I reckon so," he chuckles tightly, playing along—he can barely get his voice to work.

Mandy sidles sideways toward the stream—but then she whirls around, revealing all. "TA-DAH!" she exclaims, assuming a *Playboy* pose: hips canted, legs crossed, arms lifted seductively.

Awesome! he exults to himself, looking on spellbound. *Her bush IS light brown ... just as I thought.* She offers another pose, then another. Bryan snaps each as if he has a camera—he does, the screen of his memory: no way can he forget *these* images. He feels for a moment like he's leaving his body, a waking OBE, but he doesn't. He remains very much in the physical realm, parked on the tree stump. His hard-on pulses, as his mushrooming knob seeks more room in his Levi's. Her ruddy-nippled breasts perch proudly on her chest like a pair of gibbous moons, each just big enough to fill his hand, as he recalls from the watermelon patch. The surrounding tan lines give them a girlish and lively innocence, animated ivory.

She switches poses like a pro, but the giggles and blushing smirks, plus the averted eyes, tell him that she's still a little shy about crossing this line. Yet the contrast between her boldness and bashfulness, between her earthiness and innocence, between her darkly fertile body and puppyish, teen-maiden face makes her *all* the more desirable. She waltzes and frolics, whirling around, once, twice, then she freezes, legs crossed, one arm extended for balance, the other curled, elbow-up, behind her ponytail. Her springy, ginger-brown pubic curls adorn like a necktie the apex of this pose, accenting her cunny notch, as it cuts puffily downward a little distance before disappearing between her crossed legs. Her bush seems darker and more potent against her pale belly, that lowest, slightly pillowy, part of her torso which never sees the sun. The prim, squarish swatch of pubic hair enhances in like manner the beauty of her groin, the juncture of her inner thighs as they converge creamily upward, having less tan but *much* more allure, because of *what* they guard—*O Lord Jesus.*

After holding the pose another few seconds, Mandy scampers back into the water, and is soon crouched chin-deep in the down-stream pool. "See, babe, that wasn't hard," she chirps, lowering herself until the water is up to her nose—then she submerges all the way, staying down a good while. After coming up, she snorts and spits, pushing her wet bangs back; her hair looks dark, almost brown. "Okay, mister, I kept *my* part of the bargain. It's *your* turn now. So let's *get* those duds off." She giggles and sticks out her tongue. With her hair plastered down, her face looks notably oval, and *much* younger. The water droplets add to this impression, as they magnify her freckles. How can this little girl *in* the water, be so *adult* out of the water? "C'mon, you big jock. We made a deal? It's *your* turn." She gives her goofy grin.

Bryan, still seated on the stump, dimples, returning her grin, but the fevered awe he was feeling before has given way to self-consciousness. His penis deflates. "Okay, but gimme a minute," he replies apprehensively. "I gotta get psyched up for this."

"Awh, don't be such a party-pooper. I'll come out and help yuh if you want?"

"No, you stay there," he laughs, as he gets up off the stump. "I can handle it."

"Hey, I don't expect you to dance and pose like I did. I just wanna see whatcha got, mister, then we'll have *fun* in the water." She snickers coquettishly, no longer seeming quite so young.

* * *

MAGRUDER STATE FOREST
TUESDAY, AUGUST 6, 1991 — 3:30 PM

Using the rearview mirror, Mandy fiddles with her disheveled, towel-dried hair. Bryan looks on, engrossed. Though now calm, or relatively so, as compared to his fevered state when watching her strip by the stream, he's still fascinated by all her little feminine tasks and habits, and his interest derives from the same love and carnal curiosity, only on a smaller scale.

"My dadgum hair's beyond repair," she says, "but I reckon it's worth it, con*sid*ering the reason." She giggles and smirks. Giving up, she pops the elastic thing back around her stringy, frizzed-out ponytail then stuffs the comb into her purse. After putting on her sunglasses, she slips the keys into the ignition, but before cranking she lifts her buttocks, one then the other, so she can adjust the beach towel beneath her. She's back in her clothes of course, save for her panties, which she tossed into the picnic basket along with her softball cap. Her shorts are drier now, but not totally. Ditto for the knit shirt. "Well, babe, do your feet *smell* any better?" she quips, as she finally starts the Firebird.

He punches her playfully in the shoulder. "I'll say—you sure weren't kidding about having *fun* today."

"So you liked it, didyuh—my *Playboy* poses?"

"O God, y'were better than any *Playboy* I ever saw—least the ones that Spanky keeps under his bed. Those pro models look *way* too

142

perfect, and glossy and cold ... like mannequins."

"Porno mags: so *that's* what you do at his house?"

Bryan dimples. "Nawh, I just saw 'em once or twice—but goshdang, I wouldn't be talking after the show *you* put on."

"I practice that routine in front of my mirror, but no one's ever seen me before. That's for *darn* sure." She blushes and giggles then drops the stickshift into reverse and backs up. She pauses a moment to fasten her seat belt; Bryan does the same. "But y'really did like it, huh? Even with my fat ass?"

"Get outta here. Your ass is *just* right."

"No, it's not," she banters, as they hotrod out of the parking lot, spewing peastone behind them. "It's getting big and fat, just like Mama's." They pick up speed on the shady, tree-lined road, the tires ripping and popping, but then she quickly throttles back, to negotiate a curve. "And my thighs too—they're getting flabby at the top, even with all the running I do."

He gives a hissy whistle that turns into laugh. "Well, pretty lady, if you call that flab, I hope you *stay* flabby."

"And my tummy's getting a bit soft too. Plus, I'm bloated, 'cause my period's due ... like this weekend."

"Get outta here—stop putting me on. Your bod is A+ ... top, middle, *and* bottom ... no doubt about it." Bryan, laughing, hangs onto the door grip, as they slide a little on the gravel. "In fact, Billy Ray says they're having a wet T-shirt contest over at The Cove this Saturday ... you know, that roadhouse on the east side of the lake. Considering what I saw today—O Lordee—I reckon you'd win something if yuh entered."

"Keep it up, cowboy. I've heard about some weird contests down in New Orleans I could enter *you* in ... and we'd win *big*."

This pun sets them both to laughing. "Well, I sure wouldn't have won anything when I first got my clothes off today."

"Nope, but I think it's *cute* when it's soft. And it sure didn't stay soft, not after I came out of the water and kissed yuh."

"Yeah, you broke the rules."

"Not really—we didn't get into necking or anything. I just wanted to encourage yuh."

"Well, it's a good thing we had that pool of spring water to chill us out, or we might've broken a lot *more* rules."

"Not *me*," she chortles. "I have self-control, remember?"

"Oh yeah, I forgot." More laughter.

They soon pass Campsite #1, and Mandy turns onto the main road (no more gravel) that bisects the state park. *It IS amazing we didn't do anything,* Bryan remarks in his thoughts, *considering all the flirting, and how naked we got. Maybe this's just a dream.* Lifting his baseball cap, he runs his hand over his head. *No, I'm very much awake—and in my body. But how can I just sit here with her, and be almost relaxed, after witnessing, in living color, everything she's got? That icy water saved us. If we'd come right to the car after her stripper routine, we'd still be making out, and then some. But going home and calling it a day IS the wisest thing. She has to baby-sit anyway.* They had a fun time cavorting in the stream, chasing, splashing, laughing like a pair of naked grade-schoolers, then they rested in the deeper pool, their mood mellowing. And before getting out, they agreed to cool it on the way home, no necking, lest they end up disrobing again, with *no* ground rules, and no creek to jump into.

The forest gives way to meadows and open areas, then after passing a log administration building, they exit the park and head west on Texas Farm Road 84, which takes them back to FR 115. Bryan adjusts the fold-down visor to block the sun—he doesn't have his dark glasses. Mandy pushes the Firebird up to seventy. "That AC's too cold on my legs," she remarks, as she cuts the temp back. "These shorts are still damp, and it feels *weird* without panties." She giggles, giving him a sensual side-glance.

A warm tugging in his crotch threatens his semirelaxed mood. *She may get me going yet?* he reacts, but only to himself. *I love it when she talks about her panties, or anything down there. And she looks so cute and sexy in those sunglasses, especially with her bangs going in all directions.* He figures she's about to start another round of sporting and suggestive teasing, like she's been doing all day, but she sobers instead, focusing on the road ahead—as though she realizes, as he does, that flirting at this point is like juggling vials of nitroglycerin.

"I reckon it's a *good* thing I hafta baby-sit my little sister tonight," she laughs, lending credence to his conclusion.

"You got that right, Miss Amanda Fay."

After going another mile or so, she smiles sweetly at him. "Seriously, babe, y'didn't get too embarrassed, didyuh?"

"Nope, not really. It was just a *super*-new experience, that's all. But I'm glad we did it."

She gives a soft little laugh. "Me too."

Dimpling, he gives her a tender peck on the cheek. Then he pushes his seat back all the way and stretches out as much as he can. She pats him on his folded arms, then flips on the radio and scans the dial, stopping at Neil Diamond and "Heartlight." She doesn't normally listen to Neil Diamond, but the song fits their mood, which has shifted from frolicsome to seriously romantic—or so it seems.

* * *

This has been a dadgum weird day, like way out, Mandy says to herself, as she turns left on FR 115 and accelerates southbound. *Like totally crazy ... yet super fun.* She gives a girlish titter under her breath. *That big jock has conked out over there.* Bryan, his cap bill low over his face, hasn't said anything for several miles. *I reckon that picnic by the creek was TOO MUCH for him.* More girlish laughter, a few hushed ha-ha's. The radio's still tuned to the soft-rock station, but the mood music has given way to news: a quote from Supreme Court nominee Clarence Thomas about his upcoming confirmation hearing, then a report from Moscow on President Bush's summit thing with Mikhail Gorbachev, then something about the worsening crisis in the Balkans, the Serbs fighting to gain control of Croatia.

I wish I could just watch Bryan sleep, Mandy sighs, paying scant attention to the radio, *instead of staring at this goshdang highway. I wish I could watch him sleep tonight as well. I wish we could be together every day and every night, and never have to say good-bye. O God, why do we have to wait, and wait, and wait?* Liquid waves of affection warm her bosom, then the happy vibes move lower, and lower, becoming carnal in character. *Oh, I want him, ALL of him. We should pull off on some side road, and really get it on, like get THIS over with—no, we can't; we can't.*

The radio spouts the weather: a few isolated thunderstorms. Choppy static: this FM station is breaking up. She moves to *Country Rock 104*; they're just close enough to Sulphur Springs to pull it in. *Now that's a hot tune,* she reacts, as she gets George Thorogood and "Bad to the Bone." *But this's the last thing I should be listening to right now.* Nonetheless, she doesn't change the station—she turns it up in fact. The bluesy music makes her want to shake her butt, like she did during her striptease routine by the stream. She can't wiggle much while driving, so she drums her heel on the floorboard, her hand on her thigh, keeping time:

> I make a rich woman beg.
> I make a good woman steal.
> I make an old woman blush,
> and the young girls squeal....
> I mean to tellyuh, baby,
> that I'm *bad* to the bone....

She battles to keep her thoughts from going overboard, but this roadhouse song, with its raunchy slide guitar, chugging bass, and sexy saxophone, not to mention the sassy drumtrack and suggestive lyrics, sweeps her into the "naughty girl" realm.

Bryan shifts his left leg, stretching it out, yet despite the music (even at higher volume) he shows no sign of waking up. She glances at his long, jockish, denim-clad thighs, then at his crotch. *Oh gosh, I'd love to unzip him.* But she harks back instead to their skinny-dip session at Campsite #9, where her strip-dance fantasy finally came true. *I can't believe we actually took our clothes off—all of them. But how much longer can we play and flirt around. I can't take many more days like THIS. And it was MY idea. If Mama knew, she'd lock me in my room till I'm twenty-one.* Mandy giggles to herself.

The Thorogood song ends. She kills the radio, her thoughts now rocking as much as any roadhouse rhythm. *How can that big jock be so cute and handsome, and have those gorgeous green eyes, and yet have such a hunky, sexy bod.* She sighs hungrily. *And when his boner came up, I couldn't take my eyes off it. I was dying to play with it, but I ran back into the water instead.* She passes a slow-moving cattle truck, one of the few vehicles she's encountered since turning onto FR 115; there are more crows than cars along this stretch. She pushes the ponycar up to 75 mph. *Damn, I'd love to fondle him ... like right now. I can't stop thinking about it. Pastor Ron preaches that the Holy Spirit will deliver us from impure thoughts. I reckon he's preaching to the guys, but girls get horny too. I doubt there's any girl older than twelve who has pure thoughts all the time, especially if they know how it feels to get off—not me ANYWAY.*

She undresses Bryan in her thoughts, until he's nude again, by the stream. He performed no exotic routines, but he did playfully assume his batting stance. She pictures his naked, perfectly-toned physique, his strapping frame, his rippled stomach, his cute buns, his sturdy chest and shoulders and neck, which are brawny but not bulky, and his long muscular legs which have just enough hair to make them irresistibly virile. But the memory of his cock affects her the most, sending warm shivers to her pantyless crotch. She can't help but squeeze against them as she drives, but this offers no relief. It heightens the torment rather, arousing all the more the erotic tickle between her legs. She recalls his ruddy, robust shaft, made all the more ravishing by its blue serpentine veins and engorged burgundy head, perfectly fashioned to plumb her depths. And the dark hair at the root, through which his lowest, untanned belly showed fair and taut, added a primal, mannish potency, setting her heart to pounding—then and now.

Mandy passes a green pickup loaded with bales of hay, the small bales like Bryan was loading when she came by to get him. *I can't believe how wild and crazy I've been all day. And now my thoughts are WAY out of bounds.* She shakes her head, but she can't shake the electric buzz between her legs. *I need to do my thing. That's what it is. That's why I'm so wild today. It's been too long. I shoulda taken care of it this morning, in the shower. It's always better when I wait and wait, but now it's making me nuts.* She checks out Bryan again, noting his chiseled, whisker-shadowed jaw. *O God, I'm gonna melt in a minute. I feel like pulling down my shorts right now. I reckon THAT would get his attention. Course, the way I freak when I come, I'd run this damn Firebird into the ditch.* She laughs huskily, as they whip under Interstate 30; they're only fifteen minutes from Longley Road. *But I'm sure he masturbates as well. All guys do. I wonder what it's like for him. I wonder how often he does it?* Bryan shifts and yawns, waking up. "So, babe, how *d'yuh* deal with it?" Mandy blurts, her thoughts surfacing.

"What? Whaddeyuh talking about?"

He stretches and sits up. Mandy feels suddenly sheepish and self-conscious. She can scarcely believe she's asking him about this most risqué and personal subject. Her cheeks heat up; she knows she's blushing. Yet she doesn't retreat: "Whaddeyuh do? I mean, when we kiss and make out. We can't go all the way—so whaddeyuh do about the feelings?"

He rubs his eyes then gives her a yawny bewildered look: "I uh, I uh ... well, I—"

"Sorry, babe. I didn't mean to lay this on you when you're just waking up." He adjusts his seat, so he can sit up.

"It's okay," he replies, his voice drowsy. "Just give me a second to clear the cobwebs."

"There's a little bit of lemonade left in the thermos," she says, gesturing toward the back seat. "I reckon it's warm by now, but the sugar might help yuh." She slows to fifty, as they come up behind another pickup, a black, rusted-out wreck of a thing, with no tailgate. No hay, no load at all: this truck is simply going slow—the driver, in a cowboy hat, is most likely an old codger, and the pickup probably can't do more than fifty anyway. But this time Mandy doesn't zoom around it; there's too much going on in her head to even think about passing.

A minute later, Bryan sips lemonade, from a white cup. He dimples and smirks. "Now what's this you're asking me? I have a feeling it's gonna be *out there*, like everything else today." He blushes, his smirk growing into a wide country-boy grin.

The smile encourages Mandy, at least enough for her to proceed, though she's hardly comfortable with this subject—it's much easier to embrace taboo topics when you're lost in lustful daydreams. "Oh, I been thinking a lot while you were dozing." She gives a grin of her own. "And it's not exactly G-rated."

"No problem, pretty lady. You got my curiosity going."

"Anyway, I was wondering especially about that time at the watermelon patch—remember?"

Bryan takes a swig then gestures with the styrofoam cup. "No dadgum way could I forget *that*."

"Well, when I got home that night, I was still buzzing ... you know where. Then I had this a*maz*ing dream about you."

"Nawh, not about *me*?" he sports, his handsome face pulsing pink then pinker.

"Cut it out," she fusses playfully amid a giggle. "Lemme have some of your lemonade."

He hands her the cup. "Sorry, I'll be good now."

After taking a sip, she returns the cup. "To make a long story short: the dream got me urgently aroused, like out of my mind—we were making out in the grass by the giant oak tree, and just as we got ready to *do* it, I woke up. I was all sweaty and going crazy, so I uh ... I uh—well, I masturbated." She gives a snuffling laugh, a self-conscious snicker through her nose. "There, I *said* it. That word sounds so clinical, and I feel really bashful about saying it out loud, but when I do it, it's *any*thing but clinical." She grips the steering wheel tightly, then less tightly, flexing her hands, as the Firebird pokes along behind the black pickup.

Silence: he seems at a loss for words—at least, he doesn't reply right away. *O God, I feel weird,* Mandy declares to herself, as she glances at her sweetheart. *I never thought I'd be telling these secrets— maybe I shouldn't have?*

But his voice, when he finally responds, brims with kindred wonder. "Oh, pretty lady, this makes me love you *more* than ever." He caresses her shoulder. His touch comforts her, making her feel less self-conscious, as does his confession. "But I guess you and I are very much alike when it comes to pent-up passion, because I did the *same* thing when I got home that night, except I took care of it *before* I went to sleep."

She chuckles hushedly. "I figured you did."

"Well, it's a *real* personal thing, and nobody talks about it—oh, Spanky does, and a few other guys on the team, but they're just cutting up. They'd never bring it up at a serious moment, or in mixed company." Gulping the last of his lemonade, Bryan places the empty cup in the beverage holder in front of the gearshift. "I've wanted to ask you about it many times, but I never had the guts." He gives her a fond pat on the cheek. "So I'm sure it was a bit nerve-wracking for you to bring it up."

"No kidding. I couldn't believe what I was saying. But we've been wild and crazy all day, least I have, and we already got naked and went skinny-dipping, so I reckon we can tell our secrets too."

"Yep, I'm learning a *lot* today—O Lord, am I *ever*. And I've been curious about you for a long time, pretty lady, like ever s—"

"You curious about *me,* nawh?" she kids, giving him some of his own medicine. They laugh. They've not only broken the ice on this taboo subject, but the remaining chunks are melting fast.

"So that was the first time," he asks, "after that sex dream?"

"Not hardly."

"But, pretty lady, I thought you had *self*-control?"

"I did ... until I met *you*—no, I actually learned how to get an orgasm when I was thirteen."

"Gosh, Mandy, you're more like me than I imagined, 'cept I started when I was twelve." They both snicker. "So how often d'yuh—well, you know?"

"Now you're really getting personal, mister."

"I know, but you started this whole thing."

She senses herself blushing again, but she's too much in the groove to stop now. "Oh, it's been happening a lot this summer. The longer I wait the better, but it's not easy to ignore after a week or so, and ten days is about my limit. I reckon I'm addicted." She giggles coquettishly.

Bryan dimples. "Goshdang, pretty lady, you *do* have self-control. Heck, I hafta deal with it anytime we're together, like when I get home, like every time, almost."

"Well, that figures since you're a *guy* ... but y'could go *blind* you know, doing it that much?" More mirthful dimpling and giggling. "That's what I heard about it once, like when we lived in Arkansas." She gestures toward the pokey truck in front of them. "But really, babe, d'yuh ever feel guilty—you know what they say about it at church? You know that story in Genesis where God struck a guy dead for spilling his seed on the ground?"

"Oh, I never spill *mine* on the ground," he wisecracks. "So I'm okay." Blushing, he laughs to the point of tears, her too. He waits, getting his breath, then he continues, his tone more serious. "No, I'm quite familiar with that story, and it used to make me guilty as hell, but not anymore. In fact, I see sexual release as healthy, at least from a biological point of view. It's not good to keep all that passion pinned up. Plus, I don't have any choice."

"You got that right, mister. Once you learn how to come, it's like being hooked on drugs." Mandy giggles. "The only way to stop is to do the *real* thing. Maybe it's about time? Maybe we should take care of this 'love itch' ... like nature intended?"

"It's gonna happen, pretty lady. Not right away ... but it's *gonna* happen."

* * *

"Looks like a storm brewing behind us," Bryan remarks a little bit later, as Mandy turns left on Longley Road. "We could use some rain, but I reckon it'll miss the farm, like most." The sun has disappeared nonetheless behind the towering thunderhead, giving the dry summer landscape a grayish, almost silvery sheen.

A devilish smirk plays upon Mandy's mouth. *What's she got up her sleeve?* he wonders to himself. *She's got that look again.*

The Firebird clatters over the cattleguard and whips up the Howards' driveway, a plume of dust churning up behind. "I guess Mom Howard isn't home yet?" Mandy notes, still smirking. "I don't see that little Honda she drives, or your dad's Buick?"

"Yeah, Dad's never here before five-thirty. With Mom, it's hard to say—her schedule varies."

Mandy slows, as she approaches the walkway leading to the front porch—but then she guns the Pontiac, zooming past the house, past the barn. "Hey, where the heck are yuh going?" Bryan asks, as they jounce down the tractor trail. "I thought y'had to baby-sit your sister this evening?"

"I do, but first, mister, I gotta deliver yuh back to your hayfield—exactly where I picked yuh up."

* * *

"Oh, babe, I love you *so*," Mandy sighs five minutes later, after a furious session of kissing. "You turn me on like *crazy*." They're parked in the hayfield, beside the flatbed truck.

"I love you too, precious," he whispers, trembling with want. "I love you so much it *hurts*." His throbbing erection feels like a rake handle inside his jeans.

Striptease, skinny-dipping, sporting, flirting, have to cool it, must cool it—CAN'T COOL IT! Their unspeakable need to kiss and fondle and more, charged to excess by the still-hot impressions from this afternoon's risqué adventures, not to mention the racy talk on the way home, has blown away the no-necking pact. For that matter, their willful decision to restrain themselves has ripened their passions all the more, bringing everything to a fevered head.

He slips his hand under her shirt, but she breaks the action, to make it easier for him. Leaning forward, she whips the yellow polo over her head. Then after sliding her seat back, she reclines as much as she can, giving him unhindered access to her chest. "Your tits are awesome," he coos, as he fondles them, the left, then the right. "They're so beautiful and perfect ... more so than any porn model. O Jesus God, I've been *dy*ing to touch 'em—like all afternoon." He finger-teases her nipples; they swell and bud, turning more red than pink, as they jut upward amid the lighter-hued areolas.

"So you're glad I hung around?" she giggles hoarsely, her blue eyes sultry and trancy.

"Oh, pretty lady, I'll *never* be the same after today."

"Me neither—oh, babe, you're getting me *so* high. Oh, kiss me. Kiss me some more." He moves back to her lips and darting tongue, which still taste faintly of lemonade. As he does, she works one-handed on his belt buckle, then his zipper.

* * *

I can't believe this day! Bryan exclaims to himself, as he ambles like a drunk across the weedy, summer-brown lawn, heading for the backdoor of his house. Mandy just dropped him off seconds ago, as she departed hurriedly, on her way to baby-sit Gretchen. *O God, sh-sh-she—goshdang it all, she blows me away.* He stops and looks back, just in time to catch a last glimpse of the red Firebird charging eastward on Longley Road. He feels again her excited touch—she's in his pants, stroking, petting, teasing. Then she's loosening those pink shorts, inviting his hand. It all comes back: her dreamy face, her mews and moans, her dimpled navel, the dampish heat of her pantyless mound, the springy patch of pubic hair—then he ventured lower, discovering a hot wonderful wetness amid clammy folds of flesh. "Oh *yes*, right there," she cried breathlessly, as he fingered the biggest fold.

Bryan walks bowlegged, because of the ache between his legs, an extreme case of blue balls—they didn't go all the way, or even get off. "Oh, babe, we can't," she gasped, slamming on the brakes just as her hips began to gyrate. "That feels *so* good. But if we go any farther, I'm gonna spasm, and no way can I stop after that."

Reaching the back porch, he plops down on the steps to collect his wits. *It's amazing. How can she STOP like that?* He gives a silent whistle that turns into a chuckle. *But O God, I LOVE her when she's earthy and hot and uncorked. How am I gonna stand it in Waco? How? When? What am I uh ... I-I-I? Hold it; hold it. My damn brain's gonna blow a fuse.* He takes a deep breath to settle himself, then another. The sky is getting darker. He hears thunder. *That storm may hit us after all? Maybe I should get that hay into the barn—nawh, I can't. It'll hafta wait.* He shakes his head. *Maybe I AM dreaming?* He sniffs his hand. *No way ... I can still smell her pussy.* The scent clings to his fingers, an exotic smoky-vanilla fragrance that's wild yet sweet; it's like nothing he's ever smelled before. It intoxicates him, making him all the more smitten with her. He'll never be the same, and he may never *wash* his right hand again.

* * *

Same day, 5:50 p.m. *Oh gosh, I needed that!* Mandy pants to herself, as the shudders of orgasmic release give way to that warm, melting trance that lingers blissfully after lust is satisfied. Her heart pounding, she lies on her bed, naked save for the knit shirt which is up around her neck. *This whole day's been totally berserk. That's what he does to me, that big hunky jock.* She giggles hushedly. It's thundering outside, but the house is quiet except for the drone of the AC across the room. Turning onto her side, she closes her eyes and hugs her pillow. *Oh, I wish he was here with me now, so we could cuddle together. That's the way sex oughta be. I blew the whistle again, but I don't see how we can wait much longer.* A clap of thunder resounds above the house, as if to emphasize this point.

She gives little heed to the thunder, or to the sudden gusts of wind, or to the metallic patter of raindrops on the cowling of the air conditioner. *Oh, Bryan honey, I love you so. I need you with me—like in the same bed ... like every night forever.*

She hears noise, someone downstairs. Hopping up, she grabs her robe from the closet. She feels suddenly self-conscious, her face warming. "Mandy, I'm home!" Gretchen yells.

Putting on the robe, Mandy opens her door. "I'm upstairs," Gretch," she replies, speaking from the doorway.

"I *bare*ly beat the storm," Gretchen declares breathlessly; she's at the bottom of the stairs, or sounds like it.

"Is Toby inside?"

"Yeah, he just came in ... through the cat door."

"Good, it's raining out."

"Yeah, great big drops. I *just* made it. I was pedaling *super* fast, and the wind was blowing the trees and I saw some streak lightning— so where's Mama?"

"She's working late, remember, till nine I think. I'll be down in a bit. We can make grilled-cheese sandwiches or something."

"Okay, but I'm not real hungry or anything. Me and Molly Ann— we pigged out on chips and dip at her house." Mandy hears the TV come on: a *Flintstones* re-run, at high volume.

Closing the bedroom door, she pads over and turns the AC down a notch, then she looks out the window above it. The rain is already letting up, and the clouds are breaking to the west. This storm is moving on, after skirting the north side of Spindle. *O Jesus, I'm screwed up,* she laments, as stabs of self-disgust attack her dreams. *I'm a TOTAL slut ... and I'm corrupting Bryan too.*

She scans the rain-dampened rooftops across the street; her stomach churns. *Or maybe we're leading each other astray?*

Turning around, she can't help but focus on her disheveled bed, which testifies to her depraved plight.

* * *

THE HOWARD FARM
WEDNESDAY, AUGUST 7, 1991 — 6:15 AM

Bryan yawns, as he exits the back door on his way to tend to Millie. In addition to grazing, the mare gets horse feed and pellets. He also has to drain and refill her water trough. The shadows are grotesquely long, and the air is thick and damp, and sweet with alfalfa. Beyond Longley Road, the first rays of sun have painted the landscape yellow and orange and amber, rich buttery swatches of color, as though applied with a palette knife. Before entering the barn, young Mr. Howard pauses to stretch; he's in no hurry, as the haying will be delayed today; the fields are too wet. The thunderstorm last evening didn't dump much rain, but it added enough moisture to make this morning's dew very heavy, so much so that it drips from the eaves of the old chicken house. In addition, Billy Ray has to repair the baler.

But Bryan has bigger things on his mind than harvesting hay. *We sure broke the no-petting rule, and every other rule—well, almost all.* These same thoughts have been popping ever since Mandy departed yesterday, and they're now producing more anxiety than amazement. *We're trapped in a contradiction. I'm crazy to be with her, but then she makes me even crazier, like yesterday.* He soccer-kicks, with the side of his boot, a chunk of cement, a nugget-sized piece of an old cinder block—it strikes with a wooden *whap* the base of the barn door. *How can I concentrate on college and everything? Dear Jesus, you've given me special gifts and special powers, even a preview of death and Heaven ... plus a calling to learn all I can about it ... but right now I can't think about anything but Mandy. We should be married, but we can't get married. It's totally out of whack. I'm jerking off, when I should be with HER. It's not honest; it's not reality.* Taking off his baseball cap, he gestures skyward, as if beckoning God. *We're obeying the letter of the law, but it's so crazy and false. And I'm leaving for Waco in three weeks.* An ominous shudder works up his spine then tightens like a fist between his shoulder blades.

THE SILVER CORD

CHAPTER TEN

PLEASANT HILL BAPTIST CHURCH
WEDNESDAY, AUGUST 7, 1991 — 7:31 PM

Despite the sparse turnout, twenty-five or so (typical for an August evening), Pastor Ron preaches with undiminished fervor, on the folly of trying to fool God. Mandy sits with her mom in the third row. She wishes she was a little kid again, so she could escape to junior church like Gretchen and Molly Ann.

"Let's consider some additional verses," the pastor instructs, returning to his pulpit. Mandy, her throat tightening, follows along in her own Bible, turning from passage to passage:

> The eyes of the Lord are in every place, beholding the evil and the good.

> He that covereth his sins shall not prosper, but whoso confesseth and forsaketh them shall have mercy.

> If thy right hand offend thee, cut it off.... for it is profitable for thee that one of thy members should perish, and not that thy whole body should be cast into hell.

> For they that are after the flesh do mind the things of the flesh; but they that are after the Spirit, the things of the Spirit.... So, then, they that are in the flesh cannot please God.

> Know ye not that the unrighteous shall not inherit the kingdom of God? Be not deceived: neither fornicators, nor idolaters, nor....

He goes on reading, at least ten passages in all, and by the time he finishes, Mandy's Bible has gone blurry, from tears.

* * *

In the corner stands a grandfather clock, an odd piece to have in a modern-day pastor's office. The incessant *ticktock* bothers Mandy, as does the inscription under the face: "Only one life, 'twill soon be past. Only what's done for Christ will last." She asked Pastor Ron, right after the service, if she could talk with him, and he told her to wait in his office. She's been in here a number of times (her mother's desk is

154

just outside), though never for counseling. She sits soberly forward, a respectful ladylike pose, as though the pastor is already here. *Dear God, I hate this,* she prays, as she toys with the Velcro clasp on her purse, pulling it open, *rrrrrrr-rip,* then closing it. *But I know I hafta get back on track. And please be with Bryan tonight, and give him peace. I do love him so, but I want your perfect will to be done.* Lumpy-hot pain claws at her throat. More tears well up, but she bites her lip fighting them back. She hasn't seen Bryan, or called him, since she left the Howard farm yesterday.

She feels tacky in her stonewashed jeans and turtleneck: *I shoulda worn a skirt.* She rarely gets dressed up for midweek service but now wishes she had, though she had no idea she'd be meeting with Pastor Ron. It was a spur-of-the-moment thing. She fiddles with the ribbon marker in her Bible, a blue Scofield that Charlie gave her last Christmas. She usually brings her little white Bible, since it fits into her envelope purse, but the Scofield better matches her frame of mind. Everything in the office adds to her unease: the big official-looking desk, the diplomas on the wall, the in-box, the multiline telephone console, the computer with its blinking screen-saver (angels and clouds), the Bibles and concordances stacked on the desk, the bookshelves behind. And the triumphant buzz of the departing believers down the hall doesn't help any: how can they have such godly, dedicated lives while she's mired in carnality and selfish concerns?

Ticktock, ticktock—it's 8:10 p.m. She's only been in here five minutes, but it seems like five hours. She fingerfluffs her bangs, then her ponytail. Her hair's a total disaster, or so she imagines. She should hurry to the ladies' room and fix it, but before she can, Pastor Ron arrives, closing the door behind him. "Sorry I kept you waiting, Amanda," he apologizes, as he shakes her hand and sits down at his desk. Leaning back, he loosens his tie then interlaces his pudgy, fat-fingered hands over his paunch. "But I had a few pressing matters that came up, as they usually do after service." He gives a quick genial laugh, three syllables maybe.

"That's okay," she replies, as she plays once more with the latch of her purse. "I appreciate you taking time to see me on such short notice." She tries to appear calm and poised, but her words come out shaky and mouselike.

He gives a compassionate smile, as if he senses her distress, yet his grayish eyes scan the wall behind her with only occasional direct glances. "Well, I can always find time for you, Amanda. After all, you and your mom, and your little sister, are almost like family to me, and I must say, you've really grown up since I first met y'all four years ago." His conversational voice, though still bassy, is quite relaxed compared to his stentorian preaching timbre, and his sunny disposition—he's grinning again—gives his heavy-jowled face an avuncular character, as if he *is* family.

Mandy forces a smile of her own. "Yeah, I reckon Mama's been working for you a good while now."

"She's topnotch. I don't know what I'd do without her."

After an awkward moment of silence, Pastor Ron clears his throat then leans forward and gets right to the point—though his tone remains relaxed, and his eyes continue to roam: "So I expect you're here to talk about Bryan, you and Bryan Howard?"

The bull's-eye question shatters her ladylike pretense. She doesn't reply; she can't reply. Her thoughts race; her face burns. She looks down, her eyes filling.

"It's tough being a teenager," the pastor goes on, "but the main thing to remember, Amanda, is that God is on *your* side, and so am I, and so is your mother. We love you dearly in the Lord, and the same goes for Bryan. I don't have all the answers of course, and God's will is often difficult to discern ... but I'll gladly listen to you ... and then we can talk and pray about it."

"I-I, well, I have questions. I uh...." Mandy hesitates. "I uh ... well, Bryan and I have this—no, I can't. It's *too* personal. I'm sorry, Pastor. I can't. I just can't!" Bolting out of the office, she runs sobbing to the parking lot, to her mother's car.

* * *

"Bryan, we hafta talk, and right away," Mandy declares on the phone some three hours later.

"What about?" he asks drowsily, though he knows what.

"About *every*thing. Mama and I just had a long talk ... and, and—" She falters, as though on the verge of breaking.

"It's okay, pretty lady," he whispers, though he knows the situation is anything *but* okay. He can scarcely keep from crying himself, as his dashed dreams dissolve, trickling downward into his stomach where they turn tepid, then cold. He was in bed just falling asleep when the phone by his computer began to warble, each ring piercing his heart like an executioner's bullet. It had to be Mandy, and his mother quickly confirmed, with a knock on his bedroom door.

"We gotta talk about everything," Mandy repeats.

"You can't tell me on the phone?"

"No, I'd rather not."

"So when?"

"Like after I get off from the diner tomorrow afternoon, or maybe in the morning before I go in? But that'll be super early."

Bryan's thoughts rush in all directions, a panicked throng in a collapsing building. He must find an exit, some way out of this calamity. "I can come to your house *right* now, if yuh want?"

"No, it's after eleven, and I don't wanna create a big stir. Let's meet at the DQ in the morning, say around six-fifteen?"

"I thought you had to be at work at six?"

THE SILVER CORD

"I do, but I'll call in ... and tell 'em I'm gonna be late."

* * *

SPINDLE, TEXAS - THE DAIRY QUEEN
THURSDAY, AUGUST 8, 1991 — 6:12 AM

Slumped against the door of his pickup, Bryan sips his coffee. He brought it with him, in a travel mug—the DQ doesn't open till six-thirty. No decaf today—he needs the strong stuff. Guilt, pain, anger, remorse: he anguished all night, tossing, turning, weeping, pacing, then back to bed, then up again. He begged God, he questioned God, he fought with God. But at dawn he ran up the white flag. Mandy has chosen the only honest and godly solution to their dilemma. She hasn't said it yet, but she *will*.

His brain flutters wearily behind gritty eyelids; he can hardly think, much less plead his case, *their* case. He's parked in the back facing Bixby, his usual spot. A puff of wind drifts in his window; it smells dank and dewy, and faintly of decomposing sugar—from the unemptied trash containers. Chirping birds welcome the sun, which has risen enough to color the treetops but not the parking lot. Everything is still gray and gloomy down here, especially in Bryan's mind: *This whole thing sucks, and I need to take a leak. Those birds sound happy, like everything is normal, but this day is anything but normal.*

He groans, shifting his feet. He's wearing sneakers and cutoffs, plus a T-shirt, quick stuff. *I gotta call Billy Ray when I get home. The dew's heavy; we can't cut till eleven—how could things change so much since Tuesday? She was so happy and free, and she gave me that super picture of herself sitting under the tree? To hell with haying. It doesn't matter.* His thoughts are disjointed and depressing, yet he feels nothing below the neck save for his full bladder; his emotions have gone numb. He swigs his bitter brew. *Ugh! This stuff tastes like horse piss.* Nonetheless, he drinks some more then gestures upward with the mug. *I wish I was a goshdang bird. Then I'd be up there singing instead of sitting here waiting for the ax to fall. Birds don't have hang-ups about making love. But me and Mandy, we hafta be good, and righteous, and civilized.*

Bryan spots the Firebird coming down Bixby. No zip, no pizzazz: she drives in a listless, ho-hum fashion. She pulls into the lot, easing to a halt. Getting out, she yawns blankly, without looking at him. No smile, no bounce in her step: her mood seems just as ho-hum as her driving, though she looks angelic in her fresh, blue-and-white Goddard's outfit, and her golden locks are softly feathered. But there'll be no last-minute heroics. He's just here to capitulate, to sign off on what the Lord has ordained.

THE SILVER CORD

GODDARD'S DINER
THURSDAY, AUGUST 8, 1991 — 8:29 AM

"Amanda, you have a phone call," Marge Goddard informs her niece amid the bustle and hubbub of an August morning—during July and August, every morning is busy like Saturday. "It's your mama. But don't stay on long, 'cause I'm gonna need yuh out front. Big Wes Allen just pulled up with a party of four—no, there's five of 'em I reckon." Mandy heads into the kitchen, along with more words from her aunt: "Y'better hurry, young lady, if you want the best tip of the day."

Mandy exhales huffily. Getting a big tip from Big Wes is the *last* thing on her mind. Picking up the phone, the one in the chef's cubicle, she says hello.

"So didyuh tell him?" Helen Stevens inquires.

"Mama, I'm right in the *middle* of the breakfast rush, and Aunt Marge is freaking."

"I know, but she's always hyper. Besides, she can spare you for two minutes—so what happened with Bryan?"

Mandy's throat pangs, but she manages a curt reply: "Friends ... we agreed to be friends."

"*He* agreed?"

"Yes, Mama ... *yes.*"

"Oh, honey," Helen replies, her voice softening. "I know it's painful, for both of you. But it's a *wise* decision."

* * *

THE HOWARD FARM
THURSDAY, AUGUST 8, 1991 — 9:30 AM

Ginny Howard, standing behind her son, pats him gently on the shoulder, as he works at his computer. "Bryan hon, I have such mixed feelings about this. I love Mandy like a daughter—we got so close when you were in the hospital."

"I know, Mom," Bryan replies detachedly, as he sorts then transfers a file he'll need in Waco. He's tired, overtired.

"And it was so sudden. I wonder if Helen—no, forgive me. I know Mandy has a mind of her own, and so do you."

"That we do ... and this's a mutual thing; we both came to realize how hard it would be with me in Waco."

"But I know Mandy loves you, Bryan. I *know* it. I *know* it. She beams like a lighthouse whenever you two are together." His mom's fervency pricks his heart, getting through the numb fog. "And yet I *can* see this decision as practical and logical. You'll be unfettered in Waco, and she'll be free to enjoy her senior year, then if God wills, you can resume your steady relationship when she gets to Baylor next year."

Without turning around, Bryan takes his mother's hand and caresses it. "Yeah, that's the gist of it. Everything's on hold for one year." The words "breaking up" were never used during the talk at the DQ, but that's what they did: there'll be no more necking, no more romance, no more secret engagement.

He returns to his keyboard, his mom departing—but she stops at the door: "Yet I wonder, Bryan, if it's *possible* to be practical when it comes to love ... like in the Song of Solomon: Love is strong as death; its coals are coals of fire, which have a most vehement flame." He knows well this "vehement flame," for it's burning in his stomach, suddenly, strongly. "So when didyuh say Billy Ray would be here?" Ginny asks, shifting abruptly.

"Oh, about noon or so."

"Y'don't *haf*ta cut today y'know? Considering?"

"I know, Mom, but it's better to keep busy ... especially since I can't sleep during the day."

Ginny departs; Bryan moves another file. *I was okay with this, but now I'm not feeling so good.* Working faster, he tries to recover his sense of detachment—with little success.

* * *

Same day, 2:44 p.m. Billy Ray, taking off his hat, wipes the sweat from his brow. "I tellyuh, Bryan, it's a goddam shame. That gal of yours is one of the prettiest around, and I hear tell she's smart as well." He spits out a shot of tobacco juice. They're taking a break, before removing the mower from the tractor and hooking up the baler, and Bryan just shared the Mandy news.

"Yeah, it's a bummer," Bryan says, grabbing his Igloo jug out of the flatbed truck. He takes a long swig, then another. He can quench his thirst but not the hot yearning in his gut. It's been there ever since his talk with his mom.

Billy Ray pulls his bag of Beechnut from his overalls. "Awh shit," he growls, "this thang's empty. I reckon I'll hafta fetch another bag from my truck." His pickup is parked over on the tractor trail. He ambles toward it, dragging his bad leg.

I may not make it through this summer, Bryan remarks to himself, as he watches Billy Ray limp along. *June was a fairy tale, July was up and down, but August is gonna finish me, and it's only the eighth.* He swigs more water then grabs a towel from his work bag; he dabs the sweat off his neck and shoulders—he's haying without a shirt as usual. Before putting his gloves back on, he pulls his watch from his jeans: 2:48 p.m. *Mandy gets off work in ten minutes.* He imagines her coming out of the diner, going to her car—he even pictures her cute way of walking, that slack and slouchy saunter, her ponytail nodding like it does.

Grabbing his T-shirt from the cab of the flatbed, Bryan tears madly across the hayfield, headed for his house. "I gotta go!" he barks as he whips past Billy Ray. "I got a *big*-time emergency!"

"Go for it, goddammit!" Billy Ray hollers, as Bryan sprints up the trail. "Tell her you love her, and keep on tellin' her—and don't take no for an answer!"

His lungs burning, Bryan gulps the humid, sweet-smelling air. The blue sky above seems suddenly brighter and bigger. *I can't let this happen. I won't let this happen.*

* * *

GODDARD'S DINER
THURSDAY, AUGUST 8, 1991 — 3:01 PM

Huffing and sweating, his heart booming, Bryan guns his pickup into the parking lot. He circles around back, lurching to a stop next to the Firebird, which is parked by the dumpster. *O God, be with me. It looks like I made it. She hasn't come out yet.*

He sheds his sunglasses; he takes a deep breath. It took only eight minutes to get here, an all-time record. He smells garbage and hot asphalt, not to speak of his own BO, though he's nearly desensitized to the sweaty miasma in the cab. His T-shirt lies wadded beside him; he never put it on. He uses it to towel the sweat off his chest and neck and arms; he dabs his brow, his face.

He digs his watch out of his jeans: 3:03 p.m. *She's late,* he tells himself as he watches a truck trundle by on Main Street (Hwy. 29). *But she never gets out on time; there's always some last-minute crisis. Oh gosh, she's gonna be surprised to see me. But Billy Ray's right. I can't take NO for an answer. And Mom's right too. Love IS a vehement flame. I can't put it out—even if I wanted to. And I DON'T! Oh Mandy, Mandy. To hell with my calling. She IS my calling. I'm NOTHING without her.*

He dabs his neck again. He checks his watch: 3:04 p.m. *It won't be long now.* The backside of the diner faces east toward the abandoned grain elevator, and he feels like he's on top of it getting ready to jump off, a reeling vertigo rush akin to the dizzy elation he feels when he looks into Mandy's eyes, but this is far more scary and daring, a desperate audacity—he's risking ALL to rescue their love. He fiddles with the keys as they dangle from the ignition switch, then he checks his watch again—it's still 3:04 p.m. Pushing his hat back, he buries his face in his hands.

"Bryan *How*ard!" Mandy exclaims. "What are *you* doing here!"

"Get in, pretty lady," he tells her, boldly.

"Wha-whaahh? I thought?" she stutters, as she joins him in the truck. "What's going on?" She can't help but grin and blush.

THE SILVER CORD

She's glad I came! Bryan exults to himself, his hopes rising, his face dimpling.

"So whaddeyuh doing here?" she asks again, gesturing with upturned hands.

"Oh, I just happened to be downtown, and I thought I'd drop by to see yuh."

"Yeah, right. Y'just happened to be down here, all sweaty and hot with no shirt—oh, mister, you stink." She snickers and shakes her head, tossing her ponytail, which hangs droopy and disheveled after a full day at the diner. Ditto for her bangs. But he likes her hair when it's less than perfect—it has that tousled, country-gal look. And with her blue eyes sparking, her cheeks full of girlish color, he sees her as more adorable and puppyish than ever, and her dollface lips have that pinkish cherub pout that renders her irresistibly kissable.

His heart booms, a kettle drum in his chest. "Well, precious, let's just say I'm here on business—we have some unfinished business, you and me." She gives him a curious sideways glance, just enough to supercharge his vertigo high, to push him over the edge. Falling, falling, can't stop now: he gathers her in his arms, kissing her fervently—reckless abandon, "vehement" fire.

She kisses him back—then abruptly jerks away. "No, no. Don't, babe, no." Bryan's heart lurches then bangs berserkly, rampaging toward agony, the kettle drum now a jackhammer.

She scoots away as far as she can, pressing the door. She frowns; she hugs herself, tears rolling down her cheeks. Then she breaks into hard crying, her head rocking, her body heaving. He breaks down as well, a storm of regret shaking him, rocking him. ALL IS LOST! HE SHOULD'VE STAYED HOME! Tears blind his eyes; he tastes salt; he buries his face in the sweaty T-shirt. He feels embarrassed and devastated.

"We can't, babe," Mandy whimpers, as her sobbing subsides. "We just can't. We don't have any place to go with this. If we can't get married—and we can't—we hafta be friends for now, like we agreed this morning. We hafta put everything on hold."

Bryan blows his nose on the T-shirt. "But whaddabout that picture?" he asks between sniffles. "You just gave it to me on Tuesday. Was that some kind of a lie?"

"No ... of course not. But what can we do? We still have three years to wait—officially? And we're gonna be apart this whole year coming up. We can't be kissing and petting and going wild, and then stopping ... and feeling weird and guilty. We can't be kissing and necking *at all*, not until we're ready to get hitched. It's impossible; we've gone *too* far."

His eyes still blurry with tears, he stares blankly at the rusty dumpster, which crouches like a wide-mouthed monster to the left of the pickup. The jackhammer in his bosom throttles back amid the pulverized rubble, the shattered dreams. He doesn't want to look at her—he *can't* look at her. "So what'd your mother say to you last night? You didn't mention her this morning, but that seems to be the reason?"

"She didn't say anything I didn't already know ... or you. It's not like this is some *brand* new thing."

"That's for sure," Bryan sighs, as if addressing the dumpster. "So you see this as God's will?"

"Yeah, I reckon so. It's hard to figure what God has in mind, but I think he knows best. His way is not the *easy* way, like Pastor Ron says, but it'll be better for us in the long run."

"So you're gonna be dating other guys this year?"

Mandy sniffles. "I *don't* know. I'm not gonna be looking, but I'm not gonna rule it out either. And that's what you should do down in Waco. If we're supposed to be together next year, or whenever, then the *Lord* will make it happen." Bryan hears the glove compartment click open—he's still looking the other way, out his window. She blows her nose; she evidently found a paper napkin or something. "You and me, we're still young in the Lord. Mama *is* right about that. And she's right about not being able to control our passions."

"So y'told her about Tuesday?" Bryan asks, wiping his eyes with the T-shirt.

"Not in detail, but I told her. We talked about everything ... love and sex ... and sin ... and marriage and having babies—all of it. Plus college and basketball, and being a teacher someday, and Mama brought up Charlie and the possible move to Arkansas." Mandy blows her nose again. "And we talked about you, babe ... about Baylor and being a doctor, and your baseball injury and that terrible night at the hospital ... and how it coulda been God, like a warning or something."

"You really think God is like that?"

"Well, he does judge sinners in the Bible."

"So y'think God was judging me?"

"Not *you,* but us. And it wasn't so much a judgment, like we were wicked or anything, but it's more like the Lord was trying to get our attention ... to show us we were getting off track."

"So you're afraid he might hafta *get our attention* again?"

"It could happen? But even when God uses adversity to teach us, it's not *all* bad; it still works for good. It's like I told Mama. If you hadn't got hurt, you and I woulda never gotten so close, like heart-to-heart, and we woulda never had that wonderful talk by the big oak tree the day after you graduated. I told her all about it, about your grandfather and your childhood. I even told her about your near-death experience, and your floating dr—"

"But, Mandy, how *could* you?" Bryan blurts, as fresh tears spill from his eyes. "Baptists can't handle that stuff. She'll think I'm in *fellow*ship with Satan." Daggers of pain hack through the bridge of his nose, into the quick of his brain. He hides his face in the T-shirt once more.

"Well, you *do* have floating dreams, or OBEs or whatever yuh call 'em. It's the *truth*, and I'm tired of hiding stuff from Mama, and telling her lies and half-lies. We hafta grow up, babe; we gotta face reality." She sniffles then mews, a muted whimper. "That's why we hafta put things on hold. We hafta be friends now—it's the *only* answer."

"Well, I don't *wan*na be friends," he snaps, looking up, but not at her. "I love you. I don't wanna be your *goddamn* friend!"

Mandy, sobbing, hops out of the pickup. He still doesn't look at her, but he hears the Firebird ripping around the diner.

* * *

THE HOWARD FARM
THURSDAY, AUGUST 8, 1991 — 11:10 PM

Bryan lies in bed, staring up into the darkness. The purring AC lulls his exhausted psyche toward sleep. *This's the worst day of my life— it's even worse than losing Gramps.* Fatigue has taken the edge off his torment, but for a while this afternoon, after Mandy rejected his bold move at the diner, he felt like parking on the railroad tracks and waiting for a train to take him out.

He cried on the way home; he cried in the barn; he cried in here. He did talk briefly to his mom, through his closed door, but he didn't show his face, even for supper. *Dear Jesus,* he prays wearily. *It's like Mandy's a different person ... like she turned into her mother or something. Yet she DID kiss me back in the truck, for a second before she jerked away.* He yawns, rolling onto his side. *But maybe I'm the one that's screwed up. Maybe God is chastising me ... for putting Mandy ahead of him, and for being all caught up with my astral experiences. Maybe I'm deluded ... like deceived by the Devil—no, that can't be? Can't be?* His prayer fades into much-needed sleep.

Next thing, he's floating above the house. He feels good, almost giddy—no more heartache. A waning slice of August moon hangs hazy and low in the western sky. *I have control this time,* he remarks to himself, as he swoops low over the fields where he and Billy Ray have been cutting hay. *It's not like my near-death experience when I was drifting aimlessly above the pitcher's mound.* Reaching Longley Road, he heads east. He can discern the dirt surface below him, since it's lighter, sort of ashy gray, while the fields and woods are darker, more slate-colored. A quick mile later he turns south following Misty Hollow Road. Too fast: he slows his forward speed, simply by wishing it. *It's amazing how my sleeping brain and astral body work together. They're still connected somehow, by the SILVER CORD? It has to be the silver cord, the same tether that God severs at death. Maybe that's why I had no control during my NDE? Maybe it was severed already?*

No, can't be. If it was cut, I couldn't have gone back into my body when Doc Wilson and the paramedics were working on me. I can't figure it. The astral dimension is the realm of the soul, and I'm somehow traveling in it, and yet I'm not dead. It's metaphysical, but it's REAL. For some reason God chose me to have this capacity. But why? Why does it happen to me? It's beyond ALL knowledge—and most scientists would never believe it. But still, it's HAPPENING! And the SILVER CORD is somehow the key to understanding this mystery.

Bryan could zoom on a beeline to Mandy's house, but it's more fun to follow the roads, as if he's driving his pickup at treetop level. No cars: Misty Hollow doesn't have much traffic, especially at night, but an amber glow looms ahead, the lights of Spindle. The night air seems cooler down here in the hollow, and he can smell the mucky-dry creekbed. Sailing over the wooden bridge, which spans the creek, he quickly arrives at Butler Road, then Henley Avenue, then Colby Drive. He slows to a hover near a streetlight across from the Stevens driveway where Helen's Escort is parked behind Mandy's Firebird. He feels energized and exhilarated, not the heavenly bliss he experienced during his near-death journey, but the vibes are certainly good.

A greenish minivan passes underneath Bryan—it turns into a driveway a few houses down. Although he knows he's invisible, he waits nonetheless for the car to park and for the occupants to go inside, then he wills himself closer to Mandy's house, floating slowly across the street, then over the front lawn. As he drifts toward her bedroom window, above the porch, he pictures her sleeping peacefully in her bed, her sweet, angelic face pressed cozily into her pillow. *O Lord, I love her.*

The air conditioner in the window whirs and rumbles; the blinds above it are closed; he can't see inside. *I wonder what she's sleeping in. Shorty pajamas I bet?* Closer, closer: he reaches out to touch the AC cowling, but his hand goes right through it. *O God, I love—NO, NO, hold it. Halt. I can't. I can't.*

He commands his astral presence to retreat. Whoosh—he's back at the farm, over his house, then a second later he's back in his bed, back in his physical body: *Damn, I just had an OBE. I was at Mandy's house—or maybe I was dreaming it? No, no, it was real. And I almost went into her room, but I didn't. I was excited and happy. Still, it wouldn't be right to invade her privacy, without her knowing it, especially since we're not even GOING together anymore. Everything's on hold. We broke up.*

This awful truth comes howling back, bringing with it all the regret and agony, a crushing, binding, tightly relentless pain, as if his heart just went through the hay baler.

THE SILVER CORD

* * *

The next morning Bryan sits on the front-porch steps, munching toast and sipping orange juice. Billy Ray will be here shortly. They have a hundred bales in the barn, which need to be hoisted up into the loft, and they plan to do that while the dew dries. Across the driveway, Snowball (the cat) crouches in the grass, then she pounces and scurries in a tight circle, evidently pursuing a field mouse, then she crouches again. She still has those quick feline moves, despite her age: she's thirteen? Her long fluffy tail twitches—then she pounces again, nailing the rodent, who gives a death shriek as the white cat sinks her fangs.

Bryan feels sorry for the mouse, but this morning he sees it as futile to interfere. He takes a drink of OJ then gives a sigh. It's all part of God's natural cycle, the suffering and the dying, and the dashed hopes. Life is overwhelming and heartless, but there's nothing he can do about it. He must grow up and accept reality, a reality that does not include his Mandy dreams. *I can't believe how much things have changed since June,* he muses to himself, *but that was just a fairy tale. Real life isn't like that.*

After finishing his toast and juice, he places the glass on the plate then sets the plate on the porch. Leaning forward, he wraps his arms about his knees. The concrete walkway in front of the house looks more grassy than gray, from all the dandelions and weedy tufts of lawn which have invaded the cracks. A train of black ants snakes around one of the nearest tufts. In the midst of this train a cadre drags a dead cricket, slowly, dutifully.

Gosh, it's all around, the cold facts of life, and death. I felt so good during my OBE last night, but now I'm back to earth, and I gotta let go of my fantasies. I gotta lower my expectations. And maybe it wasn't an OBE at all? Maybe I just dreamed I was out of my body going to her house? Maybe all my OBEs were no more than night-dreams? Plus, they might not be good? Maybe God DOESN'T like the idea of soul travel, whether real or not?

The door opens behind him. "Are you okay, Son?" Henry Howard asks—he smells like Mennen aftershave.

"Yeah, Dad, I'm okay," Bryan replies without looking up.

Henry pats his son on the shoulder. "Looks like the dry heat's coming back, the way the haze shimmers on the hills. We need rain. Too bad that storm didn't give us much on Tuesday—now, Bryan, y'can lay off the haying for a while if yuh want."

"I know, but it's better to work and keep my mind occupied."

"I reckon you're right, Son," Henry drawls, his voice trailing off. "I reckon you're right."

The elder Howard goes back inside, the bracy scent of his aftershave lingering behind (he always smells like Mennen in the morning, when he's getting ready to leave for the feed store). Their brief exchange could scarcely be called a man-to-man talk, but this's how they deal with things. And the paternal pat on the shoulder conveyed as much as words ever could, if not more so.

Bryan fingers the ripped-out knee of his Levi's. *I reckon Dad has known for years what I'm realizing this week. Maybe that's why he has all those lines in his face? And I reckon that's why most older folks seem more sad than happy.*

Snowball trots over triumphantly and drops the dead mouse in front of Bryan, as if presenting a gift. He pets the purring feline, while she nuzzles the side of his cowboy boot. "You old-lady cat. I still like yuh, even if you *are* a killer." Retrieving the mouse, she disappears around the house, evidently headed for the back porch where she eats her prey. Having the cat come over makes Bryan miss his long-dead collie. *I wish Buster was still alive. He didn't care if I was good or bad or carnal, or obsessed or deceived. Maybe I shoulda gotten another dog? Too late now.* He gives a little murmur. *Buster was just happy to be WITH me. But with humans, it's like love always gets messed up by duty and doubt, and guilt, except with Gramps. I could tell him all about this, the whole banana , and he'd understand—but I can't tell him ANYTHING. He's dead, like that mouse, like that cricket.*

A dust plume appears on Longley Road; it's Billy Ray in his gray pickup. Bryan stretches to his feet. *I reckon I just hafta run with patience the race that's set before me—that verse doesn't turn me on, but it makes sense to obey it. I gotta concentrate on getting ready for college. And I should get Spanky or Roy to throw me some BP down at the school—I need to be sharp for fall baseball.* The beat-up Dodge clacks across the cattleguard and heads up the driveway. *And I need to be more diligent about praying and going to church—especially when I get to Waco. Maybe the Baptists are right for preaching patience and humility and abstinence, and for steering clear of the paranormal.* He gives a quick snort, as guilt nibbles his conscience. *I wonder if I should call Mandy and apologize for being so abrupt yesterday at Goddard's. No, it wouldn't be honest. I meant what I said.* Fear joins the guilt. *And who knows, she might not wanna talk to me now? She may've decided that any interaction between us will only encourage me to come on to her again, like I did yesterday? O God, why'd I do that? I lost my dadgum head.*

THE SILVER CORD

CHAPTER ELEVEN

SPINDLE, TEXAS
FRIDAY, AUGUST 16, 1991 — 10:05 PM

God, I miss her SO, Bryan laments, as he turns right on Main Street (Hwy. 29). *It's been eight days, but it seems like eighty.*

Grow up, face reality, trust God, go to church, get in shape, get ready for college, cut hay, do your duty, stop fantasizing, be practical—to hell with it. Despite his intentions, he hasn't been to church any more than usual, just Sunday morning, and he's only gone running once, and he never made it down to the school to take batting practice. Without Mandy he has no spark, no drive, no inspiration, no reason to do *any*thing. It's all gone, leaving nothing except a desolate and doleful ache, a relentless gnawing in the pit of his stomach—the whole world has turned gray and barren, and cold. He hasn't talked with her since their showdown behind Goddard's, and he's gun-shy about calling her. He's scared she'll be abrupt and cold, or even hang up on him. This is hardly rational—she said she wanted to be friends—but his woeful, drag-ass frame of mind is not geared for objectivity. He did see her at church, from a distance, but he departed quickly after the service, and made no attempt to interact with her—she was *with* her mother.

He hasn't shaved since Tuesday, but he did shower and slip into fresh cutoffs tonight, plus a sporty pullover, in case he runs into Mandy by chance—not likely, since she rarely goes to the bowling alley. Leaving downtown behind, he pushes the pickup up to sixty. The night air streams in his open window, normally an invigorating sensation after a day of hundred-degree heat, but on this bleak Friday the draft seems more chilling than balmy. Three miles later, he pulls into Westside Lanes, which sprawls on the north side of Highway 29 not far from Oiler Park. The gray, windowless, corrugated-steel structure looks more like a warehouse than a bowling alley. *He's here,* Bryan remarks to himself, as he parks next to Spanky's truck. *I figured as much.*

Once inside, he pauses near the shoe-rental kiosk, amid the muted clunking of pins going down. Most of the sixteen alleys are taken, so the wooden clatter is continuous, not to mention the kudos and the cussing, and the automatic pinsetters, and the balls rolling—on the alleys, in the gutters, popping up onto the return racks. It's cool in here, but the air smells better outside. This place has the usual bowling-alley odor, somewhere between a gym and a cheap tavern: hardwood and plastic, and perspiration, and mildew and beer and cigarette smoke. He spots Spanky and Roy on alley #3, but he goes to the right, toward the lounge. As he does, the smell of beer and nicotine grows stronger, along with the dank, mildewy fetor of the timeworn carpeting.

* * *

"What the *hell* is this?" Spanky Arnold drawls, as he weaves through the pool tables to the corner booth where Bryan is seated. "You're on your way to *god*dam stardom for the Baylor Bears, and you're hidin' back here with a bottle of Bud?" He gives his roosterlike cackle. "Shitfire, slugger, I don't thank I've seen yuh drinkin' since the Legion-team party at the lake last summer. And you're *by* yourself for chrissake? Where's Mandy?"

"Have a seat, Spanker," Bryan replies, sidestepping the questions for now—he gestures toward the empty side of the booth. He needs to talk, but not until Spanky winds down.

The wiry little redneck slides into the booth. "So yuh just came in here and ordered that goddam brew, like it was nuthin'?"

"Yeah, I reckon so," Bryan replies, without elaborating—he's too downhearted to care about being carded and embarrassed, but there was no problem anyhow; the Latino waitress served him without objection, though she did give him a knowing smirk.

"Well, they never ID jocks in here for chrissake; that's Frank's policy." Interlacing his hands, Spanky pushes them, palms out, until the knuckles crack. He's dressed in his usual redneck style: jeans and T-shirt, sleeves rolled—but the dingy, time-grayed shirt is too small, ridiculously so, and it seems ready to rip with every move of his wiry arms. "Plus, you're a goddam celebrity, with your mug on the sports page all during baseball season. No way are they gonna give *you* a hard time."

Bryan replies between sips of beer: "I've seen her before, the waitress ... but I don't know her name or anything."

"Well, I bet she knows yours—where is she anyhow? I could use a brew myself." He cackles, nodding with his burr-cut head toward the far corner of the lounge. "Hell, she's probably in the ladies' room smokin'. I know most of the cunts who work here, and they're all lazy and bitchy and slow, 'cept for one or two." The strong scent of Aqua-Velva has smothered all other odors, even the beer and nicotine— Spanky must bathe in the stuff. And his huge Roman nose looks more sunburned than usual, and it's crisscrossed with lines of peeling. "And likah say, they never hardly check IDs, unless it's some shitass that Frank has it out for. But still, slugger, it's a bit weird to see *you* back here breakin' the goddam drinkin' laws." More cackles. "It's a good thang I saw your pickup in the parkin' lot, or I woulda missed yuh for chrissake. I was on my way to Benny's to rustle up some pool action. The tables here are goddam worthless for hustlin'. I'm out lookin' for money action most nights ... ever since I quit Legion ball the end of June. And I'm sure glad I did for chrissake. That fartface Henderson couldn't manage a *god*dam whiffle-ball team. They got eliminated at the regionals last week. I reckon you heard about it—and they got their asses wiped both games." Pushing his tongue out, Spanky makes a juicy, sputtering, fartlike sound. "Now last year we had a *real* team, but thangs went into the goddam toilet this summer. It's good yuh *didn't* play this year; it woulda drove yuh crazy for chrissake—but you're lookin' good, slugger. I haven't seen yuh for more'n a month, since that evenin' at the DQ. So I reckon the doctors back in Dallas gave you a clean bill of health?" Spanky leans back and hugs himself, his freckled mug breaking into a wide Huck Finn grin.

"Yeah, the tests came out okay," Bryan replies, returning the grin, despite his downcast mood. He pushes his baseball cap back on his head then pours the last of his Budweiser into the glass.

"Shitfire—that's good. I may not see yuh much, but you're still my goddam fishin' buddy from way back. I'll never forget those long, hot days when we'd go fishin' down at your lake, and we always ended up in the water for chrissake, and your dog too, even your *grand*father— now he was a fuckin' rebel like me."

"Yeah, I reckon he was in a way—but Gramps never had a mouth like yours, Spank."

"Awh c'mon, I've toned *way* down."

They both laugh, then Bryan says, "So where's Roy?"

Spanky slumps sideways, his back to the wall. "Oh, he just left a few minutes ago. We did manage to scare up a little action on the lanes earlier—shit, my mouth's goin' dry. Where's the goddam waitress, any goddam waitress? Plus I got a hankerin' for a BLT. Frank may give us a break on the drinkin'-age thang, but he needs to kick some ass around here. The liquor laws are unjust anyhow. If you're *god*dam old enough to join the army, y'should be able to drink beer in public for chrissake—now there's got to be a gal somewhere? They spend half their shift in the goddam can, and most of 'em are dog-ugly and old enough to be my mother." Giving a grousing snort, he gestures toward the bar. "Shitfire, I may hafta go get it myself—but anyway, me and Roy, we were hustlin' some hayseed farts from Marlow."

"I know. I saw y'all when I came in."

"Damn, why didn't yuh come over and join us? We coulda used yuh for—" He stops midsentence as the waitress arrives, a busty, thirty-something, south-of-the border-looking gal.

"You fellows need anything else?" she asks, with a slight accent— she has coal-black hair and large round eyes almost as dark. She'd be halfway pretty, if it weren't for her bulbous, big-nostrilled nose. Spanky orders a Coors Light, a BLT, plus an order of fries, while Bryan asks for another Bud.

"She's not bad for an over-the-hill Chicano cunt," Spanky declares after the waitress departs. He shifts around to face Bryan, his elbows on the table, his voice going hushy. "And she's not as bitchy as the others. Her name's Nina. She's related to Hector, Hector Perez—she's his aunt, or cousin, or sumpthin'. I've shot the shit with her a few times. I even played pool with her one night after thang's got slow. I thank she's a part-time whore ... least I hear tell she did a mini gangbang at Benny's a couple years back. She fucked three guys on a goddam snooker table for a measly twenty-five each—after-hours of course." Spanky blushes and cackles and wags his head. "I don't know if it's actually true for chrissake. Most of the drunks at Benny's are goddam braggarts and liars, and Benny too. But that's the *hot* gossip on Nina. She looks Mexican, but she could be Puerto Rican. I thank Hector's both for chrissake. She looks like Hector, the eyes anyway—don'tcha thank?"

"I guess, maybe so," Bryan says, draining his glass; he realizes that Spanky's just getting started; it's going to be a while before he's ready to listen to anything serious, if at all.

"She's sorta chubby," Spanky continues, "and she's got a nose like a nigger—she's got some coon blood I reckon. But I'd still *fuck* her for chrissake." He grins and gives a palms-up "why not" gesture, along with another cocky waggle of his burr head. "But I'd do her *doggy* style. Her ass turns me on way more than her f—" Stopping abruptly, he sits back and puts on an innocent, little-boy expression, as Nina brings their order then departs.

Spanky takes a big swig of Coors, from the bottle—he *never* drinks out of a glass, beer anyway—then he jabs the air, with the bottle: "Yeah, Nina, would be a good fuck I bet. She probably goes berserk when she comes. Women love it the *most* when they get past thirty, especially when they're chubby and they don't get laid much. And it *really* turns 'em on to do younger guys, and her ass is so *god*dam luscious. Hell, I thank I could do almost *any* bitch doggy-style—they *all* look good from the back, even the ugliest ones, like that Cherokee whore I banged in Tyler last spring. She looked like *god*dam Tonto for chrissake, but her ass was A-fuckin'-plus, and she sure knew how to wiggle it. She's the only pro I ever had, cost me a hundred and fifty, but it was more than worth it I tellyuh." He cackles and swaggers, his cheeks turning redder than his sunburned nose.

While Spanky chugs some beer, Bryan gives a forced little chuckle, but his heart is sighing—he can only take so much of Spanky's lewd humor: *O Jesus, maybe this was a stupid idea? How can I talk to him about personal stuff? He might wisecrack about Mandy's butt? I know he has a heart, but when he gets on a roll about girls, it's like they're all whores in a porno flick.*

"Yeah, slugger, we sure coulda used you before," Spanky says, backpedaling. "Roy cain't pick up spares for shit. And yet we still had those assholes on the ropes, until the last frame."

"So how much didyuh lose?" Bryan asks, surrendering to the situation—he figures he'll finish this second beer, then go home.

"Sixty bucks, thirty each. But we woulda *won*, if that goddam seven pin had gone down. My ball was hookin' right into the pocket, like a cock into a cunt—it was perfect for chrissake. But the seven pin stayed up. It wobbled, but the fucker stayed up."

"So you got a spare?"

"Fuck no. I guttered my goddam second ball." Spanky thrusts his hand over the table to indicate the errant roll. "It was choke-city for chrissake. Hell, if this keeps up, I may hafta get a damn regular job— but I did win a few bucks *last* night ... playin' poker."

"So why'd Roy leave?"

"Oh, they have some kinda football meetin' at the gym in the mornin', then they start those fuckin' two-a-day drills on Monday. That's one sport I'm glad I stayed away from, even if they *do* get all the goddam glory."

Fifteen minutes pass, and Spanky is still doing most of the talking. He's finished with his BLT and french fries, and he's halfway through his third beer, having caught up with Bryan, who's also on his third— he decided to stay for one more, plus a couple of nachos, which he quickly downed. The background noise, the wooden clunking of pins and other hubbub coming from the other side of the building, has diminished in volume and frequency, as the crowd of Friday-night bowlers gradually thins out. The lights in the lounge seem dimmer, the air thinner. The beer is working on Bryan, warming and expanding his inner self, and his impatience with Spanky melts a little more with each swig: *Let him talk and talk. What does it matter?*

But then Spanky suddenly shifts: "So, slugger, what the fuck *are* y'doin' here tonight. I asked yuh before, but y'didn't say?"

Responding to the opening, Bryan shares his Mandy woe, the beer having also melted the fear that Spanky will take it lightly, and he doesn't. The little guy leans back and listens, his arms wrapped about his chest, his blue eyes warm and earnest. Bryan discloses almost everything regarding his ten months with Mandy with emphasis on the break-up last week, but he avoids the near-death, paranormal stuff, which would only add distracting complexity. "I gotta take a leak," he announces finally, having said what he needs to say.

"Me too," Spanky says, "but first, let's order another round." He signals Nina, who's behind the bar, on the other side.

"Goshdang, Spanker, I've already had three?"

"Well, after hearin' your story, I need at least *one* more, to get my brain in goddam gear—so I can tellyuh what I thank."

"Okay, order me another Bud—I'll be right back."

He gets back just as Nina delivers the beers. "Y'boys must be enjoying yourselves. It's a good thing Frank doesn't make us card y'all."

"Hell, Nina, I'm twenty-two," Spanky brags. "I'm just a little slow gettin' outta goddam high school, that's all."

"Yeh right," she kids. "If you're twenty-two, I'm nineteen."

"Sounds good to me," Spanky cackles. "That means you're the *per*fect age for me—we should play some more pool together for chrissake, and then y'can take me home with yuh?"

"Oh, get outta here," she giggles as she collects the empty bottles and hustles off, her hips swishing inside her short black skirt. Bryan plunks down, while Spanky takes off for the can.

"So, slugger, when're yuh leavin' for Waco?" he asks upon his return, his tone surprisingly serious. The way he was carrying on with Nina, it seemed as if he was back to his usual jesting and bravado, especially since he has a lot of beer in him.

"The first of September," Bryan replies, as he sips some Bud, from the bottle; he quit using the glass two rounds ago. "Sunday the first. My folks are coming too ... like with a carload of stuff."

Spanky rubs the top of his own bottle, his fourth, then takes a swig. "You're not takin' your goddam Chevy?"

"Yeah, I am, but I can't carry my computer stuff in the back of the truck; it's too bouncy. Besides, my mom and dad wanna see my dorm and everything. Classes don't start until the ninth, but I hafta be there early, for freshman-orientation week. And we have fall practice as well, the baseball squad."

Bryan nurses his beer, while Spanky sits back and drums the edge of the table as if he's punching numbers into a calculator. "Well, Bryan buddy, I cain't believe you 'n Mandy broke up."

"Yeah ... but we *did*. She refers to it as 'putting things on hold,' like I toldjuh before."

"In any case, I reckon it's a *god*dam good reason for gettin' drunk." He gives a mini-cackle. "So you're leavin' on the first?"

"Yep, that's right."

"Well, that should give yuh just enough time."

"Time for what, Spank?"

"To patch thangs up with her."

"Whaa-whaa? Whaddeyuh talking about?"

Spanky drums faster, working his freckled fingers. "Let's face it, slugger: the horny goddam cunts of this world are gonna drive us crazy 'fore we reach twenty-five, me anyway. They're hot 'n ripe, and irresistible, yet most of 'em are cunnin' and deceitful, and full of bitchy poison. And when they say they wanna be 'friends,' that means they doughwanna see your fuckin' face." He gives a resigned snort then sucks some beer. "But Mandy Stevens is different. She's a goddam *rare* gal—so I have a hankerin' that *your* situation ain't nearly so bad as y'thank."

Bryan's heart pops to attention. "Whaddeyuh getting at?"

"I'm just tellin' yuh the goddam facts. She's not like the typical whores and bitches we hafta deal with. She's plenty sexy to be sure—any guy knows that—but she also has a heart, and she's smart, and she's a straight shooter, and she has fight in her ... and I reckon she wants to be with yuh *all* the time, no matter what she said last week for chrissake. And I bet she's hurtin' just as much. She loves yuh dammit, and *nuthin'* can change that."

"Goshdang, Spanker, you sound like my mom. But uh, but...."

He fumbles for words, but Spanky's already tying up the loose ends: "Your mom's right—that's a *true* fact. I may joke a lot about sex and all, but whatcha got with Mandy is nuthin' to joke about—it's like a miracle for chrissake; it's like a sacred thang; it's a goddam once-in-a-lifetime thang. It's like me and Sylvia Goodman. I started lovin' her in third grade, when she was just a skinny blond with big front teeth and pigtails." He chugs some beer then gestures with the bottle. "I thank I toldjuh once, in the old days. Well, I kept on lovin' her till she moved away in the eighth grade, and I *still* love her for chrissake. When she left, she was fuckin' pretty and filled out, and she turned me on like crazy, but it was way more than a pussy thang. Shit, I never even kissed her. We skated together once, at Calvin Brower's birthday party in the sixth grade, and her hand was so soft and warm, and it was slightly moist. I'll never forget it." He shakes his head slowly, giving a wide-eyed murmur.

Bryan, amazed, doesn't reply, lest he break the momentum. He's never heard his redneck buddy open up like this.

After a quick slug of Coors, Spanky goes on: "Now don't get me *wrong*—fuckin' is still a great thang, even if yuh don't have that magical connection, and I wanna get as much pussy as I can. But I haven't got nearly as much as I let on, and the few gals I've made it with, like Carrie Sue Baily, have all turned out to be first-class bitches." He snuffles and snorts. "But really, Bryan, I cain't see how Mandy would wanna break up with yuh—no fuckin' way, not in her heart at least. Nawh, it's gotta be a goddam guilt-trip thang." He stops, as if to check his buddy's reaction.

"Go on," Bryan prods, dimpling.

"Well, the way I see it, Mandy's head is strivin' to overrule her heart, and it's a fuckin' fierce battle, so it may last a while. It's the goddam *pressure* of life, the pressure to conform, to be good, to look good, to say the right thang. It's all around us for chrissake. And when you're a winner, it gives you the big head, but when y'fail, it makes you feel like shit." Spanky drinks some Coors. "I hate it. That's why I gave up long ago. I got sickah feelin' guilty and ashamed, and rejectin' myself all the time, so I quit bowin' down to all the rules and customs and manners. So now I have a bad reputation at school. The teachers say I'm unruly and disruptive and disrespectful, and I *sup*pose I am. But I cain't obey anythang unless I see a goddam good reason." He slaps the table then paws the air—he's into it. "Now everyone sees Mandy as good and godly and top-notch, so the pressure on her is fuckin' impossible to deal with, and yet she's still tryin', and you're doin' the same thang, slugger. I reckon that's why you been goin' half crazy since you got into her panties. But it's more intense with her, 'cause she's got all that strict religion in her, from her mama. I reckon I'm the last fuckin' person to be talkin' about goddam religion. I've hardly set foot in a church since I got expelled from Sunday school at K-Street Baptist—for cussin' out Miss Dillard, the old lady who gave out those red and green stars. But I do know about shameful feelin's, and how they make us do thangs we don't really wanna do, and goin' to church stirs up those kinda feelin's more'n anythang I know of." Spanky gives an indignant snort. "I never found God at church. I never felt it anyhow. When I need to pray or thank deep about thangs, I go to Buzzard's Roost ... so I can get away from all the goddam hype and craziness of life. Like in December when the geese are comin' in to winter on the lake. They all come, honkin' and flyin' in a V. It's mag-fuckin'-nificent. Now lemme tellyuh ... that's sumpthin' y'can sink the teeth of your soul into. That's the God I want."

"Yeah, I hear yuh," Bryan responds. "I like being out in the wild too ... though I don't see church as *all* bad."

Spanky takes a quick shot of beer. "I know, I know—you're still into it. And maybe the Lord does show his goddam face at church from time to time. But *wherever* he hangs out, the true God, I don't see how he could be against you and Mandy bein' crazy for each other, or even goin' all the way. How could he? You guys are in *love* for chrissake!" Spanky drains his Coors Light, then gives an open-handed gesture, as if to say, "I reckon that's all the wisdom I got on this." But he doesn't really say it.

"So y'think I should call her?" Bryan asks, his hopes perking.

"You goddam right. If she says she wants to be friends and put thangs on hold, then *be* her friend for chrissake." Spanky grips the empty Coors bottle with both hands, as if he's wringing the neck of a chicken. "That's my take on it anyhow."

* * *

The next morning Bryan calls Goddard's Diner and boldly asks for Mandy, who's working her regular Saturday shift. He can hear kitchen voices amid the clinking and clunking of dishes and pans, but his pounding pulse seems louder.

"Hello," Mandy says a few seconds later.

"How yuh doing, pretty lady?"

Silence: she doesn't answer. Bolts of fear: *O God, she's gonna hang up on me.*

"I'm all right," she replies finally, her voice barely above a whisper. "And you?"

"Well, I've had *better* weeks, but I'm surviving."

"So why'd yuh call me?" she asks curtly.

"Well uh ... well, y'know how yuh said you wanted to still be friends and all ... and I got all upset and said no way?"

"Yeah ... so?"

"Well, I'm sorry I cussed and got so mad, and I've changed my mind, I think."

"How's that?"

"Well, I'm willing to be friends, on one condition."

"What condition? I mean we—oh, I gotta go. Aunt Marge is yelling at me." Mandy's voice sounds louder, more normal.

"No, wait. Wait a second." The sudden time crunch flusters Bryan, but he manages to blurt his offer: "I just wantcha to ride with me down to Baylor that first day—as friends, just *friends*. My mom and dad are taking my computers and stuff in their car, so you can ride back with them. The first of September ... it's a Sunday. I just wantcha to see the place, so y'can look forward to next year when you'll be coming down yourself. So how'bout it?"

"Oh, Bryan, I gotta go. Aunt Marge is wiggling her finger."

His heart hammers harder, faster. "Well, just say yes or no."

"Well, I uh—yes; okay, yes. But I gotta go now."

I don't know if she's glad or pissed, Bryan reacts, as he gazes out the window over his desk. *But it was a YES; she did say yes.*

THE SILVER CORD

CHAPTER TWELVE

INTERSTATE 35, NORTH OF WACO, TX
SUNDAY, SEPTEMBER 1, 1991 — 1:03 PM

Bryan Howard's truck cruises southbound on I-35, his dad's white LeSabre in close pursuit. Pushing his cap back, Bryan wipes the perspiration from his forehead. His spiffy clothes (spiffy for him anyway: short-sleeve dress shirt, stonewashed Levi's) feel clingy and tight, especially the jeans. The wind hisses through the barely open windows. He had his window down before, but he got tired of the buffeting. The sun seems hotter since Dallas, and brighter; he adjusts his sunglasses. The pickup gets especially warm on long trips like this (it's three and a half hours to Waco give or take). He has the vent fan going, but the tepid streams of air jetting from the dashboard ducts offer little relief.

And yet the hot cab ranks low, very low, on Bryan's list of concerns. *Oh gosh, time's running out,* he frets to himself as the old Chevy whips by a rectangular sign, white on green: Waco 22 mi. He glances over at Mandy. No change: she's still dozing, as best he can tell. She's wearing her dark glasses, but she's snuggled against the door, and she hasn't moved much or said anything for a half hour or so. *O Jesus, I wish to heck I could get inside her head. I shoulda said something before. I shoulda—no, it's best that I didn't. She has to make the first move. O God, I hate this. Maybe the whole idea of something happening today is a crock of bull manure. But how can I be sure?*

Taking a slow breath, to calm himself, he gazes at the highway, at the white lane-dividers blipping by. The weather, though sweltering, is ideal for moving stuff in an open pickup. The hazy-bright, cumulus-dappled sky still has that blank, oppressive, dirty-blue look that comes with summer heat and humidity. September could pass for July, save for the lower sun angle and that spicy, almost-smoky, dry-grass aroma which signals the approach of autumn. Bryan's stuff rides in the back, several cardboard boxes and a couple of suitcases, plus an old military trunk that Gramps gave him years ago. It's mainly clothes and books and baseball gear, plus bedding and towels, along with a few dishes and utensils, and he also has the swivel chair from his room, his computer chair. The Macintosh itself, along with the peripherals, rides in the Buick. Ditto for his tape deck and TV and VCR, and the picture of Mandy, the one of her lounging on the grass under the big oak tree, the one she gave him the day they went skinny-dipping, a day that now seems unreal, impossible, yet it most surely did happen, less than a month ago.

The double highway shimmers ahead, a pair of gray ribbons traversing the sunny checkerboard of crops and pastures. In the far distance the ribbons converge before disappearing into a vast silvery sea, or so it seems: the ocean is really a mirage created by the surface glare, a most common feature when driving on these long, straight stretches of Texas interstate. Bryan glances at Mandy: no change. *I can almost taste her lips and feel her arms about me, and yet I may never hold her again—O God.* Wearing her blue and red madras shirt plus a khaki skirt (but minus her softball cap), she looks cutely angelic, even as her blond locks wilt in the humidity—yet she's also womanly and tempting, especially her haunches, which fill her skirt potently. And her perfume, though not as strong as before, tantalizes him, as he focuses on the summery scent amid the greasy, grimy farm-truck odors in the cab. *I wonder if she's hurting as much as me, like Spanky says, and Mom? How can I know? And what can I do?*

This is the first time he's been alone with Mandy since the eighth of August, the day they broke up, and he was hoping that something wonderful and miraculous would happen as they drove along, such as a spontaneous mutual outburst of confessing and kissing and hugging, but so far nothing even approaching that has happened. Before she conked out, she did laugh and joke some—mainly about what's going on at school; Spindle High resumed classes on Thursday, the 29th—but there were also torturous intervals when she seemed reserved and distant. The signals have been mixed at best, and she's certainly said nothing which goes beyond their "just friends" understanding, nor has he.

He did talk to her at church a couple of times since she agreed on the phone to ride with him to Waco. He even toyed with the idea of taking her to the DQ for an ice cream, but when he hinted to her about it, she seemed less than enthusiastic, so he didn't pursue the issue, lest she change her mind about going with him today. So this trip is *it*, his only opportunity, and it's almost over. His heart flutters, then sinks. It's nerve-wracking enough to leave home, to start college, to compete for a position on an NCAA baseball team, but Mandy's *by far* the main reason for the anxious vibes in his stomach: *O God, this's killing me.* He can't help but notice the ruddy glow of her cheek, the girlish wisps of hair in front of her ear, the soft curve of her neck inside the collar of her shirt. *I don't wanna put things on hold. I love her NOW. I need her NOW. I feel like pulling over and grabbing her. I can't help it. She looks so kissable and precious, and yet after today, we'll be in different worlds.* As the miles click by, the pressure builds: he must wake her and blurt out his case. But he doesn't, and it's soon too late. There it is, the modest skyline of Waco looming ahead in the haze. No more farms, no more ranch land: the rolling rural landscape has given way to suburban sprawl, to contoured developments and access roads and strip malls, to Sunday traffic jockeying for position on the interstate, which has widened to four lanes, each way.

"Hey, pretty lady, we're almost there," he announces, after

swallowing his feelings. "We're gonna stop to eat in a minute." Considering the state of his stomach, Bryan has little appetite, but his mom suggested they stop for lunch first thing, before going to the campus.

Mandy yawns, sits up, then fingerfluffs her hair. "I reckon I fell asleep," she responds groggily, detachedly, without looking at Bryan. She yawns then opens her purse, the little gray one.

Waco (150,000 counting the suburbs) is puny compared to Dallas, but it's a *big* change from Spindle. After passing under Route 340 (the loop), Bryan exits onto the access road which is lined with motels and gas stations plus the usual brand-name eateries: McDonald's, KFC, Taco Bell, Pizza Hut, Denny's. He pulls into Denny's, the Buick following (he and his parents ate here back in January, when they came down to see the campus and to meet with Tom Weaver, the Baylor baseball coach). They're not actually in Waco yet but Bellmead, a suburban community. Nonetheless, the university lies only three miles away, just across the Brazos River. *Nothing I can do now,* Bryan sighs, as he gets out and stretches. He adjusts his cap then his Levi's, tucking his shirttail. Mandy, still in the truck, digs in her purse.

* * *

"I'm going to the ladies' room," Virginia Howard announces, after everyone has ordered, and the smiley-faced waitress has whisked away the menus.

"Me too," Mandy echoes. Henry and Bryan get up, so the women can slide out of the circular booth.

I wish I was grown up and settled like Mom Howard, Mandy says to herself, as she follows in the wake of Ginny's swishing dress, a pastel-blue shirtdress with a wide leather belt. *It's goshdang sucky to be a senior in high school, especially now. Maybe I shouldn't have come today? I feel weird, like outta place.* The lunchtime aromas remind her of Goddard's Diner: coffee, french fries, hamburgers, pastry. She could just as well be at work, on her way to pick up an order, but she's not. She's 160 miles away, feeling weird. Passing under a chandelier with green globes, they hang a right between the PLEASE WAIT TO BE SEATED sign and the cashier's counter.

* * *

Back at the table, Bryan sips his water, while his dad peruses the parents' info packet which arrived last week from Baylor—his reading glasses are propped halfway down his nose. "So, Son, d'yuh know how to find Fletcher Hall, your dorm?"

"Yeah, I checked the map—it's not far from I-35, where we get off. It's on the southwest corner of the campus, on Spangler Ave ... like right across from the health center."

Removing his glasses, Henry arches his eyebrows, as he does when giving fatherly counsel. "This's a big step y'know?"

"That's for sure," Bryan replies, dimpling respectfully.

"I only went to college for one year ... to East Texas State, which is less than an hour from the farm, but I got so homesick, your grandfather had to come get me the first weekend." They both laugh, though Bryan's ha-ha is tempered by regret—regret that he didn't say anything crucial to Mandy on the way down, and now it's too late. "I did get used to it," Henry elaborates, "at least enough to finish the year, but I never really liked the damn place. So it's natural to feel a bit anxious I reckon."

"I do have a few butterflies," Bryan admits, in an understatement. He figures his father knows that Mandy is the *main* reason, but they don't get anywhere near bringing it up.

* * *

"This whole situation must be very hard for you," Ginny consoles, as she exits the last stall in the ladies' room, the toilet trilling behind her. She joins Mandy, who's already working on her hair at the mirror—she fixed herself in the truck before, but the muggy heat on the way down did a job on her bangs, and they still don't look right. Ginny leans over the adjacent washbowl, fingering a blemish on her heart-shaped face, which is still firm and delicate and full of youthful undertones, despite her forty-two years. "I haven't had a chance to talk to yuh, Mandy, and I don't want to interfere with what you and Bryan have decided, but I just wantcha to know—well, uh ... I uh...."

Mandy senses her cheeks getting hot, her throat tightening. Her heart tugs her toward Ginny, who captures her with a fond gaze, their eyes meeting, in the mirror. "Oh, honey, I love you like a daughter," Ginny gushes, as they embrace warmly. "That's what I'm trying to say. No matter what happens, I'll always love you special, just like at the hospital."

"I love you too, Mom Howard," Mandy replies, tears rolling down her cheeks.

Ginny smiles, her green, Bryan-like eyes brimming—then she quickly exits the restroom, the door shushing behind her.

Returning to the mirror, Mandy dabs her eyes with a tissue. *That hug felt so beautiful and real ... but just because Mom Howard and I are close, that doesn't settle things between me and Bryan. I don't know what to think. I expected him to say something in the truck, to make some kind of move, but he never did, and yet I'm not sure what I woulda done—if he had.* She dampens the tissue then dabs a bit more. *Nothing has changed. He's still gonna be gone this whole year. We gotta get real about all of this. I shoulda said no, when he asked me to come with him on this trip to Baylor. It's just stirring up doubt and hurt and confusing feelings. But, dear Jesus, I uh, I uh—stop it. The deal is done. We hafta wait. We do.*

Tossing the tissue, she returns to her bangs. *But whaddabout all the sexy flirts on campus. I know how girls are, especially the loose, cunning types. They're just waiting for guys like Bryan. Baylor may be a Baptist school, but that doesn't mean anything. The biggest prick-teasers I know are Baptists. But it's outta my hands.* Mandy sighs resignedly. *This's all part of trusting the Lord. If we're destined to be together, no one can change it.*

Her blue eyes are dry, and her complexion has returned to its normal ruddiness. She exits the bathroom. *The pain and fear we feel is for a purpose. That's what the cross is all about. That's how we get to know Christ. It has to be? It has to be?*

* * *

FLETCHER HALL - BAYLOR UNIVERSITY
SUNDAY, SEPTEMBER 1, 1991 — 2:42 PM

Bryan Howard, his parents and Mandy a few steps behind, strides up the wide, sun-scorched sidewalk in front of Fletcher Hall, an older, three-story, red-brick building, which sits well back from the street. On their right a stately shade tree (a cottonwood?) offers some relief from the stifling heat; the temp has to be in the upper 90s, enough to make the concrete hot underfoot, and he can still detect the bitumen odor cooking up from the parking lot. With a huge parking area on one side, the area they parked in, plus another sizable lot in the back, there's more asphalt than grass around this place, and yet the Bermuda lawns out front *are* well maintained. Over the arched entrance to the residence hall hangs a sign: WELCOME BAYLOR FRESHMEN!

Hustling up the steps, the Spindle foursome goes inside. They pass through a vestibule into a large traditional-looking reception lobby. The air conditioning feels good, compared to outside, but there's a noticeable chemical odor in here, as if the carpets have just been professionally cleaned. Bryan feels a bit overwhelmed. This is the *last* stop. He's not going home—this *is* home.

"Well, howdy and welcome," a plumpish, middle-aged woman declares, pushing up from a table near the center of the room; there's also a young, geeky-looking character at the table, but he stays put. "I'm Grace Danley. I'm the residence-hall director here at Fletcher, which is just a fancy, new-fangled word for *house*mother." She gives a quick titter. "And you are...?"

"Oh, uh ... I'm Bryan Howard. I'm a freshman ... on the baseball squad. And these are my folks, and this's my friend Mandy—she's coming to Baylor next year, so she came down with us to see the campus."

"Well, it's so nice to meet you," Ms. Danley says, shaking hands all around, robustly. With dark, gray-frosted hair, a double chin, and a pair of half-glasses suspended about her neck, she looks to be fifty something, and she has a "Go Bears" name tag on the lapel of her suit (she's dressed in a peach-colored skirt and jacket). Her blue eyes twinkling, she seems genuine in spirit, yet the welcome pitch sounds somewhat canned.

"This big room is so charming," Ginny observes. "I love the oak paneling and the blue carpets, and the tie-back drapes and the high ceiling, and the sofas and love seats looks so comfortable. And that staircase reminds me of an old-fashioned hotel, with the wide banister, and the big knobby newel post."

"Yes, we're proud of our reception lounge," Ms. Danley responds, nodding her head in affirmation—her graying locks are styled in a short bob which accentuates her chubby cheeks and jowls, yet she's pleasantly attractive for her age, and size.

Ginny gives Bryan a motherly pat on the shoulder: "You're gonna feel right at home here, dear."

Henry makes a grunting sound, then he speaks up, awkwardly: "Who's that in the painting? It covers half the wall."

"Oh, that's Dr. Fletcher himself, Theodore Fletcher. He was a Baylor alumnus and a renowned Waco physician. He died during the flu epidemic ... in 1918. He remained with his patients around the clock, until he also became infected with the virus."

"So this dorm was named after him?" Ginny says.

"Indeed it was," Ms. Danley replies, gesturing like a museum guide. "In his will he left a sizable sum to the university, and they used it to build the Fletcher Science Building, now the Fletcher Life Sciences Building, and later this dormitory, in 1923."

"This dorm is *that* old?" Mandy asks, ending her mouselike silence—the sound of her voice pricks Bryan, stirring his sense of woe, which had receded a bit behind the excitement and anxiety of checking in.

"That's right, young lady," the matronly director affirms. "It's been renovated a few times over the years, yet we've done our best to retain the original decor." Ms. Danley's voice is hefty (like her figure), and she speaks with the usual Texas drawl, but her words flow steadily, precisely, with few pauses, so she can say a lot in a short amount of time—and her grammar is flawless, as if she once taught English. "But this dorm is young compared to some buildings on campus. After all, we're the *old*est university in Texas. Baylor was chartered in 1845, you know? The original college is no longer standing, but we do have a few buildings that are well over a hundred years old."

Ms. Danley escorts the foursome back to the check-in table. "This's Marvin Latrobe," she says, introducing the young, nerdy-looking character. "He's my upper-class proctor on the third floor, but we call them RA's now. RA means resident assistant."

"Glad to meetcha," he twangs shyly, as he stands and greets each of them, reaching across the long, cafeteria-style table, which is stacked with clasp envelopes and green-and-gold folders. A skinny, pasty-faced, crewcut fellow wearing a tie and thick-framed glasses, Marvin—the name fits well—looks as if he grew up down the street from Wally Cleaver on *Leave It to Beaver.*

After Bryan repeats his name, the bespectacled RA sits down and scans the roster. While he does, Ms. Danley sweeps her hand toward the empty lobby and says, "Things sure won't be this quiet around here tomorrow. We have a two-day check-in for freshmen, and I suspect most of the fellows will arrive tomorrow, at the *last* minute. Only twenty-nine have checked in so far today. That's why I'm able to give you folks my *extra*-personal attention." She laughs. "Now the upper classes don't arrive until next weekend, and we don't have that many assigned to Fletcher: fifty-one this year, plus the RA's, whereas we have 163 freshmen." Clearing her throat, she gives Bryan a nod of approval. "But I commend you, young man, for coming early. You'll have a chance to relax and get your bearings, without all the hubbub and confus—"

"Ms. Danley," Marvin interrupts, "I can't find a freshman named Bryan, on *either* list?" He speaks with a reedy voice, which likewise fits his name, and frame.

"It's not *Bryan*," she corrects him, her voice an octave higher. "The last name is *Howard.* His first name is Bryan—here, let me have a look." Slipping on her glasses, she leans over the table. "Let's see now?" She flips to the second page. "Oh yes, here you are: Bryan Howard, freshman, baseball scholarship ... Spindle, Texas ... '79 Chevrolet pickup. Let's see ... looks like you're in unit 311. That's the east wing, third floor ... Marvin's floor—so he'll be your RA. And your roommate is Steve Jordan, from Ardmore, Oklahoma; he's also a baseball player. But he hasn't checked in as yet." Marvin, working quickly to redeem himself, finds the correct envelope among the stacks plus the corresponding folder; he hands them to Bryan.

"Okay, folks, follow me," Ms. Danley instructs. "I'll take you up *my*self. I've been sitting long enough." She leads them through a steel fire-door into a hallway, which has the same blue carpet and dark-oak wainscoting. She moves just as energetically as she talks despite the extra pounds on her buxom figure, though her gait does have a duckish waddle to it. "My living quarters are just ahead—number 102. If you *must* see me after hours, you can find me here, but for *non*-emergencies you should go to Marvin. During the day, I'll be in my office out front. Now that envelope we gave you contains your key, plus your temporary ID. You'll get a permanent photo-ID during in-processing on Tuesday."

After passing a dozen doors and several frosted wall-sconces, which provide subdued lighting to the corridor, they go left around a corner, into a different wing. "The nearest cafeteria is a five-minute walk ... the Bill Daniel Student Center which is just across Waco Creek. That's also where you get your mail—they'll assign you a box. There's a map in the folder, along with your freshman-orientation material which includes your DPS form. You must register your vehicle with the Baylor Department of Public Safety, and they'll issue you a parking decal. We still have students who get by without a car, but they're getting fewer each year, and the on-campus traffic is a problem, not to mention the parking. Dean Buckley's pushing bicycles, but it's a tough sell. After all, this *is* Texas." She laughs, a hefty ha-ha-ha.

Halfway down the wing they hang a right into a motel-like vestibule where they pause at the foot of a stairway amid several vending machines. "You can bring your stuff in through this entrance," Ms. Danley remarks, pointing to a set of doors that lead outside. She then takes them up the concrete stairs, which look relatively modern. "We could've gone up the main stairs in the lobby, but I wanted to show you the side door." She's beginning to huff and puff, but her words continue to flow—relentlessly. "Now the freshman athletes normally live with the other jocks at the Quadrangle Apartments on the east side of campus, but this year they're renovating a portion of them, so we're housing eighteen of you fellows over here, mostly baseball players. But there'll be thirty non-athletes on the third floor as well, so it's not a jock section by any means, though it does have the best accommodations, since all the units were recently enlarged."

"I'm glad Bryan's gonna be here," Ginny interjects, as they pass the door leading to the second floor. "It's good to be with the regular students. And I reckon things'll be a bit more settled and orderly compared to the jock dorm, the Angle whatever?"

"The Quadrangle," Ms. Danley corrects. "The students refer to it as 'the Quad,' and you're right about things being a bit lax over there. They don't get the supervision they need, in *my* opinion, and there have been a few incidents, such as parties that got out of hand, but nothing major ... as at some schools. After all, we *are* a Baptist university, so even the jocks are more well-behaved." This sets off a collective laugh, as Ms. Danley halts on the last landing—to elaborate: "But yes, we're fairly strict here at Fletcher, and we *will* be as long as I'm in charge, and we're not as lavish and modern as the Quadrangle, but we do have more history and character. For decades this hall had nothing but tiny two-man rooms, with community bathrooms here and there. Then around 1960 they converted it to married housing, to studiolike units with their own baths and cooking areas, a total renovation. But when the couples started living off-campus, they converted it back to a men's dorm. That was 1977, the first year I was here; they still called us 'housemothers' then." She wheezes and chortles. "But that's why this place is unique. Now in the summer of '89 we modernized the heating and air-conditioning systems, and the fire-sprinklers, and that's when they remodeled the third floor, making the units even bigger—we had planned to renovate the other floors too, but the money was diverted."

THE SILVER CORD

She's like a dadgum encyclopedia, Bryan remarks to himself, as they finally reach the third floor, which still exudes an odor of newness, of paint, and wallboard, and new carpets.

"This's Marvin Latrobe's room," Ms. Danley points out, "number 303. He's not a jock, of course, but he's mature and honest, and fair. He's a junior and a theology major. He's mainly here to help with problems or questions, but he also exercises authority on the floor ... if there's too much noise late at night, or loud music, and so forth. We do have more serious infractions occasionally, but our fellows are well-behaved for the most part."

Reaching unit 311 at the end of the hallway, she ushers them inside—into a large, apartmentlike room. "This unit is set up like a small suite," she explains, gesturing this way and that, "with a sizable main room plus two cubbyhole bedrooms, and you have an open, galley-style kitchen. The bathroom is to the right of the bedrooms, off the kitchen, the door beyond the breakfast table."

"Wow, awesome, *super* cool," Mandy declares, while Ginny says much the same, using less slangy, more motherly lingo.

"This *is* awesome," Bryan adds, joining the chorus. "I don't see how the Quadrangle can be much better." Then his words go silent: *I wish this dorm was still married housing, and Mandy and I were moving in, as a couple.* The room smells new, like the hallway, but there's also a faint sweetish fragrance, as if there's an air-freshener somewhere in here, like those solid, cone-shaped Renuzit things that gradually dissolve away.

Couch, coffee table, recliner, armchair, end table with lamp: the furniture is cheaper than the stuff downstairs in the reception lounge, more like what you'd see on display at Sears, including a shelved TV stand which crouches nakedly in the corner. Yet it's rather overwhelming for a dorm room. "Man, things have sure changed since *I* went to college," Henry observes. "You even have wall-to-wall carpets, and a picture window."

"Things *have* changed," Ms. Danley agrees, "and I went to school right here at Baylor. I lived in Collins Hall down the road, but I dare not tell you the year I graduated." More hefty ha-ha's. "But most of the dorm rooms on campus are larger now, though Fletcher is a special case, as I said before, and 311 is one of our largest units, since it's at the corner of the wing." She adjusts, with her chubby fingers, a circular dial on the wall between the two bedrooms; a fan comes on, a whispery hum. "This's your thermostat. I'm putting it on 70° for now. The system is in cooling mode of course. We turn the heat on in October. And when the weather becomes more tolerable, you can open your windows—they slide open sideways."

She steps over to the kitchen area, where the floor is covered with pale-gray linoleum tiles. "Now your meals at the cafeteria are part of your scholarship, so I expect you'll be eating there most of the time, but thanks to the unique history of this dorm, you also have this cooking nook." She turns the sink faucet on and off, then she opens and closes the refrigerator. "But you'll need your own dishes and utensils and whatnot." She opens one of the cabinets above the counter. "We have a housecleaning crew who vacuums and scrubs your bathroom and collects the trash, every Tuesday for this wing, but they don't make beds, or do dishes—that's your responsibility. Same goes for laundry: we have a laundromat in the basement." Dusting her hands together, she retreats toward the door. "I'll leave you folks alone now, plus I have to check on Marvin. He's excellent overseeing the floor up here, but he's not yet up to speed when it comes to running the check-in table." She gives a chuckling laugh. "Oh, I almost forgot: we have a very strict visitation policy at Baylor, a *good* policy in my opinion, and it's heartily enforced here at Fletcher Hall." Her voice has taken on a sterner quality. "Female guests are forbidden except on Saturday and Sunday from one p.m. to six p.m., and violators must report to Dean Buckley, and the penalty can be quite severe, even loss of on-campus housing privileges. So, young lady, if you plan to come down to visit Bryan, you must be out of this room by six."

I wish, Bryan interjects to himself, as Mandy gives the housemother a little sheepish titter. *The way things stand now, I doubt she's gonna be in here after six, before six, or any time.* He tries to make eye contact with her, but she carefully avoids him, looking down, then out the window, then she fiddles with her purse, opening and closing the Velcro clasp, like she does.

"I don't expect any problems regarding this," Ms. Danley allows, "but I like to tell each incoming freshman personally, and I also must emphasize our no-smoking policy. Same goes for alcoholic beverages and illicit drugs." Her tone softens a trifle. "Like I said before, Baylor is a Baptist school, and most of the students *are* Baptists, as am I, so these rules are second nature around here, and not difficult to keep. I don't push my religion on others—but I do encourage my students to attend Sunday services, whether Baptist or otherwise."

* * *

FLETCHER HALL, UNIT 311
SUNDAY, SEPTEMBER 1, 1991 — 4:40 PM

Young Mr. Howard suffers silently in the armchair, his dad in the recliner, while his mom and Mandy are slouched back on the sofa. Like air escaping from a slow-leaking tire, the sense of newness and excitement has run its course, leaving everyone deflated. There's light coming in the window to Bryan's left, but the rest of the room is dim and shadowy. Gloomy, dreary, heavy: the melancholy mood is so strong he can almost smell the stink of it. After hauling his stuff up here—it didn't take long, with everyone helping—they toured the campus in the Buick, so Mandy could see everything, and they just got back ten minutes ago. Bryan can tell his parents are distressed, as they try to cope with the fact that he's *not* going home with them, while he's heartsick and empty, because Mandy *is* going home with them.

"I really like the tawny hue of the carpet in here," Ginny remarks— she's been talking about the decor of the dorm room ever since they got back. "It goes so well with the pale-blue walls, don'tcha think, Henry?"

"Yeah, I reckon," he agrees perfunctorily, as he checks his watch. "But we should hit the road, hon. It's almost five." And yet, he remains in the recliner, as though hoping to somehow escape the inevitable good-byes coming up.

"And that little breakfast table is so cute," Ginny continues, seemingly oblivious to her husband's comments. "I love that honey-oak finish. I wish we had one at the farm."

Her domestic chatter rings hollow, and irrelevant, yet it's her way of dealing with stress, as Bryan well knows. But he doesn't give a shit about the carpets or the walls. It's all meaningless without Mandy, who seems ready to nod off, her head back, her eyes heavy. He can't tell if she's sad or weary or bored, or all three. But she's surely not the wild and frisky filly who frolicked naked by the creek at Magruder State Forest less than a month ago. *O God, how did it come apart so fast? Let's get this over with—this whole day has been TORTURE.* He grips the wooden arms of the chair (it has cushions, but the arms are bare) until his knuckles turn white. He wishes that homesickness was *all* he had to deal with, like most freshmen, like his dad years ago at East Texas State. An awful knowing torments Bryan, a premonition, a portent—if Mandy leaves today as a "friend" so called, they'll drift totally apart, and she won't come to Baylor next year, and he'll never kiss her lips again. They'll write a few times, even talk on the phone, but then she'll hook up with someone else, and most likely he will too. That's what happens to high-school romances, just like her mom says. Yet it strikes him as totally unjust and out of whack, like realizing you've misread the sun your whole life, that it actually rises in the west, not the east.

His throat is dry, and he has a weird taste in his mouth, like straw, like hay. The rueful feelings grow stronger squeezing his chest. Too much: he gets up and looks out the picture window, which faces east (it's not a picture window in the true sense, since it's bisected vertically by an aluminum frame, actually the adjacent frames of the two glass panels which slide back and forth). A big pine tree guards this corner of the dorm (northeast corner), but it's far enough left to allow a view. The parking lots are ugly, but the grassy areas beyond are more picturesque. Ditto for the diagonal sidewalks and the footbridges across Waco Creek, one of which leads to the Bill Daniel Student Center, the student center Ms. Danley spoke of, where the nearest cafeteria is located. *I could walk over there later,* he says to himself, *to check it out, though I don't feel much like eating.* The idea of exploring by himself, the student center or anything on campus, only adds to his misery. *Maybe I'll just get something from the vending machines and crawl into bed early. Things won't be any better tomorrow, but at least they'll be resolved.*

"Are you okay, Bryan honey?" Ginny asks.

"Yeah, Mom," he lies, speaking out the window. "It's just a big change, that's all. But I doubt I'll be rushing back to the farm ... to cut hay with Billy Ray." He forces a laugh, as does his mom. She's obviously sad about him leaving the nest, but he realizes full well that she knows the truth, that he's hurting over Mandy.

She shifts back to her domestic diversions: "I'm gonna pick out some new curtains for you, Bryan. I'll mail 'em down. These gold ones they have in here look rather cheap and gaudy. I think something in brown would go good."

Bryan loves his mom, and he *will* miss her, but right now the small talk is too much to bear. "I'm gonna take my computer stuff into the bedroom," he announces, needing to escape. "I'm gonna claim the one with the window, since *I* got here first." He gives another forced laugh.

"It's time for us to go, anyway," Henry says again, though he still doesn't get up from the maroon recliner.

Grabbing his Macintosh from the kitchen table, Bryan carries it into the leftmost bedroom and sets it on the long desk. *This whole situation is SO awkward. Mandy hasn't said two words hardly since we got back from checking out the campus.*

She rode in the back with Ginny, while Bryan rode up front with his father. As Bryan pointed out the different landmarks and buildings and athletic facilities, Mandy would say "cool" or "neat," but she directed her responses more to Ginny than to Bryan, or so it seemed.

After getting the printer and a box of peripherals from the kitchen nook, Bryan closes the bedroom door all but a crack. He aches to summon Mandy, so they can talk alone, but he doesn't have the balls. And it'll take a miracle for her to come in here on her own, and he's past the point of expecting any last-minute moves by God. She hasn't given him any fond regard, even a smirk or a witty remark, since Dallas anyway. Giving a sigh, he gazes out the bedroom window, which faces the same way as the picture window in the other room. There aren't many vehicles in the parking lot, no more than fifteen or so. *We beat the crowd by coming today, but so what? I still feel like shit, worse than shit. I wish they'd quit dawdling, so we can get this over with.* He blows out a pained exhalation, a silent whistle. *O Jesus, I just need five minutes alone with her, but it's not gonna happen.*

In the sultry distance, well beyond the parking lot, Waco Creek meanders northward just this side of the M. P. Daniel Esplanade, headed for the Brazos. The shallow stream—it's just a trickle this time of the year—runs under Spangler Avenue near Neill Morris Hall, then it passes under a couple of foot-bridges before disappearing underground near Hudson Plaza which is near the Bill Daniel Student Center (the Daniel name is famous at Baylor, famous anywhere in Texas for that matter). After flowing in a man-made channel under the center of the campus, the creek reemerges near Russell Gymnasium before emptying into the river near Ferrell Field. He can't see all of this from here of course (the campus is over four hundred acres in size; he can see nothing beyond Hudson Plaza), but he knows the layout of the university.

There's a small hill on his right several hundred yards away. On top of it stands a water tower. The campus slopes gently downward to the north, toward the river, so this tower commands the highest point, or close to it. The oval tank, big and round and green, like a monstrous watermelon, has bright gold lettering on it: "Baylor Bears." The late-afternoon sun throws the egglike shadow of the tower onto Collins Hall, the nearest girl's dorm, the one Ms. Danley lived in when she was a student, though it's a stretch to imagine her as a frisky young coed. But Collins Hall *is* the nearest. If only it was next year, and Mandy was checking in at Collins with the other freshman gals. But alas, he's resigned to the dreadful prospect that she'll never check in at Baylor, next year, or any year. This torturous conclusion makes him hate God, hate life, hate being submissive and good, and dutiful and responsible—no "hate" is too strong of a word. Nonetheless, he's hardly on fire to go out and achieve great things for Christ and humanity. He gives a sigh of exasperation. *O dear Jesus, do something. I can't stand another minute of this.*

Noise, movement: he opens the bedroom door. This is it—his dad is up. "We're leaving, Son," Henry announces, as though responding to Bryan's prayerful pleas. "It's five o'clock."

"I'll walk y'down," Bryan declares, grabbing his baseball hat. He hurries ahead, as the foursome exits the suite.

Three minutes later, they're all gathered by the Buick. "We'll get through this," Bryan says, with double meaning, as he hugs his mom. He fights to keep his composure.

"I reckon so," Ginny responds tearfully, her voice quavering, "but this's even worse than that first day at Spindle Elementary years ago, when I took yuh to your kindergarten room, and I had to leave yuh there." She laughs snuffily, then holds him tightly.

"Son, you're gonna do good here," Henry declares, patting Bryan on the back. "I just *know* it."

Henry and Ginny escape quickly into the Buick, leaving Bryan and Mandy standing alone behind it. She averts her eyes, looking down. A shriek gathers in his throat, a plaintive cry, but he dares not give it life. He swallows it rather, clamming up, just as he's done all day. He spouts instead a dutiful pleasantry: "Well, pretty lady, have a good trip back."

"We will," Mandy replies in like manner—she fidgets with her hands, picking at her thumbnail.

They hug awkwardly, their lips far apart, then she disappears into the back seat of the car.

* * *

Well, that's that, Bryan declares to himself, as he dabs away his tears in the bathroom. *They should be on I-35 by now?* He practically ran back up here to his dorm room, arriving in time to see the Buick pull out of the parking lot, yet that was not the reason for his haste. He just wanted to get away from Mandy, from that awkward, lifeless hug. He wanted closure, resolution, and now he *has* it. Grabbing more toilet paper, he blows his nose then steps over to the washbowl and mirror. His eyes are still red but no longer overflowing, as they were when he was bounding up the stairs. He's glad he didn't see Ms. Danley or that geeky floor proctor, or anyone. For now at least, Fletcher Hall seems quieter than a mausoleum, this end of the third floor anyway.

After tossing the wadded tissue into the sturdy, hotel-style toilet, he turns on the faucet, collects cold water in his cupped hands, and throws it into his face. He reaches, by habit, for a towel, but doesn't find one (a pair of shiny tubular towelracks stretch along the wall behind him, but both are empty; there's nothing in the bathroom except for a half roll of TP plus a purplish bar of soap in the shower stall, floral-scented soap, the same fragrance he detected when he first entered the suite—it wasn't a Renuzit air-freshener after all). *I reckon I should dig out my towels,* he tells himself, as he dries his face with toilet paper, his hands on his Levi's. *In fact, I hafta unpack everything. It's gonna take a while, but it'll keep me occupied at least.*

Exiting the bathroom, he turns on the kitchen light, a florescent panel above the sink. He surveys the boxes and suitcases; most of his stuff ended up on the floor between the breakfast table and the back of the couch, which faces away from the galley. But before he starts unpacking, he explores the cabinets and drawers; they're made of wood, pine maybe, and they're tan in color, a blah, ugly hue, like the color of peanut butter. They're all empty except for a few rags and sponges under the sink along with a plastic bottle of Joy dishwashing liquid, an inch or so left—but he does find some graffiti, on the back of one of the cabinet doors: "ELAINE BLANKENSHIP IS A PRICK-TEASING, DECEITFUL BITCH! - - - L.L.G. / Feb. 12, 1990."

Looks like someone else had a broken heart over some gal, Bryan remarks to himself, as he checks out the narrow closet to the right of the bathroom, *and not too long ago. But I don't see Mandy as a bitch—no way.* The closet is also bare save for a broom, a blue-plastic dustpan hanging on a hook, and a plumber's helper way in the back. *It's not her fault what's happening. It's just reality that's all. And she was the first to face up to the whole situation. It's way bigger than both of us.* Giving a sigh, he goes over to commence unpacking. *Except a man deny himself and take up his cross—that's how Pastor Ron preaches it, and it's true. I must put the Lord first. He died for us, and he knows what's best.* Despite this dutiful shot of self-counseling, the gnawing persists in his gut, the queasy sense of defeat.

Two of the cardboard boxes rest on Gramps' old army trunk, while another one sits on the floor beside it. Bryan decides to start with the one on the floor; it contains the towels, if he's not mistaken. Picking up the carton, he takes it around and places it on the sofa. As he does, he notices a grayish something between the end cushion and the armrest. "What the hell?" he reacts, as he digs it out. "It's Mandy's *purse.* She left her purse."

He takes it to the breakfast table where the light is better. No doubt: it's her gray envelope purse. Before he can collect his wits enough to realize the implications of his find, a rap comes at the door. He hurries to answer it. Blond bangs, blushing grin, blue eyes beaming—it's her: MANDY! Bryan's heart bolts up into his throat, beating berserkly as though he's swallowed a helicopter: *WHOMP! WHOMP! WHOMP!*

"Ah, ah ... whaa?" he stutters, his thoughts thrashing. "I mean uh ... how'd yuh get back in?"

"I'm legal until six, mister. Don'tcha know the rules around here?" She pushes boldly by him, her ponytail bouncing, her hips rocking back and forth inside her khaki skirt. She halts near the sofa, slouching on one leg, in that adorable, loose, nonpostured manner of hers. "So, you big jock, you ... what'd yuh do with my *gosh*dang purse?" Folding her arms, she nods toward the spot where she was sitting before. She gives him the cute rabbity routine, pursing-nibbling her lips, crinkling her nose.

He looks on, stunned, but then his hopes rip upward out of the grave. To hell with closure; to hell with self-denial; Mandy's back. They may yet win this thing—in *extra* innings.

"It's on the kitchen table," he says, pointing at the purse. His wits have returned, just enough to get his words out sanely.

"We were just getting on the highway," she relates, bopping over to get it. "I felt *so* embarrassed. Your dad had to get off at the first exit, but it only took a few minutes, five at the most, to get back here. I don't know *how* I coulda left it behind like that?" She playfully spins the purse between her hands, like a wheel, then she tosses it into the air, almost to the ceiling. Twisting around, she catches it one-handed behind her back. She blushes and giggles then gives a quick, put-on curtsy and head nod, as though bowing before an audience.

Now's my chance, Bryan cries to himself. *She's not only back, but she's full of piss and vinegar.* She giggles again then pivots jockishly (point-guard style) around the breakfast table, her sneakers squeaking on the linoleum.

THE SILVER CORD

To the door: he hurries there ahead of her, holding it shut. "C'mon, I gotta go. They're down there waiting." She puts on a poker face, but it turns into a smirk. "I told 'em two minutes."

"I'm not gonna letcha go," he declares. "I've got some things to say first." Giving no reply, she looks down, her smirk curving into a coy grin—a knowing grin, or so it seems.

Bryan, gazing at his sweetheart, dimples into a smile of his own. Only inches away, he devours with his eyes her disheveled bangs, her sun-freckled nose, her lank ponytail, her tan, softly smooth neckline inside the collar of her madras shirt, which allows, a bit lower, a glimpse of bra and cleavage between the buttons. He inhales her perfume, her hair, the perspiry summer-day heat of her body coming through her clothes. He loves her beyond words, beyond thoughts, beyond time, beyond all duties and rules and social responsibilities, beyond reputation and ambition, beyond all power and wealth and majesty. This love HAS to be God—but if it isn't, he'd rather be godless.

As though reaching the same conclusion, Mandy sobers and lifts her big blue eyes. "Oh, babe, you've been crying; your eyes are red." She gives him a pat on the shoulder.

"Yeah, I guess I got a little teary-eyed when y'all left."

"Oh, Bryan honey, dear Bryan," she mews, embracing him fervently, frantically, her hot, wondrous, girl-jock heft pinning him against the door, the corner of her purse digging into his side, her face hidden in the hollow between his shoulder and neck. He hugs her back, pulling her cushiony bosom into him, into him. Giving a little gasp, she comes up and kisses him. He tastes her lips, her tongue, her unsated yearning. His knees quiver, his penis tingles; a joyous wind whips through him, a triumphal rush. Her tongue pushes deeper. He moans happily.

"Oh, babe, I love you so," she gushes, after breaking for air. "I do, I do ... but, but—" She hesitates, groping for words. "But, but ... but we...." Her eyes fill; she seems suddenly distressed and confused; she bows her head.

"But what?"

Slipping free, she slumps against the wall opposite the recessed coat closet. His joy falters then spins downward into his stomach, where pangs of doubt devour it. Shifting her weight from one sneaker to the other, she fiddles with the purse, the Velcro clasp. Tears streak her face. "Now *I'm* crying, and I swore I wouldn't. I swore I wasn't gonna let this happen." Fishing a Kleenex out of her purse, she wipes her cheeks then dabs her eyes. "Oh, babe, I'm sorry I lost control. I'm sorry. We *can't* be doing this; we *can't.*"

"Why not?"

"'Cause we can't. You know why? I don't hafta say it."

"Well, I don't agree," he counters, forging on with desperate abandon despite the awful whirring in his gut. "You don't have a *damn* thing to be sorry about." Though shaken, he can still taste victory on his lips. Besides, he's got little to lose. Just minutes ago he was alone in this room, and she was gone for good.

Taking her boldly by the hand, he leads her over to the sofa. "Now you sit down right here, pretty lady—this won't take long, but you're *gonna* hear me out." She gives a quizzical murmur but obeys, plunking down on the leftmost cushion, her purse on her lap. Swinging the coffee table out of the way, he kneels in front of her. He clasps her hand gently, but earnestly, between both of his. She looks down shyly, but not at him. Using her free hand, she wipes her sniffles with the tissue then dabs her tears away.

"Oh, precious Mandy," he commences, his voice hushed yet firm, "I love you so much it hurts. And I know *you* love me. You've never denied it through all of this, and you just told me again by the door. That's why you don't have anything to be *sorry* about. It's right and good, *and* godly, for you to kiss me and hug me. There's nothing more *right* under Heaven—at least, that's how I see it." He utters a throaty emphatic sound, almost a growl. "So I don't wanna put things on hold with you. This just-friends bullshit won't work. It's *all* or nothing, and we both know it. We *are* friends to be sure—you're my *best* friend in fact—but I also wanna kiss you and fondle you and get naked with you, and have mind-blowing sex with you, and live with you, and have babies with you, and be by your side as *much* as possible, now and *forever*." He pauses, giving her a chance to reply, but she remains silent, and still, save for the occasional eye-dabbing. "Oh, pretty lady, I've loved you ever since I first saw you at that church cookout, and it's grown stronger every day, and especially this past year. And *you* were there after my injury, loving me and praying for me and staying close by my bed, until I came to. I'll never forget your big blues eyes looking down so beautifully, as I lay in that ICU bed. It's like you're inside me living with me all the time. Yet I also see you in every sunrise, in every sunset, and I feel your presence on the wind that blows through the trees and fields. You're the inspiration for all my hopes and dreams and ambitions, and goals. You're my joy, my *reason* for living."

He takes a slow deliberate breath. She's crying again, softly. His words are hitting home, and her tears are *moving* him, along with her adorable seated pose, the canted head, the parted lips, the golden hair draped on her neck. Dropping his gaze, he studies her thumb as it protrudes from his handclasp—it's cutely small and girlish with a trimmed, unpolished nail, which sports a few of those whitish, crescent-moon spots. He loves this thumb, with its blemished, tomboy nail; he loves *all* her fingers, and all her limbs. He loves everything she has— he can't let her go. He caresses her hand, as though it's her heart. "Oh, Mandy, sweet Mandy ... without you everything turns dreary and cold, and empty and blah. It's been horrible, ever since that day behind the diner. And what set it off was that hot session we had in the hayfield, after we got back from skinny-dipping. That was the *trigger*, but it was building all summer. We were trying to be in love without getting turned on—and that's *not* possible. And our future plans seemed so far away, like half a lifetime, so we tossed in the towel so to speak, just so we could be Christian and good, and mature and responsible." Bryan snorts for emphasis. "But it's a lie to deny our love, and to run away from it, as if it's foolish and sinful and childish, and I was running just as fast as you were. Yet how can it be bad—even the lust part—when this love we share is the biggest and most beautiful thing that's ever happened to us? Now I know your mama says you should wait to get serious and romantic, but if she wants the *best* for you, then how can she oppose it? It doesn't make sense to wait and wait and wait." He sucks a quick breath. "In any case, Mandy, this isn't gonna work, this just-friends bullshit. If we leave things 'on hold,' I'm afraid we'll just end up living separate lives forever, and that's *too* much to bear. So I have a better solution."

"What's that?" she sniffles, breaking her silence.

"Let's get married."

"Yeah right," she quips, interrupting him; she shoots him a quick glance, along with a smirk. "I'm *bare*ly seventeen. Besides, Mama would *shoot* me." The whirring in Bryan's stomach whips around, moving in a good direction. Despite her mocking tone, he can tell she likes this subject. Lifting her eyes, she focuses on something to his right rear: the recliner? the lamp? She snickers hoarsely then clears her throat. "You really *are* dreaming?"

"Not a chance, pretty lady. I'm serious; I don't mean—" He stops midsentence, realizing she needs some time.

She sniffles and purses her lips. Though still gazing beyond him, her blue eyes grow wider, her brows arching. "But *how*?" she asks sincerely, no longer mocking the idea.

"I don't mean *right* away ... but next spring ... after you graduate. This way we'll only have nine months to wait instead of three years—we can deal with that, whether we have sex or not. Gosh, we can almost hold our breath that long." They both laugh—she's *with* him now. "Well not quite, but we'll survive it. And we can do away with this just-friends bullshit, and nothing will be on hold. We'll get together on weekends and holidays, whenever we can. Then as soon as school's out, we'll have a small wedding at the farm, then we'll go on our *honey*moon, which's gonna be outta this world—then we'll move down here to Waco and get an apartment off campus." He dimples and gives her a love-tap on the shoulder, a storm of delight gathering in his bosom. But he's also wary—if she rejects him now, he'll surely die. "Oh, Mandy, just think of it. We'll be husband and wife like we *should* be. And hopefully, your mom will go along, but if not, we'll wait another month, until you turn eighteen in July?"

"D'yuh really mean it, babe?"

"You dadgum right I do. I've never been *more* serious in my life." Going up on his knees as high as he can, he takes her by the shoulders. "In fact, I may as well make it official and put it *all* on the line. I've never come right out and asked, even when we got secretly engaged last April—that was more like a fantasy thing, but this's *real* life." He swallows then utters a little whine, a few nervous notes escaping. "So here goes ... Amanda Fay Stevens, will you marry me—under the terms I've just described?"

She looks right at him, her blue eyes warm and glistening. She curves her mouth, an enchanting half-grin. He *has* his answer, but she voices it anyway, softly, slowly, "Yes ... yes...."

Glory, glory, relief and glory: the joyful tempest in Bryan's bosom breaks loose, almost blowing him backwards out the window, or so it seems. She collapses into his arms, and they fall sideways onto the sofa. As they hug and kiss, she repeats her answer: "Oh yes, babe, let's do it. Let's *go* for it."

* * *

FLETCHER HALL, UNIT 311
SUNDAY, SEPTEMBER 1, 1991 — 7:21 PM

Bryan Howard, alone again but unspeakably happy and relieved, gazes out at the gray, last light of day. The lights around campus are winking on, one here, one there, mostly street lights and such—the buildings are mainly dark, aside from the Bill Daniel Student Center where the cafeteria is evidently still serving. But he didn't eat there this evening, nor did he visit the vending machines downstairs. Henry and Ginny Howard, after getting the news, were in no mood to rush back to Spindle, so they all went back to Denny's for a spontaneous celebration.

Bryan can hear, faintly, the traffic on I-35, plus occasional louder noises, like a truck downshifting. The nearest exit is almost a mile away, yet the highway itself passes within two hundred yards of this corner of the campus (the southwest corner), but his room faces the other way, so the traffic isn't noticeable enough to be bothersome. The AC fan kicks on, obscuring the highway murmur. Crossing the nearly dark room, he adjusts the thermostat, killing the AC. The dormitory suite is cool enough, too cool in fact, now that he's the only one here.

Leaving the lights off, he returns to the window. He likes this view, especially tonight, and he can see out better if the room is dark. The reunited lovebirds have already selected a date: Sunday, May 31, 1992. They'll have the ceremony outside, on the lawn behind the Howard homeplace. But they won't spread these good tidings to anyone, beyond his parents, until Mandy has a chance to tell her mother. Helen presents a potential problem to be sure, the only dark cloud on their otherwise sunny horizon, but Mandy feels she can get her mom's acquiescence, if not her blessing—but if that fails, they'll get married on July 20, 1992: Mandy's 18th birthday.

"I don't care if Mama disowns me," she proclaimed boldly at Denny's. "It's *my* life, and we're getting married, no matter what. It's a done deal now. I love her, but it's *my* life."

O Jesus God, thank you, thank you, Bryan prays, lifting his gaze skyward, up into the pearly twilight. His happiness leaps and lurches then reels and kicks, as though he has a drunk bullfrog in his bosom. God is suddenly GOOD again, and big and loving, and kind. And young Mr. Howard has been thanking him ever since Mandy said yes. He relives again that wondrous scene, which turned around this whole day, this whole summer, his *whole* life.

They necked on the sofa; they cried tears of joy; they shared countless words of affection and devotion; they laughed and chased each other; he swept her off her feet and swung her around in circles, almost knocking the lamp over. Then they necked some more by the breakfast table. "My darling Mandy, my precious pretty lady," he cooed between kisses. "We have *so* much fun together. This's like Heaven, but it's happening *now.*"

"Dear, dear Bryan," she sighed in reply. "You *are* my best friend and soulmate, but you're *gonna* be my lover and husband. You already are, but we're gonna make it official now. I was hoping something great would happen today, and now it *has*. O God, I love you *so*. And I'm so very, very proud of you."

Finally, they rushed down to tell his parents, who suspected something was up, after waiting so long. But before they left the room, Bryan popped another question, not a high-stakes query like his proposal though perhaps just as crucial: "So tell me, pretty lady, didyuh leave that purse up here on purpose?"

"C'mon, you big jock," she sported evasively, as she tickled his ribs, playfully pushing him out the door. "D'yuh really think I'd do that? It was *God*. This whole thing was an act of *God.*"

* * *

INTERSTATE 30, EAST OF DALLAS
SUNDAY, SEPTEMBER 1, 1991 — 9:54 PM

Things worked out better than I ever imagined, Mandy sighs to herself as she looks out at the passing countryside from the back seat of the Howards' Buick. *I'm just glad that Bryan took charge like he did.* The moon is out; it's fat but not full—it's just bright enough for her to see the woods and fields going by. The car is quiet, save for the Texas Rangers baseball game crackling at low volume on the radio. Ginny has conked out on her side of the front seat. During the first half of the trip, jubilant chatter filled the car, but things have finally settled. *No school tomorrow; it's Labor Day ... but I hafta go on Tuesday. It's only the second week, and it's already a drag ... and NOW it's gonna be a super drag ... but May is only eight months away. I can't wait.*

A mile or so later, a highway sign appears in the headlights ahead—it grows bigger, bigger, then zips by on Mandy's side of the car: Sulphur Springs 20 mi. A tremor of unease undercuts her joy, as she realizes they'll soon be turning off onto Highway 12—she'll be home in less than an hour. *Oh gosh, how am I gonna break this news to Mama?* she wonders, directing her thoughts toward the moon, beyond the moon. *No way can I tell her tonight. She didn't even like the idea of me riding down to Baylor with Bryan. I'll wait until she's in a really good mood, like maybe next weekend?*

Her unease grows—but then she fights back: *Why am I feeling guilty about Mama? It's MY life, and Bryan is good and honest and godly, and he LOVES me—so I don't have one dang thing to feel guilty about, especially when Mama married a bum like Charlie—not that Charlie can help it or anything.* Mandy screws her fist into her palm, silently but firmly. *I love her, and I know she loves me, but it's MY life! I'm not going to the cross just to make her happy and all. NO WAY! Next year at this time, we'll be married ... we will.* A warm rush chases the negative vibes.

* * *

FLETCHER HALL, UNIT 311
SUNDAY, SEPTEMBER 1, 1991 — 11:40 PM

I wonder if she really did leave that purse on purpose, Bryan muses to himself, as he turns over in his bed. *If so, it was a brilliant move.* He chuckles at the thought.

He's having trouble getting to sleep, but he's too elated to give a gosh damn. He's been in the sack since eleven, since he finished unpacking. He hooked up his computer, his tape deck, and his TV—he can get five channels with the rabbit ears, though he doubts he'll be watching it much. The 14-inch Sony looks ridiculously small atop the large stand in the living room. If his roommate has a bigger model, Bryan will move the Sony in here. He plugged his phone into the jack under his desk, but there's no dial tone; he has to get it turned on. He put his clothes in the chest of drawers, plus some in the closet—there's a tiny closet in the corner—then he made his bed, a smallish double bed which seems much bigger in this little room. While he was working, he played the Stevie Nicks cassette on his tape deck. The songs reinforced his sky-high, drunk-on-Mandy mood, especially "Talk to Me," their favorite. Finally, after taking a shower, he unwrapped her photo-portrait and placed it on his desk.

He already masturbated, getting off to a dreamy honeymoon fantasy. Sex was hardly a concern today, yet it quickly got bigger in his mind, and his gonads, while they were kissing and cooing. In any case, he needed his usual post-necking release, a release that normally relaxes him right into sleep—but not tonight. He's too keyed up. The wondrous words and images keep popping, and popping, in his head. He turns over again, folding his pillow. In addition, he has a hundred Baylor concerns wiggling forward from the back of his mind. He can't do much tomorrow, since it's Labor Day, though he plans to check out the caf and explore a bit. But Tuesday things swing into high gear: baseball, freshman orientation; in-processing, registration, all kinds of stuff.

He's exhausted, physically and mentally, not to speak of his frazzled emotions. Yet he's quite content to lie here basking in this warm Mandy glow, which heats him from inside. *Nothing's on hold, and we're getting MARRIED in the spring. Hallelujah! I still can't believe it!* Sitting up on the side of the bed, he switches on the desk lamp and grabs her picture. He lightly touches her sweet oval face with the back of his index finger. "I love you, my precious, pretty lady," he whispers out loud. He gazes at her for a long moment, devouring her, drinking her in.

I wish Gramps was alive, Bryan sighs happily, as he clicks off the light and gets back into bed, *so I could tell him the good news.* The oak tree in the photo brought his granddad to mind. *But maybe he knows everything that's happening down here anyhow? I sure had that feeling when I saw him in my near-death experience.*

Closing his eyes, he begins to pray: *Dear God in Heaven, I thank you for this day and for what you did for me and Mandy. Thank you for my life, and for hers, and for the love we share.* Although his talks with God are mostly spontaneous, he's reverting for this night to the bedtime routine he practiced as a lad. *Please forgive me for being so mad at you recently, and for complaining and not having any faith. But you came through anyway—and I thank you; I do. And I thank you for Jesus who died for my sins. And I thank you for healing me and saving my life back in May. I thank you for giving me a glimpse of the other side, and for my other astral trips—all of which have stirred my curiosity about the silver cord. And I pray you'll help me to investigate this mystery here at Baylor, and later as a doctor. Please help me to get used to this campus—to all the new places, and new people, and new routines. And please be with me on the baseball field. Help me make the team. And be with me on the ninth when classes start for real. And help me to get used to being away from home and everything. I thank you for my parents, and I pray you'll take care of them, and help them to adjust to my absence. And dear sweet God, I thank you so much for my precious Mandy. I pray you'll work in her mama's heart, so our wedding plans can go smoothly. And PLEASE keep Mandy safe and healthy while we're apart. Bless her as she goes through her senior year. I pray all this in Jesus' name. Amen.*

The childlike prayer does the trick, and he falls asleep, his physical self anyhow. His soul-body rises slowly off the bed. He floats through the exterior wall, through the steel and bricks and mortar. He's quickly outside, ascending above pole-mounted lights and parked cars and blacktop, while on the other (west) side of the residence, a sparse but steady stream of cars whiz by on Interstate 35.

Exhilaration, ineffable sense of freedom: at first he's startled, almost frightened, but he quickly realizes what's happening. He continues to ascend for a few seconds until he can see the whole campus plus the thicker grid of lights denoting downtown Waco to the west and southwest, but then his thought-control takes hold, and he comes back down, slowing to a hover about thirty feet above one of the goose-necked, parking-lot lamps. Above him hangs a gibbous moon among a sprinkling of stars, the ones bright enough to be seen through the late-summer haze and moonlight, not to mention the urban glow from below. *O God, I feel so good, like a geyser is going off inside me, like how I felt when Mandy said yes—I wish she was here with me now.*

Leaving the parking lot behind, he glides east over the lawns and walkways on this side of Waco Creek. Crossing above the creek, he circles over the student center then heads south above the M. P. Daniel Esplanade. Below him, a couple strolls hand-in-hand, but the campus seems deserted for the most part. Reaching Neill Morris Hall, he extends his astral arms and banks playfully to the left; his arms are invisible—even to him—but he senses their presence; his soul-body is somehow substantial, though it seems weirdly undefined, like an amorphous energy field.

He can't name *all* the Baylor buildings of course, especially from above at night, but he does recognize the more notable edifices, like Pat Neff Hall directly ahead, with its silver, capitol-like dome glistening in the moonlight, and Old Main with its helm-roofed spires sporting weathercocks, and Burleson Hall with its towering cupola. After flitting like a phantom above and around these ornate, Victorian rooftops, he swoops low over Burleson Quadrangle, picking up speed, then he zigzags to the north buzzing Fountain Mall, whipping by the Fletcher Life Sciences Building before climbing and coming to a humming-bird halt over Moody Memorial Library, a massive, columned structure that looks down upon the gushing, foaming fountain which gives the mall its name.

On the way here, he flew over two more couples and a few solitary guys, plus another pedaling a bike—students? faculty? locals? or maybe visitors? In any case, they're all late-nighters: it has to be midnight. Sunday is giving way to Monday, to Labor Day. *If they could see me,* Bryan laughs to himself, *they woulda panicked and freaked, like I was an alien or something. I guess it's good that I'm invisible.* He laughs again. Except for the athletic fields, most of the campus now lies to the south of him, sloping gently upward to the water tower. Rooftops and streets and intersections, and all kinds of lamp-posts, and grassy expanses and walkways, and hundreds of stately trees. But the acres of pavement, the many parking lots, tarnish this striking night-time panorama.

Assuming a stretched-arm Superman pose, Bryan streaks north to the Brazos River then follows the waterway to Ferrell Field, the baseball complex (a long home run over the right-field fence would almost make it to the river). Descending onto the grayish, moonlit diamond, he floats over to his usual second-base position, and crouches, as though ready to field a grounder, a strange sensation with his feet some three feet off the ground, as best he can estimate in this strange, other-worldly dimension; he can't really tell where his feet are; he just knows they're below him. Next, he zips to home plate where he takes his batting stance, an equally weird sensation, but fun to try. Departing the baseball complex, he glides over the softball fields, over the parking lots, over Ferrell Center, the home of the Baylor basketball teams, and other indoor sports like volleyball. *This's where Mandy's gonna make her mark,* he says to himself, as he circles the domed arena.

Bryan recrosses the campus, flying a little higher than before. Arriving at the watermelon-shaped water tower, he hovers near it. He thinks about continuing on to the south, to check out Floyd Casey Field, the Baylor football stadium, which is located a mile or two southwest of the main campus. But before he can complete his decision, he notices a high-flying jet in the eastern sky, its contrail ivory-white in the moonlight. *That plane must be 30,000 feet up, and I reckon it's traveling 500 mph.* As he stares at the plane, he feels a sudden urge to chase it. *I wonder?*

Concentrating intently on the westbound aircraft, he rockets skyward, as he did in his near-death experience at Oiler Park, but this time he has control, and there's no tunnel; he's not dying. Within seconds he's zooming along next to the jet, the frigid cold and near-sonic speed having no effect on him. "What the hell! Goshdang it all!" he hollers out loud—at least, it's out loud in the astral dimension. "I didn't know I could do this." (Hearing is another mysterious aspect of his OBEs. He can hear himself speaking and some sounds about him, like the roar of the jet, though the engine noise seems somewhat muted, and he could hear the traffic on I-35 when he was hovering near Fletcher Hall plus the gurgling of the fountain at Fountain Mall, but *no one* can hear him.) He's within a few yards of the jumbo jet, as it cruises through the rarefied atmosphere, which smells like ice, though he doesn't feel cold. No doubt about it: this huge, bright-silver, moonlit craft is an American Airlines DC-10 Luxury Liner, as evidenced by its red and blue lettering, and the enormous tail sporting a dark-blue eagle with double A's underneath. "This's awesome and unbelievable! I love it! I love it!"

Moving even closer, he peeks inside one of the windows—some of the passengers are reading, some are talking, but many are snoozing on this red-eye flight. For a moment he considers going inside the plane—he feels confident he can pass through into the pressurized cabin—but he quickly dismisses the idea. He's never used his astral powers to violate anyone's private space, though he almost did last month at Mandy's house. Nonetheless, he does peer in a few other windows. *If they could see me out here,* he chuckles to himself, *that would cause one HELL of a stir.* He laughs so hard he feels faint, though he doubts he *can* faint during an OBE. He retreats from the fuselage, to a position near the wing tip, near the outboard ailerons. *I wonder where they're headed? California? Mexico? Maybe Hawaii?*

Looking down, he catches a glimpse of the moon reflecting on the Brazos River north of Waco, a quick silvery flash, as if God illuminated it just for him. The lights of the city itself, including the Baylor campus, cluster thickly, like nerve ganglia, about a lower, more southerly bend of the river—while farther out, away from the metropolitan area, a multitude of tiny lights dot the countryside in all directions. It's a magnificent sight, but it's now behind him receding to the east. A frightening possibility enters his mind. *What if someone woke me up right now? Could I get back in time, or would I die? O God, what a terrible thought, especially when Mandy and I just made up and set a wedding date. I reckon I've done enough joy-flying for one night.*

Like a solid-rocket booster separating from an orbit-bound space shuttle, he falls away from the jetliner in a graceful arc. Down, down, he goes, spiraling and spinning. He spreads his arms and legs like a skydiver, a wondrous sensation, though unlike a parachutist, he feels no rush of air about him. He sees the campus coming up, closer, closer, but he's not afraid. Closer, closer—then all at once he's back in his bed, waking up.

Turning on the light, he grabs his watch; it's 1:55 a.m.

THE SILVER CORD

CHAPTER THIRTEEN

FLETCHER HALL, UNIT 311
MONDAY, SEPTEMBER 2, 1991 — 6:54 AM

After getting up to take a leak, Bryan crawls back into bed, not to sleep but to sort his thoughts. Orange dabs of sunshine play on the wall above his dorm desk, above his computer. *I fell asleep about midnight, yet when I checked my watch, it was almost two a.m. So if that was really an OBE—and I feel certain it was—it took two hours. No, that's not necessarily true. It all depends on how long I slept before, and after, and there's no way to be sure. But in any case, it was a WILD trip.* He laughs aloud. *I still can't believe I chased a jumbo jet. I reckon I won't be talking about this to anyone around here.* He laughs again, so heartily it shakes the bed. *But why do I have these powers, this gift? Why did God choose me for this? And how is it possible? We're talking about the fundamental essence of the human individual, the whole flesh-mind mystery. Where is the "me" in me? What is the "me" in me? And it's somehow related to what happens at death? My ethereal body is connected to my flesh-and-blood body—by the silver cord, and the cord links my sleeping brain to my detached consciousness, or soul, or whatever it is that enables me to see and hear and talk to myself, though I can't interact with other people. But when we truly die, the cord severs, letting us go for good. This means we DO have an ongoing eternal essence. Death is NOT the end. But it makes sense, and not just because I learned it at church. There has to be life after death. We ALL yearn for it. It HAS to be. It's a super big thing, this longing for life. I've always felt it ... but especially since Gramps died.*

The AC fan kicks on, though it's hardly hot in here. It's a trifle chilly in fact. He should get up and adjust the thermostat, but he's too deep in thought: *We ALL hafta die, but I don't know anyone else who comes out of their body when they go to sleep. I've read about soul travel and other weird stuff, but none of it is quite like my episodes. My OBEs are uniquely mysterious, yet they seem super REAL to me, and way different from regular night-dreams, which are usually chaotic and disjointed. But the main difference is one of perspective: in my normal dreams I'm always IN my body on the ground, not up in the air. And yet my OBEs could still somehow be regular dreams I reckon? But either way, I'm gonna start writing this stuff down ... like a diary, like a journal. And I'll hafta keep it locked up, lest they lock ME up.* He chuckles boyishly. *I SURE doubt that the rest of the new freshmen around here have THIS kinda stuff on their mind.*

He laughs again then stretches and sits up. He can't help but focus on Mandy's picture on the desk, the handsome leather binder opened toward the bed. *But that OBE wasn't the biggest thing that happened in the past twenty-four hours—no way!* His heart flutters joyfully. *She said YES. It's true. It's really true—we're getting married in the spring, and I'm going home to see her in three weeks. O God, I can't wait.* He sighs gleefully then cuddles back into the bed, hugging a pillow, closing his eyes. The humming AC fan morphs into violin music, a sweet serenade. *Maybe I'll call today and surprise her? I'm not sure I can wait till I get my phone turned on. I'll use the pay-phone down the hall.* He gives a happy snuffle. *No, I should wait I reckon. I don't like pay-phones, even if I do have Dad's calling card* (his father gave him, before they left the farm yesterday, a Southwestern Bell card plus a Visa card for emergencies, $1500 limit). *Plus, there's gonna be a lot of noise in the hallway today.*

The Mandy-high subsides, as college concerns squirm to life in his belly. *I don't like being brand new. I still hafta meet my roommate, this Jordan guy, and I have no idea what he's gonna be like. And everything else is gonna be new as well ... like eating at the caf ... like meeting the other fellows on this floor ... like reporting to Coach Weaver tomorrow ... like a million th—*

RAP! RAP! Someone's knocking. *RAP! RAP!*

Startled, he rolls out of bed, pulls on his jeans, and pads quickly to the door, yawning as he goes. *Who can this be? It can't be my roommate, not yet? It's only ten after seven?*

"Sorry to knock this early," Marvin Latrobe twangs. "But I'm going over for breakfast, and I thought yuh might wanna come along."

"I-I, well ... yeah," Bryan replies, feeling a bit dumbfounded.

"You're Bryan, right? If my memory serves me?"

"Yep, that's me. And you're uh ... the RA, the proctor guy?"

"I am indeed. I'm in room 303, just a few doors down. I'm officially Marvin Charles Latrobe, but just call me Marv."

They shake hands, awkwardly, Bryan reaching down—he's a head taller than the pasty-faced proctor, who has beady gray eyes behind his Buddy Holly glasses. Scars from old acne pockmark his pallid complexion. *How can anybody in Texas be this pale?* And his hideous suit (no tie) doesn't help: it's a cheap polyester thing, grayish khaki, like the color of dirty dishwater.

"I don't hafta help Ms. Danley until eight-thirty," Marv pipes—his reedy voice has a scratchy, nasal character. "And there's hardly anyone on the floor as yet, and I wanna get acquainted with the troops anyway, so I—"

"Oh uh—come in. I'm sorry; my brain's still half-asleep."

"I *know* the feeling," Marvin replies, as he enters. He gives a nerdy little laugh. "You're a baseball player, right?"

"Yeah, I reckon that's my claim to fame. But playing at the college level is a lot different than high school, you know? It's the pitching mainly. The guys up here have major-league stuff."

"They do indeed," Marvin agrees—without a clue. "I read about that, how most universities are spending more, the athletic departments, to provide their teams with state-of-the-art gear and training equipment. I'm *sure* that's the case here at Baylor."

Bryan stifles a laugh. "The budgets *are* growing I reckon."

Marvin clears then gives a smug little grin. "I've never been much into sports, but I plan to follow our teams more this year. After all, I'll be supervising you *jocks* up here." His grin grows into a chuckle, equally smug. He chops the air clumsily. "And I have more time—now that I'm done with my DB&C Project."

"The what?"

"DB&C ... Digital Bible and Concordance. I spent the last two years developing a digital Bible, so anyone with a PC can read and research God's word from floppy disks—and it's gonna be on a CD. And they're available on campus ... over at Truett Seminary. That's where I worked on the project, even though I'm still an undergrad." He gestures more vigorously, his hands herking and jerking. "Now I'm talking *all* versions: King James, Scofield, Thompson, NIV ... and the concordance is *better* than Strong's—forgive me, but I've always been into computers big time, so when the Lord led me to change my major to theology, I decided to make the most of my gifts." He gives his geeky laugh. "I didn't wanna bury my talent ... like in Matthew 25."

"Well, have a seat," Bryan says, gesturing toward the sofa. "I just hafta visit the bathroom and grab a shirt."

I'm not sure I like this wimpy little geek, he tells himself as he brushes his teeth, *but it IS nice of him to ask me to come along, especially since this's my first time to eat at the cafeteria; it's better to be with someone when you're doing some new thing.* Fresh tugs of new-student apprehension reinforce this conclusion. Leaning close to the mirror, he fingers his shadowy chin then his sideburn where it meets his close-cropped hair (he just visited the barber shop Friday). *Maybe I should shave? Nawh, not now, not for breakfast. Plus, I don't wanna hold him up. I'll do it later.*

* * *

BILL DANIEL STUDENT CENTER CAFETERIA
MONDAY, SEPTEMBER 2, 1991 — 7:41 AM

Marvin Latrobe, having finished his cantaloupe, divides his bran muffin then carefully butters both halves. Across the table Bryan Howard sips his decaf between bites of scrambled eggs and bacon. They're seated on the far side of the cafeteria near the windows. The small, squarish, restaurant-style table offers more intimacy than the long, institutional kind back at Spindle High. But save for the tables, the cafeteria looks much as Bryan expected: beige linoleum, accordion room-dividers, drop-ceiling checkered with florescent panels, long curtains (saddle brown) covering the windows. It smells typical as well—breakfast aromas, the coffee and bacon dominating. But he can also detect the floor wax, which looks thick and shiny enough to ice skate on.

When they first came in here, Bryan got that weird, fish-out-of-the-pond feeling, but after he followed Marvin through the serving line, and the chubby cashier-lady accepted his temporary student-ID, he became more comfortable. Only a small portion of the tables are open, perhaps two dozen (the rest are stacked on top of each other in the rear), yet there are plenty of seats to handle the forty-odd students eating on this Labor Day morning (half girls, half guys, most dressed casually like Bryan, some more casual: jeans, shorts, jogger sweats, sneakers, beach clogs, sandals, oversized T-shirts—but *no* suits save for Marvin).

The girls look rather ordinary, some are fat and homely, but a few are stunningly attractive, so much so that Bryan couldn't help but notice their ruddy glances, as he exited the serving line with his tray, not to mention their tempting, grade-A bods. One gang of coeds, ten or so, has commandeered three of the tables, pushing then together to make one giant table. Females seem to socialize faster, gathering in herds and flocks. It bothers Bryan that he checked out the good-looking ones. It's most natural and reflexive, yet it still pricks his conscience, especially since he's totally married to Mandy, now and forever (the ceremony next May will simply confirm this reality). In any case, he's glad he's now facing the windows, with the other tables and serving area behind him.

The front part of this (Bill Daniel) building, the foyer, the lobby area, the main hallway, has more character, retaining the original 1930's art-deco style, as do the marble floors and high ceilings. When they passed through the lobby, Marvin pointed out a set of double doors, which lead to a chapel. The cafeteria is in the rear, at the end of the wide hallway, and on the way here you pass the student post office, a bookstore co-op, other shops, plus numerous campus-activity booths—all of which are closed today. A banner, similar to the one at Fletcher Hall but bigger, hangs in the foyer: WELCOME BAYLOR FRESHMEN!

Marv pushes a piece of his muffin into his mouth. After washing it down with a swig of grapefruit juice, he gives Bryan a curious look, his beady eyes narrowing, as if he's appraising the young freshman. "I don't mean to meddle," he says, "but d'yuh mind if I ask yuh something personal?" His reedy voice has taken on a pushy-quiet tone, like that of a salesman.

"Go ahead," Bryan responds guardedly, gesturing with a piece of toast. Until now, they've talked mainly about academics and dorm life and computers, plus a bit more about baseball. When Bryan revealed he had a Macintosh, Marvin gave a dissertation on the pros and cons of the Apple operating system as compared to DOS and MS-DOS. (He's obviously a hi-tech whiz, but he remains clueless when it comes to sports.)

Marvin sips more juice then commences, "Oh, I was just wondering if yuh go to church?"

Bryan had a hunch this was coming, and he resents this kind of evangelical prying. Nonetheless, he gives an honest reply: "Yeah, I go most Sundays, or I did back in Spindle. I'm a born-again Baptist—though I don't agree with *all* the Baptist ways."

"Fine, great, praise the Lord," Marv declares, giving a toothy grin; his teeth are crowded and crooked, and yellow with plaque. "I figured y'were already saved. But lemme give yuh one of our tracts anyway. I just *happened* to have one with me." Twisting around, he fishes inside his suit coat (draped on the back of the chair) and produces a little blue pamphlet with a picture of a church on it. He hands it to Bryan. Under the picture is the name: River Road Christian Assembly. Inside, there's a schedule of services, plus the Biblical plan of salvation.

Bryan slips it into his shirt pocket (the same pale-blue shirt he wore yesterday). "Thanks," he tells Marvin, perfunctorily.

The bespectacled RA lifts his chin, proudly. "River Road is the best little church around, and it's not so *little* anymore. It's growing, and reaching out—we're working *hard* for the Lord. I help the pastor, as part of my pre-seminary practicum program. Pastor Lawrence is his name, Greg Lawrence. He's a Baylor grad, Class of '79, and a real *reg*ular guy. He got his divinity degree here as well, from Truett—the George W. Truett Theological Seminary to be precise. I mentioned it before." Marv lifts his hands, palms up, as if exhorting a congregation to sing louder. "I'm already taking a lotta Truett classes, but I feel that it's equally vital to put our faith into practice. That's why I'm enthused about helping Pastor Greg. We're interdenominational, but we do have a lot of Baptists of course. There's a map on the back of the tract; it's only *three* minutes from the campus." He nods toward the windows; his dirty-blond, '50s-era crewcut stands straight and stiff like the bristles of a brush.

Bryan gives a dutiful smile but no reply. Perhaps he will check out Marvin's church, but he considers this read-a-tract method of evangelism to be cheap and superficial and trite—the God he's in touch with is *much* too glorious to be peddled in such a fashion. An impulse, a little tug of indignation, moves him to tell this dorky zealot about his near-death glimpse of Heaven, or even last-night's OBE, but he quickly kills the idea. *No way can I talk about it,* he declares to himself, as he scoops up the last of his scrambled eggs. *I don't know him well enough. And if he's such a gung-ho Christian, I'm sure his mind is closed on the subject, like tighter than a pickle jar. Besides, I'm ready to get outta here. I'd like to walk around by myself, and check out the campus at a leisurely, ground-level pace.* He chuckles under his breath. *Yeah, it would be a bit MUCH to tell him I was skirting the rooftops last night, like Casper the ghost.* A gust of laughter gathers in Bryan's bosom, but he stuffs toast into his mouth to suppress it—all but a few syllables, which he covers with a cough.

Marvin, working on the second half of his muffin, seems suddenly subdued, no longer chipper, as though realizing that young Mr. Howard has had enough of his company.

After killing his coffee, Bryan grabs his blue Spindle Tiger baseball cap and prepares to excuse himself, but before he can, he hears a voice behind him: "Mind if I join you two?"

"Well, if it isn't Dr. Agnostic," Marvin quips. "But do sit down. With all these freshmen running around, it's good to see another upperclassman. Besides, I haven't given up on yuh yet."

A smirky, curly-haired guy with a thin mustache unloads his breakfast (pancakes, sausage, OJ, coffee). Wearing threadbare cutoffs plus an Einstein T-shirt, he looks older (mid 20s maybe). The impish smirk and mustache, along with the "Dr. Agnostic" tag, give witness to a playful, unfettered spirit, as does the spark in his brown eyes— not to mention the shaggy visage of Albert Einstein. In any case, Bryan senses on first impression that this older student, despite his slim, less-than-athletic physique, is about as different from Marvin Latrobe as one could be.

After disposing of the empty tray, he extends his hand to Bryan: "Hi, I'm Chris Hansen."

* * *

That Chris Hansen guy is quite a character, Bryan reflects ten minutes later, as he exits the student center. *And he's pre-med like I'm gonna be.* He cuts diagonally across Verner Street to get to Fountain Mall, the long, grassy quadrangle in front of Moody Memorial Library. *Plus, he sure knows how to deal with Marvin: "Awh, stop your goddamn preaching. You can call me agnostic all you want. It just means I don't know for certain, which is true ... but neither do you, despite your claims."* Bryan snickers. *And he made the point in a funny, good-natured way, without getting all huffy and defensive like most folks do when they talk about religion—like Marvin did when he argued back.*

Ambling up the sidewalk on the west side of the mall, Bryan recalls how Marvin fussed and whined, countering with the standard line: assurance comes through faith, not sight; the Holy Spirit conveys certainty, not our senses. But Chris was hardly eager for a debate, as he devoured his pancakes (after saturating them with butter and syrup). Instead, he gave the nerdy RA a mirthful pat on the back and quipped, "C'mon now, Marv; how can you be so obsessed with this religious bullshit, when we have all these sweet young darlings to look at? I must say, gentlemen, there's nothing like fresh, just-out-of-high-school pussy to get my juices flowing in the morning. And I bet some of these babes are still virgins. Now I wouldn't mind giving them a few tutoring sessions." Chris laughed heartily, while Marvin fumed. That's when Bryan, laughing as well behind a cough, excused himself.

And Chris is older, even for a junior, Bryan thinks on, as he crosses the dew-covered grass to the other sidewalk. *I reckon he's at least twenty-three. I wonder why he's here this week? He can't be an RA— no way? And he's into lewd jesting, like Spanky, yet it comes out in a more polished way—he's not hillbilly crude like the rednecks back home. He has an educated tongue, but his accent is weird, like a monotone. He sounds like Mr. Denham—Denham's from Omaha, and he has the same flat, singsongy way of talking. Maybe Chris is from Nebraska too? I wonder why he came down here to Baylor? And he's got that bizarre shirt. I wonder if he wears it for a joke, or if he's actually into Einstein.*

Bryan pauses to check his watch: 8:07 a.m. *It's sorta weird. So many students have been here, like thousands and thousands, going back to the 1800s, and yet right now I'm practically by myself.* (Today's horde of incoming freshmen has yet to arrive.) He surveys the empty quad: McCurdy Hall, Constitution Hall, Peyton Hall, Strecker Mathematics Center; granite, sandstone, purple brick, marble steps, majestic facades. The academic halls, along with the colossal library looming at the north end, speak of tradition and history and steadfastness, as do the stately trees scattered here and there: towering pines, several oaks, a pair of magnolias, a cottonwood, plus a few others he doesn't recognize.

His left sneaker is loose. Using a nearby bench as a footstool, he reties it. *I gotta do some shopping later. There's a Safeway next to that Denny's we ate at yesterday, and a Wal-Mart too. It's Labor Day, but they should be open. I wanna get some cold cuts and peanut butter, and milk and bread, so I'll have some food in my room, and I need a laundry basket and uh, and uh ... Dr. Pepper, and I gotta gas up the truck. I'll make a list.*

The hazy sky, dirty blue but cloudless, promises another summerlike day. The breeze, just a hint of wind in his face, still has that muggy feel to it, like yesterday, though it smells sweet this morning, from the dewy grass. He resumes his stroll toward Moody Library, his thoughts returning to breakfast: *Chris's cocky and full of himself, and yet he seems to have a heart. He even likes Marvin, at least enough to sit with him—which is saying a lot.* Two guys pass by, headed the other way. Bryan gives them a little salute and a howdy, as they do much the same. A pair of fellow freshmen he surmises from their youthful looks and casual garb (shorts, baggy shirts). *And Chris is always smirking ... like he's got some fun thing on his mind, like tutoring those sweet, just-outta-high-school "darlings."* Bryan laughs. *Sheesh, I'm just a green kid compared to him. I wonder how many Baylor guys haven't done it yet. Not many I reckon? Chris probably considers me a country-boy hayseed, since I was mainly quiet. He isn't super macho by any means, but he has that slender-faced handsomeness that gals go for, especially with his mustache. I reckon he's done it a lot. It's obvious he didn't come here straight from high school.*

Reaching the fountain, Bryan leans against the waist-high wall. The foamy, gurgling water spurts out of the fountainhead before tumbling into a big round pool. The bubbles and wavelets glisten in the sun. There's nobody around, just a sparrow hopping about on the concrete wall. The little gray-brown bird flits down to the water, skimming, splashing, flapping, then it flies up and perches on a lamppost which overlooks the pool. "Y'got one heck of a big birdbath, little guy," Bryan quips up toward the sparrow, who's busy preening. After watching the bird, he walks around the fountain where he discovers a bronze plaque:

In memory of James Anthony Dinsmore, Class of '21, whose generous bequest made this beautiful fountain and mall possible.

Everything on this campus was built with money from dead grads. But they don't call this Dinsmore Mall? I reckon they decided that Fountain Mall sounds better? Pushing his baseball hat back, Bryan gives a frolicsome laugh. *It's hard to believe I was actually flying over this dadgum fountain last night, and then I was WAY up there, above the library, where those pigeons are. It makes me dizzy to even look up there now.* The towering columns and Grecian capitals, plus the scrolled pediments with their relief sculpture, give the massive edifice an imposing aura, as do the marble steps leading up to the main entrance. Moody Library could almost pass for the Supreme Court Building. At any rate, it would look very much at home in Washington, D.C.

Damn, it's scary to even think about being above the roof of this library, much less six miles up chasing a jumbo jet. Maybe it WAS just a dream? But it seemed SO real? Maybe my sleeping brain was just recalling all the campus buildings and images? No, it HAD to be real? But how can I know? He sighs. *Maybe if I follow, on the ground, the route I took around campus in my OBE last night, I might find convincing evidence, something I recognize, but only from flying over it—nawh, that's a long shot. I doubt I can prove it that way.*

He takes a deep breath, filling his lungs with the humid air. *But there IS one thing I do know for sure. I love Mandy Stevens with all my being ... with all the LIFE that's in me. And as long as I have her, I can deal with anything. I just wish she was here with me now looking at this fountain. But next year she will be—and we'll be MARRIED. O God, it's gonna be awesome.*

The fountain gushes and gurgles; Bryan exults—for a long blissful moment. But then a nibble of anxiety tempers his joy, a tiny gnawing in his stomach. *I know absolutely for sure that I love HER, but maybe SHE's having doubts? Maybe she's having second thoughts now that she's home? Maybe she told her mom, and Helen went ballistic, and Mandy caved? No, nawh. What am I thinking? That's horseshit. She loves me as much as I love her. I'm sure of it. I am.* He checks his watch: 8:18 a.m. *I'm thinking too much. I should go back and get the truck ... and do my errands. But maybe I'll go check out the river first.*

He follows a walkway around the library, with the intention of hoofing it down to the Brazos, but a bank of pay-phones stops him cold. *Yes, yes*—before he has time to reconsider, he punches in Mandy's number plus the key digits from his dad's phone card. Butterflies, quickened pulse—*I hope SHE answers, and not her mom.* He hears the recorded "thank you" then the clicking and the beeps, then it rings: once, twice.

"Hello," Mandy answers sleepily.

"I bet I woke you up, pretty lady?"

"Oh, Bryan babe, it's you—no, I'm already awake, least halfway anyhow. I was just lying here thinking about you." She gives a buoyant giggle, which instantly relieves him.

"So you're still in bed?"

"Yeah, it's Labor Day ... so we're all sleeping late. Y'must be calling from a pay-phone?"

"That's right, pretty lady."

"The one in the hallway at your dorm?"

"No, I took a walk after breakfast, and I found this row of phones by the big library. I'm a long way from Fletcher Hall, but it's peaceful here; it's early, and there's hardly anyone around."

"It's peaceful here too. Mama's still asleep, and Gretchen. I like it when the house is super quiet, and there's no hurry to do anything, and I can just linger here in bed. Plus, my friend is due this week, my monthly thing, so I'm feeling extra lazy—and bloated." She gives a husky chuckle. "It's almost cold in my room, with the AC going, but I'm nice and warm under the covers. I'm sure glad I don't hafta waitress this morning. I'm back to my school-year schedule at the diner, which is good."

He adores her cozy, yawny voice with its husky undertones; it doesn't matter what they're conversing about, as long as she loves him—and she does, she does. "Yeah, this long weekend is almost over, and I got a million things to do, starting tomorrow."

"But, babe, it's gonna be super exciting down there, going to college and all, while I'm still up here at boring old Spindle High. I'm super proud of you, but I'm *en*vious too—and what is this anyhow? I thought y'weren't gonna call till Wednesday?"

"I uh ... well, I couldn't wait."

"You couldn't *wait*?" she flirts. "To talk to little ole me, up here in little ole Spindle?" They tease and laugh, several rounds.

"I *still* can't believe it," he declares, sobering. "I mean uh ... what happened yesterday."

"Me neither—and it's hard to believe it was *just* yesterday."

"So you're glad about our plans?"

"Oh gosh, babe ... I can't stop thinking about it."

He considers asking about the purse again, but decides against it, lest he set off another session of playful bantering, which is fun, but the amorous mood is getting him high. His voice softens: "Oh, Mandy, all those weeks without you. It was the worst thing. I missed you like crazy."

"I missed you too, babe. I cried almost every night. But I'm so glad I uh ... and you—well, that *we* came to our senses." She gives a cozy laugh. "Now I'm missing you again, 'cause you're far away, but this's a much *happier* way of missing each other."

"You got that right ... but just think of it, precious—next year at this time, we'll both be down here at Baylor, and we'll be *in* the same bed, instead of just talking on the phone like this."

"Yeah," Mandy purrs. "It's gonna be heavenly, and totally neat, like, like—well, it's mega-awesome. I just wish May would hurry up and get here." She gives a giddy exhalation. "Oh, Bryan honey, I can't even wait for the twenty-seventh, when you're coming home for the weekend. I got my calendar circled; it's three weeks from Friday. We can go for a walk to the big oak tree, then I'm gonna hug and kiss you like you wouldn't believe."

Dizzy, stoned, reeling: Bryan is so Mandy-drunk his knees are about to buckle. "Gosh, it's gonna be *great*. Then maybe in October y'can come down here, for one of the football games. There's even a special dorm for weekend quests."

"I'll come down in the Firebird. It'll be a super-neat trip; I just hafta let Aunt Marge know ... like a couple weeks ahead."

"So y'think your mom will let you drive this far ... alone?"

"She better; she was driving all over when *she* was my age. So I sh—oh, here comes Toby. He likes to hop in bed with me in the morning. I leave my door open a crack so he can get in."

"Can't say as I blame him," Bryan declares, tongue in cheek.

"Now, Toby, get off my boobs," she commands playfully. "You're such a *spoiled* pussycat; yes you *are*."

"Sounds like he's got good male instincts."

"No kidding. But I don't think he has any: he's neutered."

"Good thing—otherwise, I'd be *jea*lous."

More laughter. "No, his big thing is getting his back rubbed."

They joke a bit more about Toby, then Mandy shifts: "We shouldn't talk *too* long, babe. This could get expensive?"

"It's no big deal. I have my dad's calling card thing. I'm gonna pay him back, but it's okay."

"Well, we gotta be careful about money, y'know?"

"Goshdang, Mandy," he kids, "you sound like my *mother*."

"Well, we both need to save, so we can get furniture and stuff. We can't have an apartment with *nothing* to sit on."

This sets off a session of happy banter about married life, then he goes silent.

"Are you still there, babe?"

"Yeah, I was just wondering if I should tell yuh something ... something amazing."

"What? Whaddeyuh? C'mon ... you got me curious."

"Well, it happened during the night; it was incredible, like—"

"You had one of those *float*ing trips?"

"I sure did. But it's better if I tell yuh about it in person."

"Ah c'mon, tell me now. Please, I wanna hear."

Relenting, he gives her a quick synopsis of his astral journey.

"Wow!" she reacts. "That is *so* cool and awesome ... like totally far out and unbelievable. I wish I could go on one of those floating dreams with you—my life is so dadgum dull and boring compared to yours. You actually chased a jet? It's *way* out, like a scientific breakthrough ... if y'could prove it somehow. In any case, y'should be on the news or something, or at least on one of those shows about strange unexplained things."

"Maybe someday, but right now I can't tell *any*body, or they'll be coming after me with tranquilizers and a strait jacket." Dimpling, he gives a boyish guffaw.

"Well, I wanna hear more. I'm sure you left out a *lot*?"

"I'll tell yuh the rest when we go down to the big oak tree—and don'tcha go and tell your mama."

"Don't worry. I'm not gonna do *that* again." After clearing her throat, she shifts to a new subject: "So didyuh meet your roommate, that Oklahoma jock?"

"Steve Jordan: no, not yet, but I did run into an interesting guy in the cafeteria this morning."

Bryan fills her in about Marvin and Chris Hansen, which gives rise to other questions and elaborations until it's after nine o'clock. He wishes he could talk with her *all* day, but it's time to go. Besides, some loud-mouthed greaser in a *Grateful Dead* T-shirt has invaded his privacy, picking up the last phone, the one farthest away from Bryan, and he notices a lot more pedestrian traffic—the campus is coming to life. Nonetheless, before saying good-bye, he poses a key question, which has been lurking in the back of his mind, "So, pretty lady, didyuh break the news to your mom, about *us,* about our plans?"

"Get outta here. I haven't even been home ten hours, and I been sleeping most of that—but I will. I'm gonna do it. I just hafta wait for the *right* time."

THE SILVER CORD

* * *

FLETCHER HALL PARKING LOT
MONDAY, SEPTEMBER 2, 1991 — 11:53 AM

As Bryan eases the old Chevy into the side lot, he finds many cars and much commotion: students going and coming, taking loads in, coming back for more, family members helping, others giving advice, others milling about among the varied collection of vehicles, most of which have their doors and hatches (or tailgates) open wide to disgorge cargo. *This place is sure hopping now,* he tells himself, as he wheels the pickup through the buzz of activity into the back lot. *And it happened fast; there was no crowd at all when I left to go shopping.* He parks as far away as he can get, but he doesn't get out. Pushing his hat back, he leans his elbow out the window and gazes wide-eyed at the grass and trees beyond the parking lot then at the puffy clouds drifting overhead. The familiar tarlike smell of the hot blacktop wafts in, along with the confused mix of voices and other noises blowing over, on the breeze, from the side lot—but he gives little heed: he's still high on Mandy. *I wish I could go call her again, and just talk and talk. Maybe it's a good thing she's NOT down here this year? I'd be worthless.* He laughs. *Hell, I'm worthless as it is.* While shopping, he could scarcely concentrate on his list, yet he managed to get back here with two sacks of groceries and one bag from Wal-Mart, plus the plastic laundry basket.

C'mon, Bryan, get your ass in gear, he kids himself. *Even when you're married, you're still gonna have work to do and practical things. So let's get this stuff up to your room before the milk spoils and the ice cream melts—and guess what? You forgot to get gas.* He considers going out again, but decides to wait till later, after the hubbub settles. Hopping out, he heads for the dorm; he uses the new laundry basket to carry his bags.

A few minutes later, after negotiating the crowded stairway, he arrives on the third floor and hustles, basket in hand, to the end of the hallway, where he find the door to 311 slightly ajar. He pushes it open with his foot.

"I reckon you're *Bryan* Howard," booms a bassy drawl.

"That's me," Bryan affirms, as he discovers a sandy-haired fellow of ursine proportions amid a rat-nest of boxes and luggage, and clothes and electronic gear. "And you're Steve I take it?"

"Yessir, that's right," Steve replies, while Bryan places the groceries and such on the breakfast table. "I'm Steve Jordan from Ardmore, Oklahoma. I've lived there since I was five, on 13th Street NW." He gives a friendly nod, his pudgy face breaking into a wide awh-shucks grin. Stepping around and over the clutter, he comes over and extends his mammoth, thick-fingered hand. "I'm mighty pleased to meetcha, dude."

Bryan, feeling suddenly like a half-pint runt, shakes it. "It's good to meet you too."

Jordan's thick, heavy-jowled neck seems wider than his head, as though he has no neck. "I'm barely nineteen," he drawls, "but I'm already goin' bald." He leans closer, so his roomie can see the circle of whitish scalp showing through at the crown—Bryan also catches a whiff of BO.

"Well, it happens," he replies, a bit amazed at this childlike candor, "but you're hardly bald." Steve actually has plenty of hair in the back and on the sides, a tousled haystack that looks as if it was dried in a wind tunnel—he needs a good trim in fact.

"So what'd yuh thank of that *Ranger* game last night?" Steve asks, as he returns to the living-room side of the sofa—which now resembles a garage sale.

"I uh ... well, I didn't have a ch—"

"Nolan can still throw bullets, and he's forty. Damn, he's past forty. I can bring some heat, but nuthin' like he does."

"So you're a pitcher?" Bryan asks.

"Yessir, I am," Steve responds, as he goes down on one knee to search inside a gym bag.

"Well, I'm an infielder ... second base my senior year. But it's my hitting that got me here."

Jordan, his head almost in the bag, shows no sign of hearing Bryan; he seems suddenly oblivious. Dressed in workout sweats, the big guy looks more like an offensive lineman than a baseball pitcher, especially with his less-than-firm paunch. Bryan can't help but note his huge belly, but his arms are powerfully muscular, like a pair of pythons, and his thighs look thicker than telephone poles, and just as solid. *I bet he weighs two-fifty at least, and he's taller too. Damn, I may be the smallest guy on the team, but I reckon I can outrun him.*

"Ah-ha," Steve declares, as he fishes a pair of fancy-looking sunglasses out of a zippered side-pouch. Hoisting himself to his feet, he slips on the wraparound glasses then grabs his cap from the back of the sofa, a red baseball cap with an A on it—he dons the hat as well, then adjusts both. He looks almost laughable, like a hulking head coach in an absurd football comedy. "I reckon I'll catch yuh later, dude. Jamal's waitin' for me down in my Bronco. I just came back up to get my shades, my Ray-Bans—oh, if I'm not back tonight, feel free to watch the game on *my* TV." He gestures toward a big wide-screen monitor resting on the carpet in front of the TV stand. Bryan's little Sony seems to have no screen at all by comparison.

"I doubt I'll have time," Bryan replies. "But I *will* move my set into my room, so you can put yours on the stand."

"Jamal's on the football squad," Jordan goes on, again paying little heed. "Third-string quarterback and special teams. He's also from Ardmore—that's howcum we're friends. He's a sophomore, but they red-shirted him last year, so he's playin' as a freshman, for eligibility."

Steve fingers the air rapidly, as though playing a hot riff on a piano. "We're goin' out to Sizzler for lunch, then later he has practice down at Floyd Casey, not in the stadium, but at the practice fields. And I'm gonna hang around the sidelines and watch. I know one of the assistant coaches, so I don't hafta stay up in the bleachers. Then afterward, I may hang with Jamal some more. He can get chicks into his dorm room at the Quad. Course, if Susie ever caught me foolin' around, she'd whack my dick off." He gives a bassy laugh. "She's my girlfriend, but she lives in Wichita Falls now—with her grandmother. So I reckon I'll be goin' up there a lot. But she *does* know I go out and see the strippers now and then. I just need to get rid of this damn gut." He pulls up his sweat shirt and pats his blimplike midriff. "I been eatin' too many Whoppers and drinkin' too much Pepsi." He laughs again, his belly shaking like Jell-O. "But I reckon the Lord loves me as I am—now Saturday's the first football game y'know, against Louisville. It's not a conference game, but I'm still lookin' forward to it—oh by the way, Bryan, d'yuh know if we have *baseball* practice tomorrow?"

"Well, we have a meeting at least," Bryan replies. "At two o'clock. But it's just gonna be freshmen this week."

"Jamal's smart for a colored guy. Some of 'em are dumb as shit. I reckon they cain't help it, and I don't discriminate or nuthin'. Sometimes I slip and use the N-word, but never around Jamal. He's got a C-plus average, which is better than half the jocks, and he runs like a jackrabbit. He rushed for 2003 yards and 24 touchdowns his last year in Ardmore, and he caught twelve TD passes. I played too, but now I'm gonna concentrate on pitchin' only. Gotta go, dude. Glad to meetcha—and don'tcha worry about this mess. I'm gonna take care of it." The big guy lumbers out the door, without closing it.

Gosh damn, Bryan chuckles, as he puts the groceries away. *He's built like a grizzly, yet he comes across like a dadgum teddy bear. But I reckon I'll hafta set some housekeeping rules—and I doubt we're gonna get into many deep intellectual discussions.*

* * *

BILL DANIEL STUDENT CENTER CAFETERIA
MONDAY, SEPTEMBER 2, 1991 — 5:47 PM

Exiting the serving line, Bryan Howard feels a bit uneasy, as he encounters a chattering array of unfamiliar faces: girls, guys, his collegiate peers—maybe two hundred? Spotting a table in the back, he weaves through the chatter and clitterclatter, through the mixed aromas of hot food, and warm bodies—perspiry flesh mixed with perfumed fragrances. "Hey, Bryan, over here!" sounds a flat non-Texas voice—it's Chris Hansen.

"This place is packed compared to this morning," Bryan remarks upon arriving at Chris's table.

"It is indeed," Chris agrees, smirking under his mustache (the impish smirk tempers his rakish handsomeness, while the Errol Flynn mustache enhances it, as does his curly hair which spills over his collar). "A horde of freshmen, and they're all agitated and excited like a swarm of bees in a new hive. I'm almost done, but you're welcome to join me."

"Thanks," Bryan says, as he sits down. "I'm surprised you recognized me, in this crowd."

"Oh, I never forget a face, especially a distinguished one. It's not every day I have breakfast with a super-jock baseball stud, who's also a scholar." Chris snickers, his brown eyes gleaming.

Bryan blushes—his cheeks feel warm. "Well, I reckon that's debatable." He gives a bashful, farmboy laugh. "Besides, what makes you think—I mean, I hardly said ten words this morning?"

"Well, that was enough ... for an astute observer of humanity such as myself." Amid more smirks and snickers, Chris takes a bite of his dessert, some kind of pie. Finally, he elaborates, his voice chewy thick: "I realized right off that you were hot shit, and Marvin confirmed it after you left, filling me in on a few key facts ... like you graduated third in your class, and scored in the top SAT percentile, and you led your conference in hitting for three straight years, and the Houston Astros are after you."

Bryan dimples, his blush deepening. "Gosh, I don't recall telling Marvin all *that*." Cutting his baked ham, he directs his attention self-consciously to his plate. He tries to be cool, to appear poised and laid-back, but his boyish grin won't go away. He can't help but react to Chris's ego-boosting appraisal, especially since he likes, and looks up to, this puckish, free-spirited junior. He knew it this morning, and more so now.

"Marv saw your folder," Chris explains, gesturing with a forkful of pie—yellow and lumpy, looks like banana cream. "He gets the full skinny on you guys, since he's a proctor. Now that's a job I'd never want." He chuckles then eats the bite of pie. "But your record is astounding, to say the least." He sips his coffee.

"But I'm just from a little country town. There's not much competition. It's not like I—"

"Oh, please, please," Chris interrupts, toasting the air with his coffee mug—his eyes flash with cocky audacity. "Don't give me that self-effacing, pseudo-Christian humility. You're good; you're gifted; you're smart as hell—you've got what it takes to plow new ground. You'll be going places that ordinary guys can't go. It's reality damn it—so you don't have to apologize for it."

Bryan's ego swells. He sips his iced tea. "Well, I reckon—"

"And it sure doesn't hurt that you've got that good-looking, all-American, country-boy charm, not to mention the physique of a Greek god. You're a baseball star, but you could've excelled in football, basketball, any sport." Chris pauses to sip his coffee, relaxing as he does. "In any case, slugger, you certainly stand out compared to the herd—mind if I call you 'slugger'?"

"No problem. It's sorta like a nickname anyhow. My friend Spanky calls me that back home, plus a few other baseball guys."

"I like it; it suits you. It means you go for the fences, and beyond the fences. And I'm not just talking about home runs. I sense that you have more to offer than super-jock heroics."

"I'd sure like to think so," Bryan responds, as he stabs then eats a chunk of ham then loads his fork with scalloped potatoes, pushing them on with his crescent roll. His ego is still revving, but he's also a bit bewildered: *Gosh, I just met this guy ... yet he talks like he's known me since grade school.* Bryan drinks some tea then goes for more potatoes. On the way to his mouth he loses some, a few cheesy fragments tumbling onto his lap, onto his jeans. *Damn, I'm hardly eating like an all-American—and now I'm gonna have a greasy spot on these Levi's, and I just put them on fresh ... when I got outta the shower.*

Chris has likewise altered his attire since breakfast, a more noticeable change, having replaced the Einstein T-shirt with a beige golf shirt. He pushes his coffee mug toward Bryan. "Most guys who come to Baylor are just after credits and connections, and trying to get laid ... and they haven't had a fucking original thought since the ninth grade"—Steve Jordan flashes through Bryan's mind—"and the rest are Marvinish and wonkish, all brain and no dick, if you know what I mean? Not that I care to spend a lot of time analyzing the goddamn male students." He frowns, then snickers and smirks, his thin mustache curving and twisting like a gull in flight. "How could I ... with all these sweet young babes to check out? Pussy, pussy; my fucking God— it's all around us. But I won't get going on that again." He laughs some more, as does Bryan despite a Mandy-tug on his conscience. Chris returns to his dessert. "Besides, there's little chance of getting their frilly Baptist panties down anytime soon. Maybe in the winter when things get boring? Now the upper-class gals are easier, not *easy* mind you, but *eas*ier, though most of them are in relationships of one form or another, except the dog-uglies." He gives a playful sigh. "In any case, this banana-cream pie will have to suffice tonight, and it's not too bad by the way." He downs the last two bites then picks up the remaining crust with his fingers. "This student-center caf is hardly famous for great desserts, but they do okay on their pies, except for apple, which always comes out too bland; they can't get that homemade spiciness."

"Yeah, good cooking *is* a plus ... but I'm not super picky when it comes to food."

"Good thing," Chris laughs, gesturing with the pie crust. "No ... the food's actually okay here, not great but adequate. I live off-campus, but I have a meal card. I usually ride my bike over, but I walk sometimes, like today." He pops the crust into his mouth then sips some coffee. "Now if I'm hungry for topnotch cuisine, I go out to a restaurant, and I do know some good ones."

Bryan finishes his peas, then his potatoes. "So why're you here *this* week? I thought the upper classes were—"

"Oh, I'm doing data management for Dr. Richardson over at the neuroscience lab. I work part-time for him, and we were into this big project during summer session which ended three weeks ago, and I just decided to hang around. Plus, I really don't have any better place to go." This reply gives rise to other questions, but Bryan decides not to pry, not now at least.

A busboy, pushing a wheeled cart, rattles up to the adjacent table. Unlike the caf at Spindle High, you don't have to dump your tray before leaving—as Bryan found out this morning, from Marvin, who went on to explain that the busboys (and busgirls) are mainly students, working to defray their college expenses.

"Before I go, slugger, I have a question for you," Chris announces, after killing off the dregs of his java.

"What's that?" Bryan asks, recalling the similar exchange with Marvin at breakfast. *But no way is Chris gonna WITNESS to me,* he chuckles to himself, downplaying any similarity.

The puckish junior leans back in his chair, interlacing his hands behind his neck. He gives Bryan a pensive look, his rakish features going sober—he almost seems a different person without his patented smirk. Yet he says nothing.

"So what's the question?" Bryan prods after a long moment.

A hint of levity flits about Chris's mouth suggesting that the poker face is forced. "What's your thing?" he asks finally. "Your passion? I mean ... what rings your bell?"

"Well, uh ... I reckon I'm into neuroscience, like you. I'm pre-med, and I uh ... well—"

"C'mon, I want number one," Chris barks, feigning sternness. "Any goddamn nerd with a computer can do neuroscience." The smirk quickly returns, then lurches into a teasing grin. "You have a girl back home, don't you?"

Bryan dimples. "Yeah, I reckon I do."

Chris leans back further, until the front legs of his chair are off the ground. "I figured as much, the way you blush and squirm when I talk about pussy and panties." He laughs, a few smirky syllables. "But I actually envy you—so what's her name?"

"Mandy ... Mandy Stevens."

Bryan, sensing a kindred warmth in Chris despite the smirky jesting, goes on for a few minutes about Mandy, in a general but fervent manner—emphasizing the hold she has on his heart, without divulging the recent roller-coaster developments.

Chris leans forward, placing his elbows on the table. "Well, slugger, I guess you got it bad ... but I know where you're coming from." He gives Bryan a fond, buddylike punch on the shoulder, his brown eyes earnest. "I may crack jokes about girls and sex and everything, but I recognize the difference between horny bravado and true love, and you surely have the latter."

Bryan nods but doesn't reply. He senses the bond between them growing stronger, not simply because of the friendly jab, or the accolades before—he felt it this morning even, when Chris was wisecracking the whole time. There's more to it, like some kind of kinship, soul-mate thing. And the fact Chris calls him "slugger," like Spanky does, seems to fit right in.

"And I didn't mean to put down your neuroscience goals," Chris says, as he gets up. "In fact, brain medicine is what my whole life is about. I'd like to hear your take on it sometime. And I can share some valuable scuttlebutt about the pre-med program." The impish smirk returns to Chris's mouth—he looks normal again. "But I'd also like to hear more about Mandy—and I've got some love stories of my own, and a few *other* kinds of stories." He laughs and gives an open-handed gesture.

Departing the table, Chris heads out of the cafeteria, but then he suddenly reverses course and comes back. "As a matter of fact," he says to Bryan. "Why don't you come over to my place Wednesday evening, say about six o'clock, or whenever you get back from baseball practice."

"Uh ... yeah, yes—that'll be great," Bryan replies.

"We can whip up some hot dogs and then have a good long talk— here's my address and phone number." Chris jots the info on a napkin. "And I'll draw you a quick map too."

THE SILVER CORD

CHAPTER FOURTEEN

SPINDLE, TEXAS - COLBY DRIVE
TUESDAY, SEPTEMBER 3, 1991 — 2:55 PM

Mandy, home from school, hustles up the shady back steps then into the kitchen. Helen Stevens, a concerned look on her pixie face, meets her daughter at the door. "Hi, Mama," Mandy greets, despite the sudden downdraft in her stomach. She tries to act nonchalant as she drops her book-pack and car keys on the counter, grabs a bag of Friskies, and fills Toby's dish, yet she knows that something is up. At the sound of the Friskies, Toby scurries in from the living room, but after a few bites, he bangs out the cat door, as if he too realizes that *something* is up.

"So let's have it, Amanda," Helen quickly confirms, her hands on her hips, her eyebrows converging sternly.

Mandy gazes out into the backyard—to escape her mom's hazel-eyed frown. A sense of injustice burns the back of her throat. "Whaddeyuh talking about?"

"You know *very* well, young lady. I overhead you talking to Bryan on the phone yesterday morning. I didn't bring it up till now, because I needed to *pray* about it."

* * *

BAYLOR UNIVERSITY - FERRELL FIELD
TUESDAY, SEPTEMBER 3, 1991 — 4:00 PM

Coach Weaver delivers a batting-practice fastball, and Bryan jacks it out of the park, a *towering* drive that clears the 385-foot sign in left-center field. It seemed to kiss the clouds, the cauliflower cumulus which decorate the afternoon sky. "Not too shabby," the lanky, gray-haired mentor barks from the mound, "for a first-day, *pow*derpuff pitch."

Weaver, who played briefly (backup catcher) for the White Sox in the early '60s, came to Baylor three years ago but has yet to turn the program around. The Bears finished in typical fashion last season, next-to-last in the Southwest Conference. But this year's freshmen crop gives reason for optimism. He's recruited several high-school standouts, including Bryan Howard.

"So can he actually use that stick?" asks a Negro voice—it's Elmo McKinney, the hitting coach, who's just arrived at the batting cage. He and Bryan talked earlier, at the team meeting.

"He's all over my *straight* stuff," Weaver replies, chuckling, "but he hasn't seen my junk yet." The head coach steps off, going behind the mound. Bryan, as he waits, can't help but grin at Coach McKinney, a stoutly built, gruff-voiced, seventy-some-thing Baylor fixture, who could pass for Willy Mays. He never made it to the Majors, though he did play in the Negro leagues, hitting .350-plus for the Kansas City Monarchs. (Bryan learned all this from Steve Jordan.) Coach Weaver returns to the rubber. "Okay, kid ... let's see whatcha can do with this one."

Bryan instantly picks up the spin and break, but he tries to pull the pitch anyway, hitting it into the dirt—the ball ricochets, *KA-RRRRING,* off the frame of the cage. The coach delivers another deuce: same result. "C'mon, Howard! My goddam grand-daughter can stay on a bender better than that. And come next week, you'll have more to deal with than *my* broken-down arm."

I sure looked sick on those two, the Spindle superstar reacts to himself, as he steps out and wipes his sweaty palms on the legs of his practice uniform.

"Howard, try closin' your stance a mite," Coach McKinney suggests, smiling broadly. "And yuh gotta go *with* the pitch; if yuh try to pull ever'thang, y'just gonna tie yourself in knots."

Stepping back in, Bryan moves his left foot a little closer to the plate. He hopes to get another curve, and he does. Keeping his weight back, he stays *on* the pitch and hits a rope to the warning track in right center where it scatters a foursome of pitchers doing windsprints (some two-dozen freshmen, including walk-ons, showed up today). "That's more like it, kid," Weaver growls from the mound. He comes with a few more spinners, and Bryan lines each for a base hit, one to right, one to center.

"See, there ain't nuthin' to it," McKinney adds, "as long as y'get the barrel through a*head* of your body-turn. But if your weight's done shifted, you ain't gonna hit nuthin' but bleeders."

When Bryan finally leaves the cage, he feels a rush of satisfaction along with a profound sense of *relief.* Except for a brief session with his dad (at the farm the day before he left), he hasn't swung a bat since he got hurt in May. Yet his skill with the lumber seems as good as ever. His brain function has to be A-OK, plus his eyesight—his vision has *indeed* returned to normal.

* * *

MISTY HOLLOW ROAD (NORTH OF SPINDLE)
TUESDAY, SEPTEMBER 3, 1991 — 4:36 PM

A rumble of thunder joins the crunch of sneakers on dirt, as Mandy Stevens and Wendy Lewis jog up the last upslope of their three-mile run, a short, gentle hill but taxing nevertheless on this sultry afternoon. The approaching storm has chased the sun, offering some relief, as does the freshening pine-scented breeze. Reaching the crest, Mandy spots the distant Firebird, some six hundred yards ahead (to the south), down by the wooden bridge. *Goshdang it to hell!* she cries to herself, as she picks up the pace, the sandy clay giving way to peastone beneath her. *My mouth's in the gutter, but Mama makes me so fucking mad, I can't help but cuss.* Wendy tries to keep up but soon falls behind.

After the mother-daughter showdown in the kitchen, Mandy fled tearfully to her room but didn't stay there long. Putting on her running garb, she stormed out of the house, picked up Wen, and came here to Misty Hollow Road. They hadn't planned to work out today (they were just here yesterday), but Mandy had to do something with the fire in her belly.

Faster, faster, she covers the last fifty yards like a fast break on the basketball court. Reaching the red Pontiac, she whips off her Tiger cap then leans gasping against the hood, her lungs sucking great drafts of air, which now smells mucky-damp like the creekbed under the bridge. Her sweaty bangs cling to her forehead. She normally doesn't perspire profusely, but today's extreme exertion has left her downright wet, especially her T-shirt and jock-bra.

"My God, Mandy," Wendy gasps, as she staggers to a halt—she almost collapses but manages to balance herself against the driver-side door. "This isn't the damn Olympics, y'know?" Her cheeks pulse pale, then purple, then pale. "And basketball doesn't start for a bleeping month." She gives a wheezy laugh. "But I reckon my fat ass'll be looking good if I keep running with *you*. Oh gosh, I'm wicked sick. I may hafta barf." She leans over, hands-on-knees, but doesn't throw up. Instead, she goes around to the passenger-side window where she reaches inside for a towel. She wipes the sweat from her elfin, odd-nosed face. Lightning flashes followed by a peal of thunder.

"Looks like we made it back just in time," Mandy observes, as they get into the car. The first drops of rain have arrived, a fitful patter on the roof. "But I like to run when it's storming out, especially when I'm *pissed* off—I can't believe how negative Mama is when it comes to Bryan. She used to like him ... until last month."

Wendy sheds her terrycloth headband. "Oh, I'm sure she likes *him* as much as ever. It's *you* that bothers her. She doesn't like *you* liking him, and loving him, and being so serious. That's how mother's *are*. They're wicked protective and possessive."

"You got *that* right."

"Like when Jerry and I were going together. Mom was *al*ways on my case, and yet she's hardly religious at all compared to *your* mother." Wendy finger-fluffs her hair; she looks older without the braces, and her voice no longer has that wet, gravelly hiss.

Mandy gazes at the huge raindrops, as they dapple the dusty windshield. "Mama preaches a lot, and quotes her favorite verses. Yet I reckon it *is* more of mother thing."

"But she *doesn't* know about next May? I think yuh said that on the way here, but y'were in such a wicked huff, I couldn't be sure what the hell y'were babbling about."

They laugh—Mandy's feeling better. "Yeah, I reckon I was in quite a lather when I picked you up." She inserts the key, but doesn't start the Firebird. The rain has ceased for the moment, yet the sky continues to get darker. "But no, I don't think my mom even suspects that we've set a date—no way. If she did, she woulda been out here chasing me, considering the *mood* she's in." Mandy laughs louder, a snuffly guffaw. "I was planning to tell her soon, even tonight, but I sure can't do it when she's in my face with her holier-than-thou bullshit."

"But you said she overheard you guys on the phone?"

"She did, but she just caught enough to figure out that we'd patched things up ... despite all her counsel. That's what got her ticked." Mandy flicks the dangling keys. "She saw it as so *godly* and *wise* when we broke it off last month—y'know, when we decided to put things on hold and just be friends?"

Wendy twirls the headband on her finger. "God ... if she's *this* concerned about you guys going together, how the heck canyuh tell her you're getting married in May?" She rolls her brown eyes, giving a whispery whistle. "And you'll still be *sev*enteen?"

"No *kid*ding. I been asking the same question since Sunday."

"Well, like I been saying all year, kiddo—Bryan's the *best* thing that's ever happened to yuh. So I wouldn't back down on this, no matter what, even if she never gives her okay, even if you *never* tell her, even if you guys hafta run off and *elope*."

Mandy snickers. "I doubt it'll come to that, since I'll be eighteen in July."

"In any case, it's *your* life ... not hers."

A burst of righteous indignation chases Mandy's levity. "You goshdang right it is!" She slaps the dashboard. "And I *am* going through with this, whether I have her approval or not."

A blinding flash illuminates the sky accompanied by a big clap of thunder—as if God endorses her bold assertion. The rain returns, harder and steadier, a drumming downpour.

* * *

BAYLOR UNIVERSITY - FERRELL FIELD
TUESDAY, SEPTEMBER 3, 1991 — 5:14 PM

"Well, whaddeyuh thank, dude?" Steve Jordan asks Bryan, as they exit the clubhouse, heading for the old Chevy pickup.

"About what?" Bryan replies.

"Now I wouldn't be askin' just anybody on the team or nuthin', but since we're gonna be roomies an' all, I reckon we can level with each other."

"Yeah, I reckon we can—go ahead."

"D'yuh see *me* in the startin' rotation come next spring?" His tubalike voice rises an octave.

THE SILVER CORD

"Gosh, Steve, it's *on*ly the first day of fall practice, and you pitchers won't be throwing for real until next week."

"I know, but I did give yuh a few fired-up tosses, while we were waitin' for practice to start, 'fore the coaches came out?"

"Oh yeah—well, what I saw of your stuff looks A-OK."

"Y'thank so?"

"I do indeed," Bryan assures him, as they hop into the truck. "Besides, Coach Weaver wouldn't have given you a scholarship if he didn't plan on using yuh."

"But that was before I put on thirty extra pounds," Jordan counters fretfully. "I reckon I got the biggest gut on the team—and the smallest *dick*. Goshdang it all, I was almost embarrassed to go into the shower room with the other guys. It's actually *normal* in size, but my fat belly hides it."

Bryan, dimpling, gives him a playful jab on his pythonlike arm. "Don't be such a worry wart. You're *worse* than an old lady. If yuh throw heat, with reasonable control, then you'll do fine."

Steve's massive bulk dominates the cab, as does his flowery scent, which has obscured for now the greasy farm-smell of the truck. He's more fragrant than a honeysuckle bush, not from cologne but bath-talc; he powdered himself before putting on his street clothes. As he applied it, he explained with a laugh, "I get heat rash after sweatin' hard, so I gotta use lotsa this stuff, even though it makes me smell like a dadgum whorehouse."

Bryan starts the Chevy. "Besides, you're gonna be trimming down that gut of yours, now that you're working out every day. And lots of great pitchers have a tendency to get overweight—like Roger Clemens. You think *he's* ashamed to show his body?"

"Nope, I reckon not," Steve says, as he dons his wraparound sunglasses. "And come to thank of it, I *am* built like Roger." Giving a pudgy smirk, he pats his midriff then lifts his chin, extending his jowly neck until the excess flesh unfolds. "Now Roger's listed at two-twenty, but he's at least two-forty I betcha, and that's only *fifteen* less than me, and he wasn't exactly skinny back durin' his college days here in Texas, and yet he still pitched the Longhorns to the national title in '83."

While Jordan goes on about the Red Sox hurler, Bryan eases the Chevy out of the parking lot. After a few quick turns, they head south on Rigby Avenue, which skirts around the east side of the campus. It's only a five-minute drive to the dorm, but it's a bit far to walk, so they plan to take turns chauffeuring. For that matter, there'll be a caravan of freshmen baseballers commuting from Fletcher Hall to the Ferrell complex each afternoon.

Steve seems contented, absorbed—no longer fretful—as he continues to elaborate on Clemens, reciting stats from his best years with Boston then giving a detailed, batter-by-batter replay of the Rocket's record 20-strikeout game against Seattle in '86. He's a genius when it comes to baseball trivia, or football, or most any sport. As he gabs on obliviously, he paws the air with his mammoth hands, playing that imaginary piano like he does.

Bryan can't help but like this big teddy bear of a guy, but he has to tune him out, for sanity's sake. *Damn, I almost feel like his big brother,* he chuckles to himself, *or even his mother. But it's sure better than rooming with some pompous, show-off asshole, like Randy across the hall—he's a good outfielder with a mean stick, but he's obnoxious as hell. And yet, his roommate, Pedro, seems quiet and laid-back—I feel sorry for him—and he's awesome at shortstop. All the guys are awesome, yet I feel good about my chances. And I also got a lot of campus bullshit done today. I just wish Mandy was here to share all this with me. I hope my telephone's working, so I can call her tonight. That phone-company gal said it would be switched on today.*

Reaching Spangler, they hang a right, heading back into the older part of the campus. Steve is still gabbing and gesturing, but his bassy drawl has taken on a remote quality, as if it's coming over the radio. The street is rather empty, just a few cars and bicycles. There was more traffic earlier, but nothing like they'll be facing next week. Bryan likes this shadowy, tree-lined avenue; it looks very homey and residential, almost Spindle-like if you ignore the college buildings and parking lots. He thinks back to Sunday afternoon, to what his father told him: "Son, you're gonna do good here. I just *know* you are."

Yes, yes, nothing but yes, Bryan exults silently. *It's like all the questions and fears I had during the summer have been resolved—in the BEST way possible.*

"I got a powerful hankerin' for a Whopper," Steve drawls a minute later, as they exit the truck at Fletcher Hall. "I thank I'll hop in my Bronco and run over to Burger King. And I'll fetch a few extras, to snack on durin' the Ranger game, plus some fries—and you'll be welcome to have one, dude, if you're gonna watch. They're playin' the Orioles, in Baltimore, so it starts early."

Bryan grabs his jock bag out of the back. "I may watch part of it, but I'm going to the caf for supper. I like Whoppers and fries as much as anybody, but it's better to have a balanced meal. Besides, why spend money when we can eat free at the caf?"

"You're right, Bryan. I reckon I *should* have some damn veggies and whatnot. I gotta watch *my* budget too ... plus my gut. But tomorrow night I'm goin' out with Jamal. I thank I toldjuh? And then on Saturday after the football game, I'm goin' up to Wichita Falls to see Susie. She can't come down, 'cuz she has to work durin' the day, at Safeway."

"Sounds like a plan—but y'still hafta get that mess cleaned up."

"Yessir, I know. I'm gonna do it tonight in fact ... between innin's, while the commercials are on, and I got earphones too ... in case yuh hafta study or anythang." Bryan can't help but laugh.

THE SILVER CORD

* * *

Mandy Stevens, already dressed for bed (shorty pajamas plus robe) slouches over the study desk in her bedroom, doing her homework. Gretchen is downstairs watching TV, while their mom's at the church for a business meeting. Mandy has done the assigned reading in her physics text, but she now has to do the application problems. She reads, from a worksheet, the first one:

> A car moving with constant acceleration covers the distance between two points 180 feet apart in 6 sec. Its speed as it passes the second point is 45 ft/sec. (a) What is its speed at the first point? its acceleration? (b) At what prior distance from the first point was the car at rest?

Who gives a flying goshdang? she murmurs to herself. *This course sucks, and it's only the second week. How did I ever end up in Advanced Physics 412?* She swivels the office-style chair to the left, to the right, then she leans back and listens to the *shhhh* of the rain on the roof. She twirls her pencil then rubs her lower lip with the eraser. *Mr. Denham gets so excited about this stuff. He talks about Newton's Laws of Motion the same way Pastor Ron talks about winning souls. I can see getting psyched if you're gonna work for NASA or something, but I'm gonna be teaching grade school—least that's what I wrote down at my guidance-counselor interview last week. Truth is, I'm not sure about anything. I just wanna be out of high school and married to Bryan, so we can be together and have our own place, so we can make love, and make love.* She titters. *Now that's the kind of motion I wanna major in.* She drums the pencil on the desk, a little bluesy riff: tat-tat, tat-tat, rat-a-tat-tat-tat.

Proceeding nonetheless with the physics problem, she grabs the calculator from her book pack then lifts the top of the desk and pulls out a legal pad (she's had this old-fashioned school-desk since the fourth grade; her mom got it for her back in Arkansas; but she bought the swivel office-chair herself, at a garage sale down the street). She draws a rough diagram on the yellow pad. *Here are the two points, and this can be the car.* She draws a tiny rectangle with an arrow (vector) on it. *Now let's pick a formula.* She flips through her physics book, back and forth through the first chapter. Then she returns to the worksheet, reading the problem again, and again, but each word seems unbearably heavy, like lifting cinder blocks with her mind.

Giving a weary snort, she closes the textbook. *I can't do this now. My mind's all fogged up, after fighting with Mama, and running with*

225

Wendy. Hopping up, she pads over and turns off the AC; it's chilly in here. She gazes out the window at the hooded streetlamp, at the raindrops falling through the cone of light, down, down, straight down—no wind. *I can finish my homework in the morning. I'll get up early—oh, how I WISH I was outta Spindle High. It's getting SO old and boring. I do look forward to basketball, and softball, but it won't be the same, with Bryan gone. Plus, I gotta work for Aunt Marge tomorrow night. I'm tired of the diner, and homework, and dadgum chores, and going to church—and PUTTING up with Mama.*

Her mother's tirade comes back to her, from this afternoon: "Amanda Fay, you still have an *entire* year of high school ahead of yuh, and yet you act like you're *already* off at college. You used to be so diligent and caring, but over the summer you've become defiant and selfish. Well, I've had enough of it. And now you're all gaga over Bryan again. Y'just can't let go, can yuh? I declare—you're *more* like your daddy every day. It may seem exciting to disregard my counsel, but you're gonna learn, young lady; you're gonna *learn.* And your attitude toward church—it grieves me to no end. You skip every other service, and of course, you didn't go at all on Sunday, 'cause you were *gone* to Waco—Waco, Waco, Waco. You talk about it like it's paradise. Well, it's *not.* Life is not some fairy tale. This world is full of sin and suffering, and God has called us to serve and sacrifice ... to win the lost ... and to love and help people like Jesus did."

I am selfish, Mandy admits silently, as though addressing the streetlight. *But what can I do? I mean, I can pretend to lay down my life for others, and for God—I've tried it plenty—but what's the point, if it's not real? Besides, Mama's not as holy as she pretends to be. She's more like me than she lets on.*

At supper they achieved a truce, yet Mandy hasn't divulged anything further about Bryan. As far as Helen knows, they're simply going together again, and even that is somewhat limited, as Mandy pointed out so eloquently (though less than honestly) between bites of pork cutlet, since they'll only be seeing each other once a month, if that.

A huge truck, the eighteen-wheeler kind (but without any trailer), trundles by, huffing diesel smoke from its twin stacks; it's Mr. Gaylord, who lives a few houses away: he drives all over the country. The exhaust lingers in loose, rain-pierced wisps under the streetlamp. *I wish I could level with Mama, but how can I? If I tell her the WHOLE truth, she's gonna—well, I don't even wanna think about it. Like I'm really gonna catch her in some great mood, when she'll give her okay to me and Bryan getting hitched in May. No way in hell—she's gonna freak. O God, this whole situation is like a bomb ticking.*

She returns to her desk, plunking down in the chair. *And Mama's right about some things, like me being less responsible. I never loved doing homework, but I always DID IT, all of it the night before. And I never complained about the diner, until this year—I was proud to have a job—and I never missed church hardly. Maybe I AM carried away with fairy-tale notions about Waco?* Tears well up amid pangs of guilt. *Maybe I shouldn't have been so quick to say yes to Bryan on Sunday?*

Fighting back the need to cry, Mandy reopens her physics book, and determinedly scans the various equations, but her thoughts remain captive to her conscience: *Maybe I should tell Bryan that next May is WAY too soon. Maybe we should put things on hold again, like we decided last—NO, NO, a million times, NO!* She socks her fist angrily into her palm.

Her bout with doubt disappears in a fireball of indignation, silent but liberating: *Why am I blaming myself, like I'm some kind of terrible sinner, just because I love Bryan Howard? Damn, damn, damn it all! It's not ME, it's MAMA!* She slams back in her chair—it squeaks and groans. *Wendy's right. Mama should be happy that I have a wonderful, good, amazing, gifted champion of a man, instead of some soused-out, fucked-up, triple-time loser, like Charlie. AAAH JESUS! She makes me SO mad! She should be happy, even if Bryan and I get hitched tomorrow!* Mandy pounds the desk with her fist, *ka-BAAAM!* The pencil flies into the air, the calculator onto the floor. *And I'll tell her about next May if and when I damn well please. I'm not—"*

"What's goin' on up there!" Gretchen yells. "I heard a *big* noise, and it wasn't thunder ... and Toby's freaking!"

"Oh, it was just my desk," Mandy replies with a half-truth, after going to the door of her bedroom. "You know how the top slams down when you open it too wide and let go?"

"I sure do," Gretchen affirms from the bottom of the stairs. "You almost got my pinkie once."

Mandy turns, but Gretch has more: "I wanna stay up till...."

"What? What is it?"

"I wanna watch TV till ten. I'm watching 'Rosanne' now, but 'Little House' comes on at nine ... the re-runs. Can I stay down here and watch it? Mama said if she wasn't home, that I had to come up and take my *bath* at nine. And she's *al*ways late gettin' home from those dang business meetings."

"Okay, you can watch it," Mandy proclaims, boldly (and gladly) overruling her mother. "But y'better get up here quick if yuh hear the Escort in the driveway."

"Oh, I will. I will."

Closing the bedroom door, Mandy does a frisky little jig, a variation of her Indian-stomp routine, then plops down again at her desk. Her indignation has cooled, but not her resolve: *I'm not gonna FRET about what Mama knows or doesn't know. I'm just gonna look forward to seeing him—in three weeks.*

The rain comes down harder outside. The steady thrumming lulls her into sweet recollection. Closing the physics text and turning off the desk light, she harks back to last fall, to Bryan's first phone call—after he finally got up the courage to ask her out. She chuckles as she hears again his shy, less-than-polished approach, which endeared him to her all the more: "I was just wondering ... I uh ... well, you know the hayride they're having at the church Saturday night—actually it's several churches going together, the Harvest Hayride, like every year...."

The hayride was heavenly, though they did nothing but hold hands. Their first real kiss, in the barn at the farm, occurred two weeks later, then came December, and they were suddenly going steady, without any formalities—they just knew.

She recalls more recent events—from the summer, the watermelon patch in the moonlight, the picnic at Magruder State Forest. A naughty itch commences between her legs, as she thinks back to that wild day by the stream when she disrobed before Bryan, her strip-fantasy-come-true, and then he was naked too. *Oh gosh, I love him so, in every way, all the way.* She imagines him naked again, but this time they're newlyweds at a motel, and she's fondling his erection, getting it primed and ready to do its wondrous deed. *Whew, my imagination is getting away from me.* She snickers lustfully. The swelling heat between her legs demands attention. She closes her thighs, squeezing against it, but it only grows bigger. *O Jesus, I love how it builds, the horny feeling, when I wait and wait, but this's too much.* And the thought of fondling herself right here at her homework desk whets the temptation all the more, making her legs quiver—it seems especially rebellious and wanton and risky, like doing it at school. Leaning back, she unties the sash of her robe, then slips her hand inside her pajama pants, slowly, teasingly.

*   *   *

That was super nice, Mandy purrs to herself, as she snuggles under the comforter, *like WAY better than doing homework.* What she started at her desk, she finished on the bed. She hugs her pillow; she sighs blissfully then wishfully. *But how many more times do I have to do this alone, without Bryan? Maybe we shouldn't wait until we're married? I mean, what's the diff—*

The phone rings; she grabs it expectantly: "Hello."

"Well, whaddeyuh doing, pretty lady?"

"Oh, I'm just lying here listening to the rain."

"It's raining up there?"

"Yeah, it started this afternoon—oh, Bryan babe, I was hoping you'd call."

"I wanted to call yuh earlier, but I didn't get a dial tone till twenty minutes ago. They just turned on my phone, *finally*."

She gives a saucy giggle. "Well, you big jock, I must say your timing is heavenly."

THE SILVER CORD

"How's that?"

"I'm not tellin'."

"Why not?"

"'Cause you couldn't handle it? Let's just say: you've been real *big* on my mind." They both laugh. She figures he knows, but neither of them gets any more specific. Instead, he gives her his new phone number, then she abruptly shifts: "Mama and I had a big fight today, but I feel *much* better now. Plus, I don't give a goshdang what she thinks."

* * *

BAYLOR UNIVERSITY - FLETCHER HALL, UNIT 311
TUESDAY, SEPTEMBER 3, 1991 — 9:57 PM

She's in a dadgum feisty mood, Bryan declares to himself after hanging up. *But it bothers me a bit, the fight she had with her mom.* Turning off his desk lamp, he steps over to his bedroom window. The campus lights look the same, but the moon has disappeared behind a bank of clouds. A pickup lurches to a halt in the parking lot below, and three guys spill out; the lots are full now. Steve Jordan is in the big room watching the Ranger game, but he put on his earphones when Bryan came in here to call Mandy, so there's no sound save for the AC fan, plus occasional voices from Unit 309, muted voices coming through the wall, loud enough to hear but not to comprehend: Sammy and Eric, the fellows next door—soccer players. They seem friendly and laid back; Bryan and Steve met them this morning. Most of the jocks on the floor are baseballers (like Randy Burke, the big-mouth jerk across the hall), but a few other sports *are* represented.

When Helen Stevens learns about our true plans, the shit's gonna hit the fan, Bryan goes on in his thoughts, as he focuses on a swarm of June bugs and moths flitting berserkly under the nearest parking-lot light. *And she HAS to find out sooner or later, even if Mandy doesn't come right out and tell her. We can't keep this wedding a secret all the way to May. And yet, Mandy doesn't seem worried at all. She sounded confident and buoyant, almost cocky. I reckon I shouldn't fret so much about how and when her mom's gonna find out. I hafta trust God on this.*

His anxiety subsides, as eros stirs: *And when she answered, she was all cozy on her bed, in the afterglow of sexual pleasure. She didn't actually say it, but that's what she was flirting about—it had to be that.* His penis quickens inside the cut-off sweats he put on after returning from the cafeteria. *O God, she's a hot ticket, and to think that she fingers off, and craves it as much as me—sheeesh.* Lust calls, but he decides to wait. It'll be better when he's ready to go to sleep. A low-flying aircraft on the far (northeast) side of the campus helps divert his attention: *That must be a helicopter, those lights. I've seen several flying over the campus since I've been here.* He soon hears the faint whop-whop sound, confirming his assumption. *I reckon it's the state police, or maybe it's a TV-news chopper.* He chuckles under his breath. *It's amazing to think I was flying over this campus myself, just night before last. That was some wild trip.*

He follows the westbound copter until it disappears from view behind the big pine at the corner of the dorm, then he notices, a bit higher in the sky, a flash of lightning, then another. *Looks like it may rain here too?* He leans closer to the window to get a broader view of this warm September night. As he waits for more lightning, bits and pieces of the phone conversation with Mandy replay in his mind, not the crucial part about her fight with her mom, but other, more mundane portions:

"So, pretty lady, what else happened today, besides fighting with your mama, plus that other secret thing you won't tell me?"

"Get outta here, mister. You keep going back to that. You're too nosy, y'know it?"

The storm shows itself again, as bluish strobelike flashes flare upward in the clouds. It reminds him of Gramps, of the many times they watched squall lines approaching the farm.

"So y'really wanna hear about my boring life up here in goshdang Spindle—O God, I can't wait to get outta here. I'd rather hear what's happening down there at Baylor."

"Lemme hear about YOUR day first."

"Well, that won't take long. I went to school, then Wendy and I went to O'Henry's for lunch. She had two discount coupons for bacon burgers, and she gave me one. Then I went to trig class, and then study hall. I have study hall last period until basketball starts. Then later, after I got pissed off at Mama, I picked up Wen, and we went running up on Misty Hollow Road."

"I thought it was raining up there?"

"It didn't start until we got back to the car, but I like running in the rain anyhow."

"So that's it?"

"Yeah, I reckon so. Oh, after I took Wendy home, I picked up Gretchen over on Bixby, because it was raining. She goes for piano lessons at Ms. Stanley's. She hadta leave her bike there, but she'll get it tomorrow. She hates those piano lessons, even more than I did— now is this BORING enough for you?"

"Sounds like vital information, though I reckon I can get by without knowing the whereabouts of Gretchen's bicycle."

Bryan chuckles at this recollection, as he sees more lightning, several quick flashes which illuminate from within a massive, upward-boiling thunderhead. It's true that much of the stuff he and Mandy talked about was inconsequential. Yet he hungers to know everything, even about her most ordinary experiences, things no one else would take note of. And he cherishes her way of telling him, the way she inflects her voice for emphasis here, de-emphasis there, plus the giggles and snorts and snuffly mews. He could talk with her forever, and ever, without getting bored.

"So whaddabout you, babe? Didyuh see that older guy again? Chris? The junior you met at breakfast yesterday?"

"Yeah, as a matter of fact I did. He and I ate at the same table last night. And he invited me to come over to his place for hot dogs. He lives off-campus, and he's into neuroscience like me, and he's got attitude, in a good way."

"Whaddeyuh mean?"

"Well, he doesn't take shit from people. I'll tellyuh more after I see him again."

"How 'bout your roommate? Didyuh finally meet him?"

"Yeah, Steve Jordan. He got here yesterday. He's huge, like two-fifty, and he's quite a character, like a great big kid."

"D'yuh like him?"

"Pretty much. He's a bit disorganized and untidy, and he's not too keen when it comes to academics. But y'really can't help but like the big guy—I mean, he tells me everything. He's a sports journalism major. Least, that's what he chose from the list ... but he's mainly into baseball. And he's a pretty good pitcher, from what I saw of him this afternoon. He can hum it."

"You guys had practice today?"

"Yeah, it went okay—just the freshmen though. The upper-class guys don't start until next Monday."

"D'yuh like your coach, that Weaver guy?"

"He's okay, though he acts tough, like head coaches always do. But I like the hitting coach the best, Coach McKinney, Elmo McKinney—he's an old black fellow who played for the Kansas City Monarchs back in the old days, in the Negro leagues."

A bolt of lighting forks downward to the northern horizon, followed by a smothered double-concussion, the distant rumble of thunder. This thing is definitely getting closer.

"But your college classes haven't started yet?"

"No, they start next week, but we had Freshmen Orientation, and we have it again tomorrow and Thursday, plus we hafta take a bunch of tests. There's a big emphasis on making sure each freshman knows what Baylor is all about, so tomorrow we'll be breaking up into smaller groups and going around to all the campus buildings and academic departments. But the bullshit we had today was pretty dumb. We met in this huge auditorium, the Babcock Center for the Performing Arts—there's two thousand freshmen, so it takes a big place—and then different bigshots came and talked to us. But it was still dumb, since everything they told us is right out of the student handbook, like how to register your car, and of course, they went over all the campus rules

and regulations, especially the part about not having members of the opposite sex in your dorm room except on weekends, when they have to leave by six p.m."

"Yeah, babe, I reckon we know about THAT rule."

THE SILVER CORD

CHAPTER FIFTEEN

FLETCHER HALL - UNIT 311
WEDNESDAY, SEPTEMBER 4, 1991 — 5:11 PM

"Hey, dude, I gotta question for yuh," Steve Jordan drawls, as he pads out of his room in his underwear, a knit shirt in each hand. "D'yuh thank I should wear the tan one, or the blue one?"

"Which is bigger?" Bryan replies from the living-room couch where he's looking over tomorrow's orientation schedule—they just got back from baseball practice minutes ago.

"The blue one I reckon—it's triple-extra large."

"Then wear the blue one."

"Yeh ... I thank I look better in blue anyhow; it goes with my eyes. It's no big deal. Me 'n Jamal, we're just goin' out to eat." He gives a sheepish laugh, a few sousaphone notes. "Course yuh never know. We might swing by the Peek-A-Boo Club out on the 340 Loop, and check out the action. Jamal's been there a number of times." Steve laughs louder, his huge, half-naked belly shaking like it does; he's wearing an old-fashioned undershirt, the track-and-field, athletic style (the kind Bryan's father wears), but it's much too small, barely covering his chubby, cavelike navel.

Jordan disappears into his room, only to reemerge a minute later, the blue polo halfway over his head. "I got another thang to ask yuh about," he says, as he wriggles into the shirt.

"What's that?" Bryan responds.

"D'yuh thank dogs go to Heaven?"

Bryan chuckles but quickly sobers, realizing his roommate is asking earnestly. Steve's blue eyes and pudgy features express a childlike concern, pricking Bryan's heart, not to speak of his own memory of Buster, and how he asked Gramps the very same question. "Well, Steve," he replies, "it seems—"

"My dog Hardy died last week," the big guy interrupts. "I mean, we hadta put 'im to sleep, 'cause he was fourteen, and his kidneys were failin'. My dad doesn't come around much, since he 'n Ma are havin' a trial separation, so she drove me, and I held Hardy in the back seat. He was shiverin' like he always did when he went to the vet, but I thank he knew it was his *last* trip. Yessir ... I thank he knew." Steve paws the air. "Hardy was just a dadgum mutt I reckon, but he followed me *ever*'where, and he slept on my bed, and I cried when he died. Not at the animal hospital mindyuh—I kept my cool while they were giving him the shot and ever'thang—but later when I was buryin' him in the woods behind our house. We brought him home in a trash bag." Steve snorts and wags his head. "But that guy down the hall, that damn little whipper-snapper—Marvin, the RA feller: well, he said dogs don't have a soul, so they *cain't* go to Heaven. He ate at my table at lunch, and he gave me a salvation thang and invited me to church." Jordan's hand-gestures become more expansive, as if directing an orchestra. "Marvin said it's important to hear the Word, so y'can grow as a Christian. I reckon he's right about church, but it bugs me, what he said about dogs 'n cats, and the other animals. If *we* have souls, why don't they? They seem just as lovin' and all ... more so in fact?"

"I believe they *do* have souls," Bryan reacts. "Come over and sit down, and I'll give you my take on it."

Steve plunks down in the armchair where he anxiously pats his naked knees. He smells like honeysuckle, as usual, from his after-practice, bath-talc routine. Bryan feels like blasting Marvin and his imposing, hyperspiritual, know-it-all approach but decides instead to talk about Buster, about the collie's love and loyalty and their unconditional friendship, and then about that terrible day he got run over, and about Gramps, how he seethed whenever preachers or other hotshot Christians spouted that doctrine about animals not having souls. When Bryan finishes, they both have tears in their eyes. He considers sharing about his own soul-body experiences, but quickly kills the idea, lest he blow his roommate away—plus, Steve would blab it to *everyone* in Texas.

"Well, I tellyuh, dude," the big guy declares, hoisting himself out of the chair, "you oughta be a preacher yourself. Yessir ... I reckon y'got a good way of puttin' thangs—shit, it's almost five-thirty. I gotta pick up Jamal."

Two minutes later, Steve, now fully dressed, bombs out of the bathroom, grabs his red Ardmore hat, and heads for the door, but Bryan, still on the couch, stops him, speaking over his shoulder, "Hold it a second."

"Damn, I hardly have a second. But whatcha got, dude?"

"Oh, I was just gonna suggest that y'might be a bit more careful about telling folks about your private matters, especially guys like Marvin Latrobe."

"I know, I know," Steve replies, as he opens the door, with a click. "My daddy told me that a *hun'*erd times ... and my mom."

"I don't mean to butt in, but everyone's not kind-hearted and trustworthy—like *me*." They share a laugh, then Bryan shifts, "I don't know what time you're coming back, but I'm gonna be gone until nine or ten I reckon. I'm going to see that upper-class guy who lives off campus, the one I toldjuh about."

"Well, dude, I could be a *lot* later ... if y'catch my drift."

* * *

Same day, 6:02 p.m. Bryan, after exiting the side door of the dorm, strides across the puddled parking lot. The storm he was watching last night finally did arrive, with gusty winds and down-pours. The rain continued on and off through the night then gave way to passing showers, more like sprinkles, which persisted until early afternoon, but now the sun has come out, giving a cameo appearance as it sinks in the west. He inhales the balmy-fresh, after-rain aroma, a welcome change from the baked-asphalt stink that normally surrounds Fletcher Hall. It's still warm out (upper 70s), but the sweltering heat has departed, at least for today. Reaching Spangler Avenue, he heads east along the oatmeal-colored sidewalk, which also sports numerous puddles—the timeworn slabs of concrete have cracked and heaved, forming little basins. Waco Creek likewise gives witness to last night's deluge, as it roars and churns under the Spangler Avenue bridge, having grown from a trickle to a torrent. The weatherman on Channel 2 (Norm something?) said the storms were caused by an upper-air disturbance.

The Baylor freshman pauses by Neill Morris Hall to check the paper napkin, the map Chris Hansen scrawled at the caf. *East on Spangler to Rigby, then south to Eleventh, then east to Baker, then I jog south to Douglas—it's a white, two-story, number 146.* Bryan planned to take his pickup, but when the sun came out, he decided to walk. Replacing the napkin in the back pocket of his Levi's (he's wearing jeans plus a button-collar sport shirt, and his blue Spindle Tiger baseball cap), he continues on his way along Spangler, the same street he and Steve just came down an hour ago (in Steve's Bronco) on their way back from baseball; they did practice today in spite of the weather, though Coach Weaver cut the session short. Bryan played second, shortstop, and third today, as the coaches focused on defensive skills.

Save for a red-faced jogger and a lady walking a cocker spaniel (on the other side), the tree-lined avenue is empty. The huge expanse on his left, Founder's Mall, looks more verdant than a golf course, especially with the sunshine and long shadows. The rain has invigorated the grass and trees, perking up the green hues, washing away the dingy browns and grays. And the blue sky, rinsed of its haze, looks equally vivid amid the breaking clouds overhead. A puff of wind caresses Bryan's cheek, a gentle zephyr just strong enough to stir the leaves and pine needles. The beautiful evening fortifies his positive frame of mind, a happy daylong optimism anchored of course by his Mandy dreams. "It's *my* life, and we're getting married as planned, whether Mama likes it or not." That's what she said on the phone last night. And Bryan is usually upbeat after practice anyway. Vigorous exercise, especially on the baseball field, elevates his mood—not to mention the warm, heart-to-heart talk he just had with Steve Jordan back at the dorm. The big guy may not be sophisticated or intellectually impressive, but he's anything but shallow when it comes to the issues that really count in life (in that sense, Bryan misread him a country mile when they first met two days ago). To top off his glad mood, Bryan looks forward to visiting with Chris, albeit with some apprehension, since the smirky-faced junior has quickly become a significant, mentorlike figure on the academic, visionary, non-jock side of his life.

Maybe I should've worn Bermudas or something, he remarks to himself ten minutes later, as he heads south on Baker. *I dress like a dadgum hayseed square, like I grew up on a farm outside Spindle, Texas.* He laughs out loud. *But what's the point of trying to be someone that I'm not? Gramps wore overalls his whole life. And I'm sure Chris doesn't expect me to arrive in some hyped-up, preppy, Banana Republic garb—wait a minute, I'm going too far. That's Douglas Street. I'm already past it.* Doubling back, he heads east on Douglas, marching between the curbside trees and terraced lawns, his long, sporadic shadow advancing ahead of him. *It shouldn't be much farther. I'm looking for 146, and that house there is 117.* The neighborhood seems strangely quiet—no traffic, no dogs, no kids. The tree-canopied, purple-brick pavement reminds him of Coolidge Street back in Spindle, as do the traditional, pre-WWII homes, some brick, some stone, some wood, most having a large front porch and manicured lawn. And the lots are elevated three of four feet, so each driveway goes abruptly upward— and a few of the drives are the ancient, early-century kind, just a pair of concrete strips with grass between, leading to equally old-fashioned, barn-door garages.

146 is an even number, so it's gonna be on the other side. Skipping over a curbside puddle, Bryan cuts across the worn brick pavement to the other sidewalk. *Gramps said they paved with bricks during the Great Depression to create jobs ... back when the banks and farms were failing, and the price of oil was three cents a barrel, and many folks had to eat at soup kitchens and bread lines.* Bryan learned about FDR's prime-the-pump policies in history class, but he remembers best what Gramps taught him.

He soon arrives at a two-story clapboard colonial surrounded by waist-high hedges; there's a magnolia in front and a double garage to the left rear. No number—but it has to be 146, since he just passed 144. And it *is* white, or roughly so, behind a dingy yellow-gray veneer. He goes up the steep part of the driveway, just far enough to note the rundown condition of the place: weedy grass ten inches high, gutters and shutters awry, roof shingles missing here and there—and the hedges are in desperate need of a trim. Ditto for the cedar bushes guarding the large, recessed front porch. The sickly, sun-faded color of the clap-boards seems most fitting, since the place stands out like a sore compared to the other homes. Only the dark-green magnolia, tall and healthy, runs counter to this appraisal.

He studies the porch, the steps, the mailbox, looking for a number. *Maybe this isn't it?* he frets, as he advances a few more steps then retreats. *I can't just bop around to the back, if it's not the right house.* He starts to leave, but quickly reverses himself. After a bit more hesitation, he proceeds up the flagstone path which leads to the porch.

THE SILVER CORD

I'll knock on the front door and ask.

"Hey, slugger, stop lollygagging like a goddamn fool," Chris kids, as he appears suddenly in the driveway, wearing his raggedy cutoffs and Einstein shirt—plus his ever-present smirk.

"Oh, I uh ... I uh," Bryan stammers, feeling a bit embarrassed. "I was just looking for the number."

"There is one, on the porch post, but it's hidden by that big overgrown shrub—but I live back here." He nods toward the rear. "C'mon ... let's have a brewski." Bryan follows him.

A naked basketball goal, hanging askew on the garage, speaks of kids and fun, of happier years for this old house. Skirting a rain puddle, they hang a right between the house and the garage, pushing through a slatted swing-gate into a small courtyard, a concrete patio plus a rectangle of lawn, also weedy and unmowed. A tall and shaggy cedar (near the gate) shades half the patio. A set of steps lead up to the back entrance of the house, but Chris goes left, to a smaller frame structure attached to the garage.

Pulling open the spring-held screen door, *skee-eeeek*, he escorts Bryan inside, into a plain, musty-smelling, two-room apartment without much furniture, just a bed, a computer desk, a few folding chairs, a rickety kitchen table, and a long, square-armed, moth-eaten sofa, all of which are covered with books and papers and floppy disks and notebooks and binders and printouts. More books and such overflow from cardboard boxes scattered about on the bare wooden floor. The patio entrance, strangely enough, takes you into the bedroom, but the living room is larger with a kitchen in one corner, and there's a bathroom between the two rooms. "As you can see, I'm a world-class housekeeper," Chris wisecracks, as he opens a door to the right of the sofa. "This's the garage ... where I keep my wheels, my trusty steeds."

"I thought yuh rode a bicycle?"

"I do whenever I can, but sometimes I need more advanced transportation. Now that little green job on the right is my toot-around car, but the Caddy is my pride and joy." He nods smirkily toward the black, dust-covered hog. "I hardly ever drive it, but it still runs like a Rolls Royce."

"Gosh damn ... with those fins on the back, it must be thirty years old?"

"Almost; it's a '63 to be exact. It's a goddamn classic ... and it's worth twenty grand."

"So how'd yuh—"

"That's the most amazing part, slugger. I won it in a poker game ... at Oakvale Country Club." He swaggers, his mustache twitching. "From a rich old fart from Lubbock."

"You gotta be *shitting* me?"

"I *am*," Chris laughs, his brown eyes gleaming mischievously. "No way in hell is that Caddy mine ... no way." Bryan laughs as well.

"No, it belongs to Mr. O'Shea—Dudley O'Shea, who owns this property. He's a retired auto dealer, but he's in the hospital, long term, so I just see his wife, Annie, every now and then."

"But the *little* car does belong to you?"

"Yeah, that's my goddamn Chevette. It's a cramped little wreck, but it gets me around ... and I *can* fit my golf clubs in the back, if I fold the seats down—d'you play perchance?"

"Nawh, not really. I went twice with my friend Spanky ... but we just fooled around on a few holes. He used to caddy at Lester Hills, the country club, so he got into the game, at least enough to hustle the rich kids." Bryan chuckles. "But *I* never took it up."

"Well, golf's hardly a super-jock thing," Chris quips, as they retreat into the apartment. "It's more like a prick-teasing gal who gives just enough to keep you coming back." He snickers. "It's a goddamn worthless addiction, that game—but let's cut the BS and get those brewskis." He grabs two cans of Michelob from the refrigerator, tossing one to Bryan. "Being a beer-drinking Baptist, you probably go for Bud or Coors ... but I like a more sophisticated label."

More snickers and snuffles, from both. Bryan blushes, his cheeks warming. "So y'know my religious upbringing too?" he replies, as he pops open the Michelob and takes a swig.

"Without a doubt, slugger. Hell, that's the first thing Marv told me." Chris sips his own beer, then pushes the can toward the young freshman. "Not that I give a shit what church you waste time in, but it sure doesn't take a Sherlock Holmes to conclude that you're a goddamn Baptist."

"How's that?"

"Well, what else would you be, growing up on a Texas farm, and coming to Baylor for college? And having a sweetheart back home, and getting all sheepish and shy when I talk about sweet young virgins and ripe pussy?" He chortles then downs a quick slug of beer. "And y'look like a fucking country-boy Baptist, with that fifties haircut, and those new Levi's and sneakers, and that damn Ricky Nelson shirt." Pangs of shame commence in Bryan's gut, but they quickly subside, as Chris gives him a playful jab to the shoulder. "Don't pay attention to me. I got ten shirts like that in my closet, and Levi's too. And if I had a sweetheart back home, or anywhere, I'd shave this mustache in a second if she asked me to, and I'd get a damn 'Happy Days' haircut as well. Besides, anyone who rides a yard-sale bike and drives a goddamn barf-green Chevette can hardly brag about being cool and trendy. Shit, I sound like a fucking bumblebee when I drive that oil-burning clunker down the street."

They share a hearty laugh, then Chris says, "But I bet you don't drink that much, d'you—being a dedicated jock?"

"Nawh, I reckon not. Maybe a few times a year, but tonight's a special occasion."

"You fucking right it is. We're going to ponder the mysteries of the universe, and pose the ultimate questions. We're going to push beyond the last frontier. But before the damn bullshit gets too deep, let's go out back where I got my hibachi going. Here, you take my beer, while I grab the hot dogs and stuff. It's all in this grocery bag— I just loaded it up ... right before you got here."

Exiting through the bedroom, they hang a left around the garage apartment, then Bryan follows Chris through a trellis gate into the mixed aromas of burning charcoal and just-mowed grass; it's a big backyard, a half acre or so. They head for a dilapidated barbecue pit on the west side of the yard, where a small hibachi, glowing with hot coals, sits atop the larger grating. "This brick monster still works," Chris says, as he places the bag in a lawn chair next to the pit, "but there's no point in firing it up just for the two of us." Retrieving his beer from Bryan, the junior takes a swig then gestures toward two other lawn chairs a few paces away, within a square of closely cropped lawn. "Relax, slugger, and have a seat, while I put these tube steaks on." The rest of the yard is unmowed, the grass and weeds ankle deep, more so in places.

Bryan gives a snorty if-you-say-so laugh then plunks down. A mid-sized pine stands sentry over this corner of the yard, shading the mowed patch of grass. He notices, back by the trellis gate, a concrete storm cellar crouching like a WWII bunker among the weeds and overgrown bushes, and next to it (abutting the courtyard fence), there's some kind of chicken-wire pen, empty and choked with undergrowth; it's too small for chickens? It must be for pigeons, or maybe rabbits? A fair distance left of the storm cellar (perhaps forty feet), a trio of pecan trees, sun-washed and heavy laden with green pecans, command the rest of the shaggy, unkempt expanse of yard. "This's quite a place," the freshman comments over his shoulder. "It's like yuh have your own house, and yard, plus a garage for your car."

"It's actually a dump, this property, but the peace and quiet is A-plus. That's the main reason I moved off campus. I got sick of bowing down to proctors and dormitory rules, plus the noise and pranks and other bullshit, though I must confess I did my share of cutting up when I was living at Gaylord Hall, on North Campus." He gives a devilish snicker. "I'm losing money by living here, since I have a research grant that includes the dorm. If I was married, I'd get money to live here, but not as a single student, so I have to pay the $300 a month myself, plus I have to do a few chores for the landlady."

"Damn, $300 isn't bad, or is it?" Bryan asks, between sips of beer— he can hear the hot dogs sizzling behind him.

"It's a steal for Waco, for any college town ... especially in a neighborhood within walking distance of the campus—there's a jillion students looking for apartments."

"So how'd yuh find it?"

"Doc Richardson told me about it. He's the professor I study under, and I work part-time in his lab, like I told you, mostly dogwork, like filing data—that's how I get the rent money."

Removing his Spindle Tiger cap, Bryan slouches back in the chair. The whole sky is clear now, the same rich, unsullied blue. The peaceful setting relaxes him, plus the beer, chasing the remnants of his Chris-anxiety. "So your professor keeps track of off-campus housing opportunities?"

Chris laughs. "Not hardly. It was more like fate. He played a lot of golf with Mr. O'Shea, but the old fellow had a stroke a year ago ... and he ended up in long-term care in San Antonio. That's why his wife is hardly ever here. Mrs. Annabel O'Shea, but she likes to be called Annie ... says it makes her feel younger. But anyway, she rents a place in San Antone, so she can be near her husband. When she realized she'd be gone for some time, she asked Dr. Richardson if he knew of any students, who'd be willing to live here in the garage apartment, and also watch over the property. And she said she'd knock the rent down from $400 to $300, if I'd do all the yard work and everything."

"So *you're* the reason this place is so overgrown?"

"C'mon, I just mowed today ... after it stopped raining."

"Yeah, ten square feet? It musta taken all of fifty seconds?"

"About that, after I got the fucking mower started." They share a laugh. "Okay, okay—I'll take credit for the unmowed grass, and the overgrown hedges and such, but they've let this house go for years." Chris grins impishly, his mustache lifting and twisting. "As long as I mow before Annie comes to check on the house, I'm okay, and she hasn't been here since July, and I doubt she'll be back anytime soon. I do talk to her on the phone." He pauses to deal with the sizzling dogs. "I suppose she'll sell this place after Mr. O'Shea dies. But either way, I doubt she's going to invest much money in upkeep, and I expect this whole street will eventually suffer the same fate. I'm surprised the rest of the homes are still in such good shape. This old neighborhood used to be fairly well-to-do, but now it's just *old*. It's still ninety percent white, but everyone is elderly and retired. Once they die off, the demographics will shift toward Chicanos and other Latinos, plus blacks. But I'll be well outta here by then. I'll be a goddamn famous neuroscientist, and you too, Bryan Howard—now get your ass over here and grab a couple of these wieners."

* * *

SPINDLE, TEXAS - GODDARD'S DINER
WEDNESDAY, SEPTEMBER 4, 1991 — 6:50 PM

Mandy Stevens picks up two chicken-basket orders and hustles over to booth #2, where Spanky Arnold and Roy Collins are sipping on the tall cherry-Cokes she delivered earlier.

"It's been a while since I saw you guys in here," she remarks.

"Well, the grub at the bowlin' alley has gone to hell," the freckled redneck declares, as Roy nods his agreement. "And the waitresses here are *way* better-looking." Spanky cackles and blushes but quickly covers himself. "I'm not talkin' about you, Mandy. I mean uh—well, you *are* a goddam knockout for chrissake, but I know you 'n Bryan are back together, since Sunday, and we're both glad for yuh, aren't we, Roy?" Roy nods again, while Spanky attacks a chicken thigh, the crispy crust spewing in all directions.

"So where didyuh hear that?" Mandy asks casually, giving a husky little laugh to hide her curiosity—and concern.

Spanky stuffs a big handful of fries into his mouth plus half his dinner roll—his cheeks bulge as he chews. He licks his fingers, slurping, sucking. "From Wendy ... Wendy Lewis," he finally replies, his voice clogged with food. He takes a quick drink of Coke. "She was at the bowlin' alley last night with Lena Beth, and they were both feelin' pretty goddam good, and me 'n Roy—well, we sat down at their booth, right, Roy?"

"That we did," Roy affirms, as he eats—at a slower pace.

"Now y'know I'm not into gossipin' or nuthin'," Spanky elaborates, "but Wendy was goin' on about how she went joggin' with yuh, and how yuh ran her fat ass off." He cackles again, gesturing with the half-eaten thigh. "Well, you 'n Bryan quickly became the hot topic of conversation, and Wendy said that you went down to Waco with him on Sunday, and that you guys were back together—like *more* than ever. I was happy to hear it, since me 'n Bryan have been buddies from way back. Plus, I always figured you two would be gettin' married for chrissake."

* * *

WACO, TEXAS - 146 DOUGLAS STREET
WEDNESDAY, SEPTEMBER 4, 1991 — 7:08 PM

"So, Bryan, how about another brew?" Chris Hansen asks, while collecting the paper plates, the empty Humpty Dumpty potato-chip bags, and the other debris left from their hot-dog feast.

"Damn, I've already had two?" Bryan replies, as he swigs down the dregs of his second.

"So, you're not driving or anything?"

"Okay, but I gotta take a leak before I drink *any*thing else."

"Just piss on the hedge, over there," Chris replies, chuckling. He points beyond the barbecue pit toward the corner of the yard. "That's my favorite spot ... and I'll be back in a minute."

He's twenty-seven, Bryan says to himself as he urinates, *even older than I thought. And he's from Illinois, which explains his flat way of talking. He's full of wisecracks and all ... but we've hardly solved the mysteries of the universe.* While eating, they chatted and kidded but got no deeper than the grass he's pissing in, by the hedge. He shakes then retracts his ropy penis, laughing as he does. *I should tell him about the OBE I had Sunday night. Now THAT would sure get things stirred up I reckon.*

After sitting down again, Bryan gazes up into the sunset sky, now more pink than blue. He moves the lawn chair, to get a better view, around the pine. A few birds are chirping, and he can hear the traffic from downtown Waco, faint but audible. *I wish I COULD tell him about my OBEs,* he reflects seriously, *plus my brush with death. I'd like to hear what he thinks about it ... but no way ... no, no. That would be TOO much to lay on him.*

"That sky is really something," Chris observes, as he hands Bryan another Michelob. "It's pink and gold and silver, all at the same time, and it's not smoggy like most sunsets. This's the best time to be out here, if we can put up with the bugs."

"They don't seem too bad to me," Bryan responds, as he pops open the cold can, his third.

The Baylor junior plops down but says nothing—no quips or jesting. They simply sip and watch the sunset. Chris is waiting for Bryan to say something profound, or so it seems. In any case, the freshman feels again the desire to confide about his soul travel, a more compelling urge. It's still too much—he can't do it. But after a long moment, he does break the silence in that direction: "Have yuh ever wondered what it's gonna be like the very last time you close your eyes?"

"Y'mean for good? When we croak?"

"Yeah ... when we die, as we surely will in due time."

"Good god, slugger, you're going deep on me." He chuckles, gesturing with his brew. "Most folks avoid that subject like the plague, especially anyone under forty. But yeah, I've thought about it. I guess it depends on who's in charge of this reality we live in. Which God ... if any God? Maybe it's your Baptist God? Or it could be the non-religious God *I* hope for? Or maybe it's the Jewish God, which is supposedly the same as the Christian God, or maybe it's some Eastern God, like a deified Buddha?"

Bryan sips then gives a little snuffle. "I doubt the real God has a label. I reckon he *is* non-religious, like you're hoping ... but he's still the Christian God, and everybody's God."

"I agree. At least, I hope for such a God, which is all I can do as an agnostic. But if true, he has to be universal and inclusive. I can't see him as narrow and sectarian, despite all the holy-rollers and fire-and-brimstone preachers who paint him that way."

"Well, when *they* die, I doubt they're gonna be super picky about Bible doctrine."

"You got that right," Chris quips, his puckish personality

reasserting itself. "Those zealous fuckers will be begging for mercy ... as the demons of death suck 'em down into the *fires* of Hell." He playfully inflects his Illinois monotone, as if preaching himself. He takes a drink of Michelob then gives a hearty laugh.

Looks like he's back to jesting and cutting up, Bryan remarks to himself as he spots a solitary seagull soaring high in the pearly sky. "Look at that seagull," he says aloud; he points.

"Yeah, they come up from the Gulf," Chris replies smirkily. "They can smell the goddam Waco garbage all the way from Galveston." More smirks and snickers.

There's no way I can bring up my OBEs now, Bryan goes on in his thoughts. *Not with him laughing and all—but that gull sure reminds me ... and the plane.* Far above the white bird, an eastbound jet, a fiery point of light, paints a contrail across the heavens. He harks back to that day in June when he and Mandy were on her porch watching a similar high-flying aircraft—or more recently, the moonlit jet he chased on Sunday night. *Gosh, it seems so far-fetched all of a sudden ... like WAY out. Maybe I'm half crazy? Maybe I have delusions? Or maybe it was just a regular dream? No, it was real? It had to be?*

Chris gestures skyward with his beer. "That seagull has hardly flapped its wings. They can really fly high, yet they stay aloft with no effort. Now wouldn't it be goddamn amazing if we could soar like a bird ... or like that jet *way* up there?"

Bryan drinks then spits a stream of Michelob onto the grass. "I *can*," he blurts boldly. "I can—and I'm not *josh*ing you."

"You mean you fly those little Cessna planes?"

* * *

SPINDLE, TEXAS - GODDARD'S DINER
WEDNESDAY, SEPTEMBER 4, 1991 — 7:14 PM

Mandy, forcing a smile, serves dessert at booth #2: a hot-fudge sundae for Spanky, apple pie for Roy. "Thank yuh, *ma*'am," Spanky drawls, playfully exaggerating his accent, yet he quickly clams up when she doesn't respond—as if realizing her distress.

She marches back behind the counter where she dutifully wipes and replaces the tray then checks the serving window for her next order. But instead of picking it up, she flees to the ladies' room. *Oh my God,* she laments, after locking herself in the second stall. *Wendy told Spanky and Roy, AND Lena Beth. Now everybody in town's gonna know—including Mama.*

Since hearing the "gettin' married" gossip, she has willfully kept her composure, but she can no longer ignore the panging in her stomach. She gazes tearfully at the toilet, at the seat, at the water, at the chrome flush handle. She wipes her eyes with toilet paper. *Mama's gonna find out—I gotta tell her first, like tonight. Oh, Wendy, how could yuh? It's not like you to blurt out private stuff? And Lena Beth is the BIGGEST gossip in the whole f-ing school. I can hear her giggling and whispering now: "Mandy 'n Bryan are gettin' married in May. Can yuh believe it? It's a secret, but I found out." And Mama's gonna find out too. Half the checkout girls at Kroger's hang out with Lena Beth. And now I'm about to cry, and I don't go on break for thirty minutes. If Aunt Marge sees me crying, she'll tell Mama. I shoulda told her the truth right away, like on Sunday night. Or maybe I should call Bryan and tell him we can't set a date, that we gotta let all this settle down. Then I can deny, and it won't be a lie.*

The door squeaks open. She smells perfume. *Some lady's coming in.* Holding her breath, Mandy stands utterly still, as if her thoughts will be divulged if anyone notices her. She hears a snap and a rustling then water running—finally, the door again. The lady left, after fixing her face and hair, or some such thing.

Mandy takes a deep breath then dabs her eyes. *C'mon, gal, get hold of yourself. You're not gonna break. You're not gonna make a scene.* She inhales again, slowly, fully. The flush handle comes back into focus, and the toilet. *It's your life—remember? You can't let your mama affect you like this. After all, she's not GOD. Now y'just hafta hang in till your break, then you'll have fifteen minutes to think, to figure out what to do.*

* * *

WACO, TEXAS - 146 DOUGLAS STREET
WEDNESDAY, SEPTEMBER 4, 1991 — 7:20 PM

"Damn, I guess you *aren't* pulling my leg," Chris concedes, no longer laughing—except for his brown, twinkling eyes, which continue to convey amused incredulity.

"No, I'm not," Bryan affirms. "I *have* soared like a bird; at least, my soul-body has."

The seagull has disappeared, and the jet, but the contrail remains, a rosy, disintegrating double-line across the post-sunset sky. When Bryan first made his bold assertion, some five minutes ago, Chris reacted with jesting and flippant gibes; he rolled his eyes and gestured mockingly with his beer can, as though it was coming out of his chest and floating through the air. But the young freshman has finally convinced the curly-headed junior that this is no joke, albeit with some chagrin on Bryan's part, a growing sense that he's making a *tot*al fool of himself.

Chris drinks then runs his finger around the top of the Michelob can. "So tell me, slugger, does this happen often?"

"Not super often, maybe once or twice a year, since I was a little kid." A mosquito whirs near the bill of Bryan's cap; he swishes it away. "Mainly after some big emotional thing, like when my

244

grandfather died, or my dog Buster got run over, or when this kid Jeff Burton stole my new baseball glove when I was ten. But some years it didn't happen at all."

"So heartache makes it happen?"

"Not just heartache, but happy times too, like on Christmas once, and when I first rode Millie bareback—she's my horse. And later in sports, like after getting the game-winning hit in my first high-school game. And it just happened again this week."

"You've already flown out of your body since you got here?"

"I sure did—Sunday night, my first night at the dorm."

Chris gives a little moan then compresses his lips, as if trying to stifle a laugh.

He must think I'm a freak, a loony nutcase, Bryan interjects to himself, now wishing he'd kept his mouth shut. *But the shit's already out of the horse. No point in trying to save face now.*

"This's goddamn wild stuff," Chris declares—he slumps back in his chair, extending his slim, hairy, knobby-kneed legs. "It's no wonder you struck me as different from the other freshmen guys. So when did this first occur? How old were you?"

"I was four, and sick with a fever; that was the first time."

"And it only occurs when you're sleeping?"

"Well yeah ... like when I'm just falling asleep."

"So you could be dreaming ... a regular dream?"

"That's the *key* question ... yet I'm pretty darn sure I come out of my body, like ninety-five percent sure."

"This's most extraordinary, to say the least," Chris observes, arching his brows. "You float through the air without a physical body? You can see and reason? You have a distinct sense of self? You retain frontal-lobe function ... even while separated from the cerebral cortex?"

Bryan nurses his beer. "It *is* way out ... but I reckon I'm tethered somehow to my sleeping brain—that's the *big* mystery. This tether, which I call the 'silver cord,' must be the same thing that binds the soul to the nervous system under normal circumstances. But during my OBEs, it grows longer somehow, or it acts at a distance. And while I traverse the x-y-z spatial domain, my psyche remains in an astral dimension, such that I can't touch or affect the real world, and yet I *do* receive sensory input, mainly visual and audible, and I have detected certain smells, like honeysuckle and horse manure."

"So how many people know about these so-called OBEs?"

"Not many. In fact, Mandy's the only person I've really told in detail, like everything. But I have talked about it some to my parents, though not lately, and to my granddad before he died."

"So why'd you tell *me*?"

"I dunno. It just happened. Or maybe it's fate, like you talk about, or God ... like we were discussing before—or it could be the *beer*?" Bryan gives a resigned little laugh and lifts his Michelob can, as if making a toast. His new friend may well write him off as a kook, having no more scientific validity than a UFO fanatic who claims he's been abducted by aliens, but it's too late now—the shit is most certainly out of the horse.

Chris slaps his thigh, nailing a mosquito—smudge of blood: he flicks the crumpled carcass away. "So what does Mandy say?"

"Super awesome—that's how she describes it."

"She *actually* believes you come out of your body, and fly around at night?" Chris asks, inflecting his flat Illinois accent, as much as it will bend. "Like some kind of *goddamn* ghost?" He chugs down a big drink of beer, upturning the can.

"Yeah, I think she—"

"Hell, this's too much," Chris chortles, almost choking, as he succumbs to another bout of mirthful amazement. "Fuck, I'm sorry. I didn't mean to cut you off, but this's getting to me."

"No problem. It *is* super weird ... and wild and *way* out. I don't blame you for laughing, or seeing me as crazy."

"No, no—I don't see you as crazy. Hell, slugger, who am I to say whether this's real or not? You're the one who's experienced it, and you seem level-headed to me, *damn* level-headed in fact." Chris sighs, shaking his head. "As a student of science, I'm a skeptic when it comes to any paranormal phenomena, and yet I can't rule it out. Who am I to rule *any*thing out?" He sits up in the lawn chair, belching loudly as he does. "I'm open to almost any goddamn theory, but I have to see a lot of evidence before I accept it as plausible." He smirks then downs another swig; he burps again, amid a chuckle. "Of course, if we look back through history, we find that most of our great scientific breakthroughs were made by weird, way-out, fanatic types." They share a good laugh, as Chris leans forward and playfully jabs Bryan's leg. "So you don't have to hold back. You can be as *crazy* as you want around me." More laughter, as Chris slouches back into his chair, his puckish smirk remaining on his mouth.

"Well, your ghost analogy isn't too far off," Bryan chuckles, feeling reassured—their budding friendship is most likely not in jeopardy (though he's still less than certain how this is playing, from a scholarly perspective). "I can even go through walls, and people can't see me, or animals. I've flown around my horse Millie a number of times, and she's never shown any sign of being aware of my presence. I could even spy on people, but I've resisted using this to invade anyone's privacy."

"That figures," Chris quips, lifting his beer, "since you're a goddamn, clean-cut, role-model Baptist. But if I ever come out of *my* body, I'll be zooming on a beeline for the nearest girl's dorm, to check out those sweet darlings in the shower." He blushes and smirks, his brown eyes flashing; he gives a jaunty head-waggle. It's still light enough out to see the horny spark in his eyes. "Whew, goddamn it all.

Now that's a world-class way of shooting beavers ... especially the freshmen chicks. Just think of all that ripe, just-out-of-high-school pussy, and those perky cheerleader tits ... like the damn locker-room in *Debbie Does Dallas*." He snickers and crosses his legs. "Shit, this's giving me a goddamn hard-on. Let's face it, slugger, I'm already a dirty old man ... at twenty-seven. But there'd be a frustrating downside, since a goddamn ghost can't fuck in the x-y-z dimension." This punch-line sets off more laughing and wheezing, Bryan too. "But we're getting way off track here," Chris says, after sobering. "Let's get back to what you were saying before, and I'll be good now; I will. So go on: you were talking about Mandy?"

"Mandy ... oh, yeah—well like I said, she sees 'em as real."

"And your parents?"

"Hard to say. I reckon they mainly view it as dreaming, the regular kind of night-dreams. And I've never pressed the issue with my mom and dad, or even with my grandfather when he was living, since I always had doubts myself—until recently."

Chris slaps his naked knee, going after another mosquito. No blood; the insect escapes. "So what makes you more certain about it now? You said you were ninety-five percent sure?"

"Well, ever since I had my near-death experience, I've—"

"O Jesus God, don't tell me you had one of those too?"

"I sure did, last May. I almost died during a baseball game, after suffering a TBI."

"You had a traumatic brain injury? You got hit with one of those aluminum bats?"

"No, the ball."

"I thought you guys wore batting helmets?"

"No, this happened when I was sliding into home. The relay throw got me." He takes off his cap and fingers his left temple. "It got me right here; I lost my helmet rounding the bases."

"I noticed that scar tissue by your ear before, but it doesn't look all that serious."

"I also have a scar up here ... from the operation." Bryan pushes his hair back off his forehead.

"So you saw the white light and everything—like that Dr. Moody guy talks about, and your whole life flashed before you?"

"Yeah, it pretty much fits the pattern he talks about in his book, but Dr. Kübler-Ross describes it best in her writings; she worked with the dying and did lots of interviews."

"Aaah ... so this's why you brought up the whole 'when we close our eyes for the last time' discussion earlier?"

Bryan laughs. "Yep, I reckon so. But I sure didn't expect to get this far into the subject."

"Y'went through a tunnel too, and heard the whirring noise?"

"There was a tunnel but no whirring noise. I did hear music though, some kind of country song, before I entered the tunnel—a twangy tune, like Hank Williams Jr., but there were no words."

"And what did your parents say about that?"

"I haven't told 'em—not yet. I just told Mandy."

The jaunty junior wags his head, exhaling loudly—a hissy jet of air. "Damn, slugger, this's way out, like well into the twilight zone. It's no *won*der you're different—hell, I've never had a talk like this with a freshman, or *any*one for that matter. We get into far-out discussions at the lab, but nothing like this—so *this's* why you're all fired up about neuroscience. I figured it had to be bigger than academic curiosity." Hopping out of his chair, Chris hoists his Michelob toward the pearly-white sky; there's no color left save for a ruddy band hugging the horizon. "This's enough to make goddamn Sir Isaac Newton roll over in his grave, along with all the professors and preachers who ever set foot on the Baylor campus, not to mention the know-it-all doctors. I love it. I love it." He smirks impishly, emphatically, his mouth canting more than usual; his thin mustache seems ready to whip up his nose. He pats the wild-haired visage on his T-shirt. "But I doubt we're disturbing Dr. Einstein. He spent his whole life rocking the boat ... like always bringing up impossible shit that pissed all over the accepted laws of physics ... like the fact that time contracts or light bends." Chris drains the last of his beer then crushes the can. "I definitely want to hear more, but first I have to piss on yonder hedge." He swaggers over to the take-a-leak corner of the yard, chin high, his head nodding in chipper fashion, but his lean figure moves in a stiff, non-jockish manner.

Bryan laughs to himself: *I bet he WOULD zoom straight to the girl's dorm, if he ever had an OBE. He's got pussy on the brain. It even gets me going over those freshmen babes, like that gang from Collins Hall I see at the caf. I wonder how many of them are actually virgins.* A tug of guilt tempers his thoughts. *I just wish Mandy and I were gonna sleep in the same bed tonight. It's gonna be hard to wait until our honeymoon. Damn, it's only the fourth of September.* He slaps a mosquito, on his forearm, then sips his brew. He laughs again. *I can't wait to call her. I'll tell her about tonight ... about my big mouth and all.* A crow caws in the distance, its cry mingling with the diminished traffic noise from downtown. The gathering darkness has sucked the green out of the grass, and the trees, and the hedge, leaving various shades of gray. Chris zips up and heads back. Bryan chuckles. *I wonder if he still sees me as gifted and intellectually keen, like at the cafeteria Monday evening. But whatever be the case, Mandy loves me, and I love her ... so nothing can bring me down, not really—even if he calls me a disgrace to science, and chases me outta here. But I doubt he will.*

"Holy Christ!" Chris reacts a good while later, after Bryan has elaborated about his near-death experience. "That's *quite* a story ...

with a happy ending. But the first part when you were hovering over the baseball field—wow, shit, totally wild. That's enough to pucker my goddamn asshole. You *act*ually saw the doctor working on you, and everyone standing around, while you were supposedly unconscious, and these things were corroborated by your girlfriend?"

"You got it," Bryan confirms; he kills off his Michelob, a last, warm swig he was saving till he finished the NDE story.

"Well, it's no wonder that you're more confident now about your other astral experiences. Damn, this's almost enough to convince an ultra-skeptic like me."

Bryan laughs, gesturing with his empty can, but doesn't reply. A mosquito whirs near his ear. He brushes it away. It's almost dark now, and the bugs are worse. The first stars have blinked on overhead, plus a quarter moon in the west, with a brilliant star, looks like Venus, below the moon—all of which provide a fitting astronomical backdrop to their twilight-zone conversation.

"But I can also see why you don't blab this to *every*one," Chris goes on, "and I don't mean getting a crazy label from the scientific community—oh, you'd get that no doubt—but I'm talking about being a Baptist farmboy in Spindle, Texas. This near-death trip of yours hardly conforms to orthodox Christian beliefs, especially the mind-blowing elation you felt. I gather it was more like a cocaine rush, or a sexual high, than a somber, holy, religious sensation."

Bryan chuckles. "I don't know about the drug analogy, but it *was* similar to sexual ecstasy, yet bigger and *better* ... like more expansive, and consuming, and thrilling. Then when I came out of the tunnel into the Heavenly realm, into the bright fog, the feeling peaked then turned peaceful and euphoric, like I was floating in liquid waves of love, and bliss—it was inside me, and yet it was all around me too, and my senses were magnified so I felt all this a million times more."

Chris dog-paddles his shadowy, twilit hands, as if trying to swim out of his chair. "Now that's a *hell* of a good way to die," he chortles. "Y'rode a goddamn orgasm right into glory. Forgive me for being insensitive about death, but you won't hear many pastors, Baptist or otherwise, who preach that dying is better than sex."

"Y'got that right," Bryan declares amid mutual laughter. "That's another reason I keep all this to myself. Pastor Ron preaches about Heaven—he's my pastor back home—and he does talk about the joy and bliss of being in the presence of God, but what he talks about is more self-abasing and worshipful, like we'll be weeping with happiness to be there, but it's more like a great relief that we didn't go to Hell, like into the Lake of Fire. I reckon there'd be quite a hubbub in the pews if he compared it to drugs or *sex*ual pleasure, like you just did." More titters. "But if I had to pick one experience to explain what it was like, then orgasm comes closer than anything, and yet it still falls short."

The junior gives a smirky nod. "So it was better than any sex you ever had, huh?"

"Well uh ... well—"

Chris laughs knowingly. "Hell, I figured you were a virgin."

Bryan dimples and blushes, his face heating; he's glad it's too dark to see color. "Well, we've gotten to second base, maybe to third, but never all the way."

"We? You mean Mandy of course?"

"Yeh ... and she's like me. I mean she's—"

"A virgin too," Chris says, completing the statement.

"I uh ... yes, yeah. She's ... I mean, we're gonna wait until—"

"C'mon, slugger, y'don't have to divulge all your personal stuff ... just because I'm a nosy goddamn pain at times. Just tell me it's none of my fucking business. You don't have to be nice and polite you know, just because I'm older. Fuck that. Besides, I'm getting you way off track. Y'were talking about the euphoria you felt, how it was better than anything on earth."

"Well, there's not much more to say, except I coulda stayed there forever—no problem."

Chris leans back, locking his hands behind his head. "Of course, when doctors and scientists comment on this subject, they dismiss the whole idea of soul or extra-physical cognition ... or sensation. They maintain that the euphoria you felt is simply the mind's way of coping. That's how Dr. Richardson teaches it. He says that shock and trauma cause certain autonomic processes to kick in, which flood the nervous system with endorphins—you know the pain-relieving opiates that our body produces naturally ... and they create the blissful near-death high, along with the dreamy illusion of being out of the body."

Bryan rolls his empty beer can between his hands. "Yeah, I've heard that before, and it *is* plausible, except it's one heck of a coincidence that what I imagined about my unconscious body, and the paramedics, and Doc Wilson, is the exact same as what Mandy saw with her wide-open eyes."

"That's why your case is uniquely convincing," Chris replies.

"It *is* the most amazing thing that ever happened to me, and it sure makes the whole fear-of-death thing less of a downer, but I'm not anxious to get that close again, not yet anyhow." They both laugh. "I still have a lot of living to do ... down here. But another problem with the mind-coping-with-death theory is the fact that I also feel elated during my OBEs, not as strongly, but it's certainly a happy sensation, even the ones that occurred after unhappy events, like when Gramps died."

"But that's the explanation you'd get, if you got up in one of your pre-med classes and told this story—and yet you'd get even less applause if you testified about it at Marvin's church."

"That's for sure," Bryan agrees. "Now St. Paul was taken up to the Third Heaven in Second Corinthians, and he didn't know if he was in his body, or out of his body. But if I made such a claim, they'd say it was the devil deceiving me—maybe not to my face, but that's how they'd view it. This's why I have trouble with the whole church thing, even though I still go most Sundays. Of course, Paul was a first-century apostle, so they accept the supernatural in his life, but not for the modern-day Christian—we're supposed to go by the Word, and *only* the Word."

"Sounds familiar," Chris relates. "I didn't bring it up before when we were talking about God and religion, but I was brought up a Methodist back in Centralia. In fact, my dad was a deacon at our church: Hillside Wesley Methodist. I didn't become agnostic until high school—but since then I've looked at religion from a more objective viewpoint, and I've studied it ... as an observer of humanity. Anyhow, the way I see it, the closed, puritan mind-set has fucked up almost every denomination in America, especially the super-zealous types like Marvin Latrobe. I don't fault folks for seeking God, or crying out to God—I do it myself. I don't know if he hears me, but I do it. Seeking solace in the divine is a natural reaction to our dilemma: we have to face death, and life, without assurance, and that's scary. Nor do I fault believers for gathering together on Sunday. But when their leaders profess to have *all* the answers, with certainty, that strikes me as irrational and dishonest. I'd rather have *no* assurance than false assurance. I'd rather consider all things, even bizarre new things, instead of keeping my mind locked in a box—damn, I'm getting up a good head of steam here. But suffice it to say, the Bible thumpers, like Marvin, won't welcome the idea that you rode an orgasm into Heaven. They don't mix eros and Christ—even the Pentecostals. They ignore the fact that Jesus was a man, with carnal passions. They portray him as nonsexual, a self-sacrificing, super-devoted servant of the Almighty, whose only desire was to save souls and reform people. I'm not saying he was a Casanova, but I bet he had a normal sex drive, and he did hang out with whores ... like Mary Magdalene. And he frequented the seedy bars and back alleys of Capernaum, where the fishermen and tax collectors got drunk, and I suspect that's where the hookers danced and plied their trade." Chris gives an open-handed gesture. "Now I suspect he was there to win them to his cause, and it's less than likely that he was screwing these gals, but it's still a possibility. At any rate, he did declare that the harlots and winebibbers would go into Heaven ahead of the Pharisees. And of course, there's the other time, when he was eating with the local bigwigs, and a woman of the night came in and started kissing and massaging his legs and feet, a most erotic act—and she could've been Mary Mag too."

A mosquito bites Bryan, on the neck; he slaps it. "This kinda talk wouldn't get far at my church back home. It's a given—Jesus never had sex with *any*one, even a wife, much less a *harlot*."

"But it was rare to be single back then," Chris replies, "so Jesus was probably married, and I sure doubt he was celibate his whole life. But this no-sex-for-Jesus attitude just points up what I was saying before. The hard-line evangelicals, and the Catholics, all the fundamentalist religions, even the Muslims—they want us to be afraid of God, and ashamed of sex, with its rapturous, out-of-control pleasure. They want us under control—like on our face before some high and holy throne. But you saw no throne?"

"None at all. There was no throne, or people bowing down—and there was *no* fear ... just a beautiful sense of well-being the whole time, even before the ecstasy inside the tunnel."

"And that part about seeing your grandfather under the oak tree, and sensing that he was talking to you. The Baptists don't preach that I bet?"

"No, they don't," Bryan affirms, tossing the beer can back and forth, from one hand to the other. "But don't get me wrong ... I'm not as negative on organized religion as you are, Chris, and I still believe most Baptist doctrines, but I *do* agree about their narrow-minded ways. Most pastors tend to condemn new things, anything that doesn't fit. That's why I'm more open than most Christians, like more focused on Jesus himself, without putting him in a box. How could I, considering?"

"That's the problem with puritan fundamentalism," Chris declares, paddlewheeling his hands, "or any fundamentalism. You're not allowed to doubt or question; you're not allowed to consider new evidence. They demand blind allegiance to tradition and unproven theories, even failed theories. They fight against progress, just like they've done since the Middle Ages. This's my opinion anyway." He sighs and shakes his head. "All the bigshots in our society pay homage to orthodoxy; they honor the Pope and Billy Graham, and get all quiet and reverent. The politicians, the media types ... they may not be religious themselves, but they still pay homage. And if you're just a common churchgoer, you also get credit ... like brownie points. It sells to be religious—and yet it's hardly rational when you consider that Hitler was religious, along with most tyrants through history ... and almost all wars have been fought for godly causes, so-called ... whether it's the Christians, or the Jews, or the Muslims, or the Hindus, or whatever sect. And each of them sees their way as right, while everyone else is wrong. It's really an ego and power thing."

"And every religious system is crammed full of strict rules and regulations, even the cults."

Chris snorts, giving an affirmative nod of his head. "That's a fact. And it's irrational, like the Christian Scientists won't allow their sick children to visit a doctor, and the Jehovah's Witness religion doesn't believe in blood transfusions, or birthdays, and the Adventists don't use makeup or eat meat, and of course, the evangelical Christians condemn all non-believers to Hell. I can't explain all the bad things that happen, like the Holocaust, or the starving kids in Ethiopia, or the countless innocents that are tormented with abuse of one kind or another. That stuff haunts me, yet I'd say a lot of it has been caused by blind devotion to some religious system—but don't write me off as a God-hater. Just because I abhor what fundamentalist religion does in the name of God, I don't reject God dogmatically. I'm not an atheist. In fact, atheism is just as illogical as narrow-minded zealotry. I'm just uncertain that's all. Yet I do hope there's a loving intelligence behind this reality. And this God I hope for wants us to be free and unashamed, and fully alive, and he wants us to seek the truth, to test the theories ... and to place our confidence in the theories that best fit the evidence."

"Sounds good to me," Bryan interjects.

Chris leans forward in his chair—he chops the air. "I want to weigh the evidence. I want to learn by trial and error, like the scientific method. If any theory of mine doesn't fit reality, then I'll gladly adjust it, or discard it. And we should seek God, and explore the supernatural in the same manner, even though right now the answer to most metaphysical questions is: I don't know, or I'm not sure. That's why I'm an agnostic. But I'm hungry to investigate these mysteries, just like you have a passion to study the link between the brain and the sense of self ... for obvious reasons. After all, slugger, when you get right down to it, it's the passions and affections—what the preachers call 'soul'—that make our mind different from a computer. It's a mystery, but it somehow has to fit together ... the whole love and heart thing ... and the need to break free and truly live. It all has its root in neuroscience, along with the God-connection thing, and the soul thing, and the birth and death thing, all of it. Who knows, Bryan ... maybe God, or destiny wants us to explore this great mystery together someday?" He laughs. "And it'll take something *bigger* than us, the way greed and politics govern the research process these days, but who knows? To every *thing* there is a season ... and God has made every *thing* beautiful in its time."

"You quote the Bible pretty darn good for an agnostic?"

"Oh, I know the book—I just don't expect to find *all* the answers in it. But I suspect you take it more seriously than I do?"

"I reckon so," Bryan replies, slapping another mosquito. "Especially Psalms and Proverbs. And the Gospels of course. Yet there's also a lot that's weird and difficult to understand."

"I know. That's why I don't expect to find all the answers in it." Chris gives his impish smirk. "Like how you can fly around and be in your bed at the same time."

They share a laugh. "It *is* a goshdang mystery. And it *would* be neat to work with you on it someday, Chris, though right now you're *way* ahead of me when it comes to neurology."

"Perhaps so," Chris replies, his voice softening, "but I'm still in the dark on most aspects of brain function, just like I am when it comes to the creative force that made the brain. Yet being an open-minded agnostic is the only honest and logical stance when faced with a mystery, as any student of Sherlock Holmes can attest." He gives Bryan a pat on the knee. "Yet I do have hopes and dreams about God and the issues of religion, especially the idea of living on after death. It seems pointless to go through this life, loving and longing, and then to suddenly cease to exist."

"You got *that* right. We hafta live forever—it's *always* been a big yearning inside me, like the *biggest* thing about me, except maybe for Mandy, and she's connected to it somehow. It's like a quest, and my astral experiences have validated this yearning, inspiring me onward. There has to be something beyond ... for *all* of us ... there *has* to be. I've glimpsed it, but I want more."

"I must say, slugger, I share the same longing, and my hopes about the afterlife fit fairly closely to what you experienced. But it's one thing to hope; it's another to see. In that sense, slugger, you're well ahead of me."

* * *

SPINDLE, TEXAS - GODDARD'S DINER
WEDNESDAY, SEPTEMBER 4, 1991 — 8:06 PM

"Spanky Arnold and Roy," Mandy blurts to Wendy Lewis on the phone. "They were here eating tonight, and Spanky said—"

"You must be at work?" Wendy interrupts.

"Yeah, I'm at the diner, and Spanky says he knows I'm getting married, that he talked with you 'n Lena Beth. But I couldn't call yuh till my break, and then Aunt Marge made me take a party of four, and it took forever, but Spanky—"

"Hold it, hold it. Settle down, kiddo."

"Okay, okay, but it bugs me, what Spanky said," Mandy replies hushedly around the lump in her throat. She shifts her weight from one sneaker to the other, as if about to pee in her panties, but her unease has nothing to do with her bladder. "He was talking about what you 'n Lena Beth said at the goshdang bowling alley last night. I can't believe it."

"Whaddeyuh mean? What'd he say?"

"He uh ... he uh—" Mandy stops to compose herself; it hurts to think that Wendy would do such a thing.

"It's okay, kiddo," Wendy consoles. "Just take your time."

"I am," Mandy sniffles, wiping her eyes with a wadded paper napkin. "I just need a second, that's all." She was late getting her break, as usual, but when Aunt Marge finally gave her the okay, she hurried to the pay-phone by the rest rooms—she normally uses the staff phone in the kitchen for local calls, the one in the chef's cubicle, but not this time, lest Aunt Marge overhear.

"So what the hell did Spanky say that got you upset?" Wendy asks again, after a long moment.

Mandy, having regained her poise, reports the conversation that took place at booth #2.

"No, no, that's not it," Wendy assures. "I didn't tell Spanky, or Lena Beth. No way, kiddo—not a wicked-big secret like that."

"But Spanky was talking like he knew that we'd set a date?"

"Well, he doesn't know anything about that, not about next spring. I reckon he was just gabbing and wisecracking like he usually does. He's been talking about you guys getting hitched ever since you and Bryan started going together last year. I just told him that you two had patched things up ... when you went down to Baylor—and that's all Lena Beth knows as well."

"Oh, *good*; I'm glad; that's good," Mandy gushes, feeling profoundly relieved—she gives a husky little laugh. "I sure didn't think you'd be blabbing our secret stuff."

"You got that right, kiddo ... especially around Lena Beth." Girlish giggles hiss through the phone, in both directions.

"Yeah, if we told her, we may as well put an ad in the paper."

More giggling, then Wendy says, "But she can't help herself. She's gained so much weight. It's like gossip is the only way she can get attention. But Spanky's not like that. He may brag a lot, but he doesn't get off on spreading secrets. Besides, he's in your corner y'know. He's pulling for you 'n Bryan; and he'll be on your side, just like me—even if you guys break *all* the rules."

"Oh, I know, Wen. I'm sorry for overreacting. It's not Spanky. I know he's Bryan's friend no matter what, and mine ... but it's *Mama*. She's the one who gets to me. I hate to think what she's gonna do when she finds out. It's like I'm a super chicken when it comes to her. I know she has to find out, and I'm the one who has to tell her, but I keep putting it off."

"Can't blame yuh, kiddo. She sure won't be giving kudos and high five's, when you break *this* news."

* * *

WACO, TEXAS - 146 DOUGLAS STREET
WEDNESDAY, SEPTEMBER 4, 1991 — 8:11 PM

"Here, slugger, put some of this on," Chris says upon his return. He hands Bryan a squeeze-bottle of insect repellent. "This stuff smells like kerosene, but it should keep those damn mosquitoes and gnats away. We could go inside, but I like sitting out here, under the starry sky."

"Me too," Bryan responds, as he applies the oily repellent to his arms and ears and neck, and to the brim of his baseball hat. "This summer I sat outside with Mandy a few times ... like in the evening ...

and we had a contest to see who could spot the first star, then the second, third, fourth, and so on. I started looking at the stars with Gramps years ago. He was really into it."

"I've always been drawn to the sky, day or night," Chris remarks. "It inspires me and makes me feel free—so, would you like another beer or anything, or more chips? Or I could grab something sweet, like cookies, and I think I have some Eskimo Pies in the fridge?"

"No, I've had plenty," Bryan says, as he returns the insect repellent. "Besides, I should get going soon. You probably have things to do?"

"Nothing more important than this. You can stay as long as you want." Chris sits down. "It's not every day I get a chance to shoot the shit with a real-life Rod Serling character." They share a chuckle. "You were talking about Gramps, your grandfather, about watching the stars with him?"

"We did a *lot* of things together, and we were outside much of the time, and we often went back out after supper to watch the stars come out, especially on clear nights like this."

"This is good weather for star gazing, without the smog. Yet the lights from downtown still interfere, that orange glow over there. I bet you can really see the night sky back on your farm?"

"Yeah, it can be quite spectacular. Gramps knew most of the constellations, and the visible planets, like Venus and Mars, and Saturn. Venus was the brightest, and it was often near the moon, like tonight." Bryan gives a fond chuckle. "He always pointed out the Big Dipper, without fail, and he taught me how to use it to locate the North Star. It was almost a sacred thing with him."

Chris titters. "Yeah, even an irreverent smart-ass like me has to feel a bit humble looking up at the goddamn Milky Way. I can see why Van Gogh was into painting the night sky, and he always exaggerated the stars, making them big and swirly."

"Yeah, I've seen some of his paintings, in these big art books we had at school."

Although Bryan's eyes have adjusted to the dark, everything appears ashen and indistinct, including Chris in the other chair. "You talk about your grandfather a lot," he remarks, his tone becoming earnest again. "I take it you were quite close to him?"

"Yeah, I spent more time with him than with my parents."

Chris beckons upward, toward the stars, his hand moving murkily, vaguely. "It's fascinating that you encountered him in your near-death experience?"

"I'm not sure what it means, but Gramps was the main god-figure in my life, and he still *is*. I mean, he inspires me as much as ever, in my quest ... in my yearning for truth and immortality."

"I gathered as much. So you're a lot like him?"

"In my heart anyway."

"So that's why you're still a Baptist?"

THE SILVER CORD

"Well, he died when I was nine, and it's not like he preached to me, but he's the main reason I did accept Christ when I was twelve—at least, that's when I made it official and got baptized."

"Sounds like my church growing up. Most kids got saved in Sunday school, even me, but I don't see it as having any lasting effect, on most of us anyway." Chris chuckles.

"Yep, it *is* sort of a ritual in most churches. Jesus has been crucified and risen for nearly two thousand years, but the modern term 'born-again Christian' hasn't been around too long. I think it was Billy Sunday who first coined the phrase, in its revival-tent sense, and of course, Billy Graham, and Jimmy Swaggert, and Pat Robertson, all the TV preachers, have pounded it home. But for most it's just a ritual, like joining a club. That's sorta how it was in Spindle, the teen ministry and all. Of course, the Pentecostals speak in tongues to give evidence of being born again, but in many ways that's even more of a formality."

The mosquitoes are still whirring, but they're no longer biting—the repellent is working. "So what about you, slugger? Do you see it as more than a ritual, more than a catch-phrase?"

"I reckon I do ... though it's kind of far out, the teaching attached to it ... like the Holy Spirit coming in to regenerate us: If any man be in Christ, he is a *new* creature."

"Yeah, we learned those same doctrines at my church, and that whole process does seem rather incredible." Chris laughs, a few snuffly syllables. "But it's no more incredible than the idea of coming out of your body and flying around like a ghost."

"No kidding," Bryan chuckles, as he stretches and shifts in his chair.

"What about the resurrection and all that? Do you accept it as historical truth?"

"I reckon so. I've never wavered from the key beliefs concerning *Christ*. I don't put him a box, like I say, and I'm open-minded when to comes to *new* things of course. But I believe he died for my sins, and then rose from the dead, and that he's coming again. It's a faith thing that can't be proved, but that's what Gramps believed, and I trusted him *tot*ally."

"What about Hell and damnation? Do you believe in that?"

"When I was a kid, I had nightmares about Hell, especially after hearing some preacher warn about the 'unpardonable sin.' I even saw the Devil's hand at the end of my bed, or I dreamed I did. But Gramps helped me get over those dreads. He declared that the Jesus he loved would never send me to hell, even if I did bad things from time to time. I reckon he had doubts about anybody going to Hell. That was one doctrine he didn't care for, along with the one that says animals don't have a soul." Bryan gives a chuckling laugh.

"Yeah, the Hell forever thing is hard to swallow, and it's one of the main reasons I became an agnostic. I can't rule it out, but it certainly

257

seems illogical for a divine creator to damn certain people to eternal agony. I don't see any profit in it, even for the worst, most evil types. The God I hope for is into fixing and enlightening people, rather than damning them, and I sure don't buy the idea that saying a prayer with some Marvin Latrobe type is going to make *all* the difference—like forever."

"Gosh, Chris, you sound almost like Gramps. He had this Jewish friend, Michael Leavitt, a gray-headed codger who came out to the farm to play dominoes. And I heard Gramps get pissed a few times, after church, objecting to the teaching that all Jews go to Hell. He wasn't keen on the organized church, even though he went. But he loved the Lord, and I reckon I'm the same. I believe Jesus loves me, and I love him. That's the main thing I hang onto. It's not a macho thing, but it's the biggie."

"But how can you love someone you haven't hung around with? Now you don't have to answer, Bryan, if I'm getting too personal? But it's a question I often posed to myself growing up."

"That's okay; I don't mind talking about it. I reckon it's part of the whole born-again thing, which makes Jesus come alive in my heart, to use a childlike way of describing it. So in that sense we have hung around together." Bryan stands up, to stretch his legs, to get the blood flowing.

"Are you sure it's not Gramps ... your grandfather?"

"Whaddeyuh mean?" Bryan asks, as he steps over to the barbecue pit.

"Well, when you consider Jesus and the whole love-of-God thing, who's the first person who comes to mind?"

"Oh yeah ... Gramps. I see what you're getting at? But you're making my point ... in a roundabout way."

"Don't mind me. I'm just playing the devil's advocate. You may be a churchgoer, but you're a maverick-at-heart ... just like your grandfather. He sounds like a damn character, a boat-rocker in his *own* way. I would've liked him I bet."

"I reckon so ... and he woulda cottoned to you just fine, as he used to put it."

They share a chuckle, then Chris gives a resigned sigh. "But it's the close-minded types that make life difficult. The ones like Marvin Latrobe, who reject their hearts and play the expected role, to gain favor and avoid rejection—and to earn points with God. They always do the right thing, and say the right thing, and kiss the appropriate ass. They're so fucking predictable you could replace them with a robot, and no one would notice hardly. Seek ye first—you know the verse."

Folding his arms, Bryan sits side-saddle on the barbecue pit, next to the lukewarm hibachi. "I sure do. Mandy's mom is a lot like that, at least outwardly. She works for Pastor Ron part-time; she's the church secretary at Pleasant Hill Baptist; that's the name of our church. I mean,

I like her okay, and I know she has a heart, down deep, but she also scares me, her blind allegiance to the Church."

"I gather this makes for some interesting give-and-take between Mandy and her mother?"

"That's for sure," Bryan replies without elaborating, despite an impulse to do so.

Chris spreads his shadowy arms, an expansive gesture. "But it's not just religion, Bryan. We humans seem most willing to deny ourselves, our true selves anyway, to follow some cause. I suspect it has a lot to do with self-esteem ... or self-uncertainty ... and guilt of course. It's like we need approval plus a winning identity. And there's the money issue of course, which makes us all whores to some degree. It's the same in academic circles, and corporate business, and politics, and the military—I was in the Air Force for three years by the way—and I'm sure you've seen it in sports too, among your baseball teammates."

"That's a fact to be sure. Even here at Baylor already, even this afternoon at practice."

"And yet, the Marvin types are the worst, since they march under the banner of Almighty God. It's sad to me, and tragic. I sense that he's a neat person under all that zeal and hype—hell, I almost like the guy. But he's so locked up, like always worrying about sin, especially sexual sin where he plays the guilt card on people, like the puritans have been doing all the way back to Plymouth Rock. Churches exploit their members, taking their money and their time, yet they submit willingly, in most cases. This's why Jesus got crucified. It wasn't because of the Devil, or the need to pay for our sins. He got nailed because he was a rebel, who stirred people up against the religious authorities and the money system, and the oppressive Roman government. I know you believe Jesus died for you sins, and I respect your view, but I see it as barbaric and cruel to think that God would require the blood of his child before he could accept me at his supper table."

"That's all right," Bryan allows. "We certainly aren't gonna agree on everything. In fact, I'm surprised that we have as much common ground as we do."

"No kidding," Chris concurs. "But the worst thing about the hard-line evangelicals is the way they separate people in the *name* of God ... to keep the flock pure, to keep the sheep from doubting and falling away. The preacher has to warn them all the time about worldly friends, like exhorting and commanding that they reject anyone who might lead them astray, and I mean total, no-talk rejection, like shunning forever."

"Pastor Ron doesn't harp on that much," Bryan replies, as he returns to his chair, "but I sure know whatcha mean."

"That's why my mom and dad split up when I was in the tenth

grade. She couldn't deal with his sudden fervor for God, and his demand that they serve the Lord more, and give thousands to support Methodist missionaries. She was trying to raise us—I have a younger brother—while Dad was giving everything to the church, and yet after it was all over, I found out that he was secretly screwing one of the Sunday-school teachers."

"That's a hard thing to go through, Chris—and yet, I can see how it opened your eyes."

"But the God I hope for is the exact opposite of Marvin." Leaning forward, Chris points at the sky. "Just look at those stars up there. They're moving a trillion miles an hour, and they're exploding and changing and being born and dying, and they're swirling in galaxies, and they're being sucked into black holes. And the God I hope for made them all: the heavens declare his handiwork. At least, he unleashed their genesis in the Big Bang. On that I'm hardly agnostic—someone had to light the fuse. And he didn't make the stars to *scare* us, but to give us hope, to make us dream ... to inspire us to think big, and to live big, and to love big—to live each day from the HEART!"

"Whew," Bryan responds, as Chris pauses for a breath. "I must say you're one rare agnostic. Not only d'yuh know the Bible, but you're a *gosh*dang good preacher too."

"I guess I did get a bit carried away there."

"No problem. In fact, I like what you're saying."

"Well, that's my take on it. And when I look up at the sky on a night like this, it makes me realize how bound up we are down here. We yearn to be free and full of love and life, and eros and poetry, and boundless ideas that take us to new places and into revolutionary adventures. But the religious, socially correct mind-set is petrified of such things. They preach security and structure and proper behavior, and self-control. They want us to conform, to play the expected role. They applaud piety and duty ... and safety. But when we march to that drum it just makes us lonely and sad, because what we really want is LOVE—and LOVE is not orderly or secure, or predictable." Chris whaps the arm of his lawn chair. "It's risky and stormy and untamed, and when it comes, it blows our nice Christian life away."

These powerful words quicken Bryan, uncorking him. Before he can check himself, he's telling Chris everything, all about his Mandy-love, and how it has indeed been risky and unpredictable, even this week, especially this week.

When he finishes, a good bit later, Chris gives a knowing chuckle then says, "Damn, slugger ... talking with you is like watching four movies at the *same* time, and I got a feeling each one of them is going to keep us on the edge of our seats."

* * *

It's after ten when Bryan finally departs the O'Shea residence. As he hustles along Douglas Street, he hears a dog barking. It's cool enough for a jacket now, so it feels good to walk fast. He can scarcely believe how long he and Chris talked, or what they talked about. But the heartfelt sharing has bonded them.

The puckish junior did most of the talking for the last hour, telling Bryan about his life back home, his three-semester stint at the University of Chicago, his hitch in the Air Force, along with more about his parents' problems. Finally, he talked about his love life, about Jennifer Clay from Wheaton, Illinois. They lived together for one year. Then one day she left, and Chris was too heartbroken to stay in Chicago, so he joined the Air Force, and trained to be a medic, which fired his ambition to be a doctor, and that led him eventually to Baylor and pre-med.

It's amazing, Bryan chuckles, as he walks north on Baker. *Chris is always joking and carrying on about all the pussy on campus, and how ripe and ready they are, and yet he's not had one of them. He's only been with one lover ... that Jennifer gal.*

THE SILVER CORD

CHAPTER SIXTEEN

WACO, TEXAS - THE BEAR'S PAW LOUNGE
SATURDAY, SEPTEMBER 7, 1991 — 4:21 PM

"So you're all psyched for Monday?" Chris says, as he and Bryan lay claim to a table on the far side, near the raised band-dais and emergency exit. "All that Mickey Mouse bullshit is over for you freshmen. The new semester starts for real."

"Tell me about it," Bryan replies, removing his blue Spindle Tiger cap. "I got four classes Monday, and two on Tuesday." He hand-wipes his perspiry brow. "And I got enough books to start a dadgum library, like $350 worth. It was a goshdang workout, just getting 'em back to the dorm." He laughs. "I've glanced through most of 'em, but *stud*ying is another thing."

Chris wags his curly head. "I bet you can't wait, slugger. Hell, you probably get off on studying, don't you? But it figures, you being a self-disciplined, country-boy scholar, and a damn Baptist to boot." He grins teasingly under his mustache.

"Get outta here. Stop pulling my leg ... like y'do."

Their bantering voices echo strangely about the large, near-empty lounge, which is decked out with green-and-gold bunting to celebrate the kickoff of the '91 football season, along with a big GO BEARS! banner behind the bar. The Bear's Paw is a college hangout (pub and club) on Conley Avenue, not far from Floyd Casey Field where Baylor is beating Louisville—at least, they were leading by twenty points with seven minutes to go. Bryan and Chris left the game early to beat the crowd, so they have the pub to themselves, for now. The cool air in here, plus the dim lighting, offers welcome relief from the sweltering stadium, but the dank, yeasty, bar-room odor reminds Bryan of Benny's Billiard Hall back home, though Benny's is one-tenth the size, a seedy redneck rathole compared to this place with its sea of tables, along with the dais, a dance floor, and a pool-and-game room (video games) to one side.

"So where's the john?" Bryan asks. "I gotta take a leak."

"Over there, beyond the pool tables—go down that hallway; you can't miss it. So you want a beer or what? I'll order for us."

"Goshdang," the freshman responds, hushedly. "I'm only *eighteen*, y'know?" He speaks at low volume, lest anyone hear him, though no one is close enough, especially the fat bartender.

Chris gives his impish smirk, along with a jaunty little salute. "Don't sweat the small stuff. Just go; I'll get you a Budweiser."

When Bryan returns, he finds a frosty bottle of Bud Light waiting for him. "This's a goddamn college town," the puckish junior explains, gesturing with a foamy mug of draft beer. "They look the other way, as long as someone in the party is legal."

"Yeah, we got a bar back home where under-agers get served, and sometimes y'can get beer at the bowling alley, and a lot of the locals go over to The Cove—that's a dance-hall roadhouse on the other side of the lake. But I ... well, I—"

"But I'm a *good* boy," Chris wisecracks, "a good Baptist boy. I don't hang out with the rowdies and floozies and sinners. I don't get bombed on Saturday night like the hayseed hicks, who dance and howl and wave their big, sweaty cowboy hats. I don't ride mechanical bulls and bet on the goddamn mud-wrestling sluts. I take my gal to church picnics instead. I'm a good boy, I am."

Bryan dimples sheepishly, his cheeks warming. "Well, I—"

"C'mon, slugger, drink your damn beer. I'm just putting you on— like while ago, like I always do." Bryan laughs and sips his Bud, while Chris smirks, his brown eyes sparking; he grabs a few corn chips from the gratis basket that comes with the drinks. "I was born a goddamn joker; it's in my blood I guess—but I *am* corrupting you. Hell, you've probably had more beer since you met me, than you drank all during high school."

"Almost," Bryan confesses, "but I reckon a little corrupting won't hurt me none." He drinks more Bud then clicks his bottle against Chris's mug, toasting the jovial moment. (A glass came with Bryan's brew, but he ignores it, a la Spanky Arnold.)

The mustached junior takes a swig then backtracks: "It was a damn overreaction anyway, when they raised the Texas drinking age from eighteen to twenty-one. A few Waco establishments enforce it, but most have an unspoken policy to draw the line at eighteen, where it used to be. They'd never admit it, but that's the way this fucking town operates, especially the bars and restaurants that cater to college kids .... like right here." He sweeps an open hand toward the empty tables and deserted bar. The paunchy, balding barkeep has retreated, along with the waitresses, to the hostess station near the entrance. A lady with a beehive hairdo huddles with them, evidently instructing them about the post-game rush, which will commence shortly.

"There's no drinking on campus," Chris goes on, "so this place makes a bundle serving Baylor students, all the upstanding, born-again, beer-drinking Christians—except for Marvin, of course; he sips a Seven-Up, and hands out those goddamn tracts, so he won't feel guilty for being here." They share a hearty laugh. "And bands come in to play. Like later tonight, the *Kilroy Kingpins*—they're a local country-rock group. Plus, the menu's decent, mainly sandwiches, but most guys come to get buzzed and check out the chicks. This's one of the few hangouts where the girls feel comfortable. Most nights, there's more pussy in this place than a gold-rush whorehouse, but they come by the carload, or with their damn boyfriends, so picking one up is a long shot." Chris waggles his head. "You have a better chance of connecting with Baylor cunts in class, or lucking out and getting some sweet young thing for a lab partner."

Here he goes again, Bryan chuckles to himself. *But I'm sure not looking for a sweet young lab partner.* He thinks about Mandy; he shifts sideways in his chair, then forward again.

"Forgive me, slugger. I know you're getting hitched in the spring, but I can't help myself. I'm a horny agnostic son-of-a-bitch." Chris gestures with his mug, the foam sloshing back and forth. "If I can't have the girl in my heart, then I'd like to fuck them all, especially those baby-faced, first-year sweethearts." He lifts his chin in a bawdy, swashbuckling fashion. "I'm a horny bastard, I am—and I'm more irreverent than the goddamn Devil, when I get going." He snickers. "But I doubt I'll be fucking any female soon, whether sweet or sour, or young or old." He laughs again then settles. Popping more corn chips into his mouth, he quaffs his beer to wash them down. "But anyway, slugger, this place is usually perking and hopping. And the fraternities have keg-parties here, not in the main lounge, but out back in the Bear's Den—that's the new building on the other side of the parking lot. But this main pub has been here since the fifties, so it has a lot of history and tradition. I don't come here as much as I used to, now that I'm an old man of twenty-seven. But the younger students need a watering hole to escape to, especially you freshmen—they really lay it on you the first year, with all the required bullshit and the damn extra reading."

"The course load *is* bit overwhelming," Bryan replies thickly, speaking through a mouthful of chips. "It's exciting in a way, the challenge, but it's also scary. It's like they wanna weed out the weaklings as soon as possible."

"Not really; it just seems that way. The academic board has actually relaxed things in recent years, to boost enrollment. Most anyone, even C-students from podunk high schools can make it, no problem. Most professors grade on the curve big-time, so you'll breeze right to the top."

"Get outta here."

"I mean it—you're a goddam genius compared to the average Baylor freshman. Plus, you're focused ... for obvious reasons ... so you won't be distracted by all the campus falderal."

"Falderal?"

"You know, the whole Greek scene, the rushing and pledging. Baylor, being Baptist, was never a party school like UT, but we do have fraternities and sororities, though they're not as big as they once were. But jocks, of course, have their own crowd; they don't get into all that Beta Alpha Epsilon bullshit, or Beta whatever. I never got involved either, being older—it's quite juvenile if you ask me. Anyway, it's probably good that you're a baseball stud, and a good-boy Baptist with a girl back home." Chris laughs then sips his brew. "I mean, you *will* have to bust your butt a bit, to make all A's. I mean, the extra reading, and the term papers."

"Yeah, I reckon I have some late nights ahead of me."

Chris burps through another laugh. "But I doubt we'll catch your roommate burning much midnight oil. He strikes me as all-jock." (Jordan sat with them at the game.)

"You got that right."

"But they'll still pass him, as long as he shows up. They rarely flunk a scholarship athlete. And I bet he's taking the easiest courses, like Retail Math and Word Processing 101."

"His schedule *is* pretty low-key. He doesn't have a clue when it comes to physics or chemistry, or high-octane stuff ... but he's not *dumb*. In fact, he's quite sharp when it comes to the things he cares about."

"I'll say. The guy's like a goddam computer when it comes to sports trivia. Hell, he knew the stats on every player at the game, even the opposing team. I don't know shit about sports, except golf maybe. I do watch that on TV. But I didn't even know Louisville University had a fucking football team. I hardly ever go to the games here, but it's rare to get a free ticket."

"Well, don't expect one every week," Bryan kids, between sips of Bud Light. "Jordan got these from his friend Jamal, who plays on the team. You know, number twenty-four, the guy who returned that kickoff fifty yards, while Steve was jumping and screaming—I thought he was gonna break the goshdang seat."

"He does get into it."

"Tell me about it. He gets just as excited when he's watching baseball back at the dorm."

"Yet he seems to have a big heart, and he doesn't hide it at all. I mean, he kept on talking about his girlfriend in Wichita Falls, and how he was going to see her *right* after the game."

Bryan gives a fond chuckle. "He *is* a character ... like an overgrown kid. I thought at first that he was just a big airhead—y'know ... no original thought since seventh grade. But now I'm seeing a lot more. In fact, I think his simple, honest way of—"

"Hey, Chris!" comes a high-pitched voice, from the other side of the room. "Chris Hansen."

"Well, if it isn't Tracy McCollum," Chris declares, as a cute, dark-haired babe hurries over to their table. "I thought you transferred to LSU, to be with Stu?"

"No, the whole thing fell apart," she explains, as she gives Chris a peck on the cheek. "I reckon I'll be right here, after all."

Bryan, nursing his Bud, looks on awkwardly, trying to be cool and cordial without staring. And yet, he can scarcely ignore her perfumy, brown-eyed presence. She's tall for a girl, and stoutly built inside her baggy T-shirt and khaki shorts, but she does have a figure—

she's not roly-poly by any means, a little beefy in the butt perhaps, but not fat, and she's not bovine-busted, like so many of the hippish gals on campus.

"And Stuart?" Chris asks, giving his classic smirk, along with a palms-up, what-gives gesture.

Tracy snorts and tosses her head. "He's at LSU, just like he planned." She hand-combs her bangs to the side. Her short, black, wind-mussed hair frames her kitty-cat cuteness like a football helmet. "But that bastard is *his*tory as far as I'm concerned." She goes on elaborating about Stu, who must be her ex-boyfriend. She speaks with a rural twang, but it's not exactly Texas, and the pitch of her voice seems unusually high for her age and size; it's almost squeaky, more like a teenybopper than a five-nine Baylor coed—she has to be five-nine, or close. As she fills Chris in, she slices the air with her slender, honey-brown hand; her arms are surprisingly lean, and graceful.

The strap of her handbag slips off her shoulder; she pushes it back up. "But let's stop talking about him ... before I start cussing." Shifting, she cants her upper body one way, her hips the other, flexing one knee. Bryan, catching a glimpse of thigh below the cuff of her shorts, averts his eyes instantly, determinedly, but her flesh lingers appealingly in his mind, the creamy, less-tanned inside of her leg. Guilt nips his conscience, but the nibbling vibes quickly turn into longing— a longing for Mandy.

"So you're back in Collins?" Chris inquires, still smirking.

"You got it. I just moved my stuff in. Jamie's gonna be my roommate again. That's why I came in here. I'm looking for her. She said to meet her here after the game."

"Well, the after-game crowd hasn't arrived yet, as you can see, but it won't be long—oh, excuse me. I'm sorry, slugger." Chris tips his head toward Bryan. "Tracy, this's Bryan Howard. He's a freshman baseball star, and he has ambitions of becoming a neuroscience nut, like me."

After a moment of self-conscious tittering, all three of them, Bryan stands and shakes her hand—it feels slim and girlish and clammy. She blushes and gives a shy little grin, but he mainly notes her dark, Hershey-brown eyes, which have a concave Asian sweep to them, or it could be Indian blood. But her pretty Doric nose and prim mouth seem a better match for her Irish name. Ditto for her complexion, which is fair and unblemished, save for pink spots of peeling on her cheeks and nostril wings. He's taller, but not that much—she's five-nine to be sure, maybe five-ten.

"Have a seat, gal, and let me order you a beer," Chris says, after Bryan sits back down. "You may as well join us, while you're waiting for Jamie."

"Well uh ... okay. But first, I hafta visit the powder room." Before leaving, she gives Bryan the eye, a sidelong glance.

"Don't even think about it, Tracy," Chris teases. "He may be a good-looking jock, but he's taken; he's got a gal back home." Bryan blushes but hides his unease behind a sip of Bud. "He's engaged in fact. Besides, he's too *young* for you."

"Chris Hansen, you're terrible," she scolds good-naturedly. "You have *no* tact at all." She snorts then departs—but gets in another gibe, over her shoulder: "And you still dress like a bum. I can't believe you're wearing that damn Einstein shirt."

Her full buttocks shifting potently from side to side, she disappears down the narrow hallway beyond the pool tables. Chris downs some beer then pushes the mug toward the ladies' room. "She's an all-right girl, once you get to know her. We went out together a couple of times back in '89—that's when I first got here—but it was awkward and not at all romantic. She has a big-sister personality, at least around me, despite the fact I'm six years older—so we ended up friends. I still have fantasies about screwing her, but that's hardly news. I'm a horny bastard, I am. I even kid her about it, but she doesn't take me seriously."

"So she's in pre-med too?"

"No, pediatric nursing ... at least, she was last spring. She's changed her damn major three times in two years—she's a junior like me. But we *did* meet at the neuroscience lab. She takes care of the rodents, the research mice and rats, plus she does odd jobs for Doc Richardson, and she helps me when things get hectic. It's her campus job, or it was. But anyway, she ended up with my buddy Stuart LeClair. She knew him already; they're both from Louisiana, like way down in Cajun country. He was a graduate assistant for Professor Richardson, but now he's got a research position at LSU. We had a few deep discussions, Stu and me, but nothing like the other night—he never floated out of his body, to my knowledge." They share a laugh. "Stu's smart, smarter than most doctors, but he didn't have the grades to get into med school. He was more into basketball. He even got picked by the pros, drafted or whatever they call it. But it didn't work out, so he came back to Baylor to do graduate work in anesthesiology. He's brilliant, but he can also be a goddamn asshole, especially when it comes to women, so it doesn't shock me that he and Tracy broke up." Chris gestures again toward the rest rooms. "She was a basketball player herself, in high school, but—"

"She's certainly *tall* enough," Bryan interjects.

"But she couldn't make the team here. Too slow down the court—that's how she puts it." Chris gives a lewd giggle. "She's not built for speed, with that ass of hers. But it sure gives her a nice fuckable shape, and she sure knows how to wiggle it."

THE SILVER CORD

* * *

When I get back to the dorm, I'm gonna call Mandy first thing, Bryan proclaims eagerly to himself, as he hops into the stifling cab of his pickup. His heart pangs for her.

After rolling the windows down, he fires up the Chevy and backs down the driveway. They took Chris's Chevette—it *does* sound like a bumblebee—to the game, not to the game actually but straight to the Bear's Paw; you can park in their lot for free if you have a recent receipt from the bar. Traffic and parking, game-day hustling: anyone with a square of open asphalt, or gravel, or lawn, or dirt, even a few spaces, can charge top dollar when the Baylor Bears are playing at home. As Bryan rumbles west on Douglas, he feels relieved—and free. He likes being with Chris, but after Tracy joined them, and then Jamie, a skinny little blonde with grasshopper legs and *no* boobs, he found himself wishing he was out of there. Joking, gossip, another round of beer; two guys, two girls, laughter, and jesting—his conscience reacted: *Watch out. They're flirting with you, especially Tracy. You're being unfaithful to Mandy. This's like a double date.*

No it's not, he countered. *I didn't plan this. And I can't just walk out. I don't wanna be rude. And I can't help but notice Tracy's legs— she's wearing shorts. But she's not here to be with me; she's Chris's friend, and Jamie looks more like a thirteen-year-old boy than anybody's date, especially with her butchy haircut and those zits on her chin, all pasty with pink cover-up.*

Nonetheless, he couldn't quell his unease, or his longing for Mandy, not to mention the bassy blare of the jukebox and the boisterous, increasingly drunk, post-game crowd, which had transformed the once-quiet pub into wall-to-wall rollick, akin to a Bourbon Street blues joint during Mardi Gras. And Jamie, despite her scrawny figure, drinks like an oilfield roughneck, and she has this perverse way of casting her eyes heavenward, as if posing for a Madonna painting—yet she looks anything but motherly. Tracy strikes him as more intelligent, and more fun, and sexier certainly, as his conscience attests, though she too, after three beers, became rather irksome. She *does* have a bossy, big-sister personality, especially toward Chris: she pestered about the Einstein shirt, his foul language, his need for a haircut, even about his impish smirk; then she needled him about his reclusive off-campus lifestyle, and his lack of a steady girlfriend—and on and on. Too much: Bryan politely excused himself, escaping the crowd, then he hoofed it back to the O'Shea residence.

That whole bar-scene is not for me, he declares to himself a few minutes later, as he hangs a left on Spangler. *It's like a big, false, hyped-up thing, like everyone is trying to look happy, and act happy, and the booze helps them perform.* The deserted campus—there's not a soul in sight on this sultry Saturday evening—strengthens his sense of liberty. *Maybe I'm wrong? Maybe they're actually happy? But I doubt it. I think they're looking for love, even Chris, with all his wisecracks and lewd jesting ... and Tracy ... and Jamie. But once you find it, you don't have to play that game.* He sighs. *O Jesus God, I thank you for Mandy, and I'd rather be alone with her than anything ... like under the big oak tree back home. We don't need a crowd.*

* * *

An hour later, Bryan lies breathless on his bed, basking in Mandy-afterglow: heart, mind—and body. He hugs his pillow. *She was really glad I called. She loves me. I hear it in her voice; I feel it in her eyes, even when I just picture them in my mind, her big blue eyes. And she can't wait till the twenty-seventh. I can't wait either.* He sighs happily. *Gosh, what a week this has been. It was just last Sunday that we made up—hard to believe.* He gives another sigh that turns into chuckle. *I could go home sooner I reckon*—the thought gives him a rush. *Nawh, the waiting will make it better. Plus, I hafta concentrate on my studies. I wanna get off to a good start in my classes, and on the baseball field. But my phone bill's already outta sight, and I've only had the dang thing since Tuesday.* More chuckles.

CHAPTER SEVENTEEN

INTERSTATE 35 - HILLSBORO, TX
FRIDAY, SEPTEMBER 27, 1991 — 1:10 PM

Three more hours, Bryan Howard declares to himself, as he veers to the right, following the signs for 35E, which goes northeast to Dallas, while 35W goes due north to Ft. Worth. *Getting out of Waco early is a real bonus. I should be home by four-fifteen, instead of six ... like I told Mom last night.*

Rotating his cap back on his head, he slips on his aviator sunglasses. The rain has ceased, the clouds are breaking, but the highway remains wet. A cool front slid southward through the region overnight, setting off showers and chasing, for now, the summerlike heat and humidity. Bryan even wore a jacket to class this morning—it's on the seat beside him, not his high-school letter jacket, but a lighter denim one. It's not nippy out by any means, 65°-70° maybe, but the cooler, drier air mass working down from the Rockies and Upper Plains promises a fallish feel to the air this weekend. That's how Norm Gossage, the Channel 2 weatherman, explained it. And Spindle will feel it more than Waco, especially at night on the farm.

Bryan jockeys around an 18-wheeler hauling rusty oilfield pipe. A burst of road spray coats the windshield; he flicks the wipers on, then off. The fields and wooded groves lie washed and puddled, their checkerboard pattern looking more green than brown after the rain. He spurs the pickup, pushing up to 75 mph. His one o'clock English Comp class with Professor Emerson was canceled—he found out at noon, a PA announcement in the caf. Forgoing lunch, he hot-footed it back to the dorm. He packed his bag while gobbling down a baloney sandwich, then he hit the road, stopping for gas in Bellmead.

Ahead of him slanted shafts of sunshine pour through the tattered overcast. You rarely see sunbeams in Texas, and Bryan takes them as a good sign, just like Gramps always did: *O Lord, it's like you're right here with me. I can hardly believe how much you've blessed me since Mandy and I made up.*

Despite the long odds for a freshman, he's well on his way to nailing down a starting position on the Baylor baseball team, with a .416 intersquad batting average plus five home runs. Old Coach McKinney has taken a liking to young Mr. Howard and gives him many helpful pointers—plus, he said he'd cover for Bryan at practice today. Fridays in the fall are low key anyhow. Good things are also happening in the academic arena where he finds the study load well within his capabilities. There have been no *big* exams as yet, but he's aced the weekly Chemistry quizzes, along with a couple of pop tests in American History. Dorm life has likewise been a plus, despite his roommate's Oscar Madison tendencies—Steve Jordan has turned out to be a true pal. Ditto for his friendship with Chris Hansen. They've gotten together two more times, and Bryan often eats with Chris at the caf.

The only cloud in this sunny picture is Helen Stevens. Mandy has yet to tell her about the wedding, but she's going to, and Helen will surely accept the situation, once she realizes that her daughter is not *about* to retreat? And either way, they can get married in July if it comes to that. But the Helen thing is a back-burner issue right now. Bryan isn't thinking past Sunday.

* * *

THE HOWARD FARM
FRIDAY, SEPTEMBER 27, 1991 — 2:45 PM

"Hi, Mom Howard!" Mandy greets, as she rounds the house, making her way between the big cedar bush and the ten-foot mesh-style satellite dish. "I thought yuh might be back here. I hope y'don't mind me getting here early."

"Of course not, sweetheart," Ginny replies, taking a sheet off the line. "I heard yuh drive up, but I figured you'd find me, and if it was someone else, I didn't care if they found me." She laughs. "Oh, I like your blouse, and your hair—your bangs look so blond in the sunshine. You look *downright* pretty."

Mandy grins, her cheeks warming. "Thanks," she responds, pawing the grass with her sneaker. She left her softball cap in the Firebird. The shirt is new, an Aztec print, long-sleeved, a fallish tawny brown—it has a Western flavor that goes good with her faded Levi's. "And thanks for inviting me over for supper."

"You're quite welcome ... but I hope you're not famished or anything, because we're eating late, like around seven ... since Bryan won't be here until six or after."

"Well, I'm not exactly thinking about food right now."

"Nor am I, and I'm just his *mother*."

They share a giggle, as the ponytailed high-schooler hurries over to help get the rest of the laundry off the old four-wire clothesline. Ginny is dressed in her housework garb, an old gray sweat shirt plus khaki dungarees, but her ashy-blond hair looks clean and fresh, and a trifle damp, as though she just got out of the shower before coming down to bring the clothes in.

The breeze feels pleasantly warm, because of the sun. It was chilly and rainy this morning, but the clouds are gone now, aside from the puffy fair-weather kind. Mandy has been feeling good all day, and being here with Mom Howard amplifies the cozy sense of elation, as does the farm itself, the house, the barn, the fields. *I feel SO at home here,* she thinks happily, as she unpins a pillowcase. *And next spring we're gonna get married in this very yard, Bryan and me ... with the birds singing, and the grass all green, and the sun shining bright— just like today.*

"It *is* exciting to have him home," Ginny remarks a moment later, moving closer to Mandy, "even if it's only a weekend."

"That's for goshdang sure. I hardly slept last night."

They laugh, then Ginny's eyes fill with yearning, her ocean-green, Bryan-like eyes. "I don't reckon I'll ever get used to him being gone. It's only been four weeks, yet it seems like a year. But this's gonna be extra special, his first weekend home. I even got off work early. And the weather has turned out beautiful too. All that heat and humidity is gone." She beckons skyward then inhales deeply. "I love how the air smells in the fall. It's gonna be perfect for his homecoming. I already vacuumed, and I got supper all planned, plus I got his room all set, except for his bed; I had to wait for these sheets to dry. And I still need a few things from the store, and I hafta pick up Henry at five-fifteen. The Buick's down at Tom's Texaco till next week. Billy Ray's fixing the brakes or something. Henry may trade that Buick anyway ... for a new pickup, since Bryan took the Chevy to Waco ... but we might just get an old used truck, to haul hay and such."

Mandy tosses a pair of overalls into the basket then gives a girlish titter. "I got home early too. We had a team meeting for basketball, since practice starts next week, but I wiggled out of it. Coach Perkins acted tough, like she does, but then she laughed and said, 'Go on, get outta here. Y'know all my policies anyway.' I didn't tell her exactly, but I think she knew Bryan was the reason." More titters, from both of them. "So when I got home, I took a quick shower and got dressed and all, then I decided to come right on out here. Mama's at work until four. She knows I'm eating with y'all tonight, and that Bryan's gonna be here for the weekend and all, but she has a habit of messing up my plans at the last minute ... like making me baby-sit."

"So who *is* watching Gretchen?" Mom Howard asks.

"Oh, she's staying overnight at Molly Ann's, which is good. Molly Ann Heimberg—they're always together. But Gretch is almost nine, so she can be home alone anyway, during daylight."

"Well, I'm *glad* you came early. It gives me a good excuse to take a break. We'll have a snack, to tide us over till supper ... as soon as we get these clothes in. I have a dryer, but I like to put 'em on the line when I can. They turn out fresher, and whiter. So when the sun came out, I decided to take advantage of it."

* * *

While the two women in his life bring in the laundry, Bryan passes over Lake Ray Hubbard, the Chevy humming across the long I-30 bridge. He bounces his hand on his thigh, keeping time to Fats Domino and *I Want to Walk You Home*. He's tuned to KRYZ, the oldie station.

THE SILVER CORD

The bluesy rhythm stokes his Mandy-high, until his happy heart seems ready to burst out of his bosom.

Highway construction, stop-and-go traffic: he lost thirty minutes on 635, circling the south side of Dallas, but he's now cruising again. After two more tunes (*The Beatles* plus Roy Orbison), the news comes on: something about Yugoslav tanks invading Croatia, a blurb on Secretary of State Baker's West Bank ultimatum to Israel, then a report on nukes in the former Soviet Union, and how they could fall into the wrong hands, and then a local story declaring that 46% of Texas blacks live below the U.S. poverty line, which is defined as an income of $12,674 for a family of—too much: Bryan kills the radio. He does care about current events; he even has to track the news for his American History class, but right now he's thinking only of his sweetheart: *I wonder if she'll be at the house when I get there?*

* * *

Truth is, she's al*ready* at the house, having a heart-to-heart with Bryan's mom, over doughnuts and coffee and Dr. Pepper (for Mandy). "I don't blame yuh for being reluctant," Ginny says, after dunking her doughnut and taking a drippy bite. "I doubt your mama's gonna be too thrilled about this wedding."

"No kidding."

"But I reckon you'll hafta tell her at some point."

"Oh, I know," Mandy sighs, between sips of Dr. Pepper; she already downed her doughnut, and her fingers are sticky from the glaze. "It's not like I'm *twelve* or anything. I'll be eighteen next July, so Mama has to let go at some point." Mandy wipes her fingers on a paper napkin. "And she's not against Bryan; she likes him a lot in fact. But she has this super-perfect, Christian-family idea, where y'grow up and get educated and financially stable, and rooted in Christ, and then when you're twenty-four, and everything's *just* right, you can get married."

They share a chuckle, as Ginny dabs the kitchen table with her own napkin, dealing with the spilled coffee—the dark-pine piece is constructed like a picnic table, and it has benches instead of chairs. Tonight they'll be in the dining room, around the big fancy, fold-out table. "I sure don't remember us being financially stable when *I* was twenty-four," Ginny relates, still chuckling. "I was pregnant with Bryan, like big as a hippo. But I know what Pastor Ron preaches about family situations. Still, pious planning is one thing ... while love is *another*."

Snowball pads into the kitchen and meows insistently at the door. Ginny gets up and lets the old cat out. "Okay, your royal highness, okay."

"I'm glad Toby has his own door ... our tomcat," Mandy comments, with a titter, as Ginny sits back down. "Otherwise, we'd be at the dadgum door a hundred times a day."

"We had a cat door too, but I got tired of finding partially eaten mice on the kitchen floor."

"Yeah, Toby brings 'em in sometimes, but he mainly leaves 'em on the back porch."

"Well, it's instinctive, how cats behave, and that sort of fits in with what I was saying before." Ginny picks up the last of her doughnut and gestures with it. "You can't stop cats from killing mice, even though the Bible says thou shalt not kill. And God's the one who made cats with predator instincts. It's more than I can figure out, so I just have to accept it. Same goes for hearts that are in love. You can't tell a heart to stop loving. You just hafta stand back and *give* it room."

"I wish Mama saw things your way, instead being a control-freak. But after what *she* went through as a teenager, I reckon it's hard for her to have an open mind on this whole issue."

"I agree, Mandy ... but I do know Helen enough to realize that she loves you very much. She does want the *best* for you—it's just that her idea of *best* is different than yours. And to be honest with you, honey, it probably *would* be wiser if you and Bryan waited a few more years before getting married." She downs the piece of doughnut then gives a resigned shrug. "But true love is rarely *wise*. That's why it's so thrilling and romantic and scary, all at the same time. So I'm not about to play judge and jury on what you two decide to do." Reaching across the table, she gives the teenager a tender caress on the shoulder, conveying more love than words ever could. Mandy's eyes fill.

Mom Howard slides off the bench, taking her coffee to the sink where she pours the last of it down the drain. "But that's *enough* serious talk for now," she announces. "It's almost three-thirty. Let's not worry about when you're gonna tell your Mama, or what she's gonna do." Ginny steps into the big old pantry off the kitchen—it's still a pantry, but it's also the laundry room. "Let's get these sheets ironed, then you can help me make up Bryan's bed, then I gotta change my clothes and do my hair and get going ... if we're gonna have that baked-ham supper. I have a special sweet sauce I baste it with, and the flavor penetrates better the longer I leave it in. And we also hafta tend to Millie." Mandy, hustling over, helps Mom Howard unfold the ironing board. "You 'n Bryan are gonna have three happy days together—that's as far as we hafta think right now."

* * *

After giving Millie some oats, and checking her water, Virginia Howard and Mandy exit the barn. "Now, honey, y'make yourself right at home," Ginny says, as she prepares to get into her little gray Honda. "Y'can watch TV or put a movie in the VCR, or whatever. I reckon I'll be back around five-thirty ... after I do my shopping and pick up my husband. And thanks for helping with the chores."

"Anytime, Mom Howard. It was neat, the talk we had."

Ginny gives her a warm embrace. "Oh, Mandy, you're such a blessing. I knew it at the hospital. That's when I realized how devoted you are to Bryan. I love you like a daughter."

"I love you too," Mandy declares, returning the hug, "and it's an honor and a blessing for me that I'm gonna be part of your family—I feel like I already am."

"Oh, you are, sweetheart, you are. I'm just glad that you 'n Bryan worked everything out that Sunday before we came back. The love you two have is *rare* ... and beautiful. And I do hope things go smoothly between you and your mom, but no matter what, you're always welcome here. You can even live here until next May, if it comes to that." Ginny gives a motherly chuckle. "I doubt it will, and I sure hope it doesn't—for everyone's sake. But let's not fret about it now."

After Ginny departs, Mandy goes back inside. Plopping down on the living-room sofa, she flips on the TV. The guy on the Weather Channel is talking about thunderstorms in Mississippi. Then the local conditions (Sulphur Springs) flash onto the screen, plus the weekend forecast: chilly nights; sunny days. *It's ten after four,* she remarks to herself. *Two hours, at least. Dang, this's like waiting for dadgum Christmas.* She thumbs through *Satellite TV Week,* the program guide, but she's scarcely in the mood for searching through the endless choices. It's easier to sit back and surf. (At her house they still have old-fashioned TV, antenna only, six channels max, but she knows how to operate the Howards' satellite system.) Using the remote, she zaps to another channel, Court TV, which is boring, then to C-Span—ultra boring—then to a Dracula movie, *uuugh,* then to some home-repair program—*super uuugh.* Rotating the dish to another satellite, she surfs some more, then she moves to a third satellite where she finally finds a "Little House on the Prairie" rerun, the heart-wrenching episode where Mary Ingalls loses her sight. Mandy, as a small girl, was addicted to "Little House," and she still watches it a lot with Gretchen, but not today.

Zapping the television off, she heads for the stairs. No TV, no air conditioners, no one home: the house seems strangely quiet. She almost feels like an intruder as she trots up to Bryan's room, her Reeboks slapping the wooden treads more loudly than usual, or so it seems. She was up here before, helping Ginny make his bed, but now she's free to browse. She scans the rustic beams in the ceiling, the knotty-pine paneling, the huge homemade desk, the bookshelves. The books are gone, most of them, and the computer, but Bryan's pennants and pictures still adorn the walls, along with the shelves of trophies and awards, plus his gun rack and little-league bat rack. She's drawn to everything, since it all speaks of her dear babe, and his upraising here on the farm. She can even smell him in here, his manly, jockish aroma, like sweat and Brute mixed together. She also detects a faint cigar stink, or maybe it's just in her mind. She laughs, as she recalls how

THE SILVER CORD

Bryan always brings up Gramps and the cigar thing every time she's up here. Beyond the trophy shelves in fact, near the corner, hangs a large picture of Gramps and Bryan holding a stringer of orange-bellied fish, a dozen pan-sized bluegill. Gramps wears an old Texaco cap, while Bryan has a flat top, and he's smiling with no front teeth. Mandy *loves* that picture.

She goes to the desk, to the bay window. She can't help but focus on the giant oak tree, its canopy still summer-verdant in the sunshine as it looms majestically in the distance. She recalls the happy times on that hilltop, and at Ruby Pond beyond. She cherishes everything she can see from this window, all the trees and fields and trails, plus the fences and the barn, even the old weather-grayed henhouse—not to speak of the blue sky and fleecy clouds, which perfectly crown the sunny, rain-greened landscape. The striking panorama stirs a sweet yearning, a longing to know Bryan as a little boy, to know what it was like for him living here on this farm his whole life, like when he was four, or seven, or eleven. *Once we're married,* she sighs, *we'll talk and share night after night, and day after day, till we know each other as much as we know ourselves.* She's gathered bits and pieces of his boyhood life, but she's hungry for the whole story.

A buzzard circles high above the barn, its widespread wings seesawing stiffly on the breeze, a common sight yet impressive, and mesmerizing. She watches the large, dark, carrion-seeking bird, as it glides lazily around toward the hayfields where it spirals higher, riding an updraft—then the vulture goes blurry amid a wave of drowsiness. Mandy's lack of sleep is catching up to her. She yawns, her thoughts drifting like the buzzard—but then a pang of concern sharpens her focus, chasing the sleepiness. *But how canyuh get married without telling Mama? It's been a month, and you STILL haven't told her.* A shiver courses up her spine. The room is hardly cold, with the air conditioner off, but she feels suddenly chilly. Hugging herself, she turns abruptly away from the window, away from the sunny view of the farm.

Her conscience readily plays the role of Mama: *"It's just an adolescent emotional thing"*—*"Most high-school romances never lead to marriage, and those that do, usually end in divorce."* She toes the carpet with her Reebok. *"It would be nice if life was a fairy tale, but that's not reality, honey."*—*"Bryan may be a sweet Christian lad, but he's certainly not ready for a wife. And you're scarcely more than a child, Amanda."*

The negative barrage threatens Mandy's mood, the happy sense of expectation, but Mom Howard's counsel comes to the rescue: *"The love you two have is rare and beautiful.... You can even live here until next May.... You can't tell a heart to stop loving. You just hafta stand back and give it room."*

"She's right," Mandy proclaims, in a loud whisper, as she escapes the self-doubt. "I'm not gonna bow down on this, no matter what Mama says. And I'll tell her my plans when I damn well please." She stomps the floor. *I'm not a little kid anymore. Mama has to let go. Besides, she's just trying to deal with her own guilt, like she's trying to relive her life through me—but she can't. It's not HER life. It's mine ... and I'm gonna spend it with Bryan. We're gonna BE together, and we're gonna SLEEP together. Now that's the most delicious thought of all.*

Love and marriage may go together like a horse and carriage, but it's gonna be goshdang hard to wait for that buggy to arrive. She giggles. *But maybe we shouldn't wait? Maybe we should go to a motel and get it on, or the barn, or wherever. At some point nature's gonna win, 'cause love and desire: they go together like heat and fire.* She giggles louder. *Not exactly great poetry, but it's the biggest practical reality I know of. It's a good thing I got those condoms from Wendy* (they're stashed in the back of the Pontiac, plus she has one in her purse), *even though we won't need 'em right away. No way am I ovulating—my period's due on Tuesday, or is it Monday? Now if Mama was to find those rubbers, she'd really go ballistic.* More girlish titters. *And yet I'm sure she's seen plenty of 'em, even when she was younger than me. But there's not a chance she'll be looking under my spare tire. Bryan may've gotten some too, but I doubt it—he's not as practical as I am. Let's face it; it's gonna happen. Maybe THIS weekend even— probably not, but it could.*

She sashays about the room, swinging her hips, gesturing provocatively with her arms. *O dear Lord, I'm ripe and ready. I don't wanna be a virgin anymore. I love him. And I want him forever—but also NOW.* She gives a husky murmur. *Oh, Bryan babe, when you get here, I may grab you and not let go.* She dances faster, jitterbugging, twirling, reaching for the ceiling—until she's dizzy and panting. She halts, finally, beside the queen-size bed, the one they just put clean sheets on. Catching her breath, she waits for the spinning room to slow, and stop.

In tune with the rustic decor, the bed is made of pine, and sports a large headboard. Two fat, goose-down pillows are neatly tucked under the purplish, quilted bedspread, while another quilt, a blue-and-white comforter, lies folded at the foot. Mandy, like a child at play, stands erect then allows her stiff body to collapse slowly backward onto the bed. She kicks off her sneakers. *I wonder what it's gonna be like,* she says to herself, her eyes closing. *I want him so much, and yet Wendy says it hurts the first time, and bleeds when the hymen breaks. And he's got quite a package. I still can't believe how big it got that day by the creek. But I don't care if it hurts.* She gives a randy chuckle. *Gosh, I haven't kissed him for a month.* She chuckles again, the laugh turning into a sigh, an exhausted sigh. Her libido urges her onward along this track of thought, but she's feeling sleepy again, now that she's reclining. Removing the pillows from their tucked positions, she props one under her head while embracing the other, as if it's Bryan. She pulls the comforter up over her. *I'll just rest here a minute. He won't be here until six anyway.*

* * *

As Bryan turns off FR 92 onto 115, the happy balloon in his bosom inflates to the max—he's pumped with glad anticipation. His pulse quickens. Even the gray, timeworn pavement seems glad as it sings along under the spinning tires of the old Chevy. He checks his watch: 4:51 p.m. *I'm still ahead of schedule,* he chuckles, as he fishes his Brute cologne from the travel bag on the seat beside him. *I doubt Mandy's at the house yet, but I guess I should be ready anyhow, in case she runs out and attacks me.* Laughing louder, he slaps some Brute onto his cheeks, then he grabs a tube of Colgate toothpaste and sucks a bit into his mouth.

Five minutes later, he turns onto Longley Road, and the Howard homestead soon appears in the rolling distance, on the left beyond Caddo Creek. Glory to God, joy unspeakable: the old farm, sunny, sprawling, verdant from rain, seems as beautiful as the Heavenly landscape in his near-death experience. A small herd of Angus, fifteen or so, graze peacefully on the leased, west-side acreage, while the hayfields beyond ripple in the breeze.

"She *is* here," he exults, as he rattles across the cattleguard and heads up the familiar driveway. "There's her Firebird."

He parks in his usual spot near the barn. *But I don't see Mom's Honda, or the Buick? This is peculiar, but I'm sure not complaining.* Grabbing his bag, he jogs to the back porch where he pauses briefly to pet Snowball before hustling inside, into the familiar smells of his lifelong home, topped by the sweetish aroma of baked ham. "Anybody here?" he inquires in a normal tone, as he strides through the kitchen— no answer. Dropping, with a heavy clunk, his travel bag, he goes into the bathroom off the downstairs hallway. *Hmmm ... I wonder if she and Mom went to town?* he says to himself, as he empties his bladder. *Or Mandy could be hiding ... like waiting to pounce on me?* He laughs boyishly under his breath. *She's too much I tellyuh.*

Exiting the bathroom, he proceeds carefully toward the stairs, lest she come whooping out of the dining room, or the living room, or out of one of the closets. "Hey, anybody home?" he asks again, as he ascends the stairs, bag in hand. Entering his room, his heart does a happy jig, as he discovers a curious but wonderful surprise: cuddled under the comforter, his precious Mandy naps like Goldilocks on his bed. At least, her eyes are closed, and she shows no reaction to his presence. Tiptoeing across the room, he puts down the bag quietly, places his cap on the empty desktop, then quickly sheds his sneakers.

Awestruck, he studies her from a distance—no movement, steady breathing, blond ponytail curled forward under her chin. No doubt:

she's asleep. *What's going on?* he chuckles giddily to himself. *I come home from college, and there's nobody here except Mandy in my BED. When? How? What? I must be asleep myself and dreaming this?* But the questions quickly surrender to an upwelling of affection, which ushers him silently to her side. He adjusts, gingerly, the comforter, so it completely covers her denim-clad legs. Going down on his knees, he gazes at her closed eyes, her adorable, sun-freckled nose, her valentine mouth, her feathered bangs and earlocks which cutely frame her sleeping countenance. He leans closer, close enough to feel the warmth of her flesh, and to inhale the sweet fragrance of her hair plus a hint of perfume, the summer scent she wears. Warm, intoxicating vibes spin outward from Bryan's heart, coursing along every nerve and sinew, casting a wondrous spell. He longs to kiss that rosy, half-puckered mouth, but he resists for now. There's no sound, save for the slight hiss of her breathing. He studies a pinkish spot of new skin on the high point of her cheek where a bit of sunburn has peeled back amid the ruddy tan and freckles. A similar spot highlights the knob of her nose. It's almost October, but summer still reigns in her country-gal face. A budding pimple, more *red* than pink, seems ready to erupt on her chin. He loves her, he adores her, even her blemishes, and he's glad she doesn't wear that yucky, pasty cover-up stuff (like Tracy's friend Jamie). Mandy has no make-up at all, save for a light application of lip-gloss, which has cracked a trifle along the pucker lines.

Little girl, seductive woman; Goldilocks, Sharon Stone. How can she be so innocent and childlike, yet so sexually potent? He can scarcely fathom this question, much less answer it. He just knows he's powerless to resist her call, and that he has no life without her, no incentive to dream or achieve, or to do anything, like in August when they broke up. *Dear Lord,* he prays silently, his eyes filling. *This love, our love—it's the most incredible thing, like how I felt at the edge of Heaven.* Too much: he has to touch her. Ever so gently he caresses her shoulder through the quilt, then her arm, then her hip—she feels wonderfully warm and inviting. He lightly fingers her bangs and forehead. Finally, he kisses her bangs, then the side of her mouth.

Mandy stirs, her big blue eyes blinking open—she smiles tenderly. "Oh, babe, it's you. Is it six already?"

"No way," Bryan replies, dimpling. "It's five-eleven to be precise. I got here early."

"Me too," she giggles sleepily, "like straight from school almost." Turning onto her back, she stretches and yawns.

Bryan aches to kiss her—he can taste her lips—yet he resists a bit longer. "So how'd you end up in my bed, pretty lady—not that I mind?" They both laugh. "I reckon y'weren't kidding the other night when yuh said things might happen this weekend."

Mandy smirks and blushes. "Get outta here, you big jock." Throwing the comforter back, she gives him a playful jab to the shoulder then sits up on the side of the bed; she puckers her nose then fingerfluffs her hair. "No, your mom had to go shopping, then she's gonna pick up your dad at the feed store. The Buick's at the Texaco station. Billy Ray's fixing the brakes."

"Damn—sounds like you know *every*thing that's going on."

She giggles huskily. "Y'got that right, mister—but anyhow, I was watching TV, then I got bored, so I decided to come up here. And I got sleepy I reckon."

"I reckon you did."

"My hair's a dadgum mess," she fusses. "And I just washed it this afternoon. I should get my purse outta the Firebird." But the coquettish side-glance suggests she has more exciting intentions.

Bryan takes her hand; their eyes meet. "Oh, pretty lady, I missed you *so* much." She replies with a kiss, her tongue darting sensually. Lips locked, they fall sideways onto the bed.

"O God, I missed you too," she coos, coming up for air. "And I'm gonna kiss your face off—but first I gotta freshen my mouth in the bathroom. I got that blah, sleepy taste, which I'm sure you noticed." Before Bryan can say anything, she's on her way out of the room, her hips gyrating provocatively, a plume of giggles trailing behind her.

"Oh, that's *super* nice," Mandy sighs ten minutes later, as Bryan fondles her ruddy-nippled breasts. "It's like you have electricity in your fingertips." After several rounds of heavy necking, he ended up on his back on the bed, while she sits atop him, straddling his waist.

Bryan dimples. "So y'like that d'yuh?"

"O Jesus, yes," she purrs, looking down at him with trancy eyes, her dilated pupils darkly agaze: unsated lust haloed in blue. "If yuh keep that up, I'm gonna take off my jeans, and *yours* too ... but *don't* stop." She already shed the Aztec shirt, plus her bra. His balls pang, while his engorged cock, trapped like a catapult under her, seems ready to rip through the damply hot layers of fabric that separate his desire from hers.

"Oh, pretty lady, you're getting me *so* high?"

Grimacing with delight, she tucks her chin into her shoulder. "Tell me about it, mister. I can feel yuh under me." She shifts a trifle. "Ah there—that's even better." She grinds her crotch against his hard-on, slowly but intently. She gives a muted giggle, then her eyes close, her face going dreamy. Her tongue lolls on her lower lip. Uttering a throaty murmur, she picks up the pace.

O God, he cries silently. *Her pussy's rubbing me just right.*

Mews, moans, denim humping denim—then comes the gritty rumble of an arriving vehicle. "Oh shit," Mandy reacts, rolling off Bryan. "They're here."

"You okay, pretty lady?" he asks a minute later, as they hurriedly get themselves together.

"Couldn't be better," Mandy jests, as she buttons her shirt. "I like stopping *half*way. I have *will*power remember?" They share a breathy laugh. "But I advise yuh to be ready, mister ... 'cause that's just a preview of *com*ing attractions—pun intended." More giggles. "Dry-fucking is good hot fun ... but we're gonna finish this first chance we get—without any dadgum clothes." She gives him a sensual kiss to seal the deal, then they hurry downstairs, just in time to greet Ginny and Henry at the back door.

* * *

THE HOWARD FARM
SATURDAY, SEPTEMBER 28, 1991 — 7:48 AM

After feeding and grooming Millie, Bryan gives her a fond slap on the hindquarters. She whinnies then gallops playfully out of the barn into her small romp-around pasture where buttery swaths of sunshine, the first rays to make it over the pine grove, have painted the dewy grass. She whinnies again, pawing the ground, swishing her dark tail, tossing her head—her long shadow doing the same. Bryan gets the message: she wants him to come and frolic. The aging mare still has a lot of filly in her. "I can't now, old girl," he tells her. "But this afternoon we're gonna take you out for a ride, me and Mandy."

Millie, showing her teeth like Mr. Ed on TV, snuffles and snorts and shakes her mane, as if to say, "Well, I know where I rank on *your* list. But I reckon it stands to reason, since you're a horny stud, and she's in heat *all* year round."

Chuckling at Millie's antics, Bryan grabs a rake (from its wall-hook) and cleans out her stall, raking the dirty straw outside. He has on a sweat shirt plus his denim jacket, and he needs both on this fallish morn. And yet the sunshine signals a pleasant day, and he's eager to spend as much of it as he can with his sweetheart (she'll be here about noon), albeit with little prospect of finishing what they started yesterday. "Looks like we're gonna be virgins a little longer," she whispered to Bryan after supper last night, while they helped Ginny clear the table. "I got my friend; I just found out in the bathroom."

"Oh well," he replied hushedly, giving an awh-shucks grin, "it's hardly the end of the world." But his nonchalant, no-big-deal pose offered little solace. In truth, the news disappointed him more than a little, as it dashed his giddy high. Plus, he felt guilty for letting his flesh rule his emotions, when he should've been thinking of Mandy. After all, she's the one who has to put up with cramps and bleeding for four-plus days, not him.

Nonetheless, despite their drastically lowered expectations, they still escaped to the barn after the dishes were done. "My dang period would hafta come early *this* month," Mandy declared, as they strolled hand-in-hand across the dark yard, a flashlight beam dancing ahead. She gave a resigned snuffle, but it quickly turned into laugh. "I reckon

God's watching over us, huh? And I used to be so regular, like twenty-eight days, but last month it was twenty-six, and this month, twenty-*five*. See whatcha do to me, you big jock." She chortled heartily, making Bryan laugh too.

Climbing up into the hayloft, they sprawled in the straw where they kissed and hugged and laughed and teased—and tickled each other. They toyed with the flashlight, illuminating the gray rafters above, plus the roof planks and support beams, then working their hands, they created huge shadow-monsters. Finally, they studied the elaborate cobwebs in the corners and crevices until the light got weak, the batteries waning. Turning it off, they cuddled in the dark. "Oh, Bryan babe," she cooed after a while, "going all the way with you is gonna be heavenly, and I'm sorry I sorta spoiled things. But I want it to be just right the f—"

"Oh, pretty lady, it's not *your* fault. It's perfectly normal."

"I know, but what I'm getting at is uh ... well, even if we never could do it, I'd still love you forever. I knew it at the hospital the day you got hurt. God answered my prayers—but even if you had ended up paralyzed or something, I woulda still wanted to be with you my *whole* life."

Returning to the present, Bryan spreads clean straw around Millie's stall, then he replaces the rake on its hook. Exiting the barn, he heads back to the house. While waiting for Mandy, he plans to hit the books for a few hours. The dewy grass wets his cowboy boots. The air has a bracing nip to it, enough to make his breath visible. When he came down for breakfast earlier, it was 40° on the thermometer outside the kitchen window, downright cold for September. *Once we're married*, he says to himself, his thoughts going back to sex, *we'll be together every night. So it's no big deal ... that it didn't happen this weekend.*

Going inside, he finds his mother at the kitchen table, sipping coffee in her bathrobe, her ashy-blond hair still disheveled and unkempt. This strikes him as odd; she doesn't lounge around the kitchen after doing the breakfast dishes, even on weekends (it's traditional at the Howard farm to eat early and heartily, and then to get on with the day, a routine carried over from the old days when Bryan was a wee lad and Gramps was alive, and they had a corn crop, and cotton and watermelons, and cows and chickens, plenty to keep them busy from sunrise to sunset). While Bryan washes his hands at the sink, he and his mom exchange a few comments about Millie, and about the chilly weather, and how they had to turn the heat on for the first time since April—then after a pause she announces, "Bryan honey, I have something for you. I'll be back in a minute. Why don'tcha have another cup of coffee? I made a fresh pot of decaf."

After getting his brew (in a big brown mug that belonged to Gramps), he sits down, sliding onto the bench opposite his mom's half-empty cup (a small, blue mug from the set of dishes, he and his dad gave her for her birthday last month). Henry has already departed, taking the Honda to the feed store; he works every other Saturday. Snowball meows at the door. Bryan gets up to let her out. "Okay, you old-lady cat, but be kind to the mice for a change."

As he returns to the table, his mom comes back into the kitchen. "I don't care for this decaf of yours," she kids, as she tops off her cup from the fresh pot. "I need my batteries charged in the morning ... especially now that I'm pushing fifty." She laughs. "But there's no point in making more regular."

He dimples, lifting the brown mug. "Get off it, Mom. You're barely forty-two?"

"But look at my hair," she says, as she sits down at the table; she fingers a lock near her temple. "I'm certainly gray enough to be fifty?"

"I don't call that gray. It looks blond to me." He's right for the most part: despite a bit of frost here and there, her ash-blond hair remains more blond than ashy. "But even if you *were* gray, or white-haired for that matter, you'd still be the *best-looking* mom in all of Texas."

Her green eyes sparking, Ginny blushes girlishly, her heart-shaped face going pinker than the roses on her robe (a kimono-like garment she wears on chilly mornings). "You're too much, Bryan. You really know how to lay it on thick, don'tcha. It's no *wonder* Mandy lost her head over you." They share a laugh, as he senses his own cheeks warming.

Between sips of coffee, they engage in more fond mother-son jesting, then comes a quieter, more serious moment. "You said you had something for me?" he asks curiously.

She looks beyond him, her eyes pensive and wide, as if gazing into another dimension. "I do ... but it's for Mandy actually, for you to give to her ... if yuh like it. My mother gave it to me—Grandma Scott, who you barely knew. She died of cancer when you were four."

"I remember her ... sort of."

Ginny's attention returns to the table—she caresses her son's hand, giving him a tender, motherly look, her face full of yearning. "I want so much for you and Mandy to be happy. I believe in my heart that God has chosen you for each other. I've been convinced of it ever since that terrible night at the hospital. She's a remarkable gal, and I know she loves you, Bryan, with *every* fiber of her being ... but there are always obstacles that get in the way of love, especially when you're both so young—like last month, what y'went through. And I'm not gonna kid yuh: there'll be more trials and tribulations to test your devotion to each other. That's how life is; this world can be a cruel, cold place. Jesus says that a little child is the greatest in the kingdom, but most people, even Christians, *especially* Christians, are more interested in your outward performance than in the passions of your soul. They want winners at any cost; they don't want us to 'become as a little child.' So it's *never* easy to follow the heart." Her green eyes fill. "But I wantcha to know, honey, that I love you dearly, and Mandy too, and when you two get married in the spring, or whatever you two do in the name of love, I'm rooting for you *all* the way."

Bryan starts to reply, but he can't get the words past the lump in his throat. He sniffles, fighting back his own tears.

"I'm sorry to prolong this," Ginny consoles softly, as she reaches into the pocket of her robe and comes out with a small, blue-velvet jewelry box. "It should be close to the right size, but if not, we'll take it to Sulphur Springs and have it fitted."

Taking the box, he opens the spring-held top, uncovering a magnificent engagement ring. Diamonds, goldwork, perfect for Mandy: the antique setting sports a large center stone surrounded by four smaller ones—it dazzles without being overlarge or gaudy. He doesn't know much about rings, but he realizes instantly that this is *one* of a kind.

*   *   *

INTERSTATE 635
SUNDAY, SEPTEMBER 29, 1991 — 7:21 PM

I'm halfway to Waco, Bryan tells himself, as he slows for the construction bottleneck south of Big D. The hazy heat has returned, the preview of fall retreating northward. It's almost sultry. But he feels too good to be bothered by the weather, or the traffic. The sun has set; it's getting dark—the Dallas skyline on his right grows brighter by the minute. He cares little for urban settings, but the glassy cluster of square-topped buildings does have a certain beauty at night, especially the steeplelike communication spires, with their red-blinking lights.

He's still very much a virgin, and Mandy too, yet he could scarcely be happier about his weekend at home. He gave her the ring on Saturday afternoon. They rode Millie down to the big oak tree, and while the mare grazed on the side of the hill, he and Mandy spent a blissful two hours lounging in their favorite spot. The ring thrilled her, rendering her speechless, though she did manage a few slangy superlatives: wow, awesome, goshdang super! He explained about Grandma Scott, about how he barely knew her, while he never knew his maternal grandfather—he was an Army NCO (MSG Jonathan Eric Scott), who died in Vietnam five years before Bryan was born.

But Mandy also had a surprise for him: "Guess what, you big jock, I'm coming down to Baylor in two weeks, on Friday the 11th. I worked out my schedule with Aunt Marge this morning, and Mama even said it was okay, as long as I drive only in the daytime, and as long as I'm back by Sunday at six; she even said she'd sign a note so I can get outta school early. I expected her to say no for sure, but when I got home from work, she was on the phone with Charlie, and I could tell she was in a super-good mood, so when she got off, I hit here with

THE SILVER CORD

the Baylor request ... ta-dah! Maybe I shoulda gotten her blessing on the wedding too, but I didn't wanna press my luck. I reckon I'll hafta keep that a secret a little longer, till I get back from visiting you."

* * *

BAYLOR UNIVERSITY - FLETCHER HALL, UNIT 311
SUNDAY, SEPTEMBER 29, 1991 — 10:31 PM

Bryan sheds his clothes, getting ready for bed; he's been back for an hour and a half, and he just finished the last of his homework. He pads in his underwear to the bathroom. "Hey, dude, I gotta remind yuh of sumpthin'," Steve Jordan drawls, after removing his earphones—the big guy's sprawled on the sofa watching the Sunday-night NFL game (Steelers vs. Redskins).

"What's that?" Bryan asks, stepping out into the kitchen.

"Remember how I toldjuh I was goin' to Wichita Falls this Friday, since the Bears are playin' Arkansas ... on the road?"

"Yeah, y'said something about it, before I left for Spindle."

Jordan gestures with the earphones. "Well, I decided to leave Thursday mornin' instead, after my word-processing class. It's Susie's birthday, and we're gonna celebrate. So you ain't gonna see my fat ass around here for three nights I reckon."

"What about your *other* classes, and baseball practice?"

"It's no big deal," Steve replies, hauling himself up into a sitting position. He spreads his mammoth hands over the coffee table, palms down, like an umpire giving a "safe" signal. "I've only cut three classes since school started." He repeats the spread-hands gesture. "Shit, Jamal skips a couple ever' week." He gives a pudgy grin then lies down again. "And Coach Weaver knows all about my heat. I got nuthin' else to prove till spring."

"Well, this place won't be the same, but I reckon I'll be able to sit on that goshdang sofa for a change." But the big guy has already replaced the TV-earphones, tuning Bryan out.

After brushing his teeth, Bryan adjusts the AC thermostat then returns to his room, closing the door behind him. But before he can crawl into bed, his phone warbles.

"Oh, Bryan babe," Mandy gushes. "I know it's super late, but I just had to hear your voice before I went to sleep."

"Gosh, I'm glad you called," he replies. "I got back here about nine, but I can't stop thinking about yuh."

"Me neither, and I'm so excited about coming down there on the eleventh. I can't *wait*. It's gonna be the biggest, best thing that *ever* happened. Oh, babe, you make me *so* happy, and I love the ring. I can't stop looking at it, and it fits super good, and before we know it, I'll be wearing it every day ... once I tell Mama. I'm gonna tell her when I get back from Waco—that'll be the best time. But right now, I

285

got it in my underwear drawer." She giggles huskily. "Well, that's all I wanted to say. You make me so *gosh*dang happy, and crazy—I'll be out of my mind by the time I get there, so you better be ready for action, mister."

CHAPTER EIGHTEEN

SPINDLE, TEXAS - COLBY DRIVE
THURSDAY, OCTOBER 3, 1991 — 7:24 AM

Mandy Stevens, yawning, pours milk on her Cheerios. Her mom and Gretchen are still upstairs, but she's dressed and ready to go. She has to meet with Mr. Denham before school concerning her lab project, which involves the application of Newton's laws to a basketball in flight, a most familiar subject for her.

After finishing her cereal, and toast, she takes the dishes to the sink, grabs her school bag and car keys, and heads for the door, but before she gets there, a godlike voice stops her—cold: "So what's this all about, Amanda?"

Mandy turns around, her life changing forever. Time slows to a crawl, the kitchen going dark except for her mom's extended palm and the blue ring-box upon it.

* * *

BAYLOR UNIVERSITY - FLETCHER HALL, UNIT 311
THURSDAY, OCTOBER 3, 1991 — 11:59 AM

Returning to his room after his morning classes, Bryan finds his answering machine blinking wildly—he has four messages. *Dear God, what's this?* he cries to himself, his alarmed heart racing and thudding. *No one has my number except Mandy and Mom, but why would they try to reach me four times on a weekday morning? O Jesus, maybe somebody died?* Tossing his books on the bed, he quickly pushes the playback button:

> **Message #1** — Oh, Bryan babe, it's me (she sniffles, her voice breaking). I hafta talk to you ... like soon, like *now.* Call me at Wendy's house ... 319-456-4254. It's eight-fifteen but I'm not going to school. Mama and me—we just had it out. She *found* the ring.

> **Message #2** — Bryan, me again. You must be at class. It's nine o'clock. I'm still at Wendy's house. She skipped school, so we could talk. I-I uh ... I uh, I uh ... (silence then sobs).

> **Message #3** — Sorry I lost it while ago. But anyway, Mama found the ring last night while I was at the diner, but she didn't nail me till this morning.

I fessed up, but it didn't help. She says no way in *hell* is any daughter of hers gonna get married at seventeen, and my trip to Baylor on the 11th is off, then she said I couldn't go out with you at *all* until I graduate. So I said I was leaving, and she said *fine*, go, get out.... So call me at Wen's: 319-456-4254. I love you.

Message #4 — Bryan, you don't hafta call. I made my decision. I'm coming down to Waco today, like pronto. It's eleven-thirty now, so I should be at your dorm around three-thirty. Me and Wendy had a long talk, then she helped me get my clothes and stuff. I barely got room to get into the goshdang Firebird (giggles). This's one hell of a day I tellyuh, but I feel good now, like *super* free. I got *wind* under my wings, and I'm flying outta here. Oh, babe, I love you *so*.

His knees shaking, Bryan goes into the big room where he cleans up Steve Jordan's mess, the usual collection of clothes and shoes and dishes, plus potato-chip bags and Pepsi cans. The big guy evidently took off for Wichita Falls after his WP class, as planned, and the tumultuous disorder of his bedroom gives witness to a hasty departure. *Gosh, his room is a total disaster,* Bryan declares to himself, as he tosses Jordan's clothes in there then closes the door—all the way. *Even more so than usual—but why am I rushing to clean up now? Mandy can't come up here until Saturday. God, I'm losing it.*

He steps over to the window where he tries to collect himself. *O God, she left home. She's on the way. It's downright scary almost, and yet things could turn out REAL good.* Taking a long slow breath, he watches a green rattletrap pickup, as it hotrods out of the parking lot, discharging a plume of oily smoke that mingles with the heat waves rising from the pavement. Autumn heat: October has come in like September ended: sultry, hazy, summerlike. *But where is she gonna stay? And what's her mom gonna do? If Mandy's really leaving for good, we'll hafta live off campus, but how will that work if we're not married, my scholarship status? And what are we gonna—maybe I should call Chris Hansen? He's the one who told me about the guest-house dorm. Stop it. Hold it. There's no point in fishing for answers now. I don't even know all the gosh-damn questions.*

His Fletcher Hall comrades, in twosomes and threesomes, make their way toward the Waco Creek walk-bridge and the cafeteria beyond. *I better get going, if I'm gonna eat lunch and get to English Comp— no way: forget lunch, forget class. To heck with Professor Emerson. I got BIG things going on. Damn, she's gonna be here in a few hours.*

THE SILVER CORD

She's got way more balls than I do. He chuckles, his reaction firming on the positive side. *Yeah, this could turn out REAL good ... at least, in the short run. In any case, I got a feeling we're gonna end up in the SAME bed.* More chuckles. *And I reckon I'm gonna be skipping practice, unless it gets washed out by those storms they're predicting. That could be one building now.* A swelling cumulus, a baby thunderhead, shades the north half of the campus.

* * *

INTERSTATE 35 - SOUTH OF DALLAS
THURSDAY, OCTOBER 3, 1991 — 2:28 PM

Should be easy from here on, Mandy tells herself as she highballs toward Waco. *Getting around Dallas was the tricky part, and that construction cost me a lot of time.* She glances at the map on the shift console (she picked up the fold-out map at the Shell station in Sulphur Springs, where she stopped for gas). *Now that I'm on 35, it's a no-brainer to get to Baylor. I can't wait.*

Farms and ranches glide by on both sides, along with dirt roads and fences and old windmills, and cattle ponds and streams and stretches of woodland (pine, oak, cottonwood, plus willows marking the creekbeds and waterholes). Moderate traffic, mainly trucks: at least, she notices the trucks more. She whips past a slow-moving rig, an Allied moving van laboring on the slight, but long, upgrade. *I'm glad I don't have a van full of furniture. A carload of clothes and stuff is plenty, especially when I have no idea where I'm gonna be living.* Her things are piled helter-skelter in the back, and she has a bulging trash bag of stuff in the passenger seat beside her plus a suitcase wedged in front of it. Leather shoes, sneakers, fabric-softener, perfume: the car smells like her room, like her closet. She and Wendy hurriedly grabbed as much as they could fit into the hatchback coupe—the rear seats are folded down to maximize the cargo area.

Puffy clouds dapple the sky, and some have grown beyond the cottony, fair-weather stage, especially to the west and south (ahead of her) where they've joined to form a dark band along the horizon. Despite the low October sun, it's stifling out: hazy, muggy, hard to breathe. But she's not feeling the heat inside the sporty, air-conditioned Pontiac—not from the *weather* anyway. She left Spindle with the radio rocking, her mood soaring, but she now rides in silence, save for her thoughts. She has no misgivings about choosing Bryan over her mom—there *was* no choice—but the exhilarating sense of liberty and adventure has diminished somewhat, as the bigness of her decision weighs upon her, not to mention driving fatigue and drained emotions; and she misses her little sister. "I hafta go, Gretch," Mandy blurted this morning before escaping to Wendy's house; she gave Gretchen a tearful hug. "If Mama's gonna be this way, I can't live here. But I love you special, and I'll tellyuh more when I get a chance."

Mandy takes a swig of warm Dr. Pepper (she grabbed two Dr. P's while getting her stuff, plus Fritos and Twinkies). *Gosh, I can't believe how much my life has changed since this morning. No more rules. No more curfew. But it's also scary and strange.* She drinks more pop then gestures heavenward with the can. *O Lord, I'm really uncorked now. It's like I'm an outlaw escaping from jail. I'm breaking ALL the rules.*

The gathering clouds grow darker ahead, and taller: thunderstorms, a towering line. Their wispy-cirrus tops shroud the sun, muting the shadows, hushing the colors in the rolling Texas landscape. *Looks like some heavy weather? But what else is new? I've been in the middle of a goshdang storm all day.* She can't help but laugh. *I reckon I can beat it to Waco? But if not, let it rain and blow, and thunder and all. Nothing's gonna stop me now. I'm well past the point of no return.* After another tepid sip, she returns the soda can to the beverage slot at the front of the gearshift console. *Forgive me, God, for not telling Mama sooner. I know I shoulda told her about the wedding first thing. But I knew she'd freak, and she did. It's not fair, the way she came down on me. Maybe I AM out of line? Maybe she IS wiser than me. But I'm betting the other way, Lord. And I sense that you're on MY side. But even if you're not, I'm still going through with this. And either way, I need you now more than EVER. Please bless me and Bryan, and be with Gretchen back home ... and ... and—gosh, I don't even know what to pray for. I don't even know where I'm gonna be living, or how I'm gonna get money.*

The AC feels a bit chilly as it fans her Levi's. She flicks it down a notch then redirects the airflow. *And what's gonna happen with my last year of high school? And my scholarship? I sure didn't make it to Denham's lab conference to talk about Newton's laws and basketballs.* She gives a husky chortle. *My good-girl reputation is gonna be in the toilet—that's for sure. And it won't take long, once Lena Beth and her gang hear about this. But I'd rather be an honest outlaw than a goody-goody poser.* She laughs again, warily. *And I sure won't be at practice today. Looks like my Spindle hoop career is finished—O Lord, there's a thousand questions. We can't get married right away, or maybe we can? I don't know. I don't know. I don't know ANYTHING—except that I love Bryan more than ever, more than anything, and that's ALL that matters.* She presses harder on the accelerator kicking the Firebird up to eighty mph.

A Stuckey's sign looms ahead on the left marking the tiny hamlet of Maypearl. As she whips by the exit, her thoughts tumble backward to the showdown with her mother:

"This's the last straw, Amanda! I declare—you sneak around and get engaged behind my back. The heart is deceitful, and who can know it. You've probably been sleeping with him too."

THE SILVER CORD

"No, I haven't, but I'm going to, and I can't wait. And don't call ME deceitful. You're the one who snuck around my room, snooping in my stuff—that's how yuh found the ring. But y'wait till now, till I'm on the way to school to lay this on me."

"Well, I had to pray about it before I—"

"That's bullshit, Mama. Don't gimme that fucking line!"

"You watch your MOUTH, young lady! How dare you use that word!"

"Well, I'm pissed dammit! Super pissed! How can yuh be like this— you were only SEVENTEEN when you married Daddy?"

"That's how I know, young lady. I learned the HARD way. And no daughter of mine is going down that road, not if I can help it. You're not even out of school. This whole thing has to stop. I can't allow it to go on. I can't. You're just like your damn father. Selfish and stiff-necked. Here ... take your bleeping ring, but no way in hell are y'gonna get my blessing, or the Lord's."

"So you know how God feels about it, huh?"

"I sure do: flee fornication; the flesh profiteth nothing; children, obey your parents. You know what the Bible says, but you don't care— because you have no fear of God in you."

"That's for damn sure. I don't wanna be afraid of God. I wanna be in LOVE with God, just like I am with Bryan."

"Aaah-phewwwh! I'm wasting my breath. I hafta go to work. I hafta tend to Gretchen. I'm washing my hands of this. If you choose to forsake God, and your family, then go—the door's open. But mark my words: you're gonna learn the HARD way."

Mandy whips around a minivan that refuses to relinquish the fast lane. Fighting back tears, she kills off the last of the Dr. Pepper to soothe her throat. The lumpy ache has come back—she sniffles. It hurts, what happened with her mama.

But thank God for Wendy Lewis, who stayed home from school so they could talk. Wendy tells it like it is—she does: *"Well, kiddo, I guess the shit is finally hitting the fan.... It's okay. I like to skip school.... I don't blame yuh. What else canyuh do? It's your life, and you love him.... I say: follow your heart. Go after your dreams with reckless abandon. Most kids, even the rebels and rowdies, grow up and surrender their souls; their dreams drain away to nothing. It's better to crash in flames than to play it safe. It even says so in the Bible. I mean God wants us to be HOT, not lukewarm. And how can we be hot, if we're going against our heart? It's like Miss Ryder says in English Lit: "First of all, to thyself be true." I mean, it was Shakespeare who said it, or he said something like that in Hamlet—that's the play we're studying now. But he's right, kiddo—what's the point of living to please your mom, if it's not the REAL you? How canyuh be close to her, if you're just playing a role? It's like you're not there anyway.... No, she can't make you come home. You're not officially legal, but y'can be on your own at seventeen, or even sixteen, and the police or anybody won't press the issue.... It's your decision, kiddo, but I sure wouldn't give up Bryan, no matter if Christ himself came down and told you to."*

Wendy's counsel encourages Mandy—again—as does the green highway sign on her right: Waco 57 mi. *I'm getting closer.* The burning in her throat subsides. When she and Wen returned to Colby Drive (Wendy following in the Subaru), no one was at home of course, but Mandy left a note on the kitchen table:

> Mama ... we have a BIG difference of opinion on things, but I don't hate you. In fact, I love you, as I always have, and I thank you for all that you've done for me over the years. But it's time for me to live my own life. I'm not forsaking you and Gretchen, or God. I trust God more than ever. If I must learn the hard way, as you say, then so be it. I'll always be your daughter, and you can always tell me what you think, and I'll listen, but from here on I have the final say concerning ME. I've decided to go to Waco, to be with Bryan one way or another—and I'm leaving right now. I'm gonna get my money out of the bank, my three hundred dollars, and I'll get a job down there. So I'll be just fine.... Love, Mandy.

The dashboard clock says 2:39 p.m., but it seems suddenly later, like evening almost. No more sun, not even a fuzzy spot to betray its position in the sky. The advancing clouds have chased the lively hues from the fields and hollows, rendering them more gray than green, especially in the hazy distance where the rolling vista goes vague and blurry, merging with the sky. Shedding her sunglasses, Mandy pushes her softball cap back on her head.

* * *

BAYLOR UNIVERSITY - FLETCHER HALL
THURSDAY, OCTOBER 3, 1991 — 2:45 PM

It's really getting dark, Bryan observes, as he eases the pickup into the parking lot. *I'm not going to practice anyway, but if it's gonna get rained out, I won't hafta call Coach McKinney. I'll check the Weather Channel. Course, they might still have a team meeting, but baseball is WAY down on my list right now. Mandy will be here at three-thirty, or maybe earlier, the way she drives—oh gosh, I can hardly wait.* He gives a boyish yelp, as he swings to a halt in his usual spot near the back. He's a trifle nervous about her coming all this way by herself, but she's a topnotch driver, and it's virtually impossible to get lost.

She's too much, he goes on in his thoughts, a happy current coursing through him. *We can go to the Holiday Inn in Bellmead, or some other m—wait, wait, hold your horses.* Giving a laugh, he grabs the sack of groceries and hops out. They're going out for supper, but he got more snacks and such, just in case—even though she's not allowed in his room on weekdays. Besides, he had to do something to kill time after he showered and shaved, and got dressed: Levi's plus a sporty gray-denim shirt. While he was shopping, he wrestled again with the many uncertainties—but not for long. They have tonight, tomorrow, the whole weekend. They can deal with the practical bullshit on Monday.

He's taking her to the renowned Cattleman's Steakhouse for supper—it's twenty miles south on I-35, a bit north of Temple. He went there with Chris, and the food is A-plus. And Bryan is plenty hungry; he's had nothing but Ritz crackers since breakfast, and considering the wild nature of this day, he suspects Mandy is much the same. But eating is just the first inning. *O Jesus, this could be a GREAT night. I'm glad I got those condoms.* Chris gave him a handful before his trip home to Spindle last week. Bryan keeps one in his wallet, the rest in his room.

* * *

INTERSTATE 35 - NORTHEAST OF HILLSBORO
THURSDAY, OCTOBER 3, 1991 — 2:51 PM

The double highway ahead seems strangely pale, a pair of satiny ribbons converging toward the dark El Greco horizon. It's still bright behind Mandy (to the north and east), but the approaching squall line has blackened the western sky: gray, purple, inky-blue, like smoke from burning crude. *I'll be getting to the 35W junction soon,* she reminds herself, as she stuffs a Twinkie into her mouth. She glances at the map. *And I go south.* A bolt of lightning splits the brooding murk in front of her. *That storm's looking super bad. I might still beat it ... though I'm beginning to doubt it. But I've driven through some humdinger storms before, like when we went to Arkansas back in April.*

* * *

2:53 p.m. After quickly unpacking his groceries, Bryan checks the Weather Channel, but the Negro weather gal (Vivian ???) is talking about the Tropics, about convective activity coming off the coast of Africa. *I don't care about goshdang Africa. I just wanna see the Texas radar loop ... to check out this storm. Maybe there's something on the local station? I doubt it—they just have soaps during the afternoon.* Nevertheless, he zaps over to Channel Two where he finds an ad for Pampers. Tossing the remote on the sofa, he heads to the bathroom to take a leak. *I reckon I should call the clubhouse anyway, and tell Coach*

McKinney. *It's no biggie. I mean, Jordan's gonna miss two days of practice.* Bryan gives a nasal laugh. *It could be a GOOD thing that he's gonna be in Wichita Falls until Sunday. I'm not sure I have the balls to sneak Mandy up here. But who knows?* He laughs again, as he shakes and retracts his dick. *If Marvin found out, my ass would be cooked. But the way things are going, I just m*—a sudden beeping from the TV derails his train of thought.

"We interrupt this program to bring you a severe-weather bulletin from our senior meteorologist, Norm Gossage."

Bryan hustles back to the television. *Gosh, it must be serious, if HE's giving the report. He's never on this time of day. To hell with baseball practice. Mandy's out there by herself.*

"The situation has worsened since my last update," the slender, bewigged weatherman explains, showing the latest radar data. He points to a line of thunderstorms running north-south from Ft. Worth to Temple. "We have a funnel on the ground north of China Spring. It spawned from this hook echo here." He fingers a red-orange blob hanging back northwest of Waco.

"O Jesus God," Bryan whispers aloud, as pangs of fear kill the happy vibes in his bosom.

"This cell is moving northeast at thirty-five miles mph," Gossage elaborates. "If it continues on its present course and speed, it will reach Gholson within minutes, and Birame within twenty, tracking across I-35 as it goes." He places a bony fingertip on the interstate halfway between Hillsboro and Waco. "If the tornado remains on the ground, it should pass just south of Randolph ... some twenty miles north of Waco."

Bryan looks on, stunned: *If she's ahead of schedule like I figure, she could be in that area, somewhere around Randolph. Unless she's way ahead, or well behind—I hope.*

He scarcely hears the rest of the report: "And please be advised that other tornadoes could form along this squall line, which is unusually potent for autumn. We do get severe weather in the fall of course, but this set-up today is more like April than October. There's no immediate tornado-threat to Greater Waco, but the squall line itself is accompanied by hail and seventy-mph winds, along with torrential downpours and lightning strikes, so we're in for quite a storm during the next hour. But it should all be over by four p.m—that's the good news. But in meantime, please stay tuned to Channel Two, and we'll keep you informed on this rapidly developing situation."

Rushing to his room, Bryan dials Wendy to confirm Mandy's departure from Spindle: yes, she's definitely on the way; she left before noon, like twenty minutes before—just as he thought.

THE SILVER CORD

* * *

Oh damn, Mandy reacts, as she realizes she took the wrong exit. *I'm headed for goshdang Ft. Worth. I'm going north. I hafta turn around. I'll never outrace this storm now.*

* * *

2:59 p.m. Alarmed by the TV report, Bryan bolts down the stairs, taking three at a time. *Maybe she got here early?* he cries breathlessly to himself. *I hope, I hope—O GOD, I HOPE!*

Reaching the first floor, he bangs out the side door into the eerily dark afternoon. He checks the parking lot, the side lot, then the back lot. He gives a resigned groan. *There's no sign of her. But what was I thinking? With that construction around Dallas, no way could she get here by now. O Jesus! She's still up on I-35, right in the path of that tornado.* A cascading peal of thunder reinforces this dreadful conclusion, as do the menacing clouds overhead, which have so blackened the heavens that the parking-lot lights have come on.

* * *

3:00 p.m. It doesn't take long for Mandy to correct her mistake. After going two miles north, she comes to another interchange where she gets off then back on, this time headed south.

* * *

3:02 p.m. *Why is this happening?* Bryan wonders as he dashes around to the front of Fletcher Hall to get a better look at the storm. *The timing couldn't be worse. Maybe God sent this storm to stop Mandy, to keep her from coming to me, to punish her for rebelling against her mom. NO, NO—God's not like that.*

Lightning forks the western sky, followed by a resounding barrage of thunder. A billowing, gray-bellied roll-cloud, riding the outflow, unscrolls swiftly toward the campus, yet there's no wind, not a breath of air moving about Bryan, as he observes from the sidewalk, along with a few of his dormmates. It's strange, the calmness—how can it be? Time slows down, or so it seems. And the air smells peculiar as well, like sulfur, like that stinky odor after you fire a shotgun. And the dark clouds have a weird yellow-greenish tint, like swamp water.

* * *

3:07 p.m. Lightning, thunder: a strong gust buffets the Firebird. It's not raining yet, but a wall of mean-looking clouds advances toward Mandy, rolling, whirling, boiling—like purple dinosaurs grappling in the sky. It's so dark, she can barely read the sign on her right: Randolph

7 mi., Waco 30 mi. *Dear God, I hope this isn't a tornado. But whatever it is, I'm not gonna beat it. I've got thirty miles to go.* Slowing to sixty, she turns on the headlights.

* * *

3:08 p.m. A raindrop splatters on Spangler Avenue, then on the sidewalk in front of Bryan, then another, and another, enormous drops, the size of silver dollars. The other students flee for cover, but he remains. Fury and majesty: the storm awes him, rendering him small and helpless. Now the wind: it whooshes through the treetops; it swirls down Spangler Ave pelting the freshman with grit and sand. The big cottonwood roars behind him, its leafy crown swishing and thrashing in the turbulent gusts. The chilly downrush chases the heat, and the sulfur stink. The wind smells frosty and bracing, as if blowing off a glacier. A shiver shoots up his spine, partly from the chill, but mainly because of dread. He pictures the tornado approaching I-35, a fierce, smoky-black funnel bearing down on his love, his life—his precious Mandy. *O Jesus, please be with her. Help her get through this safely.*

Here comes the downpour: the icy drops pelt his back as he sprints to the front door. A brilliant flash blinds him; he stumbles on the steps. *Kerrrrr-RAAAAACK!* The accompanying thunder rips the sky in two, or so it seems. "You just made it, young man," Ms. Danley declares, as Bryan hustles inside. The house-mother gazes out at the storm, like a sea captain on the bridge of a ship. "Looks like we're in for quite a storm."

"You got that right, ma'am," he replies, tipping his baseball hat. "You got that right."

* * *

3:10 p.m. "It's coming down so hard I can barely see!" Mandy exclaims above the roar. "And the wind keeps pushing me, and pushing. This's worse than a goshdang carwash." She slows to forty, then thirty—she works the stickshift, dropping down a gear. It takes all her strength to hold the wheel. The windows are fogging; she whips the airflow lever to defrost. The fog clears, but the rain drums down harder than ever.

* * *

3:11 p.m. By the time Bryan gets back to his unit, the storm is raging full blast, the wind whining and howling. The room is dark; he flips on the table lamp then hurries to the big window. The pine tree sways violently, as if ready to break. Curtains of rain sweep across the inundated parking lot—the water looks deep enough to float a boat. On the TV, soap-opera lovers discuss some bizarre crisis, but Bryan has a *real-life* crisis: *Mandy's out there, and I can't do a gosh-damn thing to help her.* His heart flutters then sinks. The TV bothers him, distracts him. Yet he leaves the set on, in case there are more weather bulletins.

A tremendous flash and explosion lifts the building into the air, or seemingly so. "That was damn close!" Bryan exclaims. "The thunder and lightning came right together."

No more voices—the TV is dead, and the lamp: no power.

* * *

3:13 p.m. *Oh no, it's hailing too,* Mandy realizes, as she pulls off onto the shoulder and turns on the hazard blinkers. A truck whizzes by on her left, a shadowy whalelike shape in the downpour, then a car, then another. *Those folks are nuts.* She pulls farther to the right. *One of these dadgum idiots might hit me—oh shit, this is not good.* The deafening metallic clatter scares her, and the pinging on the windshield—the chunky globs of ice look big as golf balls. She kills the wipers, lest they get mangled. *O Jesus, the windshield's gonna break, and the wind's blowing so hard—the car's rocking.* A long minute later the hail stops, but the deluge continues, and the wind. *I-I ... oh why? And I'm so close, like twenty-five miles?*

A sobering verse, as if to answer this question, comes up from her conscience: *Pride goeth before destruction, and an haughty spirit before a fall.* She shifts in the seat. *Maybe God sent this storm to teach me a lesson, like he did with Jonah? The Lord sent a great wind, and the whale swallowed Jonah ... because he rebelled and disobeyed ... and tried to run away.*

* * *

3:16 p.m. Amid the lightning flashes and thunderclaps, Bryan paces to and fro in his dark dorm-suite. He nervously wrings his hands. Outside, the storm continues unabated, the wind howling and hissing. Hailstones pepper the picture window. His sweetheart is somewhere out in this monster, and he has zero information. *That f-ing tornado must've hit I-35 by now? What's going on? I need to know!* Grabbing the remote, he zaps the TV: no response. Going over to the wide-screened set, he manually pushes the button: nothing. Then again, and again—irrationally: still no response. There's no power, no news, no nothing. Giving a disgusted snort, he resumes his anguished pacing.

* * *

3:20 p.m. After wrestling with guilt and doubt for a few minutes, Mandy breaks free, then pins her conscience to the mat: *NO WAY IN HELL! I'm not going back. I'm gonna FOLLOW MY HEART. I'm going to Baylor. I'm going to Bryan—or I'm gonna die trying. If you sent this terrible storm to kill me, Lord, then so be it. But I'm not turning back. No way, not now.*

Wind, thunder, blinding rain, more hail, big hail. The tempest cranks up several notches, as if preparing to deliver the coup de grace. It's darker than midnight, louder than a jackhammer. The Pontiac shudders and sways, rocking with the gale—but then the hail ceases, the rain slacks, the wind stills. Turning on the wipers, she peers out—the sky is getting brighter. Silence, save for the rhythmic *ka-shunk* of the wipers, or so it seems by comparison.

That's more like it, Mandy declares to herself, her hopes brightening as fast as the sky. After pressing the gas pedal a few times to make sure the engine is still running, she checks for traffic then accelerates onto the highway, resuming her journey.

* * *

3:23 p.m. Desperate for news, Bryan dials the state police; he gets a recording that puts him on hold. *That twister has to be past the highway by now? Maybe she beat it ... or maybe she got delayed longer than usual on 635, and she's still back toward Dallas? Or maybe the funnel went back up into the clouds?* A sharp crackle pops through the phone, as lightning flashes outside his bedroom window, but he's still on hold. *C'mon, tell me something—O God, I hate this!* Thunder rumbles, but the rolling peal seems muted, more distant; the storm is receding.

* * *

3:25 p.m. *Where'd all this traffic come from?* Mandy wonders, as she tops a hill. Ahead of her, she sees nothing but brake lights. She quickly slows and pulls off onto the shoulder, lest she get caught in the thick of it. She kills the engine. She's come less than three miles from where she stopped before. More vehicles arrive, cars, trucks, RVs, SUVs—the traffic jam grows backwards to Mandy, and beyond. An eighteen-wheeler pulls up behind the Firebird, its engine thrumming heavily, its twin exhausts snorting and fuming. "I reckon you're not finished, are yuh, God," she quips out loud amid a laugh. "If it's not one thing it's another. But hear this: I'm still going to dadgum Waco, if I hafta get out and *walk* the rest of the way."

* * *

"I-35 is closed south of Randolph," an officer informs Bryan at 3:27 p.m—finally. "We have a multiple-vehicle accident."

"Accident?" Bryan replies aghast, his heart hammering. "You mean the tornado?"

"The details are sketchy, sir, and the cause has yet to be determined. We just know that multiple vehicles are involved, blocking the entire interstate, northbound and southbound."

"But my fiancé is on I-35 right now; she could be in the middle of all this—how can I find out more?" Shock, horror: Bryan can scarcely spit out his words. "She's blond, with a ponytail; she's driving a red Firebird, an '84 Pontiac. D'yuh have any news about a red Firebird?"

"I'm sorry, sir. We have no info on victims or vehicles. You're welcome to call later, but it will likely be several hours before we can release info to families and next of kin."

* * *

3:29 p.m. Cracking her window a few inches, Mandy squeezes her thighs against her need to pee. *This traffic jam looks impossible, but it's WAY better than being in that hailstorm back there.* She squeezes harder; her bladder's been full since Maypearl, though she's had scant room in her mind to give heed to routine needs. *I oughta get out and squat right there in the grass. I reckon that would sure catch the attention of that truck driver behind me—he looks like an old fart.* She giggles then does her rabbity routine with her mouth and nose.

It's raining once more, but just a gentle shower. The highway ahead descends gently for a mile or so then rises to another crest, with gridlocked traffic all the way to the top. When you're driving, you see the woods and creeks as you whip through the hollows, and yet you scarcely notice the ups and downs of the interstate as it negotiates the rolling terrain, but this shallow valley in front of her is quite obvious now that she's stopped.

A helicopter circles overhead. *Whatever happened is beyond the next hill. It must be super bad, if it's blocking the whole dang highway. I haven't seen any cars going by in the northbound lanes? Good gosh, if I hadn't taken that wrong exit at Hillsboro, I'd be up there myself— I reckon God's WITH me after all.* She gives a sassy little chuckle. *And I'm gonna be with Bryan tonight, one way or another.* She hears a loud warbling—sirens. A convoy of emergency vehicles, their lights flashing, zips by on her left, headed south on the empty northbound side of the superhighway—police cars, ambulances, fire engines.

* * *

3:37 p.m. The rain has stopped. Bryan hurries downstairs. He's too distraught to stay in his dark, increasingly stuffy unit. The power remains off, and the telephone frustrates him. He's been trying to call Channel Two, but the line is busy, and busy, and busy. He did get through to 911, and the Waco police, but they told him nothing new about the tornado or the situation on I-35.

After stopping in the reception lounge to ask Ms. Danley about the electricity—the whole campus is out—he goes outside to survey the grounds, which are still white with marble-sized hail amid the leaves and litter and downed branches, and puddles, and aprons of mud. The sky is clearing, and the air is refreshingly cool compared to the muggy pre-storm heat. Lightning has splintered a big pine in front of the health center across the street. Half the tree is still standing, but the charred top-section lies smoldering on the lawn. *I reckon that was the super-bright explosion that knocked out the power,* he surmises. A score of fellow students stand about in two's and three's gawking at the scene. But Bryan can only think of Mandy: *Where is she? Is she safe? Is she hurt? Is she trapped in a tangle of twisted steel?* He jogs down the sidewalk. He checks the parking lot; he scans up and down Spangler, but there's no red Pontiac. *O Jesus, it's past three-thirty. If she beat the tornado, she'd surely be here by now. O Lord, I hate this. Why'd you let this happen?*

He scampers toward his pickup, a panicky impulse urging him to race up the interstate, to rescue his dear Mandy, but he quickly veers toward the dorm, nixing the wild notion: *If she didn't make it past the accident scene, I can't get to her anyway. I'll just end up in traffic south of Randolph. And if she's okay, she might call? Yes, yes—I gotta get back to my room.*

* * *

3:46 p.m. The sun is out. It's getting stuffy inside the Firebird. Mandy rolls her window down all the way. She still has to pee, but the need is duller; her bladder is going numb like it does—thank God. Leaning close to the dash, she scans the windshield and the hood—both look okay. At least, she can't see any cracks or chips or dents from the hail, or chips in the paint. The nearby drivers have cut their engines, including the trucker behind her. There's no movement at all, except for the emergency vehicles coming and going in the northbound lanes, and she's seen three helicopters. "This's getting dadgum old," she murmurs.

* * *

3:48 p.m. The refrigerator kicks on, signaling the return of electricity to the dorm, along with the hum of the AC fan. Bryan stops pacing and zaps the television on, and sure enough, the Channel Two news-team is airing a special report on the storm. Plunking down on the sofa, he absorbs every detail.

"The situation continues to be chaotic," intones Susan Hines, the red-haired anchorwoman. "The state police have closed I-35 between Elm Mott and Randolph, an eight-mile mile stretch north of Exit 343. We'll be going there live momentarily, but again, for those just tuning in: a killer tornado touched down this afternoon northwest of Waco. The twister, first sighted at 2:51 near China Spring, cut a swath eastward slamming into a mobile-home complex in Gholson, then it roared through Cedarvale before ripping across I-35 south of Randolph. Unbelievably, there were no deaths at the trailer park, or in Cedarvale. Sadly, however, the story is far worse on the interstate, where the storm caused a massive multi-vehicle pile-up. Okay ... uh—yes, we're going live by newscam to Pam Tucker at the scene."

"Susan, we have a major disaster here on I-35," the pretty reporter (a Jessica Savage knockoff) explains—she stands on a hill in front of the scene, which could pass for a salvage yard, with the many smashed and tangled vehicles, some stacked one upon another. "Ironically, the weather is beautiful now. The sun is shining and the storm system has moved east of the area, but behind me lies the quick-and-lethal work of this killer tornado."

Bryan, his legs going rubbery, his pulse hammering, searches for the red Firebird in the pile-up, but the focus is too blurry, the colors too muddied and jumbled.

"You can't tell much from this distance," Pam Tucker goes on, "but we hope to have aerial footage soon from our News Two, Eye in the Sky Copter. We're waiting for the medevac helicopters to clear the airspace. And we can't move closer with our camera truck, because the paramedics are still extricating the victims, and the toxic-spill crews are working feverishly to clean up the spilled gasoline—so far, there have been no fires, which is a miracle to say the least."

"Spilled gasoline?" Susan Hines asks.

"Yes, Susan, we have an overturned Exxon tanker blocking the southbound lanes—you can see the foam-covered trailer at the front of the pile-up."

"So this truck was hit by the tornado?"

"In effect, Susan ... but to be precise, the driver lost control trying to *stop*, as the funnel roared onto the highway from that wooded area over there." Turning sideways, Pam points at a splintered stand of trees to the immediate west of the scene. "We have an eyewitness, Mr. Bennie Earl Cash, a maintenance worker who was mowing on this very hill." The camera pans right to include a chunky, middle-aged Negro dressed in coveralls and a greasy Dallas Cowboy cap. "Now, Mr. Cash, please tell us what happened. We understand the tanker flipped over?"

"That's right, ma'am," he affirms, the whites of his eyes growing big. "I was right over yonder on my tractor, and I looks back, and I seen the twister a'comin', and the gasoline truck put on the brakes, but he couldn't hold 'er, and she skidded sideways." He fishtails his callused hand to indicate. "Then she jackknifed and rolled over. The cars was able to stop, the first few in behind the truck, then the rain commence to fall ... so hard I couldn't see nuthin' else, nary a thang. Then I hightailed it for the gully down yonder. I reckon that's when the rest of the cars crashed into them others."

"It must've been terrifying for you, Mr. Cash?"

"Yes'm, I'm still a'shakin' I reckon."

"We appreciate your help, Mr. Cash. Thank you very much." The camera shot narrows to Pam Tucker only. "It was the blinding downpour, Susan, that caused the real mayhem, as vehicle after vehicle plowed into the stalled traffic ... a chain reaction of collisions extending back some three hundred yards. Several vehicles careened onto the median, into the grassy drainage ravine, and a couple ended up in the northbound lane, like that white panel-truck lying on its side—it's a FedEx truck we understand. But this's why the state police have closed both sides of the interstate, not to speak of the spilled gasoline which must be pumped out of the drainage ravine, before the highway can be reopened. But the foam has minimized the risk of—"

"How about?—sorry, Pam. But what about casualties?"

"Our information is incomplete at this time, Susan, but so far we have four confirmed fatalities, plus dozens of injured. The driver of the Exxon truck miraculously survived, with head lacerations and a broken leg. He's been medevacked to Hillcrest Medical Center. And we understand that the critically injured are being flown directly to Temple. Most of the injuries occurred well back in the pile-up, where vehicles plowed at high speed into each other because of the blinding rain. This information comes from Don Watrous, at the Department of Public Safety,"

"O Jesus, no," Bryan cries—he collapses on the carpet, tears spilling. He prays desperately, but fears the worst.

* * *

That was SOME storm, Mandy declares to herself as she observes the receding clouds to the east. The wispy, anvil-topped thunderheads look magnificent in the bright sunshine, but she's too occupied to appreciate their beauty. She feels a growing sense of urgency about getting out of this mess, mainly because of Bryan. She knows she's okay, but he doesn't, and the traffic in front of her hasn't budged. The dashboard clock says 4:06 p.m. *I should be there by now,* she frets. *He's gotta be worried. I wish I knew what's going on.*

Several motorists, having exited their vehicles, wander about, seeking news, trying to get a better view. Mandy remembers her radio. Adjusting the ignition switch, she turns it on and scans the dial, but she finds nothing but music on FM, and static on AM. *Those storms are still too close; they're messing up the reception. This radio's crummy on AM anyway.* Giving a sigh of frustration, she turns off the radio, and the ignition. *I sure wish I had one of those new-fangled cellphones, like the one Doc Wilson was using the day Bryan got hurt.* Slouching against the door, she hangs her arm out the window, she taps impatiently on the side of the car, then she fiddles with the exterior mirror. As she moves it, she catches a glimpse of the trucker behind her. *Speaking of cellphones, I think he's got one. He's talking on something back there.* She's not crazy about the idea of seeking help from a stranger, a truck driver no less—the truckers at the diner are always coming on to her—but she has no alternative. Stepping out of the car, she adjusts her softball cap and ponytail, then strides back to the blue-and-gray Mack truck.

"Excuse me," she announces through the open driver-side window, as she grabs the assist handle and pulls herself up onto the first boarding step—she's still a good foot below the window.

"Hello there, pretty thang," the burly, bearded, ruddy-faced trucker responds—he wears hippie sunglasses, the wire-rimmed, John Lennon kind. "I reckon we're gonna be stuck here for a good spell." Ashen shocks of hair push out from under his grimy, sweat-stained cowboy hat. The scruffy beard and mustache are just as gray; he looks old, like fifty, maybe sixty?

Pushing her cap back, she smiles up at him, politely: "I don't mean to be nosy, sir, but I noticed yuh talking on a cellphone?"

"Nawh, that's my CB ... and it's a cheap piece ah junk."

"So yuh can't call a regular phone number?"

"Not a chance, darlin'. On a quiet day, y'might get a local operator to patch yuh through, but not with all these truckers stuck here. Plus, I got no range hardly—my transmitter's weak."

"Well, d'yuh know what's going on?"

He sheds his dark glasses. "A tornado wrecked a tanker up ahead," he explains, his blue eyes twinkling. "That's the scoop, as best I can tell from talkin' to the other truckers—I got enough range for that. Plus, I been listenin' to the police channels. The damn cyclone was a monster they say. It hit the highway an hour ago, some three miles ahead of us. The tanker rolled over, and that caused a huge pile-up, a whole goddamn shitload of cars. Pardon my language, darlin', but it's a bad scene. I reckon there's gotta be fatalities—by the way, I'm Andy, Andy Biggs." He extends a greasy, sweaty hand down to Mandy; she shakes it.

"I'm Amanda Stevens from Spindle, up by Sulphur Springs. I'm on my way to see my boyfriend at Baylor. Most folks call me Mandy."

"Mighty pleased to meetcha, darlin'."

Mandy doesn't really care to be called "darling," yet it's typical redneck lingo, especially among truckers. And he seems helpful enough, and considerate, and he has kind blue eyes. "So, Mr. Biggs, d'yuh have any idea how long—"

"Ain't no reason to be formal—just call me Andy."

"Okay, Andy—so whaddeyuh think? Are we gonna be stuck here forever? I need to get to Waco, like *right* way. Bryan's gotta be freaking out, if he heard the news about the tornado; he's my boyfriend—I mean fiancé."

"Well, Amanda, I got a hankerin' we're gonna be here for a good spell. This's the worst goddam gridlock I've ever seen—pardon my language, darlin'. And I been truckin' for thirty-five years. Course, I ain't got the same urgency y'got, since nobody's gonna panic about this here load of Wrangler jeans." He gestures toward the trailer behind him. "I gotta deliver 'em to the Wal-Mart warehouse in San Antone, but I don't reckon it's gonna matter a'tall if I don't get 'em there till tomorrow." He shakes his head slowly, his friendly eyes going narrow with concern, or so it seems. "Your situation is more worrisome to be sure, with your boyfriend waitin' and all—damn, I wish I could help yuh somehow. Now if y'could get over to the northbound—nawh, this traffic's packed tighter than a herd of Guernseys at milking time. Plus, the smokeys would be on yuh. They got their emergency stuff usin' those lanes. Shit, I reckon David Copperfield couldn't even help us, not stuck way over here on the shoulder."

"I sure wish we could do *some*thing," Mandy sighs, her face falling. "Bryan's gonna be worried sick. And this's a super-special day for us—like my first visit to Baylor."

"I reckon it *must* be special," he replies, "the way you got that Firebird loaded to the gills?"

"Oh, I'm bringing a bunch of stuff for him," she fibs, as she steps back, lowering herself to the ground. She looks down dejectedly; she paws the still-dampish asphalt with her Reebok. She dares not divulge that she left home for good this very morning, though her body language gives witness. Returning to her car, she leans back against it, her arms folded resignedly.

Swinging open the door of his cab, Andy climbs down and joins her. Almost as wide as he is tall, he could pass for an oil-field drum, a bearded fifty-gallon drum. "Now, darlin', I didn't mean to throw a wet blanket on thangs. They're workin' to clear the scene ... but it's gonna take a while."

Mandy gives him a nod and a snort, tossing her ponytail, but no reply. After an awkward silence, he saunters around to the passenger side of the car then onto the short cut of grass which abuts the pavement. Mandy follows. He's shorter than her by two inches, and he'd even be shorter if it weren't for the thick heels on his cowboy boots, rattlesnake-skin boots. And his OD (military) T-shirt does a poor job covering his potbelly, which hangs over the top of his grease-smeared jeans.

This portion of the interstate is elevated, providing a bird's-eye view of the surrounding countryside. The sun is getting low in the sky, and a pleasant, almost coolish, breeze has sprung up. "You know what, darlin'?" he remarks, his eyes squinted against the sun. "I gotta wild idea."

"What's that?" Mandy asks. Andy doesn't reply—he seems suddenly absorbed. Another siren warbles by in the northbound lane, but he pays no attention. He's looking the other way, down the steep embankment. A thick growth of Johnson grass and milkweed covers the man-made slope, along with scattered chokeberry bushes and patches of goldenrod, and not far from the bottom a dirt road runs parallel to the highway.

"Y'see that farm road down yonder?" he says, finally.

"Yeah, the dirt one," Mandy answers.

"Well, I reckon it's no more'n fifty or sixty yards away, a hard sixty mindyuh, but if we can somehow get that Firebird of yours down to it, I thank y'might get yourself outta here in time to have supper with your—what's his name again?"

"Bryan ... Bryan Howard," she tells him again, her heart skittering with hope—and apprehension.

Andy wades into the Johnson grass. The tasseled vegetation looks richly green after the rain, and the clinging droplets glisten like little stars in the sunshine. "Christ, this stuff's wetter than seaweed and just as snarly, and it's near waist deep, but I thank we can drive through it, goin' downhill, but we got that level stretch at the bottom, and I'm 'specially concerned about the ditch."

"What ditch?"

"The one that drains the dirt road. Y'cain't see it very well 'cuza the weeds, but I reckon that's gonna be our *main* obstacle. Tellyuh what, darlin', let's go down and take a look." Mandy, her jeans getting soaked, follows the paunchy trucker, as he gingerly descends the embankment. The wet grass smells strongly sweet like the hayfields on the Howard farm, a pleasant change from the exhaust fumes back on top. Andy gives a labored chuckle. "Damn, Miss Amanda, I'm already huffin' 'n puffin', and this's the easy part. I shoulda gone on that diet my wife's been yakin' about the past fifteen years." He laughs again. "I don't know how in the hell I'm gonna get back *up* this hill."

More chuckles; Mandy laughs as well, yet her thoughts are sober: *This's gonna be like a goshdang daredevil stunt. Can he actually be serious? It's way out, like half crazy. But he does seem like a nice old guy, and he's going out of his way to help me ... and he's not coming on to me like the younger truckers at the diner. It's easier with old men— they seem more relaxed around girls, like grandfathers. I'm sure they still think about it, but when we're this far apart in age, it's a non- issue, which is good, considering everything ELSE that's happening today.*

"The embankment seems firm enough," Andy drawls, upon reaching the bottom. "But it's a mite soft down here where the slope levels out." Tramping about among the goldenrods, he tests, in several places, the weight-bearing capacity by pressing his boot into the spongy turf until water comes up. The yellow flowers, nodding like flames in the breeze, reach to his shoulders, some to his ears—this guy is *short*. "Yeah, gettin' across this boggy area could be tricky, but it's not quicksand or anythang, and it's only six or eight yards, ten at the most, and we'll have a good head of steam after comin' down the hill. And I have a hankerin' the ditch ain't so bad either, even though it's flowin' like a goddam creek after all that rain—pardon my foul mouth, darlin'." Breaking a branch off a nearby chokeberry bush, he checks out the water in the ditch. "Nawh, this thang's not deep, no more'n a foot or so, and it's only a yard wide. The sides are muddy as hell, and I reckon we might bottom out, but we could still make it, if we're goin' fast enough."

"You're right about the mud," she affirms apprehensively, as her sneakers squish about in the goo. Losing her footing, she almost steps into the fast-flowing water but hops across instead, onto the road. Going to Waco this way seems farfetched, like a hail-Mary shot from half court.

Andy kicks the road surface here and there with the heel of his boot. "Now this here road is nice'n solid with a gravel crown. If it was clay, like the sides of the ditch, the rain woulda turned it to goddam putty, like a lotta back roads 'round here. But we'll have no problem on this one, if we can *just* get to it. That damn ditch would be nuthin' if we had a four-wheel drive, but gettin' that Pontiac ponycar across will take a little doin'—that baby's low to the ground." Removing his cowboy hat, he wipes his brow then hand-combs his tousled, pewter-colored hair, pushing it back on his head. Despite the coolish change in the air, he's sweating profusely. Replacing the hat, he plods pensively back and forth near the ditch, as though reconsidering the whole notion.

Mandy hears another siren. Muted by the thick vegetation, it sounds weirdly remote. She could peg a softball to the top of the hill, or get it close, but the highway seems suddenly far away, like miles. Being down here is like another world. The steady buzz of crickets and grasshoppers adds to the illusion, not to mention the bright sun and blue sky. It seems impossible that a vicious hailstorm and tornado roared through here a little over an hour ago. Perhaps this whole way-out day has been a dream, starting with her mother and the ring?

Andy's redneck twang brings her back: "I still thank we can get across this ditch, darlin', but I'd sure feel better if we had some rocks or logs or sumpthin', to fill it in."

"How'bout those logs over there?" she asks, pointing westward, toward a pile of fence posts on the far side of the adjacent pasture.

"Well, I'll be damned. They're puttin' in a new steel-post fence over yonder, and right on time. Maybe there is a God?" He gives a hearty guffaw. "And I reckon they won't mind if we borrow some of those old *wood*en posts. C'mon, sweetheart, help me get 'em."

A barbed-wire fence already borders the near side of the pasture. After helping each other through it, they quickly make their way over to the pile of discarded posts. "Now we gotta watch for splinters," Andy says, as he examines them, "but they should do the trick. They're all gray and weathered, but there's no rot, and they're nice'n thick, just right for us. It'll take a few trips, but let's have at it." He grabs two, Mandy one—they're heavier than they look.

* * *

4:22 p.m. Back at Fletcher Hall, Bryan lies aching on the sofa, having surrendered to the worst-case scenario: his dear Mandy, if still alive, is badly injured and suffering, and he can do *nothing*. He stares wide-eyed at the ceiling, at the changing patterns of light coming from the muted TV. The heavy sense of impotence has sapped his soul—he has no more emotion to cry with, or to hope, or to pray, or to curse, or to make futile phone calls, or even to watch the news reports.

* * *

"That looks pretty good," Mandy says to Andy Biggs, as she helps him position the last post in the ditch. During one of the trips to the other side of the pasture, she stole away into a nearby pine grove, so she feels more comfortable, her bladder. She likewise feels better about this whole project, though she's hardly gushing with confidence.

"Yeah, that's right solid," he agrees, as he places his weight on the makeshift bridge, "and it didn't take us no more'n fifteen minutes'. We make a good team, sweetheart—you ain't bad for a girl when it comes to workin'." Mandy grins bashfully, while he gives a wheezy laugh. "Damn, I'm outta shape ... but I reckon we got twenty in there now, ten here and ten there, which gives us about a twelve-foot target, sorta like a half-assed cattleguard."

Mandy wipes her hands then pushes her cap back on her head. She crinkles her nose then gives a smirky half-grin. "So you're really serious about this? I mean uh ... I appreciate you helping me and all, but you're not obligated or anything."

"No, I ain't obligated, darlin', but I know you're anxious about your boyfriend, so if I can help yuh, then why not? You see, I gotta daughter of my own: Elsie Jo. Hell, she's got three youngins of her own now, but she was your age once, and I used to worry my head off when she first started drivin', knowin' what I know about the dangers of the road. So I have special feelin's for young ladies in distress. Besides, I got nuthin' *better* to do." Gesturing up the hill toward his truck, he gives a breathy chortle. "I'm sure as *hell* not goin' anywhere in that mother."

"But y'think we can in *my* car, like actually get outta here?"

"Well, it's your Pontiac and your decision, but with these here posts in the ditch, we have a good chance of pullin' it off. I've driven a few Firebirds in my day, and Camaros, even in competition." Andy, blushing as he brags, puffs up his chest and drums his elbows against his paunchy torso: a rooster flapping. "I used to do some stock-car racin' back home in Midland. So I reckon I can get her to this road, if anybody can."

"But what if we *do* get stuck?"

"Well, I already consider you a friend, darlin', so I sure ain't gonna abandon yuh. I'll getcha out one way or another, even if I hafta call my boss for a tow truck. But I have a good feelin'. I thank we can *do* it." He struts back and forth near the ditch, flapping his elbows again. "I'm more concerned really about that shitload of stuff y'got with yuh. It's sittin' up too high in the back. If we hit these here posts too hard, it might come flyin' forward into the front seat—I doubt that'll happen, but there ain't no sense in takin' a chance. Maybe we can pack it tighter and lower, or we might hafta put some of it in my truck. Then we'll haul it down on foot once we get your car onto the road. It's too bad y'don't have a big trunk, like on a Cadillac. That goddam three-door coupe ain't got shit for cargo space—but we're gettin' way ahead of ourselves." Giving a snort, he gestures toward the top of the hill. "'Fore you decide anythang, or we repack anythang, we hafta check the latest scuttlebutt on the traffic. If thangs are gettin' ready to move, we can forget this. I'll get right on my CB—if I have any breath left after climbin' this damn hill." More snorts and laughs, Mandy too.

She quickly scales the slope, the steep climb scarcely taxing her jockish, teen-gal physique, save for a bit of hard breathing near the top. Andy follows, at a considerably slower pace, not to mention a couple of rest stops along the way. Finally reaching his truck, he plops panting onto the boarding step. While he regains his breath, Mandy surveys the traffic jam. A helicopter zooms noisily overhead, while another circles on the far side of the gridlocked river of cars. "This dadgum traffic jam looks just as bad as ever," she reports to Andy.

"I figured as much. But lemme get on my CB. I just need a few more seconds; that goddam hill liketah finished my fat ass."

While she waits, Mandy cleans the mud from her Reeboks with a Popsicle stick she found on the pavement near the truck. More sirens: a convoy of fire engines zoom by in the northbound lane—they're headed south toward the accident scene, a copter following. "I wonder why they're bringing in more fire trucks now," she remarks. "I don't see any smoke or anything? And it's been well over an hour since that tornado hit?"

"I dunno, darlin'," the stocky trucker replies, as he climbs up into the cab, "but I aim to find out, once I get this radio fired up." A minute later the door opens again. Andy shakes his head. "I reckon this traffic ain't gonna be movin' a'tall. I checked with a few of my CB buddies up ahead, and they tell me it's gonna be four hours at least, 'cuza the benzene."

"Benzene?"

"Yeah, it took 'em a while to figure it out, but that tanker wasn't carryin' ordinary gasoline, but some kind of benzene, ethyl benzene I thank. If I remember right, it's a hyped-up fuel for race cars ... and it's highly toxic. Well, he dumped the f-in' stuff all over the highway, and it's puddled in the median, and it's in the drainage system. Those trucks we just saw—that's a special hazardous-materials team from Carswell AFB in Ft. Worth; they're comin' to clean up the site, but it could take half the night. The smokeys have rerouted all traffic between Randolph and Exit 343, but the rest of us are stuck—unless you wanna take a wild ride down that embankment with me?"

"Well, why not?" Mandy blurts boldly. "Nothing ventured, nothing gained." She laughs, giving an open-handed gesture. *I've been on the edge all day anyway,* she adds, but only to herself.

"I'll be damned," Andy growls a minute later, after Mandy pulls open the hatchback door at the rear of the Firebird. "You got thangs all twisted and tangled, hangers and all. No wonder it's ridin' so high." Perfumy teen-girl fragrances waft out, as if they just opened her bedroom closet. "Now let's get this all out, plus the stuff in the front seat, then we'll raise the rear seatbacks to their upright position, and then we'll stow the suitcases in the cargo well behind the seats, plus all these Sunday shoes, and that damn hair blower, and whatever else will fit. And the rest of it, we'll pack good'n low in the back seat, so it can't fly around. And by they way, darlin', these here clothes sure don't look—or smell—like they belong to no college guy?" He gives her a knowing grin. She returns the smile—but gives no reply.

* * *

4:48 p.m. Bryan buries his face in the sofa cushion. He considers calling Wendy Lewis again, to see if she's heard anything, or his mom, or even Helen Stevens, but quickly vetoes the idea. *If Mandy called anywhere, she woulda called here.* He has given up on God, on any good outcome. Even his agony has turned cold, a deep, dull, resigned hurt that pervades his psyche like embalming fluid. *She must be injured too badly to phone anyone—if she's still alive? I could call the different hospitals, but they'd just stonewall me like the damn police did earlier. Once they learn her identity, from her wallet, they'll notify her mother, then Helen will call my mom, and she'll call me. And there's no way to hurry this sucky process.*

* * *

4:50 p.m. Andy Biggs lowers the Firebird driver's seat to allow for his rotund belly, then he secures himself behind the wheel.

"So it's not gonna hurt anything, having me in the car?" she asks, from the passenger seat.

"On the contrary, darlin'—we want the weight balanced, as much as possible. Course, we'd need two of you to equal me, and *then* some." They both laugh, releasing nervous energy. "But if you're scared about it, I can go it a—"

"No way—I don't wanna miss this, not now." More laughter. She stays put, despite the butterflies.

After adjusting his hat, the bearded trucker slips on his John Lennon sunglasses. "Okay then, fasten your seatbelt, and make sure that shoulder strap's tight. Could be a little turbulence ahead." He starts the engine. "I reckon we're ready, once we get this baby jockeyed around into position. Cranking the steering wheel hard to the right, he pulls slowly forward, just missing the empty minivan in front of them (the Hispanic driver got out when the rain stopped and has yet to return). Andy backs up a bit, getting a better angle, then he carefully maneuvers the Firebird off the paved shoulder. Some of the stranded motorists have gathered behind them, becoming spectators. He eases forward until the front-right wheel reaches the Johnson grass at the top of the embankment; he sets the emergency brake. The car still sits at an angle, but it's ready for the plunge—it won't take much to straighten it out, once they get rolling.

With the car in neutral, he races the engine a few times: *VOOM! VOOM!* He shifts into low and releases the clutch until it grabs. "I wanna get the feel of this here clutch, and the gas, and the gear stick. It's a good thang y'got a standard. I doubt we could pull this off in a damn automatic." *VOOM! VOOM!* "I reckon this's a V-6, ain't it?"

"Yeah, it's a six," she replies, her heart *voom*-ing like the engine, or almost so.

"Well, I'm glad it ain't a V-8, for what we gotta do. Those big mothers are too damn powerful. The rear end tends to get away from yuh, even on pavement." *VOOM! VOOM!* "This baby has just the right amount of oomph. Now here's the plan: we're gonna start this run in low, then shift to second halfway down. It's like a controlled acceleration, where the geared-down engine serves as a brake to keep us from runnin' away, and yet I hafta give it enough throttle to get us up to speed in the deep grass. I reckon we gotta be doin' at least thirty-five to get across that soft area at the bottom." More curious onlookers have gathered; there's now a small crowd. "You all set, darlin'?"

Mandy's butterflies feel bigger in her gut, like sparrows thrashing. "Ready as I'll ever be."

"Tower, this's Firebird Victor 6," Andy joshes playfully. "We're ready for take-off.... Roger, 6, understand ... you're cleared on runway two-seven-zero." He snorts and cackles—he may be an old trucker fart, but he's filled with boyish bluster and bravado, like Spanky Arnold back in Spindle. "I reckon we got the green light, darlin', so here goes." Cutting the wheel another notch to the right, he releases the brake. While the crowd cheers, the Firebird slips forward with gravity, the front end swinging around—then with a roar Andy accelerates down the hill, the deep grass swishing beneath them, beating the underside of the low-slung ponycar.

"Yikes! Oh shit!" Mandy shrieks, her butterflies rushing up into her bosom, into her throat.

Hitting a chokeberry bush, the car yaws right ripping up a big hunk of grass, but Andy quickly straightens her out, working the wheel with a racer's touch. He shifts into second then gives her more gas— *VA-ROOOM!* "We're halfway home!" he shouts, as they bounce over a rough spot. "Now if we can just make it to the *god*dam road!" Reaching the boggy area at the bottom, the hard-charging Firebird fishtails through the goldenrods, the rear end whipping left then right— *too far* to the right. The consequences unfold in slow motion, or so it seems.

Reaching the ditch, the right-front tire clatters across the fence-post bridge, but the left one misses completely sending a geyser of water high into the air, as it slams into the ditch then bounces forward onto the dirt road. "Dear Jesus!" Mandy cries, pitching forward, then leftward, her safety belt tugging hard to keep her in the seat. The Firebird whipsaws, the rear end sliding hard right. Andy, wrestling to straighten her, punches the gas pedal—*VOOM! VOOM!* The back wheels whine propelling them a few more feet, but they quickly lurch to a halt.

"MOTHER*FUCK*!" he reacts, as time returns to normal speed. "We almost made it. Pardon my language, darlin', but I'm afraid we got our ass stuck in this *goddam* ditch." They face obliquely down the dirt road, the front wheels clearly across, but the rear tires remain in doubt, especially the left one, which is obviously lower than the other three, making the car tilt. Muddy water dapples the windshield and hood, from the geyser that shot up. "But 'fore we jump to conclusions or try anythang, lemme take a look." Venting a few more expletives, he hauls himself out of the car.

Mandy waits, her pulse racing. *This's all I need. Now he's gotta call a wrecker to pull me out, and we probably messed up the front end—I shoulda said no.* She watches out the back window, as Andy grabs one of the fence posts and repositions it under the rear of the car, then another.

"Yep, I reckon we're sure'nough stuck," he confirms, as he plops back into the driver's seat. "I moved two of those posts behind the left-rear wheel, but it's mired like a goddam pig in a wallow, and the right one's just barely across." He gives it a little gas—to no avail: the car shimmies but doesn't advance, the back tires spinning vainly. "Damn, we need front-wheel drive." He pauses to catch his breath. "I reckon thangs ain't lookin' too good, but don't give up on me yet, Amanda. I've still got a trick or two up my sleeve." Dropping the stickshift into reverse, he backs up a few inches, then he shifts into low and nurses the Firebird forward until the wheels lose traction, regaining the same few inches. Back, forward, back, forward: he repeats the process. Mandy, cranked around, follows the action. Back, forward, back, shifting, shifting. Faster, faster—Andy rocks the car furiously. Finally, he stomps the gas pedal. "C'mon, you fucker!" he hollers, as the rear tires scream and smoke, spewing mud and water and grit. "Y'can do it! Y'can do it!"

The high-pitched fury grows louder until the wail seems ready to explode, like a turbojet screaming past the red line, but before it does, the Firebird creeps forward, slowly, slowly—then all at once it zips ahead, as the mired wheel whips up onto the road. "YES! YES!" Mandy shouts, giving Andy a jockish high-five.

As they exit the Pontiac to check for damage, the crowd on the hill cheers and claps. Andy waves his cowboy hat and gives a theatrical bow. The huge left-side rut emerging from the ditch gives witness to his driving prowess. "Well, I reckon we did it, darlin'," he exults, as he checks out the rear end of the car; he sucks air; he's breathing hard. "It's all caked with mud back here, but it looks okay." He checks the front wheels. "Looks normal up here too, but I cain't be sure about the alignment till we get up to speed on a paved road."

After they get back into the car, he gives a winded laugh then pats her fondly on the shoulder. "Yeah, Miss Amanda, that was a *bitch* of a ditch, but we came out on top—we did. Now I'm gonna have yuh at Bryan's door in twenty minutes ... give or take."

She giggles then gives her goofy grin. "If y'wanna chauffeur me, I sure won't complain—but you're not required to, y'know?"

"Awh yes, I am. After puttin' this much effort in, I'm gonna make *damn* sure y'get there. These back roads can be tricky to navigate. Plus, I ain't got the wind to climb that hill ... not now." He fiddles with the wipers, squirting fluid, getting the muddy spots off the windshield. "And I'd like to meet you boyfriend anyhow, this young feller you're so fired up about."

"Whaddabout your truck?"

"Fuck my truck—pardon my language, darlin', but that damn rig ain't goin' nowhere."

* * *

5:19 p.m. A loud knock rouses Bryan from a near-doze. Rolling off the sofa, he hurries to the door: IT'S MANDY!—along with a short, bearded, old-looking guy in a cowboy hat. "Oh, pretty lady!" he yelps, as he gathers her into his arms. "Thank God. Thank God." His eyes go blurry: tears of relief. "I was so dang scared. I saw the tornado reports on Channel Two. I thought for sure y'were in some hospital, or worse."

"It's okay, babe; I'm fine. I was never in any real danger, but I hate it that you had to worry—oh, Andy... uh, uh ... oh, babe, this's Andy Biggs. He drove me here, using the back roads—he knows *all* the shortcuts."

Bryan shakes his hand. "Hello, Mr. Biggs ... and thanks."

"Howdy, Bryan ... but just call me Andy."

Sharing a laugh, they proceed into the suite. "If it wasn't for Andy," she adds, "I'd still be out there ... stuck in traffic."

THE SILVER CORD

CHAPTER NINETEEN

WACO, TEXAS - SOUTH FRANKLIN STREET
THURSDAY, OCTOBER 3, 1991 — 7:17 PM

"I like it how you just bopped right up to my room," Bryan kids Mandy, as he halts the pickup at a red light. "That was a bold goshdang move—like breaking Ms. Danley's *number-one* rule."

"Well, the side door was open," she chortles, "and I sure wasn't gonna go ask permission, not after what I been through today." She punches him playfully in the shoulder. "I reckon I'm done asking for permission, mister—if y'know what I mean?" Smirking, she gives him a seductive side-glance, rolling her big blue eyes. "So how much farther is this Italian restaurant?"

"About five minutes I'd say."

"Good, 'cause I'm starving."

"Me too." The light changes; Bryan accelerates. The October evening befits their ebullient mood: upper sixties, low humidity, pink twilight in the western sky—light-jacket weather, and a perfect night for snuggling. "It was *still* a bold move," he chuckles, backtracking to the dorm rules.

"Well, we didn't see anyone except for two guys, and they didn't seem surprised, since Andy was with me. They probably thought we were family members on a special visit?"

"Yeah, he could pass for somebody's dad ... or *grand*dad."

"He does look old, 'cause of the gray hair. But he's not *super* old; he's fifty-four actually; he told me on the way." She gives a snorty laugh. "But I'm sure we looked like relatives making a visit. And when we all left to take him back, there wasn't a soul around—it's like God cleared the way. But even if we had run into that Ms. Danley lady, I reckon Andy woulda smoothed it over. He's a first-class bullshit artist." More laughter.

"Y'got that right; he could talk all night. He's a character—he reminds me of Spanky, or how Spanky'll be when he gets old."

"He does for sure," she chuckles fondly. "I been thinking the same thing ... the way he cusses and brags. He even struts like Spanky when he walks."

"And there aren't many truckers, who'd go outta their way to help, like he did—course, the fact that you're a beautiful sexy teenage goddess may've had something to do with it."

"Oh get outta here, you big jock."

Before driving Andy back to his truck, they spent the good part of an hour at the dorm, sharing, laughing, unwinding—and snacking on Doritos and Dr. Pepper. They told and retold their incredible tales from this afternoon. Bryan also called home—he gave his mom a quick report on this wild, ever-changing day, and he asked her to tell Helen Stevens that Mandy had arrived safely in Waco. They offered to take Andy out to eat with them, but he declined, saying he had to get back to his truck, though the blue sparkle in his eyes spoke of a more heartfelt reason: to give the two lovebirds a chance to be alone—at last. So the threesome packed into Bryan's pickup (they couldn't fit in the Firebird because of her stuff, though it drives okay, the front end), and they retraced the back roads, with Andy directing, to the spot where the Firebird came barreling down the I-35 embankment. The blue-and-gray Mack truck still sat at the top, but the traffic had begun to move, at a crawl, yet it *was* moving—they could tell from the other high-profile vehicles. Andy insisted they all get out—he wasn't about to let his new friends go, until he told the story one more time. The paunchy old trucker, strutting and flapping his elbows, gave Bryan a blow-by-blow description of everything that happened, gesturing again and again toward the downhill track of crushed grass and muddy ruts. Finally, after exchanging handshakes and hugs—and before that their mailing addresses—Andy hopped across the ditch and made his way, huffing and puffing, up the hill.

On the way back to Waco, Bryan and Mandy took advantage of the deserted dirt roads, pulling over twice for brief but fervent sessions of necking. They kissed and hugged, sharing sweet words of love and joyous relief, their pent-up emotions desperate for each other after surviving this shocking, scary, unbelievable day. Yet they stopped short of petting and foreplay, saving the best for tonight—at the motel.

Bryan whips the pickup around a city bus that's pulling over. "I was gonna take yuh to this famous steakhouse, but it's like twenty miles away." Exhaust from the bus wafts in through his partly open window, but the odor soon gives way to a happy, intoxicating fragrance, as Mandy digs around in her envelope purse, coming out with a small vial of perfume; she puts a dab on each side of her neck, the same summery scent. (She told him the name once: Amber Dawn or something like that?) "Now we could eat at the Bear's Paw, where all the college kids hang out, but they don't have much of a menu, beyond burgers and dogs."

Shedding her softball cap, she pulls down the mirrored visor on her side. "Well, mister, I'm hungry enough to eat a dadgum horse. So most any kind of food suits me." She works on her bangs with a small metal comb—it warms his heart, her maidenly routines; it's the little things that manifest her presence most powerfully. "But this Italian place sounds *fine* for tonight," she says, as she combs her ponytail. "We can go to that steakhouse to*morrow*, and the college hangout the *next* day." They laugh giddily. "We'll eat out every night till Monday, and we're not gonna worry about money, or mothers, or school, or what's gonna happen next." More laughter, as she pops the comb back into the purse. "This's wild ... like living on the edge."

"You got that right," he agrees, dimpling. "We've sure come a long way—in less than a year?"

"Whaddeyuh mean a *year*? This all happened today, you big jock ... like since I got up this morning." She giggles and gives him more playful punches, pummeling his arm, his ribs, his thigh.

O Jesus, Bryan exults to himself. *I'm so happy I'm getting dizzy, like I'm about to come outta my body and have an OBE. And we're going to a motel after we eat. This's goshdang good.*

* * *

Mandy is thinking about the same subject: *The Holiday Inn sounds plenty exciting, but his roommate's gone until Sunday night—what if? Why not? To do it in Bryan's dorm room—now that would be a fitting climax to this crazy, risky, way-out trip.* The unspoken pun makes her giggle and snort.

"Whaddeyuh laughing at?" Bryan asks, as they turn left on a side street.

"Oh, nothing. I was just thinking about something."

"What?"

"I'll tellyuh later, after we eat." She gives a sassy snicker. "Better yet, I'll show yuh."

"Awh c'mon, y'got me curious," he persists, as he parks across from a two-story, yellow-brick building with a canopied entrance and a red-tile Mediterranean roof. Manicured squares of lawn bracket the covered walkway, along with sculptured, pillbox hedges. Script letters on the canopy give the name: **Tony's.**

"Hey, you big jock," she fusses playfully, "this place looks swanky, and I got mud on my sneakers and jeans, and my cuffs are still damp from the grass, and I got Dr. Pepper on my shirt." She points at a beige, barely visible spot on her knit shirt, the same primrose polo she put on this morning for school (a school she may never attend again). "And I need to wash my hair."

Bryan gives her a love-pat on the knee. "Don't let the fancy doorway fool you. Tony's is actually cozy and laid back." He laughs, his wonderfully green eyes sparking boyishly. "After all, I'm just a country lad right off the farm—no way am I gonna eat any place where I can't wear Levi's. Dang, I'm wearing denim from head to toe, and my jacket's denim too." He laughs louder; she chuckles as well. "And besides, pretty lady, I think you look dadgum terrific, considering what y'been through today."

Grabbing his jacket, he hops out. She gets out too, slipping into her gray-poplin windbreaker as she exits. "So you've eaten at this restaurant before?"

"Yeah, I was just here Tuesday night, with Steve Jordan and Chris Hansen, and we sure didn't dress up or anything—in fact, Steve was wearing sweats." Bryan dimples. "I'm not a big fan of Italian food, so

I ordered spaghetti and meatballs, to be safe, and it was outstanding—that's the only thing I recognized on the menu, plus lasagna ... but then they brought a buncha side dishes, in addition to the spaghetti. It's like no matter what you order, they give you *every*thing on the menu, along with tons of bread and salad."

"Well, like I say, mister, I'm hungry enough to eat a horse."

"Most Texas restaurants are into beef big time," he goes on, as he takes her hand and escorts her across the street. "Like ribs and steaks and barbecue, so this place offers a welcome diversion. And the owner is a bona fide Italian. I mean he's actually from Italy, from Naples. Antonio Pierentosi—but they call him Tony, which is a heck of lot easier to say. He used to work in New York and Boston, where he became well-known as a chef. But he moved here in '78, and opened this place the following year. He also has a restaurant in Killeen, and another in College Station."

"Goshdang, you big jock, you sound like a tour guide."

"Well, I'm just repeating what Chris said. He's an expert on all the restaurants around here."

A bow-tied host greets them inside the door. He seats the young couple at a corner table on the far side of the candlelit dining room, which is empty save for two other parties, also clad in jeans and such. Wall sconces add more light, enough to read the menu. Bryan excuses himself and heads for the men's room.

It IS cozy in here, Mandy remarks to herself, *and sorta old-fashioned, with the checkered tablecloths and paneled walls. And they have candles, which makes it extra neat.*

A waiter soon arrives, a slim twenty-something guy with a blond crewcut. "Good evening, madam," he says, as he pours the water. "How are you tonight?"

"Just fine ... now. Starving, but fine."

"Well, I can assure you, madam, that you brought your appetite to the right place." He gives a nonchalant toss of his head, a faint smirk playing about his mouth. "May I start you two off with a glass of wine?"

"Well uh ... uh," Mandy stammers, blushing—and feeling a bit stupid. "What kind d'yuh have?"

"It's all right here, on our wine list. I'll be back in a few."

Where is Bryan? she murmurs to herself, as she peruses the names. *I know nothing about ordering wine. Chablis, Chianti, Chardonnay, Cabernet, Burgundy, Tuscany, Barolo, Madeira, Merlot, Soave—damn, this's all Greek to me. Wendy's mom ordered wine that time she took me and Wendy out to eat in Sulphur Springs, for Wendy's birthday. It was red wine; no it was white—but I don't have a clue about these names. Where IS Bryan? Why's he taking so long? I'm a dunce when it comes to worldly things. It's like I've been living under a rock all these years, a Baptist, country-gal rock. But why'd that waiter offer me wine in the first place, without asking for my driver's license. No way am I legal, but he calls me "madam" like I'm thirty-five or something.* She titters. *I know I've grown up a lot today, but I'm STILL seventeen. He can't think I'm twenty-one?*

The waiter returns. "So have you decided, madam?"

"Well uh ... what would you suggest? I mean just for a small glass, like enough to sip on?"

"Oh, I like the house Merlot ... or perhaps our Chardonnay."

"I was sort of hoping you just had some red or white wine."

"Well, we have a red Merlot, and a white Chardonnay." The waiter blushes, trying not to laugh, but he can't help it. Bryan suddenly appears, laughing as well.

"So this's all a set-up," Mandy huffs good-naturedly, her face going hot. "You big jock, you."

"I'm sorry, precious," Bryan snickers sheepishly. "This's Ernie. He's Chris's friend. He waited on us Tuesday night, and he's handling these last few parties tonight. I ran into him on the way to the men's room, and that's what got this started."

After more mirthful guffaws, Ernie says, "Don't tell anyone, but I'm going to serve you folks some wine anyway, in honor of your engagement—Bryan tells me *every*thing. No, no, that's not true, but he did say that you're recently engaged."

* * *

"I wanna propose a toast," Mandy declares, halfway through their sumptuous dinners (Bryan has lasagna, while she, in keeping with her daylong abandon, chose an exotic shrimp entree, which turned out to be delicious—she gave him some. As for the wine, they both chose Chardonnay).

"Well, I must say," he kids, "for a country-town Baptist, you're really getting into the swing of things." They laugh.

She lifts her tulip-shaped wine goblet, which Ernie recently recharged, and Bryan does the same. More titters and smirks. "C'mon, mister, be serious."

"Okay, I'm sorry."

"To Bryan Howard and Amanda Stevens," she blurts, after regaining her composure. "To the secretly engaged couple, who won't be a secret after *today*." She giggles in spite of herself. "May they be happy, healthy, and live long lives—and may they have a bunch of screaming kids."

They clink their goblets together, then Bryan says, "Hold it, I have a toast as well." But before he can get his words out, their eyes meet, and lock. No more kidding; no more banter. *O Jesus God,* his heart sighs. *I got that vertigo feeling, like I'm gonna fall into those big blue eyes.* The warm heat of her gaze melts him, rendering him helpless and vulnerable, but oh so happy. He gestures with the white wine. "To

317

my dear, dear Amanda," he whispers earnestly, "to my love, to my future wife ... to my very life. May *all* our dreams come true, now and forever."

They gently touch their glasses. "And to Bryan," Mandy adds, her eyes glistening in the candlelight, "to my sweetheart, and *best* friend ... to the love of my life. And I wantcha to know that I don't regret the choice I made today. It was a super-big decision, but I'm *so* glad I made it. Now we're gonna be together ... no matter *what*." They click their glasses, for the third time.

They conclude the toasting, but their hearts continue to overflow. Bryan leans closer, taking her hand. "I know it hurt to leave your mama, and I pray you two can reconcile somehow. But it's time for *us* to be together. We're more grown up, and more ready, and more in love than our parents give us credit for. And I believe the Lord wants us together. I was *so* scared today. I feared the worst, and I had doubts about everything. But God brought you safely to me, and that makes it *all* good."

"Oh, Bryan," she coos, her eyes filling. "Some real bad things happened to a lot of people out there on the highway. It's sad and tragic, and we don't know why. But God took care of *us* for a reason. So we should follow our hearts and have *no* fear."

* * *

FLETCHER HALL PARKING LOT
THURSDAY, OCTOBER 3, 1991 — 9:31 PM

Bryan slows to a halt next to the Firebird. Mandy has to get some things out of her car before they go over to the Holiday Inn, and he needs to pack an overnight bag as well. "I'm just gonna whip up to my room to get my toothbrush and stuff," he tells her, his soul aglow with anticipation. "You get what yuh need outta the Firebird, and I'll be back down in five."

She grabs her cap and purse but gives no reply—then BANG, she's out of the truck, sprinting toward the side door of the dorm, a plume of giggles trailing behind her.

"Mandy! Mandy!" he cries, chasing after her. "You can't go in there. It's going on ten o'clock. If you get caught—" He stops midsentence, lest anyone hear him.

Reaching the dorm, he bolts up the stairs, but she's well ahead of him, almost to the third floor. *Oh shit!* he exclaims to himself. *If she runs into Marvin—Do not pass go! Go directly to jail! And she has to go right by his door to get to mine. O Jesus God?*

Bryan arrives on the third floor expecting the worst, but he finds the corridor deserted save for his sweetheart laughing hushedly in front of Unit 311. "Hurry," he whispers, as he unlocks the door, and they rush inside where she collapses giggling upon the sofa.

THE SILVER CORD

He can't help but laugh as well, as he switches on the end-table lamp plus the kitchen light. Removing her softball cap, she twirls it on her forefinger then sails it like a Frisbee onto the armchair across the room. "Well, now that I'm in here," she gushes, her cheeks redder than any Merlot, "I reckon I'll hafta spend the night, or Ms. Danley might see me, or that *Marv* guy."

"Goshdang, that was risky," he declares, feigning discontent; he's actually elated at this turn of events. "I could get kicked outta the dorm." He tosses his jacket onto the recliner.

"Well *good*," she banters sassily. "We'll get an apartment, and that'll take care of one big decision ... like where I'm gonna live. Besides, I *like* breaking rules, and I'm getting goshdang good at it. Plus, I'm getting you back for that trick you played on me at the restaurant." She snuffles and snickers, and kicks off her sneakers. "And your roommate's gone, so why waste money on a motel?" Shedding her jacket, she sticks out her tongue at him then does that rabbity routine with her face. "This's elementary logic, mister. But since I can't show my face in the hallway, I guess you'll hafta go down and get my stuff outta the Firebird."

"You're too much," he exults, pouncing upon her. "You wild thing, you."

Mandy giggles and yelps, as he tickles her ribs then her legs, but she quickly retaliates. "You're in for it now!" she shrieks.

"Not so *loud*," he laughs, as he wrestles with her, trying to pin her arms—with little success. "Someone might hear yuh, and you *sure* don't sound like a guy."

"Let 'em hear me," she huffs amid more titters. "It's a *stu*pid rule anyway." She does notch down the volume however—but not her counterattack. Gaining the upper hand, she paws his midsection until he's begging for mercy.

Bryan finally escapes, hopping to his feet, while she sits up and loosens her ponytail, removing that elastic thing. Silence, bashful silence—their mirthful play gives way to the realization that they're here for the night, alone with their love, and lust. They'll be sharing the same bed, like newlyweds. She fingerfluffs her unfettered locks; they flop limply about her ears, her cheeks, cutely framing her puppyish face, with its warm maidenly glow, no longer crimson but softly pink and pulsing. Rotating the coffee table out of the way, he leans over her, as if doing a push-up on the back of the couch. She grins up shyly, knowingly, but her eyes beckon boldly under her disheveled bangs, twin pools of blue topped by a curtain of gold. Bryan leans closer. He rubs his nose on hers then pecks the top of her mouth. He smells Chardonnay and garlic and lip gloss, along with the contrasting aromas of perfume and perspiration, a stimulating contrast.

Giving a giddy little moan, Mandy nibbles his mouth, while caressing his cheeks, his neck, his hair. Then she kisses him fervently, her wine-flavored tongue darting and probing. Currents of desire course zipper-quick to his crotch. His penis stiffens, but his knees go wobbly.

"Oh, pretty lady, you're getting me stirred," he whispers after another long kiss. "You're making me shake all over."

"That's the whole idea," she sports hushedly, sensually, her voice going husky like it does, her grin no longer shy but alluring and hungry, matching her eyes.

He devours her trancy gaze until dizzy with delight. Too much— he collapses onto the sofa beside her. But before he can gather her into his arms, she's on her feet, fluffing her hair, blowing into her cupped hands. "Yuck," she titters, "I got Italian breath. How canyuh stand kissing me?"

He dimples. "I've suffered worse things." The mirthful mood has returned, though now with a decidedly erotic character. "I reckon I can endure it."

"Oh get outta here, you big jock. But before we go any farther, I need to—"

"So y'think we're going farther, d'yuh?"

Mandy smirks coquettishly. "Doesn't matter to me, mister. We can be *good* Christians if yuh like, and pretend we're on a church hayride. We'll just kiss—and obey the nothing-below-the-neck rule. I have *will*power, remember?" Giving a sporty laugh, she nods her head toward the bathroom. "But either way, I gotta take a shower. I'm *all* sticky."

"I'll bet you are," he teases.

She laughs despite herself, her blush deepening. "You're such a *gosh*dang know-it-all, but you don't know as much as y'think." Fishing her keys from her purse, she tosses them to Bryan. "And by the way, hotshot, you're not exactly calm, or maybe that's a *flashlight* in the pocket of your jeans?"

"Could be, miss priss. But I have a hunch you'd like for me to put it in *your* pocket."

"Whew-*whee*, y'really have a way with words, for a country-boy Baptist." More titters, both of them. "But before you can put anything in my pocket, y'gotta catch me." He bolts off the couch, trying to grab her, but she flees giggling into the bathroom, closing the door all but a crack. "I can still outrun yuh, big boy." She crinkles her nose in playful defiance then closes the door all the way.

"Hold it. Lemme in a second. I gotta brush my teeth."

"No way, mister; I know your tricks. Now you be good ... and go down and get my stuff while I'm getting into the shower. I just need my purple barrel bag; it's in the cargo hatch. And see if yuh can find my madras shirt. My clothes are stuffed behind the front seat. And get my blow-dryer too."

O God, she drives me crazy, he murmurs happily to himself, as he hears her clothes coming off, the muted *rrrrrrp* of her zipper, the rustling of denim, the jingle of her belt buckle, the *swish* of cotton, along with a few intimate pops and ticks.

"Are yuh gonna get my bag, or what?" she asks, as if she can see him dawdling outside the door.

"Oh yeah ... I'm on the way right now. But I'm gonna getcha *good* when yuh get out."

"I *hope* so," she chortles in reply.

* * *

I goshdang hope so, Mandy repeats to herself a minute later, as she checks her chin in the mirror; last week's pimple is gone; ditto for her period: it ended yesterday—thank God. Giving a titter, she peeks out the door, halfway expecting Bryan to still be there, but the room is empty. She doesn't close the door; she opens it wider in fact. Now that she's naked, save for her panties, it excites her to leave it open. She gives a sassy wiggle then pops the elastic on the blue hip-huggers.

Returning to the mirror, she cups her breasts, admiring their girlish firmness and uplifted perch, and yet they're womanly enough to leave no doubt about her sexual potency, especially the areolas and nipples, which adorn the tips like pinkish polar caps. *It may hurt if we go all the way,* she reminds herself, *but I'm more than ready—and way more than sticky.* She titters again. *I'm goshdang wet in fact—from kissing him.* She slips the damp undies over her hips then rolls them down to her ankles. She fingers her bush then lightly strokes the whiskery sides where she shaves it. *We may not consummate this first time—I don't wanna put him under pressure or anything—but I'm MORE than ready.* Stepping out of the panties, she spins giddily about then does a little jig. *Oh gosh, I'm so hyped I'm about to pee on myself.* After another playful whirl she plops down on the john. *I bet I'm the only gal who ever peed in THIS toilet. Especially with the door open. I don't even do that at my house.* She giggles but quickly sobers. *Gosh, it's NOT my house any more. I left this morning—for good.* A pang of homesickness, tinged with guilt, tugs on her heart. *It's just Gretchen and Mama living there now.* As Mandy wipes and flushes, the enormity of this truth threatens her frisky, uncorked mood. *I'm just seventeen, and I'm out here on my own. And I'm on the verge of having premarital sex ... Mama's super-big NO-NO ... plus God and Pastor Ron.*

But by the time she steps into the shower stall a minute later— after waiting for the water to get hot—the honeymoon vibes have regained control. *I woulda been leaving next spring anyhow. And Mom Howard called Mama to tell her that I got here okay, despite the storm, and I'll call home myself in a day or two. It's not like I hate Mama or anything, but I had no choice.* She lathers up with an orange bar of soap that smells zesty wild, like daisies and clover. *I don't care if I'm only seventeen. Mama was doing it with my real dad at sixteen, maybe fifteen. And young girls used to get married all the time ... like it was totally normal in the old days.* She gives a determined snort. *Plus, I don't care if it's a sin—but it's not. No goshdang way. I can't see God coming down on us just because we don't have the paperwork. In his eyes we're married already.*

No washcloth: she scrubs with her hands. As she does, she pictures Bryan's wonderful green eyes loving her, wanting her, possessing her—like at the restaurant, like a few minutes ago on the sofa. The thought makes her nipples tingle. Ditto for her clitoris, as it pushes out from its soapy hiding place. *It's a good thing I got those condoms in my purse,* she snickers, as she rinses off. *I doubt he ever got any. My period just ended yesterday, but it's still better to use one—if we get that far tonight. I should go on the pill, now that I'm out from under Mama's nose.*

Mandy checks the shampoo in the rack, a cylindrical bottle of Suave. *Where is Bryan? I need MY shampoo. This cheap stuff's okay for short hair, but it'll wreck mine.* More snorty laughs. *He has no clue what girls go through.* She cranks up the hot water a notch. *Oh, that feels good on my back. I hope it doesn't run out.*

* * *

Upon his return, Bryan finds the bathroom door ajar, the suite filling with steam and the fragrance of soap. "Here's your stuff," he announces above the *shhhh* of the shower. Knowing she's naked behind that gray shower curtain thrills him; a hot wind whirls in his gut. "I got the purple bag plus the hair-blower, but I couldn't find your madras shirt ... so I just grabbed a white polo—it's beige actually, now that I can see it."

"No biggie ... but what I need now is my shampoo. It's in the end-part of my bag, a white plastic bottle."

Unzipping the pouch, he pulls it out—then reads: "Pantene Pro-V. Shampoo Plus Pro-Vitamin Conditioner. For Normal—"

"Okay, okay," she giggles. "Just give it to me. Y'don't hafta do a dadgum TV commercial."

"I like to be pre*cise*," he quips, handing it too her—without opening the curtain. They sport and laugh some more, then he heads for the closet off the kitchen. "I got a fresh towel for you, pretty lady, and a wash rag," he tells her, as he reenters the bathroom. "I shoulda given these to yuh before."

"Thanks. It's a bit late for the wash rag, but y'can leave the towel on the counter by the sink. I'll be done in ten minutes."

After quickly brushing his teeth, Bryan departs, closing the door behind him. He checks his watch: 9:59 p.m. *She'll be out by ten after— O Jesus God, I'm almost shaking.* The AC fan kicks on. Going to the thermostat, he kills it then slides open the big window several inches, letting in the pleasant night air. He likewise cracks the window in his room. While in there, he splashes Brute onto his cheeks, then he unbuttons his shirt and applies some Ban roll-on to his underarms. He even puts some on his belly, Ban and Brute, and around his crotch, reaching down inside his Levi's. He leaves his shirt unbuttoned, his shirttail out. He showered this afternoon, but that seems a week ago, considering.

He slips out of his sneakers and socks then pads back to the living room. The shower has stopped in the bathroom, and Mandy's blow-dryer has commenced. Bryan plops down on the sofa, but he can't sit still. He goes to the window. *It looks so normal out there,* he chuckles to himself, as he gazes out at the parking lot and the campus lights beyond. *How can it look so normal on a night like this? after a day like this? And I reckon everyone's doing their homework and getting all set for classes tomorrow. But not ME.* He adjusts his jeans to give room to his ropy, semi-erect dick. He circles the sofa, drumming his fist against his open hand. He's giddy but nervous; he has butterflies; he's amazed, he's wired, he's anything but tired—in spite of the exhausting and tumultuous ordeal he endured today.

10:06 p.m. He kneels near the TV stand; he flips on the stereo, tuning to KOZY 99.4 (soft-rock FM): where John Denver is singing "Sunshine On My Shoulders." He'd rather put in the Stevie Nicks tape, but it's down in the truck. While on his knees, he catches a whiff of foot odor. *My dadgum feet stink from being in those sweaty sneakers and socks. I shoulda showered again tonight, but it's too late now.* He has Desenex but goes instead to the kitchen sink, where he washes his feet with dishwashing soap, left then right, balancing clumsily on one leg. Almost falling, he laughs hushedly; he's tall, but it's still a stretch. He hurriedly dries on a towel from the closet then kills the kitchen light, leaving only the table lamp on, the one in the living room.

10:11 p.m. *O Lord, she'll be out soon.* But the hair dryer is still going. He paces a bit more then plunks down in the recliner, after moving his denim jacket to the back of the armchair, above Mandy's blue-and-white softball hat. *She must've just gotten over her period,* he surmises, shifting to the practical realities related to mating. *She got it last Friday, and it lasts four or five days. This means she can't get pregnant, or does it? She can't right before her period, but afterward, I'm not sure? It has to do with ovulation. Damn, I'm a dunce when it comes to female things.* He chuckles. *But I reckon it's better to be safe. We sure don't need a pregnancy now—we have PLENTY going on.*

Hustling into his room, he turns on the elbowed desk-lamp then grabs a condom from his top drawer; he hides it under the Macintosh mouse-pad, within reach of the bed. He adjusts the arm of the lamp, and the shade, until the lighting is just right. *We're all set. I can't think of anything else.* But his mind is too keyed up to rest. *I gotta be gentle. It hurts the first time for a girl, when she breaks her cherry, as Spanky calls it. But who knows? We may not have actual intercourse this first time? I just hafta be sensitive. And whaddabout me? Spanky says some guys get so excited they lose their hard-on, or they ejaculate too soon, and some mess up the mood while fiddling with the rubber.* Bryan retrieves the packaged condom, trying to remember how to open and unfurl it, like the one Spanky showed him in tenth grade.

C'mon—stop freaking. Y'can't cover all the bases or plan out every detail. Besides, she's gonna be my wife; we have our whole life together. It's not like we gotta be perfect the first time. Nonetheless, he's still concerned about the rubber. He studies the foil packet under the lamp: TROJAN PLUS, LATEX CONDOM, LUBRICATED. He also reads the small print concerning AIDS and pregnancy. *This should do the trick, and I've got a bunch more in my drawer, plus one in my wallet.* Closing the bedroom door behind him, all but a crack, he returns to the big room; he looks out the window. The blow-dryer goes off in the bathroom. *She's done with her hair. It won't be LONG now.* The radio seems a bit loud (*Foreigner* and "I Want to Know What Love Is"). Bryan turns it down a notch. It's far from his favorite song, but the mid-'80s hit certainly fits the moment.

Plopping down on the sofa, he places his bare feet on the coffee table (after repositioning it). He hears clinking and clunking in the bathroom then the water goes on, then it goes off—then the door clicks open, and Mandy marches out wearing a baby-doll nightgown and a blushing grin, but no ponytail. The perfumed fragrances from the bathroom accompany her. Her freshly shampooed hair, beautifully blown and feathered about her puppy-cute face, glistens like spun gold in the soft lamplight. The shorty nightgown hangs to her thighs like a large V-necked T-shirt, though its frilly blue fringe makes it prettier, and more feminine than *any* T-shirt, as does the bowed ribbon at the neck.

"Well, babe, whaddeyuh think?" she flirts, strutting like a model in front of Bryan, her pert uplifted breasts lusciously evident, as they press out against the cottony gown.

"Very nice, pretty lady," he replies from the couch, in an understatement. "Very, very nice."

After giving him a toothpasty kiss, quick but sensual, she prisses back to the center of the room. As if on cue, a faster tune plays on the radio, John Cougar Mellencamp and "Crumblin' Down." Mandy shimmies like a stripper, rocking her butt like she did that day they went skinny-dipping. Canting her hips one way, her shoulders the other, she gestures seductively, her eyes darting humid fire under her feathery bangs—blue heat. She skips and spins. She gives a saucy smirk then wags her head, tossing her golden locks. Halting near the coffee table, she gyrates in place, her hips seesawing to the music. She slowly lifts the baby-doll gown, showing more leg, higher and higher, teasingly so, until he catches a glimpse of tan-lines and darkish crotch: pinkish fissure, pubic beard—but quickly *gone.* Dropping the frilly hem, she twirls away toward the picture window.

THE SILVER CORD

Her audacious carnality entrances him, blowing away his honeymoon anxiety, as a hot wind clears the fog on a summer morn. He drinks her in, his boner quivering inside his jeans. He's obsessed with the female form, especially hers. Her goosefleshy, bewhiskered underarms fascinate him, as do the fine halos of blond hair on each thigh, which end abruptly at the shave-line just above the knee. Her flesh teems with youthful vigor, yet she's not one bit craggy or brawny, like a guy. Her strength is packaged rather in graceful, flowing lines and soft, cushiony, hairless flesh. Her shoulders are gently rounded inside the clingy gown, not square like his, and her arms and wrists and hands are lithe and swanlike, and her waistline is higher up and smaller, accentuating the outward curve of her hips. Her teen-gal physique is *so* striking and elegant and beautiful and different—it lures him, astounds him, stirring his carnal curiosity again and again. And yet his desire, though forever unsated save for what she has under that nightie, goes beyond the flesh. He yearns to know *all* of her, her glory, her girl-woman mystique, to discover all the facets of her femaleness, all the secrets of her gender.

Lifting her arms and closing her eyes, she boogies to the beat. *She's really unleashed,* he chortles to himself, dimpling. *Those lyrics about walls coming down are right on target.*

By the time the song ends, she's on his lap kissing him. A new song is playing, but Bryan has tuned out everything but Mandy, Mandy: her tongue, her lips, her hot toothpasty breath, her randy gaze, her downy locks, her mind-altering aromas. She's still wearing the nightie, but he can feel her naked crotch, her hot dampness pressing upon his legs. She sits on his knees, her legs straddling, as he slouches, hips forward, on the sofa. To achieve this intimate posture, they had to move the coffee table—again.

"Oh, babe," she purrs breathily after another session of torrid mouth-to-mouth action. "You really know how to light my fire." Reaching inside his open shirt, she caresses his chest, his abs.

"Well, pretty lady," he whispers, as he lightly touches her breasts through the gown. "You don't do too bad yourself. That dance was enough to arouse any red-blooded guy. She gives him a proud little grin along with a wanton roll of the eyes. Too much: he can no longer resist her fleshy, widespread thighs. Reaching under the nightie, he probes the pantyless heat until he finds her bush and that most singular secret of nature that resides under it.

"Jesus, yes, right *there,*" she exults, as he fingers a clammy fold of engorged flesh then explores the hotly moist slit leading downward from it, just like he did that that day in the hayfield. She closes her eyes, her face going dreamy, her cheeks flushing. "Oh, mister, you've got *magic* fingers."

He withdraws; she gives a little moan. "So y'want more?" he flirts hoarsely, his words catching in his throat—he's so high he can barely talk, and his dick's harder than it's ever been.

"I'm okay," she boasts coyly, giving a naughty-girl smirk, deliciously protracted. "I have *will*power y'know?"

He laughs. "That's right; I forgot. Well, you let me know, ma'am, if I can be of service."

For a long moment, she gives no response except for more smirking and a sassy nodding of her head. Finally, she says, "I can live without it y'know?" Her lewd bragging stirs Bryan all the more, especially since she can't hide the husky undertones in her voice or the flames in her big blue eyes. She bites her upper lip then wets the lower one with her tongue, working it slowly, alluringly from side to side. He can't help but kiss her.

Quickly becoming the aggressor, she kisses him back, her tongue flitting then pushing deep. After coming up for air, she helps him out of his shirt, then she dances her fingertips on his shoulders, down his biceps, upon his chest. Her touch gives him delightful shivers. Closing his eyes, he leans back and enjoys the attention, mewing now and then with contentment. She nibbles his ear, then licks the inside of it. She pecks him on the forehead, the neck, the shoulder. She lightly sucks his nipples. With the back of her fingers, she caresses his chin, his cheek, the scar at his temple. She has clearly taken charge of the lovemaking.

Hopping up, she takes his hand. "Okay, big boy, let's move on to act two—and I reckon the script calls for a bed."

"I thought y'could live without it?"

"I can," she sports, as he gets up. "You just wait and see."

The soft rock on KOZY follows them into his bedroom, but it's now fainter, hardly noticeable. After pulling back the covers on Bryan's bed, and fluffing the pillows, Mandy sheds her nightie then hugs him from behind, her erect nipples pressing deliciously against his naked skin. She gives him a tender kiss on the neck, on the shoulder. Then with a few skillful motions, her arms about his waist, she unbuckles and unzips his Levi's.

While he slips out of his jeans, she hops onto the bed where she sits Indian-style on the far side near the foot, a smirk on her cupid mouth, her cheerleader calves crossed in front of her nude body, which so captivates him that he pauses, pants in hand, to stare, to gaze, to gather her in. It may be October, but she's still more tan than white, save for those private female zones, which render her most different from him. Girl, woman, maiden goddess: he devours her nubile curves and slopes and nooks and crannies, and tan lines, and shadows, and dabs of lamplit flesh. Her rose-nippled tits hang so beautifully, so whitely, two ripe unplucked pears. And he finds her belly dimple most singular, the way her navel stares out from the shadows like a recessed screw. But her ginger-brown bush beckons most powerfully of all, and he soon fixes on it with all his attention. "Hey, you big jock," she quips, snapping him out of his trance. "I'm ready and waiting." Extending her hand, she adds a humorous line from their August frolic by the stream, "Come on in, babe; it's not *that* cold."

* * *

"Oh, Bryan honey, I love your bod," she coos a few minutes later, as she kisses his naval then nibbles the masculine ribbon of hair below it. Still wearing his underpants, he lies on his back, both pillows under his head, while she straddles his legs on her hands and knees. His eyes closed, he dimples, giving her a sex-drunk grin, but he doesn't say anything.

Taking a deep breath, she inhales his presence. He smells of Brute and anti-perspirant—she recognizes the familiar scents—and there's a bit of BO working through, a most virile pheromone which quickens her desire like an aphrodisiac. Moving down, she kisses his calf, the muscle, tasting salt, licking hair. She pecks his knees, one then the other, then she works up the inside of his long, stout thighs, and before she knows it, she's kissing the white fabric of his jockey shorts. *O Jesus,* she declares to herself, gazing wantonly at his rock-hard shaft, as it stretches against its cottony cocoon. *I'm getting so wet—I may not outlast him after all. I've had his cock on my mind ever since that day by the creek, and now it's only inches away. O dear God.*

Rather than rushing right to intercourse, with its possible pain and awkwardness, and potential loss of self-esteem for Bryan, it's her plan to get him off first, while holding back herself, and holding—until her teen-gal hormones have taken her higher than she's ever been. Then, it will only take a few finger flicks from him, and she'll be going off like a roman candle. It'll be super for both of them, even if they don't go ALL the way on this first night, and if they do, she'll be lubricated as much as any virgin. Wendy talks about it too, how it's wiser for lovers and newlyweds to start with manual and oral stimulation, so they can satisfy each other without the pressure of actual coitus. And it makes sense to Mandy (despite how preachers condemn it more than fornication, calling it sodomy and perversion, the oral part); in fact, she's practiced this honeymoon scenario in her recent fantasies, but she had *no* idea it would happen this soon, and she needs all her willpower to pull it off. It's one thing for a horny gal to pace herself while masturbating alone, it's another to have a hunky, A-plus, chiseled-jaw male right on the scene, hotly virile, his cotton-clad boner throbbing within reach. And speaking of masturbation, she hasn't since week before last, and then she had her period, so she has a healthy store of horniness, not to mention the reckless abandon she's been riding all day. She could come *really* good right now, like in three minutes (fast for her), if she simply strokes her engorged clit, a most delicious temptation, but she determinedly resists.

Mandy shifts instead to the side of her man, sitting back on her heels. Her carnal curiosity raging, she pulls back the elastic waistband of his underpants, freeing his erect penis, which springs upward, bowing majestically over his belly, over the manly ribbon of stomach hair she was kissing before. She can't help but fondle his hard-on. It feels hot and veiny. He gives a throaty moan, pushing his undies down farther until they're around his thighs. She plays in the dark-brown thicket of pubic moss at its root—his bush is a few shades darker than hers, potently so—then she fondles his testicles, his swollen goosefleshy bag, which seems as big as a softball. Finally, she runs her finger up the length of his stalwart cock, following one of the bluish serpentine veins. He utters a series of little murmurs and mews. She loves to touch this wondrous machine, and she loves, even more, the realization that it's getting him higher, and her too, unbearably so.

"Oh, *mis*ter, let's get these underpants completely off."

"Do what yuh need to do, ma'am," he replies—he smirks but remains remarkable passive.

After quickly sliding his briefs down his legs and over his feet, she returns her attention to his cock. She finds the broad, ruddy-violet mushroom head especially captivating; it's spongy firm and hot, and it pulses with every beat of his heart. *Damn,* she sighs to herself. *I may come just from looking at it.*

She teases with her finger the sloping edge of the engorged glans; Bryan gives a sigh of his own: "Whew, gosh ... O God. If yuh do that much more, I may lose control."

"That's the whole point," she flirts huskily. "Y'just enjoy the ride, big boy. I'll take care of gettin' yuh there." Gripping his one-eyed stallion, she jacks it gently up and down, as if her hand's a pussy, and he's slow-fucking it. His expression goes dreamy, his cheeks radiant. She has no idea how guys hold themselves when they jerk off, but his broken moans and mews tell her that she's doing A-OK, as does a clear drop of pre-cum after ten or fifteen strokes.

Going down on him, she treats herself to his 'sweetness' with a kiss and a lick, then she dances her tongue down his shaft and over his turgid nuggets. He gives a needy whimper, and so does she, as her own excitement has reached that sweetly agonizing plateau where 'going over the top' is the only way down. She adheres nonetheless to the plan. Taking his big cock seriously into her mouth, she develops a slow and steady blow-job rhythm amid his fevered mewing and panting.

Picking up the tempo, she soon senses the coming eruption. Removing her mouth, she finishes with her hand, pumping him fast and furious, and it doesn't take long. He arches his back, his haunches going rigid—then with a dispatching thrust and a long groan, he comes, spewing glutinous strings of jism high into the air. He ejaculates again and again, covering her girlish fingers with the hot milky liquid, plus his chest and stomach, even his neck. Finally, his body goes limp, his penis deflating, while he lies panting in a near-stupor.

THE SILVER CORD

Mandy can scarcely digest this amazing event, and it stokes her own fire to the torture point. *O Jesus, he just kept on coming and coming, like forever. And it still feels warm on my hand.* She sniffs. *It smells exotic yet wild, like musky dank.* She giggles under her breath. *It woulda been neat to get off just as he did, but I'm glad I didn't—this time. Now he can fondle me to orgasm just like I planned. I doubt there'll be any penetration tonight, since he's already shot his wad— to say the least. But I wanted to get him off, and I DID.* She gives a wanton sigh, a delicious shiver coursing through her nude high-schooler bod—she's cocked and ready: hair-trigger hot. *O Jesus, I'm so goshdang high. I love it, how lust feels when it's almost painful—the need. I know I'm gonna COME like crazy, but not quite yet.*

She notices Bryan stirring—his panting has subsided. He reprops the pillows under his head. "Wow, babe," she declares. "Was that something, or what? So how'd yuh like it?"

He dimples and blushes. "Oh, pretty lady, where'd yuh learn to do that?"

Mandy snickers, her face warming as well. "Oh, it's just one of my *many* skills."

Bryan gives a boyish snort, his blush deepening, his green eyes still blissfully entranced. "Well, it was *tot*ally awesome."

"You got that right," she agrees, grinning and rolling her eyes. "Oh, babe, you're a mess. Let me get something to wipe you off." She pads to the bathroom where she washes her hands then dampens a towel with hot water. As she does, she senses her own dampness oozing down her inner thigh, not to mention her clitoris, which stretches to her knee, or so it seems.

"Where'd all this come *from*?" she asks upon her return. She dabs the semen off his warm, well-sated flesh. She finds more on the sheet, on the pillow, even a spot on the headboard. "Girls get wet, but we sure don't spew like *that*—I never saw anything so wild. And it spurted so high, the first few shots anyway, and then it just kept pouring out, like it was never gonna stop?"

"I reckon it's just been waiting for this night, so *you* could let it out." He comes up and gives her a peck on the cheek.

She kisses him back on the lips, hungrily, sensually, then she smirks. "Well, if I was a guy, and I came *right* now, you'd need three towels, at least, to clean me up, not to speak of the walls, and the ceiling, and the window." She giggles. "I've been horny to the limit before, but *nothing* like this."

"Oh, precious, I shoulda taken care of that," he declares, pulling her into his arms, as she lies down beside him—he gives her one of the pillows. His eyes go warm, filling with affection.

"No, no, honey, I'm glad," she assures, as they snuggle face-to-face, pressing their naked flesh together. "I coulda fingered myself off while I was doing you, but I'm glad I didn't—I woulda missed the show." She titters. "Plus, I wanted to satisfy you first. I sorta planned it out this way, for our honeymoon. I just didn't expect to be on any honeymoon *this* soon."

He grins and dimples. "No kidding."

Mandy, lying on her right side as he lies on his left, fingers the sparse sprigs of chest hair about his paps. "But anyway, I figured for our first time, it might be better to get each other off, you then me, instead of rushing right into the real thing. Besides, the *longer* I wait the higher I get. Y'know, I toldjuh that day in the car." More wanton giggles. "But let me warn you ahead of time, big boy: I may never stop once I let myself go—girls can climax more than once, y'know?"

"That's what I hear," he chuckles, as he fondles her left breast then plays with the nipple, sending feverish currents to the core of her womanhood.

Grimacing against her need, she licks her lips then his. "It's like I got a million hornets buzzing inside me, and they all want out *super* bad. I can't get your cock outta my mind, but right now your hand will do quite well."

"Y'mean like this?" he flirts, reaching between her legs.

Mandy, giving an excited little murmur, rolls eagerly onto her back, spreading her thighs, closing her eyes. She feels his fingers combing through her pubic hair, then he teases her groin on each side of her aroused vulva. Her pulse skitters erratically.

"So, ma'am, how's your self-control now?"

"Just fine ... sir," she fibs, without opening her eyes—her voice is so tight and full of husky breath, she can scarcely get her words out. "I can ... *live* ... without it ... y'know—O Jesus God."

Spurred by her saucy bravado, Bryan ventures to the heart of the strike zone where he strokes her clit, slowly but firmly, then faster and faster. "Oh, babe; oh, babe," she whimpers between panting breaths, her heart hammering in her chest. Her hips begin to gyrate, to rock n' roll, as when she was dancing in the big room, but this time she has no power to stop them, for the hot stings of pleasure take her quickly to point of no return. She pictures his ruddy cock, the purplish mushroom, the bluish veins, the hot throbbing, the drop of pre-cum, the wondrous ejaculation: X-rated images that fuel the final, thundering charge to the summit, sealing her deliverance. Nonetheless, she fights the gathering tumult, trying to prolong that ultimate high just this side of letting go, but she's *way* too primed to win this battle, and she quickly yields to the mighty intoxication.

"O *Jesus*," she sobs, "I'm coming. O Jesus, *fuck* ... O *GOD!*" Throwing her arms wildly about, she stretches her legs and gives a convulsive gasp, as the hot spasms of rapture deliver her into that melting swoon where pleasure dies by pleasure. A soft shudder ripples through her limbs, then she lies motionless, limp, and breathless, dying with sheer delight.

THE SILVER CORD

A minute later: Bryan, his head propped on his hand, looks on with loving awe, while Mandy, her eyes closed, her cheeks flushed, recovers her breath, and her senses. She remains on her back beside him, though she's assumed a more modest, crossed-leg position. The heat from her exercised body wafts up along with the aroma of her arousal and orgasm, that sweetish, smoky, ferny-wild fragrance that comes only from a girl's pussy. His fingers are still wet with her juices. A smirk plays upon her mouth, as though she's proud of her sexually potent, teen-gal cunt, with its power to rapture her—and him. "So, was it worth the wait?" he asks, as he fondly toys with her belly dimple.

Her smirk widens into a wifely grin. "O God ... was it *ever*." She comes up and kisses him then plops back onto her pillow.

"Well, precious, the feeling is certainly mutual, and I'm more than glad to accommodate you—dang, gal, you blow my mind. I love it, that look you get on your face. It's like—well, I can hardly believe this's really happening, that you're really here. It's like a dream, yet it's better than *any* dream, way better."

"You got that right, mister."

He chuckles. "I guess we're still virgins, *tech*nically speaking. But I'm sure not complaining."

Mandy blushes and giggles. "Me neither, but I'd say our days are numbered, if we keep *meet*ing like this." More giggles, then she paws the air playfully above her naked breasts. "Gosh, babe, it's mind-boggling. I mean, I got up this morning thinking about next year, how we'd be sleeping together every night, then all of a sudden we're here in the same bed. Who could believe it? It's wild and super awesome ... like presto magic." She purses her lips, wrinkles her nose—the cute rabbity routine. A warm upwelling floods his bosom, until he's faint with affection, and wonder.

He pulls her to him, a tender hug. They share a few more laughs, then silence overtakes them, a sweet serenity. She nestles into his embrace, while he caresses her back and kisses her hair, inhaling her shampoo plus that singular mink-oil Mandy-scent, which authenticates her identity. This is not just any female in his arms, not just some sweet-smelling twat—but his love, his life, his one-and-only, his dream-come-true, his reason for being. This really *is* Amanda Fay Stevens lying here in his bed, in Unit 311, at Fletcher Hall on the south side of the Baylor campus.

Giving a cozy sigh, she snuggles closer. *Thank you, God,* Bryan prays in his heart, as he joyfully overdoses on her warm honeymoon presence. *This IS better than any dream. It's like Heaven, like the love I felt after I got hurt at home plate, like going through that tunnel, and gliding over those green fields. We're still in our bodies, but the feelings are somehow the same. It's a mystery, but loving and dying are somehow connected.* He kisses her on the head, the top of her bangs. "Oh, pretty lady," he purrs, his thoughts surfacing, "you make me *so* happy."

"Me too, babe. You make me happier than I *ever* thought possible." Her breath feels hot on his neck, blissfully so. The nude lovebirds go on cuddling and cooing for a while, then she gives him a nibbling peck on the chin, followed by a lustful, lip-locking kiss, which refires his own desire. "Looks like you're coming to attention again," she sports. "It's kinda normal for girls, but I didn't know guys could get it up again so soon."

"Usually true, but I reckon y'got me under a *power*ful spell." He laughs, rolling unto his back.

Mandy, her blue eyes sparking, sits up, as if she wants a closer view of his resurrected member. She gives a bawdy smirk. "But you better be ready, mister ... 'cause I *really* get wild the second time around." Bryan has a flirty reply, but her touch renders him speechless, as she runs her finger up the full length of his boner. She presses it back against his stomach, then lets it spring up. "Boing," she kids girlishly, as she does it again. "This thing is *so* neat, babe. I love to play with it—and I got something for it."

She scampers into the other room, returning with her purse. After hopping back onto the bed, she pulls out a foil packet, a condom. She laughs blushingly, a high-schoolish titter. "Wendy gave me a bunch. Most of 'em are stashed in the Firebird."

The pause in the action has no ill-effect on Bryan's hard-on. The girlish frolic stirs him all the more in fact—not to mention the rubber in her hand. He jabs her playfully on the shoulder. "Well, gal, I reckon you *are* serious about losing your virginity?"

"Let's just say, I believe in being prepared." More giggles.

He dimples. "So do I. In fact, I'm one step ahead of yuh."

"Get outta here."

"Yeah, I got some—from Chris Hansen. And I put one on my desk while you were in the shower; it's under the mouse pad."

Mandy, her tits jouncing, crawls across him then scoots off the bed. "Ah, here it is," she announces after a quick search of the desk. She compares the two packets under the lamp, her curvaceous shadow growing to monstrous proportions on the walls and ceiling. "I can't believe you actually *have* one ... but *mine's* better." She laughs, tossing his back onto the desk. "Yours is just a plain old Trojan, while mine's a Saxon Gold Ultra Lube, the best rubber y'can buy ... according to Wendy, and she works at a drug store y'know?" It excites Bryan to hear Mandy say "rubber" just like a guy. "Plus, it says right here that it's been electronically tested. Wen knows all about rubbers, and not just from her job—she's been screwing since ninth grade, like I toldjuh before. And she says the more lube the better, especially for rookies." This assessment elicits more laughs, from both.

"Okay, pretty lady, you've convinced me," he concedes, looking on with his hands behind his head. "So now what?"

She mounts him, her knees astride his thighs. "I'll show yuh *what.*" Her springy bush, more brown than ginger in the shadows, looms potently above him, marking the seal of her womanhood, the seat of her lust and satisfaction. His fingers, still sweetish with her scent, give witness that she just got off with a gasping, bed-shaking, hand-job climax, but she wants more—or so it seems. She wiggles forward a trifle until he can see the smile of her pussy, a darkish, slightly canted slit between her pinkish labia, which are still a bit swollen and agape from before. This X-rated sight reinforces his erection, until he's throbbing to penetrate that pouty grin. "Okay, babe, lets put this thing on Mr. Happy here." Ripping the corner of the packet, she removes the oily, beige-colored condom. "I doubt I'm ovulating, but we better use it I reckon. And this kind smells good too, not like the cheap ones that stink like a burnt balloon." She giggles. "I don't mean your Trojan, but the super-cheap, unlubricated kind that Wendy showed me last summer."

"I'll be danged, gal, you know more about rubbers than I do."

More giggles and smirks. "Well, that's not saying much." Her demeanor remains girlish and playful, but her dilated eyes and throaty voice tell him that her intentions are most serious, as does her fixation with his pulsing cock. Before proceeding with the rubber, she fondles him. "Goshdang, mister, you're bigger than ever, even more so than while ago."

Her touch thrills him; he closes his eyes. "Oh, pretty lady, you have *magic* fingers."

"I like to play with it. It's hot, and it turns me on like *crazy*. Gosh, you're so big I'd hafta use two rulers to measure it."

"I doubt that," he chuckles, without opening his eyes.

"Well, it's at least nine inches anyway, which is *way* bigger than most guys."

"So how does a *nice* Baptist girl know such a thing?"

She titters. "I'm not telling. You don't hafta know *all* my secrets. Now, let's see ... this little pouch goes on top, on the outside, and it unrolls this way."

Electricity: Bryan feels the condom unscrolling down the length of his cock. "Gosh, gal, you handled that like a pro. How didyuh learn to do that?"

"I'm not telling that either," she teases, as she moves up and gives him a lingering kiss, her tongue jitterbugging in his mouth. He finds then fingers her dangling nipples; she moans.

"Oh, precious," he whispers, "I want you."

"I want you too, honey ... like *right* now." She kisses him until he's shaking with anticipation. "Jesus, my clit's big enough to hang a hat on. O God, I need to come again ... but this time I want you in me." She sighs wantonly. "Lemme get on my back. That'll work best. But

I'm plenty wet ... believe me."

Trading places, Mandy assumes a missionary-wife posture in the middle of the bed, legs spread, knees up, both pillows tucked behind her head. Taking Bryan's hand, she pulls him to her.

"Okay, precious, I'm gonna take it real slow," he assures, as he kisses her lightly on the lips then brushes back her bangs.

"C'mon, you big jock," she brags coquettishly, "I can handle what you got. In fact, I reckon I'm hot enough right now to take on your whole goshdang baseball team. I could outlast 'em all."

Her X-rated bravado heartens him, as does the lust in her eyes, more azure heat. *She sure acts ready,* he tells himself, while he teases the fleshy periphery of her pussy mound with the head of his dick, one side then the other. Nonetheless, he resolves to be gentle, to take it easy and slow.

"C'*mon,*" she urges, her voice hoarsely tight. "You're gonna drive me mad." Closing her eyes, she flicks her tongue over her top lip. Bryan moves center stage, parting her cunt lips with his rubber-clad knob, just enough to get it oozy wet. He's eager to enter, to push deep, but he restrains himself. He slides his glans up and down then rubs it against her fully aroused clitoris, pinkish-red folds of flesh, swollen to the size of a child's thumb.

Tucking her chin, she gyrates her haunches. "Now, babe ... now. It's okay." Bryan, pressing for entry, sinks his shaft an inch, then two. His shelving mushroom disappears into her hotly wet, but insufficient, orifice. She gasps then whimpers with pleasure, or is it pain? He advances deeper, helpful motions from her meeting his measured but steady pushing. "Owh!" she cries out, wincing. "Oh, babe ... you're *so* big." He's now securely inside her, halfway at least, but he's stuck, and he dares not thrust again, lest he split her asunder.

He hugs her tenderly, their hearts beating as one—pounding, racing. "It's okay, precious. We don't hafta do it the first night."

But after catching her breath, Mandy gives him a kiss plus encouraging words, "Don't stop now. It hurts, but it feels good too. Oh my God, Bryan, it's so good to have you inside me, after waiting so long." She gives a labored giggle. "You're stretching me, but it's *more* than worth it." Her vagina has stretched indeed, dilating to accommodate him. It's still tight, but he's no longer stuck. He withdraws his stanchion, all but the head. He pumps her gently, without going deep, thrilling him, and her. "Oh, babe, that feels good now, *super* good. O God—but I need *all* of you."

Bryan renews his advance, as she shifts and wiggles beneath him. At first, he makes no further progress, then comes a tearing release, and he's suddenly there, all the way in.

"Ouch!" Mandy shrieks. "That one ripped me I think."

"Sorry," he says, as he pecks her cheek.

"There's *nothing* to be sorry about, you big jock. I had to lose my cherry one way or the other, and now it's done. Besides, the hurt's going away."

He waits, holding her close. "Let's just lie here a moment."

Mandy utters a throaty sound, a little growl. "Oh, babe, I got those hornets inside me again." She playfully squeezes his shaft with her sphincter muscle, urging him on. Getting the message, he commences the love grist, gently, deliberately, a piston in slow motion—then he picks up the pace. "Oh! Oh!" she cries.

He halts. "Am I hurting you, precious?"

"O God, no ... you're not, you're not. Don't stop. I love it."

* * *

FLETCHER HALL, UNIT 311
FRIDAY, OCTOBER 4, 1991 — 12:37 AM

"Well, pretty lady, I still have a question," Bryan says, as the two lovers cuddle under the covers.

"Go ahead, fire away," Mandy replies, speaking away from him. They lie butt to gut (her butt in his gut).

"How *did* you learn to put a rubber on like that?"

"Oh, I've practiced on *lots* of guys."

"Cut it out," he reacts, feigning displeasure, yet he can't help but laugh. He tickles her ribs; she squeals and squirms. He's still nude, while she's back in the baby-doll nightgown, yet it hardly covers her wondrous ass. He loves the warm heft of her naked backside, but he's exhausted; he'll not be getting it up again. Thrice in two hours: bliss, bliss, and more bliss. They made love till midnight, past midnight. They even used his condom, the Trojan on the desk. And it's not just his pecker—after this long, emotional day, his whole being is bushed. Same goes for Mandy. They're *over*tired in fact, making it difficult to get to sleep, but the cozy pillow-banter *is* helping them to unwind—finally.

"No, I actually learned with a carrot," she recants a moment later. "At Wendy's house ... the day she gave me the condoms."

"A carrot?"

"Yeah, a long thick one from her garden ... like *you*."

"Well, I'm hardly long and thick right now."

"I know; I can feel you against my butt. But I like it when it's soft and dangly too. It's so amazing and *cute*."

"Sounds like you've got a bad case of penis-fascination?"

"Y'better believe it, mister—like ever since I learned about boys. Your plumbing is *way* neater than mine, like totally."

He gives a snorty guffaw. "Not to *me*—no way."

Shifting onto her back, she giggles but doesn't reply. The room is dark save for the campus lights sneaking in the window, along with the night breeze, a coolish zephyr that makes the shade move now and then (Bryan opened the window wider after their second round). There's just enough illumination to see each other, grayly. With the window open and the AC off, Bryan can hear the trucks on I-35 more than usual, but Fletcher Hall seems deathly quiet. His dorm mates have all turned in, none of whom have a goddess in their bed like he does—*very* unlikely anyhow. He figures Sammy and Eric, the soccer guys next door, must've heard the moans and shrieks, the orgasmic cries. It's no biggie, since his days in the dorm are numbered, considering. He laughs to himself, especially as his thoughts shift to Marvin Latrobe down the hall—no way in hell does he have a girl in *his* room.

Bryan rolls away from Mandy, onto his back. A tattered plume of light flits across the ceiling: a car in the parking lot. "But getting back to Wendy," he says, "you mean to tell me, she actually had yuh put a condom on a carrot?"

"Yep—in fact, I did it twice, using her cheap stinky ones, to make sure I was unrolling 'em right. She must have a hundred rubbers. She keeps 'em in a big coffee can, in her closet."

"Damn, she's worse than Spanky."

"I wouldn't go *that* far, though she is rather liberated in her thinking ... yet it makes sense." Mandy gestures for emphasis, her girlish hand fanning the darkness. "They should teach us how to put 'em on in school, least by the time we're in tenth grade."

"They do in some schools ... but no *way* in Spindle."

"Mrs. Snodgrass mentioned them in Health & Homemaking 101 last year, but she didn't have any to show us. And she refers to them as *pro*-phylactics. It's all so clinical, like it has nothing to do with the girls in the class. When it comes to sex and birth control, she harps about abstinence ... and talks some about the 'pill.' It's like condoms are *way* too suggestive to deal with."

"That's for sure. It's a super-taboo subject ... though Pastor Ron has preached about it a few times."

"Yeah, I was there ... but he's *mainly* negative. He says they encourage fornication. He doesn't yell and scream about it like some preachers, but he's definitely in the *abs*tinence camp. He says that birth-control devices are for married couples only, and that teenagers shouldn't be allowed to have 'em, since it gives 'em the green light to go all the way."

Sudden silence. *That's us,* Bryan tells himself, feeling a bit weird. *Pre-marital sex—we just did what he preaches against.*

Mandy clears her throat. "So, babe, d'yuh feel guilty ... about tonight?" Her words confirm she's thinking the same thoughts.

"Uh ... well, well ... I uh—"

"No way!" she exclaims, answering for both. "I'm not gonna let anything mess up this night." She chops the air, her hands whipping up and down then all around, like a pair of darting bats. "We've done *nothing* to be guilty about. I don't care what they say at church, or what Mama says. They can call it fornication, or sodomy or whatever, but what we have is *way* more than that. We have *true* love. It's the greatest, most super love any couple can have, and we're gonna be together forever. We've waited so long, *too* long. How can we be in love and *not* go all the way? Besides, we're *gonna* get officially married ... when it's time." *Whap!* She smacks her palm with her fist. "But it doesn't *matter* if we're *legal*. How could the Lord be all concerned about some ceremony, and some license from the state? *He's* the one who gave us this love. And *he's* the one who saved you last May. And *he's* the one who got us back together when we tried to break up, and *he's* the one who saved me from that tornado. If I hadn't taken the wrong exit in Hillsboro, I woulda been right in it."

Her fervent resolve relieves Bryan, and she seals it with a kiss, as they roll into a tender embrace. "I love you, precious," he whispers. "You've got more fire in you than *any* preacher. And as far as I'm concerned, we're *al*ready married—that's why it was so natural and awesome, and *godly*, to lose our virginity to each other. And we didn't actually *lose* anything, but we gained a wonderful thing. It's what the Bible means when it says we leave our father and mother and cleave unto each other, and become 'one flesh.' Oh, Mandy Stevens, I love you so."

"I love you too, Bryan Howard," she coos, her tone softer but just as emphatic, "and that's all that matters. That's why I left and came down here, and that's why I'm staying, even if I hafta live in my goshdang Pontiac." She gives a muffled laugh. "I'm not gonna bow down to Mama anymore. I love her, but she has to let me live my own life now."

"So whaddeyuh think she's gonna do?"

"I reckon she'll try to persuade me to come home, once she gets off her high horse. She won't do anything for a few days, to save face—that's how she is when we have a fight. Besides, she knows I'm not dead or anything. But I'll probably call her first, like on Saturday or Sunday. I'll be nice to her, but I'm not gonna budge on this one. She's gotta accept the fact that you and I are gonna be together—and I reckon she will, once she realizes how final this whole thing is." Mandy chuckles then kisses him on the shoulder. "But either way, you're stuck with me, you big jock."

No more words, but none are needed, as this silence brings peace, and joy, and sleep to Mandy. She falls into a beautiful slumber, her breathing hot and steady upon his shoulder, her lips parted in a faint but angelic smile. Her soft, maidenly, nightie-clad bosom presses cozily against him, their hearts beating as one: *ka-thump ... ka thump.*

O dear Jesus, thank you for this, Bryan prays, as he watches his sweetheart sleep, her disheveled hair framing her face. *I've yearned so long to hold her all night like this, and now she's here.* Brimming with affection, he gazes at her until his own eyelids get heavy—then all at once, he's above the bed, looking down at the two lovers, as they sleep in each other's arms.

THE SILVER CORD

CHAPTER TWENTY

FLETCHER HALL, UNIT 311
FRIDAY, OCTOBER 4, 1991 — 8:28 AM

Gosh, what a dream, Mandy reacts, as she awakes alone in the sun-splotched bed. Squinting against the brightness, she yawns and stretches. The room comes into focus. She gazes at a sunny reflection on the ceiling, a shimmering birdlike shape that flaps its wings every time the window shade moves with the breeze. After a brief, befuddled where-am-I sensation, everything comes back with a happy rush. *No, that wasn't a dream. I really AM in Waco, in Bryan's bed.* Her sore body, especially in the pelvic regions, confirms this glad realization, albeit with a remaining bit of mystery concerning Bryan. He's nowhere to be seen, and the bedroom door is closed, all but a crack. *Maybe he went to class?* Turning onto her side, she pulls the sheet and blanket back over her shoulder—the air coming in the window smells spicy fresh, like fallish, and it brings with it a refreshing chill.

The sound of Bryan's voice in the other room establishes his whereabouts. *He's talking to someone? Maybe Marvin, the floor-proctor?* Mandy has to pee, but she waits, lest she cause a scene. *Now that Marv guy would really flip if I came waltzing out in this skimpy gown.* She laughs, muffling with the pillow. *Maybe he overheard us last night? But so what? I reckon we're gonna be getting our own place anyway. What else can we do?* She listens closely, trying to pick up the conversation, yet she doesn't catch anything, except Bryan saying something about Monday.

She hears a cupboard opening, closing, then water running—then he comes into the room, and plunks down on the edge of the bed. He has on his jeans but no shirt, and his chiseled chin sports a manly shadow. He dimples, giving her a big awh-shucks grin. His green eyes beam with boyish mirth. "So, pretty lady, you woke up," he says, as he gives her a peck on the cheek. His whiskers tickle her, and his breath smells like orange juice.

"Yeah, I did," she replies, giving a gruff giggle, her voice still thick from sleep. "And it sorta blew me away at first—until I realized where I was. I thought for a moment it was *all* a dream."

"I *did* have a dream," he declares, his grin twisting curiously. "Not the regular kind—least, I'm pretty sure."

She jabs him playfully upon the arm. "You didn't—not one of your floating trips?"

"Yeah, it happened as I was falling asleep. I was suddenly up there, looking down at us." He flutters his hand toward the ceiling. "I mean, I was hovering above the bed, but somehow I was still with yuh under the covers. That's the great mystery."

Mandy stretches and yawns. "And then what?"

"Nothing much. I just smiled, or my astral face did, and then *zippo* ... I was back in my regular body; I didn't wanna leave yuh. I hafta *will* myself outside, if I wanna go on a *long* trip."

She paddlewheels her hands. "Gosh ... I wish I could go on one of those OBE trips with you. That would be *super* wild, especially if we could have sex with our soul-bodies. And we could do it anywhere, and *no* one could see us. Wow-wee, super wild."

Her ribald response sets off a fit of laughing and snorting, until Bryan's eyes are watering. "You're too much, pretty lady."

"So who were yuh talking to while ago?" she asks.

"Oh, I was on the phone. I had to catch Coach McKinney before he left for the fieldhouse to teach his nine-o'clock class. I didn't wanna wake yuh, so I used Steve's cordless."

"I thought maybe someone was out there with you, like that Marvin guy." More titters, as Bryan lies down beside her, without getting under the covers.

"If you're hungry," he says, "I have toast and cereal in the kitchen, and orange juice."

"There's no rush, babe. I'd rather just lie here with yuh." She snuggles close, walking her fingers over his sturdy chest; she inhales his manly odor. "You smell good, you big hunk. I think I like your raw unshowered smell best of all."

"You don't smell too bad yourself ... though I reckon you do need to brush your teeth."

Mandy, blushing, wrinkles her nose then sticks out her tongue at him. "Well, whaddeyuh expect? I don't sleep with tic tacs in my mouth. Besides, we gotta get used to each other ... messy hair and morning breath, and burps, and farts ... like all of it."

"Whaddeyuh mean?" he teases, clasping his hands behind his head. "I never belch or fart."

She tickles his ribs. "Get outta here. I remember you gassing up your hayloft ... like enough to *blow* up the barn—and it *sure* wasn't from me, or Millie."

After more laughter, he backtracks: "I reckon we did make some jungle-like noises last night." He gives a silent whistle. "So how d'yuh feel?" She snorts but doesn't reply. "That good, huh?"

Unable to resist his green-eyed smirk, she gives him a nibble on the chin then a serious, heartfelt kiss. "Oh gosh," she coos, "I've never felt so happy and contented ... though I *am* a little sore." She giggles. "In fact, I'm a *whole lot* sore, but it's a 'good' sore, like how I felt when I went horseback riding at camp back in Arkansas. But the horse I rode last night was *way* better-looking." She giggles again then clears her throat.

"That last time *was* outta sight ... with you on top." He grins, rolling his eyes. "Dang, gal, you're getting me stirred."

THE SILVER CORD

"Me too. But let's wait—oh, this's *so* neat, being able to do it any time we want ... but I like to let it build up, the sex urge."

"You *do* have amazing restraint ... even when we went to extra innings." He grins wider, showing his teeth.

"But you liked it, huh?"

"O Jesus," he replies, blushing, "it was A-plus ... five stars."

"I must say, we did all right ... for a couple of virgins. But we're not virgins any*more*. That blood on my leg was the proof, not a lot ... but I reckon there might be some on these sheets."

"So it *did* hurt?"

"Just when you broke through, but after that—O God." She laughs thickly then clears. "But we better change the subject, if yuh *know* what I mean—so why'd you call your batting coach?"

"I'm more comfortable talking to him than Coach Weaver."

"I know, you told me ... but why'd yuh hafta call at all?"

"Oh, I hadta tell him I wouldn't be at practice today, and—"

"Goshdang, babe," she cuts in, going up on her elbow. "You don't hafta miss practice on my account. I'll come and watch." She pushes her sleep-mused locks off the side of her face.

"Y'could, except it's already canceled. Coach McKinney said the storm left big erosion gullies in the infield, so they hafta haul in a truckload of special dirt from Dallas to repair the damage. It's gonna take all day—so there's no practice till Monday."

"Well, I *do* wanna come and watch, and y'don't hafta drop everything, just because I'm here. Y'still have college, and all?"

"It won't kill me to miss class today." He smirks boyishly. "No *way* can I think about American History or Calculus 201, or English Comp (Emerson's class meets M-Th-F). Plus, we hafta find a place to live, you and me."

Mandy likes the ring of those words, as she plunks back onto her pillow. "But your scholarship? Canyuh live off-campus?"

"Yeah, I reckon so. We have a few freshman guys on the team, who live in town. As long as I hit home runs, I can do what*ever* I want." He laughs. "No, I'm gonna tell Coach Weaver that we're engaged. It's no biggie with him. In fact, I can still live here officially, but unofficially off-campus with you—that is, if you don't get me kicked out today." More laughing.

"This's *so* wild ... how much my life has changed, and *fast*."

"That's for sure. This time yesterday, I was in class. I didn't have a clue, till I got back and checked my answering machine."

Mandy giggles. "Yeah, I reckon I filled that baby up." She rolls off the bed. "Gotta pee. I'll be right back."

* * *

She didn't close the door, Bryan observes a moment later, as he hears Mandy, the hissing trill that girls make when they tinkle into the toilet.

It's like she doesn't hide ANYthing from me. It's so neat. I love it. Still on the bed, he yawns, stretching toward the ceiling. *It feels sorta weird skipping class, but I'll be there Monday. And maybe by then, we'll have our own place.* The toilet flushes, then he hears her brushing her teeth, then the water stops, but she doesn't come out. A minute passes. *What's she doing in there?*

He soon gets his answer, as she pads back into the room, grinning goofily, her left hand hidden, obviously, behind her.

Bryan smirks. "Okay, gal, whaddeyuh got there?"

"What makes you think I got something?"

"'Cause y'got that crazy grin on your face?"

"Ta-dah," she declares, revealing her hand, which sports, on its third finger, their engagement ring. Antique goldwork, star-bursts of reflected light: the diamonds looks especially dazzling in the sunny room. Extending the hand, she admires the ring.

"So where yuh been keeping that?"

"In my make-up kit. I hid it there, after I got it back from Mama. I can't believe I didn't think about it until now."

"Well, we don't hafta hide it any longer."

"Oh, I know—isn't it pretty? I can't stop looking at it."

Rolling off the bed, Bryan hugs her, gives her a playful kiss on the bangs, then he heads for the bathroom.

"We should get *married*," she announces.

"Whaddeyuh talking about?" he replies from the bathroom. "We're gonna ... next spring, maybe sooner? That's why you *have* that ring."

"No, I mean today. Let's get married *today*."

* * *

INTERSTATE 10 - EAST OF BEAUMONT, TX
FRIDAY, OCTOBER 4, 1991 — 7:07 PM

Bryan, with Mandy at his side, jockeys his pickup through the traffic, and the rain, his heart still charged with happy abandon, an exuberant spontaneity that blew them out of Waco eight hours ago. "Well, Mrs. Bryan Howard," he kids, his face dimpling; he can't stop grinning. "D'yuh feel better ... now that you have *two* rings on your finger?"

"You betcha," she chirps, as she scoots closer and plants a kiss on his bristly cheek. He took a shower before departing the dorm, but there was no time to shave. She kisses him again, her breath still spicy from the Big Mac she had at McDonald's. After leaving the chapel in LeMire they stopped to eat, not in LeMire itself but right before they got back on the interstate. It's murky enough for headlights, but it's not dark yet. The steely-gray clouds are still visible, as they scud by overhead. Grimy spray from an 18-wheeler peppers the windshield. He spurts some fluid to clear it, then the wipers resume their normal rhythm. Showers, muggy air, occasional thunder: the notorious weather front (the one that spawned yesterday's I-35 tornado) has stalled out along the Gulf Coast, albeit without the severe weather.

They got married at the Beauregard Parish Chapel in LaMire, Louisiana, just across the Sabine River from Daleyville, Texas. Shyler Comstock, the local justice of the peace, runs the LeMire operation. A beige-suited, silver-haired gent, he could pass for Colonel Sanders, the fried-chicken baron—he even has the same beard. "Ah declare, we get a lotta kids from Texas," he drawled, as he scanned Bryan and Mandy's paperwork: license application, affidavits of age and citizenship, blood-test results. "In fact, that couple out in the waitin' room—they came over from Houston." (The on-site, thirty-minute blood lab is right down the hall from the small chapel, both of which are in a new wing behind the old domed courthouse.) When Bryan produced the $280 fee (four $50s, four $20s), the jocular JP quickly stamped their application APPROVED, amid a hearty guffaw. "Now our licenses are just as legal as any, yet we do hafta charge extra for out-of-state couples. But the fee covers ever'thang, includin' the bloodwork, and a quatah of it goes to our parish food-and-shelter program. Same for speedin' fines, mindyuh. We call our counties parishes over here, and it does add a godly quality to our name, but we're not connected with the Catholic church a'tall ... or any church. Yet we do respect the sacredness of matrimony."

It took Comstock a minute or so to read the marriage-ceremony blurb, from a timeworn, dog-eared book, while Bryan and Mandy, clad in their usual jeans and such, stood hand-in-hand before him, along with a single witness, an olive-skinned, Creole-looking fellow named Sergio, who tends the courthouse grounds and stands in when needed. Upon being pronounced "husband and wife," the happy groom kissed his bride, then they exchanged wedding bands, rings bought hurriedly this morning at Friedman's Jewelry Shoppe in Waco before they zoomed out of town. Bryan paid for them ($375 for both) with his *Visa* card, but he got the $280 cash from his local account, at the Brazos Savings Bank on Kyler Street—he actually withdrew $500, so they'd have plenty for gas and food, and so forth.

But how the heck did they end up getting hitched in LeMire, Louisiana? Chris Hansen is the answer, plus Tracy McCollum. When Bryan realized Mandy was dead serious about eloping, like *pronto*, he called Chris at the neuroscience lab. The puckish junior declared a zero chance of getting married in Texas before next week, because of blood-test laws, but then he went on to say (amid the usual wisecracks) that they still have a few JP wedding mills in Louisiana, if Bryan wanted to "drive his ass off."

Chris didn't have details, so he grabbed Tracy out of the rodent room: "I grew up in Louisiana, y'know ... and they still have some shotgun ways of doing things." She giggled. "But if you guys are serious, there *is* a place ... not far from I-10. Stu has a friend that eloped there. It's a rip-off, but I reckon it's legal."

As they hum through Beaumont, Bryan spurs the pickup into the leftmost lane. He's had the old Chevy maxed out the whole trip. "So, pretty lady," he chuckles, "what was all that last night about ceremonies being eyewash for society?"

"They are. At least, the big fancy weddings. It's more honest ... how *we* did it. It was just you and me; it wasn't like a big show or anything, and I'm super glad we did it this way ... even though I had to *lie* about my age, on that affidavit thing."

"Well, in any case ... this's been one heck of a fun day, like *wild* and uncorked ... racing down here like we did."

"I'll say. It's *super* wild ... and yesterday, and last night." She giggles. "It's like a *million* things have happened in the past two days." More laughter, both of them.

Bryan cuts the wipers back to intermittent mode—the rain has stopped, and the clouds have begun to break up.

"Look at that sunset," Mandy remarks a couple minutes later— she gestures over the dashboard. "The sky's so red and beautiful; it's like God put a Christmas ribbon around this special day." She cuddles against him, nestling her head into his neck.

A blissful silence reigns for several miles, then she comes up and kisses him lustfully. He returns the kiss then pulls away.

"You're no fun," she banters kiddingly.

"Well, once I start kissing yuh, I may not be able to stop."

"*So?*"

"So we could have a wreck ... if I can't see?"

"Well, there's *some*thing else I could do, and it won't take your eyes off the road one bit."

They share a bawdy laugh, then she fiddles with his zipper. "Don't even think about it, Amanda. That'll wreck us for *sure*."

"But, babe, I can't wait till we get to Waco."

"Me neither ... but that's *one* thing we can't do at 75 mph."

She tables the subject until they exit I-10, swinging north on 287: "No, babe, let's go the other way. Let's go to *Gal*veston."

"But uh ... what uh. We gotta—"

"No, we don't hafta do *any*thing, not tonight anyhow. It's too far to Waco, like *five* hours. Let's go to Galveston instead ... to a motel, and afterward we can walk on the beach, in the dark. It'll be super neat, like a quickie honeymoon. We can go back to Waco tomorrow afternoon." She giggles girlishly. "Let's do it. It's only an hour from here." Tucking her chin, she rolls her big blue eyes, a coquettish side-glance. Bryan, needing no more persuasion, takes the next exit, so they can reverse direction.

THE SILVER CORD

* * *

WACO, TEXAS - 146 DOUGLAS STREET
SUNDAY, OCTOBER 6, 1991 — 3:47 PM

Before taking another load inside, Bryan pauses in the driveway beside his pickup. Lifting his Spindle Tiger cap, he wipes his perspiry brow— it's ninety degrees, plenty hot enough for short sleeves and cutoffs, but the humidity is tolerable on this happy October afternoon, certainly not as muggy as Galveston. Chris Hansen returns from the house, his patented smirk playing under his mustache. He hefts a box of books out of the back of the truck. "I must say, slugger," he quips, giving an elfish head-wag, "you two don't waste much time when it comes to big decisions; that's for *damn* sure." They share a robust laugh, as Bryan grabs his 14-inch Sony—by the handle—plus a lumpy trash bag containing clothes and shoes and such. He follows the puckish junior through the slatted gate which leads to the patio.

Mandy exits the back door, her face beaming girlishly below her softball hat, which is cutely reversed, bill backward, on her head. "Good job, guys," she encourages, retreating to hold the door. "Just a few more trips then we can start on the Firebird—gosh, this place is *so* neat. It's *hard* to believe."

Hard to believe but true: the newlyweds are moving into the O'Shea house, the second floor. As it turns out, they spent *two* nights in Galveston, making love, and making love, and making *more* love. They had no time, or energy, to think about practical things, but when they got back to Waco around noon today, they learned that Chris had been working on their behalf. Bryan had mentioned, on Friday morning (during the Louisiana, get-married conversation), that they needed an off-campus apartment, but he had no idea that Chris would have one waiting upon their return.

Chris left a message on Bryan's answering machine at the dorm. He returned the call, and Chris explained the situation, peppering his good news with the usual cracks and gibes: "I talked with Annie O'Shea, and based on *my* recommendation, she said you can rent the upstairs part of the house, three rooms and a bath, plus you can use the kitchen downstairs, and the washer and dryer in the garage. She says she'll probably be putting the house on the market in the spring, barring a miracle with her husband. But you can live here until it's sold. The rent will be $300 plus electricity, as long as you help me with the yard work"—Bryan couldn't help but laugh when he heard this—"and you can use her furniture if you like. You're welcome to move in immediately, and no deposit is required, as long as she gets the first month's rent by next Friday. I have the key to the back door, and I'll make a copy for you. She wants you to use the back entrance only, but that gives you access to the stairway, and the kitchen."

Bryan said yes on the spot, a decision his new bride heartily endorsed when he got back down to the parking lot—they had planned on spending the afternoon *looking* for a place. Mandy fell in love with the house at first sight, despite the shabby exterior and overgrown yard, though she did remark that the basketball goal on the garage needed attention. And once inside, she raved about the roomy, 1940s-era decor.

They're soon done with the pickup; Bryan moves it out onto the street. Mandy then backs the Pontiac up the drive. Exiting the Chevy, Bryan stretches. Next door, old Mr. Lipski mows his lawn, the strip by the street; he wears a wide-brimmed straw hat. The newlyweds met him earlier, shaking hands across the hedge by the garage, but the eighty-something widower is so deaf they had to shout, and he's totally emaciated, a skeleton with skin, but he does a *hell* of a job with his yard; it's a ten: lawn, flowers, trees, shrubs—in stark contrast to the O'Shea property. The neighbors on the other (east) side, Mr. and Mrs. Foster (also elderly) keep a manicured lawn as well, but they don't fraternize much, according to Chris, and they travel a lot in their RV.

My whole life has changed in three days, Bryan exults, as he looks down the shady street, *and ALL for the better.* He stretches again, reaching for the milky, cumulus-dappled sky, what he can see of it between the leafy crowns of the trees. Waco basks in a hot, sun-bright haze, but the weaker light and longer shadows, along with the spicy, dry-grass aroma of the breeze, give witness that the seasons are turning, as do the trees along Douglas Street. Green still prevails in the overarching foliage, but a yellow tinge to the cottonwoods speaks of autumn, as do the wispy-delicate seeds floating down like airy little parachutes. The oak leaves have dried and curled a trifle, showing their pale undersides, as they do before finally fading to brown in November. The magnolia on the front lawn sports in like manner the red-splotched cones exclusive to this time of year. Texas does not undergo a majestic foliage season, with a dramatic display of color. Fall is fickle down here, but the signs of change are there nonetheless, if one cares to note them.

* * *

Same afternoon, 4:51 p.m. While Chris and Bryan cook hamburgers on the hibachi in the backyard, Mandy dials the phone in Chris's apartment, her festive mood tempered by the prospect of talking to her mama for the first time since she left home on Thursday. Anxious butterflies: one ring, two rings.

"Hel-*lo*," comes a chirpy, exuberant voice—it's Gretchen.

"Hi, Gretch—"

"Mandy! I knew it—I *knew* you'd call today. I just knew it."

"So whaddeyuh doing?" Mandy asks, her throat tightening.

"Oh, I'm playing video games with Sandy Lucas, but right now she's in the kitchen putting the potatoes in the oven. She's baby-sitting for me. You know her; she's the frizzy redhead who always sits up front at church—she's in the eleventh grade, like one year behind you. I can beat her at Donkey Kong, but the dang joystick is still freezing up ... so we hafta restart a lot."

"Oh yeah, Sandy ... so where'd Mama go?"

"She had to go to Kroger's ... for some inventory thing, and then she's going to Pastor Ron's staff meeting, and then to evening service ... so she won't be home until nine-thirty."

"Well, I just wanted to touch base with her ... to let her know that I'm okay and everything. I'm gonna be living with Bryan now (Mandy leaves out, on purpose, the eloping part). We just got our own apartment here in Waco. It's actually a house, the second floor. We even have a y—"

"Wow, super neat. Can I come and visit? Can I? And I'll bring Molly Ann too. That'll be *so* cool."

Mandy laughs. "We'll see ... after we get settled and all."

"Toby killed a *mouse* today," Gretchen announces, in her tell-all manner, "and he left the head and the guts on the back steps, like usual. When Sandy saw it, she screamed like Godzilla was in the backyard or something." Gretchen giggles. "And she's scared of bugs too, and when she tries to throw the softball, it shoots out sideways— she can't fire it to me like you do. She's a real *wimp* when it comes to sports, but she makes good brownies, and we're gonna have pork chops and scalloped potatoes for supper. But we're gonna eat late, 'cause we just had brownies and ice cream at three-thirty. After supper we're gonna watch *Life Goes On*, and *Murder, She Wrote*, then I hafta do my vocabulary words—ugggh—and then I hafta take my bath at nine."

"Well, tell Mama I called," Mandy says, taking opportunity while her sister pauses to catch her breath.

"Oh, I will. I will."

"We'll be getting our own phone soon, I'll call her then—and uh ... well, there's one last thing I wanna tellyuh, Gretch."

"What?"

Mandy hesitates, the tightness in her throat growing thicker and hotter and more prickly. "I just wantcha to know that I love you no matter what ... no matter where I live, or what's going on between me and Mama."

"Oh, I know—and I love you too. But I'll love you super extra special if yuh come get me and Molly Ann in your Firebird, so we can come down there for a visit." This eager retort causes a fit of laughing that consoles Mandy. She's still chuckling in fact when she hangs up the phone a long minute later.

It would be fun to have her come down, she remarks to herself, as she takes off her softball hat and fiddles with her ponytail before going back outside. *That's the one downside to all of this, having to leave her behind ... even though I woulda been gone next year anyhow. But still, it bothers me to have that super-priss, Sandy Lucas, baby-sitting in my place. Oh, I guess Sandy's all right, but she acts so goody-goody all the time.* Mandy sighs. *But I'm sorta relieved that Mama wasn't home. This way she'll know I'm A-OK with a place to live, and yet I can save the BIG news until later in the week, after we get our phone.*

* * *

146 DOUGLAS STREET - UPSTAIRS BEDROOM
SUNDAY, OCTOBER 6, 1991 — 10:14 PM

"Oh, sweet babe," Mrs. Bryan Howard coos to her new husband, as they cuddle in bed, amid the blissful afterglow of orgasm. "You make me *so* happy." Her eyes glimmer with glad tears, reflecting the dim illumination from the streetlamp outside.

Bryan kisses his young wife on the forehead. "You make me happy too ... more than I could ever say. I never realized how much till this week. It's *big* ... like a supernova inside me."

"I know, honey—it's inside *both* of us; it's like we feel everything together, like ... like ... well, it's like—"

"We've become one flesh."

"Yeah ... just like God says. Our love makes us *one*, and it's forever, because it comes from Heaven." She sighs dreamily. "Ever since I was a little girl, I just knew love had to be bigger than what they talked about at Sunday School. All my teachers talked about 'God is Love,' especially Ms. Kenison when I was eight. She made us recite the whole verse: 'He that loveth not knoweth not God; for God is love. I John 4:8.' But the *love* she talked about seemed more like an obligation, like doing your duty ... like Christ was so *high* and holy, and we had to worship and bow down and fear him, because we're sinful and unworthy. But I never accepted *that* God, not in my heart—oh, babe, this's the only God I want, the God I feel when I'm in your arms."

"Me too, precious. Me too." He inhales her fragrant, freshly shampooed hair. "Gosh, I feel so good, I thought for a moment I was gonna float right up to the ceiling, like on Thursday night, but I'm glad I stayed down here ... with you."

"Oh, I wish I could go with you on one of those trips," she whispers, as she nuzzles between his neck and shoulder.

Bryan caresses her back. "It *has* to be God, this love we have ... because the only thing close to it is how I feel when I'm out of my body, and especially when I got my glimpse of Heaven. It's somehow the same ... like we've talked about before."

"It *is* the same ... yet it's beyond all understanding ... like a big awesome mystery. That's why it's so neat that you're gonna study all about it, and I'm gonna help yuh." She sighs, her breath warming his ear. "I'm gonna be teaching school kids, but I'm also gonna help *you*.

It's the greatest purpose I can think of ... to love people, and show 'em that death isn't the end."

"I sure can't think of anything better. I've had a longing about it my *whole* life, even before the near-death experience ... like a *deep* yearning about living forever. It has to be ... but there's still so much uncharted territory. It *is* an awesome mystery, like way out there, and yet, it's somehow connected to what we have, the love ... like I say. In any case, I wanna learn *every*thing about it ... and try to find the answers."

"And I'm gonna help, and we're gonna do it in an honest scientific way, without all the fear and narrow thinking that messes up the religious approach, even though there's a lot of truth to what we learn at church ... if they'd just open their eyes and grab a hold of this love we're feeling. Oh, babe, you make me *so* happy. Just hold me ... just hold me."

They've chosen the guest room for their love-nest (Jason's room). Chris explained that Annie's son, Jason, lived at home until six years ago, when (at 38) he finally married and moved to Phoenix where he bought, with his father's financing, his own GM dealership. But the business failed, as did the marriage, as did his relationship with his father. He remained in Phoenix, going to work for a real estate company. Annie begged Dudley (Mr. O'Shea) to reconcile with Jason, but he stubbornly refused, so his son never came home, not even for a visit. The O'Sheas also have a daughter, Margaret—she's younger than Jason, though she left home long before he did, moving to San Francisco in 1968 where she dabbled at college (UC, Berkeley) while smoking dope and protesting the war. Margo's rebellious phase soon gave way to conformity however, as she married a yuppie lawyer and moved to Washington, DC. She rarely makes it back to Texas, though she did fly down when Dudley had his stroke last year. Her old room, across from the bathroom, is now an upstairs TV lounge—the Howards intend to use it as their living room.

Chris related all this scuttlebutt while giving Bryan and Mandy a tour of the off-limits part of the house, the dining room, the living room, Mr. O'Shea's home office, plus a large den, which was added on in 1956 (fifteen years after the house was built. There's also a basement for extra storage, though the Howards have little if any to store. Chris says that Annie likes to sip beer and chat when she's up, and she has a salty, gossipy side once she gets going. (There's a picture of her on Dudley's desk: she's plumpish and white-haired yet attractive for her age; she's just as Irish as her husband Chris says, second generation.)

"Time out," Mandy announces, as she rolls out of Bryan's embrace. "I gotta pee." Plucking her nightie from the braided rug, she pads to the bathroom, sidestepping the various boxes and bags, some empty, some full, some partially unpacked.

Bryan, sitting up, fishes around for his undies. He notices, again, a faint tobacco smell in the room, not a sweetish, homey aroma like Gramps' cigars, but the acrid, ashy odor left by cigarettes, yet it's too weak to concern him much. When he hears Mandy returning, he heads for the toilet himself.

"We're getting pretty good at this sex thing," she quips a couple minutes later, as he rejoins her in the bed. "Least, for a couple of rookies—gosh, it's a*maz*ing how many times we've done it in four days, less than four days."

"I'll say. You're wearing me out, gal. I may not live through this, but I can't think of a *better* way to go." They laugh, then she crinkles her nose, purses her lips, doing her rabbit thing.

"Well, practice makes *per*fect, as they say. And we sure got *plenty* in Galveston." More titters, as Mandy turns onto her side, to assume their familiar butt-to-gut pillow-talk position. "It's a good thing we went to CVS and bought more Trojans. Course, I doubt I'm ovulating anyway, like I been saying."

"Maybe so, but we *sure* don't wanna get pregnant, not yet."

She doesn't reply, but after a long moment she giggles.

"What's so funny?"

"Oh, I was just thinking about the song and dance you went through ... at CVS before you bought 'em."

"What song and dance?"

She fans the murk with her hand. "Y'know, how yuh had to make sure no one was around before you snuck up to the condom rack and slipped the blue box off the hook thing, and then yuh filled up that carry-basket with razor blades and toothpaste and shaving cream and paper clips and Scotch tape, and Juicy Fruit, and breath mints, and three bars of Dial soap, and other stuff, until the Trojans were buried at the bottom."

"Well, whaddeyuh expect? No way was I gonna go waltzing up to that lady cashier with just a box of *rubbers* in my hand."

"But I offered to do it, and you wouldn't let me?"

"I know, but it's *my* responsibility."

More giggles. "Oh, Bryan Howard, you're *so* much a male ... like strong and tough and proud, and yet you're still a little boy underneath it all. It's so cute, how yuh carry on."

The breeze rustles through the magnolia tree outside, making the leafy shadows on the wall quiver a bit. Ditto for the window curtains, as they wiggle gently. The AC was on earlier, but the dry October heat disappeared with the sun, giving way to a pleasant night. So Bryan opened the windows, the south-facing ones. They have windows on three sides, two facing south, two facing east (which bracket their bed), and one facing north, but the north window is plugged by the AC, an old Whirlpool.

"So whaddeyuh think about Chris?" Bryan asks a while later.

"Well, he's sort of a sarcastic wise-ass," Mandy responds, still speaking away from her husband. "But I reckon it's mostly for show. I can tell he's a nice guy underneath it all ... and he seems super smart, and he *cer*tainly knows how to get attention, the way he's always smirking and joking around. Plus he wears that weird Einstein T-shirt, and he says the F-word almost as much as Spanky." She chuckles into her pillow. "I even caught him giving me the eye a few times ... out by the barbecue pit."

"Well, I can't blame him. You're the most awesome gal in Waco, now that you're here, especially compared to those *old* Baylor girls on campus. They're like *over* the hill."

She elbows him playfully. "Cut it out, you big jock."

"Well, you *are*—but getting back to Chris: he does put on quite an act, yet he was low key today. You shoulda heard him that first day at the caf ... popping off about all the 'fresh pussy' on campus, and how he'd love to give 'em some private tutoring. But he hasn't made it with any of 'em, or even tried very hard."

"Why not?"

"Because he's still in love with Jennifer."

"Jennifer?"

"She's the girl he lived with back in Illinois before he joined the Air Force. He told me all about her. We talk a lot—he's older, but he's the best friend I have down here, except maybe for Steve Jordan. Chris calls himself an agnostic, but he really believes in God ... at least, the God we were talking about before."

"Well, he *has* to have a good heart. I mean, he's really gone out of his way to help us ... even cooking hamburgers. But this whole house deal is big, and he vouched for us with Mrs. O'Shea and everything. Gosh ... it worked out *super* good for us."

"You like this place, d'yuh?"

"Oh, babe, I love it," she declares, twisting onto her back—she paddles the air for emphasis. "I figured we'd end up in some apartment complex, with fifty other off-campus couples. That woulda been okay, but this's like having our very own *house*."

"But it's sort of dumpy don'tcha think. The outside?"

"I reckon so ... but it has *char*acter, and I love the inside, the old-fashioned furniture and all. They even have one of those big, stand-up radios down in the living room. And the wood floors are beautiful, especially with the oval rugs, and I like the priscilla curtains ... and the walls too ... especially the little pink tulips in the hall and down the stairway. And the bathroom is neat, with the cast-iron tub on legs, and the circular shower-curtain thing, which was obviously an after-thought—but it's a good thing, since I know how much you *hate* taking baths." She laughs.

"C'mon ... I've taken plenty of baths."

"Not since *I've* known you." More laughing. "But I'm not super psyched about these tan curtains in here; they look kinda blah and rumpled, like they're made outta tow sacks, and they smell like cigarettes, and the walls are painted instead of papered ... and the brownish color is blah, like super-weak cocoa. This whole room is sorta blah compared to the rest of the house, but I reckon that's because her son lived in here."

"So, y'like the *big* master bedroom better?"

"I do like that fancy four-poster bed"—Mandy gestures, as if holding a miniature version of the bed—"and the blue wallpaper with the white lilies, plus the extra closet space, but I think we'll be more at home in here. This room is *plenty* big, least compared to your bedroom back at Fletcher Hall."

"That's not saying much," Bryan chuckles.

"And I can always put new curtains on these windows."

"Or we can use the ones at the dorm, the brownish ones Mom sent me. I forgot 'em this afternoon. Jordan won't mind. I doubt he ever noticed we had curtains." They both laugh.

"So didyuh talk to your roommate?"

"Yeah, I finally got him—I used Chris's phone, while you were up here taking your bath. He was all anxious and hyper like he gets— he thought I moved out because of the big *mess* he left behind when he took off for Wichita Falls last Thursday. But when I told him I was married, he said he couldn't blame me for running off and all ... yet he hopes I won't move out officially, 'cause he might get a *hard-ass* roommate who won't let him eat Whoppers on the coffee table when the Cowboys are on the tube." More laughter, louder and harder.

"He *does* sound like a big ole kid, like yuh say—but the curtains at the dorm should work in here. They're sorta copper colored, so I reckon they'll go with these walls. There's no point in moving down the hall to the big bedroom. But it'll be a good place to escape to ... for studying and all."

"As long as there's a lock on the door ... to keep *you* out."

"*Me*?"

"Yeah, you. No *way* can I study with you around." He nibbles her ear, then her neck, tickling her—she squeals. "How can I concentrate, gal ... if you're unzipping me, like tonight?"

"Well, I reckon you'll just hafta learn to *con*centrate better."

They sport for a while, then Mandy goes silent. "Whaddeyuh thinking about?" he asks, realizing her mood has sobered.

She fidgets, picking at her thumbnail. She replies, speaking toward the ceiling, "Oh, I was just wondering about something."

He shifts onto his back as well. "About what?"

"Didyuh ever go to that church y'talked about? The one Marvin goes to, the floor-proctor guy?"

"No, not yet. He keeps on inviting me and giving me tracts, and Steve Jordan—he's after him too ... but we've never gone."

She gives an openhanded gesture. "What kinda church is it?"

"It's non-denominational, but from reading the tracts, I'd say it's similar to ours. We can go sometime, if you want. It's just a little ways from the campus, down by the river."

"Oh, I dunno ... but maybe we should? It's sorta weird."

"Weird?"

She stretches upward, interlacing her hands. "Yeah, it seems weird," she elaborates, her words riding a sigh that grows into a yawn. "I mean uh—well, I get to make my own decision about it ... instead of having Mama bugging me, and bugging me."

"It *will* take some getting used to I reckon."

"Oh, I'm sure not complaining, but it's a big dadgum change I tellyuh." She sighs again. "I'm not crazy about church ... but we shouldn't give it up altogether. I don't mean every service, like Mama goes ... but we could go on Sundays most of the time."

"Sounds like a plan—and if we don't like Marvin's church, we can find another one."

"Yeah, I'm sure Mama's gonna ask about that ... once we're talking to each other again."

The church talk tugs on Bryan's soul, a bothersome call to duty. Same goes for Baylor. "Well, pretty lady, we better get to sleep. I gotta be in class at eight o'clock, and I still have some reading to do before I leave here. I'm like two days behind."

"Heck, you'll catch up in no time ... but I reckon things *are* gonna be different." She uplifts her knees, a sign she's *not* ready for sleep. "It's like we hafta come down to earth, least in the daytime." She gives a subdued chuckle. "I have all kinds of things to do myself ... while you're in class. Then at three I'm gonna come over and watch yuh practice." She snuffles then clears her throat. "But I hafta finish unpacking, and we need groceries and stuff, and I wanna arrange these rooms as much as possible, plus the kitchen downstairs ... and I gotta start looking for a job, and I hafta call the phone company, and I also hafta check out my school situation ... but I can do that later in the week I reckon."

"So I should give yuh some money ... for shopping?"

"Nawh, I still have the two-fifty I got on Thursday ... before I left. I was gonna close the account, but I didn't have time, so I left fifty dollars in the bank."

"Good," Bryan jests, his spirits lifting momentarily. "That'll give us something to *fall* back on." He playfully slaps her raised knees, through the covers.

She titters, but it seems half-hearted. "I used my *mon*ey to buy the Firebird. You know all about it ... so don't play dumb." He can't tell if she's serious or being funny, so he doesn't reply. "But once I get a job, I plan to save up again, as much as I can."

Giving a tired murmur, he clasps his hands behind his head; this money talk is getting heavy—it weighs on him like his unfinished homework. "You don't *have* to get a job, you know?"

"Oh yes, I do."

"Why?"

"'Cause we gotta pay the rent, that's why, and we hafta eat, mister ... and we hafta put gas in the car, and the truck, and a jillion other things ... plus it's gonna be boring around here, if I'm just waiting for you to get home from class and all ... but it's mainly the money. We gotta *pay* the bills."

"But we *have* money," he reminds her. "I still have eight thou left, even after all we spent—though I guess it's more like seven, considering what I owe my dad on the credit card."

Mandy drums her uplifted thighs. "Yeah, but that won't last long, not even six months." She gives a silent whistle—no doubt she's serious now, worse than serious.

Bryan senses a tension between them, a testiness surfacing—it's hardly a fight, yet it feels almost painful, compared to the high they've been riding since Thursday night. "But we can eat at the cafeteria, you know? I'm still on scholarship, and officially living in the dorm, so I can eat there for free, and it doesn't cost much for you, like three bucks maybe."

"You can live in the dorm ... and here at the same time?"

"Well, not forever, but maybe for the rest of the semester. I'll still get money after that, as a married jock on scholarship ... like food, *and* rent." Going up on his elbow, he folds his pillow then returns to a supine position. "That's one advantage of being legally hitched. Now they *could* change my status sooner, like at the end of the month. It's up to Coach Weaver. I'm gonna give his secretary a copy of our marriage paperwork this week."

"Okay ... so we can save money by eating at the caf. That'll help, but I still wanna get a job."

Bryan gives an openhanded gesture. "But whaddabout high school? You still hafta graduate?"

"I can work *part*-time, like weekends, and after school. Plus, I only need a handful of credits to get my diploma. Maybe they have night school here in Waco? I gotta check on it."

"They're gonna wonder why you're not with your parents?"

"I'll tell 'em the truth—I'm living with my husband."

"Speaking of parents, you never got a hold of your mom?"

"No, just Gretchen, like I said. But I'll call Mama as soon we get the phone hooked up. I doubt she'll accept all this like Mom Howard did ... but I'm gonna tell her anyway."

"Yeah, my mom *is* rather open-minded, but she did say she wished we'd waited until next spring ... like we had planned. Yet she understands *why* we eloped."

Mandy extends her legs and scoots closer to Bryan, though

remaining on her back—he feels suddenly better. "Your mom *is* open-minded," she affirms, her tone softening, "and she's kind and sensitive, and easy to talk with. She doesn't expect everyone to agree with her. I can't help but love her—like she's my mom too, and I guess she is ... in a way."

"You got that right, pretty lady. You're very much part of my family, whether we eloped or not, but I'm sure glad we did."

"Me *too*," Mandy declares, giving a warm grin that melts the remaining tension between them. He gathers her into his arms. "Let's have a party," she adds a moment later, "to *cel*ebrate."

"What ... a what? I though you hated parties?"

"I don't mean a big hoopla reception—y'don't do that when you elope, thank *God*." She giggles. "Just our special friends, like a handful. We can cook steaks in the backyard."

* * *

The next day (mid-morning), Mandy scribbles a letter to Wendy:

> You should have my postcard by now, the one I sent from Galveston. It's true: we're married, and we just got our own apartment here in Waco, actually a house, the upstairs. We got hitched in Louisiana. I'll call and tell you all about it. We'll have a phone on Wednesday—I just talked to the telephone lady. But I'm sending this to you now, because we're having a little get-together on Sunday afternoon, the 13th, to celebrate. I'm talking super laid back, just a cookout in the backyard—yes, we have a yard! I know it's short notice, and a long drive, but I hope you can make it. You can stay over if you like. Monday is Columbus Day I think? Bryan plans to ask Spanky, and maybe Roy Collins. You can all drive down in one car? Plus, we're inviting a few of Bryan's new friends from the college, but there won't be a crowd or anything. He'll be calling Spanky, but you can tell him too, if you see him at school. I'll tell you how to get here when we talk. Thanks again for helping me last Thursday. You're right about LOVE! We can't give it up no matter WHAT! It's been crazy and wild, like you wouldn't believe, but everything has turned out SUPER GOOD!

I gotta remember to mail this letter, Mandy reminds herself some five minutes later, as she eases the Firebird down the driveway. *I'm glad Bryan had some stamps. And I gotta put some gas in this car.* Heading west on Douglas, she glances at the directions on her lap (Bryan wrote them down for her). *Once I get on the interstate, I'll be okay. I remember that Safeway; it's not far from Denny's. And there's a Wal-Mart too. I should get a new net for that basketball hoop on the garage. And we need to tighten it, so it'll hang right.*

* * *

WACO, TEXAS - 146 DOUGLAS STREET
WEDNESDAY, OCTOBER 9, 1991 — 2:40 PM

As Mandy Howard slips into her brown and yellow Denny's uniform, the phone rings in the TV room (living room). Hustling down the hall, she grabs it, her heartbeat quickening as she hears her mother's voice: "I got your message, Amanda."

"I didn't uh ... well uh," Mandy stutters, trying to corral her emotions. "I mean uh ... gosh, Mama, I just left my number on your machine five minutes ago, after they hooked up our phone. I thought you'd be at Kroger's?"

"I am, but I called home to get my messages." Now comes an awkward pause. Mandy, her heart thumping, twists the coiled handset cord around her finger. "Now, Amanda Fay, I can't talk very long," Helen goes on, after ten seconds or so—seconds that seem like minutes. "I have two new checkout girls; they're due any minute, and I hafta process their paperwork ... but I had a long conversation with Ginny Howard."

Mandy gulps. "So uh ... you know? I mean uh—"

"I know *every*thing, and I'm not thrilled. But Ginny had a lot to say, and I agree with her ... at least, for the most part."

"You *do*?"

"She's not too happy about this either, but now that it's done, she feels that we should accept your decision." Helen gives a breathy sigh. "Love covers a multitude of sins, so I reckon her advice makes sense. But I'll need some time to let this sink in."

"I know, Mama," Mandy replies, feeling profoundly relieved.

"Or to put it a*noth*er way: I tried to stop this, but I couldn't, so I reckon there's no point in fighting yuh now." She sighs again, but this time it turns into a laugh. "I declare, young lady, you're even *more* stubborn than your daddy, running off and eloping ... in some hick town in Louisiana." Mandy laughs too. "It's quite bold I must say, though I didn't realize there were still JPs around who do shotgun weddings, without parental consent."

"Well, seventeen is the legal age over there," Mandy lies, lest her mother dig farther.

"Whaddabout school? Are you enrolled ... or what?"

"I sure *am*. I signed up this morning, at Newcomb Tech on the west side of town. I start tomorrow, and I get to go at night, like three nights a week. It's a special kind of high school, and they have evening classes for students with weird circumstances, like me. And I can graduate in January, if I work my tail off."

THE SILVER CORD

"Didyuh ask them about your basketball scholarship?"

"I mentioned it, but that's a Baylor decision. Coach Ames may still keep me on her scholarship list for next year, even if I don't play at the high-school level *this* year. I hafta set up an appointment with her, so I can explain all the changes in my life. If I was gonna play this year, I'd hafta go to a regular high school full time, and that would be hard. Besides, I need to concentrate on getting my diploma—that's the *main* thing."

Helen gives an approving "hmmmn" then says, "So, how're yuh fixed for money?"

"We're doing okay I reckon. Bryan has money saved up, plus his scholarship, and I just got a waitress job at Denny's, and we have a super-nice apartment for three hundred a month."

"Yeah, Gretchen told me ... the upstairs at a house."

"That's right ... and we have *gobs* of room. Y'should come and visit. I know Gretchen's anxious to come down."

"Let's not get ahead of ourselves, Amanda. Like I say, I need some *time* to let this sink in."

* * *

Mama always quotes that verse when she's ready to sign a truce, Mandy chuckles to herself, as she brushes her teeth five minutes later. *Love covers a multitude of sins. It's like she has to get in the last word—like she's so godly and right and I'm the sinner. But any way you spin it, this's definitely progress. And she didn't bug me about going to church or anything.* Helen didn't bring up the subject, but her daughter did; she told her mom about Marvin Latrobe's church, and the fact that she and Bryan planned to go. Mandy was anxious to share any- and everything positive, and she did. The lie about Louisiana bothers her, albeit not enough to dampen her positive reaction to the conversation as a whole.

Pulling up her waitress skirt, she drops her panties and plops down on the toilet to pee. *It's like everything's working out, ever since I escaped that tornado. And Ms. Rodriquez at Denny's said she'd only schedule me on Wednesdays and weekends, and she's giving me this Sunday off, so we can have our cookout, and she won't normally put me down for any Sunday morning, so we can check out Marvin's church—but not this week, with the cookout.*

THE SILVER CORD

CHAPTER TWENTY-ONE

146 DOUGLAS STREET
SUNDAY, OCTOBER 13, 1991 — 3:37 PM

Sunny, warm, azure sky: perfect weather for a cookout. Bryan Howard, his arms folded, his bosom happily aglow, rests back against the barbecue pit, the side opposite Chris Hansen. A puff of wind ripples through the trees: the leaves flip and flutter about the clusters of almost-ripe pecans, pale-green pods that will soon dry and split open, disgorging their hard-shelled fruit. A butterfly flits overhead, a big, tiger-striped Monarch making its southward migration, as they do each October. Another one zigzags above the storm cellar, flapping its orange-and-black wings then gliding over the fence into the courtyard. Bryan inhales the rustic aroma of the hot charcoal. He's supposedly helping with the fire, but Chris seems to have everything under control. Ever since the jaunty junior heard about this Sunday get-together, he's played an active, take-charge role; he even volunteered to make the baked beans in his own kitchen, and the cake—Tracy McCollum came early to help him. (Bryan and Mandy were glad to include her; she's not only Chris's friend, but she also supplied the crucial information about the wedding chapel in LeMire.)

"Okay, slugger, this fire's ready," Chris declares smirkily. He forks each of the raw T-bones, moving them from the platter to the spacious cooking grate. After sprinkling Lawry's salt on the sizzling steaks, he covers them with a homemade hood, a steel trash-can lid, bent a bit to give it more volume. "It takes longer to get this big pit going, but now the coals are just right, so these fuckers should cook nicely."

Bryan nods, but his attention is elsewhere. He can't help but adore his fetching bride, as she hovers about the serving table, a collapsible campsite thing next to the makeshift picnic table (a plywood panel propped on cinder blocks—the plywood came from the O'Shea's garage, as did the camp-table, while Chris and Bryan lugged the cinder blocks up from the storm cellar). The pine tree in the corner shades both tables. Since the steaks are a bit tardy, Mandy is covering the food with aluminum foil to keep the steamy dishes warm, to keep the bugs out of the potato salad. Wendy Lewis helps her, while Tracy arranges the lawn chairs and folding chairs around the picnic table. Bryan is glad that everyone (except Roy Collins) is here to celebrate—Spanky and Steve Jordan are out front playing basketball—but he's looking forward most of all to bedtime, to another night of conjugal bliss.

Mandy, wearing her primrose polo plus stonewashed cutoffs, steps over to the main table; she stretches over it, straightening the white-plastic tablecloth. Her cutoffs ride up in back giving Bryan a glimpse

358

of that creamy, less-tanned flesh that deliciously cushions her upper thighs, and yet her supple girl-jock arms thrill him almost as much, as do her maidenly hands, and her feathered bangs, and her bouncy ponytail, which cutely protrudes out the back of her softball cap. Drunk, bonkers, honeymoon high: he's discovered, in ten wondrous days, her wanton secrets and lustful fury, yet her girl-woman allure is still irresistible, not to speak of her country-gal demeanor, familiar yet sweetly endearing—that slouchy, tomboyish way she moves and gestures and nods, like right now. Mandy, Mandy, Amanda Stevens— no, she's Amanda Howard. But either way, she's more vital to Bryan than the air he breathes, than the blood flowing in his veins, than the heart that keeps it flowing—she even trumps in importance his own mind and soul, the great mystery of self, which enables him to feel and know this undeniable fact of life. As if sensing his gaze, she gives him a blush and a grin, her big blue eyes sparking with fond mirth. Geysers of delight—Bryan feels an urge to rush over and throw her onto the grass, to make glorious love right here and now, a daringly outrageous act that would certainly test the limits, even among this open-minded group.

But Mandy breaks the spell: "Oh, honey, can yuh get the steak knives? I forgot 'em, and the ketchup, and the A-1 sauce."

Bryan jogs across the freshly mowed grass, headed for the house. Entering the courtyard area, he meets Steve Jordan going the other way. The big guy's breathing hard; beads of sweat dapple his face and jowly neck. "I know it's a sin to gamble," Steve mutters, his sousaphone drawl tinged with frustration—he shifts his eyes back and forth behind his wraparound shades. "But I thought *sure* I could beat that little fart." He pats the air with his thick-fingered hand, as if still dribbling a basketball.

"Whaddeyuh talking about?" Bryan asks.

"I just lost three bucks to your buddy from Spindle, shootin' hoops."

"Oh no, I shoulda warned yuh."

Steve's gaudy attire (turquoise, floral-print, Hawaiian-style shirt plus plaid Bermudas) gives witness that he dressed himself, not to mention his bright, poinsettia-red (Ardmore) cap—he no longer has Bryan at the dorm to coordinate his clothes. He smells quite floral as well, from the perfumed talc he uses; it obscures, for the most part, his perspiry BO. Removing the hat, he wipes the sweat off his brow then gives a pudgy grin. "Yessir, I got taken I reckon ... but it serves me right for goin' against my *dad*gum principles. I never bet on sports, whether I'm watchin' or playin', even if it's just a pick-up game." His frustration has given way to jolly self-deprecation, his default emotion.

"That's a *good* rule to follow," Bryan laughs, pushing his own (Spindle) cap back on his head, "especially when Spanky Arnold's in town. He's got a good heart, but he's a hustler."

"Tell me about it, dude. He kept on sayin' he was a *base*ball pitcher like me, and he never played basketball 'cuz he was too short, and while we were warmin' up, he didn't sink a *dad*gum thang. Hell, he was puttin' up airballs. And he staggered around like he had polio or sumpthin'." To illustrate this point, Jordan crumples his hat into a ball and shoots a make-believe shot, rocking and reeling afterward—like a drunk. "But once we started the game, that little fart couldn't miss. He blew me away ... like 21-13. He moves like a cat. I mean he's more shifty than a goshdang runnin' back; he's got better moves than Jamal even." Shaking his jowly, no-neck head, Jordan clears his throat, a thunderous rumble; he paws the patio with the toe of his size-15 sneaker. "And yet, I still shoulda beat 'im ... considerin' I'm a foot taller. *Heck,* I got every damn rebound almost."

"Well, why don'tcha demand a rematch after we eat?" Bryan interjects, giving the big fellow a consoling pat on the shoulder.

"I reckon I might. I just wish I hadn't put on these *ex*tra pounds. It slows me down, and gets me all tuckered. Yessir, I'm up to 261 now, like I toldjuh at practice on Friday. He lifts his shirt, displaying his mammoth, floral-scented gut as it balloons nakedly over the waist of his shorts. "I pigged out too much up at Susie's last weekend. Her grandma made all kinds of pies and stuff, and I couldn't resist. The Lord loves me like I am, but if I'm gonna start for Coach Weaver next spring, I gotta get down to two-thirty at least. It doesn't hurt me on the mound"—he executes an abbreviated version of his wind-up and delivery, his wadded hat now serving as a baseball—"but it sure cuts down on my quickness when I'm fieldin' my position, and that's why Spanky ran circles 'round me shootin' hoops just now. But don't get me wrong, dude: I'm still gonna chow down today." Unfurling his hat, he slaps it against his thigh, giving at the same time a gusty guffaw. "No *sir*, I can't diet with those dadgum steaks abroilin' out there; they smell *mighty* good I tellyuh."

"They do indeed. Chris just put 'em on the fire. I'm helping him, but I had to run into the house a minute."

Replacing his crumpled cap, Jordan gives another belly laugh then lumbers on, toward the charbroiled aroma, but Bryan stops him: "Hold it a second."

"Whatcha got, dude?"

"Oh, I just wanted to tellyuh that Mandy and I are glad you made it over today."

"Well, thanks for invitin' me. This's quite a weddin' party ... with the steaks'n all. Heck, it musta cost y'all a hun'erd bucks."

"I wouldn't call it a *party* exactly—it's just a get-together for our most-special friends."

Steve blushes, a rare event. "Awh gosh ... well, I reckon you guys are special to me too. And I like your house and ever'thang. Plus, the Cowboys won't be on till eight, so I got plenty of time. They're playin' the Giants back East—on ESPN." He fingers the air like he does, but more compactly, as if drumming on a bongo. "I'm sorry I didn't bring you guys a special present or nuthin'. I was gonna give yuh one of my new videos ... *The Natural,* that Robert Redford baseball flick. Y'know, we watched it a couple weeks ago. But then I decided I better keep it for inspiration. Yessir ... I *love* that dadgum story. It sorta reminds me of you, Bryan, 'cept the guy is older. But you do *hit* like him."

"I *wish*," Bryan laughs. "But don't worry about getting us—"

"I *did* kick in eight dollars," Jordan interrupts, "to Chris ... for the mugs and the Mr. Coffee that everyone's gettin' yuh—oh *shit*, I shoulda kept my mouth shut I reckon."

Bryan gives his ex-roomie a friendly jab, on his pythonlike arm. "No biggie. I overheard Chris and Tracy talking about it."

Jordan hikes up his Bermudas then adjusts his genitals, like a batter getting ready to hit. "But I *can* keep a secret, dude—like back at the dorm. I haven't told Marvin a dadgum thang. I just said y'were gonna be away a lot ... seein' your girlfriend."

"Well for now, I'm still officially living at the dorm, but I think Coach Weaver's gonna change my status at the end of the month." Bryan chuckles. "So y'might get a new roommate."

Steve resumes his bongo-drumming, at a faster tempo. "Well, I hope I don't get any *dang* roommate. If I cain't have you, I'd just as soon have that place to myself—but I don't blame yuh or anythang. Heck ... I reckon Mandy's one of the prettiest gals I ever laid eyes on, and she's got an ass on her that could *raise* the dead. Pardon me for lookin', but her caboose would put most any stripper to shame. Course, I could *never* say anythang like this in front of Susie." They both laugh.

I sure can't argue, Bryan remarks to himself after Jordan disappears into the backyard. *She DOES have an ass that could raise the dead, and we're gonna be sleeping together this very night, and every night forever—but I better stop daydreaming and fetch those steak knives.* (They bought the knives at Wal-Mart this morning, a last-minute afterthought.)

"Hey, slugger!" Spanky Arnold shouts from the driveway.

"Yeah!" the happy bridegroom replies, halting halfway through the back door.

"How'bout a quick game of one-on-one! I just whomped all over your goddam roomie!"

Bryan does an about-face in the doorway. "That's what I hear! But I gotta get some stuff outta the kitchen!"

"C'mon for *chris*sake!" Spanky insists cockily. "It won't take me five fuckin' minutes to beat your goddam collegiate ass! We'll just go to eleven. And w'can play for fun. I know you're not keen on bettin' or anythang."

I'm tempted to play him for twenty dollars, Bryan laughs to himself, as he swings open the slatted gate, joining Spanky on the driveway. *I should teach him a lesson, for Steve's sake.* (They've played one-on-

one a number of times back at Spindle High, when the baseballers had rainy-day workouts in the gym, and the wiry loudmouth only beat his taller teammate once.)

Spanky, dressed in his usual too-tight T-shirt with the sleeves rolled, passes the ball to Bryan, who dribbles twice then spins in a lay-up. "Damn, Spanker," he banters good-naturedly, as he puts in another set-up, "can'tcha let go of your pool-shark ways for one day even?" Bryan tries a fall-away shot but misses.

"So Steve toldjuh?" Spanky replies, as he grabs the rebound and pumps in a twenty-foot jumper: nothing but nylon—*whoosh*. (Mandy put a new net on the goal and tightened the bolts.) The ball bounces into the open garage where it caroms crazily off Chris's Chevette; it rolls down the driveway, going under Bryan's pickup. The freckled redneck chases the wayward ball.

"Yeah, he said yuh worked him for three bucks."

"So, what the fuck?" Spanky fusses, as he slides halfway under the truck to retrieve the ball. "He's a goddam giant for chrissake. Like ten inches taller than me."

"I know, but he's also gullible when it comes to gambling."

The little guy doesn't reply, and Bryan's feeling too good to pursue the matter. They take turns shooting freethrows. Spanky seems to have lost his sense of urgency about going one-on-one, and Bryan soon realizes why. "So, slugger, are yuh gonna tell me or what?" Giving a cackle plus a head waggle, he lofts a long shot from well down the driveway. The ball wheels around the rim, but doesn't go it. Bryan grabs it, puts in a lay-up, then tosses it back to his Spindle buddy, without answering the question.

Spanky cradles the basketball under his arm. The salve on his huge wedgelike snout reflects the sun, making the nose look even larger and redder. "C'mon, Bryan, let's hear it for chrissake."

"Hear what?" Bryan teases, dimpling into a grin—he realizes now why Spanker was so anxious to get him out here.

More cackling. "You know goddam what?"

"No, I don't."

Spanky comes closer until Bryan can see the scalp freckles amid his blondish burr-cut hair. "Don't gimme shit," he grouses hushedly. "Y'don't hafta tell *ever*'body, but we been friends since kindergarten for chrissake. So what was it like, gettin' into that wild young thang? Does she get all *crazy* and wet? Does she make animal noises? C'mon, you lucky *god*dam bastard ... tell me."

* * *

Meanwhile in the backyard, Wendy Lewis pursues a similar line of questioning, though in a more grown-up fashion. "So, kiddo, has it *really* been good?" she asks Mandy, as they stroll under the pecan trees. Tracy and Chris are watching the steaks, while Steve Jordan chugs his second can of Pepsi at the ice chest, which also contains Mountain Dew and Michelob beer, and Dr. Pepper of course. "You were *wicked* happy on the phone, plus your letter?"

Mandy blushes, her face warming. "Well, I don't see how things could be much better." She does her fidgety nose-mouth routine, crinkling, pursing, puckering, biting her lip.

Wendy smirks, rolling her dark-hazel eyes. "So you're happy ... *and* satisfied?"

"I'll say," Mandy declares, grinning girlishly.

"I figured as much. Gosh, I bet y'could write a book."

"That I could, but it might be banned, least by the Baptists."

They share a giggle, as Wendy gives Mandy a high-five. "Well, kiddo, from what I know about the horny Baptist girls back home, they'd be the first ones to read it, especially the ones on the basketball team. God, they're wilder than ever."

After a bit more jesting, their mood sobers. Wendy fingers a dried zit on the side of her bulbous nose, yet her complexion *has* improved since the summer. "I reckon I finally followed my heart," Mandy offers, giving a happy little titter. "Like *you* been telling me this whole year." She picks up a green pecan and hurls it toward the back fence. "But it was *my* decision of course."

"Oh, I know ... I know," Wendy replies, sweeping her bangs to the side. She's not wearing her Tiger cap, not now anyhow (the disheveled state of her mouse-brown mop suggests that she wore the hat on the way—she and Spanky drove down in her Subaru to save gas). "It's easy to *give* advice, but it takes real guts to do what you did, kiddo." Shaking her head, she gives a snuffly laugh then grins broadly, showing her pretty teeth. No braces, fewer zits: she's certainly prettier than last year. "It's wild and amazing, this whole thing—but it's wicked neat, how yuh pulled it off." Stuffing her hands into the back pockets of her jeans, she kicks a weedy tuft of grass with her sneaker—the lawn doesn't grow very well over here under the pecan trees.

Mandy fiddles with a loose piece of bark on the furthest tree. "It *is* hard to believe. It's like my *whole* life has changed ... but it's good that things are settling down now, so Bryan and I can get on with our schooling and all. And finding this house was really a godsend."

Wendy sweeps a maidenly hand toward the O'Shea home. "Oh gosh, this *is* a great place. I love your apartment, and this yard is wicked big." She snorts for emphasis. "But it does strike me as peculiar that your mom backed off ... when she was totally *pissed* before. I mean you're *still* seventeen?"

Mandy breaks off a piece of the loose bark. "Well, she's certainly not thrilled about it. But I reckon she's accepted the situation, at least enough to call a truce between us."

"So does she know that you lied about your age?"

"Not a chance. You're the only one who knows, and Bryan of

course." A visceral tugging pesters Mandy. She fidgets with the piece of bark, tossing it from one hand to the other. Yet her conscience has no chance of dampening her spirits—not today.

Wendy shrugs. "Well, you know your mom better than me. But it still seems weird. But either way, kiddo, it's *your* life, like I been saying all along. And I'm glad for you."

"So what was it like riding down with Spanky?" Mandy asks, changing the subject to get her mind off her mother. She tosses the bark onto the ground.

"Oh my, he's a damn character ... as you well know. He's a world-class bullshit artist, and he never stops talking hardly, and my car's gonna smell like shaving lotion forever, and most of the time he's bragging... about baseball, or bowling, or shooting pool, or about poker games, or his be*loved* truck. At first, he toned down his cussing, but by the time we got to Dallas he was using the F-word every other sentence." She laughs and throws up her hands. "I'm no angel when it comes to gutter talk, but he's off the chart. And yet y'can't help but like the guy. He even flirted with me a little, which I thought was cute—that was the only time he acted shy at all."

That would be something, Mandy interjects, but only to herself, *Wendy and Spanky.*

"But like I said before," Wendy goes on, "he thinks the world of Bryan, and you too, and he sees things like I do ... I mean about you running off to be with Bryan and all, and he—"

"Hey everybody!" Chris reports, loudly. "It's time to eat!"

* * *

Mandy, having finished her steak and salad, relaxes back in her chair. She sits at the end of the table, the place of honor in Chris's seating scheme, with Chris on her right, Bryan on her left. Sipping her Dr. Pepper, she gives her husband a loving glance. Bryan, engaged in an ongoing conversation with Spanky and Steve (concerning the Baylor gridiron loss to Texas Tech in Lubbock yesterday), doesn't notice. *He's so goshdang cute,* she sighs to herself, *the way he dimples and talks with his hands—it's SO amazing that we're married now, and I'm living here in Waco.* She takes another drink of her pop. *I like that new shirt—it gives a bluish tint to his eyes.* (She got him the shirt this week, a blue, paisley-print, button-collar chambray.) Her giddy heart does a cartwheel. *Oh gosh, I feel like kissing him right now.*

But before her yearning becomes obvious, she returns her attention to the table, to her role as bride, and hostess, a most non-traditional combination. "Y'want more potato salad?" she asks Steve Jordan. "There's a lot left?"

"Don't mind if I do," the big fellow drawls around a mouthful of beans—she passes the bowl.

"How'bout you, Spanky?" she says, after Jordan has taken a huge helping.

"Nawh ... thanks, but I reckon I'm done. I gotta save room for dessert ... and more *brewski*." He cackles and snorts, and pats his gut. "It's a good thang I'm not drivin' for chrissake." The empty cans by his plate give witness that he's on his third brew. He and Chris, and Tracy, are drinking beer; the rest have pop, even Wendy—because she *is* driving. She has to work tomorrow (Columbus Day), so they're going back to Spindle tonight.

Mandy, stretching, returns the bowl of potato salad to the serving table behind her. Steak, potato salad, tossed salad, corn on the cob, baked beans, Texas toast: the two newlyweds and their five guests have just downed one heck of a backyard feast, and Jordan is still going strong. Chris whispers to Tracy, and she excuses herself from the table.

It's nice of her to help out, Mandy remarks to herself, as Tracy sashays through the trellis gate. *And she looks good in that blouse and culottes. Bryan says that she and Chris are just friends, that she's stuck on some guy at LSU. She IS chunky, especially her hips, yet it's not so noticeable on her tall frame. And she's pretty in the face: she has that chipmunky cuteness that guys like. But she didn't make the Baylor hoop team, and she's way taller than me? So maybe I'm looking at long odds? But there's no point in worrying about it ... till next year.*

Tracy soon returns, a grin on her mouth, the wedding cake in her hands, not the traditional three-tiered variety but an ordinary cake—yet the icing *is* white, and it does sport a miniature bride and groom. Chris hops up to help. She places it on the table, as he makes room in front of Bryan and Mandy. Tracy then returns to her seat across from Steve, who's giving scant heed to all of this as he finishes his baked beans, sopping up the sauce.

"Before we cut the cake," Chris announces, standing behind his chair. "I'd like to propose a toast." He lifts his Michelob. "But first, I want to say uh ... well—"

"Oh no, not a *god*dam speech," Spanky taunts kiddingly, gesturing with his own beer. This outburst sets off a series of guffaws and giggles, as Spanker bows theatrically. Chris laughs as well but quickly puts on a poker face, a rare expression for *him*. His attire seems equally rare—he looks remarkably stylish in fact, having traded his shabby ragbag duds—no Einstein shirt to be sure—for a snappy pullover plus khaki slacks, Dockers no less. He waits for everyone to settle.

Mandy, grinning bashfully, wonders what he has in mind. *I can't tell if he's gonna be serious or what.* Her cheeks grow warmer, her blush deepening. Her husband obviously feels the spotlight too. He shifts in his lawn chair; he gives a little cough then dimples into a country-boy smile. Taking off his baseball cap, he fiddles with the bill. Mandy gives him a knowing glance plus a quick roll of the eyes, as if to say, "I wish this part was over ... but it'll be neat talking about it after we make love tonight," though she doesn't actually say it.

When it's finally quiet at the table, enough to hear the leaves rustling, the birds chirping, Chris lifts his hands as if feeling for rain. "Dearly beloved, we are gathered here today—" Too much: he breaks, along with everyone else. The laughter comes in waves feeding on itself, loud, choking ha-ha's, and wheezy snuffles and snorts, and it goes go on and on until the whole party is weak and released and near to tears. The curly-haired prankster leans on the back of his folding chair, to keep his balance.

"Get outta here for chrissake," Spanky reacts, turning beet red like he does.

"I thought y'were gonna preach a *dad*gum sermon," Steve Jordan blurts naively—the big guy is a master at understatements.

Mandy, feeling bolder about being the center of attention, leans into Bryan, as he gives her a playful one-arm embrace plus a kiss. Chris wags his head impishly, his Errol Flynn mustache dancing above his smirky mouth like a black, sidewinding flame. "That's the only thing I remember from Speech 101," he relates, his brown eyes still twinkly wet and full of mirth. "You have to loosen up your audience ... then gain their attention. I guess I'm *half*way there." More laughter, exhausted titters. "To tell you the truth, I'm actually shy about talking in front of people."

"Yeah, right," Tracy pipes, in her piccolo voice—she tosses a wadded napkin at her Baylor buddy. "You're the *biggest* show-off I know." This quip elicits a few last ha-ha's, like the final *ka-pops* in the microwave before taking the popcorn out.

"What kinda cake is that?" Jordan asks bluntly, obliviously. "I hope it's chocolate under that icin'. I don't care much for white cake or the yellow kind, 'cept for Twinkies."

"Don't worry," Tracy assures. "It *is* chocolate, Betty Crocker dark fudge to be exact. You'll see when we cut it."

"But give us a minute, Steve," Chris adds. "We still have to finish this toast."

No more laughter, no more banter—Steve's self-absorbed, childlike question about the cake has sobered the whole group, or so it seems, including Chris. *He's still smirking some,* Mandy notes to herself, *but I think he's gonna say something serious.*

"Most folks see me as a joker and a cut-up," Chris offers, confirming her silent conclusion, "and I guess I am. But I uh ... well, I want you to put that aside for a moment, because I see this cookout as a very special event." Clearing his throat, he takes a drink of beer then places the can on the table, suggesting that he's going to need more than a minute. "Now we've all been to church weddings before, and receptions and all that, and I frankly don't care much for them, as I'm sure you could tell from my mocking little parody before. It's not that I'm against marriage ... not at all, not true marriage anyway ... but I *am* against pretense, and that's the big problem with traditional weddings. First of all, most of the guests show up out of a sense of obligation, and yet they act so damn happy and hyped. It's a lie. I mean, how can we get excited about putting on a coat and tie, and sitting rigidly in a stuffy, solemn church, just so we can see Cousin Jane get married? Especially, when we hardly know her, or her groom, much less the nature of the love they share, if any. And yet we grin and nod, and act like it's so great. But in truth, we'd rather be on the golf course, or at the lake, or at the mall, or watching a movie, or slurping ice cream, or taking a nap on the couch—hell, we'd rather be at the dentist, almost."

Laughs and snuffles, a muted cackle from Spanky—but the mood remains serious. "Then at the reception," Chris elaborates, "we have to say, 'Good to see you,' to the fifty other pretenders, their faces all pasted with shit-eating grins. It's like everyone tries to act polite and cheerful, with no regard for what they're feeling inside—and it's not just weddings, it's all around ... like on campus, or at work, or in politics, or in religion, or in families, or wherever we turn. To *hell* with the heart. We have to conform to be accepted. But the fucking result is lying and loneliness, and I'm talking about the worst kind of loneliness, which is being alone in a crowd, alone behind our masks and put-on routines."

His sincere words astonish Mandy. Can this be the same puckish wise-ass, who's always jesting and joking? Chris steps back from his chair. "Sorry to get so damn long-winded, but this's why this cookout is so special to me." He gives an open-handed gesture toward the group. "Now there's not a big crowd here today, or a lot of hoopla and hype, but each of us, all *five* of us—we're here because we truly care for Bryan and Mandy. We're not just a collection of relatives and acquaintances doing their duty ... and that's goddamn important if you ask me. And we each realize how much they love each other. Let's face it: they've overcome some long odds just to be together."

Everyone looks on in wide-eyed wonder, even Spanky, especially Spanky. Chris takes a sip of Michelob then gestures with the can. "Now I've only known Bryan for six weeks, yet I realized at once that he was special, and gifted, and smart. But most of all, I saw his heart. He has a big, beautiful heart, and that's the main thing to me. There's a Bible verse—now I'm sure Mandy could quote it better than me." Restrained laughter ripples around the table. Mandy grins. "Well, I'm not going to quote the damn thing, but it essentially says that if you don't have love, you're a sounding gong, no matter how great you are in all other respects. But this's why I felt drawn to Bryan that first day. I knew he was smart, but being bright is nothing, if you don't have a heart. I knew he was a gifted baseball jock, but being a superstar is nothing if you don't have a heart." Shifting the beer to his left hand, Chris chops the air deliberately with his right, to emphasize each point.

"I knew he was young and strong, and healthy and handsome, and I knew he was highly esteemed among his peers back home, but being a popular goddamn country-town stud is nothing ... if you don't have a heart, and I knew he had a great future ahead of him, in neuroscience or philosophy, or anything he put his mind to, but achieving greatness in a professional career means nothing, if you don't have a heart."

Bryan, blushing, looks down shyly. Mandy can tell he's touched. "And one of the first things I discovered about Bryan's big, wonderful heart," the mustached junior goes on, "was the love he had for a girl back home. It was obvious he was gaga over her, the way he blushed and grinned when he talked about her. And now that I've had a chance to get to know Mandy"—Chris gestures toward her with his beer—"I can understand why. Not only is she young and beautiful and bright, and a jock to boot, but she also has a big heart like her husband. And yet the most amazing thing, something we don't see often ... I mean ... well, she has the courage to follow her heart, and she's followed it through some very difficult circumstances, not to mention the fucking tornado she drove through to get here. That was a killer storm to be sure ... and it aptly symbolizes the other storms that she and Bryan bravely faced to get to this day. We all know the story by now, and I'll not repeat it, but suffice it to say, they put love ahead of duty, and that's why we're here. And that's why I'm proud to have them as my friends." Mandy's eyes fill.

"Now, you guys from Spindle, I mean Spanky and Wendy—you could do a better job of saying what I'm saying, since you've known them both for many years. And, Steve, you could say a lot more about Bryan, since you lived with him at the dorm, but what I've said is from my heart, and I know Tracy is likewise amazed at all of this—so let's toast our bride and groom."

"Hear, hear!" Spanky exclaims, shooting up out of his seat. The others stand as well, holding their drinks high over the table: Wendy, Tracy, even Steve Jordan with his Pepsi.

* * *

146 DOUGLAS STREET
SUNDAY, OCTOBER 13, 1991 — 5:22 PM

As the sun sinks in the west, Tracy helps Mandy clean up the picnic area, while Wendy and Chris wash the serving dishes and such, in his apartment. The other three guys have returned to the driveway for more basketball. "I appreciate all you've done this week," Mandy says, as they clear the paper plates and beverage cans and other disposable debris off the table. "And I wanna thank you for the Mr. Coffee, and the mugs."

"Oh, that was from *every*one," Tracy replies, emphasizing the "every" with her high-pitched voice. She gives a ruddy grin.

THE SILVER CORD

"I know, I know. But you're the one who did the legwork, and you and Chris made the cake and all." Mandy gives a happy little snort as she secures the trash bag with a twist-tie. "It still blows me away, what Chris said today; it was sweet of him. And he's usually such a *smart*-ass. I can't believe he was so serious."

"It *was* amazing, and *I*'ve known him two years. He's got a heart, but he's a big-time show-off, and a cynic to boot." Tracy snuffles and shakes her head, a wispy curl tumbling onto her cheek; she sweeps it back. Her darkish hair is parted off center and styled into wings. "He has surprised me a few times, but it takes an atomic bomb of feeling to overcome his wise-guy personality, so you and Bryan must've really had an effect on him."

"And I've only been living here for a week."

Tracy's dark-chocolate eyes go fondly warm. She pats Mandy on the shoulder. "But he *meant* what he said about you guys, and it's true ... and I'm happy for both of you."

Mandy, blushing, doesn't know what to say, so she just gives a wide smile, her goofy grin, as she wipes the plastic tablecloth (it's the kind you keep) with a damp sponge.

"So I understand you're a basketball player?" Tracy says, shifting the subject.

"Yeah, I reckon so ... though I won't be playing this year."

"But y'had a Baylor scholarship? Before all this happened?"

"I think I still do. I just found out this week that Coach Ames is keeping me on the freshmen list for '92, as long as I get my diploma. I'm going to night school ... over at Newcomb Tech."

"Hope it works out. I'm a hoopster too ... but I got cut."

Mandy gives a sigh. "That's what I hear. But if you couldn't make it, my chances are low. I mean, you're way taller than me."

"Yeah, but Coach Ames is a speed freak. If y'can't get your ass down the court, she doesn't have much patience, and that's my weakness, because of these thunder thighs God gave me." Tracy laughs squeakily, her piccolo timbre going even higher.

"Don't be so hard on yourself. You have a super-nice figure."

"Get outta here ... but thanks." More giggles. "I'm too busy to play basketball anyway, now that I'm working so many hours at the lab. And I didn't even think I was gonna be at Baylor this year—you know, a boy-thing."

"Yeah, I sorta heard about that."

* * *

Bryan, meanwhile, leans against his pickup—he looks on, as his redneck Spindle buddy maneuvers against a lumbering, sweating, hard-breathing Steve Jordan. Spanky head-fakes left but dribbles right, leaving Jordan reeling off balance, and before the big guy can recover, the ball arcs through the air, popping the net, a crisp jump-shot delivered from the top of the circle (or where the circle would be on a regulation court).

"That's it!" Spanky crows, doing a footloose victory jig on the cracked concrete. "11-8 ... I win. You owe me another goddam dollar." He swaggers and struts about like a male grouse in mating season. "Y'came a little closer that time, but y'gotta remember that I got a six pack in me for chrissake. I'll give yuh another chance ... *after* I beat Bryan."

"Nope, I reckon I've had enough," Steve pants, as he pulls his wallet out of his Bermuda shorts; he fishes inside with his huge sausagelike fingers. "I gotta get back to the dorm. The Cowboys are on tonight." Giving a bassy belly-laugh, he finally gets the dollar out and hands it to Spanky. "I'm glad we made it a dollar this time. It's not really gamblin' if it's just a dollar."

"Okay, slugger," Spanky brags, after Steve has departed in his Bronco, "it's *your* turn to go down."

"Let's just shoot around," Bryan replies. "I'm too stuffed. Besides, I don't wanna take a chance on spraining my ankle or anything. We have a big intersquad doubleheader tomorrow."

"But tomorrow's Columbus Day?"

"I know, but it's like a fall tradition, with real umps and all."

"C'mon, slugger, don't be a such a *god*dam wimp. Let's play to eleven ... for small potatoes, like five bucks, or three even?"

"Nawh, let's just play another game of HORSE."

"HORSE. You mean HORSESHIT. I'm sick of that cocksuckin' game. I want some *real* action. And I'm willin' to put my money where my mouth is."

"So you want some action, d'yuh?" Mandy banters, as she appears suddenly, along with Wendy and Tracy. "How'bout *I* play yuh one-on-one ... for ten big ones?"

* * *

146 DOUGLAS STREET
TUESDAY, OCTOBER 15, 1991 — 7:47 AM

After giving Mandy a kiss, Bryan grabs his book bag and hustles down the stairs. He's soon in the truck chugging west on Douglas. A chilly fog shrouds the neighborhood, obscuring the treetops, rendering the old homes gray and ghostly, as they crouch in the mist behind their terraced lawns. Autumn murk rules Waco on this back-to-class morning, but Bryan sees nothing but sunshine and color, and dreams coming true. *She's been with me for twelve days now,* he exults to himself, as he hangs a right onto Baker Street, *and things keep getting better and better.*

As their love prospers, so does everything else: his grades, his baseball hopes, Mandy's job at Denny's, her night school, her scholarship situation for next year, Bryan's scholarship status *this* year (he'll be getting a married-athlete housing allowance starting in November)—and Mandy's mother (Helen, though hardly enthused, seems to have accepted everything).

On the baseball front, he feels quite upbeat about making the starting nine in the spring, and his stellar performance in the big doubleheader yesterday didn't hurt his chances. Going five for eight plus two walks, he led his team (the gold team) to a sweep. His three-run homer in the bottom of the eighth iced the second contest right before it started to rain. And he whacked it to the opposite field (a two-strike curve on the outside corner), a hitting feat that drew kudos from Coach McKinney, *and* Coach Weaver, who rarely gives praise.

Harking back to Sunday, to the cookout gathering, Bryan can't help but chuckle as he thinks about Spanky. *Mandy sure closed his big mouth. And then came Tracy, and Wendy.*

As it turns out, the wiry redneck lost three successive one-on-one games, bowing to each of the girl-jock hoopsters, costing him twenty bucks total. "Goddam it all!" he howled, after losing the last game to pint-sized Wendy under the lights (the driveway floodlight). "I *must* be drunk for chrissake, lettin' three girls beat me." He hurled the basketball angrily into the next yard (the immaculate Lipski yard), but after climbing over the hedge, and returning with the ball, he cooled down and paid Wendy her three dollars, which she said could count toward his gas money.

Before he and Wendy left for Spindle, Spanky took Bryan aside and gave him private congrats and fond wishes. Yet it was Chris Hansen's Bryan-Mandy speech that touched the Baylor freshman the most, encouraging him greatly concerning the legitimacy of their love-nest happiness. After all, there aren't many folks who would applaud their decision to elope.

THE SILVER CORD

CHAPTER TWENTY-TWO

146 DOUGLAS STREET
THURSDAY, OCTOBER 17, 1991 — 9:34 PM

Bryan Howard, at his makeshift desk (a small dropleaf table with the leaves up) in the master bedroom, ponders a calculus problem involving artillery shells fired at various angles and muzzle velocities. He explores several approaches on his scratch pad then gives a resigned sigh and leans back in his chair. He rubs the eraser-end of the pencil against his lower lip. The wind outside rattles one of the loose shutters; the weather turned abruptly cooler this afternoon. Hopping up, he heads for the bathroom, padding along in his socks and tattered jeans. Before reaching the toilet, he hears the Firebird.

She's home from school. After quickly relieving himself, he hides in the hall closet with the intention of jumping out and grabbing her as she comes up the stairs. He can't help but give a boyish yelp, as he anticipates her surprise, to be followed most surely by tickling and laughing, and perhaps a torrid session of lovemaking. He waits yet hears nothing, no footsteps on the stairs. One minute, then two: where is she?

Leaving his mirthful glee in the closet, he steps out into the hallway. He listens—nothing. He bops down to the kitchen where he finds her green book bag on the counter but not her. *Maybe she did some shopping, and she went to fetch the sacks from the car?* He expects her to come in, but she doesn't, nor does he hear anything. Puzzled, he grabs a pair of sneakers from the back porch. Slipping them on, plus his baseball windbreaker, he hustles out to the driveway, but she's not in her car. A gust of wind whips around the garage, chilling his face— it's cold out here.

Maybe she had to talk to Chris about something? Bryan trots back around the house. But Chris's apartment is dark. *He must be working late for Dr. Richardson, like he does.* Going back inside, he checks the downstairs, the closed-off rooms—no sign of her. *Where the heck is she? She wouldn't be down in the basement, or in the garage? I can't see why?*

Downstairs, upstairs, then outside again—he finally locates her in the backyard, near the barbecue pit. "Whaddeyuh doing, pretty lady?" he asks, as a burst of wind whips with a low roar through the trees.

"Oh nothing, babe. I'm just looking at the moon."

Her answer baffles him all the more, yet he doesn't press. "It's cold out here. Y'should have your winter jacket."

"Nawh, I'm okay. It's not *that* cold."

The north wind has chased the clouds, and haze, leaving crystal-clear skies overhead. The waxing, almost-full moon, a pale-blue orb suspended above the pecan trees, floods the big backyard with cold, silvery light making the grass look like snow, save in the black shadows cast by the trees. Bryan embraces his wife from behind. "It *is* pretty," he remarks, trying to focus on the night sky rather than why she's out here under it, "and I can see why they talk about the 'man in the moon.' I mean, I can make out a mouth and eyes ... maybe a nose."

"Yeah, me too," she replies. Then after a brief silence, she adds, "I wanna make a promise on the moon."

"Whaa ... whaddeyuh talking about?"

"I wantcha to promise me that every time you look at the moon, you'll think of me with all your heart, no matter where you are, or what you're doing—and I'll do the same."

"It's a deal," he agrees matter-of-factly, despite a growing sense of unease; this whole moon thing not only perplexes him, but it's giving rise to pricks of apprehension. "But I reckon we're mainly gonna be looking at it together."

"Yeah, but it's still special, knowing that this very moon will always connect us—oh, honey, just hold me. Hold me close."

A few minutes later they stroll hand-in-hand back to the house. As they do, Mandy says, "I think we should go to church this week, like we been talking about. I don't work until three."

* * *

Same night, 10:16 p.m. Bryan slouches back on the faded, timeworn sofa in their upstairs living room. He watches with little regard the ten o'clock news on Channel Two:

> UN inspectors disclosed this week that secret Iraqi documents seized at the Al-Atheer weapons center 40 miles south of Baghdad indicate that Saddam Hussein's nuclear program has successfully produced small amounts of lithium-6, a chemical used only in H-bombs. The existence of this material was never reported to UN officials despite the requirements of last April's cease-fire agreement ending the Persian Gulf War. President Bush again reiterated his zero-tolerance policy pertaining to Iraqi weapons of....

Mandy, her book-pack at her feet, reads in the corner chair, a shabby, brown-corduroy, overstuffed piece which looks nothing like the plaid divan. The other rooms in the house, even their bedroom (Jason's room), contain matching sets of furniture (old but in fine condition, and consistent for the most part with the 1940s-mood of the home), but when Annie converted this room to a TV lounge, she furnished it with garage-sale stuff, not to mention the water-spotted coffee table and the rickety mate's chair. Only the oval rug and priscilla curtains resemble the rest of the house. But the newlyweds like the room—it's cozy and comfortable, though somewhat crowded, especially with the O'Shea's 27-inch Magnavox, in its oak, swivel-base cabinet. Needless to say, Bryan's little Sony ended up in their bedroom.

Mandy flips through a textbook, reading then turning, then turning back. She purses her dollface mouth then strokes her top lip with her tongue, an abbreviated version of her rabbity move. Bryan catches a glimpse of bra and cleavage through her button-front blouse, refiring his hopes for frolic and lovemaking, yet she seems far from eager at the moment. For that matter, she has shown him little attention since they came upstairs after watching the moon in the backyard. "So whaddeyuh reading, pretty lady?" he asks, trying to get something going—he pokes her fondly with his big sock-clad toe.

"Nothing really," she replies nonchalantly, without looking up. "It's just a book on writing techniques, with samples from well-known authors."

He sits forward on the sofa. "What authors?"

"Oh, the usual famous ones ... like Steinbeck, and Dickens, and Thomas Hardy, and James Joyce ... plus a few contemporary writers too. It's not like a literature course where you study the whole story and all that. Mr. Self—he's my teacher—he just wants us to see how different writers use the language ... but I don't hafta do it now, since we don't have class again till Monday." Closing the book, she gives her husband a side glance, along with a little twist of the mouth, a knowing smirk. "So why the sudden interest, mister? I thought you hated English Comp?"

Her response encourages him; he dimples. "No way. I love to construct paragraphs and write essays, and look up w—"

"Get outta here," she giggles. "I reckon that's why y'never made better than B, while y'made A's in everything else?"

He laughs as well. "No, it was Mrs. Sparger, not me—that old biddy never gives A's to the guys in her class, especially jocks. It's a lot better *this* year, with Professor Emerson. It's more relaxed at the college level." Bryan laughs louder, giving himself away. "I actually like to write. In fact, I may write a novel, a steamy one about a seductive country-gal from a small Texas town who runs away to be with her handsome lover."

Mandy blushes. "C'mon, you big jock; you're just *try*ing to get me going. It's not hard to tell what's on *your* mind." The flirtatious quip gives him a rush, but before he can respond, she stretches to her feet and pads out of the room.

On the TV Norm Gossage gives the weather: "Now this ridge nosing down from the Panhandle"—he points at a blue H inside a large amoeba-shaped isobar—"will give us a sunny, fallish day tomorrow, a nice change from the blustery conditions ushered in by today's frontal passage, though it *will* remain seasonally cool for mid

THE SILVER CORD

October, and the—"

Mandy yells something, but Bryan can't make it out. He mutes the TV. "What'd you say, honey?"

"You *peed* on the toilet seat again," she repeats from the bathroom; he hears her quite well this time—she obviously didn't close the door; she *never* closes the door.

"It wasn't *me*," he fibs kiddingly, as he recalls his hurried trip to the john before he hid in the closet earlier.

"Well, who was it then?"

Bryan chuckles. "Gosh ... beats me? Maybe old Mr. Lipski got lost ... and wandered in?"

"It's not *fun*ny," Mandy declares, also giving a laugh, though he can tell she's less than amused. "How'd you like it if I peed on the seat in the morning, before you come in to sit down? Well, I hafta sit *every* time."

"I know, hon ... I'm sorry. I was in a rush, but I *did* lift it, as soon as I realized. The bathroom light was off."

"Well, y'should turn on the light ... especially during the middle of the night. That's when it mainly happens."

Bryan, his frolicsome hopes tempered by this wifely fussing, clasps his hands behind his head. "Gosh, Mandy, it's not *that* big of a deal. And it couldn't have happened more than *twice* since we've been here, or maybe three times?" He tries to maintain a congenial, laid-back tone. "But y'gotta realize that the seat was *nev*er down when I lived at the dorm. So it takes a while to get used to things. And I *do* turn on the light ... *most* of the time."

"Yeah right," she counters above the gurgling rush of the flushing commode. "I tellyuh what. You c'mon in here and clean it up. All y'gotta do is spray the seat with that foamy stuff under the sink, then y'wipe it off with TP—it's the canister with the green top. Y'may as well clean the whole dang toilet." She gives a sassy guffaw. "This's gonna be the rule, mister, from *now* on."

"No problem," he quickly agrees, as he makes his way to the bathroom. He'd just as soon get this issue behind them—even if she does sound like his mother.

* * *

Forty minutes later, they're in bed, not sleeping but discussing things: his schedule, her schedule, the winding down of fall baseball, Marvin's church, the Baylor Homecoming on Saturday (she reports to Denny's at six p.m., so they *can* go together to the football game). Then they shift to money concerns. After weighing their assets and liabilities, a familiar exercise, they agree that things will work out okay, once Bryan's housing allowance starts in November. Finally, they go silent.

Despite the bland nature of the pillow talk, Bryan remains confident that his wife's saucy, flirtatious side, which he glimpsed before the toilet-seat incident, will appear again. Embracing her tenderly (they're in the usual butt-to-gut position), he waits for her to make the first move. Whether in bed, or out of bed, she usually initiates the foreplay (fondling, a french kiss, lewd banter, exposing a provocative breast), but tonight she remains on her side, facing away. After a couple of minutes, he kisses her neck then nibbles her ear, while he works his hand underneath her nightie. "No, babe, don't," she tells him sleepily.

A little knife stabs his ego. "What's wrong, pretty lady?"

"Nothing ... nothing at all. I'm just not in the mood."

"Is it the toilet-seat thing?"

No answer.

"Mandy, I'm sorry about that. I didn't realize."

Still no answer.

O God, I hate this, he declares to himself, trying hard to not overreact. *I hate it when she clams up.* "It's okay, hon," he offers aloud, giving her a gentle peck on the cheek, "we don't hafta have sex tonight ... but if it's be*cause* of me, I'd like to know."

Zilch, no reply. Aside from his pulse *ka-thumping* into the pillow and the north wind buffeting the house, he hears nothing. Her silence torments, until he's ready to yell, to start a big, loud, cussing fight, but before he does, she finally responds, "No, babe, it's not you; it's me. I'm just tired, that's all ... *just* tired."

Her answer seems evasive, yet he dares not dig.

* * *

Next morning, 8:49 a.m. *I feel bad about last night,* Mandy confesses in the tub, as she settles back into the foamy-white bubblebath. *Not that we hafta do it every time we get in bed, but I gave him the cold shoulder, my bitchy side.* She swishes her hand through the perfumed suds; they have a fruitlike fragrance, like apricots. *I never felt right yesterday. It's like my heart had the flu or something.* She gives a determined snort. *But today's gonna be better, like super good, especially with the surprise I'm planning for him. I gotta go to Safeway, then I'll get the candles at Wal-Mart. And I hafta bake the cake.* She tilts her head back, soaking her unfettered locks. Coming up, she grabs her shampoo, the Pantene, but she doesn't open it. *I'll do my hair in a minute, but right now I'm just gonna let this hot water soak into me.*

* * *

BAYLOR CAMPUS - FOUNTAIN MALL
FRIDAY, OCTOBER 18, 1991 — 8:56 AM

No honeymoon lasts forever, Bryan reminds himself, again, as he strides down the wide sidewalk on his way to American History 101. It's a chilly morning and jackets abound. *Even the happiest couples hafta come down at some point.* He gives a sigh that ends with a snort. *But she was acting weird last night, like looking at the moon, and making that promise. Maybe she thinks we won't last? No, no—that's bullshit! What's wrong with me? It's normal to have a blah day occasionally.*

She was still in bed when he left for his first-hour chemistry lab, where he made little progress on his two-week, boiling-point-elevation project. Larry Fellows, his lab partner, didn't show, so Bryan had little incentive. He did get the Bunsen burner lit, yet he spent most of the hour staring at the blue flame, as if it could enlighten him somehow about Mandy, about marriage.

A fat coed lumbers by the other way, her cowlike boobs jouncing and quivering, as if she has huge water balloons stuffed inside her tacky sweat shirt. *I hafta accept the bad with the good. It's how marriage is. I mean, Mom and Dad—they've been together forever, and they love each other, and I'm sure they still have sex, yet they're laid-back for the most part. That's how life is. It's not some kind of wonderland. I can't expect each day to be mind-blowing like a goshdang OBE.*

But then comes the wee knife, another stab: *Gosh, last night was the FIRST time we didn't do it.* A shiver wiggles up his spine. *And it's not the sex—that's not it. Something was bugging her?* Hanging a left at Peyton Hall, he jogs up the steps, slicing through the crowd of students emerging, coming down. Dr. Reid's history class convenes in the amphitheater lecture hall, and you enter from the second floor. There's room for two hundred, but Bryan likes to grab a seat down front, and he has to hustle down the aisle to get one.

* * *

146 DOUGLAS STREET
FRIDAY, OCTOBER 18, 1991 — 9:13 AM

"But, Mama, we've been through all this be*fore*," Mandy reacts, finally. She fidgets with the telephone cord; she shifts her weight from one bare foot to the other. Her face stiffens.

"I know, young lady," Helen harps on, "but it's still true. It takes *more* than love. You're not gonna waltz through life, just because you're in *love*." She gives a motherly murmur. "I know how life works, Amanda. Romantic feelings aren't enough. The world's a cruel place, and you're *hard*ly old enough to face it. You're inexperienced and naive. Same goes for Bryan. Roses may look pretty, but they have thorns too."

Cradling the phone under her chin, Mandy ties the sash of her robe then pushes her still-wet hair back. "I doughwanna talk about this. I just got outta the tub; I hafta blow-dry my hair."

"Well, this's a bit more important than your dadgum *hair*. How canyuh get by with a part-time waitress job when you have rent and food and two cars? I mean, you're hardly in a position to keep that

Firebird. Y'should sell it, and put the money in the bank. You hafta think ahead, Amanda. You hafta make a budget and stick to it." Helen grunts. "I tried to let go of this, but I can't help but worry. I pray for you, and for Bryan, but it's hard to get peace about this. I fear you're falling away from the Lord, but it's *more* than that. I worry about your finances, and your health, and your ability to cope. After all, I *am* your mother, and I know a heck of a lot more about surviving than you do. You're only seventeen, don't forget? I mean, it's ri*dic*ulous to have two cars. And you're paying insurance on that Pontiac. And that mutual-fund money was supposed to go toward college. But now, all *this* has happened, and you're finishing your senior year at night school, like some kinda delinquent dropout. And how canyuh get a scholarship, when you're not even *play*ing this season?"

"Mama, stop it! I may be seventeen, but I'm not stupid. Plus, I'm *married* now. It's a totally done deal." She sighs, as a tug of daughterly compassion tempers her anger; she softens. "I know you mean well, Mama, and I don't blame yuh for worrying. But we're doing okay ... like *super* good."

Helen hesitates then says, "I reckon I must seem like a real pain in the butt, but I *do* want the best for you, Amanda." Her disturbed-mother demeanor has likewise moderated. "I don't mean to pester, but I *have* learned many things the hard way."

"I know, Mama ... I know."

"Besides, it's hard to get used to this. I mean uh ... well, the house seems so empty with you gone. Gretchen feels it too; she just *mopes* around. It's not the same. But I reckon we're gonna adjust. Besides, it's not in *my* hands anyhow ... like it says in Ecclesiastes: there's a time to get, and a time to lose ... but God makes everything beautiful in *his* time."

"That *is* a special verse, and I reckon we oughta trust in it—but I really gotta go now, Mama. I'm off work today, but I hafta go shopping ... plus a jillion other things, like the laundry—we get to use the washing machine in the garage, and the dryer, but it still takes time to fold it and all. And I'm gonna try to make it to Bryan's practice this afternoon; they only have one week left of fall baseball. But I'll call yuh on Sunday, after we get back from church. We're going this week, like I toldjuh before."

Mama can change so quickly, Mandy remarks to herself, as she blow-dries her hair before the bathroom mirror. *One minute she's all pissed and superior, and the next she's sad and saying she's sorry, or as close as she ever gets to saying it.* As she works on her bangs, a wave of homesickness aggravates her shaky mood, her heart slumping off center. *Now I'm feeling sucky again, sorta like yesterday, but not exactly. Why'd she hafta call today?* Mandy kills the blow-dryer. She gives a whispery little moan, as a sense of failure joins the yearning for Spindle. A knot forms in her throat; her eyes fill. She feels mediocre, worse than mediocre, like C-minus—not quite "delinquent" but close, and she could pass for a "dropout," considering what she left behind. And her teachers back home must surely see it that way, and Coach Perkins of course, and her basketball teammates, not to speak of softball. Mandy feels like sobbing, but she fights it off. She fiddles with the switch on the blower without turning it on. *And I was feeling good in the tub. Why can't I take things in stride like Bryan does? He's always so positive. I wish he was feeling sucky TOO. No, no—that's just my selfish side talking. Forgive me, Lord. But why can't I get rid of these negative vibes? Rejoice in the Lord always; and again I say rejoice—bullSHIT! Maybe it's because I stopped going to church? Or maybe God's chastising me, because I lied about my age in Louisiana?*

Blue eyes, bleary eyes, condemning eyes: her conscience frowns back at her from the mirror, or so it seems. She looks down. *Let God be true but every man a liar. There is nothing covered that shall not be revealed. Goshdang it all—why are these Bible verses coming into my head? I haven't read the Bible in a month at least—THAT could be the reason. Man does not live by bread alone, but by every word that proceedeth out of the mouth of God. This's weird. Maybe it's Satan? No way: it's God that concerns me, not the Devil.* She sniffs back her tears. She wipes her nose with the back of her hand. *Children, obey your parents. Honor thy father, and thy mother. But how can I? I love Bryan forever. I can't change my heart. But I DID lie about my age. And yet it's not the paperwork that counts. O Lord, I can't think about this—it's driving me nutty.* Grabbing a wad of toilet paper, she blows her nose, then she resumes drying her hair.

* * *

STRECKER MATH CENTER - CLASSROOM 422B
FRIDAY, OCTOBER 18, 1991 — 10:06 AM

Mr. Gary Cook, Professor Edelstein's teaching assistant, scrawls a definition on the blackboard (it's actually *black,* not green like most of the chalkboards on campus):

> **Simple Harmonic Motion:** oscillatory motion during which a point moves at regular intervals from one end of a line segment to the other, and then back again. If the line segment, of length 2b, extends from $x = -b$ to $x = b$ on the x-axis....

Bryan, hurrying to keep up with the left-handed, fast-writing, fast-talking instructor, scribbles everything on a legal pad. He'll amend and refine these notes later when he transfers them to his calculus notebook. He feels rushed, as he usually does in this class, but he's occupied at least—no time to fret about his personal life, as in chemistry lab earlier. He sits on the right side (near the windows) of this outmoded classroom, which smells of chalk dust and floor wax and banana blackboard oil. Decades of foot traffic have worn down the hardwood planking, especially near the door. The fourth floor of Strecker Hall is right out of the '50s, having never been renovated, unlike most areas on campus.

Mr. Cook, a red-haired, freckled, type-A personality with horn-rimmed glasses (a twenty-something Princeton grad who came here to pursue a doctor's degree), covers for Prof. Edelstein most every Friday. Jacob Edelstein, the renowned mathematician (renowned for Baylor), spends most of his time doing research and giving seminars; teaching Calculus 201 ranks well down his list. His research includes an inter-departmental project at the neuroscience lab where (according to Chris) he applies exotic, cyber-math modeling techniques to biophysical phenomena.

Biology, chemistry, physics: these disciplines demand mathematical rigor, a fact which whets Bryan's appetite for calculus, for matrix and set-theory, for statistics and probability, for any tools that will help him unlock the brain-soul mystery, a calling for which he lacks academic training (compared to his teachers, or even Chris Hansen), though he surpasses them all when it comes to fervor and personal knowledge concerning his quest.

After filling up the leftmost chalkboard, Mr. Cook continues on the middle panel where he draws a circle (radius = b) on an x-y coordinate system with the center of the circle at point O (0,0). He denotes point Q on the circle plus point P directly below Q on the x-axis, while Θ denotes the angle between the ray OQ and the x-axis. Finishing the diagram, he moves to the rightmost panel and begins to cover it as well:

> Point P executes simple harmonic motion (-b to b) when it's the projection on the x-axis of point Q, as Q moves around the circle $x^2 + y^2 = b^2$ with constant angular velocity $d\Theta/dt$. If x is the abscissa of P, then x = b $\cos\Theta$. If we denote the angular velocity by ω, then we have $\omega = d\Theta/dt$, and....

As Bryan hastily records all this on his legal pad, the words and math lingo suddenly go fuzzy, hard to read. He shakes his head trying to clear his vision, to no avail. *Oh shit,* he declares to himself *Don't tell me my eye is getting weird again. I haven't had any problems since June.* He covers his bad eye (left eye) to check, and sure enough, the blackboard comes into focus. It is the same one, the eye that was out of whack for a month or so after his head injury. *Dear Jesus, this's all I need. I'm already strung out over Mandy, and now I can't see right, or maybe it's the anxiety that set it off? Or maybe you're teaching me a lesson ... for doubting her. No, no-that's not how you are. But what the fuck is wrong with my eye? And why'd it happen now?*

To hell with calculus: he must regain his sight, somehow, and quick. He scans the old classroom with its high ceiling, peeling paint, paneled wainscoting, and scrolled molding, all of which appear indistinct to his binocular vision but crisply clear when he uses the right eye only. Ditto for the suspended globe-shaped light fixtures, which resemble giant, illuminated, upside-down Tootsie Roll Pops. Abandoning the classroom, he looks outside where, to his relief, the cool but sunny morning registers clearly on the screen of his brain, but when he focuses intently (with both eyes) on the puffy clouds, they go fuzzy. *Oh shit.* Same goes for the microwave antennas atop McCurdy Hall, and the big pine on the other side of Fountain Mall, and the sloping cornice of Moody Library in the distance. *Dammit all—now I'll hafta get those special glasses that Dr. Nadler talked about. It's not life-threatening, but he warned me that this might happen, that I might have lingering visual problems. O Jesus, how can I hit a curve ball with fucked-up eyesight?*

He watches in dismay a gray-winged blur above the columned facade of the library, a pigeon most likely. The bird flaps higher then sails, swooping toward the roof of McCurdy Hall. *THANK YOU, JESUS!* The fowl comes into focus, distinctly, revealing that it's a crow not a pigeon, that it's black not gray. Bryan can see perfectly again, even when he concentrates on the parted tail feathers, spread like a fan, as the winged scavenger glides in for a landing on one of the dish-shaped antennas.

* * *

146 DOUGLAS STREET
FRIDAY, OCTOBER 18,1991 — 12:37 PM

After downing a baloney sandwich and a Dr. Pepper for lunch, plus an apple, Mandy dutifully unpacks the rest of the groceries then puts the laundry away. As she places a pair of jeans into her dresser, she notices her blue Scofield Bible in the rear of the drawer. Digging it out, she takes it down the hall to the master bedroom, to the study desk. She opens to the Book of Psalms:

> Have mercy upon me, O God.... Wash me thoroughly from mine iniquity, and cleanse me from my sin.... Create in me a clean heart, O God, and renew a right spirit within me.... Restore unto me the joy of thy salvation....

THE SILVER CORD

* * *

I reckon I'll report to practice early today, Bryan tells himself, as he exits Professor Emerson's English Composition class. *I just hafta swing by and get Steve at Fletcher H—no, wait a minute, I gotta get my bat, the new one I took home with me last night. I forgot it this morning. I just hope my eye doesn't go wacky again, or it won't matter what bat I use.*

Leaving Draper Center, amid the usual gaggle of students, he hoofs it across Founders Mall headed for the parking lot behind Alexander Hall (off Spangler). He parks there when the campus is crowded. Warm sun, grassy space, spicy autumn aromas: as he strides along the diagonal sidewalk, he feels suddenly confident about his eye, and baseball—especially since they play an intersquad game almost every session now: *Coach McKinney says I can hit well enough to start in the spring, and I reckon I can buttress that opinion with some good licks today.*

* * *

146 DOUGLAS STREET
FRIDAY, OCTOBER 18, 1991 — 2:18 PM

Grabbing her gray-poplin windbreaker, Mandy Howard hustles out the back door. It's warm out compared to this morning, upper 60s at least, but it could be breezy in the bleachers at Ferrell Field. Bryan's already in the truck. She didn't expect to see him until *after* practice, but now she can ride with him back to campus instead of taking the Firebird. She hops in.

"A weird thing happened today," he tells her, after starting the engine. "It sorta bugged me at first, but not now." Pushing his Spindle Tiger hat back, he dimples, giving an awh-shucks shrug.

"What was it?" she asks, wadding the windbreaker in her lap.

Cranking his neck, he shifts into reverse. "Wait a minute."

It has to be less than good for him to bring it up, Mandy concludes to herself, as he backs the truck between the hedges then down the incline onto Douglas Street. The prospect of some new problem places additional drag on her own spirit, which has been fighting a headwind since her mom called this morning. She even has mixed feelings about her plans for tonight, the surprise for Bryan. It's like yesterday all over again, though so far today she's hid her blah, out-of-kilter mood from her husband. That's not saying much, since they've hardly been together, just the ten minutes he's been home from class, yet she did mention, matter-of-factly, the telephone conversation she had with her mother.

"C'mon, you big jock," Mandy presses, as they head west on

382

Douglas, "whaddeyuh talking about?"

"Like I say, it's weird; it happened in calculus class."

Between Douglas and Fletcher Hall, he tells his wife about the brief episode of blurred vision, the gist of the story then the details. Arriving at the dorm, they park by the side door.

"It's probably a fluky, one-time thing," Mandy offers, giving an upbeat smile and nod, tossing her ponytail. She scarcely feels upbeat, but she hopes her mood will rise to match her pretense, though it's an uphill struggle, and *most* out of character. "After all, babe, you've been super healthy ever since you got out of the hospital, and all your tests have been—"

"Well, dude, this's what I *like* to see!" Steve Jordan booms, his bassy drawl stopping her midsentence. "Y'got the wife with yuh ... and Coach Weaver says he's givin' me three innin's of work today." He tosses his bag into the back then hauls himself up into the truck. Mandy squeezes over toward her husband as much as she can. Jordan guffaws; he snuffles and snorts; he rubs his nose; he laughs some more—he sounds like a horse slobbering. She snickers as well, Bryan too.

Maybe this day's gonna turn out good after all? she tells herself. *It's hard to feel depressed while Steve's around.* The afternoon seems suddenly brighter, sunnier. She remains less than ebullient, but eighty percent sure feels better than the forty-sixty funk she's been in since her mama called.

"I appreciate the ride, dude," the big guy goes on, as they head east on Spangler, "'specially since I haven't been able to return the favor this week." He gives another belly laugh. "But the guy at the body shop says my Bronco'll be ready on Monday, so I can give yuh a ride if yuh need it—'course, I reckon the fall season's gonna be over next Friday, but I'll still come by to see you guys from time to time. Yessir ... and I'll bring that movie, *The Natural*, and we can watch it again on your VCR." Removing his red Ardmore cap, he shakes his shaggy head, shaggy save for the balding top. "It's damn amazin' that I could do $1900 worth of damage in the parkin' lot at Burger King. I reckon I shoulda paid better attention. I never saw that dadgum dump truck when I was backin', and 'fore I knew it, my back window was shattered and ever'thang was crumpled up, and the Whopper I was eatin' was *all* over me. Good thang I got insurance."

Replacing the hat, he slaps his massive thigh. "But I'd rather thank about today's intersquad action. Now, Miss Mandy, I'm gonna show yuh some *real* heat, even more'n last Monday, plus I been workin' on a split-finger job that drops faster than a tur—I mean uh ... it drops *dang* fast." They share a laugh, as he rubs up an imaginary baseball over the dash then demonstrates the split-finger grip. "Now Clemens has a great splitter, and he positions the seams just like I do. It's a *gosh*dang shame he hasn't made it into the Series since '86, and they blew it that year. Y'know, when Mookie Wilson hit that grounder through Buckner's legs ... but I don't thank it's fair to put *all* the blame on Buckner. It was Bob Stanley too—he did a piss-poor relief job. The Red Sox are fickle I tellyuh, but the Rangers are even worse. And this year we gotta watch dadgum Atlanta and Minnesota. Yessir ... we gotta damn mediocre Series agoin'—so y'thank the Bears can break their losing streak tomorrow at the Homecoming game? *Heck,* I know high-school football teams that play better defense, like the Ada Cougars back in Oklahoma, and Jamal agrees. *Ard*more might even give 'em a tough time—but Baylor should be able to beat the damn Rice Owls." Jordan laughs, another tubalike haw-haw-haw; he paws the air. "Heck, Mandy, you smell *real* good. Didyuh just get outta the shower or sumpthin'?"

"Not hardly," she chortles. "I just naturally smell rosy and sweet, which is more than I can say for *you* guys."

* * *

FERRELL FIELD COMPLEX
FRIDAY, OCTOBER 18, 1991 — 5:37 PM

Exiting the clubhouse, Bryan hustles over to his pickup. Jordan left with Jamal (the football team had a short workout, so Jamal came over to watch his Ardmore buddy pitch three shutout innings). "Well, mister," Mandy banters as Bryan gets in, "your eye sure worked this afternoon. You nailed *every*thing they threw up there. Dang, I wish I could hit ropes like that."

He dimples. "Yeah, I felt real good at the plate, and in the field too. I mean, I saw the ball as sharp as ever."

She grins as well, her goofy grin; her blue eyes beam. "But I reckon it's good that Steve pitched for *your* side. He may have a gut, but he can sure bring it. He'd be hard to hit no matter how good you're seeing the ball. Heck, he'd be hard to hit with radar." They both laugh, as the old Chevy chugs across the parking lot.

"It is *weird* though, what happened in calculus today."

"I doubt it's serious. It's probably just a lingering part of the healing process ... but y'hafta go for a check-up anyhow?"

"Yeah, I'm supposed to see Dr. Nadler in Dallas the first week of November, the sixth I think."

"Well, I'll make sure I'm off that day, so I can go with yuh, then we can do something after, like going out to eat. If I have classes that night, it won't hurt to miss—I haven't missed *any*."

As they accelerate southbound on Rigby, good vibes well up in Bryan's bosom. Mandy seems back to normal: frisky, affectionate, cheerful—unlike last night.

THE SILVER CORD

* * *

A minute or so later, they turn right on Verner Street. "Where yuh going, babe?" Mandy inquires.

He nods toward the center of campus. "To the cafeteria."

"Oh, I wanted to eat at home tonight. I toldjuh, re*mem*ber?"

"But we *al*ways eat at the caf," he replies matter-of-factly, "except on weekends?"

"I know, honey ... but I wanna *make* supper tonight."

Bryan gives an open-handed gesture. "What's the point? We can eat for practically *nothing* here—gotta stay on budget."

Mandy's mood crumbles. *I can't handle this,* she declares to herself, as Bryan continues west on Verner. A simple spilling of the beans about the surprise she's planning will surely change his mind, but she has bigger monsters to deal with; the cafeteria thing has merely called them back on stage. While watching the practice game, she thought she'd triumphed over her anxious discontent, but it's now coming back. Tears well up; she fights them off. *He doesn't get it. He doesn't know what I'm going through.* She aches to confess her angst, to tell everything, but she can't, she can't. She can't get the plug out of the keg.

"I wanna go *home*," she complains out loud, venting genuine emotion but evading the beasts. Bryan proceeds nonetheless, pulling into the parking lot behind the Bill Daniel Student Center. Mandy blows out a muted whistle, a perturbed *pfou!*

Easing to a halt in front of a medium-sized oak that stands sentry at the near corner of the lot, he cuts the engine, but he doesn't open the door, nor does he remove the keys from the ignition. She cracks her window a couple of inches. The air rushes out of the cab leaving *ice* in its wake—frosty silence.

I wish it was last winter, Mandy yearns to herself, as she fiddles with the zipper on her windbreaker. *Things were simple and straightforward then—for both of us.* A blue jay flits about amid the lowers branches of the oak tree. *Why can't I be bouncy and free like that bird?* The jay, cocking his crested head, gives Mandy the eye, as if tuning into her thoughts. *He feels right at home on this campus, like happy and bold. It doesn't bother him that he's not a student, or that he hasn't been to church in ages.* A nervous *rat-ah-tat-tat* draws her attention back inside the Chevy. Bryan finger-taps the padded, blue-vinyl dash, playing a few one-handed riffs—he leaves dark prints in the grayish veneer of Texas dust. After a last *rat-ah-tat*, he slumps back, stretching his jockish arms toward the windshield; a thread dangles from the frayed half-sleeve of the old underjersey. Giving a quick grimace, he grips the top of the steering wheel with both hands, as if trying to wring water out of it. Mandy sighs ruefully, but her words remain silent: *He's sure being stubborn about this cafeteria business. His mood has CERTAINLY soured since we left the baseball field—but SO has mine.* Biting her upper lip, she makes a hissy, sucking sound. The blue jay takes flight, thrashing skyward amid a series of strident shrieks: a bugle call confirming that hostilities have commenced.

Bryan fidgets with the bill of his cap; he twists his mouth, pursing his lips to one side then the other, as if about to issue his complaint, yet he issues nothing but a breathy little murmur. After rotating his posture a trifle, to face more toward his wife, he arches his brows, giving a look of baffled apprehension. His beautiful green eyes appear darker, duller, almost gray, like the ocean on a cloudy day, a sure sign he's troubled, as she's learned over this past year. She looks away. Her silence is hurting him, and things have to get worse before they get better.

Some campus litterbug has discarded a McDonald's cup in the scrubby strip of grass alongside Verner Street. It still sports a plastic lid and straw. She pictures stagnant water inside, from melted ice. She wishes she was carefree like the blue jay, but she identifies more with the out-of-place cup. The breeze sighs at her window. It smells like October, that dry, tangy, corn-husk aroma she associates with the start of basketball each year, especially *last* fall, when the days were growing shorter, and cooler, and then the phone rang—Bryan. But she won't be playing basketball this year, and the spicy fragrance of autumn makes her sad, not glad—ever since yesterday. *Oh gosh, I don't wanna think about it.* And then came the Harvest Hayride, and the necking sessions in the barn. Their love-story caught fire, consuming all, growing more wonderful with each chapter, even the hospital chapter, and then—*No, no, I can't think about it.*

A mustard-colored Volkswagen putts by on Verner, an old-fashioned beetle conveying a pair of laughing coeds to some happy destination, or so Mandy surmises: *Those college gals look so cool and hip. But I'm just seventeen. I'm not even out of high school.* She hears again her mom's voice on the phone: *"You're finishing your senior year at night school, like some kind of delinquent dropout. How canyuh get a basketball scholarship, when you're not even playing this season?"*

Mandy's throat burns. *Life sucks, and I have no one to blame but myself. No, it's partly his fault too. We shoulda waited until next July. I'm not eighteen; I'm seventeen. Let God be true but every man a liar—Mama's right; I have fallen away.* Beyond Verner Street, the imposing facade of Moody Library looms at the far end of Fountain Mall; it looks yellow-gold in the fading sunlight. The majestic edifice, with its mall and fountain, brings to mind the Book of Revelation, the New Jerusalem, the Great Judgment. *I'm not eighteen. It was a LIE to put it down on that marriage thing. I'm outta control, and it's a sin to LIE. God is not mocked. Whatsoever a man shall sow, that shall he—what the hell's wrong with me? I'm freaking and going hyperspiritual.*

THE SILVER CORD

Or maybe it's really God ... and he's trying to tell me something?

* * *

Bryan drums his fingers some more, this time on the steering wheel. The knife has returned, from this morning, chasing *all* the good vibes he was feeling at practice. Mandy continues to look the other way, out her window. No goofy grin, no beaming eyes. He can't see her face, but he can feel her scowl. *I wonder what she's thinking?* he says to himself. *But no way is she gonna tell me, not when she's in this pissy kind of mood.*

"I'm sorry," he offers aloud.

No reply.

"Really ... I am. We can eat at home if yuh want."

No reply.

He extends his hands in a beseeching, palms-up manner, a futile gesture, futile because she can't see him. "But, Mandy, there's no reason for us to get all huffy with each other?"

No reply—she turns more toward the window, giving him the coldest shoulder possible.

O Jesus God, not this again, he laments to himself amid stabs of pain, the knife hacking deeper. *And she was just laughing and smiling a little while ago.* Giving a wounded murmur, he fiddles with the keys, flicking them with his finger. They jingle and jangle clangorously— off-beat cymbals and chimes and cow bells, or so it seems in the frigidly silent pickup. *There IS something bothering her? It's the same as last night. I mean, she was out there looking at the damn moon.* He abandons the keys; the clangor ceases—but the demons remain, the same dagger- wielding devils he wrestled all morning.

"We can eat at home," he repeats, staying with the supper issue. "It's no biggie." He dares not divulge his deeper fears, lest she confirm them.

She rolls down her window all the way, but gives no response.

"C'mon, Mandy, I didn't realize."

No reply.

"Let's go to the house. C'mon ... I didn't realize."

Still no reply.

Shit, I hate this. I wish she'd say something, anything. Her stony silence threatens, reinforcing his bathyal dread. He gazes at her disheveled ponytail as it drapes the collar of her shirt, her tawny-brown Aztec shirt. Then he focuses on the pink, baby-soft flesh at the nape of her neck. *O Jesus, I can't live without her.*

Spasms of rage wrench him. He needs to shriek and cuss, to cuss God, to cuss her, to cuss himself. He needs to smash something, the dash, the windshield, the tape deck, but he refrains. He goes gentle instead, caressing her back. She stiffens at his touch: a shapely block of granite. She twists away all the more, contorting her neck muscles.

His heart keels over like a torpedoed ship: "Oh, pretty lady, why're we fighting over *this*?"

* * *

Because we need a REASON to fight, Mandy replies, but only to herself, *and we're not ready to put the real REASONS out on the table. And I reckon you know this just as well as I do.*

His bottled-up anger heats her neck, or so it seems. She senses his resentment and vexation. For that matter, it vexes *her*, her coldness, her turning away, her turtlelike manner of withdrawing, of hiding inside a shell of silence—all of which adds to her guilt: *He should YELL at me, and scream—I deserve it..*

Yet he offers again the olive branch: "C'mon, honey, let's go to the house. I'm sorry."

Mandy scarcely hears him, as she wallows: *I'm a sorry excuse for a wife. I'm a pissy-faced bitch, a stiff-necked witch, a selfish oversexed brat, and a big-time LIAR.* A country song—Waylon Jennings and "Good Hearted Woman"—wafts across the parking lot on the breeze, emanating from some nearby dorm. She normally likes this song, but not today. *Mama's right. The heart is deceitful above all things ... and who can know it?*

Removing her softball cap, she wads it and twists it. Moody Library melts in the distance, as fresh tears well up, a few spilling down her cheek. A tell-all confession gathers hotly in her bosom.

* * *

"It must be your *mother*?" Bryan argues huffily, as he slumps against his door—he's given up on the contrite approach, yet he manages to keep most of his indignation in the bottle. "The telephone call this morning ... it musta *pissed* you off, what she said about selling the Firebird?"

Mandy puts her hat back on, but she says nothing.

"Well, maybe you should *listen* to her. After all, she *is* more experienced about running a house and keeping a budget." Forget his true feelings, forget the unfairness of this attack, to hell with his conscience—he's ready to hype and spin, to lie and half-lie, whatever it takes to end this dreadful silence, even if he has to spout Mama-knows-best bullshit.

No reply from his ponytailed wife—her loosely replaced cap sits atop the ponytail; it's not hanging out the back like usual.

"Let's face it, Amanda, she's *right*. We can't be foolish when it comes to spending. That's why we eat at the caf in the first place. And I'm sure we could manage with *one* car."

Silence, nothing. He's pressing all the buttons, to no avail.

"WHAT THE FUCK IS EATING YOU!" he howls, slapping the dash—*KA-WHAP!* He hits it so hard he loses all feeling in his hand.

THE SILVER CORD

"You're acting like a GODDAM *RE*TARD!"

Instantly regretting, he fears the worst. But instead, she falls sobbing into his arms, her hat tumbling off behind her.

*   *   *

Same evening, 6:28 p.m. "Now, I wantcha to go *right* upstairs," Mandy commands mirthfully at the house, as Bryan follows her into the kitchen. She giggles then sniffles. "And y'can't come down until *I* say."

Tossing the truck keys onto the counter, he can't help but dimple. "Gosh, pretty lady, you sound like my mother."

She blushes, doing her cute nose-crinkling routine. Her eyes gleam happily despite the puffy redness left behind by the sobbing. "And y'better not sneak down, mister, or peek around." She gives him a smirky kiss along with a fond pat on the behind. "Go on, get outta here." She pushes him playfully into the stairwell vestibule, closing the kitchen door behind him.

As he hustles up the stairs, his conscience chides: *Y'were a stubborn ass about the caf. You shoulda remembered about tonight—she DID tellyuh, yesterday, or was it Wednesday?* He heads into the bathroom, being careful to turn on the light, and to *lift* the seat. *But things are A-OK now.* After emptying his bladder, he goes down the hall to their room. Sprawling on the bed, he gazes happily at the ceiling, at the glassy unlit light fixture which resembles a soup bowl. The gathering darkness outside has grayed the windows—it's almost night but not quite.

I smell something good, he tells himself dozily some twenty minutes later, *and it's making me hungry—damn, this has been one heck of a day, up and down, down and up. It's like two weeks ago when the twister hit. Nawh, it was hardly that bad ... then again, in some ways it's more scary.* Yet he never did confess his fears, nor did she; they just hugged and cooed while her sobbing subsided, then she snuggled close as they drove home.

*   *   *

Later—7:29 p.m. Bryan, working on his forth pork chop, grins boyishly at his bride, his green eyes sparking in the candlelight. A giddy rush floods her bosom. She can scarcely contain her joyous affection, not to mention her swelling desire, as she watches him eat, his fingers and lips getting all greasy. Putting down the chop, he wipes his fingers on his napkin then dabs his mouth. Turning to his string beans, he finishes them off: three quick bites.

She's almost ready to pounce on him, to take him down on the braided rug, right here in the O'Shea's dining room, with its polished-walnut table and chairs, and matching china hutch and high-legged buffet. But wherever they do it, it's going to be *super* good. The anticipation makes her quake. She loves him so, wants him so—the sobbing fit in the pickup unlocked a secret depth inside her, a chamber of unchecked delight. *Jesus,* she exults to herself, *I feel like I'm on a drug. I may come out of my body—my first OBE.* She giggles aloud at the thought.

"Whaddeyuh laughing about?" he kids, scooping the last of his mashed potatoes and gravy with his fork, aided by the crescent roll.

"Oh, nuthin'. I'll tellyuh later. Better yet, I'll *show* yuh later." More laughing, both of them. Her cheeks go warm. He blushes as well, dimpling into a big grin. He gestures with his half-eaten roll. He's got the message, the gist of her flirting. He sips his wine. She does the same then shifts—to cool things a bit: "So y'like my surprise d'yuh?"

Bryan takes a bite of roll then attacks again his last pork chop, getting the tender part near the bone. "Oh, pretty lady, this supper is *de*licious," he replies thickly, his mouth stuffed. "Y'really got a good 'do' on these chops. They're spicy and crusty yet tender—I love 'em."

Mandy grins with pride, nodding toward the kitchen. "Awh ... it's just Shake'n Bake."

"Well, my mom never made 'em this good, and it's awesome to eat in this room, and y'got candles and wine to boot. I just feel bad about the fight we had. I shoulda remem—"

"C'mon, you big jock, stop apologizing. You already did, like five times." She pushes her roll at him—she's done save for the roll. "All things work together for good ... 'member? That spat just makes us appreciate our two-week anniversary *all* the more."

"So tell me, Mrs. Howard, how'd you pull this off? This's dadgum ballsy, even for you, eating in this off-limits room, and sipping white wine?"

She lifts her goblet. "It's not just *any* wine, my dear. This's Robert Mondavi California Chardonnay, the best white wine in the USA. Some even rate it above French Chardonnay."

"Goshdang, pretty lady, you've come a long way since we ate at Tony's ... that first night."

"Well, I must confess I did have a little help—from Chris, and Tracy."

Bryan laughs. "I figured as much."

"No, I told Chris that I wanted to do something special to surprise you, to celebrate our first two weeks, and he suggested we use this dining room—he said Annie wouldn't mind, for just one night. He says she's a hopeless romantic anyway—down deep. He also got the candleholders out for me, from that buffet behind yuh, plus the linen tablecloth and the goblets."

"And the wine? No way would any store sell it to *you*?"

"Tracy got it for me. She just turned twenty-one, so she's legal. And she also gave me the recipe for the icing?"

"Icing?"

"Yep, wait a second." Mandy disappears through the swinging door into the kitchen (there's usually a stop under it, so it won't swing). She returns with a lemon-colored cake. "Happy anniversary," she announces. "It looks like lemon icing, but it's actually banana—that's the recipe she gave me, and she suggested I get marble cake, which is a Betty Crocker mix."

* * *

"Oh, babe, I don't wanna ever fight again," Mandy purrs four hours later, as the exhausted newlyweds cuddle in their bed.

"Me neither," Bryan sighs wearily, but happily, amid the still-warm aromas of marathon sex, a perspiry mingling of sweat and musky pheromones, male and female. *O Jesus,* he adds to himself, *I never knew she could go so long ... or me.* They've just recovered from a third session of screwing. They commenced on the sofa, while watching TV (*Perfect Strangers*, on ABC), then they moved to the living-room floor for round two. The third, unexpected, fit of passion started in the bathroom and culminated in their bed.

Rolling over to face him, she smirks in the dim light. "But then again, Wendy says that sex is always better after making up. She and Jerry used to boff their brains out after fighting all day."

Bryan gives his wife a fond pat on the butt, through the covers. "I'd say she's pretty much right. At least about you."

"*Me?*"

"Yeah, you. I never saw you so wild, not even in Galveston."

"Well, mister, y'weren't exactly *calm.* I reckon this's what happens when we *skip* a night." They share a muffled laugh.

"It's hard to believe you're only *seven*teen. Gosh, Spanky says that girls don't reach their peak until they're in their thirties. Shhh-eesh, gal ... you have thirteen years to go, before you even get to thirty." Rolling onto his back, he stretches and yawns. "You wore me out. It's like you were *in*satiable."

"And I'm *still* hungry," she flirts, giving him a catlike nibble under the chin. "In fact, mister, I bet I can get you up again."

"No way. My spirit may be willing but my flesh is *done.*"

A patchy sheet of light shudders across the ceiling, as a car slows on Douglas Street then buzzes up the driveway. "That must be Chris," Mandy says.

"Yeah, there's no mistaking that Chevette of his."

"I hope y'left him room." (They park their vehicles well to the right, so Chris will have room to get into the garage.)

"I did. It's hard to get the rear of my truck all the way over, where the driveway narrows, but he's good at getting around me."

"It must be midnight, or after. I wonder where he's been?" She gives a devilish giggle. "Maybe he has Tracy with him, and they're gonna do *it* in his apartment?"

"What'd you say?"

"Y'know? He's gonna boff her, screw her—they're gonna *fuck* ... just like we been doing."

"Wow-*wee*," Bryan chortles, sweeping his hand above them, like a circus barker. "You *are* ballsy tonight, saying the f-word, and serving wine, and going wild on me since nine-fifteen."

"C'mon, we did rest some."

"Yeah, like five minutes ... while I was in the shower."

"So y'want me to act modest and de*mure* ... like a good little *Bap*tist wife?" Snuffling and laughing, they wrestle and tickle and paw each other, tangling the covers, twisting the pillows.

After settling, finally, Bryan backpedals, "No, I reckon Chris was working late at the lab. He does a lot of late-night analysis for Dr. Richardson, when the mainframe is free and working fast. And I don't reckon he's sleeping with Tracy. Last I heard, she's still nuts over that guy at LSU. Chris dated her a couple of times after they first met, but it never worked. He's in love with that Jennifer girl. But this's *old* news ... I toldjuh all about it."

"Yeah, they do treat each other like siblings ... and yet she *does* come over here a lot?"

"Well, I reckon they give each other emotional support?"

"So do *you* find her attractive?"

"Get outta here," he laughs, despite an instant recollection of Tracy's flesh, from that first time at the Bear's Paw when she came over to the table, in her baggy T-shirt and khaki shorts.

Mandy giggles. "I'm just putting you on, you big jock—but she's not bad looking for a tall, chunky ex-hoopster."

She's certainly fuckable, Bryan agrees, but only to himself. *She has sexy thighs to be sure—yet there's no way in hell, pretty lady, or heaven, that she could MATCH your mating skills.* He's tempted to repeat this out loud but quickly decides against it.

"She got cut from the Lady Bears y'know?" Mandy goes on.

"That's what I hear," he replies, sleepily, innocently.

THE SILVER CORD

CHAPTER TWENTY-THREE

146 DOUGLAS STREET
SATURDAY, OCTOBER 19, 1991 — 5:53 PM

Bryan Howard, clad only in his briefs and baseball underjersey, stands at the kitchen counter, a peanut-butter-and-jelly sandwich in one hand, a mug of milk in the other. He ate a hot dog at the football game (Baylor finally ended their losing streak, beating hapless Rice 21-13), then he had a burrito at the Bear's Paw, plus nuts and chips and two beers, but he's hungry anyway, almost faint, after another torrid session with his spunky, sex-crazed wife, who just rushed off in the Firebird, racing for Denny's.

"Oh, babe honey, I want you *now*," she confessed breathily, huskily, as he kissed her good-bye at the top of the stairs. "No way can I wait till ten o'clock." She unzipped him, found him, fondled him. "O Jesus God, you're *so* big, your knob. I love it, how it pulses and turns purple." The next thing he knew, she was in the living room, in the overstuffed chair, hips forward, her panties on the floor. "Hey, big boy, lemme show yuh what I got." Teasing like a stripper, she slowly raised her waitress skirt to reveal her secret furrow, as it nestled pinkly amid the springy, ginger-brown moss, darkly potent pubic moss.

Bryan chuckles then finishes off the sandwich.

* * *

6:22 p.m. Young Mr. Howard, now dressed save for his sneakers, tackles a chemistry problem in the master bedroom:

> A cylinder contains 200 moles of an ideal, mon-atomic gas at 0°C and 100 atm. It expands until the pressure is 1.00 atm. If the expansion is adiabatic and reversible, what is the final temperature?

Finding the formula $\{3/2R \ln (T2/T1) = -R \ln (V2/V1)\}$, he puts in the data then reaches for his calculator, but the LCD display fades and flickers. He slaps it a couple of times, to no avail. He removes then reinserts the two AAA batteries—still bad. *These dadgum things are shot. Maybe Chris has some? I should go down and ask him. Nawh, he's probably still at the Bear's Paw. I never heard that buzz-bomb Chevette come in.*

No problem: he's actually glad the calculator died. It gives him a good excuse to ignore his homework. He'd much rather think about Mandy, how she moaned and shuddered and clawed his back when she climaxed on his lap. He ended up under her in the overstuffed chair. *Spanky's right. Girls DO crave it. You'd never suspect it, the way all the babes back at Spindle High always acted so modest and under control, plus the girls at church. But Mandy has SURE taught me a thing or two.* He gives a happy whistle, a whispery hiss. *It's like our honeymoon has resumed full blast, after hitting a few speed bumps Thursday and Friday. For that matter, it's better now than EVER. And it's gonna be good, this whole year ... our whole life in fact.*

Closing the chemistry text, he teeters back in the chair. *But right now I can't think past ten-fifteen ... when she gets home. She's so sassy and uncorked, ever since we made up last night—even in PUBLIC.* He chuckles, as he harkens back to the Bear's Paw this afternoon where Mandy caressed him beneath the table between sips of her beer (yes, she had beer; Tracy and Chris ordered a huge pitcher of draft, enough for all the under-agers). The others must've noticed the newlyweds in action; there were seven in their party at the big corner booth: Bryan, Mandy, Chris, Tracy, Jamie (Tracy's roommate), Steve J. and Susie (Steve's girlfriend who came down from Wichita Falls). A big-busted redhead with a thousand freckles on her face, Susie seems a perfect match for Steve, mothering him, waiting on him, listening to him, and listening to him. And despite the freckles, she's cutely attractive, in a cowgirl sort of way. The Howards were the first to leave, since Mandy had to go to work.

* * *

Next morning, very early, 4:44 a.m. Bryan, up to relieve himself, savors the dream he had while asleep—*No, that was no dream,* he corrects himself. A warm upwelling reinforces this realization. *It actually happened, starting the moment she got home from Denny's.* He hid in the closet again, to surprise her, and this time it worked wildly and wondrously. Continuing a good part of the night, it even surpassed their first glorious encounter, that honeymoon night after the tornado. He didn't leave his body, but she surely took his soul, and flesh, on a rapturous flight.

I never saw her so happy and free, he declares to himself, as he flushes the toilet. *It's like she's lost all her inhibitions since Friday when she cried in the truck.*

* * *

WACO, TEXAS - RIVER ROAD CHRISTIAN ASSEMBLY
SUNDAY, OCTOBER 20, 1991 — 11:31 AM

I don't really care for this guy, Mandy reacts to herself, as Pastor Greg Lawrence reads from Second Samuel Chapter Twelve. *Why the heck did we come here anyway?* She follows the text nonetheless, in her little white Bible which is open on the lap of her dress, her lavender shirtdress—this's the first time she's been out of jeans since she got to Waco. Ditto for Bryan, as he sits beside her in a sport shirt and slacks.

THE SILVER CORD

Amber brick, arched beams, high windows, oak paneling: the church looks and smells new, like Pleasant Hill Baptist, but this sanctuary seats twice as many. "God judged King David because of his great sin with Bathsheba," Pastor Lawrence intones, continuing his sermon. Fair-cheeked and very blond, the sturdily-built minister looks Scandinavian, though his drawl is definitely Texas. "And yet, verse fifteen tells us that the judgment also fell on the babe, the son that Bathsheba bore unto David."

Eager-faced young adults (Baylor students no doubt) abound in the polished-oak pews. Marvin Latrobe, the most eager of all, sits on the other side of Bryan. The bespectacled floor proctor has been with the Howards ever since he spotted them out front before service. "Praise the Lord!" he exclaimed proudly. "Look who's here. This's surely an answer to prayer." He laughed and grinned and beamed, showing his disgusting yellow teeth.

The pastor pauses to sip water, from a green-tinted glass. "If you're a New Covenant believer, born-again and washed in the blood, you cannot lose your salvation; you cannot suffer the second death, the Lake of Fire in Revelation 19:14. That being said, God never ignores iniquity and lukewarm devotion. If you stubbornly defy the Lord, you can, and will, suffer chastisement in Hebrews 12:7. This's not a judgment in the legal sense, because every believer possesses imputed righteousness forever based on the blood transaction at Calvary. It's more like a fatherly spanking, a divine action designed to get you back into God's army, back into his perfect will in Romans 12:2." The blond minister preaches with a drawl, yet his diction is precise, his tone intimidating. "Only when you 'seek *first* the kingdom of God,' in Matthew 6:33, can you experience the fullness of Christ and the peace and joy of the Holy Spirit. If you stray, the Lord must do whatever is necessary to correct you. Chastisement may well result in personal pain ... depression, humiliating defeat, financial ruin ... or sickness or injury. God brought such consequences into David's life ... as the Psalms surely attest."

Pastor Lawrence does not pace like Pastor Ron, but as he speaks, he scans the congregation with a penetrating blue-eyed gaze in the manner of Billy Graham: "If you refuse to repent after God has chastised you personally, he may be forced to bring painful, even dire, consequences to your loved ones, as he did with David when he struck the child with sickness unto death. This may seem drastic and unfair, but God's ways are not our ways, nor can he deviate from his nature, which is *per*fect love. He likewise cannot deviate when it comes to instilling eternal values in his children." The pastor pauses to let the words sink in. "So if you defy the Lord, beyond *pers*onal chastisement, don't be surprised if bad things start happening in the lives of those dear to you, as it did with King David."

THE SILVER CORD

* * *

Giving Marv a good-bye salute, Bryan eases the pickup out of the church lot. "That sermon sucks," Mandy declares, as they accelerate on River Road. "I don't wanna go *there* again."

"Fine with me. It was *hard*nosed ... like over the line."

No reply from his wife.

Passing under I-35, they turn right on Dutton Street, entering the Baylor campus, the quickest route home—still nothing from Mandy. He offers a few more remarks concerning Marv's pastor, but she remains mute, her eyes gazing straight ahead. Alarm bells, sinking feeling. *Oh no,* he laments, as they turn left on Verner, *she's shutting down again ... just like Friday—we're even on the same street. And this weekend was going so good.* He fears that her silence is directed at him, a less than rational fear, but love and reason cannot exist at the same time—or so it seems.

* * *

Same day—5:06 p.m. The Cowboys score again, increasing their lead over the Broncos to 31-14 with eight minutes to go. *I'd say Dallas has this one safely in their column,* Bryan concludes, as he mutes the post-TD commercials. *I reckon I gotta get my ass off this sofa anyhow. I got four hours of homework.* Sitting up, he kills the TV then downs the last handful of chips from the Fritos bag. *But considering what's going on around here, it's mighty hard to concentrate on gaseous expansion or the goshdang Articles of Confederation.* He laughs boyishly, as he pads to the bathroom. *Oh, Mandy, Mandy, you're too much. Sheeesh ... did I ever misread you in the truck today.*

As they drove home from church, Bryan feared her silence, but once inside the house, she was anything but moody. They never even made it up the stairs, as they mated madly on the kitchen floor—a first!—amid their hastily shed Sunday clothes.

Flushing the toilet, he proceeds to his desk in the O'Shea's bedroom. He laughs. *Good thing she's working a double, or I wouldn't have time to do this.* Back to chemistry—dead batteries, no LCD display. *Dang, I forgot. This calculator doesn't work.*

* * *

"Yeah, med school is like boot camp," Chris Hansen quips a few minutes later, as he searches for batteries in the bottom drawer of his computer desk, "not to mention the goddamn application process. I've been working on this for a week, and I'm still not finished, and I have Dr. Edelstein's string-theory modeling exam tomorrow." He gives a smirky laugh. "I may be up the whole damn night." When Bryan knocked on the door, he found the mustached junior hunched over his kitchen table, filling out at a stack of forms from Harvey Cushing Medical School in Houston.

"I reckon it *is* like joining the Army," the freshman replies, giving a snuffly chuckle. "I can see that I have a *long* road ahead of me ... before *I* become a doctor."

"You got that right, and I still have to get all my references lined up—it's also political, like who you know. I'm just glad I scored well on my M-cats."

"M-cats?"

"M-C-A-T ... Medical College Aptitude Tests: it's like the SATs, but for medical school." He searches a third drawer. "Ahah ... I knew I had some triple-A's." He grabs an unopened package of four. "Here," he says, nodding his head impishly like he does, "take the whole pack."

"Thanks, I'll buy some for yuh tomorrow, to replace these."

"Ah fuck, don't worry about it. Stop being so goddamn fair and equitable. We've got bigger things ahead of us than making sure we're even on batteries. At least, I hope so." Bryan dimples, his face heating, his usual reaction to these good-natured put-downs. Chris, his brown eyes twinkling, gives the freshman a friendly punch on the arm. "You just can't get that Baptist sense of duty out of you, can you?" They share a laugh, as the puckish junior returns to his paperwork. Bryan heads for the door, but Chris stops him. "You know, slugger, you don't have to be a goddamn MD to study the mysteries of the human mind."

This comment elicits a few questions from Bryan, which lead to an extended conversation about the pros and cons of a medical career versus that of a research scientist, along with a few smirky digressions, by Chris, into sex and young pussy, how med students get a lot, then he shifted to the crop of "sweet young things" at the Bear's Paw after the game yesterday—no way can he avoid this subject for more than ten minutes at a time.

It's past six when Bryan finally departs, with Chris's counsel (the serious part) still warm in his mind: "Now, slugger, don't sell yourself short. You're gifted, and you have a passionate self-interest in the whole physical-metaphysical issue, for obvious reasons.... Why bog yourself down with the demands of being an MD, much less a neurosurgeon? As a pure scientist, you'll have a better chance of discovering the brain-soul link, the 'silver cord' as you call it, not to speak of the other big questions related to the existence of a transcendent reality. And you could stay right here at Baylor. Doc Richardson's graduate program is one of the finest in the country."

As Bryan heads across the patio toward the back door, he runs into Tracy McCollum coming through the slatted gate, an Arby's bag in one hand, a book satchel in the other. "Howdy, Bryan," she chirps. She smiles and blushes; she tosses her head, whipping her bangs to the side. He smells french fries.

"Oh, hi," he responds, returning the grin, and the blush—he feels himself dimpling and warming, as if they're back at the corner booth yesterday, and Mandy has her hand between his legs under the table.

"I was just out there with Chris. I had to borrow these batteries." He shows her the pack. "He's filling out a bunch of paperwork for medical school."

"I know. I'm gonna help him, then we're gonna cram for Dr. Edelstein's *big* exam." She sighs, shaking her head. "And I don't even *need* that course, now that I'm back to nursing—so you're looking swell, Bryan. But I reckon y'should, considering." She twists her prim Irish mouth into a smirk—it grows into a titter. "I really *like* Mandy. She's young ... yet smart and fun to be with, and I can tell she doesn't take any shit ... pardon my language. But you guys have a *good* thing ... I can tell."

* * *

Next day (Monday), 12:40 p.m. The phone rings. Mandy answers. It's her mom, who gets right to the point: "Amanda Fay, I'm putting my foot down. I've prayed about all this, and I no longer have *any* doubts. It's not God's *will* for you to be in Waco—and what's more, I know you *lied* about your age in Louisiana. Y'gotta be eighteen. Charlie called Baton Rouge." Hot pangs of guilt: a freight train lumbers through Mandy's brain. Her legs go wobbly; her cheeks burn; tears well; she can't breathe. "Your marriage isn't legal," Helen goes on, her words propelled by a self-righteous hiss. "So there's no point in prolonging this fantasy. You can't run from reality ... or from God."

Mandy snuffles, catching her breath. "I don't care, Mama. I'm staying here with Bryan, whether it's *LEGAL* OR NOT! It's my goshdang life, not *YOURS!*" Slamming down the phone, she rages tearfully around the makeshift living room; she stomps the floor; she jabs the air. Bolts of emotion explode like napalm in her head, red, gold, florescent orange. She collapses on the sofa, her reaction turning gray and impotent. She embraces herself; she feels sick and chilly. Sniffling, she gazes at the Dr. Pepper can on the coffee table, then at the paper plate with its wadded napkin and crusts of bread, the remains of her baloney sandwich. Grabbing the napkin, she dabs her eyes, her cheeks, her runny nose. She snatches one of the sofa pillows (a blue-quilted, raggedy thing); she hugs it to her bosom.

Outside the sunny, wide-open windows, the old neighborhood simmers in the midday heat. The curtains sway gently, moving with the breeze. October has turned summerlike again but without much humidity—so the 85°-plus temps seem almost delightful. And only minutes ago, Mandy shared the summery mood of the day, feeling cheerful and laid back and pleasantly warm, warm enough for a tank top and bike shorts—but now goosebumps dot her arms, her thighs, her knees. She's blah and shiverish. She stares at the magnolia tree, as a burst of wind stirs the leaves, making the purplish, egg-shaped cones swing to and fro.

A lawnmower fires up, Mr. Lipski next door? *Gosh, that old geezer is mowing again,* she remarks numbly to herself. *He's always working on his dadgum yard. But that's all he has left I reckon. This whole neighborhood is old. But not ME. I'm just seventeen. I hate it. Why can't I be eighteen NOW? I said I was, but I'm NOT! I'm a—*

The phone rings. "If you're gonna be like that, young lady," Helen admonishes, "we'll just have this whole thing annulled, Charlie and I." She pauses. Anginalike pain grips Mandy's chest. The magnolia tree goes blurry, a greenish blob framed by the window. "Pastor Ron says we have the authority to annul, as parents of an underage child." Helen exhales loudly, a bothered *phewhhhh.* "This *can't* go on, and Charlie agrees. We've talked and prayed, but now it's time to act, for your sake, for Bryan's sake ... for our sake. Pastor Ron calls it 'tough love'—he says we should make an appointment with Burt Allenby. He's the lawyer who handles the legal affairs for the ministry."

"It doesn't matter *what* yuh do, it's still my life," Mandy responds indignantly, her voice wavering then firming—she doesn't break, despite the hot tears in her eyes. "Plus, you got no right messing in my business. And Charlie's *not* my father, so stop saying 'we' all the time, like he's so damn concerned. He's full of bullshit, Mama, and you *know* it."

"But, Amanda, you hafta get your thinking straight. God is not the author of confusion. This nightmare *must* end. You're barely seventeen. The Lord is calling you to come h—"

"I said I doughwanna talk about it. You have *no* right—"

"Whaddeyuh mean I have no right! I'm still your mother I have you to—" *BANG*—the accused bride hangs up again.

I hate HER! Mandy huffs to herself, as she wipes her tears. *She's so dang mean and unfair when she gets into one of her "God told me" moods, and Charlie makes it worse—no, I don't hate her I reckon ... but we sure can't talk when she's like this.*

To the bathroom: she grabs a wad of toilet paper and blows her nose. She feels feverish. The bathroom seems cold and dank. She sniffles then blows again. She needs to let go, to sob out her confusion and hurt, but she willfully holds back. *No way am I going home just because she says it's God's will. I mean, how can she know God's will for me? It doesn't matter if she's my mother. If God has something to tell me, then he can tell me DIRECTLY. He doesn't hafta go through HER.*

After retreating to her bedroom, to pull on a sweat shirt (her yellow one), she paces up and down the hall; she runs her hand along the oak railing, which guards the stairwell. *Honor thy father and mother. Children obey your par—shit. Stop it. Stop quoting the same old verses. You can't go back now. It's a done deal ... whether the paperwork is legal or not. It's the heart that counts. There's no authority higher than love. In fact, God is LOVE.*

Back to the living room: Mandy plunks down in the over-stuffed armchair where, on Saturday, she teased Bryan with her sexy moves, but that all seems in a different universe now, as does her homework— she was reading in this chair when the phone first rang, Charles Dickens from the anthology of famous authors. *I don't feel like going to class tonight. I don't feel like doing anything.* She gives a sigh. *I wouldn't be surprised if Mama calls a third time ... to give me her "kind mother" routine.*

Mandy snorts, her conscience reacting again, as she harks back to yesterday morning, to Pastor Lawrence's sermon: *If you stubbornly defy the Lord, you will suffer chastisement, and if you still refuse to repent, God may bring painful consequences to your loved ones, as he did with King David—stop it. That church sucks. I can't think about this.* She stretches to her feet. *I gotta get outta here. I'll go shopping; I'll buy a winter jacket, or I can look for curtains, for our bedroom. Those copper ones from the dorm are too short, and the color's too loud. They look weird. Then I'll go to Bryan's intersquad game. This's the last week for baseball.* She dons her softball cap, grabs her envelope purse, but before she gets to the stairs, the phone rings—a third time.

"Honey, I didn't mean to come down so hard," Helen offers, her tone still motherly though calmer and more entreating, "but we hafta be realistic. You're not even out of school." Her voice softens another notch, becoming almost tender. "I'm not saying that you and Bryan won't end up together. You probably will, in God's due season. The Lord is not against you. He wants the best for you and Bryan, and so do I. But right now...."

* * *

Same day, 5:21 p.m. *I wonder why Mandy didn't make it to our practice game,* Bryan asks himself, as he chugs east on Douglas amid the long shadows cast by the sinking sun behind him. Yet he's still too high, over his last-inning, game-tying triple, to fret about her absence. *She probably went to get those curtains, like she's been talking about.* Pulling into the driveway, he eases to a halt behind the Firebird. *But she's home now, and we better get a move on it, if we're gonna eat at the caf—she has school tonight.*

Hopping out of the truck, he bops into the house. "Hey, pretty lady!" he hollers, while bounding up the stairs. "You missed a *great* game today. I'll tellyuh all about it—but we gotta get going, if we're gonna eat before you go to class."

Whoosh! Punctured balloon—he deflates, as he finds his wife weeping in their bedroom. Bra, jeans, white socks, whiff of perfume. She sits half-dressed on the side of the bed, her face in her hands. Her tank top and sweat shirt lie crumpled on the floor, plus her spandex shorts: pink and yellow tangling with gray. He kneels beside her. "What's the matter, precious?" He caresses her naked back, naked save for the grayish, washed-out brassiere strap. On the bed behind her a fresh shirt, her madras shirt, suggests that she was getting ready for class, as does the perfume.

"Mama called," she sniffles. "She knows I lied, but I don't wanna talk about it ... not now."

"How'd she find out? I mean uh ... did she *just* call or what?"

"I *said* I doughwanna talk."

Her abruptness hurts him, the surly "I *said*," but he persists nonetheless—he dreads silence more than hostility. "It's gonna be okay, honey. We don't need your mom's approval. We don't need *any*one's approval. We just hafta step back and look at—"

Mandy bolts midsentence from the room. Bryan follows, but she runs into the bathroom, locking the door behind her.

"C'mon, pretty lady, don't shut me out. I *love* you. I don't care what your mama said ... it's gonna be okay."

"That's easy for *you* to say," she sobs through the door. "You *always* say it's gonna be okay ... but y'don't know what it's like to be me. You have no *f*-ing clue!" She snorts and wheezes, choking on her sobs.

He waits, his pulse thumping, his thoughts scurrying to deal with his fears, which loom large again, even larger than Friday night when they argued in the truck. A clotty ache burns his throat. He's near to breaking himself. He gazes tearfully at the grainy hardwood door, which smells like varnish and sports a number of knots, two of which stare back at him like raccoon eyes—no, it's more like a demon, a devil, a fiend from Hades. "C'mon, Amanda!" he cries out—he slaps the door, smashing the demon. "How can I know *anything*, if yuh won't talk about it?"

"Y'WANT ME TO TALK!" she wails, pummeling the other side of the door—*whap! whap! whap!* "OKAY, MISTER, YOU ASKED FOR IT!" She pops the door again. "Well for starters, you have a good mama, not a first-class bitch like mine, and you have a real dad, not an asshole stepfather like Charlie Stevens. They're gonna have our marriage annulled—that's what she said. That bastard Charlie called Baton Rouge, and—"

"But, honey, it doesn't matter. They can't change our h—"

"LEMME FINISH!" Mandy shrieks, so loud the closed door vibrates. "OR I'M GONNA STAY IN HERE *ALL* NIGHT!" Tears streak Bryan's face, as he surrenders, leaning against the door jamb. "YOU DON'T KNOW WHAT I GO THROUGH! I don't agree with Mama, but then again, how can *we* know God's will. You heard that preacher yesterday at Marvin's church. Maybe God *IS* CHASTISING US! It's confusing and scary, and you're gone all day doing great and wonderful things, while I'm here washing dishes, and cleaning THE DAMN TOILET!" She sobs loudly, and sobs, then she snuffles even louder, sucking air. "Y'go to class like a normal person, but I go at night like some kind of weirdo dropout. And I feel freaky on campus too, like I don't belong. And this neighborhood is weird too. There's nobody within fifty years of my age—and they all stare ... when I drive by. And I hafta work at Denny's every weekend. It sucks! But you've never had to wait on tables, so how can yuh know? And our money's gonna run out. No *way* can it last! We're running low on everything, except SEX!" More loud snuffles behind the door. "And I doughwanna go to class tonight. I don't care if I graduate. I'm sick of going to school with HALF-WITS AND DRUGGIES! It sucks! Everything sucks! So don't tell me it's okay ... because it's *NOT* OKAY!"

*   *   *

Next morning (Tuesday), 8:23 a.m. Mandy gives her husband a quick but sensual kiss on the back steps. Her lips taste like butter and syrup—they just had frozen waffles for breakfast. She blushes and smirks. Bryan dimples; he drops his book pack. "What are *you* looking at?", she sports.

"Whaddeyuh think?" he replies, as he can't help but focus on her braless breasts, as they nestle bunnylike inside her half-open bathrobe—pink flannel framing tan lines and nubile flesh. She grins goofily then kisses him again, longer, more tongue.

She giggles, her blue eyes warm and trancy. "Y'better get going, mister, or we may end up on the kitchen floor ... again."

"Not a bad idea, but y'*wore* me out last night. Dang, I better not hit any triples today. I doubt I could make it to third base."

More laughter. "So you're gonna pick me up?"

"Yeah ... I have a free hour before practice, like I toldjuh."

O Jesus, she's too much, he exults a minute later, while wiping the dew from the windshield of the Chevy. Needless to say, they made up last night. And yet they shared much more than their bodies. They cuddled and talked for hours: about her mom, about their marriage, about sex and God and guilt, and money and death and Heaven, about *every*thing. They confessed their deepest hopes and dreads—finally. And again and again and again, they confirmed their love for each other.

A wonderful tranquillity comforts Bryan, a sense of relief and finality: they've put the mood swings and craziness behind them. They can now concentrate on the future, on their shared dreams.

*   *   *

11:24 a.m. The phone rings in the Howards' living room. *Oh no,* Mandy chuckles, *it's probably Mama. Let's not go through this again.* Dropping the load of laundry, dirty clothes plus the sheets she just pulled off the bed, she hurries down the hallway. *But this time I'm ready for her.*

It *is* her mama: "Mandy honey, I didn't call to harp—there's something bigger, more urgent. I'm at the hospital. Gretchen got hit by a car."

THE SILVER CORD

* * *

1:18 p.m. Bryan, arriving home, finds a note taped to the back door—his wife's curvy, fat-lettered way of printing seems more loopy than usual, suggesting haste:

> Bryan,
> I left a message at Coach Weaver's office, but I doubt you'll get it before you come home. I got bad news. Gretchen was hit by a car. Her leg is broken, and she has a concussion, and she may have serious internal injuries. Mama called from the hospital, the big hospital in Sulphur Springs. I'm leaving immediately. It's 11:30 now. Gretch was riding her bike in front of Molly Ann's house—that's when it happened. There was a teacher's conference, so they didn't have school today. I'll call you as soon as I can, probably from the hospital.

Stuffing the note into his jeans, he runs back to the truck but doesn't get in: *There's no point in rushing up there myself. I'll wait until she calls me ... then I'll decide. But no way can I make it to baseball today. I reckon I should let Coach McKinney know.*

* * *

2:41 p.m—whipping by the first Greenville exit, Mandy flips on the wipers. She hasn't seen the sun since Waxahachie, and now the rain has commenced, a thick drizzle actually, a foggy mist that shrouds the trees and pastures, obscuring the horizon, the rolling hills ahead of her. Gray, chilly, gloomy and oppressive: the weather, and her thoughts: *If you refuse to repent after God has chastised you personally, he may bring painful consequences upon your loved ones ... loved ones ... loved ones.*

* * *

She's gotta be there by now, Bryan surmises, as he closes his American History text. *It's a quarter to five.* Exiting the big master bedroom, he pads around the corner into the living room where he plops down on the sofa next to the telephone. He zaps on the TV—they can't afford cable, so he only gets the network stuff (Oprah et al) plus a few UHF channels.

Five minutes, ten, then twenty, then a couple more. "Gosh," he whispers out loud, "she shoulda called by now?" An Archie Bunker rerun on Channel 27 holds his attention for another few minutes, but at five-fifteen, he mutes the TV and begins to stride to and fro about the apartment. *This's really getting weird.*

5:35 p.m. He closes the living-room windows. It's turning cooler

403

outside and clouding up; a front must've gone through? Too much: he grabs the phone and soon hears the recorded voice of Helen Stevens, then a beep. After blurting a message, he resumes his pacing. *Just cool it. They're probably still at the hospital? Maybe Gretchen had to be operated on.* A terrible thought, but it actually relieves him. He feels a stab of guilt, yet a bigger pang for doubting Mandy, especially after their tell-all pillow talk in bed last night.

5:50 p.m—down to the kitchen. He makes two hot dogs, grabs a Dr. Pepper and a bag of chips, then goes back up and eats at the coffee table, as he watches the six o'clock news: a story about a teen suicide (hung himself) in Hillsboro, a bus-truck collision north of Temple (two fatalities), then a follow-up on the Clarence Thomas confirmation to the Supreme Court, sound-bites from his supporters countered by clips of feminist leaders who are furious over the 52-48 vote in the Senate, then a piece about Congress sustaining President Bush's veto of the $6.4 million unemployment-benefits bill along with a reminder that his record for sustained vetoes remains perfect: 23 to zip. Bryan cares little for these stories, but he's busy downing his dogs and chips. Plus, it makes the time pass faster, as he waits for the phone to ring—he figures she'll call any moment now.

After a break, the news team airs a more-provocative piece, a special eyewitness report on last week's mass murder in nearby Killeen, a nation-shocking rampage that left 23 dead:

> As the lunchtime crowd jammed Luby's Cafeteria last Wednesday, a blue Ford pickup tore across the parking lot and barreled through the plate-glass window. A few startled customers ran to help the driver. To their horror, a muscular young man in a green shirt sprang from behind the wheel with a semiautomatic pistol. "This's what Bell County did to me!" he raged, pumping bullets in all directions. "This's payback day!" One of his first victims was an elderly man who was struck by the truck and shot in the head as he tried to get up. He then killed 71-year-old Al Gratia, who ignored his daughter's pleas and rose to confront the madman. As screams pierced the air, the gunman fired into the crowded serving line. Pausing only long enough to push fresh clips into his two pistols, a Glock 17 and a Ruger P-89, he worked methodically around the beige-colored hall. Mere chance determined who lived, and who died. The killer spared a mother and child, barking at her to get the youngster "out of here." An elderly woman put her arm around her wounded husband. As the gunman approached, she looked up then bowed her head, and he shot her. One woman survived by hiding in a freezer;

she was later treated for hypothermia. Food preparer Mark Mathews, 19, escaped by hiding inside an industrial dish-washer. He was so frightened that he didn't come out until Thursday....

That guy had to be crazy, Bryan declares to himself, as he downs the last of his Dr. Pepper—he burps then heads for the bathroom. *No normal person could freak out like that. Or maybe he was demon-possessed? But I'm not too keen on the whole idea of demons, especially when some preachers claim that OBEs are caused by demonic energy.*

Returning to the living room, he catches Norm Gossage, who confirms that a cold front did slide southward through the region this afternoon, bringing with it clouds and a few light showers. But when the News Two meteorologist mentions the rain and drizzle over North Texas, Bryan kills the TV, his thoughts returning to Spindle, to Mandy and Gretchen. The massacre piece distracted him, but his sense of unease has returned: *Damn, it's six twenty-five.*

To the phone: he dials. He expects the machine again, or maybe Helen herself, or Mandy, or Charlie even—but he gets instead a chirpy "Hel-*lo*."

"Who's this?" Bryan asks.

"Oh hi, Bryan—it's Gretchen. I figured you'd call back."

"But uh ... but, but," he stammers. "I thought you were in the hospital ... with a broken leg and all."

Gretchen giggles. "No *way* ... I'm at home playing Donkey Kong with my dad. He even *fixed* the joystick." More girlish laughter. "I was never *in* the hospital, like you ... but I did ride in an ambulance today. They took me to the emergency room in Sulphur Springs ... and it's my *foot* that's broken, not my leg."

Bryan is anxious to talk to Mandy, but his conscience urges him to be patient and sympathetic: "Well, Gretch, I'm sorry about your foot, but I'm sure glad you're okay." He chuckles. "So you *act*ually got hit by a car?" He instantly regrets the question.

"Well, sorta ... but it was more like I ran into *it*. I was over at Molly Ann's, and we were racing on our bikes ... like *down* the street and back." Her little-girl voice rises to that ebullient tell-all timbre— Bryan plunks down resignedly on the sofa. "I was pedaling *super* fast when all of a sudden Mr. Feeny came backing out in his fancy green Cadillac. He's half blind, so he didn't see me or nothing. I swerved and skidded, but I still sideswiped his door, then I crashed and burned against the curb. That's when I fell off and bumped my head. I saw stars ... and then Mrs. Heimberg was looking down at me—that's Molly Ann's mama—and then a policeman, and then an ambulance came. Molly Ann said old-man Feeny ran over my foot, but I don't remember that part. The lady medic looked into my eyes with a little flashlight, and then she took my blood pressure with one of those Velcro things that squeeze your arm ... like *super* tight. And Mr. Feeny was cussing about the big scratch on his door. My dad might hafta pay for it ... or maybe Mama's insurance?"

"Gosh, that's wild," Bryan interjects, hoping that she's running out of gas. "What a sto—"

"And *then* they put me in the ambulance," she goes on, "but they didn't have the siren going, 'cause it wasn't *life* or death. My foot was aching, but nor super bad, and I had a bump on my head. When we got to the emergency room, they took X-rays, then I had to lie on a bed, and there were greenish curtains *all* around, like giant shower curtains, and then Mama came, and Pastor Ron, and then my dad. *Finally*, this doctor guy said my foot was fractured, the metashaft bone or something like that. It was no big deal really ... but I did get crutches, and I hafta stay home from school until *Mon*day. And then later, after Mandy got here, we all went to O'Henry's to eat, even Pastor Ron." Giggles, labored inhalations—she's out of breath, at last.

"So why was Pastor Ron there?" Bryan asks, apprehensively.

"Oh, he came with Mama to the hospital, 'cause at first they thought I was hurt *super* bad. And we invited him to eat with us."

Bryan's pulse accelerates. "So is everyone home now?"

"Nawh ... just me and Daddy. He's going back to Arkansas tomorrow. He *was* gonna leave today, but then I got hurt."

"So where's Mandy?"

"Oh, she's at the church with Mama—and Pastor Ron."

* * *

Same evening, 7:07 p.m. Bryan's heart thumps faster than the pistons under the hood—or so it seems. *She's at the church with her MOTHER ... and PASTOR RON. This is NOT GOOD!* He slams the pedal to the floor, but the truck has no more. The needle flutters touching ninety-five mph then falls back in response to the upgrade. He's not far from Hillsboro.

Streaming darkly past his window, the rainy night hisses like a banshee above the rhythmic *ka-shunk* of the wipers and the maxed-out hum of the V-6. *If things were normal, she woulda called me first thing ... to tell me that Gretchen was okay. But she DIDN'T.* A vehicle looms ahead in the fast lane. Bryan hits the high beams, low beams, high beams. The intruder, looks like a Jeep Cherokee, retreats to the right lane. The pickup whooshes by amid a burst of grimy spray. Gramps' old Chevy commands the fast lane, zipping easily past the moderate northbound traffic. *She was already spooked by that fucking preacher, and now THIS. Her sister got hurt—and Mandy sees it as a warning from God. That's gotta be it ... even though Gretchen's injury turned out to be much less serious. Shit—we shoulda never gone to Marvin's church.*

Hornets swarm inside his chest, attacking then stinging his heart.

THE SILVER CORD

The taillights go blurry ahead: haloed dabs of red. Grief mounts in his throat, thick but dry. He weeps without sobbing, the worst kind of ache; it cuts, it burns, it parches his craw. Unfair, unjust: the ache turns to wrath. He socks the dash panel—the tape deck rattles violently. Then again, and again, and again, until his knuckles are bloody and numb, from the knobs. He claws at the passenger seat, trying to rip the vinyl upholstery—without success. His baseball underjersey clings to his sweaty armpits.

The miles clip by: Hillsboro, Milford, Forreston. The rain gives way to drizzle. The wipers squeak as they sweep the film of tiny droplets. "THIS SUCKS!" Bryan shouts, as he attacks the dash again, now slapping with an open hand the padded overhang, *WHAP! WHAP! WHAP!* He pants, he groans, he growls—he inhales the pungent reek of his own BO.

Waxahachie, Red Oak, Route 20. Exiting I-35E, he rockets northeast on 635, the wide but busy loop that circles Big-D. 85 mph, 90 mph: he's gotta make time now, before he hits that stretch of road construction some ten miles ahead. He jockeys from lane to lane, weaving through the traffic. To his left, the urban skyline glows eerily in the gloom. Muddy spray coats the windshield; he squirts washer fluid; he's suddenly behind a purple Plymouth, a little hatchback Horizon hogging the fast lane—at least, it looks purple in the yellowish, sodium-vapor light coming from the pole-mounted lamps. Bryan slows to sixty-five, fifty-five. He works his high beams—to no avail. *Damn, why won't he get out of the way? I reckon he's a poky old hayseed, considering that cowboy hat he's wearing, though I don't know many hayseeds that drive purple cars.* Bryan passes on the right. *Hell, that's no hat; that's hair, a goshdang Afro!*

The hatchback veers into Bryan's lane. "WATCH IT!" he screams, as he swerves to avoid the Plymouth. The pickup slides sideways, losing traction on the wet asphalt. Honking cars pass on both sides. The Baylor freshman battles the wheel, turning into the skid, regaining control just short of the breakdown lane where he eases to a halt. He shakes his bloody fist at the black driver, who continues on, obliviously. "You almost got us *both* killed, YOU GODDAM COCKSUCKING NIGGER!" He gives the now-distant vehicle the finger. "Why don'tcha go back to the fucking Mod Squad where you belong!"

Bryan eases the Chevy back into traffic, then he stomps the pedal, accelerating like a dragster, 55, 65, 75—but before he gets to eighty, he brakes then downshifts, getting off at the next exit, Exit 473 in Hutchins. He pulls into a McDonald's and parks in the back. *God, what's wrong with me? I never cuss like that. I haven't said "nigger" since seventh grade.* He slumps against the door. Bigger drops pitter-patter on the windshield; the rain has returned. *I was mad enough to shoot that guy.*

He blows out a silent whistle that turns into a murmur. *Just because she went to the church with her mom doesn't mean she's—well, I'm jumping to conclusions. I shouldn't doubt her until I have evidence. I shoulda stayed home. She probably called right after I left. I bet there's a message from her on the answering machine right now.* He sucks a long breath, trying to settle himself. *I'm WAY out of control, like foaming at the mouth. I'm no better than that maniac at Luby's Cafeteria—NO, NO, no fucking way. I'm NOT like him. I'm just afraid that's all ... afraid of losing Mandy. O Jesus God—but I'm jumping to conclusions. I'm not being reasonable. Besides, even if she did decide to leave me, what could I do about it? God's the one who brought us together, so it's up to him to keep us together. I don't have ANY control, whether I'm mad, or calm ... so I may as well stay calm. And there's certainly no point in going to Spindle tonight. I don't even have a toothbrush with me, and I stink worse than Millie after a hard gallop.* He chuckles, in spite of his pain. *God, I just took off, and drove like a lunatic.*

He feels a chilly draft; the windows are fogging. He fires up the engine, turns on the defrost. He checks his watch: 7:58 p.m. *Gosh, it's only been an hour and fifteen minutes since I left the house. I've never made it to Dallas this fast.* He chuckles again. *I reckon I had this baby moving. I doubt Gramps ever drove like that, even when it was new.* More laughter. *But then again, he probably did ... at least once, to see what she'd do.*

To think about his granddad makes Bryan feel better, as does the laughing, and the decision to go back to Waco. *But before I head back, I need gas—I'm almost empty. And before that I gotta piss.* Hopping out, he strides across the puddled McDonald's lot. The rainy-damp breeze has a fallish nip to it. *Dang, it's getting cold out here.* He shoves his hands into his jeans.

*　　*　　*

9:32 p.m. Bryan, back at the house, checks the answering machine: *O Jesus, that which I greatly feared has come to pass.* He stares wide-eyed at the black Radio Shack device, its steady red light giving the verdict—no calls. *I figured something was wrong ... ever since last Thursday when she was out there looking at the moon.* He gives a throaty little moan. *I reckon it's OVER ... at least for now ... and I can't do a dadgum thing about it.* The threatening cloud has condensed into hard evidence, a cold and convincing rain, much colder and heavier than the rain outside. *It's over; she's not coming back.* The icy knowing soaks his soul, until it collapses like a stricken tent about his heart. *But there's no point in calling her tonight. We can resolve this whole split-up thing tomorrow.*

Silent devastation. No panic, no pounding pulse, no mad dash to the truck—this time he swallows his hurt, containing his pain, save for a rueful sigh, and the toss of a sofa pillow. He sails it across the room then plunks down onto the couch. Hugging the other blue pillow, he lays his head back. He closes his eyes, trying to escape the utter sense of loss. *O Jesus, I hate this feeling ... but what can I do? I need someone to talk to, someone who knows what I'm going through—I wish Gramps was alive.*

Hearing a car, he hurries to the window in the big bedroom. It's two cars actually, Chris' Chevette then Tracy's Tempo. *I knew it wasn't Mandy—she's not coming back. It's a done deal.*

Returning to the living room, he thinks about calling his mother, but nixes the idea: *I'll talk to Mom tomorrow, after I confirm this whole business with Mandy.* He snorts resignedly. *I reckon I'll be moving back into the dorm.*

* * *

146 DOUGLAS STREET - CHRIS HANSEN'S APT
TUESDAY, OCTOBER 22, 1991 — 11:50 PM

"Wow, that's *quite* a tale," Tracy McCollum twangs in her high-pitched Louisiana voice. She gestures at Bryan with her beer, a shiny can of Michelob.

"It is indeed," Chris quips, giving a burp plus an elfish head-waggle. "Let's write it down and change the names. It'll be a goddamn best-seller." They share a beery laugh, all three.

Tracy slouches on the sofa, Chris in his desk chair, while the heartbroken freshman sits on the floor, his back against the wall. He takes a big drink of his third brew, almost killing it. His pain melts a little more with each swig. A gas stove heats (overheats) the small apartment adding to the woozy effect of the alcohol. The room smells of beer and mozzarella, and faintly of perfume, a roselike scent, Tracy's? Bryan tried to survive the Mandy thing alone, but he couldn't. He needed to talk, so he came out here about eleven. Chris and Tracy were snacking on pizza while editing computer files for Dr. Richardson, but they seemed glad for the interruption, as if looking for a good excuse to stop working.

The puckish junior swivels his chair and gets up. "So, slugger, you want another one?"

"Yeah, why not?"

Chris opens the fridge. "How about you, Tracy?"

"No, I've still got plenty left ... but I reckon I *will* have a smoke—if you guys don't mind?"

Chris gives his vintage smirk. "Hell, I thought you quit last year—but go ahead."

Tracy grins sheepishly, as she digs her Salem Lights out of her shoulder bag. "Well, let's just say I cut *way* down ... but after hearing Bryan's news, I need a good shot of nicotine. It reminds me of my own love-life, the whole *Stuart* thing." Lighting the cig, she takes a draw then nods toward the freshman. "I'll tellyuh about it sometime, Bryan, but right now I reckon y'got enough romance drama to deal with." Her words ride a smoky plume—the acrid, burnt-tobacco aroma joins then trumps the other odors in the stuffy apartment.

After handing Bryan his fourth brew, Chris disappears into the can. Tracy takes a long draw on her Salem then exhales, the smoke curling upward about her black helmet of hair. A bit of ash falls on her skirt, a denim skirt. She brushes it off then shifts on the sofa, folding her legs under her. As she does, Bryan catches a glimpse of thighs, crotch, panties, pale-blue undies. *Now if she came upstairs and went to bed with me—that would help ease my mind.* A pang of guilt accompanies this wayward thought, but he kills it with a swig of beer. *My mind's guttering out, but I gotta tranquilize myself with something, anything, even if it's just a dadgum beaver-shooting fantasy. No way am I gonna be doing anything with her—but the beer IS real, and I'm gonna drown myself in it, until I can't remember my goddam name.*

Tracy departs at one, but Bryan and Chris continue talking until three-thirty. When the freshman finally staggers out, Chris follows him onto the patio. "Now, slugger, I may be drunk," he stammers, putting his arm around Bryan, "but I know what it means to have a broken heart. Believe me, I know ... like I been saying the last hour. I may be a horny, dirty-mouthed bastard, but I still love Jennifer. And there's no goddam cure for true love."

THE SILVER CORD

CHAPTER TWENTY-FOUR

146 DOUGLAS STREET
WEDNESDAY, OCTOBER 23, 1991 — 9:39 AM

As Bryan Howard soaps up in the shower, the awful knowing gnaws upon his psyche, but the pain remains passive, inert, a resigned ache—or perhaps the cobwebby hangover has fouled his senses. Ten minutes later, after shaving, he calls Mandy's house. Gretchen answers. He gives her the message, quickly but calmly. To the bedroom: he dons fresh jeans and a button-collar shirt then descends to the kitchen where he downs a hurried but hearty breakfast of Rice Chex and sausage and frozen waffles.

This's definitely weird, he remarks to himself, as he places the dishes in the sink. *My worst nightmare is coming true, yet I'm dealing with it. And it's not just the beer I drank last night. It's like my emotions are unplugged or something.* Slipping on his denim jacket, he ambles out to the truck. It's still misty and cool, though it's supposed to clear up today.

Reaching the interstate, he cruises along relaxedly, doing sixty to sixty-five, a far cry from last night's berserk race to nowhere. The drizzly rain ceases; he turns off the wipers.

* * *

MISTY HOLLOW ROAD - NORTH OF SPINDLE, TEXAS
WEDNESDAY, OCTOBER 23, 1991 — 2:41 PM

Bryan chugs along the shadowy, tree-lined road under a blue fair-weather sky. A pinkish envelope lies on the seat beside him. He knows the contents, even without opening it—yet he does plan to open it. "Mandy said to give this to yuh," Helen Stevens declared when Bryan knocked on the door. "And I *do* hope you'll respect her wishes." Helen was low key and polite but curt, Bryan equally so. He had hoped to confront Mandy herself but accepted the letter instead. The Firebird was not in the driveway, yet he didn't ask regarding his wife's whereabouts. His composure continues to amaze him.

Reaching Longley Road, he takes a left then a right onto the two-rut trail that runs into the woods on the east side of the Howard farm. He squeaks to a halt among the conifers near Butler Creek. Hopping out, he stretches and yawns. The pine-scented breeze smells like paint thinner, and it feels crisp and bracing, quite fallish, especially in this shady hollow. He urinates on the humpy, turtle-shaped rock, the same rock he pissed on back in the summer, after he and Mandy argued on her porch, a minor tiff compared to this life-changing crisis—and yet he was much more distraught on that warm Sunday, the last day of

THE SILVER CORD

June.

I reckon it's time to get this over with, he sighs to himself a minute later, after climbing back into the cab. He shifts a little to get comfortable then opens the envelope. He recognizes the loopy, teen-gal penmanship—no doubt it's from Mandy:

> Dear Bryan,
>
> It was wrong for me to lie about my age. We can't be together now. We're too young. We can't put God to the test. Gretchen's accident could've been worse. And even though the Lord healed you back in May, He was trying to tell us to cool it, like I said before. We must get our lives on track. We have to trust GOD, not our feelings. True love is a decision, not a feeling. And I'm not sure about your OBE dreams. It could be a deception from the devil. Please don't chase after me. This's for the BEST. We have to follow Christ. I need my clothes and stuff. Maybe you can bring 'em up. If not, Mama said she and Charlie will come to Waco. He's going to stay here until Sunday, to help out. I was wrong about him. He's walking in the Spirit now—it's not an act. The license we got isn't legal. Mama has to send a notarized letter, and then it'll be annulled. I still have the rings, but I'll mail them back to you. I didn't put them in this letter, since they might've gotten lost.
>
> Mandy

Bryan fires up the pickup. *I sure wish Gramps was alive,* he yearns. Yet he remains unruffled—despite the heart-ripping note.

* * *

THE HOWARD FARM
WEDNESDAY, OCTOBER 23, 1991 — 3:42 PM

"Thanks, Mom," Bryan says, getting up from the kitchen table, "for the sandwich, *and* the advice."

Ginny Howard gives her son a hug plus a peck on the cheek. "Well, hon, I wish I could offer more assurance. But when it comes to love, it's hard to figure what's gonna happen next. I reckon we just hafta accept that we're not in control, that we can't *make* things happen. And you and Mandy are very young, so this whole situation doesn't shock me. But I still believe she loves you, like I've said all along. It could be a while ... but I have a hankering that this isn't the last chapter in this saga."

Bryan dimples then sobers. "I hope not ... I hope not."

412

Her green eyes filling, Ginny takes him by the shoulders. "Now y'don't hafta be strong and manly through this whole thing. It's okay to lose it when you're hurting. In fact, it's normal." She embraces him again. Her hair smells like Halo, the yellow shampoo that sits on the corner of the tub in the upstairs bathroom, just like it did when he was three, and six, and eight, and thirteen. The fragrance reminds him especially of those tender times at night, bedtimes long ago when she'd come to his room to tuck him in.

The mommy sensations move him, making his throat ache, but the daylong detachment quickly reasserts itself. "I know it's normal," he replies, as he turns to leave. "But somehow, I'm dealing with it, at least today." He chuckles. "Or maybe it hasn't hit me yet, that she's actually doing this."

"It *is* strange ... how our emotions work. When my dad got killed in Vietnam, I cried for a month, but when Mom died, your Grandma Scott, I hardly shed a tear, and yet I was *clo*ser to her."

Bryan opens the back door. "Yeah, it's a mystery to be sure—oh, I think I'll go say hello to Millie before I take off."

"Good idea; I'll walk with yuh. Just lemme get my jacket. That wind's a mite chilly."

"It does feel fallish out ... especially in the shade."

"D'yuh really hafta rush off?" she asks, as they stroll to the barn. "Why don'tcha reconsider and spend the night?" She gives a quick titter. "You already said no, but I wish you'd stay."

"Nawh, I reckon I better get right back. I've already missed a lot of classes, plus two days of practice, and this's the last week of fall baseball. Besides, there's a good chance I'll be coming up on Saturday ... with Mandy's stuff. That reminds me—will you call Helen Stevens and tell her that I'll take care of everything, so they don't hafta come down to Waco?"

"Sure thing, honey. I'll call her ... as soon as I see you off."

* * *

INTERSTATE 35 - APPROACHING HILLSBORO
WEDNESDAY, OCTOBER 23, 1991 — 6:23 PM

The sun setting ahead of him, Bryan rolls along at a leisurely sixty-five. KRYZ, the Dallas oldie station, plays at low volume on the radio: some Motown doo-wop number. He doesn't care for doo-wop, but on this coolish October evening, he's paying scant attention to the music.

Steering with his arms, he slips his wedding band off and puts it in his pocket. *I agree with Mom. I hafta let go of this. I hafta trust God. Mandy's note sucks, yet she could be right about the age thing. And she also talks about trusting the Lord, but I can't cozy up to a God who uses fear to make us obey. When I got hurt in May, there was no fear, just incredible love and acceptance—course, she says all that could*

THE SILVER CORD

be from the Devil. Sounds like her mother talking? But what can I do? I'll take her stuff back on Saturday, and that will be it. I'm not sure I even want to see her, considering, but I have no control over that either.

He removes his aviator shades. The orange, impotent sun resembles a giant egg yolk, as it hovers in the haze near the horizon (the autumn winds have scoured the air except downwind of Dallas). On the other side of the highway headlights pop on amid the steady but sparse stream of oncoming traffic. He turns the heat on. The sun warmed the cab for most of the trip, but now it's cool. It's going to be a cold night, perhaps frosty even? He studies the sinking sun—it suddenly goes blurry, and not from tears. Ditto for the horizon, which looks like a long ink smear. *I'll be doggone. My left eye's messing up again, like last week.* He gives a passive snort.

* * *

Some four hours later, Bryan turns off the bedside lamp and crawls into the sack, after putting on a tattered baseball underjersey, an old one from high school that he sleeps in on cool nights. It's 10:20 p.m—he's exhausted, so he's turning in early, to make up for last night. He pulls the bedcovers over him, plus his blue-and-white comforter. A burst of light skitters across the ceiling, as a car passes in front of the house.

His left eye is okay again. It cleared up before he got to Randolph, to the spot where the tornado roared across the interstate three weeks ago. *It's amazing how much has happened since that twister hit,* he remarked to himself, as he whipped by the site, a scene now indistinguishable save for the landscaping work in the median strip. But even the memory of that traumatic-then-joyous day failed to stir him—his heart remains detached, as if this tragic love story is happening to someone else, and he's looking on from a distance.

When he got home, sometime after seven, he ate a light supper—toast and peanut butter, three pieces, plus milk, plus an apple—then he paid a visit to Chris. No beer, no Tracy, no late-night lamenting: Bryan simply related the news about Mandy's letter, and they talked a while, mainly about other things.

Folding his pillow, he curls onto his side. The sheets were cold at first, but he's now quite warm. He didn't turn on the furnace when he got home, so the house is chilly. He's tired, and sedate, so he has no problem falling asleep.

* * *

A noise awakens Bryan—the back door? *Who can that be at this hour?* he wonders groggily. *It must be two a.m. or after?* He sits up on the side of the bed. Flipping on the lamp, he reaches for his watch on the night table but can't find it. Footsteps resound on the stairs. His mind clears: *Mandy, Mandy—it's gotta be her. She's come back!* Before he can move, he gets confirmation.

Blue eyes, bike shorts, golden locks, yellow sweat shirt—it *is* Mandy. She waltzes into the bedroom, her softball cap backward on her head. Sitting down on the side of the bed, she hugs him, clings to him. She kisses him tenderly then fervently, knocking her hat off. Breaking for air, she gazes at him, her face beaming, her blue eyes filled with tears and yearning. "Oh, dear babe," she whispers. "I'm *so* sorry. That letter I wrote was *so* mean, and hateful. I got spooked I guess. Our love is so big and *scary*—it makes me crazy. What we have is *way* bigger than just being married or having good sex. God has made us *one* ... so we can help people and love people, and discover super-great things together. We're a team. I'm sorry I hurt you. I'm sorry."

"It's okay, pretty lady," Bryan coos, his heart cartwheeling inside him. "I love you for*ever* ... no matter how many times you run away from home."

He dimples, while Mandy giggles and blushes. Her cuddle-bunny breasts nestle cutely inside her sweat shirt. Lifting the shirt, he fondles them, one then the other—she's not wearing a bra. "Oh, babe," she sighs. "I love you so. I want you so. I need yuh to hold me. Please hold me, and hold me, and *never* let go."

Pulling her to him, he hugs her, squeezes her, until she squeals with joy. He strokes her hair, her back, her curvaceous, girl-jock legs. Her razor-stubbled flesh feels hot to his touch, delightfully so. Closing his eyes, he inhales her presence, her hair, her flesh, her perfume. "I heard yuh at the back door," he says, without opening his eyes, "but I didn't hear the Firebird?" He strokes her back some more—it feels strangely plump.

"That's because I left my car in Spindle. I rode Gretchen's bicycle—all the way. And that's why I'm wearing these shorts."

"Get outta here," Bryan sports, opening his eyes—no light, no wife, NO MANDY!

Hot daggers rip his bowels, then they hack upward into his bosom, into his throat. He's embracing the other pillow, *her* pillow. It's a dream, a trick, a *hoax* from God, a dreadful lie save for the Mandy-scents on the pillowcase which only magnify his torment. Throwing the covers off, he sits up and turns on the light—for real. His watch sits where he left it beside the lamp—11:16 p.m. *Gosh damn,* he laments to himself, *I've only been asleep an hour, but that was long enough to tear me apart. O God, why?* He whimpers and moans; he buries his face in his hands. Lumpy fire scorches his throat. Tears well up; he sniffs them back. *C'mon, Bryan—you have classes tomorrow. Get a grip on yourself. You're BOUND to dream about her. But y'gotta let go. Mom is right. Y'gotta let go.*

The heartache subsides a notch, then another. He yawns and stretches. He's hardly feeling detached or serene, as during the day, yet the pangs of disappointment are receding—but then he notices her *yellow* sweat shirt hanging on the closet door, the *same* cottony shirt!

* * *

FARM ROAD 115 - NORTH OF SPINDLE, TEXAS
THURSDAY, OCTOBER 24, 1991 — 3:09 AM

Bryan bombs through the near-frosty night, doing eighty on a stretch of farm road that's rough at fifty. The piney woods and pastures pan swiftly by under a gibbous October moon. The silvery moon, though humpbacked and waning, remains full enough to wrench, again and again, his pain-wracked soul:

"I wanna make a promise on the moon."
"Whaa ... whaddeyuh talking about?"
"I wantcha to promise me that every time you look at the moon, you'll think of me...."

But the pain now spurs him onward. "I just gotta talk to her. She can't deny me. She can't!"

Barreling across Caddo Creek, the pickup flies into the air, as it hurtles the sunken section of pavement at the far end of the bridge. The old Chevy comes down with a clattering bang, the cargo bed and tailgate rattling violently. Bryan, not wearing his seatbelt, bounces behind the wheel, but he's past the point of being careful. He presses for more speed rather, slamming the pedal to the metal. The truck shivers and shimmies, but he gets her up to eighty-five, despite the bumpy upslope. "I may have lost part of my load," he snuffles hoarsely. "It's piled back there like a rat's nest, but I don't give a shit if I scatter her stuff over the whole goddam state." The fits of sobbing ceased before he got to Dallas, but he still has a runny nose, and his face feels blotchy tight from dried tears.

The Howard Farm sleeps minutes away on his left, but he's got *urgent* business in Spindle. *Blip, blip, blip*—the utility poles zip by like fence posts. Faster, faster, he whistles past Longley Road at 88 mph, the asphalt smoothing out under him (they recently repaved this part of FR 115). The straining V-6 seems ready to explode, to shatter—to expel its pistons like a barrage of howitzer shells. Not a problem for the Baylor freshman: let it blow, let it go, let it shower the cold moonlight with fire and shrapnel. His life has already detonated like a bomb, a few hours ago after awaking from the Mandy-came-back dream.

But it was the yellow sweat shirt on the door that triggered the blast, a blast which obliterated the false sense of peace that protected him all day yesterday (Wednesday). Wailing and flailing, he bolted across the bedroom: "I DON'T WANT HER GODDAM STUFF IN THIS HOUSE!" He ripped her clothes from the closet, hangers and all, tossing them onto the floor. Ditto for her shoes. No wife, no Mandy, no reason to live. Then he attacked her dresser, emptying the drawers. Ditto for the bathroom, the living room, the kitchen downstairs. No boxes, no bags, no effort to pack or sort—he threw *all* her things into the back of the truck, loose armload after armload. And it didn't take long, no more than twenty minutes. Then he tore-ass out of Waco. No traffic, no troopers, no stops—except for gas (at an all-night Texaco in Greenville). As he left the gas station, his rage gave way to reckless determination. *She loves me. I can't let this happen. And I WON'T let this happen! I gotta take charge.* He shook his fist for emphasis. *God helps those who help themselves. I gotta rescue her, no matter what. I shoulda left her stuff back in Waco ... but that's a goddam detail.*

Now within minutes of Spindle, he shakes his fist again. *I just want her back. And I plan to GET her back!* Popping through a plume of ground fog, he whips across Butler Creek, *bump, bump,* a much smoother bridge, then he attacks the slope on the other side. Topping the hill at eighty, he whizzes by the little-league fields, the pear-shaped moon keeping pace above the trees. *If any cops are out, I'm dead,* he chuckles to himself, a sniffly chuckle. He wipes his nose on the back of his hand. *But I reckon they're still too lazy to patrol this late.* No hankie, no hat, no jacket, no bag, no nothing—he's still wearing the tattered jersey he sleeps in, though he did remember his jeans and wallet and sneakers. Yet the cab seems plenty warm. He's sweating in fact, though not from the temperature. He hangs a left on Bixby, screeching around the corner; he uses part of the Dairy Queen lot to make it. But the DQ's dead, and the neighborhood—the whole town. *I left rubber on that turn I reckon. Mighta roused somebody, but so what? If I made it this far without getting stopped, or killed, God HAS to be on my side. To HELL with fear and guilt. I'm not gonna let misdirected religious fervor steal her from me. She LOVES me. And I'm coming to TAKE her home!*

Veering onto Colby, he slows to forty-five then shifts down, *vaah-ROOOM!* He brakes, skidding to a halt in front of Mandy's house. Three cars crowd the driveway, including the Firebird. He sprints across the lawn to the front porch, hurtling the steps. *Bamb! Bamb!* he bangs on the aluminum screen door, the frame. Nothing. He bangs again. Nothing—then noise: he hears someone. The porch light pops on, the yellow bug-lamp in its lantern-like fixture. The front door swings open. "Bryan!" Helen Stevens exclaims hushedly through the screen. "What're *you* doing here? It's three in the morning?"

"I wanna see Mandy," he declares fearlessly, breathlessly.

"Well goodness knows ... you can't see her at *this* hour. This's *not* the time." Helen fingerfluffs her sleep-mussed hair then adjusts the sash of her robe (a terrycloth robe); the ochre light gives her complexion a sickly cast, as though she's suffering from jaundice. "Besides, I reckon she said all she wants to say in the letter. But if yuh phone in the morning, we'll see if we can work something out. I'll be here until ten, then I'll be at Kroger's after that."

"But I hafta see her *now!*" he demands, nearly shouting.

"Hold it *down.* You'll wake the neighbors."

"I don't give a shit! I'm her husband. I have a right."

"The marriage isn't legal, Bryan. You know that—and *watch* your language." Helen gives an annoyed snort plus a flip of her hand, though she maintains an air of restraint, of civility, her features betraying little emotion. A shadowy figure lurks behind her—Charlie? Bryan can't make out his face, but it *is* a man.

"C'mon, Mrs. Stevens," he persists. "This isn't *fair.* Lemme in. I *hafta* see her." He tries to open the screen door, but it's locked. Charlie comes closer, though he still doesn't show his face. Bryan lets go of the handle.

"Now let's not make a scene," Helen cautions, closing the main door all but a few inches (the thick wooden door is painted gray, but it looks tan in the yellow light). "We must resolve this in a calm ... and rational manner. God is not the author of confusion. So go to your house and get some sleep. I'll consider your request. Call me in the morning, like I say."

"I shouldn't hafta go through you—it's not *right.*"

"Well, as long as she's under-age, that's how it's gonna be."

"But she *loves* me! What about that? Doesn't the heart count for *anything?*"

"You're not being reasonable, Bryan. You don't even have a coat on, and it's *free*zing outside. What would your parents think, if they knew you were banging on our door ... at three a.m?"

A storm of hurt gathers in his bosom—he realizes his cause is lost. "I don't give a damn what time it is. I HAFTA see her!"

"Stop this *craz*iness!" Helen snaps, her pixie face contracting into a scowl—her eyes narrow, her nostrils flare: no more facade of civility. "If yuh don't leave now, I'll call your father." She closes the door, firmly. He pounds angrily: *Bamb! Bamb! Bamb!* "You better leave!" she warns from inside the house. "Before the neighbors call the police. You have no further *business* with my daughter ... except to return her belongings."

"You *want* her stuff! Fine! Y'can HAVE IT!" He rushes to the truck, vaulting into the back—he attacks the tangled pile of clothes and such. Sobbing and shrieking, he flings her things toward the house, her jeans, her shirts, her softball glove, her skirts and dresses, her night-school books, her blue jumper, her sneakers, her pumps, her panties, her bras, her bike shorts, her big Thompson Bible, her pink-flannel robe, her socks, her saddle-bag purse, her pajamas and nighties—plus a softball, two basketballs, and a small suitcase. The clothing settles onto the lawn, but the shoes and such fly farther, some hitting the porch, some thumping against the gray clapboards. The softball flies over the entire house, while one of the basketballs rebounds all the way to the street. Three of her shoes end up on the porch roof, below Mandy's bedroom windows, which remain darker than death. She hasn't shown herself—at all.

His sobbing gives way to sniffles and wheezing, but the throwing fit continues until the cargo bay is empty, save for a bottle of shampoo, her Pantene shampoo. He gazes tearfully at the plastic cylinder. It's white, but it looks darker than gunmetal in the dim light. He hears a few dogs barking, but there's no human reaction to his tantrum, from the Stevens house, or the neighbors. At least, he notices none. He's panting and sweating, but the cold night has raised goosebumps on his bare arms; he hugs himself. Memories play on the screen of his mind, heavenly memories turned hellish:

> *"Here's your stuff. I got the purple bag plus the hair-blower, but I couldn't find your madras shirt ... so I just grabbed a polo."*
> *"No biggie, but what I need now is my shampoo. It's in my bag, a white plastic bottle."*
> *Unzipping the end-pocket, Bryan pulls it out and reads the label: "Pantene Pro-V. Shampoo Plus Pro-Vitamin Conditioner ... For Normal—"*
> *"Okay, y'don't hafta do a dang TV commercial."*

Picking up the shampoo, he pulls it to his bosom. His heart dies for the hundredth time amid another spasm of weeping. He reels and stumbles, almost falling over the tailgate. Spikes of pain rip upward under his rib cage, again, and again.

"GODDAMMIT, IT'S NOT *FAIR*!" he howls, as he pegs the Pantene on a low trajectory toward the porch. *KA-WHAP!* A perfect strike: the tumbling projectile nails the bottom panel of the screen door. The whole house vibrates, the whole neighborhood, or so it seems. The plastic cylinder rolls backward off the porch. "IT'S NOT FUCKING FAIR!"

Gasping, choking on tears, he jumps down onto the lawn, having regained enough of his wits to realize his jeopardy. After a quick upward glance at Mandy's still-dark windows, he hustles around and hops into the cab. No time to waste. They could be on the way—the cops? the sheriff? Peeling out, he guns the Chevy down Colby to Henley, then north to Butler, where he heads east at 75 mph, racing ahead of the moon. Reaching Misty Hollow Road, he takes a skidding left down the hill into the fog (a thick layer of ground fog shrouds the low-lying hollow).

As he trundles across the one-way bridge, *thump, thump, clatter, thump,* he glimpses a flash in the rearview mirror, bluish light. *O God, they're after me!* Dropping down a gear, he slams the throttle to the floor. The truck charges ahead, the headlights probing the eerie, moonlit fog. He shifts—fifty, sixty, seventy. He rattles over a stretch of washboardy roughness—it jars him violently. Rocks and gravel pelt the underside of the old pickup.

Halfway up the hill (the long slope where he used to jog), the fog disappears. He slows to thirty-five. His heart banging, he looks for the flashing blue light, for the police, but he sees no one, just trees, and the moon—and the fog which occupies, like a pearly flood, the low ground behind him. He resumes his speed. *Maybe I just imagined it? It coulda been the lights from the town glowing through the fog? Or the moon even? In any case, I gotta get home. Or maybe I better hide down by the watermelon patch. No, I'm overreacting. I should go to the house. I don't even know if anyone called the police. The neighbors might've? But I seriously doubt Mrs. Stevens did—she doesn't like to make a scene. I doubt she wants the whole town to know about this.*

Sixty-five, seventy—the Chevy swerves a bit but recovers. Reaching the end of Misty Hollow, he fishtails onto Longley Road, taking the turn at fifty, or close. Too fast, scary moment, but fifty seems like twenty, after going full-throttle all night. A minute later, he whips past his house, without stopping. *No way can I go home now. Mom'll understand my situation, but Dad's gonna need an explanation that makes sense, and I don't have one. Waco, Spindle, Waco, Spindle. I've been back and forth twice in less than a day. He'll never see it as sane—and it ISN'T.* Bryan gives a snort of self-disgust. *And if the police arrest me, they'll charge me with disturbing the peace, or some such thing. I don't know the goshdang laws. Still, it's not like I committed murder or anything. They don't jail people for this, but I'd hafta go to court and pay a fine, and I could get my picture in the damn paper. SHS BASEBALL STAR GOES BERSERK AFTER ELOPING WITH RUNAWAY TEEN. Dad would freak, not to mention Coach Simms and all my teachers. BRYAN HOWARD CHARGED AFTER HIGH-SPEED CHASE. But what does it matter, if I don't have Mandy?*

As he approaches FR 115, he slows to a crawl. *I got homework due. I can't miss any more classes. I need a jacket. I gotta take a piss.* He clicks on the heater fan. *I made one helluva scene, screaming and throwing stuff, but she didn't even come downstairs.* He checks behind him, ahead of him—no lights, no squad cars, no cars whatsoever. *But even if I don't get in trouble with the authorities, I got big problems back at school. I even missed my calculus exam. SPINDLE GRAD LOSES BASEBALL SCHOLARSHIP. It's like Mandy's possessed by her mom or something—this whole thing about "love is a decision and not a feeling," like you can turn it on and off. Not me. It's not a goddam decision for me. And she says my OBEs are demonic—that doctrine stinks too. BAPTIST HONOR STUDENT CLAIMS HE LEFT HIS BODY, LOSES FAVOR WITH GOD.*

Halting at the end of Longley, he gets out to pee. *I don't see anyone.*

THE SILVER CORD

It's like I'm the only person in Hollis County, who's not in bed. He shakes and zips. *Damn, it's cold. I can see my breath. I gotta get back to Waco. I've missed practice all week—almost. I gotta snap out of this. It's futile. No way is Mandy gonna see me. If I hurry, I'll make my classes tomorrow—I mean today.*

But when he gets back into the truck, he turns left toward Spindle. *Oh, Mandy, Mandy ... I don't give a shit about school ... or making the team. Not now.* He wheezes and snorts. *I'll call Helen Stevens, like she told me. I'll call from my house ... after Dad has left for the feed store. But that's four hours from now?*

* * *

HIGHWAY 29 - WESTSIDE LANES
THURSDAY, OCTOBER 24, 1991 — 3:44 AM

Shifting down, Bryan Howard wheels into the large, well-lit lot, the sandy gravel popping under his tires. The goose-necked parking-lot lights shine brightly, but the bowling alley itself closed hours ago. *This's ridiculous and nutty,* he laments to himself, as he parks in the shadows beyond a row of cedar trees on the far left side. *What am I thinking? No one's here.* Giving a snort, he jerks the keys from the ignition. *I gotta cool it. I gotta get my head straight. O Lord, give me peace. I was doing good until I had that dream. But now I've BLOWN it big time. And Mandy was probably watching from her room? Maybe I should give up? No, I gotta talk to her, even if I hafta chase her down at school. Shit, I doubt she's back in school—not this quick?*

He mewls. *She says we hafta follow the Bible, but it seems like the only way to do that is to kill off your heart: "The heart is desperately wicked and who can know it?" Preachers always harp on that verse, but it seems hellish to me ... like it makes everything a duty and a sacrifice. But what good is love if it's just a performance? The love I have for Mandy is bigger than anything, and right now it's killing me. I couldn't will it away if I tried for a million years.* He sheds a few more tears, the few he has left. The sobs have gone dry—the pain has no release. *O Lord, why'd you send me back when I almost died last May? Death was so awesome compared to this nightmare. And Gramps was there waiting for me. If Mandy's gone for good, what's the point? O dear Jesus, I thought you had great plans for us. Why won'tcha ANSWER me? Why won'tcha talk to me? It's not fair. I wish Gramps was alive. I want HIS God, not some mean God who makes us kill our hearts, not some God who uses fear and dread to make us obey. And Gramps was there at the end of the tunnel, under the oak. Or maybe it was all just a dream? Maybe all my OBEs are false illusions from the Devil, like Mandy says, but it's not really Mandy—it's her mother?*

He shivers. His arms are freezing; he needs a coat. He could turn on the heater, but he has no energy, or inspiration, to replace the key

421

and start the engine. The growing volume of her absence has sapped his life force. *Gramps is dead. I can't get through to him ... but God is supposed to hear me—O Lord, if you love me like the Bible says, why won't you answer me?* Bryan waits, and waits, but God says nothing.

Stumbling out of the truck, the Baylor freshman trudges over to the pay phone by the main entrance. He punches in the number, as best he can remember it, putting the call on his Southwestern Bell card. He hopes that Spanky answers—he does.

"I'm in deep shit, Spanker," Bryan snuffles hoarsely.

"You must be for chrissake," Spanky drawls sleepily. "It's the fuckin' middle of the night."

"Mandy left me. I was just at her house. I freaked. It's a big fucking mess I tellyuh."

"Where are yuh now?"

"I'm at the bowling alley."

"The bowlin' alley? What the fuck are yuh doin' there?"

"I'm not sure. I guess I was looking for yuh."

"Well, I *was* there ... last night, playin' pool, then I went to Roy's for a poker game—where I lost thirty fuckin' bucks. But we left the bowlin' alley at ten-thirty. You musta lost your goddam mind to thank I'd be there now."

"Y'got that right, but that's *old* news." Bryan gives a pained chuckle. "Can yuh meet me at Crockett Lake, at South Beach?"

"Shit, slugger, that's a goddam hike. Why don't we meet at the diner, or behind the DQ?"

"No, the police might see me if we stay in town ... if they don't spot me here first? I freaked ... so they could be after me?"

"The *po*lice. My fuckin' God, slugger ... this's goddam mind-blowin' for chrissake. You're a damn jock-scholar? So what h—"

"I'll tellyuh all about it at the lake."

"I'll be there in thirty. No, make it forty for chrissake."

* * *

4:25 a.m. Parked facing the lake, Bryan waits. Ghostly vapors drift over the calm water, while the sandy, moonlit beach looks surreal, sterile-white like bones in an X-ray. Hope struggles for a place in his mind, but with little success. He fingers the stubble on his chin; he takes a deep, shuddering breath. His throat pangs, but his grief remains dry and staunched. Despite the closed windows he detects the mossy-fishy odor of the lake, which deepens his woe, as it brings to mind that happy June day, when they frolicked here, laughing and running and swimming and splashing, and she cleverly snatched his trunks—right off him. He restarts the engine to get some heat then slumps against the door.

Headlights, crunch of gravel, Spanky: *VAH-ROOOHM! VAH-ROOOHM!* There's no mistaking that souped-up Ford.

"So you're a *god*dam outlaw on the run," he cackles, as he climbs into the Chevy. "I cain't wait to hear this story for chrissake." Shoving the hood of his parka back (it has to be cold, if *he*'s wearing a coat), he yawns then rubs his hands together. He smells like Vaseline and yeasty breath and stale Aqua-Velva. "Shitfire, I didn't get to sleep till one, and it's freezing outside, colder than a witch's tit. I even had some frost on my goddam windshield—so what the fuck is goin' on for chrissake?"

"Well, I left Waco before midnight, driving like a nut. When I got to Spindle, I went straight to Mandy's house, and—"

"She took off, did she?" Spanky cuts in. "Goddammit all, that's a *downer*. And she seemed downright happy when we had that cookout in your backyard. I still cain't believe she beat me shootin' hoops, and that tall gal too—Tracy ... that's her name. She's big, but she's got a *nice* fuckable shape. I couldn't take my goddam eyes off her ass, while she was makin' her moves to the basket—that's why I lost." He snorts and laughs and waggles his burr head. "I'd love to do *her* doggie-style, though I'd probably need a bench to get up to her pussy for chrissake. Course, if she got on *top* of me, she might cru—"

"Would yuh shut the fuck up," Bryan objects—he's having second thoughts about calling Spanky.

"Sorry, slugger. I'm bein' goddam insensitive. So go on."

"Well—"

"Oh, I almost forgot. I got sumpthin' to sweeten this deal." Spanky pulls a Snicker and a Baby Ruth out of his jeans. "Here ... take your choice."

"Thanks," Bryan says, choosing the Snicker despite its semi-crushed condition.

While they munch, the Baylor freshman relates his woeful tale, the fifteen-minute version.

"It sucks for chrissake, the Mandy thang," Spanky responds. "But no way in hell are the cops gonna come after yuh, not over a bit of yellin' and throwin'. Shit, when I was a sophomore, I got drunk at Benny's, then I grabbed my twenty-two outta the truck and shot out the goddam street lamps on Caddo Street, all four of 'em. He raises an imaginary rifle to his shoulder, shooting at the starry sky, which appears less starry because of the moon (it's sinking behind them, but it's still there). "And the cops didn't do a fuckin' thang ... 'cept give me a warning a few days later, and they got on Benny's ass for servin' a minor. I did agree to pay for the light bulbs and labor, like forty bucks ... but there were no charges or anythang. What you did was goddam nuthin'. I don't reckon Chief Simpson will give a damn, even *if* someone called."

"Yeah, I guess I shouldn't worry about being arrested, but that's just a side issue, really."

"Y'got that right," Spanky says, his tone warming. "I don't know what to tellyuh." He gives Bryan a pat on the shoulder. "I know she loves yuh ... like I said in August. But I reckon her mom has a bigger hold on her than I thought—and religion."

Now comes silence, a heartfelt silence, but the sincere mood quickly turns awkward. Spanky shifts uneasily. Ditto for Bryan—he's not used to tender moments with his redneck buddy.

"A *god*dam case of Coors would sure help thangs," Spanky quips, ending the uncomfortable interlude. "That would ease your mind for chrissake, or maybe a street-pack of weed."

"Maybe so, Spank, the Coors anyway." Bryan gives a mewly laugh, a few pained syllables. "But nobody's gonna sell me beer, not without an I.D. Plus, I look drunk and wild already, with my face and eyes all red ... and this raggy thing I got on. I mean, I look like I just escaped from a goshdang asylum." More titters, from both of them. "Oh dang, it *hurts* to laugh."

"Yuh do look a mite rough around the edges, slugger. Hell, you almost look ugly enough to hang with me and Roy." More chuckles and cackles. "But back to the beer—I reckon Billy Ray can getcha all the goddam brewski you need, and then some ... if yuh got the money. Course, he's hard to find durin' the day, but he shows up at Benny's most ever' evenin', like by five o'clock or six. And I got other ways of gettin' it to, though I cain't miss school today. I skipped on Tuesday, and they called the goddam house, and my dad almost took my truck keys away. But I'll be around after three, if yuh need me. Plus, I'm sure that Chicano cunt will still serve yuh at the bowlin' alley ... Nina."

"Well, I can't think that far ahead. Plus, I gotta be sober ... if I'm gonna be talking to Mandy's mom. I doubt anything'll come of it, but I'm gonna call her at nine o'clock, like I toldjuh."

"It's a goddam long shot ... goin' through her mama. But whaddeyuh got to lose? Or maybe Mandy'll answer herself? She hasn't been to school yet—least, I haven't seen her."

"Well, it was just Tuesday when she got here, so she's probably starting back to school next week?"

Spanky cackles. "Yeah, that would really be a fuckin' scene ... if you came bustin' into the high school to get her. There's been a lotta gossip, since she ran off to marry you, but that would really set off a firestorm for chrissake. Like the movie *Reckless*, when the greaser guy rode his motorcycle into the school, but he won—she left with him. So it could happen for chrissake."

* * *

5:35 a.m—Spanky, minus his parka, backs his Ford around, then *VAH-ROOOOOHM!*—he peels out of the South Beach lot, spewing gravel and sand behind him. He insisted that Bryan keep the hooded coat for today at least.

No more stars or moonlight. Beyond the lake, the first signs of dawn brighten the eastern sky. Bryan gazes wide-eyed at the pinkish glow, sleepiness overtaking him. He drifts, then *whoosh*, he's above the pickup looking down, a sense of elation welling up within his astral body. "No, no, not now, not without her. I'd rather feel the agony—it's more honest." *Bang*—he's instantly back in his body behind the wheel, his sleepy heartache resuming.

* * *

When Bryan awakes at 7:55 a.m., he's down on the seat. Cold feet, his first sensation, gives way to blinding sunshine, as he sits up. He rubs his eyes; he yawns and stretches. The ascending sun hovers just high enough to possess its full brilliance, and it's not yet hindered by the gilded bands of cirrus streaming above. As he pisses beside the truck, pangs of hurt remind him that nothing has changed—not yet. But the two-hour nap, plus his talk with Spanky, has renewed his determination, his bold resolve.

We won against big odds before, he declares to himself, as he fires up the truck, *on that first day at Baylor, when she came back for her purse, and we can DO it again.*

Arriving at the farm, he sees no cars; he expected his dad to be gone, but not his mom; she evidently had to go in early today. After eating toast and cereal, he heads upstairs; he brushes his teeth then washes in the sink, just enough to get rid of his BO. He puts on a fresh T-shirt plus a flannel shirt. He fishes in his closet for an old windbreaker. He plans to return Spanky's parka later. He paces, to kill time.

9:05 a.m. His heart racing, Bryan calls Mandy's house, using the phone on his wide, wooden-plank study desk (now bare save for the phone). He expects to get her mom, but he gets no one, not even an answering machine. 9:14 a.m. He calls again: no answer. 9:21—he calls again: no answer. By ten o'clock he has called eight times, without getting anyone.

What the hell's going on? he agonizes to himself, as he looks up the number for Kroger's. *Gretchen should be there at least—she's got a broken foot? And there's usually an answering machine. Maybe Mrs. Stevens killed everything, even the ringer, to put me off? But she's the one who said to call? She said she'd be home till ten, then after that she'd be at Kroger's.* He dials the number for Kroger's. *I know I'll get someone this time.*

A female answers: "Kroger's, can I help you?"

"I'm looking for Mrs. Stevens ... Helen Stevens."

"Oh, she's outta the office the rest of the week; she'll be back Monday. Can I take a message?"

* * *

10:24 a.m. Bryan knocks on Mandy's door: no answer, nothing. He sprints around to the back door: no cars, nothing. He knocks: no answer.

He pulls on the screen door—it's locked. No more sunshine: a cool wind buffets him. The house is shut tight, even the cat door. He peers inside but sees no one—then something moves: it's Toby. Trotting across the kitchen, the feline comes to the door, as though realizing that Bryan's a friendly human.

* * *

1:51 p.m. Thunder rumbles across the Howard farm. Bryan paces in his room. 1:54 p.m. He calls Mandy's house for the upteenth time—still no answer. *This's super weird. And I gotta feeling it's not good ... whatever's going on?* He wrings his hands; nervous sweat dampens his undershirt. He resumes pacing. He steps into the bathroom to take a leak. At 1:59 he calls again—no answer. *O God, how can everybody just disappear?* He's gone to Colby Drive three times. He also cruised by the high school, and the church, looking for the Firebird, for Helen's green Escort—to no avail. He called Wendy Lewis twice, getting her machine; he left brief but urgent messages, plus his home number.

He gazes out the window above his wide, naked desk. In the distance, the giant, still-leafy oak looks strangely pale against the darkening sky. More thunder, then the rain commences, a whisper on the roof that quickly grows to a roar. Bryan considers calling the high school, a ballsy move, yet decides to phone the diner instead, to check with Mandy's aunt, also bold but more private. He checks his wallet (ever since the tornado, he's carried a list of key numbers on a folded 3x5 card, especially those associated with Mandy). He punches the number into the phone, then quickly hangs up. *No, lemme try Wendy Lewis ... one more time.* After a few rings, the answering machine clicks on, to his dismay: *Damn, she's still not home, but it's crazy to think I'm gonna catch her in the middle of the af—*

"I'm here; it's me," she declares, interrupting the machine.

"Wendy? Is this Wendy?"

"Yeah, it's me," she chortles breathlessly, "the *real* me."

"This's Bryan, Bryan Howard—O God, I'm glad I gotcha."

"And just barely. I only came home to get my knee brace, before I go to basketball practice. So you're lucky."

"I'm not sure *lucky* is the word," he quips, despite his nerve-wracked state.

They share a quick laugh, then he explains his situation, the two-minute version.

"Yeah, I heard about it. That was wicked wild I gather, that middle-of-the-night scene—but didn't yuh get the news?"

"What news?"

"I think it *sucks* ... but Mandy's on her way to Arkansas—like all of a sudden. She left early this morning ... with her stepfather. She called me right before they left. She's gonna be going to a Christian high school in Newfield? or Northbury? or some such place? It's run by a Bible college."

Rainy silence, an awful pause. A black sense of doom, blacker than the storm outside, has rendered Bryan speechless.

"It's a wicked *bummer*," Wendy proceeds, "but she uh, she uh ... I mean, she wouldn't *lis*ten at all. It's like she's a *diff*erent person or something." These hellish words hack to death his desperate, last-ditch hope, which cowers like a condemned animal in the pit of his stomach. "Her uncle has the Pontiac, the guy who owns the diner; he's gonna buy it. Her mother went to Arkansas too, and Gretchen, but they're coming back Saturday. They're moving also, but not till Christmas."

Now it comes, the blast, the breaking dam. White-hot pain blares like a foghorn in Bryan's head. Dropping the phone, he tears out of his room, bangs down the stairs, careens through the kitchen, then bombs out the back door, scarcely touching the steps. Amid the rain and thunder, he flees in agony around the barn, racing full-bore toward the hayfields. Tears blur the dark, boiling sky; the wind takes his breath; the cold downpour stings his face. He sprints down the rain-swollen tractor trail, his sneakers squishing and splashing.

The pine grove looms in the squally murk. He tumbles headlong over the barbed-wire fence then sloshes through the storm-lashed stand of conifers, his flesh smarting, and bleeding, from the fence barbs. A low-hanging limb *whaps* him in the head. He stumbles, reeling sideways, but regains his stride. Exiting the woods, he charges madly up the hill toward the big oak tree.

The scream erupts from the core of his soul, a bellowing bansheelike lament that rips open the black Texas sky. No air, can't breathe—the keening cry sucks him dry, but it does not die. The wailing goes on and on, merging with the wind, the shrieking gale. His lungs burning, he gasps and chokes, losing his balance. He falls on his face; he tastes mud; he flails and flounders, clawing for air like a swimmer caught in an undertow. Thunder booms. Bryan catches his breath, along with the chilly aromas of rain and grass and miry soil. The Johnson grass clutches him like seaweed, soaking his shirt, his jeans—he shivers and shakes. "Dear God, why? Why? O Jesus, I hate this *FUCK*ING world!"

Clambering to his feet, Bryan staggers on, his clothes clinging heavily. He wipes the rain from his eyes, and the tears. Onward, upward—to the giant oak, where the wailing wind has taken on a deeper timbre: the roar of a tortured lion. It rages through the leafy crown, whipping the branches, making the limbs creak and sway. But he attacks the source. Sinking to his knees, he pummels the massive trunk, as if battering the face of God. The bark lacerates his hands. Yet he continues the assault until his fists are hamburger, his arms limp, his eyes cried out. Collapsing onto his side, he assumes a fetal position amid the roots and weeds. He shivers and whimpers. The blaring pain in his head recedes to a raw and distant whir. *O Jesus, let me die. Let me die.*

THE SILVER CORD

CHAPTER TWENTY-FIVE

146 DOUGLAS STREET
SUNDAY, OCTOBER 27, 1991 — 2:58 PM

Propping the pillows behind him, Bryan Howard sits up in his bed. He's been napping on and off, but he's now alert. *I'm almost a week behind in my classes,* he frets. *And fall baseball is over. I must explain to Coach McKinney, or go see Coach Weaver even. And I need to shave.* He rubs his bristly, four-day beard. *And this room's a mess. I got clothes all over. I need to do laundry. I'll get Chris to show me how to use that washing machine. Mandy knew how, but I never learned.* He gives a tortured murmur, as a Mandy-pang binds his chest. *O God, I hafta let go.* The goose egg on his head has diminished, his hands are healing, the lacerations and abrasions and bruises, and the barbed-wire punctures (hands, arms, chest) have scabbed over. Tracy McCollum removed the gauze bandages from his hands last night, replacing them with Band-Aids. She has attended to him day and night, especially Friday night when he was delirious with fever.

This has been the WORST week of my life, but a NEW week starts tomorrow, and I gotta make up for lost time. Bryan grabs his history text from the bedside table. *Maybe I should move back into the dorm? No, not yet. I'm paid up here through November 10th. I'll decide later. I already got plenty to deal with. And I hafta see Dr. Nadler on the 6th. I'm glad this knot on my head is going down.* He chuckles. *No, Doc, I was running berserkly through the woods in a thunderstorm.* More pained chuckles. *No way ... but I do hafta tell him about my eye.*

Opening the history book, Bryan flips to Chapter Eleven: RAILROADS, STEEL, AND ROBBER BARONS. But instead of reading about post-Civil War America, he gazes out the open window, focusing on a crow, as it preens itself atop the utility pole at the end of the driveway. The satiny-black scavenger looks almost blue in the bright sunshine.

Despite his pleas, Bryan didn't die at the oak tree Thursday in the storm. But the cold rain did put him in bed with the flu. Or maybe he got it because of his Mandy trauma, the emotion and sleep loss and fatigue. Whatever got the germ going, he hasn't been out of bed since Friday afternoon, except to visit the toilet.

After the hilltop clash with God, he lay weeping in the wet grass till the gale subsided to a damp rustling of leaves, the thunder to a distant echo. Drenched, drained, and defeated, he hauled himself numbly to his feet. The winterlike breeze had backed into the north. It chilled his bones, as he trudged back to his house where he took a shower and put on fresh clothes.

Leaving a note for his mom, along with Spanky's parka, he headed back to Waco, wearing a pair of cotton field-gloves to protect his lacerated hands. He could have stayed at the farm, or looked for Billy Ray and a binge of drinking, or Spanky, but something compelled him to return to Douglas Street, a vague calling, an uncanny but persuasive conviction that Spindle was no longer his home, that his month with Mandy had changed him forever. Yet as he drove, he purposed once more to accept the situation, to turn his attention to his studies, to his neuroscience goals, to making the team in the spring.

When he arrived at the house, he visited with Chris and Tracy (they were editing another batch of research files). Bryan, exhausted and ready for bed, gave them a quick report, but Tracy insisted on doctoring his wounds; she used the nurse-kit she keeps in her Tempo. She also made toast and chicken-noodle soup for Bryan, in his kitchen (O'Shea's). He was able to hold a spoon and such with his bandaged hands, but it was like eating with mittens on. While he slurped and munched, she joined him at the table, sipping on a Dr. Pepper (one of Mandy's from the fridge), but Chris stood arms-folded by the sink, offering occasional words of wisdom. Few smirks, no jesting, no hopeful spin—the mustached junior seemed downright melancholy. "We never get over it, not really ... but life does become half-tolerable again."

Bidding them good night, Bryan hauled himself up the stairs, where the ringing phone gave him a Mandy rush, but it was just his mom; he assured her he was okay, despite all. Yet he wasn't okay, and on Friday morning he woke up feverish and nauseated.

Bryan, the textbook still on his lap, notices a second crow outside. It lands on the neck of the streetlight a few feet away from the first crow. After a bit of hopping and cawing, the two birds take flight together, winging west above the trees which line Douglas Street. Bryan sighs. *Mandy, Mandy ... oh, pretty lady ... it's still hard to believe that you're actually gone.*

He returns to his homework, but after fifteen restless minutes, he gives up. *I can't concentrate. It's like I'm reading the same page over and over. Jay Gould, James Fisk, the Erie Railway, the Panic of 1869. I'll hafta learn this stuff for the midterm, but right now I'm still dealing with the Panic of 1991.* He titters, a resigned ha-ha. Throwing the covers back, he yawns to his feet then slips out of his pajamas. He rarely wears pajamas, but he got vomit on his last (clean) sleep-jersey when he threw up in the bathroom on Friday morning. He only barfed once, but he felt like death that whole day and night.

After pulling on jeans and a sweat shirt, he pads out of the bedroom, his legs still a bit shaky. He smells Tracy in the hallway, in the bathroom, her perfume, a sweet floral scent, like rose nectar. *I reckon she went back to her dorm,* he tells himself, as he brushes his teeth, vigorously. This two-day flu, or whatever it was, has left a roadkill taste in his mouth. *I haven't seen her since she brought those waffles up this morning. That was the first food I felt like eating. And I'm hungry again. I reckon I'm getting well. Maybe I'll eat at the caf tonight. I haven't used my meal card since Tuesday. But I'll hafta shower and shave first. I stink like a pig sty.* Stepping over to the toilet, he empties his bladder. As he flushes, the phone rings above the gurgling john. His heart leaps: *Mandy, Mandy.* He scoots into the living room, sobering as he goes. *No way ... it can't be her.*

"Oh, it's you, Bryan," Ginny Howard reacts, after her son answers. "I expected your friend Tracy again; you must be feeling better?"

"Yeah, Mom, I reckon so. In fact, I'm outta bed now."

"Well, I've been real concerned ... ever since I called Friday afternoon, and she told me you had a fever ... and when I phoned yesterday, she said you were asleep."

"I *did* have a fever, but it's gone now."

"So who *is* this Tracy? And how'd she happen to be there this weekend? I mean uh—"

"Oh, she hangs out with Chris—Chris Hansen. He's the guy who lives in the garage apartment. I toldjuh about him."

"Yes, I think you did—so is she a student at Baylor?"

"Yeah, she's a junior, like Chris. She works with him over at the Neurology Department, the research lab. She lives on campus ... but she's over here a lot, so Mandy and I got to know her." A pang accompanies his words; it hurts to say "Mandy and I."

"Are Chris and Tracy? Y'know, are they uh—"

"Nawh ... they're just friends. She treats him like a brother."

Ginny clears her throat. "And she just *vol*unteered to take care of you ... while y'were sick?"

Bryan laughs. "I reckon she has *strong* maternal instincts. No, she was over here anyway, helping Chris. They do a lot of computer work in his apartment. Plus, she's studying to be a nurse, so it was sorta second nature to her."

"Well, it was very kind of her to *nurse* you—but, Bryan honey, you shoulda stayed here instead of rushing back down there. You need some time at home, to get well ... and to get over this whole heartbreak situation. You can relax here at the farm as long as you like, even *this* week."

"I can't, Mom. I hafta get back to class, like I toldjuh. I *was* planning on going back Friday—but then I got the flu."

A bit later, after saying good-bye, he slumps back in the sofa. A wave of Mandy woe wells up inside him. *Mom will always see me as a little kid, but things are different now ... very different.*

Silence, solitary silence—the empty apartment magnifies the ache in his bosom. Locking his hands behind his head, he gazes at the blank TV then at the armchair where Mandy sat so often, her feet curled under her. His eyes fill. *O God, I hate this, yet I can't go home. I can't go back in time ... even though Mom would take care of me forever.*

THE SILVER CORD

And Dad loves me too, but it would hurt him if I dropped out of college and turned into a farmboy bum.

Pushing up from the sofa, Bryan steps into the hallway. He checks out the O'Shea's master bedroom. *Yeh, Tracy's gone back to Collins Hall. Her stuff is gone, and the bed's made.*

Three minutes later, after putting on his sneakers, he's outside knocking on Chris's door. No answer. He knocks harder: still no answer. To the driveway: he strides around his truck. The gray Tempo is gone, Tracy's car, but the ugly, pea-green Chevette squats in the open garage, in its usual spot. *Chris went with Tracy, or he might've taken his bicycle to campus?* A vacant space to the left of the Chevette confirms the last explanation.

Empty, lonely, panging heart. Bryan slumps against the side of his pickup. He feels desolate, forsaken, like the last soul on earth. He needs to get his mind off Mandy, but how can he, when he's all by himself drowning in the reality of her absence? Gone, gone; she's *gone*—everyone's gone. Even the weather has left town: no wind, no clouds, upper 70s.

He's soon upstairs again, dialing the phone. *I doubt I'll catch him on a Sunday afternoon.*

"Goddam, slugger, I was wonderin' if I'd hear from yuh," Spanky drawls, after saying hello and a few other things—he *is* home (winning brownie points; he was in the backyard washing his dad's Silverado when the phone rang). "So what the fuck happened on Thursday, after I left yuh at the lake?"

Bryan fills him in.

"Yeah, I heard the scuttlebutt ... about her movin' to some horseshit town in the Ozarks. That's a downer for chrissake. But we can still go drinkin' if yuh like, and we might even find some pussy." Spanky cackles. "I'll even come down there. I wouldn't mind checkin' out some of those horny Baylor cunts that Chris was yakin' about. Shit fire and save matches. That college is a goddam gold mine of legal snatch." More cackling.

"C'mon, Spank," Bryan objects, though he can't help but chuckle at the bawdy offer. "I'm not even officially single ... not yet. Besides, I'm hardly in the mood for carousing around."

Spanky softens. "Sorry, slugger. I'm just runnin' off at the mouth ... my gutter-mouth."

"No biggie—but we *can* get together. I hafta go to Dallas to see Dr. Nadler on the sixth, like a week from Wednesday. If yuh wanna meet me afterward, we could go for a pizza or something."

"My fuckin' God," Spanky reacts, despite his gutter-mouth apology. "There's enough booze in Dallas to float a goddam aircraft carrier, not to speakuh the swingers and whores, and you wanna settle for a *pizza*?" He wheezes and chortles.

After a little more bantering about Dallas, Bryan says, "Oh, by the way, your parka's at my house. My mom has it."

"Who cares about that goddam hooded thang? It makes me feel like a monk for chrissake."

* * *

Same Sunday, 4:22 p.m. Bryan heads back to his room, smelling of soap and shaving cream. He's showered and shaved, but his enthusiasm for supping at the caf has waned. The chat with Spanky allayed his gloom, but it's now back. *I feel like crawling back into bed,* he laments, as he pulls a pair of clean Levi's out of his bottom drawer. *But I reckon I should go eat. I gotta get back into real life.* He puts on the jeans plus a knit shirt, then after slapping on some Brute, he plops down on the unmade bed to put on his sneakers. As he does, he hears a car pull in. His heart jumps: *Can't be—it's not the Firebird. Gosh damn ... I'm going crazy. I gotta stop expecting her.* The Mandy-hurt digs, but then his reaction shifts. *That must be Tracy?* This conclusion distracts him, mollifying his woe. He soon hears the back door, then sounds in the kitchen, then footsteps on the stairs.

"Well, *look* who's up," she declares upon entering the room, her teenybopper timbre climbing another octave—it *is* Tracy. "I came back to look in on yuh, but I sorta figured you were better, after you ate those waffles this morning."

Bryan laughs, looking up from his untied sneakers. "Yeah, I reckon I'm gonna live. Plus, I got tired of lying in this dadgum bed." He catches a whiff of her rose-scented perfume, fresh and pungent, as if recently applied. "Your stuff's gone, so I figured y'went back to your dorm?"

"I did, to freshen up ... but I wanted to check on yuh anyway. Besides, I had to fetch a box of floppy disks that I left on Chris's computer desk. He's at the lab; he rode his bike over—oh, I also got yuh some bread and milk, and cold cuts, and more waffles, and some Dr. Pepper too."

"You didn't hafta do that."

"Well, I've been helping myself to your fridge for two days."

He detects nicotine, a faint cigarette smell working through the cloak of perfume. She cants her hips, shifting her shapely heft from one sandal to the other, then she retreats to the doorway where she leans against the jamb. Giving a shy smirk, she pushes her bangs to the side. She looks like she did that first day at the Bear's Paw. She's even wearing the same khaki shorts. The T-shirt is different—barely: it's pale gray instead of white. She's been in Bryan's bedroom a dozen times since Friday, but this's the first instance where he's noticed her clothes. No, he also noticed her Baylor sweats this morning, the jockish warm-up suit.

"I appreciate your help," he says, returning to his shoelaces. "I didn't plan on crashing like I did. I hope I didn't ruin your weekend."

"Nawh, we had to transfer a jillion files for Doc Richardson, like I toldjuh ... so I didn't have any plans." She giggles. "Besides, it was a treat to sleep two nights in Annie's big four-poster bed. And it's good to escape from the dorm, especially when Jamie's on one of her horror-movie kicks. She went out on Friday and rented every vampire movie in Waco." More laughing, him too.

"Well, you do a darn good job as a nurse. I haven't been *that* sick for a while."

"I'll say," Tracy agrees, gesturing with her girlish, suntanned hands (she still has her summer tan, a tawny, honeylike hue a notch darker than most fair-skinned gals, yet she'd still be considered fair). "Chris and I considered taking you to the infirmary Friday night, but then you fell back to sleep."

"I'm glad you didn't. I reckon I've already done my hospital time for *this* year."

"Yeh ... Chris told me you got hurt playing baseball. He said you had some kind of metaphysical experience too, though he didn't elaborate."

"*Good*," Bryan responds, dimpling.

Tracy grins as well, giving an open-handed gesture—her palms are ruddy pink. "So *what* happened? What was it?"

He grabs one of the bed pillows, placing it on his lap. "I'll tellyuh ... *one* of these days."

She smirks but doesn't press for an answer. Instead, she rolls her chocolate-colored eyes, giving him a sidelong glance. She crosses her legs, one way then the other. Bryan can't help but check out her thighs, as he did the day he met her. He quickly shifts his attention, looking down at the pillow on his lap, but he can't sidetrack the twinge of desire under the pillow, the first he's felt in a long while. He pictures her panties, the blue glimpse of crotch he caught in Chris's apartment, when she was smoking the Salem Light. He wonders what panties she's wearing today, under those khaki shorts. His face warms. Tracy gives a frolicsome titter, as though tuning into his thoughts. He senses her kitty-cat face blushing back at him. Grinning sheepishly, he looks up to confirm. She *is* blushing, but she's looking down at her feet, at her leather sandals. She crinkles her Doric nose then purses her prim Irish mouth, not the rabbity move Mandy makes, but it's close enough to unleash a torrent of guilt and hurt in Bryan's gut. No more lust, no more dimples. *Forgive me, Tracy,* he reacts, but only to himself. *I love Mandy. She was my whole life. I need her. I want her—but you're NOT her.*

Tracy lifts her eyes, meeting his wistful gaze. "Oh, Bryan dear," she blurts, as she hurries over and sits down beside him on the bed. She takes his hand. "I understand. I do ... I do. I know you're devastated over Mandy. It's a crushing thing, and now that you're well again, it's hitting you *hard*. It's a fucking heart tragedy—pardon my French—

but I *do* understand." To hear such grown-up solace coming from this childlike voice seems bizarre, not to speak of her potent sexuality and the cigarette smoke on her breath (she actually smells good, the rosy perfume, but the nicotine comes through when she talks; she must've smoked a Salem in her car on the way here). She caresses his back in a tender, sisterly fashion. "I can't fix it ... and there's no way that I, or anyone, can take Mandy's place, but I do know what you're going through. I went through it with Stuart. So even though we can't com*plete* each other ... we can con*sole* each other."

Bryan doesn't reply, but he slowly nods—he gets the message, and it *does* console him.

"We both have great potential," Tracy goes on, "if we can somehow survive the aching and longing. And I feel closer to you after these past two days, even though we've scarcely talked. But I do wanna talk and share and be friends. I wanna hear about your experiences, and your ideas. I'm not super religious, but I do believe in God, *and* destiny. There's gotta be a purpose. So I think we can help each other ... as *friends*. And Chris too. He's a wise-ass, but he's been wounded by love as well."

"I know," Bryan says, as they embrace. She lays her head on his shoulder. Sister, mother, nurse, nubile coed—he's glad for her company, for her kindness, but *no way* can she fill the gaping chasm in his life, the great abyss of Mandy's absence.

"Chris is still hurt over Jennifer," Tracy elaborates, as she stretches to her feet. She fluffs her hair, then adjusts her shorts where they've ridden up. "He lived with her back in Chicago."

"Yeah, he told me about Jennifer."

Tracy yawns. "So, Bryan, whaddeyuh gonna do for supper?"

"Oh, I figured I'd eat free tonight, at the cafeteria."

"Me too. Mind if I join yuh?"

* * *

BAYLOR UNIVERSITY - FERRELL FIELD COMPLEX
MONDAY, OCTOBER 28, 1991 — 2:25 PM

"Where the hell you been, Howard?" Coach Elmo McKinney growls, as Bryan Howard enters a small office near the entrance to the Baylor locker room. The coach, seated at his desk, wears a green-and-white gym-instructor shirt but no hat. "I ain't seen yuh for a goddam week. You called on Tuesday, but that's the last I heard from yuh?"

"Well, Coach ... I uh ... I uh—"

"Stop stutterin' and sit your white ass down."

Bryan quickly obeys.

McKinney frowns sternly, as if ready to come down hard on the AWOL freshman, but then he grins, showing his tobacco-stained teeth which gleam with gold amalgam. "Y'can relax. I already covered for yuh. I told Coach Weaver y'had a death in the family, and y'had to go to uh—"

"Spindle."

McKinney rakes his gray, tightly kinked hair. "Spindle, yeah. So that's what that S stands for on your cap?"

"Yes sir," Bryan replies, after removing the blue hat—he feels more comfortable, somewhat relieved. The stuffy windowless office smells of sweat and tobacco, chewing tobacco, and the desk (small, gray, steel-fabricated) could pass for military surplus.

The old batting coach leans forward, steepling his thick hands. He gives a throaty grunt. "Now I told a *white* lie to save your *white* ass, but I need to know the goddam truth." He gives a quick laugh. "There weren't no death in your family I reckon?"

Bryan fiddles with his cap, fingering the nub. "No sir."

McKinney rolls his eyes, the whites slipping sideways, as they shine out of his black, leathery face. "And you're not on drugs, or in trouble with the law?"

"No sir."

"So this has to be a pussy problem. I mean a *girl* situation?"

Bryan blushes, his face warming. "Well, I had the flu Friday ... but it's mainly a girl thing."

The coach sits back, the chair squeaking under him. "The ole lovesick *blues*. Shit, I reckon that's worse than death."

"No kidding."

"So yuh broke up with your hometown sweetheart?"

"Yeah ... but she was my wife too, for three weeks."

"Ah, that's right. You got married and moved outta the dorm. I saw your paperwork."

Bryan gives the necessary details, the five-minute version.

McKinney asks a few more questions then says, "I feel for yuh, Howard, but gettin' your heart broken is all part of growin' up. It happens to all of us. Hell, I musta cried over twenty gals in my day, and I was married to three." They share a chuckle. "But your sweetheart could come back y'know? There ain't no way of predictin' what a woman's gonna do." More chuckling. "So there ain't no point in redoin' your paperwork or movin' yuh back to the dorm till the end of the semester. We'll talk again in January. For now, you'll be listed as married and off-campus." The coach, giving a sigh, swivels toward the side wall, toward a collection of framed pictures and news clippings. He points at the nearest one, a faded photo of a black player holding a skinny old-fashioned bat. "See that feller there—that's Cottonseed Walker. He holds the Negro League record for most hits in a season ... 286."

"That's quite a feat," Bryan replies. "No modern player ever got close to that ... even Pete Rose, or Wade Boggs."

"True, and he did it in a shorter season, like a hun'erd thirty games—yet I reckon you ain't never heard of Cottonseed?"

"No sir, I never did."

"That's my point, Bryan, and I hope you're listenin'. Y'got great baseball potential, and I reckon you're a shoo-in to make this mediocre goddam team, and I know the Astros been scoutin' your ass. But chances are, you'll never get any more fame than Cottonseed up there. There's too many thangs that can happen."

Like my left eye going wacky, the freshman interjects, but only to himself.

McKinney swivels to face Bryan. "I may be wrong, and you might be lucky ... lucky enough to make it to the big show. But it's a goddam long shot. So I hope y'got other goals too."

"I do, sir ... I've got other ambitions."

Picking up a large paper clip, the coach taps it on the arm of the chair. "Like what?"

"Neuroscience ... brain research."

"That's right, you're in pre-med, a goddam honor student. So y'wanna be a doctor, d'yuh?"

"Yes sir, that's the plan ... though I'm now leaning more toward the research part." Bryan dimples. "But I hope to make the Astros too ... or some team. That would be super neat, plus it'll give me financial freedom to pursue my other goals."

"Shit, you really *are* a dreamer—but I've said my piece. Now get your white ass outta here. We'll be startin' weight trainin' on November 11th. I'll see yuh then."

* * *

I'm back on track, Bryan tells himself a few minutes later, as he drives south on Rigby. He lowers his window the rest of the way; it's hot again, like eighty-five. *Thank God for Coach McKinney. And my academic situation is gonna be okay too. I just have reading to catch up on, and I missed my calculus exam ... but Mr. Cook didn't seem concerned. He said I could take it Wednesday afternoon, in Dr. Edelstein's office.* Bryan wheels the Chevy onto Verner—he has to check his mail. *And the whole thing with Tracy helps. She does tend to mother me, and big-sister me, like last night at the caf, but she IS older and wiser about things.*

He eases the pickup into the sun-baked parking lot behind the Bill Daniel Student Center. He ate here at noon, but he forgot to stop by the student post office. Steve Jordan lunched with him, and Bryan gave the big guy the news concerning Mandy. Jordan seemed to be listening concernedly, between huge bites of meat loaf, but then he abruptly took over the conversation, his bassy drawl clogged with food: "Heck, y'missed my best showin', dude ... in Thursday's practice game. Yessir, I had six no-hit innin's, with *ten* Ks. And yuh shoulda seen Jamal on Saturday against Texas Tech. He ran back a punt 64 yards for a TD. We lost 49-13 ... but Jamal should get more playin' time. Then later, me and Jamal ... we went to the Peek-A-Boo Club. Heck, y'should come with us sometime." Jordan gave a big belly laugh. "That would lift your spirits, dude, seein' all those boobs and naked butts."

Bryan works the combination on his PO box then pulls out the mail, campus junk, plus his phone bill—plus a letter with a Spindle return: COLBY DRIVE. But the postmark says AR. That's ARKANSAS! Fever—hot flash. He rips it open:

> Bryan,
>   I'm sorry I missed you yesterday. I had to leave unexpectedly, so I wasn't at home, or at Kroger's. In fact, I'm still in Arkansas helping Mandy get settled at her new school. I'm returning to Spindle on Sunday, and you're welcome to call me, but what I'm saying here covers pretty much everything.
>   Amanda has moved here to Newbury. She's chosen a Christian high school (Newbury Christian Academy), and next fall she'll be entering NCB (Newbury College of the Bible). It's her decision, and I ask you to respect it. Please don't make a fool of yourself again.
>   In a month or so, you'll receive the annulment papers from Louisiana. As you know, the marriage was never legal. I harbor no hard feelings toward you, Bryan. You're a fine young man, but we must put FIRST things first. You're way too young for marriage, and Mandy's not even out of high school. I pray for you, with fond regards.
>
>   Helen A. Stevens

* * *

146 DOUGLAS STREET
MONDAY, OCTOBER 28, 1991 — 4:56 PM

Bryan, breathing hard, dials the high-school dorm in Newbury. He got the number from Wendy Lewis, who got it from Gretchen. One ring, two, then three. His heart hammers in his chest.

"Newbury Christian, Bethany Hall," comes a matronly voice, the housemother?"

"I uh—I'm looking for Amanda Stevens. She just moved in."

"Whom should I say is calling?"

"Bryan ... Bryan Howard."

"One minute please ... I'll see if I can find her."

He waits, his life hanging. *Maybe I shoulda said that she's my wife—no, nawh ... no way. That woulda caused a storm.*

"She's not in her room," the housemother tells him, finally. "I expect she and her roommates have already gone over to the cafeteria—they start serving at five. But I'll leave a message."

* * *

8:09 p.m. Bryan sprawls dejectedly on his living-room couch, waiting for the phone to ring. Except for a trip down to the kitchen for a baloney sandwich, he's been here all evening. He's called Newbury three more times, but he's never gotten Mandy. *Gosh damn ... she's gotta have the message by now? This sucks, all of it. Coach McKinney's right. It IS worse than death.*

He's tempted to call one last time, but before he can, the phone cries out with its electronic warble. Bryan's heart bangs upward, so hard it knocks him off the sofa. "That's gotta be her." He scrambles to answer—but it's only Tracy.

"Bryan dear," she says. "I just got a cool idea. Chris and I are still at the lab, but we're thinking about going down to the Bear's Paw. Why don't we stop by and pick yuh up. It'll be damn good for yuh to get out. In fact, it'll be good for *all* of us."

* * *

Same night, 10:22 p.m—the Bear's Paw Lounge. "Have another one, slugger," Chris exhorts, as he pours more Coors draft into Bryan's glass. "You're not driving tonight, nor am I, so we can drink as much as we want." Giving a smirky laugh, the mustached junior lifts his own glass. "But let's give a toast to Tracy, our designated driver, who's kindly agreed to stop at three beers. She's the best big sister I know of."

"Thanks a lot, guys," she fusses playfully, as she sips her third. After swallowing, she sticks out her tongue at Chris, but she gives Bryan a cute, semi-mischievous side-glance.

When they picked him up, in Tracy's Tempo, Bryan told them about his up-then-down day, with emphasis on the *down* part, as he related his panicky, call-Newbury reaction to Helen's letter. And they've continued to address the issue off and on, but with less and less soberness—thanks to Adolph Coors.

Chris burps. "Ex*cuuuse* me ... but I want to toast our baseball star, neuro-genius, who's gonna change the world with his wild theories, if we can just keep him, and us, from going stark-raving mad over lost lovers." They all laugh, hilarious ha-ha-ha's.

* * *

DALLAS PRESBYTERIAN - FERGUSON WING - FIFTH FLOOR
WEDNESDAY, NOVEMBER 6, 1991 — 3:51 PM

Bryan checks out a recent *Sports Illustrated*. He notes, with zero interest, a blurb on Greg Norman, the Aussie golfer. He's already digested the NFL news and the baseball BS. "If you can be here by eight a.m., we should have your test results by four p.m." That's what the lady said when he confirmed things last week. After he sees Dr. Nadler, he's meeting Spanky in the main lobby, at five o'clock. The Baylor freshman has thumbed through fifteen mags (from the table in the small waiting room), he's gone down for lunch, he's walked the grounds; he even visited the Trauma Center ICU, saying hello to Nurse Johnson and a few others. He has exhausted all the time-consuming ideas, leaving just him and the clock and his Mandy-woe, a cold empty feeling in his bosom, in his stomach, cold, empty, and sinking. He received, last Friday, a second letter from Helen Stevens: "Mandy has made her wishes very clear. If you call Newbury again, I'll have no choice but to get a court order, to restrain you."

He's tried to focus on college, with little success. He does show for class, but he's falling behind in his reading and homework, and he made 58 on his calculus exam a week ago. He fears he's on his way to an F in the course. But he can't stand to study, because it's painful to be alone with his thoughts, like right now. He needs interaction, and stimulation, and alcohol. He's downed more beer in the last nine days than in his previous eighteen years. He drinks mainly with Chris, but some with Tracy, and some with Steve Jordan and Jamal. He drinks in Chris's apartment, in his kitchen, at the Bear's Paw, at the Peek-A-Boo Club. Yes, he went to the strip joint on Loop 340, an experience that excited and revolted him at the same time.

Without doubt he's horny enough to respond to female flesh, Tracy's thighs included, but when he masturbates, his heart won't let him fantasize about anyone but Mandy, and lately, he's been too drunk for sexual release anyway. He stays up late, shooting the shit with Chris, sipping and swigging, until the Mandy-hurt disappears in a beery fog. Except for last night when he forced himself to retire early, so he could hit the road by six-thirty.

"Bryan *How*ard," a female voice announces ten minutes later. He follows the nurse to a small, beige-walled consulting room. "Please have a seat. Dr. Nadler will be with you shortly."

He soon arrives, a packet of X-rays in hand. "Bryan, I have good news and bad news, and the good outweighs the bad." He sits down at the desk; he strokes his chiseled face then slips on his glasses. I'll show you the scans in a minute, but I must say that I still view your recovery as remarkable, and there's nothing negative in today's data regarding primary neurological function and vitality—now that's the *good* news." Taking off his glasses, he pushes a black spit-lock off his forehead.

"And the bad news?" Bryan asks.

"I'm afraid the left-eye problem, the sporadic blurriness you talked about during our brief talk this morning ... it will most likely be with you the rest of your life, and it may get worse."

THE SILVER CORD

MESQUITE, TEXAS - SUNSET MOTOR LODGE
WEDNESDAY, NOVEMBER 6, 1991 — 9:17 PM

Bryan fishes two more Budweisers from the cooler in the bathtub. He tosses one to Spanky, the can shedding water as it flies across the room. "My fuckin' God, slugger ... you're drinkin' more than me. And I thought yuh just wanted to get a pizza in Dallas?"

"That was ten days ago," Bryan replies, as he pulls open his beer: *kurrrr-RUP*. He plunks down on the nearest bed (opposite Spanky). "But now I don't give a goddam shit." He flips the pull-tab toward the trash basket beside the TV; it misses.

"Well, it's a good thang I got a whole case from Billy Ray. I was just gonna bring a six-pack or two for chrissake. And you musta charged fifty bucks on your credit card at that restaurant ... for those ribs and all ... not to speakuh this motel."

Bryan, mellow but still coherent, gestures with his Bud. "It's not wise to drink in the truck, and we'd probably get carded if we went to a bar. Plus, I don't give a shit if I spend my whole damn credit limit." He's nowhere near happy, but the Mandy-ache gets duller with each sip, as does the nagging anxiety about his eye (no way can he make it to the Astros, or even play at Baylor, if Nadler is right about the blurry spells becoming more frequent).

Spanky swigs then cackles. "Well, I reckon I'm makin' out like a bandit, even after payin' goddam Billy Ray. But gettin' a room was a fuckin' good idea. There's just *one* thang missin'."

"What's that?"

"Pussy. We need some babes for chrissake."

"Nawh ... not me," Bryan snorts, stepping into the bathroom to piss. "That's the *last* thing I need ... the dadgum last." As he zips up, he hears Spanky on the phone. "Who yuh calling?"

Same motel, 10:21 p.m. "I can't believe you actually did it," Bryan chortles, as he kills off his fifth Bud. The foamy liquid is doing its job. A hot-water balloon has inflated under his heart, or so it seem, a warm and fuzzy buoyancy, his inner-self expanding. "And yuh only got one? This could turn out *super* weird?"

"Stop frettin' for chrissake," Spanky snorts, lifting his own beer can. "It's no big deal, but she's gonna be here at ten-thirty, so you better brush your goddam teeth, and comb your hair."

Same motel, 10:50 p.m. A little *rap-rap* sounds at the door. Butterflies wiggle in Bryan's gut—they're too drunk to fly. Spanky smirks but doesn't budge. "You answer it, slugger."

"Why me?" Another *rap-rap*. Bryan pads to the door.

Kinky blond hair, pink lip gloss, big gray eyes black with mascara. "Are you Bryan Howard?" she asks. Halter top, thigh-length cocktail skirt, fishnet hosiery.

"I uh, well yeah—that's me." He shakes her hand, clumsily.

"I'm Ginger, from Elegant Affairs," she announces, tiptoeing into the room, or so it seems with her high stiletto-heels. "Sorry, I'm late." She trails a plume of nostril-clearing perfume.

Spanky bounces to his feet. "I'm Curtis Wayne Arnold"—he bows to the hooker like a Confederate Colonel. Coming up, he pulls his wallet and gives her a $50 plus five $20's. "Now I'm outta here." Grabbing his beer, he heads for the door.

"Whaa ... what uh?" Bryan stammers. "Where the heck are *you* going?"

Spanky cackles—he gestures toward the door with his beer. "I'm goin' to my truck to relax with this goddam canah Bud. I owe it to yuh, slugger. I'll see yuh in an hour. Y'all have fun."

* * *

146 DOUGLAS STREET
THURSDAY, NOVEMBER 7, 1991 — 8:22 AM

Bryan Howard, his head throbbing, hauls himself up the stairs. "No way can I go to class today," he murmurs under his breath, yeasty, foul-smelling breath. Sprawling fully clothed onto his bed, he pulls the comforter over him. It's actually warm outside, but he's almost cold enough to shiver.

He departed the motel at six. He wanted to leave at midnight, after Ginger left, but Spanky grabbed his keys: "You're gonna kill y'self if yuh try to drive now. Y'gotta sleep it off, slugger."

The escort encounter was more educational than erotic. She rubbed his back, she did a little strip dance, then she spread for him on the bed, displaying her mustached pussy, a delicious sight for horny eyes, not to mention her pink-nippled breasts. Yet he got no farther than a bit of kissing and fondling. Finally, they sat up and talked—about the sucky state of love on the earth.

Folding his pillow while pulling the other one over his head, Bryan falls asleep amid pangs of self-disgust, not so much over Ginger the call girl, but because of the overall downward spiral of his life: his academic performance, his sense of responsibility, his attitude toward God, his hopes for the future, his sobriety—he's sick of getting wasted on beer, but it's the only way to cope.

THE SILVER CORD

* * *

Same day, 1:02 p.m. Bryan wakes up horny, his dick like steel. *I musta had a sexy dream, but I don't remember it.* He rolls over. The room seems hot; he's sweating. He throws the comforter off. Mandy, Mandy: she flashes onto the screen of his mind, the teasing routine in the armchair when she pulled up her Denny's skirt, displaying her crotch. *Pussy, pussy,* he sighs. *I can't stand it. I want your pussy, pretty lady.* But she morphs into Ginger at the motel, then into Tracy, who he's never seen—yet he imagines her naked on Annie O'Shea's bed. *God, I'd gladly fuck her, even her skinny roommate ... or Wendy Lewis, or the girls in the cafeteria. I'm ready to bang any ripe and juicy cunt. Horny cunt. Creamy thighs. Hairy cunt. Oh, shit, I'm REALLY in the flesh!* He considers jerking off, but a gust of self-revulsion stops him. Rolling off the bed, he sheds his rumpled clothes, grabs some clean underwear, and pads toward the shower. *God, this sucks. I can't even control my animal urges, but the hurt I'm dealing with is WAY bigger than getting my rocks off.*

After a cold, then hot, shower, he puts on fresh clothes and descends to the kitchen for a bag of Fritos plus a can of Coors, then another. Tears well up. *God, I'm a useless bum. I need help. Maybe I should go see Marvin's minister? No, he's an asshole ... but maybe some other pastor? I need something, anything to get my life back on tr—*A car pulls in: Tracy?

"Damn, it's the middle of the afternoon," she kids, as she bops into the kitchen, "and you're *already* tanking up." Bryan doesn't even look up from his beer, but the rose perfume and squeaky voice confirm her presence. He stands; he totters, he stares at the floor. "Oh, Bryan dear," she responds, realizing that he's on the edge. She wraps her arms about him, hugging him.

He finally looks at her. "Gosh, Tracy, I'm a mess. And I don't even like beer that much ... not getting smashed anyhow."

"I know ... I know," she consoles, stroking his head, his back, his shoulders. She gives him a peck on the cheek, then she finds his lips, kissing him passionately. She tastes like cigarettes.

"Forgive me," she sighs breathily. "I uh ... I uh."

"It's okay," he sniffles, caressing the small of her back. "I reckon you're just what I need ... to ease my mind." Dropping down, he grips her chubby buttock through her culottes.

CHAPTER TWENTY-SIX

FIVE MONTHS LATER:

146 DOUGLAS STREET
TUESDAY, APRIL 14, 1992 — 11:15 PM

It's a balmy spring night in Waco, warm but not hot. Bryan flushes the toilet then pads naked down the hallway, returning to the bedroom. He smells tobacco smoke, a now-familiar odor he's learned to tolerate. "So tell me, Miss McCollum," he remarks, as he opens the windows a little wider, "whaddeyuh think about my frontal-lobe theory?"

Tracy, her kittenish face still flushed from ebbing passion, takes a drag on her after-sex cigarette. "Damn," she needles him, "y'were just going on about my *thighs*; where'd this brainy BS come from?" Exhaled smoke accompanies her words. The plume drifts toward the night table where it disintegrates in the soft light cast by the lamp. She crosses her long legs under the sheet. Her haunchy, lady-hoopster physique fully occupies her side of the bed, and then some.

Yes, young Mr. Howard and Tracy McCollum are living together, an unconventional coupling to be sure, but one that rescued his sanity— and hers. The arrangement has raised eyebrows, including their own, and yet they've achieved a surprising degree of compatibility, despite all.

She rolls her Hershey-colored eyes, a smirky side-glance. "It sure didn't take long for you to shift from eros to *neuro*science."

"Well, I *am* a guy," he chuckles. His arms raised, he tightens his biceps, posing like a Bow-Flex model beside the bed.

Tracy laughs too, a smoky chortle. "Yeah, I've noticed." The laughing lifts her voice another octave, yet she sounds less chipmunky than last fall, her speaking timbre having mellowed since she started smoking again. Her breasts sprawl flaccidly under her T-shirt, diverging off her chest, as they do when she lies on her back. The overlarge shirt, one of several she wears to bed, sports a "Mardis Gras '89" banner. Though barely bigger in the bosom, she needs more support than Mandy, and the flesh under her chin shows the puffy first signs of doubling. He can't help but compare, and Tracy can't help but come short, body and spirit. He has no complaint however, aside from the smoking. And yet the cigarettes, in provocative contrast to her voice, befit her status as an older, more worldly, more seasoned gal, a status he finds profoundly alluring when she's horny, and comforting when she's not; he doesn't mind the big-sister tendency. At this crazy juncture in his life he *needs* a big sister, someone who shares his young-adult perspective but has traveled a bit farther down the road. After all, he can't become a kid again and go home to his mama—too much has happened. Tracy, like Chris, has learned the ropes, and pitfalls, regarding Baylor and Waco, the whole student scene, not to mention the neuroscience, pre-med landscape. She can *never* fill the Mandy-void—a fact fully accepted by both—but neither can he replace Stuart, the prince in *her* saga of lost love.

"Scoot over," Bryan joshes, as he joins her in the bed—he dimples boyishly. "You're hogging the dadgum middle."

"No way, I'm well onto my side. This bed's too dang small."

"It's a queen-size for gosh sakes. It's plenty big ... if you'll just get your ass over." He bumps her teasingly with his own hip. She surrenders a couple more inches amid snickers and mews, from both. "Thank yuh kindly, Miss McCollum."

"You're welcome, Mr. Howard." (When she first moved in, they considered changing bedrooms, moving down the hall, but he vetoed the idea, not wanting to make a Mandy shrine out of Jason's room. They have made love on Annie's big bed a couple times, fulfilling Bryan's November fantasy—but he and Mandy did it on the four-poster as well, so it's not unique to Tracy.)

Folding his pillow, Bryan settles onto his back, to match her supine position under the sheet—they usually do much of their bedtime talking with the lamp on, so she can find the ashtray and such. "Seriously," he backtracks, "what *d'yuh* think? Y'know, what me and Chris were talking about on the way home from the caf this evening—my latest silver-cord hypothesis?"

Retrieving her Salem Light from the ashtray, she sucks on it then slowly exhales. "Y'gotta be patient. It's f-ing fantastic, what you've experienced and all, but we can't jump to conclusions. Most researchers, even Dr. Richardson, dismiss the whole idea of extra-physical perception. They say it's illusory compensation taking place within the cerebral cortex itself."

"So y'don't believe me, all the dadgum stuff I toldjuh before you moved in, back when I was freaking, and we started meeting in the afternoon, and we had those long talks afterward?"

"Oh, I do believe you. I do—at least, I damn sure want to. We're talking about the *key* question here, the *ultimate* hope. It's the *biggie* ... and no one can ignore it. We all hafta face death, whether we like it or not. Just like Mr. Lipski next door—Chris says he's in the ICU at Hillcrest."

"His prostate cancer ... or the heart trouble?"

"Neither—he caught a bug, and it turned into pneumonia. He's old, and he's probably gonna die, but *we* hafta face it too ... someday. The reaper's gonna come for *all* of us. So we're *all* desperate—to be blunt."

"No shit. We sure don't hafta theorize about that."

She takes a hit of nicotine then gestures with the cig, as she holds it gingerly betwixt her first two fingers, softly curvaceous female digits, still girlish yet noticeably stained by the dirty habit, not to speak of the tacky, uneven nails (she tends to nibble them in class, at the lab, anytime she can't smoke). "I hope it's true, Bryan, all your OBE secrets ... and when you shared them with me, it made me feel a hell of a lot closer to you, like it confirmed that we have more than sex between us. Not that getting laid isn't a great thing—shit, that horny gang at Collins Hall would hop into bed with you in a moment, even if yuh never opened your goddam mouth, the Baptists included." She giggles.

"Sounds like a good project for a backslider like myself, but you'll have to set up the scheduling." Dimpling, he stretches toward the ceiling.

Tracy giggles some more then sucks her Salem. "Yeah right," she banters smokily. "I better get off this subject before I give you the big head." She takes another draw. "But y'can only screw for so long, then y'hafta leave or find something else to share. So we're talking about trust here. I mean, coming out of your body is not something you just spout around campus."

"I'll say," he snickers, pulling the sheet up, to cover his naked chest. "You and Chris are the only ones at Baylor I've told—but whaddeyuh getting at, about jumping to conclusions?"

Tracy flicks the ashes from the stubby cigarette, tapping it against the inside of the ashtray. "My god, Bryan, you're only a freshman. Y'gotta read all the literature, and take *all* the courses. Y'gotta consider it all, even the prevailing idea that we *have* no soul. They could be *regular* dreams, your astral experiences—I hope not, but we can't take that possibility off the table. Y'hafta get fucking intimate with that monster before you can slay it."

Bryan gives an open-handed gesture above the sheet. "But whaddabout my head trauma? I was *up there* looking down. I saw Doc Wilson working on me, and the paramedics. I was soaring on a wave of love and elation—it *had* to be real, a spiritual thing, and then I zoomed through that tunnel toward the light. And Gramps was there. Y'know, I toldjuh about it? Gosh, it was *so* beautiful, like beyond words. It *had* to be God, not the scary, do-your-duty-or-else God that Marvin talks about, but the *real* God."

"I know—that near-death trip is f-ing hard to explain away."

"Y'got that right. It was gosh-darn real, as real as anything." He gives a breathy murmur. "Maybe it's solvable, the mystery of the soul? Or maybe not? But there *has* to be more. I mean ... we *hafta* be more than flesh and blood that *rots* in a casket. There has to be life after death, and not just *life*, but love—*love* after death, and I've seen it, at least a big dadgum glimpse of it."

"That's *it*. That's what we're desperate about ... when it comes to dying. But the bigshots will still dismiss your NDE as the product of shock-induced opiates, like Chris said in the car. That's why y'gotta pay your dues before yuh open your mouth. It's a fucked-up system, but if y'don't, they'll shoot yuh down as an amateur. They'll attack yuh anyhow, but if y'know your shit, y'can stand your ground."

"Goshdang, Tracy, you make it sound like a war zone."

After a last drag she extinguishes the butt in the ashtray, clicks off the light, then reassumes her position next to Bryan; she pushes her disheveled bangs to the side. "It is ... it *is* a war. For every pure heart seeking the truth, there's a shitload of egocentric assholes pushing their pet projects, even if they hafta spin the data to make it fit. And even the sincere researchers, like Dr. Richardson, come across as cold and sterile much of the time." She gives a sigh in Bryan's direction—her breath is still smoky smelling. "That's why I changed to pediatric nursing. It's not a glorious calling—there's no fame to be had—but it has a human face at least. Plus, I got sick of trying to keep up with all the contending theories, and all the big words. Hell, they speak in a hyped-up, ego-driven language that would make even Einstein throw up. I'm *out* of neuroscience, except for the lab job."

"Y'think it's better to be a doctor than a research scientist?"

"I don't see much difference, unless you're gonna be a PCP, or a shrink, or an ER doc. A fat-cat neurosurgeon doesn't spend shit-time interacting with his patients. It's all remote and high tech. We need to get back to real people, and real-life hopes and fears. That's why your astral experiences are so cool. You can help other people who are dying, or fear they are." She snorts for emphasis. "But the scientific community leaves little room for such considerations. It's cruel and heartless, and just as intolerant as religion, like Chris was saying. And it's money-driven to the extreme. I even feel sorry for the *mice*. Those little critters have feelings too, and I can't help but get attached to 'em. Most of 'em survive their experiments, and do okay, but a few get *shit* on. It's unjust and sad, but it's a lot like life." She snorts again. "It's a shame we can't pursue knowledge without losing our humanity. People need more than tubes and drugs when it comes to terminal disease. That's why so many folks cling hard to religion ... to get them across ... even my own parents."

Tracy sucks air through her teeth, a wet hissy sound. She has a slight, barely noticeable gap between her incisors, and she has a habit of sucking air through her teeth, when she's not smoking a cigarette. "We didn't go to church much," she goes on, "not like your family— y'know, I toldjuh about it—but my mom prayed in tongues and my dad's a Catholic. It's bizarre. He's a seismologist with Halliburton, but he still claims that the Pope is infallible. I hardly ever see him since he and Ma split up—he spends most of his time helicoptering over the Gulf."

"So where's your mom?"

"She's still in Catahoula?"

"So which is it? Catahoula or Lafayette? Y'talk about both?"

THE SILVER CORD

"I grew up in Catahoula, but Lafayette is the nearest city."

The faint illumination on the ceiling, from the streetlight, shifts and stretches as the window shade responds to the breeze. "Well, Tracy, I reckon I'm a lot like Gramps, like I said before. He felt closer to God out under the stars, or watching a storm blow in. It's gotta be bigger than wearing a tie, and praying that *prayer*, and trying to live up to the Bible. I mean, if Marvin Latrobe is the *high*est form of godliness— shit, we're all fucked."

"Y'got that right," Tracy agrees, after a spasm of laugher.

"Marvin used to intimidate me, like when I was drinking and freaking last semester, and hurting over Mandy. But I'm now passed the point of confessing and groveling before some mean God, who uses scare-tactics to make us obey. Just because Mandy gave in to it, finally, doesn't make it right ... and I can't see her buying into it forever. I know I'm not perfect, but I don't see myself as ungodly, just because I don't go to church like I used to. My Jesus is *way* bigger than sermons and Bible verses—yet he'll always be my Lord and Savior. And the Heaven I glimpsed during my NDE is the Heaven I'm hoping for."

Tracy gives him a peck on the cheek. "Oh, Bryan dear, you have such a sweet, innocent spirit, and your honesty still amazes me. I wish I'd known your granddad. Y'talk about him a lot."

Bryan responds with more talk about Gramps, and God.

"I feel much the same," Tracy replies. "I understand why people need religion, but the blind-faith part bothers me. I do believe in God, but I'm also like Chris in some ways. To be honest, I hafta say that I'm *not* sure ... and yet there seems to be a design to the reality about us, even to our lives—that's why destiny seems very plausible, if not probable. It's like we have this knowing when things happen, like we knew it was coming and we couldn't change it ... like the weather."

"Tell me about it. I've had no control this whole dang year."

"Me neither. I thought I was gonna be at LSU. Instead, I'm here in Waco ... living with a hayseed freshman from Spindle, Texas." She gives her teenybopper giggle: a happy piccolo.

"C'mon, Louisiana's hardly high-brow, not what I've seen of it— but we're getting well off the subject. You were talking about the war zone, and egocentric assholes?"

"Yeah, that's what we're up against ... in science ... or medicine ... or religion. They'll shoot you down in a moment ... to advance their own selfish goals. The Church won't accept new evidence, while science won't accept a metaphysical reality. But there *is* hope in this war."

"There is?"

Tracy chops the air, her hands a gray blur in the darkness. "Jesus, God ... yes. Just think of it, Bryan ... if you can discover the science behind your astral trips, you have the potential of bridging the gap, of allaying humanity's worst fear, but even if the science remains less than complete, you still have the first-hand experience, the OBEs and the near-death thing. Whatever it is, you've actually ex*peri*enced it—and that makes you unique. That said, you still can't jump the gun. You have to patiently endure ... until you're ready. To everything there is a season, and a time to every purpose under heaven." She giggles. "I reckon I do know a few Bible verses. Course that one is so common, it's pretty much a secular saying. Chris quotes it a lot."

"Me too," Bryan replies, clasping his hands behind his head. "It's a goshdang good verse, no matter if it's overused." He gives a sigh that turns into a yawn. "But whether it's now or later, it still makes sense to me that the silver cord has to somehow tether to the frontal lobe, if that's where the capacity for awareness rests." Tracy, hissing through her teeth, turns onto her side, facing away from him. *She must be dozing off,* he tells himself when she doesn't reply. He listens to the crickets outside.

"So d'yuh feel like you're being unfaithful to Mandy?" Tracy inquires a minute later—she's still awake.

"Uh ... well uh ... some I reckon. Yeah, sometimes. Not so much now, since I'm used to having you in this bed, and it wasn't *me* that ran off to Arkansas. But I did feel guilty back in January after you first moved in. Any way you slice it, this doesn't fit the accepted pattern, us being a couple ... not that Mandy and I *did*."

"Yeah, I went through it over Stuart. I didn't whore around, but I did go out with a couple of guys, like I toldjuh, and when I met you—well, things happened." She gives her piccolo giggle but quickly sobers. "It's different for us, yet it's *now*, and it's getting us through. And I'm learning that the heart rarely conforms to religion or society ... or even to our own convictions."

"That's for sure. This year has turned me inside out. My attitudes are *way* more tolerant now, like everything has changed from black-and-white to gray. I thought I could never be with anyone but Mandy, but here we are. My love for her hasn't changed, even though it looks like she's gone for good. She's never returned my calls, or answered my letters, and now I can't contact her at all, not legally anyway, and Helen Stevens and Gretchen are living in Arkansas too. It's *all* changed."

"It *is* quite a discovery when we realize we can have feelings for more than one person, less intense, more intense, in between, but valid in each case."

"Gosh, I can't imagine many couples talking openly like this about their former lovers, fairy-tale lovers no less. Damn, it's hard to believe I was a virgin just six months ago. I thought I had life figured out, but reality demolished my notions, most of 'em."

Tracy laughs. "Well, I lost my virginity way before you, like when I was fifteen, but that's a whole 'nother story."

"You mean with the Cajun hunk at your high school, the one who used to come over and play the guitar for you."

"Yeah, how'd yuh guess?"

"Well, it doesn't take goshdang Perry Mason to figure that."

More laughing. "But back then I was a bratty know-it-all. It wasn't until I met Stu that I got *my* notions demolished."

"And Chris ... you never uh ... well—"

"We never got past kissing, and we only did that once."

"Y'think he was shocked when y'moved in with me?"

"I reckon he's a wee bit jealous ... but not shocked. He knew right away, like that first day at the Bear's Paw, that you rang my bell." Tracy laughs then makes that hissy-sucking sound. "So whaddabout your *parents*? Y'think they're okay with this whole thing now. They seemed very supportive that weekend we spent at your farm ... especially your mom."

"It's been wild, what I've put *them* through. Gosh, I go my whole life being a straight-laced kid, and then I go off to college, and I'm suddenly married to Mandy who's only seventeen, and then I'm drinking and freaking and flunking ... and now I'm living with an older woman—*outside* of marriage."

"Get outta here," Tracy chortles. "I'm only twenty-one."

"But they saw you as wanton and worldly—until February, when they met yuh in person."

"So why didn't they put up a bigger stink?"

"My dad did. He lectured me hard. He almost pulled me out of college altogether. I felt terrible for letting him down ... but Mom was more open-minded. She had a hunch that you could get me past the Mandy crisis, and she was right I reckon." Bryan chuckles. "Nawh ... it wasn't because she's open-minded, though she *is* for a Baptist, but after my Christmas-week binge, she was *des*perate for anything that might settle me down, even if I was living outside the limits of permissible behavior."

The last month of 1991 almost destroyed the Baylor freshman, his psyche anyway, and the pummeling commenced well before Christmas. On Monday the second (12-2-91), he received the official annulment papers. This refired his Mandy woe, spurring another barrage of calls and letters to Newbury Christian Academy. No contact, no response: he never caught up with his wife, ex-wife, non-wife, but he did, with Helen Stevens' help, gain the eye of a Hollis County magistrate, who issued (on 12-6-91) a restraining order forbidding *any* communication with Amanda Fay Stevens.

The same week he got a visit from Marvin Latrobe: "I just dropped by to invite you to our midweek service tonight. Pastor Lawrence is doing an amazing series on the Last Days. We've missed you at church, Bryan, though I realize you're going through a rough time ... uh ... the situation with your wife. But God loves us with a love that passes knowledge in Ephesians 3:19." The nerdy little dorm-proctor proclaimed the grace and kindness of God, but the evangelical pitch quickly shifted to sin and lukewarm attitudes, to the Lord's concern for his wayward children, then to divine discipline, a less-than-subtle assertion that Bryan was simply reaping the consequences of his own iniquity—as Mandy *had* before she got right. Guilt, hurt, gut revulsion: the whole idea sickened Bryan, adding to his misery, yet he lacked the self-confidence, or inspiration, to contend with Marvin. Perhaps he *did* bring it on himself? Still, he didn't go to Marvin's church that night. He went drinking with Chris and Steve Jordan instead. They started at the Bear's Paw, continued at the Peek-A-Boo Club, and finished at the Purple Pegasus, an all-night roadhouse west of Waco on Route 84.

When Bryan got home at daybreak he fell into a fitful sleep filled with naked boobs and butts. Tattooed honeys twirled in his head, a dozen dancers, all strangers save for Wendy on the far side, and Jamie (Tracy's skinny roommate) in the middle. They sported around their stripper poles, giving X-rated glimpses of their wares. The sex dream degenerated into a kaleidoscope of gyrating cunts, whiskered cunts and heaving midriffs. The nearest bush loomed larger, and larger, until he recognized the springy, ginger-brown curls with their neat side-trim—Mandy, Mandy, has to be Mandy. But just as he reached out to her, she morphed into a beer can, as did all the strippers, giant aluminum cans with sexy legs: Bud Light, Miller Lite, Coors, Busch, Michelob.

Bryan awoke long enough to masturbate amid pangs of self-disgust, then he fell back to sleep with no intention of going to campus—that day, or any day. He sank rather into black despair, skipping school, skipping his weight training, even skipping his erotic trysts with Tracy. He skipped everything except his beer drinking. He felt sad; he felt guilty; he felt dirty, he felt like a failure. Add to this agony his eye problem. His vision worsened (as Dr. Nadler had feared), going blurry for several hours most every day. On the 18th, the day before Christmas break, he finally returned to campus, only to learn (from Coach McKinney) that he was on academic probation, and his scholarship status was being reviewed by Dean Buckley's office. By the time the freshman arrived at the farm on December 19, he was more than ready to drown his sorrow, Spindle-fashion. With Billy Ray and Spanky helping, he managed to get drunk every night, except Christmas Eve, the spree finally culminating in a three-day binge that left him passed out with a prostitute in Billy Ray's trailer.

* * *

BAYLOR UNIVERSITY - FERRELL FIELD COMPLEX
WEDNESDAY, APRIL 15, 1992 — 10:42 AM

Fishing the last items out of his locker, Bryan stuffs them into a gym bag, socks, jocks, underjerseys and such. It's not a locker actually but a large, airy, wire-mesh cubicle. No teammates, no jockish banter, no steamy hiss from the shower room: the eerie silence haunts him, reinforcing the pangs of regret that vex him anytime he's near the Baylor Bear baseball field (or any baseball diamond). The walls and stalls taunt him, as does the stale stink of sweaty practice garb. Ditto for the rubbery carpet underfoot and the long wooden bench behind him, with its thick coat of green paint. October memories: he can't help but hark back to his fall-season heroics, with Mandy looking on from the stands. Giving a resigned sigh, he zips up the bag and heads for the back exit. "Hey, *Howard,* hold it!" comes a familiar growl, as Bryan pushes open the door. "What the hell? You ain't skippin' your goddam classes again?" It's Elmo McKinney, Coach McKinney.

"No sir ... no way," the freshman answers, as he retreats into the clubhouse, the door clicking shut again. "I haven't missed a *single* class this semester." He blushes and dimples.

The Negro coach, pushing his cap back, flashes that Willy Mays grin, his teeth and eyes shining whitely. "Well, y'better not ... or I'll be on your white ass."

"No, I got outta statistics early, so I shot over to clean out my cubicle." Bryan pats the gym bag. "The last of my stuff—I already got my glove and bats and shit ... on Monday."

McKinney drops his eyes, pawing the brown carpet with the toe of his ripple-soled coaching shoe. "I wish I could change thangs for yuh," he says, his tone softening, becoming almost paternal, "but I reckon baseball ain't worth cryin' over, not for long no how." He chuckles gruffly. "Y'just remember what I toldjuh 'bout Cottonseed Walker."

"I know," Bryan says. "Y'gotta have bigger plans than making the *show* ... and I do."

Elmo looks up, his eyes glistening—he clutches Bryan's shoulder, a firm, thick-fingered grip. "I'm sorry I couldn't get Coach Weaver to keep yuh on the list. I was hopin' we could carry yuh through next fall ... and pray for a goddam miracle or sumpthin'. Hell, y'might make this team with one eye, as a goddam walk-on ... if yuh give it another try."

Bryan, his own tears welling, fiddles with the zipper on his bag. "Awh ... it's no use. I could hang around and be a flunky, but it's too hard ... if y'know what I mean." His throat tightens.

The elderly coach pats him on the back. "Yeah , you ain't kiddin'. It does hurt when y'cain't do what yuh used to do. It does hurt ... even after *all* these years—but you ain't gonna go broke and drop outta school now?"

"No, I'll make it," the freshman assures, a laugh pushing past the lump in his throat. "I'll work, I'll beg, I'll borrow ... I'll pick up bottles ... but one way or another, I'll *be* here."

Five minutes later, he's in the Chevy on the way back to center campus. He has Biology 252 at eleven. *I can't help but like Coach McKinney,* he remarks to himself as he turns right on Verner. *He sorta reminds me of Gramps, and he saved my ass more than once, especially in January, even though we both knew I'd never be able to hit again ... not like before.*

In February, Dr. Rosenblatt, an eye specialist at Dallas Presbyterian, confirmed Dr. Nadler's November prognosis: "Your oculomotor nerve is damaged resulting in sporadic malfunction, or to say it another way: your focusing apparatus has a short in it, electrically. Glasses will help, but the correction will be rough at best, and we want to grind them for reading, even though your visual clarity may fail at any distance, whenever you try to focus intently." Bryan got the special glasses two weeks later, three pairs, and they do help some, though his attempts to hit college-level pitching with them has proven futile, C-minus at best.

He parks behind the student center; he's meeting Tracy for lunch in the caf when he gets out of biology. After the December disaster, Bryan needed a rally in January, and he got it. Not only did Tracy move in, but Coach McKinney argued on his behalf before Coach Weaver, *and* Dean Buckley, preserving his scholarship status (through May) on the condition that Bryan pass all his first-semester courses. And he did. With Tracy's help and inspiration, he busted his butt making up the back work and studying for his finals. He still got a C in English Comp, but he made B or better in all his other courses, a clutch comeback that likewise put an end to his academic probation.

* * *

Minutes later, Bryan strides along the crowded Fountain Mall sidewalk toward the Fletcher Life Sciences Building, his book bag (a knapsack actually) slung over his shoulder, his shirt clinging to his perspiry torso. Hazy-blue sky, puffy cumulus, eighty-plus temps—it should reach ninety or better this afternoon, as the first heat wave of the season bakes the region. He wears the usual jeans plus a knit shirt, but the hurried throng about him, especially the gals, could pass for a beach crowd on a Galveston pier: bike shorts, Bermudas, cutoffs, tank tops, halter tops. The sticky air smells beachy as well, from the sunscreen— almost everyone is working on a tan. After this tumultuous year, young Mr. Howard has bigger things on his mind than browning his muscles, and yet his new conditioning regime (he started Monday) should do just that. No more baseball—but he plans to run most afternoons, on the footpath along the river.

Reaching the LS building, he spots a crewcut geek coming out: coat and tie, attaché case. *Oh shit,* Bryan declares to himself. *It's Marvin Latrobe. I hope that little prick doesn't see me.* Bryan hustles, head down, up the far side of the steps—to no avail.

"Hey Bryan, wait a second," comes a reedy twang.

"I can't shoot the shit, Marv. I got biology—like pronto."

THE SILVER CORD

"Nor can I," the bespectacled RA replies, grinning smugly. "I have Church History, over at the seminary." The grin widens, splitting his pasty pockmarked face (not a chance *he*'s working on a tan). "But I wanted to offer you some encouragement."

"About what?" Bryan asks curtly, his gut tightening.

"About your eye problem and everything. Steve Jordan told me you had to quit the team."

"Yeh ... so?"

Putting down the briefcase, Marvin paws the air, awkwardly. "Well, I just wanted to remind you about the power of prayer. In fact, Pastor Lawrence is preaching on that very subject tonight."

"Fine, fine ... but I gotta go."

"But the Lord can cure your eye problem, *all* your problems in fact." He beckons toward the clouds, as if he's Elijah calling down rain. "Surely he has borne our griefs, and carried our sorrows. He was wounded for our transgressions ... and bruised for our iniquities ... but with his stripes we are *healed*."

Bryan flexes his fist. He's ready to deck this beady-eyed twerp, but he willfully resists. "Thanks for your concern, but I gotta split ... really."

The freshman proceeds up the steps, but Marvin follows, zealously, tenaciously. "All we like sheep have gone astray. That's why so many prayers aren't answered. Iniquity gets in the way. That's why backsliders can't get victory. If we have sin in our lives, we can't receive God's healing. And that's why bad things happen ... like your *wife* leaving yuh. God is not m—"

"Dammit, that's enough!" Bryan exclaims, just short of shouting. "Who the hell gave *you* the right to judge *me*! Or *any*body for that matter?" Grabbing Marvin's geeky tie, along with a fistful of dress shirt, Bryan pulls the zealot close—close enough to smell his cheap citrus cologne.

"Uh ... uh ... whaa." Marvin stammers, his face turning red, his beady eyes no longer beady behind the Buddy Holly glasses.

"Now hear this, you little fart," Bryan commands, speaking in an angry whisper. "You're not my shepherd, so *stop* pestering me like you're some kind of Old Testament prophet. I know the Lord as well as you do, better I reckon ... so get *off* it. And if I wanna come to your church, I'll *come*. If not, I *won't*. It's goshdang obnoxious, the way you bother everybody, and judge everybody. It's enough to make people *hate* God!" Bryan loosens his grip, giving him air. "Now I have no desire to fight with you, Marv, so just cool it, okay. But if you open your f-ing mouth one more time ... about my sins, or what I'm going through, or who I'm with, or *anything* in my life, I'll wring your goddam neck!"

* * *

THE SILVER CORD

Same day, 12:39 p.m. "Tracy's right," Chris remarks between bites of cherry pie. He and Bryan sit alone near the windows on the far side of the caf; Tracy departed already, to go care for the lab rodents. "You can't jump the gun with such a twilight-zone theory. We can't even prove we have a soul, much less pin down how it's married to the physical brain ... and if I had to pick a tether point, I'd chose the goddamn stem ahead of the frontal lobe. But no way can I pick. It's still *way* out there, any such knowing. Hell, I hope we do have an astral self, which transcends the flesh. Yet hoping is a far cry from finding the silver cord." Chris smirks and nods. "But I must say, slugger, that *is* a catchy name: 'the silver cord.' I can see the fucking headlines now: Spindle farmboy escapes from his body, proving existence of Biblical 'silver cord'."

Laughter, hearty laughter—then Bryan responds: "But seriously, Chris ... I've experienced it. Like many times." He gestures with a spoonful of ice cream, mocha-chip. "I *know* there's more than flesh and blood ... and bones and gray matter."

The jaunty junior takes another bite of pie then a drink of coffee. "But those astral journeys could've been mind-trips," he counters, his Midwest monotone clogged with dessert, "including your near-death thing. I hope not, but we have to play hardball with our aspirations. Tracy's right: the cutthroat bastards who rule the research world will give you zero credibility, not to mention the money factor. If you don't have your shit together, they'll dismiss you as a kook, even Dr. Richardson, though he's more tolerant than most."

Bryan finishes his ice cream then sips on his iced tea, the sweet lemony dregs. "Well, I reckon I can't be *ab*solutely sure. I'd like to be, and it's *super* crucial to me, and everyone, the whole life-after-death thing. It varies ... but I'm about 90% sure, to put a number on it ... which leaves ten percent for lingering doubts. But even if I *can't* prove we have a soul, or prove that *my* soul comes out of my body, we do have consciousness—that's a *fact*, and it has to come from somewhere."

"Exactly ... and that's where we have to start. But the exploration of consciousness involves the whole banana ... philosophy, religion, psychology, psychiatry, neurology, biology, even goddamn quantum physics, and tons of way-out math and modeling techniques, and who knows what else? So you have fifty courses to take, with a mountain of textbooks, and thousands of journal articles, before you can open your fucking mouth—plus all the unpublished reports and dissertations."

Bryan rattles the ice cubes in his empty glass. "But there must be *some*one who's proposed the idea of the soul plugging into the frontal lobe?"

"Well, there's always Dr. Ratey."

"Who?"

After a final bite of cherry pie, Chris pushes the small plate to the side. "Dr. John Ratey—he's a professor of psychiatry at Harvard Medical School."

"Well, *he* should be respected enough I reckon?"

Chris kills off his coffee, some dripping onto his shirt, a tacky sweat shirt, tan with the sleeves cut off. "Goddamn, I need a bib," he fusses, as he dabs the darkish spots with his napkin.

Bryan rattles his ice a little more then pops a chunk into his mouth. "So tell me about this Harvard psychiatrist."

Chris erases his smirk with the back of his hand, becoming quite serious. "Well, Dr. Ratey claims he had five OBEs during his tour as a combat shrink in Vietnam, and he had two near-death encounters as well, after he got wounded by mortar fire during the Tet Offensive— that was January '68. And he postulates that the soul resides in the prefrontal cortex."

"Jesus," Bryan declares, gesturing wildly with the iced-tea glass, so much so that ice flies onto the table. "Let's go talk to this guy. He's like *me*—God, shit, he's the *ans*wer!"

Chris gives an impish grin that turns into a laugh, his mustache twitching, his brown eyes beaming. "Gotcha, slugger."

Bryan dimples. "You *li*ar," he reacts good-naturedly. "Stop your goshdang leg-pulling."

"I couldn't help it. I couldn't." Hugging himself, Chris sits back and puts on a sheepish face. "Truth is, I don't know of any respected theory that actually deals with the soul, but Dr. Ratey does talk about short-term memory being a key component to consciousness, or working memory as he calls it." The curly-headed junior pauses, as if allowing the teasing mood to pass completely. "And studies show that this working memory is a significant part of the executive function of the prefrontal cortex, which fits *your* theory, slugger." Chris gives a thumbs-up.

Bryan chomps ice. "Sounds good," he responds, amid a swelling sensation in his bosom, vibes of pride.

"Now working memory holds data, motivations, and ideas," Chris elaborates, "but only for a matter of seconds, until we swing our attentional spotlight to something else. This means the frontal-lobe memory systems must rely on long-term memory to encode the new info in the hippocampus and other parts of the cortex, a process that's constantly ongoing, as long as we're awake. It's like what happens in a computer, and our working memory is our brain's RAM, or random-access memory. With it we conceptualize immediately occurring events, while we use long-term memory to direct the present and plan for the future. Now all areas of the cortex emit a steady level of noise, the 40 Hertz oscillation—that's forty cycles per second—and some areas of the cortex hum in phase, which means that the neurons perform in synchrony because they follow a kind of musical conductor in the brain, and the prime candidate for this leadership job is the collection of intralaminar nuclei—"

"The what?" Bryan interrupts, feeling suddenly stupid and overwhelmed—no more pride.

"The intra*lam*inar nuclei," Chris repeats, fingering the air like Steve Jordan. "They're located deep within the thalamus—so there's more to consciousness than frontal-lobe function, which means that your theory is lacking."

"I *guess*," the freshman sighs in an understatement; he fiddles with his spoon, twirling it like a tiny baton. "But go on."

Chris extends his left hand, as though holding a brain—he points with the right. "Well, these intralaminar nuclei receive and project long axons to many areas of the brain. They take in information, reply to it, and monitor the neuron's response to their replies, creating a feedback loop. The info flowing back and forth modulates itself, manifesting the forty-Hz oscillation, the synchronized beat. Meanwhile, the thalamus—"

Bryan can't help but laugh. "Hold it, hold it ... goshdang it all. You're *way* ahead of me."

"Forgive me, slugger. I guess I got carried away there."

"Jesus, I feel like a dumbhead dork. You're so far ahead of me, I can't even see your taillights."

"That's no biggie. It's just a matter of time. You're plenty bright enough. But this does reinforce my point—you have a hell of a lot ahead of you ... a lot of digging and learning"

"It's wild stuff ... like another language. I wish it could be said in simpler words."

"Well, Dr. Ratey does that in a way, when he compares consciousness to a music symphony ... where this recurrent network between the cortex and the thalamus serves as the conductor. But he readily admits that this analogy still comes short of explaining what consciousness actually is, so there's still room for a metaphysical explanation like the existence of the soul. They may dismiss the possibility, but they can't rule it out, just like you can't rule out the possibility that your OBEs are regular dreams."

"Yeah, I reckon we're still in the dark." Dropping the spoon into the melted remnants of his ice cream, Bryan gives a self-deprecating laugh. "I am for *sure*. I feel like a Neanderthal."

"But you do have first-hand knowledge, so you have a unique advantage. Even if you never figure out what's going on in our heads, or what dimensions we actually exist in, you still have the OBEs, whatever they are. Not that you want to blab all this to Dr. Richardson first thing, or to the other bigshots in the field." Chris snickers. "But certain people need to hear about it. I mean, you can help folks who are facing the grave. Even if you can't explain it, you did experience something wonderful while you were unconscious on the baseball field that day."

"Yeh ... Tracy says the same thing, about counseling folks that are dying."

"Old-man Lipski even ... but he's too goddamn deaf." Chris titters. "I shouldn't make light; he's critical with pneumonia."

"Yeh ... Tracy told me. I hardly know the guy, except to wave to him, and we did talk a couple times across the hedge."

"Same for me—but I must say, he does a hell of a job on that yard of his, the grass and flowers."

Bryan chuckles. "Better than *us* ... anyway."

"Come on ... our lawn's looking okay."

"Get outta here. My horse Millie could do better ... *way* better." Guffaws and titters.

"But getting back to the counseling thing," Chris replies a moment later, "that *is* something to consider." He toys with a remnant of pie crust on his dessert plate. "Neuropsychology— that's what they call it ... neuro-nuts who also do therapy ... like Dr. Ratey." Chris snickers, his wise-ass nature still perking. "Or hell, slugger, maybe you should become a minister?" He smirks, his mustache twisting one way then the other.

"No church would have me, certainly not *Marvin's*."

Laughter, from both. "So you actually told him off?" Chris says, leaning back in his chair.

"I reckon so. At least, I got my *point* across."

"God, I wish I'd been there. He can be fucking obnoxious. But it's good training for you. The neuroscience hotshots don't hand out tracts, but they're always out selling their ideas. It's all push and hype, squeaky wheels fighting for grease—so have you had any *new* ones?"

"New what?"

"Soul trips. OBEs ... whatever."

"No, none that I haven't toldjuh about."

"So that one in the snow was the only time ... since you and Mandy split up?"

"Well, I did have a brief OBE at Crockett Lake the week she left ... but the only long one was that one on Christmas Eve I toldjuh about. It snowed off and on that whole day. The flakes were big and wet, and they reminded me of last year, when Mandy and I chased each other in the snow, and that really tore me up." Bryan gives a thumbs-down gesture, both hands. "I tried to call her, but I couldn't get through—as usual."

Chris leans forward, steepling his hands under his chin. "But you have a restraining order?"

"I didn't give a shit, not that day. Then I tried to get Helen Stevens, but the phone was disconnected. That's when it hit me, the realization that everything had changed, that I had no contact. I freaked inside, but I couldn't get drunk, not on Christmas Eve. When I went to bed, I could barely get to sleep, and then I was suddenly out of my body zooming through the snow, headed for Arkansas. I willfully resisted, forcing myself back to Spindle."

"So you actually have control during these astral journeys?"

"Yeh ... I just hafta concentrate on where I wanna go."

"So what happened next?"

"Well, I was feeling no pain—it's like a drug, the OBEs, an exhilarating drug. I buzzed my house like I was Santa Claus coming in for a landing." Bryan laughs. "It was bizarre ... with the slushy snow on the roof. We hardly ever have snow in Spindle, much less on Christmas. The big oak tree on the hill was heavy with snow. I flew over it, then I followed a pickup halfway to town. It's sorta like being a ghost I reckon. But when I woke up back in my bed, I felt awful, worse than ever, and starting late on Christmas day, I went on my three-day binge with Billy Ray."

Chris smirks. "Like I say, you have first-hand knowledge."

Bryan checks his watch. "Hafta go. I got a class at one."

"Me too. I have to organize Doc Richardson's slides, for his afternoon seminar—but Tracy'll help me, once she's done with the rodents." He chuckles. "It's amazing how things happen."

"What?"

"You arrive last September, a lovesick virgin from some hick town, and you're married in a month to your high-school honey, but then you end with Tracy in your bed—while I'm celibate the whole goddamn time." Chris laughs. "The Lord is with you, slugger. He *has* to be ... whether you find the silver cord or not."

*   *   *

Two days later, Friday, 6:23 p.m. Bryan sits at the study desk in the master bedroom previewing his weekend homework load. Thunder rumbles outside. He goes to the window to check the squall line, which promises to chase the three-day hot spell (that's the Channel Two scoop from Norm Gossage). A bank of clouds looms ominously to the west, inky dark save for occasional streaks of lightning. The telephone rings in the other room.

"Steve Jordan's on the phone," Tracy announces.

"Hello," Bryan says ten seconds later.

"Hey, dude, y'wanna go to the Peek-A-Boo tonight? Me and Jamal are goin'."

Bryan chuckles. "Nawh. Thanks for asking, but I think not. I'm being good now days. Besides, I sowed enough wild oats this year to last a *life*time ... until Tracy settled me down."

"Susie's comin' down next week," Steve drawls on, seemingly oblivious to Bryan's response, "but this weekend I'm single ... if y'catch my drift." He gives his sousaphone laugh. "I doubt I'll get past lookin', but the lookin' is *mighty* good. Plus, I cain't stay out late, 'cuz we're playin' Rice tomorrow."

THE SILVER CORD

"I know," Bryan says, amid pricks of baseball regret. "Tracy and I may come over and watch."

"Good ... but I doubt *I'll* be pitchin'. Coach Weaver might call me outta the bullpen, but it's not likely. I hurled on Wednesday night up at TCU. We won, but I got *no* decision. The main day for you guys to come over is next Thursday. The Longhorns are gonna be here, and *I'll* be startin' for sure—oh, I forgot to tellyuh, dude: Coach McKinney had a heart attack."

"No shit! Uh ... whadduh? I mean ... where, when?"

"Yesterday ... in the shower ... like right after practice."

* * *

HILLCREST MEDICAL CENTER - INTENSIVE CARE UNIT
FRIDAY, APRIL 17, 1992 — 7:15 PM

"I ain't done yet," Coach McKinney growls weakly, his gruff voice barely audible above the thunder outside—the storm has arrived. "It *was* a mite scary yesterday ... like a goddam horse stompin' on my chest, but I didn't pass out, even durin' the worst part." An oxygen tube snakes up his nose, but his mouth is free—no ventilator. "I got too much to do. I ain't done yet."

"I know," Bryan encourages—he takes Elmo's thick hand, the right one; the left one has the i.v. gizmo taped to the back.

The coach gives a grin that turns into a grimace, his eyes closing. "I got shit to do, so I'll be outta here soon." But his tight grip on Bryan belies the confident words. "The good Lord may want me. But I'm not ready. No fuckin' way ... not yet."

* * *

Gosh, I told him everything, Bryan reflects an hour later, as strides across the wet hospital parking lot toward his pickup. Moved with compassion, he couldn't help but offer Coach McKinney assurance, and more assurance, which led back to last May and his own brush with death. *He may think I'm crazy or something, but what else could I tell him, considering?*

Before departing the ICU, Bryan stopped by Mr. Lipski's cubicle, but the old geyser was unresponsive, and he was plugged up with tubes—he *is* done. He's dying ... no time left.

* * *

THREE WEEKS LATER:

146 DOUGLAS STREET
SUNDAY, MAY 10, 1992 — 2:45 PM

Old-man Lipski didn't die after all, Bryan observes to himself, as he

459

trims, with handshears, the hedge along the driveway. Lipski was weeding his flower beds until a minute ago when he went back inside his house. *Gosh, he just got outta the hospital last week, yet he's working hard on his yard.* Elmo, Coach McKinney, is also home but remains incapacitated. *It's weird, Lord, how things turn out. It's like you always surprise us. I wonder about Mandy. I mean, she's never written back, or returned my calls, but she still has the rings—nawh, it's nothing. Get off it.* (He also has his wedding band of course, in the top drawer of his dresser.)

While Bryan deals with the hedge, Chris mows the lawn, and Tracy works the far side, raking the cut grass into a pile beyond the magnolia tree—she already trimmed, with weed scissors, the walkway and porch steps. Annie O'Shea is on the way, and her Douglas Street tenants are rushing to finish the yardwork (she called Chris this morning, and they've been working ever since). The sunny afternoon smells grassy sweet like the hayfields on the Howard farm, and they *could* make hay from the knee-deep lawn if they had a baler handy. They haven't mowed for weeks, and the unruly mix (weeds, grass, you name it) grows fast this time of year, especially the Johnson grass and clover, not to mention the dandelions and chicory.

Removing his cap, Bryan wipes the sweat off his brow. He looks forward, with some apprehension, to meeting Annie, finally. She has visited once since he's been living here, right after Christmas, but he was in Spindle (good thing considering his wild December binges). He surveys the last hedge, the one out front, then he commences, *chup, chup, chup*, clipping off the foot-long sprouts, squaring the edges. Behind him the popping roar of the old rotary mower advances then recedes along with the gas-engine fumes.

"Hurry up, slugger," Chris exhorts a while later, after killing the mower. "We have to rake now. I'm on my way to get the wheelbarrow, as soon as I put this fucker in the garage." Bryan has never seen him this motivated about their yardwork duties.

After a fit of furious raking and a dozen wheelbarrow loads, all the excess grass has been removed, to the huge pile behind the barbecue pit—and just in time. *Va-ROOOM!* A big black SUV wheels up into the driveway, a Jeep Cherokee. Chris hurries over, but the plump, white-headed landlady exits before he gets there.

"So you must be Bryan?" she barks huskily, as she waddles around the rear of the Cherokee—she speaks with the usual Texas twang, but the years have roughened her voice.

"Yes ma'am," he affirms, shaking her hand.

"And this must be your wife?" Annie says, taking Tracy's hand.

Tracy blushes. "No, I'm Tracy ... but I do live here now ... with Bryan ... and uh—"

"It's sorta complicated," Bryan intercedes—he dimples, his face warming. "Like a *long* story."

Annie dimples as well, her tawny eyes twinkling. "Oh my ... I see we have some real-life stories to share." She gives a gruff chortle, to Bryan's relief—they all laugh.

Wrinkles surround her eyes, yet Annie's face remains more cherubic than puckered. No doubt she was a cute Texas gal in her day—with a more-than-ample bosom which now hangs almost to her waist under her blue pullover. Yet her hips and legs, though bulbous to be sure, still retain a female shape inside her tannish jeans. A golfing-style visor binds her gray hair, a chin-length bob fringed with bangs, a rather bold hairdo for a senior lady. Ditto for the blurb on the visor: "Lucky Swinger."

I reckon she IS a character, Bryan remarks to himself.

Annie moseys up the walkway. "Yard looks good, Chris."

"Thanks," he replies. "We're trying to stay on top of things this year." Bryan chuckles over this whopper of a lie.

"So how's Mr. O'Shea?" the mustached yard-chief asks, as they pause near the porch steps.

"No change. He has good days ... and bad days." Annie's face clouds. "The worst part is the un*cer*tainty of it all, the god-awful uncertainty. I'm a Catholic ... not devout mindyuh, but I do believe, and Dudley too. Still, it's *hard* to deal with." Looking up at the old house, she sighs, then her countenance brightens. "But let's not dwell on things we can't control. Hell, Chris, I may be seventy, but I'm still a thirsty gal. I could sure use a damn beer, and I bet y'got a case in your fridge?" She gestures toward the driveway. "But two's my limit ... since I'm going back tonight."

CHAPTER TWENTY-SEVEN

SIX MONTHS LATER:

BILL DANIEL STUDENT CENTER
THURSDAY, OCTOBER 29, 1992 — 10:55 AM

Maybe I should go back to the farm and cut hay? Bryan Howard murmurs to himself, as he exits his truck to check his mail. He has biophysics lab at eleven (Fletcher Life Sciences Building), but he feels no sense of urgency. Giving a sigh, he plods through the muggy air and sprinkles of rain to the steps behind Bill Daniel. It's hot for October, but the showers signal that fallish weather is on the way. The familiar aromas of floor wax, refrigerated air, and baking bread (from the caf) greet him as he pulls open the door to the student center. *I reckon I know more about the gosh-dang brain than any sophomore on campus, but that's not saying much. And I haven't even gotten my required classes out of the way. I'll be a dadgum junior before I get into neuroscience itself, like Dr. Richardson's courses.*

Discouragement weighs upon his soul—no, he's not even sure he has a soul, or a brain. Prefrontal cortex, limbic system, motor cortex, somatosensory cortex, the 'great divide,' anterior cingulate gyrus, testosterone, neostratium, olfactory tubercle, cortisol, dopamine: he has studied and read and pondered to the point of exhaustion, leaping well ahead of his regular classes. Chris lent him a collection of advanced texts, and Bryan has slogged his way through most of them. He's also brainstormed many hours with the Baylor senior, digging, sifting, questing (Chris is a senior now, Bryan a sophomore). He's absorbed a lot from Tracy too. Yet he feels more overwhelmed than enlightened, as a forest of questions accompanies each sapling of truth, not to mention the jungle of medical jargon, the bewildering semantic undergrowth he must hack through before he can even see the trees.

And Dad's paying for everything now. Not a problem if I'm gonna be a brain surgeon. I'll be rich, and I can pay him back, but it's looking less likely that I'm going that route. I reckon Chris's right, and Tracy. My best potential lies in death counseling and research. Coach McKinney is even beating that drum. (Elmo, having recovered over the summer, has returned to his coaching duties.) *Yet it ALL seems out of reach today.*

Seconds later, Bryan finds a curious letter in his mail box. He doesn't recognize the handwriting on the envelope, but it looks girlish, the fat-lettered printing. His left eye goes blurry, as it does anytime he tries to read nakedly. Pulling the gray-framed glasses from his shirt pocket (the special ones he got from Dr. Rosenblatt), he slips them on then opens the letter:

> Bryan ... I hate to send sucky news, but I just found out that Mandy's engaged to a guy named Russell. Her Aunt Marge told me. It's totally shitty if you ask me, and unjust! He's older, like late 20s, and he teaches at the Bible college. The wedding's in June.
>
> I'm still living at home and working at the drug store. The Class of '92 didn't exactly excel when it comes to college-bound graduates. Spanky didn't go either, I'm sure you know—he's working at the bowling alley, and helping Billy Ray some, with his day-labor farmwork jobs.... Luv ya ... Wendy

Stabs of Mandy-hurt assault Bryan. *O Jesus God,* he laments to himself, stuffing the letter into the back pocket of his Levi's; his eyes smart; his throat aches. *This's ALL I need.*

Avoiding eye contact with his fellow students, he hustles to the parking lot, to the privacy of his pickup where he slaps the dashboard, *ka-WHAP*, his distress generating more indignation than tears. *This sucks! She's gonna marry some super-religious guy who's ten years older.* He strikes the dash again, and again, a series of blows. His hand buzzes, throbs, then goes numb. Slumping back, he gazes at the rain-dappled hood of the Chevy. The droplets shimmer and sparkle in the sunshine, the shower having passed while he was inside getting his heart wrung. *I'm living with Tracy, but I'm hopelessly in love with Mandy. I'm totally fucked-up. To hell with biophysics lab—I'd rather belt a few beers.*

* * *

THREE MONTHS LATER:

BAYLOR UNIVERSITY - FOUNTAIN MALL
MONDAY, FEBRUARY 1, 1993 — 8:54 AM

Bryan Howard, his Spindle letter jacket buttoned against the icy, wind-driven mist, hustles across Verner Street then strides with purpose up the west side of Fountain Mall, joining his hurried peers, the hourly, two-way swarm of students. Bryan shifts his book pack to his right shoulder then buries his bare hands in the pockets of his jacket. A full-fledged norther roared down from the Panhandle during the night dropping temps into the upper 20s, a fifty-degree drop from yesterday.

Muted chatter, white plumes of winter breath, ruddy cheeks and hands, bundled-up bodies moving quickly, urgently—most everyone has donned their cold-weather garb: parkas, jackets, sweaters, ponchos, poplin vests. A few have on ski hats, gloves even, but not the majority;

why bother with the extras unless you're working outside all day? Cold spells don't last long here, so there's little point in going whole hog. Bryan wears the usual headgear: his old Spindle Tiger baseball cap.

The air smells like snow, and the gray seamless sky reminds him of snowy days back home, but so far the arctic blast has produced nothing but freezing drizzle, not enough to glaze the roads, though he did have to scrap a razor-thin veneer of ice from the windshield of Tracy's Tempo before they left the house; they decided, just in case, to take the front-wheel-drive Ford instead of the pickup. A gust buffets him, stinging his face, yet he finds the cold exhilarating, just as he did years ago when he and Gramps would go to the big oak tree to watch a norther blow in—with its black, dust-spewing clouds, gale-force winds, and muddy rain changing to sleet and snow. They're infrequent (once or twice a year) yet unforgettable. Gramps called them "blue" northers.

Yet on this midwinter morn, Bryan has more than frigid temps to invigorate him. It's the first day of the second semester, and he's on his way to Neurology 301, Dr. Richardson's introductory treatment of neuroscience, a course normally reserved for juniors and above, but Bryan's A+ academic performance earned him a waiver. Chris helped too, attaching a glowing recommendation to Bryan's request then hand-carrying the paperwork to the doctor for signature. And to make matters better, Bryan received, just last week, an Elizabeth Daniel Alumni Scholarship, an honor-student grant which covers almost as much as his baseball scholarship, including meals in the caf.

Needless to say, Wendy's October news concerning Mandy's engagement did not send Bryan back to the farm. It did cause a week of depression plus a couple of beer binges, but then the pain turned positive, a fire igniting within him, creative fire, relentless fire, visceral desire, an unspeakable determination to pursue and discover the silver cord—for his sake, for Mandy's sake, for humanity's sake. The renewed zeal enabled him to ace his fall courses, as he achieved a 4.0 grade-point average.

It doesn't matter if Dr. Richardson puts down the whole idea of astral phenomena, the sophomore exhorts himself as he sidesteps a crippled fellow in a powered wheelchair. *At least, I'm gonna be in the arena where the nature of the mind is being addressed. I don't expect this brain guru to endorse OBEs or NDEs, or even the existence of the soul. Even though we're a Baptist school, it's like Chris says: the science professors rarely bring up religious or spiritual stuff in the classroom. Maybe that's why Jerry Falwell declared Baylor to be apostate. But I reckon the teachers at HIS school are even more close-minded. He may accept the reality of supernatural experiences, but if they don't conform to the Bible, he attributes them to demons, like most preachers. It's weird how the science types and the religious types avoid each other. After all, there's only ONE reality, even if none of us have it figured out. I just want the TRUTH, whether in church or in college, or wherever I hafta go to get it.*

He veers left across the lawn, a shortcut to the neuroscience lab, which is officially called the Fletcher Neurology Wing, yet everyone calls it the neuroscience lab, or simply "the lab." One of the newer structures on campus, the two-story edifice sprawls behind the Fletcher Life Sciences Building. It's not a wing really, but it's part of the Fletcher complex, hence the "wing" designation. In addition to lab facilities, it houses the department admin offices along with classrooms. Bryan is headed for one of these classrooms, #119 to be exact. He's been in the building many times, with Chris, and lately with Tracy, though they usually enter from the other side, the entrance off Dutton Street which leads directly to the rooms housing the rodent cages. Chris even introduced Bryan to Dr. Richardson one evening when they met the professor in the parking lot.

Bryan's silver-cord fervor not only inspires academic endeavor, but it also provides a strong center of gravity for *every*thing in his life. No more indecision, no more complaining to God, no more "woe is me" resentment, no more drinking to kill pain. He still downs a couple of brews with Tracy and Chris on occasion, or when watching football with Steve Jordan, but not to *escape*. He's focused and rooted, a latter-day Sherlock Holmes sleuthing the biggest of all mysteries—and he hopes to comfort and help people as much as possible in the process. Mandy still convulses his heart from time to time, making him weep, yet he now accepts their separation as necessary, but *not* permanent—necessary for him, for her, for God's perfect plan. It doesn't matter if she's getting married; all these things are destined. Same goes for baseball, and his career-ending eye problem. Ditto for him and Tracy. He's no longer conflicted about the intimacy they share. Their love, though less consuming, is just as perfect and essential and on time as the setting of the sun. To everything there IS a season. Same for his major—it's not something to fret about. Neuroscience with a minor in psych seems the best fit, but all this will likewise fall into place, when it's time.

* * *

Same morning, fifteen minutes later. "Neurology is the scientific study of the structure, function, and abnormalities of the nervous system," Dr. Frederick Richardson commences, after welcoming the two-dozen students (19 guys + 5 gals) and dealing with a few administrative formalities. "Such a study would take a lifetime, many lifetimes ... and would require input from all fields of academia, from biology to physics to philosophy ... to anthropology and who knows what ... so we obviously must limit the scope of this course. With this in mind, we will attempt this semester to survey the structure and function of

THE SILVER CORD

the human neural apparatus with emphasis on the brain itself, and we'll save nervous-system pathology for other courses."

A slight, balding, fair-skinned gentleman with Nordic-blue eyes behind tortoise-shell glasses, the professor speaks with a precise patrician accent befitting his New England roots. He grew up in Connecticut where he acquired two degrees at Yale before embarking on his medical career. Coming to Texas in 1946, he entered Harvey Cushing Medical School in Houston (where Chris is going in the fall). After graduating, Dr. Richardson served on the surgical staff at the hospital (now Harvey Cushing Medical Center), rising from intern to resident to renowned surgeon and teacher. He never left Harvey Cushing except for a brief stint as an Army captain, a front-line M.A.S.H. surgeon during the last year of the Korean War. Then in 1979, at the age of fifty-five, he gave up the surgical practice in Houston to take his current tenured position at Baylor, and he became the department head in 1985 upon the retirement of Dr. Elwood Lansing. Bryan learned most of this from Chris, some from Tracy.

"For our course text," the professor continues, "I have chosen *Human Neurology*, a basic work by Michael Rutter. But that's just a tiny part of the required reading. Let's look for a moment at the syllabus. It's in the blue folder I gave you earlier." Grabbing his copy from the lectern, Dr. Richardson makes a few quick comments about the monstrous three-page reading list then proceeds to the course outline. As he does, he paces slowly back and forth behind the spindly lectern, his James Joyce spectacles propped upon a prim, slightly aquiline nose.

Bryan, removing his own glasses, quickly cleans them with a cloth he keeps in his book bag—the specs are a must when he's taking notes. *This's weird. I bet I'm the only sophomore in here.* He's seated in the fourth row, the next-to-last row. *I recognize a few faces, but I don't know anybody, except that red-haired guy up front. He was on the baseball team last year, but he got cut. Frank ... that's his name. He's a senior.* Bryan returns to the syllabus on his desk (each of the theater-style seats has a small desktop that you pull up to write on). He gives an eager snort, hiding it behind a cough. *Dang, I wonder what Dr. Richardson's gonna say once he gets going. He looks sorta frumpy, like he slept in that suit last night.* The bow-tied doctor wears a rumpled seersucker outfit, which is *way* out of season on this wintry morning, and the gray hair remaining on the fringes of his bald dome spills over his collar; he could use a trip to the barber shop. No doubt about it: he looks more like a professor than a brain surgeon, a professor from the old school where dowdy looks were a badge of genius, as with Einstein. But he does have the hands of a surgeon: graceful, uncallused, almost feminine.

Stepping over to a portable blackboard, Richardson stares at the blank expanse. Like the antiquated chalkboard (obviously from elsewhere on campus), he seems out of place in this ultra-modern classroom with its track lighting, tiered seating, acoustic carpets and walls—plus high-tech gadgetry: computers, monitors, sound systems, various screens and projectors. The room smells like an airliner and sports almost as much electronic gear, but he uses old-fashioned, low-tech chalk, as he scrawls, left-handed, a pair of big words: REDUCTIVE MATERIALISM.

"Why is reductive materialism crucial to brain science?" he asks rhetorically, as he resumes his slow pacing—he clasps his hands behind him. His Nordic eyes spark behind the small, round, odd-looking spectacles—no more preliminaries: he's now into his element like a bird taking flight. "We'll answer this question in a moment, but let's first take a panoramic view of the landscape."

Bryan checks his watch: 9:27. *Good, we have lots of time.*

"In neurology," Dr. Richardson explains, "we have *hard* problems and im*poss*ible problems." He gives a wry chuckle, a throaty *yeck-yeck.* "For example: it's a difficult feat to dissect, categorize, and explain the physical structure of the brain ... but it *is* possible. Same for some aspects of brain function, especially now ... with our high-tech neuroimaging methods such as color-coded PET depictions, or positron emission tomography ... and functional magnetic resonance—that's a special MRI process. In fact, we can actually observe the difference between wakefulness and sleep. We can likewise measure the 40 Hertz signature of an awake mind, or we can follow the pain in our toe, as it registers in the cerebral cortex, or we can observe how motivation is tied to neurotransmitters such as serotonin and endorphins, or how dreaming relates to memory retention, or how images on the retina take dual pathways to the visual processing region of the cortex." He halts near the first row, near redheaded Frank. "But when it comes to the ultimate neurological challenge, to explain *consciousness* itself, we move from 'hard' to 'impossible' or *near*-impossible." He chuckles, another *yeck-yeck,* giving a toss of his bald head, then he retreats to the skinny, plastic-looking lectern, which could pass for a space-age music stand.

Some of the students seem less than engaged, as evidenced by shifting and yawning and stretching of limbs, but Bryan looks on with rapt attention, hanging on each and every word. He may've missed the big leagues in baseball, but not when it comes to the ultimate mission of his life. He's still a rookie, but he's *here.*

"This's the *biggie*," the professor elaborates, chopping the air slowly, deliberately. "We do not understand why and how conscience experience arises from flesh, or how environmental stimuli provoke subjective knowing and pondering, which leads to an awareness of *self*."

O God, he's nailing it, Bryan interjects silently, near to wetting his jeans.

"Now Dr. Francis Crick maintains that consciousness equals

attention times working memory. To be conscious of something, we have to give attention to it, and keep giving attention to it. Gerald Edeleman at the Scripps Institute takes a similar position. He agrees that we're always perceiving things, but he holds that we only become conscious when we relate our perceptions to our inner categories of experience. On the other hand, theologians define the mind as the apex of the God-created soul, while the Roswell crowd explains it as an astral uplink capacity engineered and energized by the aliens that placed us here ... and to include a primitive view, the South American Yekuana tribe says the mind emanates from Wanadi, the highest sky. Wanadi sent down his son Seruhe, who shook his rattle, chanted, and used quartz charms to conjure from the jungle the collective consciousness of the Yekuana people." Richardson throws up his hands. "Are these ideas acceptable? Who the hell knows? Pardon my language, but when it comes to consciousness, we can't rule *any*thing out ... and the theories run the entire gamut, though most fall into one of two camps: the reductionist opinion that the mind is the same as the physical brain ... and the supernatural view which identifies the mind as a metaphysical agency transcending our gray matter, an ethereal entity, such as a soul, which oversees the operation of the fleshy machine called the brain."

He's actually talking about the SOUL! Bryan exclaims to himself. *He's not as rigid as Chris led me to believe.*

The professor, pacing, rolls the chalk between the palms of his hands. "I surmise the truth lies somewhere between, wherein the mind is an emergent property of the brain—it's what results when the mind runs. Yet the process remains a mystery, a point all *honest* scientists agree on, and yet there are many different approaches to the problem, approaches as varied and extreme as the theories themselves." He does his wry chuckle, his throaty chuckle; he sounds like a crow clucking (in addition to *cawing*, the big blackbirds utter a guttural *yeck-yeck* sound just like the professor, somewhere between a quack and a warble, especially when they're on the ground gleaning the naked hayfields after the harvest back at the Howard farm). "So what's the point of this fifteen-minute excursion to far side of neurology on the first day of the course?" He sweeps his hand toward the blackboard. "Well ... I want to drive home the crucial relevance of reductive materialism, if we hope to make progress in brain science. When seeking truth, we must have rules of engagement, lest we get lost in chaos and irrational confusion, and I want you to know *my* rules from the outset. I *am* a reductive materialist, and I think it's the most logical stance. Edelman and Crick agree, as does Dr. John Ratey from Harvard. Reductive materialism maintains that *all* aspects of neural function can be explained by physical laws, *without* resorting to metaphysical phenomena. Thus, all biological and mental events are re*duc*ible to matter and energy."

He draws a circle on the board. "During this course we'll be staying in here, within the realm of matter and energy." He taps the chalk inside the circle. "But what about faith, the soul, and God? What about the theories that operate in the nonmaterial dimensions, so-called? There are persuasive arguments to include supernatural agencies in any explanation of the human mind, as you'll learn in your philosophy and religious classes. After all, there are some loud Baptist voices still speaking on this campus."

"No kidding," responds a male voice behind Bryan. Guffaws and titters ripple through the class, including the lone sophomore from Spindle, but he's more amazed than amused, and profoundly relieved: his whole quest for the silver cord seems suddenly more valid than ever, like WIDE OPEN.

"I'm an agnostic Episcopalian myself," the professor allows, as the class settles. "That may sound like a contradiction ... but I do hope there is some reality out here, Christian or otherwise." He taps the outer portion of the blackboard. "But if we open this box, we'll have to include *all* metaphysical possibilities ... no matter how farfetched ... like all the whackos and psychics and UFO abductees, and the time-travelers and necromancers, and the ghosts and gremlins and demons and angels, and—well, you can see where this would lead." More laughter. "So if God is going to get into this course, he has to manifest himself *in*side the circle. Perhaps he does? Perhaps he doesn't? But either way, reductive materialism is the *best* approach we can muster, and it's teaching us a lot about consciousness, though I'll be the first to admit that we've only scratched the surface of this great mystery."

Richardson returns to his notes. "So now that I've previewed the fantastic side of neurology, let's retreat for the remaining minutes to the neural development of the human fetus ... in chapter one of Rutter, the primary textbook for this course."

* * *

My theories are as good as any, Bryan exults, as he exits the neuroscience lab and heads for Moody Library—he doesn't have a ten-o'clock class. *We can't rule ANYthing out. That's exactly what he said. And he hopes there IS some kind of reality outside the circle. Well, that's where the silver cord comes into play. It connects the stuff inside the circle to the stuff outside the circle. It's the key to unlocking the whole goshdang mystery.*

Exhaling clouds of winter breath, he makes his way around the Fletcher Life Sciences Building returning to Fountain Mall. His peers come and go about him, but he scarcely notices. *This thing is still WIDE OPEN. No one can shoot me down, not even Dr. Richardson. I don't have a solid theory, but my ignorance concerning the silver cord is no worse than his. And it doesn't bother me that he reduces everything to materialism or whatever he calls it. I probably would too, if it weren't for my personal experiences in the astral realm. It's not something I can bring up in class. No way José ... but still, it all happened.*

The Dinsmore Fountain is a frozen pond. The spigot itself is shut off, but a layer of ice covers the standing water in the basin, and it won't melt much today. As Bryan strides by the fountain, he detects in his peripheral vision a windblown snowflake. *Hey, I think it's starting to snow.* He stops to confirm, gazing at a big pine tree adjacent to the mall until another flake flits by against the darkish-green background, then another, and another. *Yes, it IS snowing.* Boyish excitement reinforces his already exuberant mood. *I hope we get ten inches. That would be super neat.*

* * *

Delving through the science stacks on the third floor of the library, Bryan locates several of the titles on Dr. Richardson's list: *Principles of Neural Development* by Dale Purves and Jeff Lictman; *The Three-Pound Universe* by Judith Hooper and Dick Teresi; *The Cerebral Symphony* by William Calvin; *Memory's Voice* by Daniel Alkon; *Driven to Distraction* by John J. Ratey. The long reading list elicited groans from many of the neurology students, but Mr. Howard can't wait to dig into these books, as many as he can. *I may never get to the end of the rainbow on this,* he declares to himself, as he comes down the stairs, *but I sure as hell got the pedal to the metal—plus a full tank of gas.*

After checking out, he exits Moody Library, his knapsack slung heavily over one shoulder, heavy from the extra books. He hustles by the stately columns then down the wide expanse of Washington-like steps, where he finds, to his delight, the air thick with snow—huge wet flakes which have transformed the campus into a Christmas card. The sidewalks and streets are just wet, the snow melting on the warmer pavement, but a slushy inch blankets the lawns, cloaks the pine trees, and gilds the naked limbs of the hardwoods—plus the telephone poles and utility lines and fences and signs and stair rails and benches.

Pausing near the fountain, he gazes up into the falling snow, the big flakes tumbling and pirouetting as they swirl down about him. A few land on his face, tickling his cheeks. He catches one in his mouth. *O Lord, this's SO beautiful. Why have something so wonderful, like snow, if we're just flesh and blood headed for nothing but death, a slow rot in some coffin? It can't BE.* A surge of conviction grips him. *Dear Jesus, I KNOW you're with me. I know it. I know it. And I know Mandy's with me too. I feel her now. I do!* Upwelling love warms his bosom. *Gosh, oh gosh—it's so big and wondrous. And yet it doesn't diminish my feelings for Tracy. It's like everything is perfect and rightly related, even these many months of separation since my pretty lady ran off to Arkansas. It's all necessary and perfect. I don't know how you're gonna resolve things, but, dear God, I trust you. And I believe in you more than ever ... even though I don't go to church much.*

470

THE SILVER CORD

* * *

THREE MONTHS LATER:

BAYLOR UNIVERSITY - BRAZOS DRIVE
WEDNESDAY, APRIL 14, 1993 — 4:37 PM

Having completed their jog along the river, Bryan and Tracy catch their breath near the steps leading up to the parking area. A large cottonwood, its leafy new crown thick and verdant, shades this part of the footpath—welcome shade, as Waco basks in a sultry, early-season heat wave. Though Bryan has given up on baseball, he remains in tiptop condition. The aerobic exercise also sharpens his mind, enhancing his studying ability each evening. Same goes for Tracy, who's preparing for her big RN exams. She's also trying to quit smoking again—it's been ten days.

"Y'wanna catch the end of the game?" he asks a few minutes later as he eases the pickup out onto Brazos Drive. "They're playing SMU, and Jordan's pitching. He made a special point of telling me in history class—like *three* times."

"Yeah, why not?" Tracy replies, as they share a laugh over Steve's self-absorbed antics. Bryan gooses the old Chevy then shifts, then shifts again, accelerating until the wind is rushing in his open window. The truck runs as good as ever.

"I must say, Bryan dear," she sports, speaking loudly over the draft blowing in—she gives a wifely smirk. "You *really* smell like a man, or maybe a horse." She giggles, her chocolate eyes sparking under the yellow headband she wears when she runs.

"Well, you don't smell too fresh yourself, Ms. McCollum."

Still laughing, she pulls a towel out of her gym bag and wipes her face. She then dabs perfume on her neck and wrists. The rosy scent is quite familiar now, yet it still stirs his malehood, as do her smirky giggles and sweaty haunches, not to mention her nubile bosom slowly heaving inside her T-shirt and jock bra. It's been a few days, and she's *in the mood*—her flirting gives witness, as does the glint in her eyes, and she surely won't have to twist his arm. He looks forward to bedding her, and he no longer frets over whether he's being unfaithful to Mandy. The strong sense of purpose burning in his gut, for the silver cord, for everything, has resolved such conflicts. It's not an issue of morality, but of *destiny*. No matter what he does with Tracy, it can never change what he has with Mandy, just as Mandy's upcoming marriage to Russ Snyder can never alter God's perfect plan (it's still on for June, says Wendy L.). The Lord makes everything perfect in HIS time, and this knowing comforts Bryan, settles him, ushering in a sense of profound tranquillity. Ditto for baseball: a year ago he couldn't go near a Baylor game without feeling robbed and resentful, but now he can enjoy watching the team, *without* envy.

"O Jesus, somebody got hurt!" Tracy exclaims, as they pull into the Ferrell Complex; her voice goes chimpmunky, like it does when she's excited. An ambulance, its lights flashing amid a throng of players and fans, is parked near the back entrance to the home-team clubhouse. Bryan jockeys the Chevy toward the EMT vehicle, but they can't get close enough to see much.

"It *must* be bad if they stopped the game," he declares, as he prepares to get out, but before he does, he spots Steve Jordan lumbering toward them.

"Hey, dude, glad yuh came over," the big guy drawls. "And you too, Tracy. I got a shutout through six, but the game's held up ... till they get him into the ambulance and all."

"Who is it?" Bryan asks.

"It's Coach McKinney—he was waving Pedro home, and the next thang I know he's face down in the coachin' box."

* * *

HILLCREST MEDICAL CENTER - ICU
THURSDAY, APRIL 15, 1993 — 2:35 PM

"It's true," Elmo McKinney whispers faintly, without opening his eyes, "ever'thang you said lash year." He grips Bryan's hand. "I was floatin' over the damn infield, then I was back home in Alabama ... above the cotton fields. And I was feelin' good ... like I was drunk on Jack Daniels." He coughs, losing his breath.

"Take it slow," Bryan counsels, giving his mentor and friend a pat on the shoulder.

"It *has* to be the Lord. It's almost a year to the day since my first attack ... but this time he took me up. It was brighter than the sun, and I saw my mama smilin' at me."

* * *

Gosh almighty! Bryan reacts, as he climbs into his hot pickup in the hospital parking lot. *It's REAL. I'm NOT the only one.*

THE SILVER CORD

CHAPTER TWENTY-EIGHT

FLETCHER NEUROLOGY WING - CLASSROOM 119
FRIDAY, APRIL 16, 1993 — 9:54 AM

"Oh, Bryan, wait a minute," Dr. Richardson calls.

The sophomore, on his way out, quickly responds, his heart banging to attention. "Yes sir," he responds respectfully, after reentering against the flow.

"Do you have a free hour this afternoon, say three o'clock?"

"Yes sir, I reckon I do."

"Good ... I want to have a chat with you ... up in my office." His Nordic eyes twinkling, he gives his star student a parting nod.

* * *

Same day, same building, 2:54 p.m. Bryan ducks into the men's room at the top of the stairs; he tucks in his shirttail. Before coming over, he showered and put on fresh Levi's plus a sport shirt. He runs a comb through his shortish haircut—he left his hat in the truck. Finally, he sniffs his underarms. No problem: the Ban roll-on is doing its job despite the 85° heat outside. His stomach buzzes, an anxious but eager churning. As he exits, he takes a last deep breath to settle himself. The second-floor hallway smells new, like the whole building, the same acrylic aerospace aroma, and the bluish carpet soaks up noise—no echoes. *Gosh, I wonder why he wants to see me? Maybe he found out about my OBEs, and he thinks I'm a whacko? No, there's no way. Chris would never do that, or Tracy.*

"I have a three o'clock appointment with Dr. Richardson," he explains to the forty-something receptionist outside the suite of administrative offices. "I'm Bryan Howard." He catches a whiff of her perfume, an aggressively fragrant scent that reminds him of Steve Jordan's body talc: honeysuckle plus.

"Okay ... give me a sec," the bespectacled brunette replies perfunctorily, clicking her keyboard. Chubbily attractive, she has wide-set cowish eyes, short bangs, and boobs big enough to bowl with. He's seen her before, in the parking lot. "Yes, here we are ... Bryan Howard, three p.m. Please have a seat." Giving a polite smile, she nods toward the empty waiting nook.

Maybe he sees me as too outspoken for a sophomore? Bryan thinks on, as he plunks down on a vinyl sofa. *Maybe the other students feel I'm showing them up? Sheeesh, God—what would they do if I shared EVERYthing?* Laughing, he grabs a magazine from the end table, the February issue of *Scientific American*. It feels stuffy, as if the AC's turned down.

473

THE SILVER CORD

Muted commotion: the tomography lab disgorges its students at the far end of the hallway. Bryan watches, as they disappear down the stairway leaving silence in their wake. Slipping on his glasses, he comes back to the magazine, flipping the pages. A few stranglers exit the restrooms—then more silence. He checks his watch: 3:01 p.m. He fidgets; he shed his glasses. He rolls the mag into a baton. He pops it against his palm, his thigh, his knee. A black chick emerges from the wide door behind the receptionist, a modish sister sporting dreadlocks and wrap-around sunglasses. After whispering to the busty brunette at the desk, she sashays toward the stairs, a pinkish book-bag bouncing on her hip.

3:08 p.m. Bryan checks the receptionist hoping for a signal. Nothing—she's busy at her computer. *Maybe she never buzzed him? Or maybe something came—*

The professor suddenly appears, looking very casual: no suit coat, no bow tie, sleeves rolled. "Forgive me, Bryan ... I was on the phone with Dean Buckley. But do come in ... come in."

Bryan follows down a corridor past several doors, some open, some not, one filled with cubicles and clicking keyboards. *Gosh,* he reacts to himself, *I never expected him to come OUT to get me.* He towers above the diminutive doctor, above his bald knob which glistens waxily under the florescent lights.

Reaching the last office, Richardson gives a go-in gesture: "Please have a seat. I'll be right back."

Bryan sits down in a mate's chair adjacent to the desk, which is buried under books, magazines, and student papers, plus floppy disks and old print-outs. Ditto for the computer table under the window where the jumbled piles of stuff dwarf the Dell PC and ink-jet printer. A blue-corduroy suit-coat drapes the PC chair, a worn, winter-weight garment with leather-patched elbows.

New England Journal of Medicine, American Medical News, Surgical Rounds, Clinical Neuropsychology, Applied Radiology, Journal of Neurology, Applied Diagnostics—the magazines are all medical, aside from a *Golf Digest* lying upon the multibutton phone console. "That's right, he's a golfer," Bryan whispers. A putter behind the door verifies this, along with three golf balls nestled in a practice cup, the kind with flip-down sides for carpet practice. More dot-matrix output lines the wall opposite the desk, massive time-yellowed stacks, the same perfed, continuous-form printer paper. *There's enough goshdang output in here to fill my truck. And it has to be old. They do analysis on-screen now.* Time has likewise ravaged the wooden desk— he notes a missing leg plus water damage to the side panels, blotchy areas of swelling and peeling suggesting outdoor exposure. A pile of books supports the legless corner. The file cabinets (frog-green, lawyer-style) are equally ancient. All this makes the office seem much older than it is, as does the musty paper-and-ink odor, and the naked window:

there's a tan roll-up shade but no curtains.

"Frederick Winslow Richardson," reads the biggest diploma on the wall, or maybe it's an MD certificate? Bryan can't tell, and he'd rather not put on his glasses. An open lunch bag rests on the pull-out shelf plus a wadded napkin, a Pepsi can, and a coffee mug. Three other mugs guard the PC on the far table. A hint of cheese joins the mustiness, from the brown bag? He chuckles, feeling more relaxed. *The doc is definitely not into appearances.*

"Now, Bryan, I've been wanting to talk with you for some time," Dr. Richardson explains after his return and the exchange of a few pleasantries. He shifts about in his desk chair, getting comfortable. He picks up the beige cafeteria-style mug from the pull-out shelf and takes a left-handed sip. "Oh, would you like a soda or some iced tea ... or a cup of coffee? I can buzz Connie?"

"No sir, I'm fine. But thanks." *Gosh, he's treating me like a BIGSHOT,* the sophomore adds delightedly but only to himself.

The doctor, snickering, gestures with the mug then sets it on the shelf. "I drink *too* much coffee myself, but this's Diet-Pepsi ... another way of getting my fix, but it took a while to acquire the taste. I've also developed a taste for ice tea, which is saying a lot for a New England Yankee." More titters. The puckered laugh lines and liverish bags under the eyes give witness that Richardson is in his late 60s, but the eyes themselves retain a youthful spark: gray-blue, bright with vigor. He grabs the phone, after moving the *Golf Digest* plus a stack of quiz papers. "Adele ... would you please kick the AC up a notch. It's a bit clammy back here."

He must have two secretaries, Bryan surmises to himself. *He said Connie before, but now he's talking to Adele. Or maybe Adele is the big-boobed receptionist out front?*

"But back to what I was saying," the doctor remarks after replacing the phone—he wads the lunch bag and tosses it into the trash. "I've had many students in my fourteen years at Baylor, but I've never seen *any*one with such a hunger for neurology, and you're a *soph*omore no less." A happy geyser bathes Bryan's ego—no doubt now: he's here to be *commended*. He can't help but dimple into a grin. He adjusts his position, crossing his legs ankle-on-knee. The professor, creaking back in his own chair, removes his glasses, the James Joyce spectacles with the tortoise-shell frames. "I'm not talking about acing the exams, although you've surely done that, but there's something in*tangible* going on here. Chris said you were unique, and he's *more* than right. I uh ... I uh—" Pausing midsentence, he massages the bridge of his nose then his eyebrows, bushy, pepper-colored brows, still more dark than gray, in contrast to the silvery hair on his head, the monkish fringe he has left. "Let's consider for example your term paper." Replacing the glasses, he picks up a folder and fishes inside it, coming out with a stapled treatise that Bryan recognizes as his own. "Now the assignment called on the class to justify reductive materialism ... as it pertains to neurological research. And I must say you did a remarkable job proving my point ... without resorting to a stale recitation of my class lectures." His blue eyes twinkling, he gives a fond nod plus a laugh. "Hell ... you quoted Edelman and Ratey, and Purves and Crick, and Calvin and Teresi and Greene, even Einstein and Harvey Cushing himself. No doubt, you've done your reading—that *alone* sets you apart." More laughter, both of them. Bryan is so excited he can hardly keep his seat. "But what I found most creative, and thought-provoking, was the closing disclaimer ... your bold dissent. Most of my colleagues would consider it impudent for a novice to issue such a challenge, but I find it curious, and most intriguing." He flips to the last two pages. "Like what you say here." He reads:

> The case for reductionism, as stated above, stands as proven before any jury of neuroscientists. And this limiting principle does assure consistency and apparent rationality, as we attempt to explain the working of the human mind. It keeps everyone on the same playing field, with a high fence to keep out all metaphysical factors, which might introduce confusion and contamination. By heeding the limits of physicalism we have achieved much progress, especially toward identifying and mapping neural function, and malfunction. Yet despite its strong points, reductive materialism fails to answer the ultimate neuro-question: How does a physical brain produce consciousness and a sense of self?
>
> If RM fails here, it must be deficient. How does gray matter, millions of physical neurons, produce ME? I exist. I KNOW I exist. I love, I hurt, I hope, I fear, and I talk to MYSELF. It's ME. I'm real. I feel. But what is ME? Does the physical brain equal the beginning and end of ME? Am I purely matter and energy, as the reductionists insist, or does my "self" go beyond the physical? Do I possess a soul (or spirit) that will transcend death, or does my life end when my EEG goes flat? Is it possible to be ME without my flesh? Is there a more fundamental realm, an astral realm? Does astral matter exist? and astral energy? And if I do possess a soul-body, how does this astral ME tether to my gray-matter brain? And does this tether allow us to venture into the astral dimension. Is it possible to travel this realm—apart from my physical body? Do the recent advances in subatomic physics (*string theory*, etc.) open the door to a new reality, a reality where the

metaphysical has BECOME the physical?

Although my yearning for life cries out within me, giving witness that we're MORE than macro-physical beings, not to mention the convincing testimony of personal experience, I cannot as yet answer these questions with certainty—I cannot make the leap, not honestly, not yet. To use a religious term, my faith is incomplete, yet hopeful. Most neurologists would admonish me for tainting scientific inquiry with faith, yet it's much the same. The Church calls on us to accept the dogmas of our ancestors, while refusing to consider any contrary evidence that might shake our belief system, while brain scientists call on us to accept reductive materialism despite its narrowness. I see it as BLIND and DISHONEST, in both arenas. To erect a wall between God and science is ABSURD!

And we exercise this BLIND DISHONESTY when we rule out metaphysical explanations during neurological research, especially when we know that our long-accepted physical laws fail in various circumstances, as when we approach the speed of light, or when we introduce anti-matter, or dark matter, or parallel universes, or when we diminish the space-time scale to the quantum realm where Newtonian mechanics break down IAW with the Heisenberg *uncertainty principle*, where matter can exist at different places at the same time, and it can pass through walls. Even quantum mechanics and Einstein's *theory of relativity* ultimately fail in the berserk supermicro universe, as John Schwarz shows in his *superstring theory* at the California Institute of Technology. So if we carry reductionism to its extreme, we end up with weird phenomena that would be considered supernatural on a macro scale, like people flying through walls. And ALL neural processes are supermicro, if we dig far enough.

Enough is enough! What appears logical on a macro scale becomes illogical on the subatomic scale, and I submit that the interaction between gray matter and consciousness must ultimately occur on such a scale. THUS—TO RULE OUT NONPHYSICAL CAUSES BEFOREHAND IS IRRATIONAL AND PREJUDICED, AS MUCH AS ANY NARROW-MINDED RELIGION! The true physical realm of nature is wider than we can even imagine. So we can't fence things out just to keep the wheels on the wagon, just to maintain the tidy status quo. If the RM approach fails to answer the ultimate neuro-question, we must draw a BIGGER CIRCLE, even if it makes the process messy and whacko and confusing. Genuine confusion is better than contrived order. Let's get HONEST about what we know and what we don't know, whether it's a minister preaching, *or* a neuroscientist.

As for me, I want to see ALL the evidence. I don't recognize the many fences that limit and separate us. There's only one REALITY, and that's what I'm looking for! That's my quest!

Dr. Richardson shakes his head in seeming wonder then hands the paper to Bryan, whose heart beats proudly, his cheeks going warm. A red-ink A+ adorns the first page (a trifle blurry without his glasses), and yet the sophomore's gladness has nothing to do with grades, *no way*—his argument has hit home with the doctor. That's what counts, even if he proceeds to rebut it.

Richardson sips from the mug then shakes his head again. "That's a *power*ful piece of writing ... from a student. Hell, I rarely see balls like this among full-fledged surgeons."

Bryan's blush grows warmer. "Thank you, sir."

"How old are you, anyway?"

"Nineteen ... but I'll be twenty in three weeks."

"*Damn*, you're not even old enough to buy liquor, and you're challenging the foundational principles of brain research ... and you talk about the metaphysical realm with such audacity and authority, as though you've *actually* been there."

"Sheeeeeesssh ... shhh," Bryan reacts, covering with a cough.

"I'd like to know where you get your audacity. I see it in class too. You've studied your ass off, but stuff like this is *too* compelling to come from books alone." Gesturing left-handed with the mug of Pepsi, he gives a smirk, along with a roll of his Nordic eyes. "Like I say, there's something *intangible* going on. I suspect you have a story to tell." Leaning back, he strokes his stubbled beard, his dimpled chin: a crevice notches the apex, a la Kirk Douglas. "Yeck-yeck"—he quacks like a crow.

* * *

"It hasn't happened for eighteen months, since December '91," Bryan relates a good while later, as he settles a bit in the mate's chair, having told his tale. "But it's always there, the knowing." Buoyed by the doctor's ego-boosting kudos, along with Coach McKinney's testimony yesterday, he couldn't help but share *every*thing: his OBEs, his near-death episode, the Mandy part, the Gramps part, the God part, the jetliner part, the Tracy and Chris part, his parents, his boyhood, Buster, Millie, Jeff Burton, Spanky, baseball, Pleasant Hill Baptist, Dr. Wilson,

THE SILVER CORD

Dr. Nadler, Dr. Rosenblatt, the eye problem—all of it. Save for a few clarifying questions, the professor has said nothing, while slowly killing off his Pepsi. "And like I say, I haven't told many people ... no way. Chris and Tracy know, but it's not something you can blab to just anyone." Bryan gives a throaty laugh then goes silent.

Taking off his glasses, Dr. Richardson rubs his nose. He swivels toward the computer table; he stares wide-eyed out the window, as if gazing at the large sun-splashed pine tree behind the old science building. The needled boughs nod in the breeze. He gives a soft sigh that turns hard: "Hmmmm-umm."

Pangs of doubt dampen the sophomore's confidence. He picks up the term paper from beside him on the chair. He fiddles with it, dog-earing the corner. While sharing his story, rushes of adrenaline spurred him on, but now it's out there, hanging naked in the air. *O God, he must think I'm a nut, a whacko fruitcake.* He feels suddenly childish and silly, out of his league. He waits for the professor to dismiss him, to send him on his way.

"So tell me, Bryan," the doctor finally responds, still gazing out the window. "What's your favorite soft drink? Or 'pop' ... as they call it down here?"

"Uh ... uh ... Dr. Pepper," Bryan stammers, taken aback.

"Diet?"

"No sir, the regular. I mean uh ... well uh ... the diet stuff's tolerable, but Mandy hated it. I can drink it, but uh ... she always stocked our fridge with the regular kind."

"I see ... I see."

The sophomore doesn't reply except to himself: *Why's he asking me about pop, if he thinks I'm whacko? And I'm hardly helping things. Gosh, I'm stuttering like a dadgum idiot.* He looks down sheepishly; he checks his watch: 4:03 p.m. He rolls the term paper into a tube.

Dr. Richardson grabs the phone: "Connie, would you give Chris Hansen a ring down in the mainframe lab. I'm supposed to meet him at four-thirty to go over the Droznik simulations, but it'll be five before I get there. And when you get a chance, please bring us two sodas, from the faculty lounge, another Diet-Pepsi for me, and a Dr. Pepper for my guest."

The professor excuses himself, sidling from behind the desk. He retires to his private washroom beyond the file cabinets.

Bryan waits, feeling somewhat relieved: *He may doubt my story, but he evidently wants to discuss it.*

Richardson emerges. As he does, a petite redhead enters the office tray-in-hand, a gray-eyed, slightly familiar, middle-aged gal in a rose-colored suit. "Thanks much, Connie," the doctor says, taking the barhop tray, which bears the sodas, plus napkins and two styrofoam cups filled with ice. "So you got a hold of Chris?"

She gives a paste-on smile. "Yes; he says five is fine."

"Good, good—oh, this's Bryan Howard. He's new to the department this semester, but I expect we'll be seeing a lot of him— he's only a sophomore."

She nods ladylike from the doorway. "Glad to meet you."
She then exits, closing the door softly behind her.

"So, Bryan, what did Chris say about these astral experiences?" Richardson asks a bit later, after exchanging a few more comments about soda-pop and such—while opening their cans.

The sophomore chuckles, gesturing with the chilled can of Dr. Pepper, which is wet with condensation. "Well sir, he gave his usual smirks and wisecracks, but then he got more serious. He finds it mind-boggling, but he didn't banish it from his universe. He even brought up the Einstein thing."

"Einstein what?"

"Oh, the whole thing about time contraction and light rays bending, and how all the bigshot physicists back then scoffed at these wild ideas ... and yet he turned out to be right."

"That he did ... that he did. Chris sees Einstein as a saint, but he didn't get *every*thing right, as you pointed out in your paper." The doctor sips fresh Pepsi from his mug; neither of them used a cup. Yet the ice didn't go totally to waste, as the professor shook some into his mug. "So did Chris read your term paper?"

"Yes sir. He thought it was dynamite, the last part ... but he wasn't sure how you'd react to it?"

"How so?"

Bryan sips then chuckles. "Well sir, I reckon he sees you as rather strict in your views." More titters, from both.

"So he didn't encourage you to divulge your OBEs and such?"

"Not *hardly*. He said I had to pay my dues before I open my f-ing mouth. Tracy says the same. But it's too late *now*. Y'can't get the stink back into the skunk, as we say on the farm." More mutual laughter. The upbeat mood heartens Bryan.

"Well, I wouldn't call it a *stink* exactly, yet it is my nature to play the devil's advocate, and I *am* rather strict, until I see good reason to broaden my view. But most neurologists would give you a cooler, more clinical reception—if at all. To even discuss soul-travel is *way* out of bounds ... like your Dr. Nadler in Dallas. I know Joe. He did his residency under me in Houston. He's an outstanding surgeon, perhaps the best right now, but I can't see him sitting in on this." He laughs then sips and sobers. "But allow me to pose a question, one of my favorites, for challenging metaphysical notions like yours."

"What question, sir?"

"If we have a soul ... where does it go during a coma?"

Bryan chugs his Dr. Pepper. "Well sir, I just toldjuh where mine went."

"That you did. But what about the rest of the time you were

unconscious? The many hours?"

"That's a *super*-crucial question, no doubt about it. And I don't have the answer ... not *yet*."

The professor squeaks back in his chair; he clears his throat. "With your intellect and zeal, you have *great* potential in this field, whether you go MD, or research, or psych ... or whatever. And your arguments questioning reductive materialism are most persuasive." His patrician voice has taken on that precise Yankee timbre he uses in the classroom. "All this having been said, I still have to challenge the validity of your astral experiences."

"I understand, sir," Bryan responds, nodding respectfully.

"Now if you weren't such a diligent young scholar, I wouldn't give any attention to it. The tabloids at Safeway are full of such tales ... plus the Sci-Fi channel. However, I trust *you* as a witness. That makes everything more provocative, since I *know* you're not hyping up your testimony just to create a sensation."

"No sir."

The professor lifts his mug, a left-handed toast. "Still, I must play the devil's advocate, especially concerning the OBEs, most of which, if not all, occurred as you were falling to sleep. How do you know these trips weren't regular REM dreams?"

"I can't be *tot*ally sure, sir ... as you can gather from my paper." He pats the term paper, now unfurled on his lap. "But my OBEs *are* different from ordinary dreams."

"How so?"

Bryan sips his Dr. Pepper. "Well ... during an OBE the world remains authentic and substantial, never absurd like in a regular dream. And the flow of events makes sense for the most part—the only fantastic thing is *me*. My perspective is *vastly* different. In a normal dream I'm always *in* my body on the ground, while in an OBE I fly around in an astral body—and I can go this way, or that way, like a ghost." He demonstrates with the can, making it swim through the air. "And *reg*ular dreams are often disjointed and confused, and the setting can be surreal, like the dream I had last week: we were in my truck in Galveston, Mandy and me. It was brutally hot, and all the beachfront hotels and shops started to melt, and the piers, and then we were suddenly driving in the ocean like a speedboat, and a great white shark, the one from *Jaws*, was chasing us, but we escaped onto a long bridge— and then I was alone on the bridge: no truck, no Mandy, no traffic. I saw Tracy coming out of a phone booth, and we started jogging, but then *poof*—we were back at Baylor running by the river."

Richardson titters. "That's REM ... without a doubt."

"And the emotions are different. During an OBE, I always feel super good, like elated, whereas in a regular dream, I might be happy, or sad, or scared, or frustrated ... like the baseball dream I've had a number of times: I'm trying to get to some ballpark for a big game, and I can't find the right street, or the truck won't start, or I can't find my uniform shirt—stuff like that."

"The differences *are* noteworthy ... but I'm still skeptical." The doctor sips then casts his eyes briefly upward, as if checking the florescent lights, a pair of recessed rectangular fixtures in the drop ceiling. "So how do you navigate during these astral trips?"

"I just concentrate on where I want to go, and the thought propels me in that direction."

"That *is* wild. How about time travel? Can you do that?"

"You mean like *Back to the Future* with Michael Fox?"

"Yeah?"

"No sir. But time *is* hard to measure, and if I concentrate intently, I can travel so fast it seems instantaneous. If I could look at my watch, I might learn more about how time behaves in that realm. But I can't see my wrist and arm as a separate limb. Maybe I could, if I really tried, but my soul body is more like an amorphous entity, without sharp definition."

"Damn, this *is* fascinating ... yet I remain very doubtful. To be *blunt* about it, I'd rate the probability at twenty percent or less." He gives a chuckle, his wry crowlike chuckle. "I don't rate the odds of even having a soul much higher, speaking as a scientist anyway, so it's a hell of a leap to accept the idea that your soul comes out of your body, possessing conscious cerebral function while your brain's still sleeping in your bed." More chuckles. "No, no, it's *too* much. I don't buy it. I can't. These experiences *have* to be regular dreams, or maybe illusions."

"Well, there's always the baseball-glove incident?"

"Oh yes, when you were in little league. That lends credence, but he never confessed, your friend?"

"No sir ... my glove just appeared at practice, in the ball bag. Jeff denied taking it, then he moved away to Tyler, but I still believe he did it, and I caught him ... during that OBE."

"Believing is one thing, but convincing *me* is another."

"No problem, sir," the sophomore replies between sips of soda. "I reckon the OBE thing *is* hard to prove." He pushes the Dr. Pepper toward the professor. Condensation drips from the sweating can onto his knee making a dark spot in the stone-washed denim. "But whaddabout my near-death experience, when I saw my own body sprawled on the ground, and everyone was gathered at home plate, including Mandy and my parents, and Doc Wilson was working on me, and yet I was floating happily above the mound, and then I shot upward through that tunnel?"

"The tunnel Dr. Moody and Dr. Kübler-Ross talk about?"

"Yes sir."

Leaning forward, the doctor pours more Diet-Pepsi into his mug— it foams and hisses. "I respect Kübler-Ross; she's thorough in her reporting methods. But Dr. Raymond Moody is another story. His latest thing is making contact with departed spirits in mirrors and crystal balls, and his approach has become decidedly unscientific. He's no longer credible, in my opinion."

"Chris mentioned that ... or it mighta been Tracy?"

"Moody's gone around the f-ing bend so to speak ... but your near-death thing has more validity than the OBEs. In fact, I've heard similar NDE reports ever since I was in medical sch—"

"And I know another one," Bryan blurts, almost choking on a swig of pop. "Forgive me, sir ... but he just told me *yes*terday."

"Who?"

"Coach McKinney, the batting coach—he gave me a lot of attention back when I was on the team, and we sorta became friends. Anyway, he had a heart attack on Wednesday, while coaching 3rd base during the SMU game—his second attack."

Richardson nods. "Oh yes, the old black fellow who assists Coach Weaver. I heard about his coronary ... from Richard Wallrath at the country club. He's the head cardiologist at Hillcrest; I played nine holes with him yesterday evening. So your coach friend had some kind of metaphysical episode?"

"Yes sir, he did. I had confided in him before, about my own NDE—he's another one of the few I've told—and he said his experience was very much the same as mine, the pattern anyhow. He didn't tell anyone but me, of course."

"Yes ... yes ... most intriguing. And like I say, I've heard similar reports for decades, even from my own surgery patients. A few could describe actions and conversations in the OR at a time when they were clearly out. It's rare, but we can't disregard it, and there could be others who didn't dare bring it up."

Bryan dimples. "So you accept my NDE as a true event?"

Richardson laughs. "I didn't say *that*. Besides, it's a long shot that we even *have* a soul." More titters. "I suspect that these near-death experiences have a neural reality ... but I submit that they take place *inside* the brain, just like your OBEs. What happened to you, and the coach, can't be dismissed, but it *can* be explained ... short of endorsing extra-physical consciousness."

"How's that, sir?"

The professor swivels toward the sunny window. "Well, let's take the state of euphoria. I say it's a defense mechanism. When we suffer a critical injury the pleasure centers of the brain, the hypothalamus, the septum, and the nucleus accumbens, are flooded with endorphins, serotonin, and dopamine, creating a narcotic-like high. We've confirmed this in rats and monkeys. The cause of this response is still being debated, but the intralaminar nuclei play a role, from deep within the thalamus ... the same nuclei that maintain the 40 Hz synchronizing oscillation necessary for consciousness. But in any case, a lethal injury or a vital-organ malfunction might well give rise to a state of euphoria."

"You're losing me, sir ... but I do get the gist of it, the idea that trauma induces a morphine-like high. I've heard about that, and Chris talks about it too, as a possible explanation—but how about the floating sensation, and seeing myself on the ground, with everyone gathered around?"

"That's tougher, but a plausible possibility is 'unconscious perception,' the theory that our sensory systems still function to a limited degree even when we appear to be completely under. Or we could write it off as active imagination, or good guessing."

"Now *that* seems a bit far to me, even more of a stretch, sir."

Placing his mug on the pull-out shelf, the professor laces his hands over his chest, over his white dress shirt, which appears a trifle yellowed with age, like the computer print-outs. "Yes, I'm afraid that *is* somewhat of a stretch. That's why I see your near-death thing as more plausible than the OBEs, though they're much the same, and they both require the existence of a soul."

"Yes sir, a soul that somehow connects to our physical body, a soul that leaves at death, upon the severing of the silver cord."

The doctor removes his glasses; he rocks in his chair. "And desire shall fail; because man goeth to his long home ... and the mourners go about the streets; the silver cord is loosed ... then shall the dust return to the earth as it was, and the spirit shall return to God, who gave it."

"Goshdang, sir ... I didn't realize you knew the Bible."

Richardson laughs. "Not like you Baptists ... but I've always been fond of Ecclesiastes. It tells it like it is ... All is vanity and vexation of spirit. And yet it doesn't rule out the spirit returning to God. It sort of sums up my agnosticism—I *am* a member of the Episcopal Church, you know?"

"Yes sir, I've heard you mention it in class."

"I'm a hardballed skeptic, but I still hope for a good ending."

"Me too, sir?"

"And I haven't ruled God out of my universe. In fact, God seems more likely than the soul, because of cause and effect regarding origins. Yet most theories of evolution don't include God. Lacking reductive evidence to the contrary, most scientists see the universe as cold, godless, and unknowing, a place where only the fittest survive, and love is simply an animal urge that guarantees the transmission of our genes, or at best an emotion that bonds us with others for mutual benefit ... as in the age-old marriage compact where humans pair off for mating and security and the raising of offspring ... or when the early hunter-gatherers increased their chances by living together in clans." The doctor replaces his spectacles, propping them halfway down his aquiline nose. "I hope that love is *more* than that, and I also hope for God. And I *do* see him as plausible, if not probable ... as the first cause. It's a leap to assume that reality evolved from *nothing* ... and the Big Bang occurred spontaneously. And yet God could be a higher *alien* intelligence. And just because there's an intelligence who created this reality and supervised the evolution of it—well, it doesn't mean that God is loving or personal, or that we have a soul, or that he has a paradise for us. Those are all separate issues. Still, I hope for a loving God, and a good ending."

"I agree, sir. The existence of God does not guarantee love *or* eternal life ... even though the Bible says that God is love."

"The Bible is one thing, but there are myriad theories ... like the Omega Point Theory, which postulates eternal life ... without a soul ... and without violating the principles of reductionism."

"The what?"

"The Omega Point Theory. My friend Frank Tipler came up with it—he's a physicist at Tulane, and he's doing a book on it. I read the working draft. It's quite complex, but it promises eternal life through resurrection reconstitution, as opposed to soul continuity. Translation: God has everything about us digitally recorded and mapped, every thought, every action, every detail of our physique, past, present, future, every aspect of our identity, so at the end of time, so-called, we can be recreated to experience eternal bliss, along with everyone else."

"That would certainly be better that ceasing to exist or going to hell—but I reckon I'm partial to the idea of having a soul."

They share a quick laugh, then Richardson says, "That stands to reason, Bryan, though I guess the critical question is whether we get a happy ending or not ... regardless of *how* we get there."

"Right you are, sir. I call it 'love after death,' and that's the *cru*cial thing. Life after death is *not* enough in itself. We must have *love* on the other side to make it a good ending. It's been my hope, and obsession, ever since I can remember. And yet, I do have strong convictions on *how* we get there ... so that omega thing doesn't ring my bell."

The professor retrieves his mug and takes a drink. Bryan sips his Dr. Pepper as well, the tepid dregs. Silence, then Richardson responds, "But just because we *hope* something doesn't mean it's true. I have to be evenhanded in weighing our chances. We must look honestly at the evidence, and right now I don't see enough to get into court, much less convince a jury. And I don't care to hype things like an evangelist ... just to feel good."

Bryan pats his bosom, his heart. "But still sir ... we have the *yearn*ing. And it *has* to come from somewhere. I mean, the whole dream of Christianity is getting into Heaven ... like the rich young ruler who came to Jesus. It's the *biggie*: what shall I do that I may have eternal life?"

"Is this a faith thing, because of your Baptist upbringing?"

"No sir ... I reckon I'd have this yearning whether I went to Sunday school or not, or church, or I ever read the Bible. Like when I was a kid and I'd ride Millie bareback all around our farm, and the alfalfa was blowing in the wind, and the clouds were like popcorn balls in the sky. I sensed an awesome connection to the wind and sky, and to my horse. It was so powerful ... like an ache, an ultimate need, inside me yet coming from nature too, the life around me—a longing to live forever." Bryan swigs the last of his pop then gives a resigned snort. "I knew about death of course, especially after Gramps died, but the whole idea of ceasing to exist never sat right with me, and it *still* doesn't. It seems like *such* a waste to live and love, and have dreams and hopes, and to bond with friends and lovers and kindred spirits, and then to have it *all* end in a coffin. I ache for more, the eternal 'more,' and it's *way* bigger than church." He gestures with the empty can. "Don't get me wrong, the pastors and teachers at my church did nourish my faith ... but they also made me afraid when they taught about judgment and hell. But my grandfather was more like me. He felt closest to God when he was out in the weather, like in the woods and fields, and around animals—"

"Yes, your grandfather. You talked about him before."

"I was super close to Gramps, but he died when I was nine."

The professor swivels toward Bryan—he gives a warm grin. "I'm old enough to be your grandfather, you know?"

"Yes sir, I reckon you are."

"I rarely discuss God and such, especially with a student. I do talk with Chris some, on the golf course, or drinking beers at the clubhouse, but nothing like this." He laughs. "But back to your granddad: maybe he's the reason you long for life after death? I'm playing the devil's advocate again. And from a Freudian perspective, it might've given rise to your OBEs, or special REM dreams as I see them, and even to the near-death episode." He gives a one-handed, why-not gesture. "These yearnings may have governed how your mind coped with the TBI. Perhaps your NDE was simply wish-fulfillment riding a good shot of dopamine?"

"I believe it was more than that, but I can't rule *out* the dopamine explanation. And to be sure, Gramps did deepen my longing for 'love' after death, but I think we *all* long for it."

The professor pushes back from the desk, his countenance clouding. He gives a reflective murmur. "Yes, Bryan ... we do. But as a doctor and scientist I'm expected to deal with the whole death issue in an objective, lab-coat fashion, as though it's not going to happen to me, or to my loved ones." He pauses; he takes a slow drink of Pepsi. "But to be honest, I must confess a fear of death, or at least a fear of the *great* unknown, and I can't help but cry out for something beyond." He wags his head, his eyes growing large—his voice becomes wistful. "I lost my wife two years ago ... Martha ... breast cancer, a long painful battle."

"I'm sorry, sir."

"And about the same time, Dudley O'Shea had his stroke. You know, my golfing buddy who owns the house where you guys live." The doctor rolls his bald head, as if trying to get a crick out of his neck. "It's one thing when your parents die, or your patients, but when your own little group starts kicking off, it *really* hits home. I mean the death-clock is ticking, and it never stops." He sighs. "And what about hell? I mean, you're a Baptist?"

"Yeah, but—"

"The Anglicans now teach it as a *symbolic* thing, but the Bible-thumpers around here—they're all Baptists, and they still preach about hell as a real place. I've even heard of near-death testimonies where sinners have gone to hell and back?"

"I've heard of it too ... where people contended with demons and sank into fetid blackness and saw Satan himself torturing the damned. I reckon it could be true—can't rule it out ... yet most of those testimonies occur at soul-winning revivals, which sorta makes me doubt their veracity. But *I* didn't experience anything remotely hellish or bad. It was all wondrous and happy."

"But at your church ... they did teach that hell is real?"

Bryan partially crushes the empty Dr. Pepper can. "Yes sir, they did ... but that's one doctrine I have trouble with."

"I can see why, after your NDE ... and the longing you have. But even from a detached view, it makes no sense. Why create a life, just to make it suffer forever? How does God profit?" Bryan nods but doesn't reply. Richardson pours Pepsi, the last of it, then creaks back in his chair. "These are powerful questions, and yet we can't find the answers in our labs ... or simulate them on the computer." He rubs his chin, the Kirk Douglas dimple. "So tell me, Bryan ... have you developed a theory? For the silver cord I mean? That is, if I grant you the existence of the soul?"

"Not really, sir. I've sorta backed off trying to get specific. I've considered the frontal cortex, and the pleasure centers, plus the musical-conductor nuclei that Ratey speaks of, the 40 Hertz hum. Chris suggests the stem as the tether point, and it could well be. And it also might be connected throughout the brain, like harmonizing in the astral realm with general neural function ... language, emotions, thought, self talk, memory, cognition. It could be anything. It's *wide* open, like you say in class. So I've decided to simply soak up as much knowledge as I can ... till the light bulb goes on."

"Well, whether it does or not, you're still way ahead of your peers, if not your *teachers*."

* * *

4:48 p.m. Exiting the neuroscience lab, Bryan strides happily across the sunwashed parking lot. In addition to the heart-to-heart exchange, the doctor offered him a job, Chris's job, after he graduates and departs for Houston. *I think I'll swing by and see Coach McKinney again,* Bryan decides, as he gets into the truck. *Tracy won't be done with her rodents for another hour.*

*   *   *

146 DOUGLAS STREET
FRIDAY, APRIL 16, 1993 — 11:36 PM

"So did Coach McKinney say anything else about his near-death experience?" Tracy asks, as they converse in bed.

"Oh yeah, once the nurse was gone. He's talking good now. He also said I should become a counselor ... again."

"Dr. Richardson said the same thing, didn't he?"

"Not exactly. He just said I should consider neuropsychology. That way I could stay here in Waco for grad school ... and then I could go into therapy or research ... or whatever."

"I still can't believe you were in his office so long. I don't think he's ever talked with me more than five minutes."

"But you're a *girl*."

"Get outta here. What's that got to do with anything?"

They share a mirthful laugh, then Tracy cuddles close. "The seasons ... they are changing," she remarks soberly, after a long silence. "You know ... like the song."

"I reckon time *is* passing. But things should be pretty much the same for us, since y'got accepted for your nursing thing here. You don't hafta go to Houston or anywhere ... like Chris."

Tracy sighs. "Yeah, it's sure gonna seem strange around here ... without his smart-ass teasing."

CHAPTER TWENTY-NINE

EIGHT MONTHS LATER:

INTERSTATE 35E, SOUTH OF WAXAHACHIE, TX
WEDNESDAY, DECEMBER 15, 1993 — 1:51 PM

Bryan Howard cruises north in his Chevy pickup, heading home for
Christmas break—two days early. A high overcast dims the sun, while
a dingy pall obscures the far horizon: Dallas smog. His mom called
yesterday, saying Millie was in bad shape; she has a severe kidney
infection, so severe she can't stand up. Dr. Page gave the eighteen-
year-old mare some powerful antibiotics, but the prognosis remains
doubtful. Bryan cranks up the vent fan another notch then cracks his
window an inch—a tepid draft hisses in. It's unseasonably hot for
December, low 80s at least—but not for long: cold weather's on the
way.

The Millie news hurts of course, but he accepts it as destiny, just
as he's accepted the other big developments. Mandy did in fact get
married in June, and Chris departed the same weekend for Houston—
and Tracy departed the following week for Louisiana. Yes, she's gone
too, forsaking grad school for a nursing position at a pediatric clinic in
Lafayette, not far from her mom's place. The parting was sad yet
sweet—they both knew it was time.

So he's now alone at the O'Shea house. He thought about moving
back onto campus to save a few bucks, but quickly nixed the idea. The
quiet solitude at 146 Douglas provides a far better atmosphere for
study and contemplation, and the money he earns working for Dr.
Richardson (eight dollars an hour) more than makes up the difference.
For that matter, the lab job plus the scholarship grants give him enough
(with his frugal lifestyle) to bank a hundred a month, not to mention
the $25 extra Annie knocked off the rent when he assumed all the
yardwork duties. Although alone, the Baylor junior (he's now a junior)
has little time to feel lonely, as he continues his quest for the silver
cord, in a sober, less-naive fashion—reviewing the literature, absorbing
all he can, in class, out of class, and especially from Dr. Richardson
himself (he also learns from the lab job, though it's mainly dogwork:
data entry, file consolidation, etc.).

Cortical fissures, cybernetic modeling, temporal lobes, brain-stem
malfunction, nanotech analysis, plasma, hemoglobin, the Parkinson's
gene, amygdala, Sydenham's chorea, Alzheimer's, autism,
psychobiology, quantum chemistry, cerebral symphony, quantum
biophysics, neutrinos, electrons, strings, developmental
neuropsychiatry, quantum quirks, anomalous enigmas, up-quarks,

489

down-quarks, muons, astral flight, parietal-lobe circuitry, self versus non-self, perception, cognition, limbic response, gluons, photons, neurogenesis, hypnotism, superstrings, T.O.E. (The Theory of Everything), nano-consciousness, the cerebellum, EEGs, MRIs, CT-scans, gut feelings, seat of personality, soul-travel during meditation, Buddhist PET patterns, neurotheology, neuropsychology, SPECT imaging of the praying brain, quantum consciousness, the social brain, God's neural footprints—enough, enough! Bryan's hunger for truth remains undiminished, but the soul-tether possibilities within this neurological stew grow in number with each morsel he consumes, and each newborn idea quickly becomes iffy and elusive, absurdly so, like ten thousand June bugs swarming about a streetlight on a summer night.

The sheer magnitude, and complexity, of the silver-cord problem forces him to admit the prospect of never discovering a soul-body link. And yet the astonishing nature of the brain convinces him all the more that only the Lord could have designed it. And if God engineered a brain that loves, he must be loving, and if he's loving and good, he must have a purpose for putting us on this planet, a purpose that works everything for good, even the suffering and malice and unspeakable tragedies, a purpose that transcends the grave. If death is the end (or hell), then we *lose*, no matter how purposeful our years on earth. To give us a heart and mind that longs for Heaven (love after death) without *giving* us Heaven would be cruelty, the opposite of love, so we *must* exist beyond death, and that means we have a soul (dismissing for the sake of argument the reconstitution proposals such as the Omega Point Theory), and if we have a soul, it must have some kind of astral-physical tether that severs at death.

Hence young Mr. Howard, though less naive about his quest, remains adamant concerning its validity, a conviction that also brings him closer to God, not in the churchy sense but via neuroscience, as he sees the Lord's handiwork in the realm of the mind. He does go to church on occasion, not to Marvin's den of pharisees but to Hilltop Baptist with Steve Jordan, a laid-back ministry out on the 340 Loop. It's just a good shout from the Peek-A-Boo Club, a strange location for a house of worship, and yet that's how Jordan discovered it. When he met Ken Spence, the pastor, the big guy confessed his strip-joint lust-problem. Rev. Spence counseled him to abstain but didn't condemn him, plus he teaches that dogs go to Heaven. That did it for Steve; he's now a regular; he even goes to Sunday School.

Dogs have a soul, humans have a soul: Bryan is convinced beyond *reasonable* doubt. Yet he can't shut the door entirely on the nihilistic conclusions of reductive materialism. He'd love to have more OBEs for research purposes, but he's had no first-hand astral episode for two years, most likely because of his relaxed faith in God's plan. The Mandy ache remains, but it's now a confident ache, a hopeful sense of resignation which has long since replaced the torment that drove him to the edge of insanity after she left him in '91. He also misses Tracy, but it's nowhere the same. She came in due season, a kindred spirit dispatched by God to get him through his darkest night; that's how he sees it. Besides, they still talk, on the phone.

Zero sex life: yet he's not seeking or dating. He still notices the Baylor babes, in class and elsewhere, and he's on a first-name basis with a few chicks (he even fantasizes about the cute ones when he's horny at night), but his heart is fixed on Mandy. He works with Debbie at the lab (Deborah Lincoln, who now tends the rodents), a short, hippish sophomore with red hair and freckles and squinty eyes, aqua eyes. She's a bit spacy, and she talks with a lisp, but she's certainly sexy enough to screw, especially when she laughs and jokes and rolls her eyes. He banters with her but nothing more. Things are different now. The silver cord, Mandy, Mandy—it's all or nothing, no more consolation.

Jordan comes over now and then to catch the Cowboys on TV, or the Rangers, or to watch a movie. Sprawling on the sofa, he clutters up the room with enough pop cans and beer cans and potato-chip bags to fill a dumpster, not to speak of the candy wrappers, and popcorn on the floor. Bryan enjoys his ex-roomie in limited doses but has no desire to live with him again, nor does he go with him to the Peek-A-Boo Club: "Awh c'mon, dude, a guy's gotta get his dadgum batteries charged." The big fellow had a sensational sophomore year on the baseball diamond, leading the Bears to a second-place finish; he likewise drew the attention of major-league scouts, including the White Sox and Rangers.

Bryan has returned to diamond stardom himself, not baseball but slow-pitch softball. Dr. Richardson persuaded him to play for the Neurology Department in the campus league. They only won half their games, but that surely topped the 0-18 record the prior summer, and Bryan made most of the difference, batting .467 and smashing thirteen homers. His impaired vision proved quite adequate to deal with the bigger, slowly pitched ball, once he learned how to wait on the high-arc, underhand delivery. His eye does hinder him at shortstop, but as an ex-jock, he still has a better glove than the other ragtag collection of players, half of whom are nerds or semi-nerds. Even Doc Richardson—he's the coach and the pitcher—can outplay many of the younger men. Student-faculty softball is hardly big time, but Bryan needed an outlet for his competitive juices, and playing on the professor's team has given them more opportunity to interact.

Lord, please get Millie through this, he prays silently, his thoughts coming back to the present, to the farm, to his ailing equine friend. *I reckon we all have a time appointed, even horses, but she's not really that old.* Pushing his cap back, he wipes his forehead, his bangs—it's a dry heat, but he's still perspiry damp under the sweatband. *Lots of horses live to twenty-five or more. Old Buck must be thirty-five now, the Palmer's rodeo stallion.* He gives a boyish chuckle. *Millie's hardly famous, but I reckon she's just as smart. Heck, she did everything but talk when I used to ride her bareback, and she does talk in a way, with her neighs and whinnies. And she never galloped under trees. She was agile and fast, but she never placed me in jeopardy despite my foolish urgings.* The fond memories warm his bosom. *It's not in my hands, God, but I have a good feeling about this. I do.*

Turning on the radio, he punches the KRYZ button finding Wilson Pickett and "Mustang Sally." The lively tune bolsters his confidence concerning Millie, and Mandy, and the silver cord. He taps the steering wheel to keep time—happy fingers. Then the news comes on, the latest on the Long Island Railroad massacre:

> "When the shooting began," Esther Confino says, "I got down low and covered my head with my handbag, then I prayed." Prayer may stop a Black Talon, but a purse won't. The bullet is designed to unsheathe its claws once inside the victim's body. That's what Colin Ferguson had in his 9-mm Ruger, as he walked backward through the third car of the 5:33 train to Hicksville. He killed five and....

It's like the mass murder at Luby's. It's amazing how many people are getting blown away, not to speakuh the Branch Davidian fire last April, and that was close, like right outside Waco. These tragedies are horrible, but they STILL work together for good. They HAVE to. Otherwise, everything is senseless and nil, and the reductive materialists are right, and yet the very laws of nature they espouse argue for meaning, for purpose, for divine design. That's why my quest is super relevant to every person on this earth. Death is coming for all of us, whether violent or quiet.

He listens with scant attention to the other stories: the rebounding economy, Clinton's budget, the LBJ tapes, NASA's mission to fix the Hubble telescope. He considers punching to another station, but waits instead for the weather: "An arctic cold front, surging southward from Oklahoma, will bring windy, *much* colder conditions to North Texas later this afternoon. A few showers may develop along this front, with temps behind it dropping sharply into the...."

* * *

3:40 p.m. As Bryan approaches Sulphur Springs, he kills the radio, the *Mamas and the Papas*, so he can concentrate on the low, black bank of clouds rolling in from the north, along with numerous whirls of dust. A strong gust buffets the Chevy almost blowing him onto the shoulder. No more warmth—the air streaming in the window feels as if it came straight from the Yukon. And it smells frigid as well, pure, piercing, ozonic, yet exhilarating, like inhaling the highest sky, like the bracing scent of the stratosphere the night he chased that DC-10 in his first Baylor OBE. He rolls up the window. Muddy rain dapples the windshield. He switches on the wipers then the headlights. The pinging of sleet joins the rain. He turns on the defrost. *It's hard to believe I was baking most of the way.*

* * *

THE HOWARD FARM
WEDNESDAY, DECEMBER 15, 1993 — 7:04 PM

Wearing a parka and ski hat plus work gloves, Bryan strides down the tractor trail. The flurries have ceased, but not the icy wind; it bites his face. The racing clouds offer occasional glimpses of the moon. When he arrived at the farm, he found Millie on her feet, to his great relief. Dr. Page was still here—he said the antibiotics are working. The old mare is weak, but she was still excited to see Bryan, enough to whinny and thrash her tail like she does. The Howards celebrated with a sumptuous pot-roast supper followed by chocolate pie. After a relaxing time around the table with his mom and dad, Bryan excused himself, to embark on this hike.

By the time he reaches the giant oak, with its wind-tossed branches and sparse rattling leaves, the clouds are gone, leaving only the full moon, plus a rippled clone in the pond below. As he gazes up at the huge silvery sphere, his heart heaves: *Oh, Mandy, it doesn't matter that you're married. Oh, my sweet pretty lady, our time is coming. There's a reason you kept the rings. It's fate and destiny. The world may be cold and desolate tonight, but our day is coming as surely as the spring, as surely as the spring.*

* * *

NINE MONTHS LATER:

WACO, TEXAS - 146 DOUGLAS STREET
WEDNESDAY, AUGUST 10, 1994 — 2:20 PM

Spring did arrive, and summer, but the "our day" Bryan sighed about on that cold night last December has yet to come. Mandy, now married more than a year, remains in Bible school, while he still abides alone in Waco. He gets occasional news from Wendy Lewis, but he doesn't press her. By the way, Wendy and Spanky are now living together, in the apartment above Byer's Drug Store, a development that's hardly shocking. Spanky still cusses and brags as much as ever, but the little redneck has given up his carousing, and most of his gambling—for Wen.

THE SILVER CORD

Bryan, seated at his make-do desk in the master bedroom, feeds another floppy into the drive. He's extended the table, adding a leaf, to accommodate his new Macintosh and laser printer. Behind him, stumpy stacks of books and magazines and print-outs crowd the floor, along with Dr. Richardson's boxes (research data, etc.). He reaches for another disk, but Mandy stops him, her picture, the photo-portrait she gave him by the stream back in the summer of '91. After she left that fall, he couldn't look at it—it hurt too much. But he now keeps it close, so she can love him, inspire him, and give clear focus to his dreams, dreams she inhabits as the sun inhabits a summer day. Her doll-face lips and big blue eyes convey an adorable, slightly pensive emotion beneath those soft blond bangs—it never fails to melt him, as does her ponytail with the blue bow, and her girlish hand holding the daisy, and the oak tree of course, their magic place. "Oh, pretty lady," he whispers, "I love you *SO*."

Back to the Mac: he works a bit longer then shuts down. He pops a rubber band around the batch of floppies then puts them in the side pocket of his book pack. Exiting the study chamber, he drapes the knapsack on the banister, lest he forget it. He must drop the disks by the lab on his way to the softball game, the last and most crucial game of the year. A gut-rush excites him, as he hustles into the bedroom to don his uniform, a green-trimmed T-shirt over gray spandex shorts, plus a limpish white cap with a too-short bill; the rinkydink hat looks old-fashioned, like Ty Cobb era. The T-shirt sports the department logo, a smiling motor homunculus (the distorted little man with huge hands, lips, and feet used in class to show how much brain space is devoted to specific body areas) along with the team name: "WIZARDS."

If we win today, we get the trophy, he exhorts himself, as he plops down on the bed to put on his Pony softball cleats. *We'll be 15-3, if we can nail those Truett Seminary bastards—damn, I'm more worked up over this dadgum softball league than I was back in my baseball heyday.* He gives a boyish laugh.

*   *   *

Same day, 8:54 p.m. Dr. Richardson takes a hearty swig of beer, then he lifts the mug lauding Bryan, again: "Hell of a clutch hit, slugger. Two outs, two on, extra innings, down by two. I couldn't have *written* a better script." (He now calls Bryan "slugger," while Bryan uses the fond tag of "Doc" when addressing the professor.)

"That's for *sure*," Adele adds hoarsely, scooping up the last handful of corn chips from one of the gratis bowls. "This's the *great*est thing that ever happened to our team."

Bryan gives no reply, just an awh-shucks grin, as he pops a morsel of hot-dog bun into his mouth. He's been barraged with kudos since he blasted the game-winning dinger, and he's trying to keep his ego in

494

check: slamming a big, white, Worth Red Dot slow-pitched at twenty mph hardly compares with hitting Steve Jordan's heat, yet it did give him special satisfaction to beat the Truett gang, and Marvin Latrobe especially. The bespectacled little pharisee, now well into his seminary training, played right field briefly but mainly mouthed off from the bench.

"That shot cleared the fence by fifty feet I bet," Adele hypes on, her worn-out voice now clogged with chips. "And it sure shut their damned holy mouths. Serves 'em right, the way they pray before the game, and during the game, like God's on their side and all." She sips Miller Lite (a bottle) then gives a beery laugh, her hefty bosom heaving under the extra-large uniform shirt. "But the Lord gave *us* the victory." She pats the trophy in the center of the table—there are several tables actually, pushed together to form one long one, yet the brassy prize, topped by a swinging batter, stands proudly at Dr. Richardson's end. The line of squarish, knotty-pine tables stretches emptily toward the bandstand dais, empty save for beer bottles (Bud Light, Coors, Miller Lite) and beer mugs, and empty pitchers, and soda cans, and wadded napkins, and paper plates smeared with ketchup, mustard, and hot-dog relish, not to mention the terra-cotta corn-chip bowls, some empty, some half full. Everyone has departed the post-game celebration except for Bryan, Dr. Richardson, and Adele Trotman, the big-boobed receptionist.

The Bear's Paw is slow tonight anyhow—summer session is drawing to a close, and August is always a slack month. But the pub smells the same: dank, yeasty, hint of cigarette smoke—plus *more* than a hint of sweetish scent, from Adele's perfume. She must've put more on in the ladies' room. She keeps the team scorebook for the doctor, and she collects the dues, and she calls the guys when necessary, and she's also the one who ordered the uniforms. Richardson likes the little-man logo on the shirt, the motor homunculus, but nothing else. In fact, he rarely wears his uniform. He pitched today in his golfing duds: khaki Bermudas, a white polo, a blue Oakvale Country Club cap. His golf outfits are almost stylish, a far cry from the dowdy suits he wears to class.

The professor sheds his glasses, placing them on the table. He leans back in his chair; he rubs the bridge of his nose. "Yeah, that was *quite* a scene to behold." Removing the cap, he massages his bald dome. "Pastor Henniker sure got his clock cleaned ... with one swing ... and they were so *cocky* after they scored those two runs in the top of the eighth. Damn, what a *great* way to end it." He gives his crowlike chuckle, his Nordic eyes twinkling.

Bryan sips some Michelob draft—he's legal now, though it hardly matters here. He salutes the professor with his uplifted mug. "Well, Doc, you had a pretty good game yourself. Only one walk in eight innings of pressure pitching, and y'got on twice."

"Yeah, I walked twice, and got forced at second twice. Hell, I can hardly run on these old wheels of mine."

"I think yuh move pretty well, sir," Bryan counters.

"That's right," Adele chimes in between sips. "I reckon I'd pass out if I had to run around the bases, and I'm only—well, let's just say I'm forty-plus." She chortles huskily then rolls her eyes toward Richardson, big, round, yellow-green eyes. "Besides, Doctor, you have nice legs ... for *any* age."

The professor, grinning, clasps his hands behind his head. "Flattery will get you *no*where," he laughs dismissively, but the pinkish glow on his fair-cheeked face tells Bryan that he liked her semi-flirtatious remark, while the lack of precision in his Yankee accent gives witness that he's less than sober. Bryan feels mellow as well, though he's proceeding at a more modest pace. "But back to you, slugger—it's not just your performance on the field, but you've also done more coaching than I ever did. Hell, this whole softball thing was a joke when we joined the league back in '89, and I only did it because Dean Buckley kept on pestering." Leaning forward, he grabs his mug and takes a sip. "Hell ... we were almost laughed off the campus that first year."

"That's for *sure*," Adele giggles, as she grabs the scorebook plus her handbag. "This's fun, but I gotta run. Duane's bowling tonight, but he'll be home at nine-thirty." Giving another giggle, she departs, her hips gyrating heavily inside the spandex shorts.

"She's got an ass like a goddamn hippo," the doctor declares, as she disappears beyond the bar. "And tits to match. She's fat ... but I'd still *fuck* her if I got the chance."

Bryan gulps, almost choking on his beer. "Well uh ... well—"

"Sorry, slugger, I didn't mean to shock you ... but I still have blood in my dick, even at seventy. And she's not *ugly*; she's got a cute face in fact. Besides, I'm half drunk ... *more* than half."

They share a macho chortle, as Richardson raises his mug. Bryan clicks it with his, toasting the moment. *Gosh,* he reacts silently, *the doc's still hot for chicks ... like a regular guy.*

Richardson fiddles with his James Joyce spectacles, folding, unfolding, clicking plastic against plastic. He smirks. "I bet she's good in bed too. I'm not into big-busted women, but she gets me going with her teasing and such." The blue twinkle in his eyes goes boyish, as if he's eighteen again. "Connie's more fuckable actually, despite the extra years. She's got that prim, choir-lady appeal, but she's off the goddamn radar. Hell, she's more strait-laced than Queen Elizabeth." They laugh. "And she's married to Sherm Crenshaw, the university comptroller. He's just as tight-assed." More laughs. "But Adele's another story. She's anything but prim and proper. She's a horny wife in need of a good lay. She's forty-six, but she acts younger, and she's still vigorous and robust. She's hefty, yet she carries it well. Most gals her age have a pro*nounced* sag, top and bottom." He clucks like a crow. "But still ...

THE SILVER CORD

I doubt she'd cheat on Duane, despite the fact he's a zero who shows her no respect. He's a tire salesman—he works for his uncle, at Girard's over in Bellmead. He reminds me of Fred Flintstone ... in intellect, *and* looks." More titters "You've seen the guy; he's been to a few games, and he always volunteers to cook the burgers at the department cookout each spring."

The jesting gives way to sipping, then Richardson says, "I've been celibate a long time." His tone has turned pensive, and his countenance. "I flirt with Adele, and a few others ... like Caroline at the club—she's older, but *well* preserved and a goddamn good golfer. And I've even sported some with my female students. I'm talking about girls your age, which is *way* off the pussy chart of course, except in fantasy land." He snorts, his eyes going remote. "Let's face it: I'm just trying to recapture something that's gone for good. I loved Martha, and I was never unfaithful, and yet we slept in separate bedrooms our last ten years. Life is like that. The wanting doesn't change, but the *having* surely does. And it's not just sex; it's everything. I mean, it's a *bitch*, getting old."

"You're not old, Doc, not really."

"Yes I am, Bryan. Fifty-five may not be old, even sixty-five, but seventy is *over* the hill. My peers and classmates are dropping like daisies after a frost. I get news on someone every week or so. I'm healthy, knock on wood, and I can still hit a golf ball 240 ... and break 85. I can even walk eighteen when I need a workout, and I can still teach; my mind hasn't left. But I hear the clock ticking." The doctor refills their mugs, killing off the pitcher of Michelob. "That's why your work is so crucial, slugger. You're very young, and still naive to be sure, and it's a hell of a long shot that you're going to prove we have a soul, or a silver cord that severs at death, or any of the bizarre stuff we talk about—but whether you find it or not, I sure *hope* we have a soul ... or *some*thing that beats death. It's easy to write off those astral experiences ... but I hope there's something *real* going on. I can't bet on it as a scientist, not without more evidence, but I sure can as a human being. Hell, I'm betting on it with my life ... like *all* the rest of us, especially us old farts. I mean, when death is breathing down your goddamn neck, we *all* become desperate for new life ... for Heaven or whatever ... no matter how you label it, or preach it at church." Gazing into his warm beer, he gives a rueful sigh. His face seems whiter, especially about the eyes, which look strangely naked without the glasses, like Zorro without his mask. "I've had many years of college and multiple degrees, and I've worked in the world of medicine and science for forty-five years ... with a measure of success and renown—and yet I know *nothing*, or almost nothing about what really counts."

"I share the same hopes and dreads, Doc. Be*lieve* me I do."

"It's tragic, but even the most cheerful child must grow old and die. Why? It's such a waste, if we don't get more ... for me, for Martha, for you, for *all* of us." He gives his young disciple a pat on the shoulder. "I don't mean to get all morose with you."

"It's okay. I've yearned about this since I—well, you know?"

"We have everything labeled and categorized, but when it comes to life itself, how it manifests itself out of matter, we're the guardians of a few facts plus a trillion assumptions. I mean, we're all banking on God, whether we admit it or not ... that he's real, that he's good, that he'll get us across to the other side. And yet we have no solid ground to stand on. We know *NOTHING* for sure, or at least not much. All we have is faith and hope, plus a lot of wishful theories ... which all boil down to the same thing when we lie down on that last bed or gurney. There's no more wheeling and dealing, no more buying or selling, no more carrot and stick, no more goddamn games." *Ka-whap!* He smacks his palm with his fist (left socking right). "We go helpless into that dark night, just like we arrived here ... screaming and needy, the bloody fruit of our mother's womb. We were defenseless and utterly dependent. Anyone could've killed us, with a quick plunge of a knife, or a snap of the neck ... but we made it through that time." His face brightens; he replaces his glasses. "Our parents loved us and nurtured us, or whoever, with little or no input from us. And that's a *hope*ful sign ... when it comes to dying."

Bryan gestures with his mug. "Gosh damn, you're *nail*ing it."

Richardson inhales, through his nose. "That's why I applaud your idealistic fervor, even if naive. You may not've discovered the silver cord during your eighteen months in the department, or even approached the point of proving a metaphysical reality beyond the reductionist model ... but let me assure you, slugger—you're as *far* down the road as any of us ... if not more so." He nods, slowly, affirmatively. "And it's good to confide ... now that we trust each other. Of course, we can't do this *all* the time, since I'm not supposed to show favoritism when it comes to my students." He sips then gives his wry chuckle, which grows into a beery guffaw. "But you *are* my favorite, goddamn it." He pushes his mug toward Bryan. "And it's not a teacher-student thing—oh, it is in a way. But it's more like a foxhole-buddy thing."

Bryan dimples, his cheeks warming. "Thanks, Doc."

"Hell, I'm fifty years older, but I can talk to you with more ease than to my peers and colleagues ... many of whom are liars to the core." More laughs. "And I like the relaxed atmosphere in here. I wear a coat and tie all week, so it's good to come to a place like this where you can keep your hat on without feeling like a goddamn hayseed." The doctor taps the visor of his white golfing cap, which is now lifted a bit, showing more bald head.

The Spindle native swallows, nodding his agreement. "Yeah, I feel more at ease when I'm wearing some kind of headgear." He has on his old Tiger hat, having left the floppy Ty Cobb thing in the pickup. "I reckon it's the farmer in my blood. Gramps was the same. He had this old Texaco cap that he wore *all* the time."

"Nothing wrong with farm blood—I like it, I trust it. Besides, I need someone to talk to, now that Chris's down in Houston with those Harvey Cushing assholes. They're not all bad, but the senior staff is arrogant as hell, a lot of them. I don't miss it."

"Yes sir, I've talked with Chris on the phone a few times, and he says pretty much the same."

"He'll do fine nonetheless; he's sharp, and he knows how to play the goddamn doctor game, but it's still a shame, that healing people gets pushed well down the list of priorities."

Bryan sips then responds, "He likes most of his teachers, the younger doctors, but he says the bigshots are obnoxious posers, especially the head of general surgery, some guy named Spigler?"

"Oh, Barry Spigler ... Dr. Barry *Eugene* Spigler. I know him well ... at least enough to detest the bastard. He was an up-and-coming sycophant when I left Houston, but since then he's kiss-assed his way to the top. He's not the head however ... and I'd hardly call him a surgeon, though he *is* technically. He's the deputy director of HCNP, which is mainly an admin job."

"HC what?"

"HCNP: Harvey Cushing Neurosurgery Program. It's a bowl of spaghetti, their organization. They have thirty-plus treatment programs and sixteen medical departments. And to make it more confusing, the medical school is intertwined with the hospital. Most everyone wears two or three hats. It's a damn mess."

Bryan laughs. "Goshdang, Doc, you know *every*thing about Houston, all the inside stuff? It's like you never left?"

Richardson gives his patented *yeck-yeck*. "I talk to Omar on the phone ... Omar Rishad—he heads the Neurosurgery Program. He's a recent widower like me. We even get together for golf when we can." The doctor sips. "We've been friends since med school. He's an Indian chap, the country of India, but his family came to America when he was ten. He's the best old-school surgeon I know of ... or he was. He's getting on now ... though he's younger than me, five years or so." Richardson shakes his head. "But Dr. Rishad is unique. He still puts the practice of medicine ahead of money and politics, which is more than I can say for most of the leaders down there ... and Barry Spigler is the worst of all. He's deficient as a doctor, so his ego has a big time hard-on, and he gets off by lording it over the underlings, when he's not out raising *mon*ey. Plus, he's ugly as a donkey's ass." The professor gives a resigned titter; he gestures with his mug, the dregs sloshing about. "That's what we're up against, Bryan. And it's not just Houston. It's *all* over the country, all over the world. Money rules. It's goddamn whoredom on a grand scale."

THE SILVER CORD

* * *

THREE MONTHS LATER:

SHADY LAWN CEMETERY - WACO, TEXAS.
TUESDAY, NOVEMBER 15, 1994 — 11:32 AM

Rain dapples the windshield. Bryan flips on the wipers, plus the heater. The trees along Cemetery Road stand guard amid the chilly gloom, keeping silent vigil as the vehicles which arrived in procession depart one by one. A few cottonwood leaves flutter down ahead of the pickup, dirty gold and damp. The oaks, though turning brown, let go of their foliage reluctantly, shedding some in December, some in January, some not at all, while the pine trees stay green all year, new needles replacing the old which now carpet the ground around their trunks, amber carpets plus cones.

The mood in the truck remains subdued. No talking, a rarity for Steve Jordan, as is the suit he's wearing (cheap, muddy-gray, too-small, adorned with a paisley tie, but a suit nonetheless). On the other hand, he smells familiar, like Glade air-freshener, like oversweet honeysuckle. Bryan wears no suit or sport coat, but he does have on a tie inside his Spindle-high letter jacket. He gives a sigh. He'll surely miss his leather-faced, big-hearted mentor, yet he feels more reflective than sorrowful. Coach Elmo McKinney died Saturday night, after suffering a third coronary. *I wish we'd had more time,* Bryan remarks to himself—he didn't make it to the hospital before the coach expired. *And yet we had some good talks, even this year.* Reaching US 77, the old highway, they head north. As they do, he makes the decision: *I'm gonna be a counselor. No more waffling. Psychotherapy from a neurological perspective—it's the best thing I can do with my life.*

"So, dude, whaddeyuh thank?" the big Baylor senior asks, breaking the silence (they're both seniors, finally).

"About what?" Bryan replies.

Jordan loosens his tie, then he fingers the air like he does. "D'yuh thank Coach McKinney's with the Lord?"

"Yeah, I reckon he is. Death is actually beautiful ... when you're going through it. More beautiful than *anything.*"

Steve paws more fervently. "How the hell canyuh be so sure? I *know* what the Bible says and all, but I'm weak when it comes to faith ... just like I'm weak when it comes to lust and all." He gives his belly laugh, an abbreviated version.

"Faith *is* hard ... but I'm talking about more than faith."

"Whaddeyuh gettin' at?"

"Let's go to Denny's for lunch, and I'll tellyuh. I don't have any afternoon classes, and I'm not due at the lab till three."

"Sounds good, dude. I need a break from the caf anyhow, and I

500

don't give a dadgum if I miss Broadcast Media 441."

* * *

1:57 p.m. Bryan drops Jordan at Fletcher Hall. The star hurler—he's on the Ranger short list—still lives in the same dorm, same suite (Unit 311), having turned down numerous chances to move in with his super-jock peers at the Quad. As Bryan heads east on Spangler, the honeysuckle fragrance in the cab dissipates, giving way to the default smell, that greasy, gas-fumy, farm-truck odor. The old pickup is pushing 85,000 miles, but it still runs A-OK.

I reckon Steve's gonna tell everyone, he chuckles, as he chugs along the leaf-littered, weakly shadowed avenue. The rain has stopped, and the clouds have thinned just enough to let the sun seep through. *But it doesn't matter, not really. He's a true friend, and I've wanted to tell him about my near-death experience for a long time ... all the way back to that first week on campus when he was anxious about his dog Hardy.* Bryan gives a fond sigh..

Spangler, Rigby, Eleventh Street, south on Baker to Douglas. He has to grab a box of floppies at the house before going to the lab, and he negotiates the various turns without thought, having made this trip a thousand times—unlike his first walking visit to have hot dogs with Chris three years ago. The memory tugs on his heart, but as he reaches the house, it gives way to surprise. A black SUV sits in the driveway: Annie O'Shea. *Dang, what's she doing back? She was just here on Saturday?*

He finds her in the backyard. Clad in tan sweats and a raggedy cardigan, plus her "Lucky Swinger" visor, she leans against the barbecue pit, looking to the west, as if studying the clouds, the thinning overcast. She glances at her young tenant then returns her gaze to the heavens. "Dudley died yesterday," she announces huskily. "And I've come home to bury him."

2:10 p.m. Bryan grabs her luggage from the Cherokee. Old-man Lipski is raking leaves next door. The Baylor senior waves, shouting, "HELLO!" But Lipski doesn't hear. *Gosh ... that deaf geezer was halfway in the grave with pneumonia, but now he's outlived Elmo, and Mr. O'Shea. God's a dadgum master at pulling off the unexpected when it comes to death—and love.*

* * *

TWO MONTHS LATER:

146 DOUGLAS STREET - THE GARAGE APARTMENT
THURSDAY, JANUARY 19, 1995 — 9:02 PM

"It's cold enough out to freeze a well-digger's ass," Annie O'Shea declares, as she kills off her third bottle of Busch Bavarian, "but this stove does a hell of a good job. I always joked with Dudley that we should live out here in the wintertime ... to save goddam money." Tossing her hoary head back, she gives a gruff chortle. Her bangs fall over her eyes; she pushes them to the side. "But I reckon I better excuse myself. I'm a bit overtanked on this cheap swill. Still ... it's got more taste than Coors." Sidling between the wall and the table, she heads for the bathroom.

Going to the window, Bryan turns on the backyard light. It's still raining, freezing rain—no, it's sleeting now, or both. The wind-driven pellets ping against the panes and the aluminum frame. The heavily iced trees thrash in the wind. Fallen branches litter the frozen lawn. *Sleet's better than glaze. I doubt these trees can handle much more ice without losing some BIG limbs.*

Annie, deciding to keep the house, moved in the Monday after Thanksgiving, while Bryan retreated out here. She likes to chat over a six pack (her Busch B.), and he enjoys their talks as well. In fact, he's confided about his astral adventures plus the whole Mandy saga. Annie has 72 years of stories and such, and she likewise holds nothing back— or so he thought.

"I have a secret to tellyuh, young man," she announces, after exiting the bathroom. She steps over to the stove to warm her back side. She slips her wrinkled hands into the back pockets of her jeans, cowgirl style. "Remember those way-out soul trips you told me about? And the one at the baseball park?"

"Yes ma'am, I sure do."

"Well, it also happened to Dudley ... the day be*fore* he died."

* * *

While Annie shares her secret in Waco, Mandy (Stevens) Snyder talks with Wendy Lewis on the telephone: "Yeah, it's snowing super hard. I bet we have six inches already."

"It's not doing much here in Spindle, just a little sleet, but my mom says it's wicked icy down in Mineola, and Billy Ray told Spanky that it's snowing in Sulphur Springs, so I reckon we may get some snow ... but we don't usually get a lot."

Mandy titters. "Well, we're in the *O*zarks y'know. We get more winter up here." (To be precise, she's in faculty apartment #9, Newbury College of the Bible, Newbury, Arkansas).

More titters, from both, then comes an awkward silence. You can only talk so long about the wintry weather. Mandy sighs in her thoughts: *Maybe I shouldn't have called? This's sorta weird.*

But Wendy rescues the conversation: "Oh, Mandy, I'm so glad to hear your voice ... after all this time. You'll always be my best buddy. And I'll never forget all the fun times we had."

Mandy chortles—to keep from crying. "Me neither."

"I guess y'heard about me and Spanky?"

"Yeah, I found out from Aunt Marge. That's a *riot*—but I'm not really shocked about it."

Wendy giggles. "Well ... I doubt I'll be getting a new name right soon—like *you*. Goshdang, kiddo, you've had three last-names since I've known yuh."

"And I've had *four* in all, if you count Miller—that's my real dad. I toldjuh about him."

"Yeh ... the cropduster pilot, who looked like James Dean?"

"You got it. And Mama says I'm like him ... though you'd have trouble telling lately."

Silence, then Wendy: "So, kiddo, what made yuh call me?"

"Oh, I dunno—I reckon I got tired of watching TV. Russell's in Little Rock for a fund-raiser, and it might be hard getting back tonight, in this snow. We're going to Peru this summer—that's why we're raising money; it's a missionary thing."

"That's wicked wild, Mandy ... but it's hard for me to picture *you* as a missionary."

"No kidding."

"So you didn't go to Little Rock?"

"No, I had basketball practice. We have a team, but I doubt we could beat Spindle High." They both laugh. "Russell took a vanload of students, the usual routine. If it keeps snowing, they can stay at the church down there. It's like camping out indoors. I've been to plenty of fund-raisers ... believe me."

"So where's you mother, and Gretchen?"

"Just down the road with Charlie ... no more'n a half mile. In fact, I was gonna call Mama, but when I picked up the phone, I dialed directory assistance instead ... to get your new number."

"I'm sure glad you did. I miss you a *lot*, a wicked whole lot."

Mandy struggles to keep her composure. "I miss you too."

"Anyway, kiddo, I wantcha to come see us sometime. D'yuh ever come to Spindle any more?"

"Not often—Mama visits Aunt Marge and Uncle Billy, but I haven't been back for a long time. Russ and I are super busy ... with school and the ministry ... and the whole Peru thing."

"Well, if y'guys ever get down this way, you're invited over for supper. We live on the square, right above the drug store."

"Yeah, that's what I heard from Aunt Marge."

CHAPTER THIRTY

THREE MONTHS LATER:

SPINDLE, TEXAS - WESTSIDE LANES
FRIDAY, APRIL 14, 1995 — 4:44 PM

Bryan Howard, seated in the far corner of the lounge, nurses a Bud
Light amid the *thump* and *hum* of bowling balls running on hardwood,
the clap and clatter of falling pins, the occasional *womp-womp-womp*
of a gutter ball—yet he gives little regard to the sparse crowd of late-
afternoon keglers: *Dr. Richardson is right ... what he says in his new
book. The reductionists dismiss the metaphysical realm, so it only gets
attention from kooks and con-artists who make wild claims about ghosts
and seances ... and charms and spells and telepathy and UFOs and
aliens. The sci-fi writers are more tech-savvy, but their fantasies are
still a mega-leap into the future ... like "beam me up" on Star Trek.*
Coaxing the last few chips from the bag, a shiny blue-green, snack-
size bag (Wise potato chips), he washes them down with a swig of
Bud. *We hear about it at church of course, about angels and demons
and miracles, and there's no doubt among Baptists about the existence
of the soul ... yet we don't call it science, we call it faith.* He snorts
resignedly. *But to seek the silver cord using clinical methods—that's a
goshdang different ball game. And yet I KNOW what I know.*
     French fries, hamburgers, hint of nicotine, fresh beer, stale beer,
yeasty spills and stains: the Westside lounge smells like the Bear's
Paw except for the mildewed carpet. *And Elmo had an NDE too, and
Dudley O'Shea.* Bryan sips then gestures heavenward with the brown,
half-full bottle. *And all this is connected to God, and to Mandy. It's
somehow the same, the love we have. It doesn't matter that she's
married ... or where she lives, or what she's doing, or if she's a mother.
I doubt she has a baby. I woulda heard ... from Wendy, or Spanky, or
Mom. But the love we share is WAY bigger than all of it. It's bigger
than paperwork or vows or sex, or money and career goals, or how
many kids.* A warm fount floods his bosom. *It's BIGGER. It's God.
And God is LOVE ... a love that turns tragedy into triumph, a love that
makes evil work for good, a love that destines us for glory, a love that
leaves NO ONE out. It can't die and disappear into the ground. It
can't be damned to hell. And the silver cord binds us to the soul, the
seat of this wondrous love—and therefore it binds us to God, and to
each other. It's the most crucial of—*
     "What the hell, slugger?" Spanky drawls, as he arrives at the corner
booth; he plunks down opposite Bryan. "This's a *god*dam surprise,
havin' yuh here on a Friday afternoon for chrissake?"

"Well uh ... I uh," Bryan stammers, dimpling, as he returns abruptly to earth, to an awareness of where he is.

"I couldn't hardly believe it when yuh came boppin' up to the counter while ago ... but I'm fuckin' glad to see yuh. Hell, let's celebrate. Where's that new-bitch waitress?" Spanky looks weirdly formal in his olive-drab Westside uniform. He even has a name tag: CURTIS ARNOLD. Less freckles, no sunburn, no ointment on his nose—and his hair's a trifle longer (crewcut instead of burr-cut), and he's added a few pounds, maybe ten. Wendy has tamed him down, though he still uses too much Aqua-Velva.

Bryan, chuckling, sips his brew. "Like I say ... I only had one class this morning, so I got home early. Good Friday isn't a big deal with Baptists, so it's not an official holiday at Baylor, but a lotta profs cancel, which was good for me." Nodding toward his longtime buddy, he grins bigger, his face warming. "I must say, Spanker, you look *dadgum* spiffy in that outfit."

"C'mon ... it's like I'm back in the Boy Scouts for chrissake. And my hands stink worse'n shit from rentin' out sweaty shoes."

They share a laugh, as Bryan glances at his watch: 4:49 p.m. "Dang, it's almost five. I thought y'got off shift at four-thirty?"

"Clyde was late. He's a *god*dam hayseed bastard who doesn't give a shit." Spanky jabs the air, two lefts and a right. "Plus, he screwed Wendy when she was fifteen. She's never confessed to me, or anythang ... but he *did* fuck her. I heard the scuttlebutt back in those days."

Bryan chuckles knowingly—he gestures bottle-in-hand.

The wiry little redneck gives a cocky head-waggle. "But that was six years ago, like ancient fuckin' history—pardon the pun. She was young and innocent. She didn't realize he was a goddam pussy-huntin' poser—and he still *is* for chrissake." Loud cackles, then Spanky spots the waitress, a short redhead with sexy hips and a so-so face: "Hey, sweetheart! I need a Miller Lite."

Spanky, after ordering, heads for the can. Bryan sips, chuckling to himself: *Maybe I should discuss Doc's book with Spanky? I never told him about my OBEs or anything. I wonder if Wendy knows? Mandy mighta told her, and she mighta told Spanker?* Bryan chuckles aloud. *Nawh, better to wait, unless HE brings it up ... and that's damn unlikely, considering his kick-ass mood.*

"It's amazing ... how things've changed," Bryan remarks a bit later, after his crewcut buddy has returned.

"I'll say," Spanky agrees between slugs of beer—he ordered the Miller Lite plus a tub of fries. "But you're graduating from college ... while I'm still stuck in this goddam po*dunk* town."

"Yeh ... but I'll still be at Baylor for two more years."

Spanky stuffs a handful of fries into his mouth. "Shitfire, slugger," he replies thickly, greasily. "You're gonna have more goddam degrees than Mr. Denham."

"But diplomas don't mean much, Spanker ... not really. It's like that talk we had right here back in '91 ... before I left for Waco." Bryan nurses the dregs of his beer. "What you said then was great stuff, like better than any college, and don't forget that wacky night ... when you met me out at the lake."

"How could I? I liketuh froze my *god*dam ass." *Smack, slurp, smack.* Spanky sucks ketchup from his fingers. "You were love-crazy in those days, and I reckon you still are for chrissake." His tone softens, his blue eyes warming. "It's fuckin' weird I tellyuh ... how Wen and Mandy were best friends, and I ended up with Wendy, while Mandy marries a goddam missionary." Chugging some Miller Lite, he wipes his mouth with the back of his hand. "Don't get me wrong ... me 'n Wen, we have a *good* thang. But you 'n Mandy—well ... it's like off the fuckin' chart." Spanky leans forward, elbows on the table. "Anyhow ... now that we opened this can, there's sumpthin' y'should know. She's in town—she came over to our place for supper last night."

* * *

An hour later Bryan rumbles through Spindle on FR 115. Passing Coolidge Street, he gives a sigh. Aunt Marge lives on Coolidge, and Mandy's there—according to Spanky: "She came down for Easter, with her mom and sister. They're visitin' relatives, the ones that own the diner. But the missionary guy didn't come. He's spendin' Easter in South America for chrissake. They're both goin' down in June. It's a fuckin' shame if you ask me."

Back in '91, Bryan would be at the Goddard's house banging on the door, but things are different now, *very* different.

* * *

SPINDLE, TEXAS - THE HOWARD FARM
SUNDAY, APRIL 16, 1995 (EASTER SUNDAY) — 11:41 AM

Clouds drift overhead: bleached cotton against a vivid blue sky. The air smells sweet: April alfalfa, Johnson grass, the scent of wild flowers. Bryan, carrying a draft of Dr. Richardson's new book, slips through the barbed-wire fence adjacent to the tractor trail. His shirt (the usual bum-around baseball underjersey) catches on a barb, but he frees it without pricking himself. He didn't go to church with his mom and dad. After reading the doctor's book until the wee hours of the morning, he was too tired. Besides, he feels *much* closer to God out here. He likewise turned down an invitation to go to Aunt Lydia's in Longview. Lydia, his mom's older sister, has a get-together every Easter, and she marshals all the relatives she can. Henry and Virginia rarely attend, but this year they promised, so Bryan has the farm all to himself.

Striding into the pine grove, he shifts the manuscript (in a green ACCO binder) to his left hand, so he can push aside the over-hanging boughs along the trail. Before leaving the house, he took a shower to wake himself up, so he feels rather perky, and the pine scent invigorates him all the more. A chipmunk chirps excitedly, as it scampers along a fallen tree. The black-striped rodent hides in the shadows then playfully reappears. The Baylor senior, giving a fond laugh, pauses to watch the little critter.

Brain Science and the Limits of Reductionism—the doctor's latest work (much broader in scope than his previous books on neural pathology) affirms his allegiance to RM yet addresses the crucial issues. In fact, the most profound passages echo the discussions he and Bryan have had over the past two years. Bryan got a (draft) copy on Thursday, and he's been reading it ever since, even at 4:30 this morning when he finally fell asleep.

After three hours of shut-eye, he hauled himself out of bed. Down to the kitchen—he ate breakfast with his dad: scrambled eggs and sausage, plus pancakes, heaping piles soaked in butter and syrup, plus OJ and coffee and cantaloupe. They ate heartily but talked little, just a few comments about the warm weather, and the spring alfalfa, and Millie's new diet, a special feed for older horses (that Bryan gave her later when he fed his equine friend). He does share with his mom, more candidly than ever, and she offers her opinions, though with a decidedly maternal bias which comes down on his side on most everything, even his astral trips—yet she does caution about leaping to conclusions.

Giving a final chirp, the cavorting chipmunk disappears under the tangle of exposed roots at the end of the fallen pine. Bryan proceeds along the trail, the carpet of needles softly silent under his old Nike running shoes. *That little guy was almost tame. It was the same with Gramps. The animals trusted him.*

Exiting the woods, he ascends the grassy, sunwashed hillock. The big oak looms ahead, fluttering gently in the wind. The same breeze caresses Bryan's face; it's balmy out, perfect weather. The azure sky seems almost liquid in character, rich and deep like the blue of a melted Crayola. It's wondrous to behold, much like that gorgeous Saturday back in '91 when he and Mandy hiked up here. He was just home from the hospital, and he told her everything.

As he settles at the foot of the oak, getting comfy on a wide root, he can't help but ache for his dear pretty lady, a bittersweet yet *beautiful* longing. When she took off for Arkansas on that black and stormy Thursday in October of '91, he pummeled the massive trunk behind him until his hands were like hamburger, but the steadfast nature of the old tree now comforts him, reminding him that the Lord moves in his own good time, no matter the pleading. *What God doeth, he doeth it forever. Nothing can be added to it, or taken from it. That's from Ecclesiastes ... just like the silver cord.* Below him, to the east, Ruby Pond lies glassy calm except for ripples near the dam. He stares wistfully at the water, then he pushes his old Spindle cap back on his head and opens the green binder, to his favorite chapter:

> The process by which conscience experience arises from matter remains a mystery. Dr. Francis Crick attributes consciousness to attention times working memory, while Gerald Edeleman (Scripps Institute) defines it as memory reacting to perception. Others venture beyond the reductionist model, maintaining that the mind is completely separate from our gray matter, a metaphysical agency which oversees the operation of the physical machine called the brain.
>
> RM has taught us a great deal, yet the enigma of consciousness is still unexplained. In fact, the door is *wide* open. To keep out superstition and pseudo-science, we reject the notion of God plus all paranormal phenomena, and yet this broad dismissal may well sweep the *answer* off the table a priori, especially when the boundary between supernatural and natural blurs when we delve deeper into the nature of matter and energy (i.e. the quantum realm or Einsteinian velocities). Perhaps the supernatural is actually quite *natural*, once we grasp the....

He finishes the short chapter in less than twenty minutes, though he has to fight off waves of drowsiness. He scoots away from the tree, five feet or so, to the thicker, softer grass; he sprawls on his back. Folding his arms, he gazes up at the oak leaves fidgeting in the breeze. They have that moist, tender, early-season look, a lighter green like wood moss, as opposed to the darker hues of July. A cricket chirrups nearby. Bryan closes his eyes. A crow caws in the distance, in the distance, in the distance.

* * *

Something bounces on Bryan's arm. He fishes it out of the grass: an acorn. *What the heck? Acorns don't fall in April?* Rubbing his eyes, he yawns and sits up. He studies the brownish little sphere. *Nawh, this's old. It doesn't have the top part, that cap-looking stem thing.* He chuckles. *Maybe a squirrel dropped it?* He checks his watch: 1:37 p.m. *Gosh, I was dozing a good hour.*

Retrieving his baseball hat, he puts it on. *Pip*—another acorn pelts him, pinging off his shoulder. *Dang, what's going on?* A third lands near his left foot. He whips around, checking behind him, but there's nothing unusual, just the massive tree, the deep-treaded trunk. He scans the foliage above searching for a squirrel, for any clue—to no avail. The giant oak offers no explanation as to why its nutty fruit is falling in the spring.

Bryan looks to the east, toward the droning of a small plane. He spots it, a yellow-winged speck amid the cumulus. He yawns and stretches, then he laughs. *It's like this old tree is playing with me, like Gramps used to do. It harbors his spirit somehow. He loved to come here—it was his special place, a place to dream and wish and pray, a place to commune with God, the God of love and nature he believed in, the same God I'm feeling right now.* The feeling intensifies: God, Gramps—Mandy. The longing shifts back to his dear pretty lady, as when he first arrived here two hours ago. The warm vibes flood his bosom until he's faint with emotion. *Goshdang ... it's like she's inside me, her spirit.*

He gazes at the small airplane until it diminishes to a pencil point against the clouds, against the blue heavens. Twigs crunch behind him—then a VOICE: "Hey, you big jock."

Elation, alarm! His heart bolts, while his stomach knots. He dares not look. "Jeeeeesh ... I'm losing it," he whispers in denial. "I-I ... God, she's even talking inside my dadgum head."

"Whaddeyuh mumbling about?" Mandy chortles—SHE'S REAL! NO FANTASY! He jumps up, his pulse thundering. His face goes hot; he gasps until breathless. She leans against the big oak, a smirk on her face, her hips cocked cowgirl fashion—yet she has on Easter attire save for grayish sneakers, old sneakers. A canvas handbag rests at her feet, a strapped shoulder bag.

His thoughts race: "I uh ... I uh ... I-I ... whaaa?"

"Relax," she giggles, "I'm not gonna *bite* yuh." Shouldering the bag, she comes closer. They shake hands, awkwardly, then she pecks him on the cheek, just missing his mouth. He catches a whiff of perfume, the same scent as the old days. A shiver shoots to the quick of his soul. She acts composed, but her big blue eyes spark with nervous excitement. Bryan notices, and she quickly looks down, covering with a laugh. Retreating a step or two, she fiddles with the Velcro clasp on the shoulder bag.

He dimples, his pulse settling a bit as he realizes she's also less than calm. "So *you're* the one who tossed those acorns?"

"What a *brilliant* deduction," she quips, without looking up.

"So whaddeyuh doing—I mean uh ... what brings you out to the farm? And how didyuh know I was up here ... up on the hill?"

Mandy grins, her cheeks coloring, but she gives no answer. A puff of wind ruffles her bangs. No softball cap, no ponytail, but the feathered chin-length hairdo seems much like before, when she wore it down for church, and the golden sheen has lost none of its lustre. Blue-pleated blouse, pinkish, calf-length skirt, spring pastels: she looks vigorous and wholesome, wifely angelic; she'd have little trouble convincing anyone she's married to a pastor, especially in these Sunday duds—but the averted eyes and smirky blush tell a different tale, as does her PRESENCE. Mrs. Russell Snyder would not be here under this special tree, not on Easter Sunday, not on *any* Sunday, or any day for that matter. More shivers bolt down Bryan's spine. He paws the grass with his Nike shoe. "I heard you were in town," he says.

"Is that right?"

"Yeah ... Spanky told me."

Rrrrrrrp. She separates the Velcro, as she continues to fiddle with the clasp of her bag. "You keep *tabs* on me, huh?" Her blush deepening, she gives him a side-glance then looks down again.

"Let's just say, I have a vested interest."

She giggles. "Oh, you *do*, d'yuh?"

He feels drunk—a bona fide Mandy-high. *O Lord,* he prays silently, as he drinks her in with his eyes, *don't let this end badly.*

Her face is a trifle firmer, her figure a tad fuller, her freckles less evident. Her country-gal features have matured, yet despite her collegiate age (she'll be twenty-one in July), she could still pass for a high-schooler, especially when she blushes, like right now. As though sensing his gaze, she purses her mouth, bites her lip, crinkles her nose, doing several reps. This most-familiar routine makes his heart pang. She's radiant and holy and adorable and choir-girlish and saintly, yet she's sensual and sexy and vibrant, and ravishing and succulent. He aches to hug her, to kiss her, to hold her tight. Yet he willfully resists.

Giving a little laugh, a knowing laugh, she advances down the hill into the sunshine, going several yards past Dr. Richardson's manuscript, which marks the spot where Bryan was napping. "I see y'brought some heavy reading with yuh," she remarks, as she plops down in the grass, tucking her legs under her.

"I reckon it *is* kinda heavy," he replies, without shifting his attention. "It's Dr. Richardson's new book." Bryan remains fixed on her—on her sunshiny hair, on the collar of her blouse as it nestles the nape of her neck, on her girlish ankles and cottony socks which cutely protrude from beneath the skirt. His eyes advance up the small of her back where he can't help but note the raised contour of her brassiere strap, quite evident through the pale-blue cotton. His knees go rubbery.

"C'mon, you big jock," she calls over her shoulder, "take a load off your feet."

"Okay ... but first I hafta water a tree back yonder."

More girlish giggles. "What the heck, babe? Y'don't hafta disappear on *my* account. I've seen yuh *pee* a hundred times."

He hustles to the other side of the hill anyway, wading into some deep grass. *I can't believe this. And she's killer cute, more so than ever.* His soul sings, but his legs feel all the more wobbly, as if he's standing up in a rowboat in the middle of the pond.

* * *

While Bryan takes a leak, Mandy pulls a pack of Juicy Fruit out of her bag and pops a piece into her mouth. *This's WAY out,* she laughs, as shots of sugar bathe her tongue. *I reckon I'm breaking a lot of rules. And yet it's like ... so spur of the moment. It hasn't been thirty minutes since I asked Uncle Billy if I could take a spin in my old Firebird, and Mama was too busy yaking with Aunt Marge to even notice.* More laughter amid smacks of gum. *That car always did stir up my wild side. I'm glad he didn't sell it.*

"Y'want some gum," she offers, as Bryan plunks down on her left, facing her obliquely.

He takes a stick from the yellow pack. "Don't mind if I do."

Gosh, he looks good, she reacts to herself, as he gets started on his gum. *He didn't shave. I love his chin when it's whiskery dark. But he must've showered—he smells like soap ... and Brute. **O God** ... I reckon we better stay at arm's length.*

Bryan dimples, as if reading her thoughts, then he gives a snuffly guffaw, his wondrous ocean-green eyes laughing as well. "What?" she inquires juicily, her gum popping in her mouth.

"You never answered my question? I mean, here you *are* ... like all of a sudden? And on Easter Sunday, of all days?" More dimples, a big blushing smile—his eyes beckon, casting their spell, but she escapes shifting her attention to the acorns in her skirt pocket, the handful she gathered before but didn't toss from behind the tree. She pulls one out, fingering it delicately. "And how didyuh know I was up here by the tree?"

She feels his gaze, but she concentrates on the little brown orb, holding it twixt thumb and forefinger, as if it's a precious jewel; this one is complete, stem cap and all. "Oh, I dunno," she replies finally. "I went to church with Mama and Gretchen and Aunt Marge, and then we had a big Easter dinner at their house, and then I asked Uncle Billy if I could take the Firebird for a—"

"You drove out here in the Firebird?"

She works her gum loudly. "Yeah ... and it runs good as ever." She laughs. "I'd buy it back from him, if I had the money."

"So y'just decided to drop by ... to say hello?"

She tosses the acorn into the air then catches it. "That's pretty much it."

"So how'd yuh know I was home from school? Didyuh talk to my folks at church?"

"I saw 'em from a distance, but we didn't talk to 'em."

"So how?"

She smirks then sticks out her tongue at him. "I have my sources— just like *you*." She tosses and catches the acorn again. "No one came to the door when I knocked, but your old pickup was there ... so I *knew* you had to be up here by the tree."

He goes down on his side, his head propped on his hand. He dimples. "Well, I reckon you *know* me pretty dang well."

"You got that right, mister."

They both laugh, then they shift to less-volatile subjects: his upcoming graduation, Dr. Richardson's book, the Tracy thing (which Mandy knows all about), the Bible college, her calling, her summer mission to Peru, the fact she and Russ are waiting a few years before having kids. They likewise talk briefly about Helen and Charlie and Gretchen, and a few other things.

Mandy raises her right knee, folding the other leg under. She smoothes her skirt, as it drapes the knee. The breeze sneaks under, tickling her thigh. She wonders if he can see her panties. The idea thrills her, despite her conscience. She focuses on the acorn in her hand, but she can't quench the tingling between her legs. *C'mon, gal, cool it. Maybe someday, but NOT today.*.

* * *

Looking under her skirt, Bryan homes in on the cottony, pale-yellow crescent lurking amid the shadows and creamy nooks. He *can* see her panties. Hot blood charges into his dick—it stretches tuberlike down the leg of his Levi's. Covering with a cough, he lifts his eyes, lest she catch him staring. *She has to be thinking what I'm thinking?* She digs inside her big purse, coming out with a pen. "Whaddeyuh doing?" he asks.

She grins goofily. "I'm making a *present* for yuh." After drawing eyes on the acorn, plus nose, mouth, ears, and a goatee, she gives it to him. "Looks like a little man, don'tcha think?"

"Yeah, like a little artist in a beret. In fact, there's a French-language teacher at Baylor who looks *just* like this." They snort and giggle, then he slips the acorn into his pocket. "Thanks," he says, stretching his leg to make his prick less conspicuous. As he does, he catches another glimpse of yellow panty crotch. He's crazy-hot to kiss her, but after trusting God this long, he's not about to take control now—and he doesn't have to. Removing her gum, she tosses it down the hill into the grass. She blushes and gives a devilish grin. "What are *you* grinning about?" he asks.

"Oh, I was just thinking about Galveston."

His pulse picks up, as the conversation finally locks onto the target. "What about it?"

"Oh, nothing really. But that *was* a super-good weekend."

"I'll say."

She smirks but doesn't reply. His mouth goes dry. He fiddles with the tattered sleeve of his jersey. She plays with the strap of her shoulder bag. The electricity in the air grows stronger, charging, charging—a spark would obliterate them. "So did you and *Russ*ell go to Galveston ... by chance?"

"Not hardly," she blurts, hugging her upraised knee. "Oh, we went on a trip ... to St. *Lou*is ... and I reckon it was okay." She gives a moth-wind flutter of her hand.

"So you didn't uh—"

"Goshdang, you big jock," she chortles, her cheeks now scarlet, "you really *are* prying."

"Well, you brought it up?"

"I know, but uh ... but uh."

"But what?"

She giggles but gives no reply. Shifting, she straightens her legs in front of her. She pushes her skirt down, covering all but her socks and shoes. No more view, but their sporting more than compensates, making everything about her just as carnal, and glorious, as her crotch— the fevered blush, the silly grin, the blue stars in her eyes, her nubile hands and arms, the womanly shape of her bosom inside the blouse, even her ankles and old sneakers.

"So Galveston *was* better than St. Louis?" he presses.

"Get outta here. You're being *way* too nosy." Grabbing her bag, she places it on her flattened lap. She fidgets with the Velcro buckle, as before by the tree.

O Jesus, don't let it stop here, he prays silently.

"Russ and I get along okay ... but I reckon he likes marriage for other reasons mainly. We did it ... I mean we *do* it ... but he doesn't *need* it as much."

"As much as who?" Bryan sports—he's got her now.

"Who d'yuh think?" she giggles, her face even redder.

"So it's been a good while since—"

"I'm not *tell*ing," she sports. "But I *am* a healthy, normal gal, with a healthy, normal s—" She stops midsentence, her face blanching, her brow knitting. She springs to her feet.

"What's wrong?" he reacts, his hopes stalling then falling.

Squinting against the sun, she nods up the hill toward the tree. "Oh, I dunno. I'm not sure I should even be here."

Bryan, still reclining, takes her hand. "It's okay, pretty lady. I understand. You don't hafta stay. I love you either way. I'll always love you, no matter what." She looks at him, her eyes now glassy with tears—the tears move him, but he stays put.

Seconds tick by: ten or so. "Oh, *babe,*" she blurts, falling upon him. "I love you—I love you *forever.*" She kisses him, her tongue joining the Juicy Fruit in his mouth. She enraptures him, taking his breath, throwing his psyche into wanton chaos. Space-time dissolves taking with it *all* caution, *all* inhibition.

She strokes his erection through the denim; she attacks his belt buckle, her girlish hands flailing. He takes over on the belt, while she urgently sheds her undies, one leg then the other. The yellow panties catch on her sneaker—she kicks off the shoe. Before he gets his jeans past his knees, she's on top of him.

"Don't rush," she commands in a suffocated whisper, as they merge into physical union, her skirt covering their coupling like a pink tent—she's still dressed for Easter except where it counts. He gulps in happy amazement, almost swallowing his gum; he spits it out instead. She squeezes his cock with her vagina, teasing him, but she holds onto her hips: no gyrating or humping.

She gazes down at him, her blue eyes wide and wanton under her bangs, and trancy with need. His dick cries for permission to thrust, to satisfy her, yet he willfully holds back, letting her have the lead. Hot wetness soaks his balls, his pubic hair. He smells perfume mingled with sweat and musky female desire.

Unbuttoning her blouse, she lifts her bra, allowing her tits to dangle over him as she leans forward. The surrounding tan lines, though less tan than before, give just enough contrast to animate their whiteness. They're still ivory vanilla in hue with rosy-pink areolas—no way could he forget. Ditto for her swelling nipples, which are darker pink, like raspberries. He can't help but fondle them. She mews in response, her eyes dilating all the more. Her pussy draws him deeper into her, and deeper—until his engorged mushroom beats like a second heart inside her. Time passes in slow-motion. Mandy grimaces, fighting the tethered beast. The throbbing between them grows and grows—fevered thunder.

"Oh, I *can't*," she whimpers.

Rocking her haunches, she rides him frantically, while he pulls in unison, gripping her fleshy hips through the skirt. Her tits jounce; her bangs fly about. She cries openly, sobbing his name. Faster, higher, desperate fire—oh sweet torture: she utters a shriek, stiffens, and slumps upon him, gasping with relief. He comes seconds behind her, giving a final dispatching thrust.

* * *

Bryan and Mandy cuddle in the grass. Carnal rapture has given way to tender words and now to blissful exhaustion. She nuzzles under his chin, her eyes closed, her breath warm on his neck. She's dozing, or close. Her pillowy bosom presses upon his arm, a wondrous weight; he feels her heart beating. She holds his hand like a little girl. Heaven has come down on the Howard farm.

The leafy shadows cast by the oak have advanced over their grassy nest, but the afternoon remains balmy. All is quiet save for the crows plus a distant down-shifting truck. Mandy, dear Mandy: her disheveled hair frames her angelic face, while her lips, slightly parted, express a faint smile. Love and wonder—the feeling expands, becoming boundless, like the stars on a moonless night.

Drowsy, drowsy: he's drifting off, but his heart continues to soar—no, it's *more* than heart. He's having an OBE. His flesh is down there with Mandy, but his astral "self" ascends toward the clouds. The big oak dwindles below him, and the pond, and the watermelon patch. He levels off among the cottony cumulus; he can see his house and the barn. *This's SO mind-blowing. I'm up where that yellow plane was before. I just wish she was up here WITH me.* Ruby Pond, green in the sunlight, looks like a rain puddle. *This hasn't happened for three years. I should fly around and test my limits, for the sake of my silver-cord research. This's my laboratory.* Descending, he jets toward Spindle— but pangs of love quickly arrest him. *No, I can't. I can't go, not without her.*

Amid a rush of trees and sky, and fields and shadows, a video in reverse, he zips back to the oak tree, where he's suddenly back in his body snuggling with his dear pretty lady. *Thank you, God. This's where I belong today.* He yawns then nods off again.

* * *

4:29 p.m. Bryan, waking up, kisses Mandy on the cheek—but it's not her; it's the green ACCO binder, Dr. Richardson's book.

"O God, no!" he cries, bolting to his feet. "Where is she? Don't tell me this *whole* thing was a dream? Mandy, oh Mandy ... where are you!" No answer, no sign of her. He races down to the pond. "Mandy! Mandy!" Still nothing.

His hopes ebbing, he trudges back up the hill toward the oak tree. He scratches his arm, a chigger bite, a little welt. *Gosh, it seemed SO real, but y'can't control what yuh dream.* He yawns and stretches then gives a resigned shrug. He pushes his hands into the front pockets of his jeans. "YES!" he shouts, as he discovers the acorn, the little French artist in a beret. "It *wasn't* a dream. She *really* did give me an acorn with a face on it." He does a quick little jitterbug in the Johnson grass. "But why'd she leave, without saying good-bye?"

He sighs, his joy moderating. *I could call the Goddard's, but maybe I shouldn't? In any case, I hafta get back to the house.* He picks up the manuscript. A piece of paper flutters out from inside the binder. *I'll be danged. Looks like a note:*

> Bryan—sorry to sneak off, but I'm super late. We're going back tonight. But you SURE made my day, you big jock you. Like the BEST Easter ever! I reckon we got a jillion chigger bites, and weed-rash to boot, but it was MORE than worth it! I'll be in touch soon. I love you forever ... Mandy

So that's why this green binder was in my face when I woke up.

CHAPTER THIRTY-ONE

BAYLOR UNIVERSITY - BILL DANIEL STUDENT CENTER
THURSDAY, APRIL 20, 1995 — 11:51 AM

Before exiting the truck, Bryan looks again at the newspaper, at the disemboweled carcass of the Alfred P. Murrah Building, its facade blown away, its honeycombed innards exposed amid a tangled curtain of cables and shattered flooring and Sheetrock and reinforcing rods— all dangling down onto a still-steaming heap of pancaked concrete, the remains of the nine collapsed floors. He's not into newspapers (and it's been on CNN nonstop), but this's a headline to save, so he got a copy of *USA Today* on his way to campus this morning, at the 7-Eleven on Rigby Ave.

They said it was Muslim terrorists, he remarks to himself, as he enters the student center via the back entrance. *But now they say it's a home-grown plot, something about a Ryder truck. I just wouldn't wanna be trapped underneath. It's hard to figure why God allows such horror, just like the massacre at Luby's. But there has to be a reason? There has to be?* He sighs. *I've seen the beautiful side of death, but they can't show that on the tube. They can't show the souls rising up out of the rubble.*

Finding a beige envelope in his PO box, he forgets the OKC bombing. Butterflies—he slips on his glasses. *It IS from her.*

> I don't regret what happened. It was <u>awesome</u> and beautiful. But after praying about everything, I must accept the reality of my situation. I cannot change my life right now. I've decided to stay the course, to continue on with my calling. I've made promises and commitments, as you know.
>
> Russell goes back in June, and I'll be with him. I'll be teaching at the missionary school in Huarás. I'll finally be able to use all that Spanish I took in high school, and here at NCB.... Buenos dias. Cómo está usted? Me llamo señora Snyder. Of course, I'll sound super weird with my hicktown Americano accent—ha-ha. Most everyone down there speaks Spanish, but Russ says I'll also have to learn some Quechua, the Indian language, since the ministry operates outreach stations in the highlands, and in the Moñtana (the rain forest). They have a plane that flies the team around, the kind that can land on water, or regular runways. Gosh, I reckon I'm rambling—sorry, babe.

THE SILVER CORD

We'll be there for three years. Who knows what the future holds after that? In any case, you'll be in my thoughts and prayers.

The butterflies in his gut swarm downward into his bowels. His face heats; his eyes fill. *Bad news. I lose.* Unzipping his book bag, he drops the letter inside. *Gosh, Lord, I thought it was time, but I reckon I was wrong. Looks like THREE more years—at least. Who knows what the future holds? That's what she said.*

He's tempted to rush home where he can lament alone in his garage apartment, where he can soothe his hurt with a six-pack of Bud Light. Yet as he exits the post office, he fights back the tears and heads for the cafeteria, concluding among other things that he's still hungry enough to eat lunch. *She did say it was AWESOME ... with no regrets. I hafta think. I can't overreact.*

* * *

12:48 p.m. Fountain Mall. *We can't rush destiny,* Bryan reminds himself, as he strides along, his bookpack slung over his shoulder. A dank breeze fans his face; it's still cloudy, but the air is mild, no longer chilly. *But still, she's gonna—I mean, Peru is SO far away.* He sidesteps a gray, heavy-jowled, mid-life student pushing a bike. The mall isn't thronged, like between morning classes, but there's a steady flow going each way. The day dawned blustery and damp (after overnight showers) calling for windbreakers and sweat shirts, but short sleeves now predominant, save for a few cold-blooded types plus the usual coats and ties, the Marvinish nerds (though Mr. Latrobe himself departed last year, electing to finish his training at Dallas Theological Seminary, the renowned, strait-laced school for ultra-conservative evangelicals).

Feathery cirrus, tattered rows of altocumulus, windblown scud. Bryan glances at the sky; it looks awesomely cool, all nacreous and swirly and gray, with rips here and there. A clearing trend, from the west, eats away at the overcast giving it a chaotic yet majestic character, like the clouds in a Winslow Homer seascape. The fast-walking senior overtakes an ambling trio of coeds, three maidenly butts rolling and shifting, two in jeans, one in shorts. Detouring onto the grass, he passes on the right. Chris H. would surely hang back to savor the view, while whispering wisecracks about all the sweet young pussy on campus, but he's long gone (to Houston), and Bryan has too much Mandy on his mind. A youthful crowd congregates near the benches in front of Peyton Hall, no doubt waiting for a big one-o'clock class. Bryan weaves through the chattering gang of freshmen beyond which the pedestrian traffic diminishes to a trickle.

Finding a gap in the overcast, the sun sidles out—it turns the grass green, the shadows dark, the breeze warmer. *But she did come out to the farm looking for me ... on Easter Sunday no less. I just hafta trust*

517

the Lord on this. He chuckles under his breath. *But it may drive me f-ing crazy, after what happened at the oak tree.* Rotating his hat back on his head, his old sweat-stained Spindle cap, he pauses on the near-empty sidewalk. Gesturing plaintively, he gazes at the gray medley of clouds then at the wide azure swath to the west. *Dear Jesus, you sure know how to paint a sky. It's awesome, even in the middle of the day. I just pray you'll do an equally creative work with my life. I may never solve the silver cord, but I HAVE experienced it.* Stepping to the edge of the oatmeal-textured concrete, he toes the damp grass with his sneaker. *Just like all those folks and little kids who got killed in Oklahoma City yesterday. It can't be the end of them. I mean, where does love come from, if yuh just throw us away at the end of the game? I'm not crazy. I have transcended the flesh. And it's somehow the same, Mandy and LIFE, the yearning for Heaven ... for "love after death." It's all tied together, and it's crucial for everyone. We're ALL desperate when facing the grave. But, Jesus GOD, I've seen it, how love wins over death and grief. Life does have a purpose. It's more than cruel chaos that defeats us all at the end. But Lord, you hafta show me the rest. You hafta CONFIRM my faith. And I'm not talking about church.* He sighs then continues walking. *In any case, I'm well across the Rubicon on this. I can't turn back now.*

The sad-letter blues have given way to acceptance, to the same be-still sense of resignation that has kept him sane since Tracy rescued him four years ago. The sunny switch in the weather also helps, as did his lunchtime encounter with Steve Jordan. Bryan mentioned Mandy, but Jordan was totally into himself, no surprise. Bryan felt hurt at first, but it's hard to stay down when the big guy is *up*, and he was especially ebullient, beaming, laughing, waving his oaklike arms—with good reason: he just pitched a no-hitter yesterday, a 1-0 gem over Texas Tech, giving the Bears a hammerlock on first place; he'll soon be graduating (with a degree in sports media), and then he'll be leading Baylor to the College World Series in Omaha; after the CWS he reports to the Florida Rookie League, to Winter Haven, a Red Sox farm team (the Sox drafted him, not the Rangers). And to top it off, Steve and Susie are getting married in July.

Reaching the Fletcher Life Sciences Building, Bryan hops a puddle then veers off the sidewalk. He hustles across the sun-splotched lawn, his usual shortcut to the neuroscience lab in the rear. Blooming shrubs and beds of spring flowers frame the grassy rectangle. He inhales the fragrant aromas: lilacs, honeysuckle, bluebonnets, begonias, damp grass. He's not headed to class but to pick up some disks from the tomography lab. He has to condense and consolidate them for Dr. Richardson, and he'll be doing most of it at home. No more clock punching on the job—he comes and goes as he wishes. The doctor trusts Bryan to keep track of his own hours, which he submits each week to Connie, and he's getting a promotion to graduate assistant this summer.

*   *   *

"Sounds like you had one *hell* of a week," Dr. Richardson says, without taking his eyes off the color-coded PET scan on the large Macintosh monitor. "And there's no *road* map when it comes to love." The image on the screen looks a bit fuzzy to Bryan, who's not wearing his glasses. Yet he can tell that it's another rat shot, from the shape, another rodent from XB93, the latest Johns Hopkins TRP (tumor-reduction project: chemo vs. angiostatin). Baylor got a slice of the NIH funding (National Institute of Health). Much of Bryan's data dogwork involves the XB93 files. The bow-tied doctor, clad in a frayed dress shirt plus tacky suit-pants (blue corduroy), sits at the keyboard, his disciple in a pull-up chair. No class, no students: the lab is deserted except for a technician calibrating the gamma-ray detectors in the main room. "Let's face it, slugger, women are outside the reductive circle. I don't have a *god*dam clue, and I lived with Martha for forty years ... bless her heart. She drove me crazy, she did." He gives a double snort, a ha-ha through his nose. "It's im*poss*ible enough to figure the neurology of a rodent"—he gestures toward the rat brain, with its red and yellow sectors, and green areas, plus a band of brilliant purple at the top)—"but this's nothing compared to predicting the human female."

"You got *that* right," Bryan chortles.

When he arrived forty minutes ago, he found the doctor at the new Macintosh workstation in this glass-walled office at the rear of the lab. Seizing the moment, he told him all about the Mandy situation. While he confided, Richardson continued to work the keyboard and mouse, using the advanced Adobe software to check, compare, and manipulate the animal scans (rats and mice, plus a few monkey shots). But the professor was tuned to the Mandy news, as his witty response about women attests.

Richardson, leaning back, laughs again. "I just hope you get *over* this in time for softball. We start practice in three weeks, you know?" He massages his bald dome then clasps his hands behind his neck, his graceful brain-surgeon fingers half hidden in the gray thatch that shrouds the back half of his head.

Shedding his baseball cap, Bryan gestures with it—he dimples. "Get off it, Doc. You're worse than me when it comes to sports. But it *does* give me hope ... the fact that you can still run at your age—or should I say trot?"

"Better watch it, slugger ... or I'll take you out to the golf course and teach you a *real* sport, a *true* gauge of athletic talent."

"Yeh ... y'been saying that for two years."

Richardson doesn't respond save for his wry *yeck-yeck*, his crow-chuckle. Removing his James Joyce spectacles, he rubs the bridge of his nose. Silence: the mood sobers. "I didn't mean to make light of the whole Mandy thing," he finally replies, his voice going gentle beneath the patrician accent. "I know she's the apple of your eye."

"It's okay, sir. I understand."

"It's a strange thing, actually."

"What?"

"How we deal with painful subjects." He slowly shakes his head, his eyes widening—naked blue, no glasses. "You pour out your heart, and I make a wisecrack about women. It's a defense mechanism ... just like at the golf course yesterday. We were in the clubhouse watching the Oklahoma City bombing, and all the guys were reacting with John Wayne bravado ... about catching the bastards and castrating them ... and hanging them, and so on. We didn't *joke* about it certainly, but we did deflect the idea that it could happen to us. It's our nature to depersonalize things, lest the truth hit home—especially with men I think."

Bryan replaces his cap. "Yeah, I reckon you're right."

"You *reck*on?" the professor teases, his playful side taking over again. "Hell, slugger, you're supposed to know *all* about defense mechanisms and phobias ... now that you've taken all those damn psych courses, plus the ones we offer on the shrink side of our department. Five years ago, I'd never even heard the term 'neuropsychology,' but now the two departments are joined at the hip. Hell, we have seven neuroscience majors going on for the double master's program ... and *you*'re leading the pack."

Bryan blushes and laughs. "Well, it was *your* idea too?"

"Yes, I suppose ... but don't forget I was trained in the old open-and-fix school." He nods at the rainbow-colored rat brain, still big on the monitor. "I'm more into *hard*ware than software, if you get my point ... though we now have more subtle ways of going in. We don't have to use the damn can-opener as much as we used to." He gives a quick nasal laugh, more snorting. "Plus, you kids are *way* ahead these days. Hell, we're teaching stuff to undergrads that I didn't get until my third year of med school ... if at all." He waves the tortoise-shell specs then puts them back on. He fingers his notched chin, the Kirk Douglas dimple.

"I gotta get going," the Baylor senior declares, slapping his thighs; he stretches to his feet. "I reckon you're too quick for me, Doc ... and I don't mean running the bases."

Amid more snickers and snuffles, the doctor escorts Bryan into the other room, the large tomography room, which is now empty, the technician having completed his work. "Oh, I forgot to ask ... my manuscript? Did you have a chance to read it?"

"You bet, two times almost. It's great, like right on target."

Richardson, his Nordic eyes twinkling, gives his disciple a pat on the arm. "Well, I'm sure you noticed that a lot of the things we talk about made it into the book."

THE SILVER CORD

Bryan gives an awh-shucks grin. "Yes sir, I did."

The professor gestures toward the tomography equipment, which could pass for something out of *Star Wars*. "I must say ... it's downright scary how my views are evolving, and you're the *main* reason." He gives his throaty *yeck-yeck,* a few repetitions. "That's why I'm taking you on as a graduate assistant ... so you can *rewrite* all my class notes." More laughing and chuckling.

* * *

ONE MONTH LATER

146 DOUGLAS STREET - GARAGE APARTMENT
SUNDAY, MAY 21, 1995 — 10:04 PM

Bryan, sipping a Dr. Pepper, watches the Texas Ranger baseball game on his 14-inch Sony, which sits atop a knee-high stack of yellowed computer print-outs. The most doggy part of his dogwork job is moving stuff from the low-tech, dot-matrix sheets to floppies and Bernoulli disks (library files), so he has reams and reams of the old print-outs. The small apartment remains much as it did when Chris lived here, with the same O'Shea furniture (moth-eaten sofa, wobbly kitchen table, folding chairs, metal-framed double bed). Chris took his computer desk, but Bryan scrounged up another from the Neurology Department, plus he hauled an easy chair and hassock up from the basement, with Annie's help. He's in the cushiony overstuffed piece now—it's quite comfortable but still smells of cellar dank which adds to the overall musty odor. Annie suggested he clean the chair, and sofa, with her Woolite carpet foam and then scrub the woodwork and floor with Murphy Household Cleaner. She also said he should paint the walls, after removing the ancient floral-print wallpaper. Time and grit have grayed the paper. She even offered to pay him eight bucks an hour, since it's her property. But it's hardly an urgent priority to Bryan. Maybe next winter? He has plenty to do *outside*, with the grass growing like crazy again. Besides, he figures he can live with the mustiness, just like Chris did.

The Yankees lead 6-1 after six, with Andy Petite on the mound. The lanky southpaw has shut down the Texas offense save for a solo home run by Pudge Rodriguez. A commercial comes on, Budweiser and the frogs. If Annie was home, he'd go have a chat—he enjoys confiding in her—but she's down at the American Legion hall playing bingo with her geriatric girlfriends, the usual Sunday-night routine. She even takes old-man Lipski along, though he can't hear the caller, so she has to play his cards. Bryan teases her about their aged, green-thumbed neighbor: "Hell no," she grouses, "we're just friends. I've known him forever, and Stephanie, 'fore she died, his wife. He's always been too old for *me* ... and now that deaf fart is *way* over the hill." She laughed and rolled her eyes. "I've still got a lot of playful chick in me, but if I came on to him, it might kill him for god's sake."

Bryan zaps off the power on the cable set-top box, returning the TV to antenna-mode; the ten o'clock news is playing on Channel 2, a wrap-up segment on the Oklahoma City bombing:

> The Ryder-truck blast in our heartland reveals the paranoid life of accused bomber Timothy McVeigh ... with a local angle. According to sources close to his defense team, McVeigh visited more than once the burned-out Branch Davidian property outside of Waco. He was grieved and enraged by the events that took place here two years ago. Like many anti-government extremists, he had an obsession with April 19, the day of the disastrous federal raid on David Koresh's compound, which may explain why the alleged bomber chose this date to bring down the Alfred P. Murrah Building, and....

Bryan gestures with the half-empty can of Dr. Pepper. *The Waco connection is interesting, but I've heard all this already. And they've shown that scene of McVeigh in his orange jailhouse duds a hundred times ... where he's coming out of some jail with an army of guards and officers all around.* Back to baseball: the score remains 6-1 in favor of the Yanks. He gives a weary murmur; the Rangers stink.

The Baylor senior graduated yesterday afternoon, a formal affair with green robes and mortarboards, the whole bit. It took place on Founder's Mall, where staging was set up along with a vast array of folding chairs, enough to seat the 1700 graduates plus an audience of ten thousand, give or take. Dr. Richardson sat on the stage with the other dignitaries. Bryan's parents came down for the day of course, and Annie attended the ceremony as well. In fact, she chauffeured his folks over to the campus in her Cherokee. Congressman Tom DeLay gave the address, a long-winded oration that included all the proper congrats and urgings and admonitions, plus he took opportunity to laud the ongoing Contract with America, the Newt Gingrich agenda that gave the Republicans the majority in the '94 mid-term elections.

Sitting in the steamy sunshine amid the sea of green and white mortarboards (green for guys, white for gals), Bryan quickly lost interest in DeLay's canned speech, which brought to mind Billy Ray Campbell's oft-repeated assessment of elected officials: "Money runs this goddam country. All the politicians are on the take; it's a *fuck*in' system of legalized bribery." And Dr. Richardson says much the same, though more discreetly, and it takes a few beers to get him going. Bryan agrees to a point, though as with the church, he hasn't given up entirely on the ideals he's learned since grade school. He's quite aware of the corruption and influence peddling—but he'll certainly take *this* country over any other. He's like his granddad, deeply patriotic but not blindly so. Gramps was a populist, a free-thinking farm-country skeptic who questioned authority, and yet he always got tears in his eyes when he saluted the flag on the Fourth of July.

The proceedings yesterday did not move his grandson in such a fashion however. Though proud of his magna-cum-laude record (3.93 GPA) and his Bachelor of Science degree (neuroscience), his reaction was lukewarm at best as he marched across the stage to receive his diploma, and he feels equally impassive about it today, partly because the degree seems anticlimactic after what he's been through, partly because he's staying here at Baylor for grad school, partly because the biggest challenge lies ahead, the mystery of the silver cord which may well prove impossible to solve—and MANDY'S NOT WITH HIM. Now that's the BIG reason for his blah emotional state.

And he's been in this semi funk since he got her letter last month. No daggers, no fiery hurt: he's not in agony, as when she left in '91, but he's weary of waiting, of trusting God, of holding onto his dreams. The perpetual sense of resignation has sapped him, dulled him, dampened his affections, rendering him torpid, like a cloudy day without rain. He's getting to the point where he'd rather *have* pain. At least, he'd know his heart was still alive and beating. He loves her; he wants her; he needs her—no change here—and yet he *knows* it more than he *feels* it. Letting go has saved his sanity, but over time it has also desensitized him.

His folks, conversely, were anything but torpid yesterday. They beamed and blushed, all gaga with parental pride. Before they left for Spindle, Bryan took them to the Bear's Paw for burgers and fries. Annie and Dr. Richardson came too. Henry and Ginny seemed quite taken with Annie despite her salty manner. They also enjoyed the professor, whom they met last fall when they came down for a football game. Bryan will be going home to the farm himself the first ten days of June, after he completes the various application procedures involved with his grad-school grant, which he hopes to have in time for summer session.

In the top of the eighth, Paul O'Neil goes deep, a two-run shot into the right-field stands which extends the lead to 8-1. "The Rangers are *pa*thetic," Bryan declares, after killing off his soda pop. "Jordan's right. They're not worth watching."

* * *

Twenty-four hours later, we find Bryan in the same chair, tuned to the same game, or so it seems. Except the Yankee lead is 7-2 in the seventh, and he's drinking an RC Cola instead of a Dr. Pepper. In the top of the eighth, Paul O'Neil homers again, another two-run shot. *Why am I watching this?* Bryan asks himself. *It's like déjà vu all over again, as*

THE SILVER CORD

Yogi Berra would say. I feel like Bill Murray in that movie GROUNDHOG DAY. Giving a sigh, he switches to the ten o'clock news. No Tim McVeigh, but he gets plenty of O.J. Simpson. *I've seen enough O.J. as well, but it's a change at least from last night. So I haven't lost my mind—not that it matters much, considering the rut I'm stuck in.* He takes a swig from the blue can. RC tastes sweeter than Coke, and it was almost as popular as Coke when he was kid, along with Pepsi and Dr. Pepper and Nehi Grape.

A tepid draft blows through the room, billowing then sucking back the window shade. He had the air conditioner on earlier, but it makes such a racket that he turned it off as soon as it got dark, opening the windows and door instead. He prefers fresh air, yet he needed the AC when he got back from softball this afternoon, since it was 95° out. (Practice started last week for the Wizards, and Doc Richardson is fervent about defending their campus title, much more than Bryan, considering his blah emotional state.)

After Norm Gossage gives the weather, more heat with thunderstorms midweek, Bryan surfs the channels looking for something better than the Ranger game, anything. He finds a movie on HBO, *Some Kind of Wonderful* starring Eric Stoltz and Mary Stuart Masterson, a teen romance where a tomboy rebel (Masterson) is nuts over an after-school mechanic (Stolz), who also happens to be her best buddy since third grade. But he's after a gorgeous, well-to-do chick (Lea Thompson), who has a hot-shit reputation plus snobbish friends. Bryan vaguely recalls this flick but decides to watch it anyway, since it's more than half over, and the rich girl is named Amanda, as the rocking soundtrack song "Amanda Jones" quickly reminds him.

The story moves predictably toward a happy ending, yet despite the simple (some would call it corny) plot—or perhaps because of it—the movie captures Bryan, and it's not the flashy Lea Thompson "Amanda," who gets him but the rebel tomboy. It's no longer Mary Stuart Masterson on the tube, but Mandy Stevens of old, *his* Amanda from Spindle High. Feisty Mandy, adorable Mandy—golden locks, cut-off jeans, slouchy saunter, cupid lips, witty quips: she's all there save for the light-hazel eyes which he sees as *blue* of course. And by the time love wins at the end, ushering the happy couple down the long avenue of life, Bryan is wiping tears from his eyes.

His heart breaking loose, he bails out of the easy chair and rushes outside, banging through the screen door, *skee-eeeek.* He runs into the backyard where an enormous moon commands the sky above the pecan trees. He snuffles; he wipes more tears; he feels love and hurt, and gladness and sadness—*all* at the same time, the vacuum of his soul inhaling new life. "Oh, Mandy!" he shouts, his arms outstretched toward the moon. "It's still there—the fire! I feel it! I feel it!" He weeps shamelessly, agonizingly, the hot tears streaking his face. His heart expands with such force that it almost knocks him down. He staggers; he chokes; he grabs his neck where a painful knot has rendered him breathless and silent. The storm finally abates. *O Jesus!* he gasps. *I'm weak all over, like I just threw up. It hurts ... but it's better than being blah and numb.* The night-breeze rustles the pecan leaves. The balmy air feels good on his face, stanching his tears.

The moon looks down upon him, as if about to speak, to give him counsel—and then it does: "What the hell, young man?" No, it's not the moon, but Annie O'Shea, her gruff old voice giving her away, as she waddles into the backyard. "Whaddeyuh doing? I heard yuh from the house ... hollering like a goddam coyote."

"I'm just keeping a promise I made once ... on the moon."

"With Mandy I reckon?" Annie replies, her tone softening.

"Yes, ma'am. It was four years ago ... right before she left."

She sidles up next to him, her own eyes glistening under that visor she wears. She pats him on the back. "Well, young man, after everything y'told me, I can't see the Lord closing here. He can't let this story end now ... not if he's worth a damn."

*   *   *

SIX WEEKS LATER

146 DOUGLAS STREET - GARAGE APARTMENT
SATURDAY, JULY 2, 1995 — 2:44 PM

While the AC drones noisily in the background, Bryan Howard sits at the rickety kitchen table trying to fathom a cutting-edge paper (journal article) by theoretical physicist Brian Greene, a work Dr. Knudsen calls the Rosette Stone of string theory. On Dr. Richardson's advice, Bryan is taking Knudsen's (Dr. Lars Knudsen) string-theory elective during the summer session, in addition to his other graduate-level courses. Dr. Edelstein, the math genius, also provides input to the course, having developed the algorithms necessary to solve many of the string-theory equations. Stymied by the myriad dead-ends in his quest for the silver cord, Bryan is now digging into the nature of matter itself (in class, on his own) in hopes of discovering evidence of the astral dimension hidden among the quarks and electrons and gravitons and photons. *This stuff is WAY out,* he sighs to himself between sips of Bud Light. *I could read this goshdang paper a hundred times ... and I'd still feel like a dunce.* Nonetheless, he returns to the beginning:

> Within superstring theory, musical metaphors take on a stunning reality, for the theory suggests that the microscopic landscape is suffused with tiny strings whose vibrational patterns orchestrate the evolution of the cosmos. Thus the winds of change gust through an aeolian universe. By contrast, the standard model views

the elementary constituents of the universe as points with no internal structure. Although every prediction about the microworld made by the standard model has been verified down to a billionth of a billionth of a meter, this model cannot be complete or final, because it excludes gravity. And attempts to incorporate gravity into its quantum-mechanical framework have failed due to the violent fluctuations in the spatial fabric that appear when delta-x is less than Planck length.

String theory offers a profound modification to our theoretical description of the ultramicroscopic properties of the universe—a modification that alters general relativity in just the right way to make it compatible with quantum mechanics. In string theory, the elementary ingredients of matter are not point particles but tiny filaments, much like infinitely thin rubber bands, vibrating to and fro. These strings are *more* fundamental than atoms or quarks or any particle. They are the "stuff" that *all* particles are made of—the observed properties of each elementary particle arising when its internal string undergoes a particular resonant vibrational pattern. SST promises a wonderful unifying frame-work, a single, all-inclusive, unified description of the universe: a theory of everything (T.O.E.). And yet, this has not panned out in reality, because of some major dimensional hurdles.

Bryan sheds his glasses. *So far so good.* Pushing up from the table, he heads for the bathroom. *I just hope I can make sense of the rest of it this time.* On his way back he grabs a bag of chips. After downing a few, he forges on—five minutes, ten minutes:

If the circular dimension were to grow, "inflating" Lineland into the Garden-hose universe, your life would change profoundly. Take your body, for example. As a Linebeing, anything between your eyes constitutes the interior of your body. Your eyes play the same role as skin for an ordinary human. Thus, "surgery" in Lineland takes place through the eyes. But let's imagine that Lineland has a secret, curled-up dimension which expands to an observable size. Now one Linebeing can view your body at an angle and thus see directly into its interior. Using this dimension, a doctor can operate on your body by reaching inside—no cutting at all.

"Gosh *damn*," Bryan fumes, shoving the manuscript across the table. He removes his glasses; he shakes his head. "This's where I got bogged down before. No way in *hell* can I understand this 'Lineland' shit. There has to be a *simpler* approach?"

Pushing to his feet, he paces back and forth. *I'm looking for something that can't be found. It CAN be experienced—by me anyway— but it leaves no trail in the material world.* The AC compressor kicks on, making the window and wall vibrate. It's the noisy vibration that bugs him, but it's a hundred degrees out. He extends the range of his pacing, going beyond the easy chair into the small bedroom, which opens on the courtyard. Pausing at the closed, glass-windowed door (no fresh air today), he gazes at the heat waves rising from the sunbaked patio. *It's naive to think I can solve this mystery. No one else has ever explained the human soul, or even proven that we have one. Still, I can counsel people, based on my actual experiences.* He sighs. *I just wish Mandy was with me. Life is getting SO lonely without her.*

He resumes pacing. Love and longing warm his bosom, a sweet yet painful melting, like the heat rising outside. *O Lord, I miss her SO,* he laments silently, gesturing upward toward the cobwebby ceiling light in the living room, a rarely used dishlike fixture which could pass for a flying saucer. *And she's gone for good, or she may as well be.* The yearning grows, becoming unbearable. His eyes go blurry with tears. Grabbing his Bible from the computer desk, his glasses from the rickety table, he collapses into the easy chair. He flips to Psalm 69:

> Save me, O God; for the waters are come in unto my
> soul. I sink in deep mire, where there is no standing....
> My throat is dried; mine eyes fail....

When the longing overwhelms him, Bryan goes to David's poetry for solace, a recourse he's employed since the Mandy-ache returned full force on that moonlit night back in May. He finds the psalms a saner and more soothing refuge than getting drunk, though he does drink some, mainly post-softball beer with Dr. Richardson, and here with Annie O'Shea. With Tracy and Chris gone, and now Steve Jordan, Bryan's two main friends are three times his age, and then some. He has many semi-friends and acquaintances (like Debbie Lincoln at the lab and Frank Gaylord, the red-haired baseballer who also stayed on at Baylor to do graduate work in the Neurology Department), but Annie and the professor are his only remaining soulmates—and King David of course, with whom he feels a unique kinship.

He goes next to Psalm 86. As he reads, the heartache softens, becoming more tender than agonizing. Then he backtracks to Psalm 30, where the ninth verse intrigues him, his thoughts shifting back to the silver cord: "What profit is there in my blood, when I go down to the pit?"

THE SILVER CORD

It's not so much the verse, but the ball-point scribbling next to it, a note left by his grandpa. This old, leather-bound KJV Bible, like the Chevy pickup, once belonged to Gramps, and he left notes in the margin, not a lot, just here and there. This one says: "Blood = life. No blood = death. See Lev. 17:11."

Gosh, I never noticed this before, Bryan says to himself, as he turns to Leviticus 17 where he finds the eleventh verse circled with the same pen: "For the life of the flesh is in the blood."

"It's the blood!" he yelps, springing to his feet. *No blood, no soul.* He paces. *And the tether can't sever, as long as the cardio-pulmonary processes are supplying blood to brain. It's not like I have the answer— no way. Nor do I see the Bible as a medical text, but this gives me a FRESH approach—thanks to Gramps.*

* * *

Three hours later: Bryan makes supper, two baloney sandwiches plus more potato chips, having decided to eat at home instead of going to the caf. As he pours a glass of milk, the phone rings.

"Hello," he says, picking up.

"I need yuh to come get me, you big jock," Mandy declares, her voice giddy and animated.

"Whaa uh ... whaa—what?" he stammers in disbelief, his pulse racing berserkly.

"I'm at the Amtrak station over in McGregor ... like twenty minutes down the interstate. I rode the train from Little Rock."

"But uh ... whadduh? I thought y'were in South America. I mean uh ... your calling?"

"Well, mister, it looks like I have a *higher* calling."

Joy unspeakable. He isn't sure what's going on, but he senses that it's VERY GOOD. "What higher calling?"

She giggles buoyantly. "Parenthood—I reckon I'm pregnant, and *you're* the daddy."

CHAPTER THIRTY-TWO

FOUR YEARS LATER

MAGNOLIA, TEXAS
WEDNESDAY, AUGUST 4, 1999 — 9:27 AM

After kissing Mandy and Amy, Dr. Bryan Howard exits the side door off the kitchen (off the pantry nook). The sultry, pine-scented morning cloaks his face like a steamy washcloth. He descends to the driveway, his wing-tips clopping on the plank stairway. Tossing his attaché case into the back seat of his Chevy Blazer, he grabs a rag (an old T-shirt) from under the front seat and wipes the dew off the windshield. They have a double garage, but Mandy's Mustang is in there plus a jillion other things. He notes a few pine fronds in the yard, another on the roof of the attached garage. The gray split-level (22 Sherwood Circle) sits well back from the street, nestled among the conifers. *Gosh, it's hard to believe we just had that big storm yesterday,* he remarks to himself, as he peels off his sport coat, a pale-blue lightweight item. *It's like a sauna out here, and the sun's so bright ... like the sky's on fire.* He lays the coat in the back atop the brief case; his tie is inside the case. His clinical psychologist post at Harvey Cushing calls for a coat and tie, but he waits to put them on.

As he gets behind the wheel, Amy pops out the front door of the house. "Daddy! Daddy!" she shrieks, charging down the walk as fast as her little legs can carry her. "I wanna 'nother kiss, and a hug." Bryan meets his wee daughter halfway, sweeping her up into his arms. He pecks her cherub cheeks, her blond locks, then he horse-nibbles her chin and neck. She giggles, her big blue eyes beaming happily. "Oh, Daddy, your beard *tick*les."

"She got away from me," Mandy laughs from the front stoop, her eyes sparking in like manner, the *same* blue eyes.

* * *

HOUSTON, TEXAS - HARVEY CUSHING MEDICAL CENTER
WEDNESDAY, AUGUST 4, 1999 — 10:04 AM

"Well, look who's here," Dr. Chris Hansen teases smirkily, as he pokes his head into Dr. Howard's cramped little office on the third floor of the Easley Wing (the new five-floor edifice housing the Department of Surgical Medicine). "You finally decided to come in this morning?" At thirty-five, Chris seems little changed from his Baylor days, aside from nascent crows-feet about his eyes, the same brown and lively, mischievous eyes. He was always older but acted younger, and impish, and that remains the case behind his starchy-white Harvey Cushing consulting coat.

"No, I'm not here *actually*," Bryan quips. "You're talking to my hologram, which I programmed from home."

They laugh then Chris sobers. "Alex wants you to see Mrs. Weinstein again ... Sarah. The new chemo isn't doing a damn thing. So it looks like we'll have to go in. He's looking at October, but it's her decision of course. And it's a bit hairy ... the procedure ... so she's quite anxious, needless to say."

Bryan gestures with his reading glasses (a smaller-framed, re-calibrated pair). "So when d'yuh want me to see her?"

"Right away—as soon as she gets back from the lab. Sorry for the short notice ... but I'll have Edyth buzz you." (Edyth Culligan, the frizzy-haired, waiting-room receptionist—she's the closest thing Bryan has to a secretary; ditto for Chris, who's still a resident.)

After Chris departs, Bryan sorts the distribution items he just picked up down the hall (memos, mail, therapy records, a couple of professional journals, drug-company brochures). Trashing the junk (he can't prescribe anyway, except through Chris), he shifts the rest to his in-box, though he does take a moment to note the September surgery schedule from Alex (Dr. Alexander Goodwin), plus there's a staff-meeting notice signed by Dr. Rishad, the big boss on the second floor—but it's actually from Barry Spigler, as Bryan well knows. He swivels to the right, to face the adjoining computer desk. *That dang Spigler is always looking for a forum.*

Dr. Howard checks his e-mail, all junk (the PC is a Dell; he keeps his trusty Macintosh at the house, in his home office). He clicks on the calendar: *Let's see, Clara Robinson at one, Hershel Billingsly at two, and then we have that damn Spigler meeting which will drag on forever, and then I have to make my rounds. I won't be home till seven, but the traffic should be light by then.*

On the wall above the computer, three diplomas give witness to his Baylor education, including his double MS and double Ph.D. (neuroscience plus clinical psychology), which he completed in a record thirty-six months. He's a Ph.D., not an MD, yet he's still "Dr. Howard," a title that took a little getting used to for a farm-boy from Spindle. Another certificate, from the Texas Board of Clinical Psychologists, declares his competency to practice. He passed the TBCP licensing exam in June, culminating his one-year internship under Dr. Sterling (Laura Sterling), his immediate mentor here at Harvey Cushing. Certification also gives him a big salary increase, enough to balance the family budget, finally. The hefty mortgage and Blazer payments had put them in the red.

Removing his glasses, Bryan rubs the bridge of his nose. *But tomorrow I don't have any appointments at all, just a ton of paperwork ... and I can do that at home.* Happy vibes warm his bosom, as he thinks of home, of Mandy and little Amy.

The phone warbles, a local light; he picks it up: "Yes?"

"Mrs. Weinstein is waiting in 4B," Edyth tells him.

Dr. Howard, after a quick visit to the latrine, knocks and enters room 4B (a counseling chamber that could pass for a small living room). "Mrs. *Wein*stein, so good to see you again."

"Good morning, Doctor." Seated on the sofa, she extends her wrinkled, thickly veined hand. He shakes it.

"Dr. Hansen asked me to—"

"I told you to call me *Sarah*," the 73-year-old widow scolds, her puckered face breaking into a smile; her dark eyes grin too. "I can't have a handsome young doctor addressing me *form*ally."

Bryan dimples. "Okay ... *Sarah* it is."

She nods her approval. "That's better, dear." Her voice has that ex-smoker roughness, while her coal-black hair, obviously dyed, gives her an aging-movie-star quality. Ditto for the thick mascara and rosy lipstick. But she's not a celebrity, nor is she wealthy. Her husband Benjamin was a watchmaker in Toledo. She moved to Texas after his death. Dr. Howard sits down in the easy chair, facing her. A chill wind blows through the room, and it's not the AC. Sarah's face goes long, her eyes damp and wide, a rueful faraway look. "I'm trying to be brave," she confides. "But I'm having a tough time. Dr. Goodwin showed me the latest X-rays ... and I talked with Dr. Hansen too."

"I think I can help yuh sort this out," he offers, amid pangs of compassion. "But first—d'yuh like doughnuts and coffee?"

"Coffee and bagels I like better ... and cream cheese. I *am* Jewish, remember?" She gives a restrained laugh.

"Bagels ... of course."

"Please, Doctor, don't order anything on my account. I'm not that hungry ... considering."

"I understand. But I don't mean here. Let's go down to the cafeteria for a coffee break, or whatever you want. It'll do you good, and me too, and it's easier to talk down there. This room is comfortable and all, but it's still a bit formal if you ask me."

* * *

Same Wednesday, 11:14 p. m. "Oh, babe, that blew me away," Mandy pants, her eyes dreamy with afterpleasure.

Bryan feels just as dreamy. "Ahhh ... gosh ... *me* too."

Her cheeks still pulsing, she gives a wifely smirk, then she pecks him on the chin. "We've done it a jillion times, but my cunny still tingles whenever y'come through the door, or even when I see yuh outside mowing the lawn. And it's better with the goshdang light on." More smooching, then she sighs. "It's like—well, I just love you ... I *love* you."

"I love you too, precious ... more than *ever*."

THE SILVER CORD

Her face goes pink on the pillow then pearl then pink again, ruddy-pink like a tropical sunset. She smiles. Propping his head on his hand, he touches her smile then fingers the tip of her sun-freckled nose. She giggles. He caresses her shoulder, her arm. She closes her eyes. Bathed by the glow of the bedside lamp, her sex-mussed locks look like spun gold as they spill upon her temple, her cheek. "Oh, babe, just hold me. Hold me." Bryan embraces his dear pretty lady, as she presses her naked body into his. She's enchantingly warm and alive, and fragrant from bubble bath. No fears, no pressure, no growing old, no death—no tomorrow even. No more *was*, or *maybe*, or *will be* or *what if*. They have escaped together into the eternal *IS*, into the everlasting *YES*.

* * *

Ten minutes later: Mandy stretches-yawns then gets out of the queen-sized, Ethan Allen bed. "Gotta check on Amy." She grabs her robe from the chair in the corner, giving an intimate titter. "Plus I gotta *pee* ... and clean myself up. That's the downside to the pill. I end up with all your goo." Bryan, still naked, dimples boyishly from the bed, his legs crossed, his hands clasped behind his head, his ropy penis drooping sideways upon his thigh.

I bet I could get him up again, she chuckles to herself, as she ties the sash of her robe (a tawny-beige lightweight thing). His hunky bod awes her as much as ever—even after sex.

After a few minutes in their bathroom (off the bedroom), she pads into the hallway, the carpet soft and silent under her bare feet. "You be quiet, Elmo," she whispers, as she hears a canine mewing behind her. "You'll *wake up* Amy." She pauses to pet their black-lab pup, who's hardly a puppy anymore—he's ten months old, and he's always johnny on the spot when it comes to getting attention. He has a comfortable, upscale, fifty-dollar dog-bed down in the rec room, but he sleeps at night in the living room, lest he miss anything, like Mandy going to check on Amy.

After a fit of licking and tail-wagging, Elmo retreats to the living room, while Mandy tiptoes into her daughter's dimly lit room—there's a plug-in night-light. The little girl sleeps on her stomach, her goldilocks pressed into the pillow, her arm around Pooh Bear. Mandy watches her sleep, a soulful gaze. *Dear God, please take care of little Amy forever. The world is such a cruel place, yet you've blessed us SO much. Please help me too. This IS the highest calling. It's the heart that counts, not what you do at church.* Stepping closer, Mandy pulls the summer blanket up a little, to better cover her daughter, then she gently kisses her on the head. As she does, she notes a darker, dampish area on the pillow near Amy's cherub mouth. *Gosh, she's so much like me—it's almost scary; she even drools like me.*

The young mom backs out of the room, pausing at the door. The blanket covering Amy rises then falls. *It's okay. She's okay.*

* * *

Bryan waits in the bed. He made a quick visit to the bathroom himself, donning his undies on the way. The AC fan kicks on, but the blue-papered bedroom remains comfortably warm, warm enough to keep the covers off. They adjust the thermostat at night, lest it get too cold in Amy's room.

"She's all right?" he asks, upon Mandy's return.

"She's fine, just fine. And she's funny too."

"How's that?"

Mandy laughs but no reply. Shedding her robe, she wiggles into her skimpy nightgown, a baby-doll item like the one she wore back in '91, on their first night together. But this one is pink. As she crawls back into the bed, she explains: "The way she cuddles Pooh. She has twenty stuffed animals, but she won't let go of that old teddy bear of *yours*. She claimed it when we went home to see your folks last month, and she's slept with it ever since." Mandy fluffs the pillow and settles onto her back.

Bryan dimples. "I reckon she has good instincts ... like me."

"Get outta here."

Turning onto his side, he lifts the pink nightie.

"Hey, mister, whaddeyuh doing? Y'ready for *ex*tra innings?"

"Not a bad thought ... but I was just looking at your stretch marks. They fascinate me." He traces with his finger one of the whitish bands of scar tissue. She squirms and laughs.

"That *tick*les ... and I sure don't see 'em as fascinating. Turn off the light. I'm still *fat* ... from carrying Amy. And it's been three years ... three and a half. I never got back to normal."

The light stays on. "C'mon, I love your bod just like it *is*."

She *has* kept a few extra pounds, just enough to make her midriff pillowy soft amid the stretch marks, but most moms would take her figure in a flash. She's a full-time mother and part-time teacher (at Hatfield Elementary), and yet she still plays softball (on the girl's Easley Wing team at the hospital), and basketball in the winter. Bryan has likewise maintained his physique, not quite NCAA fitness but close—he jogs often, and like Mandy plays softball, on Dr. Yau's team (Dr. Yau, the surgical residency director, drafted him as a ringer).

The tummy-talk dies out, then Mandy says, "It's hard to believe Amy's gonna be four this winter ... and we've been in this house more than a year. Where did it go ... the time? Plus, we spent three years in Annie's garage apartment."

He laughs. "Yeah, a lot has happened since you called me out of the blue ... from that Amtrak station in McGregor."

"That was wild ... not crazy-wild like '91, but it *was* a big goshdang change." She caresses his hand. "But I have no regrets, no regrets. And I'm proud of you ... about today."

THE SILVER CORD

"Today? About what?"

"Y'know, the session with that Jewish lady." She kisses him on the cheek. "It was right, honey. What you did was right. I'm sure God sees it that way ... at least, the God I believe in. And I'm glad y'told me ... even though that's against the rules too."

* * *

MAGNOLIA, TEXAS - 22 SHERWOOD
THURSDAY, AUGUST 5, 1999 — 1:22 PM

Mandy swigs her Dr. Pepper. Sitting at the kitchen table in her bikini, she smells like cocoa butter, from the sunscreen. She just came in from the deck. Amy was outside too, but she's now down in the rec room watching her Barney video. *I should do my nails,* Mandy tells herself, as she lifts her hands, the left one sporting the rings Bryan gave her back in '91. *They're getting crummy-looking.* She sips more soda. *School's starting soon. I reckon I won't be lazing around like this much more.* She chuckles. *But I did work my ass off this morning.* She laughs again, as she recalls Amy's eagerness to help with the vacuuming, and the little lass did okay, as long as Mandy pulled the Kenmore canister along.

Elmo clicks up from downstairs, a tennis ball in his mouth. "No, Elmo, I can't," Mandy tells the black lab, as she pats him on the head. "I just *came* in. It's too hot out. Y'shoulda come up before." Elmo, his tail swishing, whines around the well-chewed ball, his yellow-green eyes wide with yearning. She can't help but laugh. "Plus, I gotta take a shower." Killing off the Dr. Pepper, she pads out of the kitchen. Elmo follows. She goes into her bedroom. Elmo follows. Grabbing clean panties and bra, she heads into the bathroom; she closes the door but quickly opens it again. He's right there with the ball, his big soulful eyes gazing up at her. "Oh, my big *baby*," she gushes, as she drops to her knees and hugs the hound. "You *never* give up, d'yuh?" He wiggles excitedly, his tail thrashing. "Okay, but just ten throws ... from the deck." She knows full well it'll be thirty—at least.

* * *

CHARLOTTE BAYOU GOLF LINKS - DOTHAN, TEXAS
THURSDAY, AUGUST 5, 1999 — 2:35 PM

The sultry afternoon remains sunny, but the sky looms darker to the southeast, toward the Gulf. Taking a four-iron, Dr. Howard prepares to hit his second shot on the par-four tenth. Ankle-deep rough clutches his ball, a Titleist 3 sliced off the tee—no, it was more of a fade than a slice, a power fade, yet it did land *far* to the right. Pressure: he steps back. He actually nutted the drive, out-hitting Chris by ten yards, but the older Baylor alum found the fairway, as usual. Doc Richardson taught Bryan the basics back in Waco, and he can drive the ball 275+, but like most baseballers who play golf, his scattergun power is wildly unpredictable: he pushes, he slices, he hooks, he tops, he pulls, he fades, he draws, he smothers, he pops up. And when it comes to iron play, Chris destroys him, like right now: the mustached MD got on with his second, a tough feat on this 435-yard hole. He hit a three-iron, a high, perfectly struck shot that settled right in the middle of the large kidney-shaped green which sprawls just beyond the water hazard, a wide, dammed-up stream dappled with lily pads, and guarded on both sides by kudzu weeds.

Kuh-rip. Bryan loosens then fastens his golf glove, the Velcro flap. He adjusts his hat, his Baylor baseball cap. He rolls his neck like José Conseco. "Come *on*, slugger," Chris prods. "I'm turning to goddamn stone over here. Plus, there's a storm coming—and forget that fucking long-iron; you can't get on from here, not out of that cabbage. Just take a nine or a wedge, and lay up short of the bayou. You may be strong, but you're no *Tiger* Woods."

"Hold your damn horses. I may never break ninety, but I can still beat yuh on *this* hole ... if I play my cards right."

"Fat chance. *I'm* on in two." The flag flutters near the back of the green, a difficult pin, but Chris does have a birdie putt."

Bryan snorts then readdresses the ball. "I think I can hit it clean. It's sitting up a bit, like a hen's egg in a loose nest."

"Well, you should know, being a goddamn farmer—but I still say you should lay up."

Ignoring the advice, the Spindle native inhales then takes a slow backswing. *Swish! Thwack!* The Titleist shrinks to a sunny pinprick against the dark clouds. Clearing the water by ten yards, it lands well left of target but kicks right, scooting between the bunkers—it rolls onto the putting surface, closer, closer, *way* back, almost to the pin. Bryan yelps with delight, but not Chris: "You lucky psycho bastard. That shot was on a beeline for the trees, but instead, you get inside me with a goddamn gimme putt!"

"Luck had *nothing* to do with it," Bryan taunts, rejoining his partner in the golf cart. "Just be glad we don't play for money yet." They both laugh, as the puckish neurosurgeon guns the cart as fast as it will go—down the fairway, across a little bridge, then up the trail to the right of the green. (To be precise, Chris is a neurosurgeon-in-training; he's officially a doc but not a surgeon; he assists in the OR, working with Dr. Goodwin's team, but he still has three years to go on his residency.)

The storm catches them on the par-three 16th, a windblown downpour. Quickly putting out, they escape to a water-keg hut behind the 17th tee; it's floorless, so they're able to back the cart inside, with room to spare. Ragged thunder resounds overhead: a muted rumble. "What'd you get on that hole, slugger?" Chris asks, after toweling the rain off. He pulls the pencil from the scorecard holder. He smirks, his brown eyes full of teasing.

"You know *gosh*dang well what I made."

"Oh yeah ... an eight ... and I got a three."

"Don't rub it in, A-hole," Bryan laughs, as he dabs his neck and arms with his own towel. "I was *rush*ing to beat the rain."

"Let's see ... that fucking snowman puts you 22 over. But you can still break a hundred, even if you double-bogey the last two ... and who knows ... you might finish par-par?"

"Oh, whoopie do. I'm just killing the gosh-damn course."

"Well, you are—for a guy who's only been playing two years ... with one good eye. This's a *real* sport, remember? It's not an easy jock-thing like football or baseball. I'm sure Doc Richardson reminded you of that key fact back in Waco."

Bryan tosses his towel at his cocky pal. "Get *outta* here."

Chris studies the card, his tongue playing out the up-twisted corner of his Errol Flynn mouth. "Hell, I'm leaking oil myself. I'm *six* over after sixteen. I might not break eighty today."

Removing his cap, Bryan massages his perspiry hair. "Oh, my heart *bleeds*—but don't forget hole *ten* ... where I beat your ass." He rubs in the miracle four-iron, and the birdie putt, a firm five-footer which dropped dead center (it wasn't a gimme). And the dapper MD made a *five*, three-putting from twenty feet.

The banter diminishes, as does the thunder, but the rain continues; it drums loudly on the corrugated-fiberglass roof (which is greenish and translucent). Chris grabs a Hershey bar from the carry-cooler in the cart basket. Breaking it, he gives Bryan half. They munch for a while, then Chris poses a question, his voice clogged with chocolate: "What the hell did you tell Sarah Weinstein yesterday? I hate to bring up professional shit in a sacred place like this, but I'm feeling a little heat on my ass."

"From who?" Bryan replies.

Chris pushes his golf visor back. He smirks, his mustache canting one way then the other. "Spigler. He was pissing and moaning about it, but Alex was gone—he's teaching today, over at Loma Vista. And I got out of there before the bastard could corner me." He snickers. "When the shit hits the fan, I play golf." More snickering then Chris sobers. "But he was babbling something about irresponsible counseling. I doubt it's anything serious ... but I guess I should know what's going on."

Bryan's mood goes heavy; he looks down. He shuffles his golf shoes on the floorboard of the cart dislodging shreds of wet grass and mud from the soft-spiked Footjoys. He exhales noisily, a sputtering snuffle, yet he says nothing.

Wadding the Hershey wrappers into a ball, Chris throws it toward a trash basket in the back corner of the shed next to the water keg—it misses, rolling outside into a puddle. The structure has walls, but they don't reach all the way to the ground.

Bryan stares at the wad of paper, all white waxy and brown as it lies in the swath of rain water, a long puddle that collects the runoff from the pitched roof. The dirt-floored hut smells like a hillbilly root cellar: earthy and sweaty damp. Yet it's perfect to shelter a cart, maybe two if you squeeze. But on this murky, rainsoaked afternoon they have the course to themselves. The thunder (danger, instant death, run like hell!) has sent everyone else scurrying for the clubhouse, and yet the electrical side of this cloudburst was quite benign, just occasional peals of thunder, and most were distant, like dynamite going off in the next county. The rain is the problem, not the lightning.

Carts, no carts; lightning, no lightning; golf, no golf, break ninety, shoot 110—it matters little to Dr. Howard. He has more pressing concerns. He waits; the rain hums; the roof sheds: *drip, drip, drip*. The 17th fairway stretches grayly before them, the standing water and stormy gloom dulling the verdant hues. It's a B-plus public course but well manicured. The wind has subsided, but it still buffets the trees now and then, shaking the water from the needles and leaves. Pines, oaks, cottonwoods, magnolias: Houston has the same trees as Waco except the pines are huge and more numerous, and the warmish climate also supports palm trees, not the tall, skinny, coconut kind but smaller, fan-leafed palmettos which dot the course, especially around the clubhouse.

Chris sighs then digs: "Now, slugger, you didn't get into that near-death, soul-body shit with Sarah?"

"Well, sorta," Bryan equivocates, amid pangs of unease—he feels guilty yet offended.

"Oh shit, this sucks. Alex will cover and keep it low key, but I'm sure Spigler will tell Dr. Yau ... and Laura Sterling too."

"I reckon I did push the envelope, but she's facing a scary—"

"Is this the first—I mean, you haven't crossed this line with Hershel or Emily, or Hector Torres, or any of the in-patients?"

"Well, there was Candace Ledbetter last year. She had quite a story to tell, but I was a rookie intern, so I just listened mainly."

"I know about Ledbetter; she told me too. But you haven't confessed this near-death stuff yourself ... except with Sarah?"

"Nawh ... she's the only one. But it was the best therapy I could give her. She was hyper anxious, like on the verge of—"

Chris gestures with both hands, palms-up like a Pentecostal praying. "So what'd you tell her? You said sort of?"

Bryan blows out a surrendering sigh. "No, it wasn't *sorta*, or *part*ly. I told her *ever*'thing. The whole damn story ... about what happened to me back in '91 ... when I got nailed at home plate."

Chris shakes his head, his countenance going gloomy, like the sky, like the 17th fairway, a far cry from his usual chipper self. He rubs his thumb on his lower lip. "Oh ... shit."

"But what *else* could I do?" Bryan snorts, his mixed emotions veering toward indignation. "She was almost frantic?"

"Well, there's diazepam, and lots of other benzo-dope?"

"I can't *pre*scribe medication," the young psychologist huffs, being intentionally difficult.

"Get off it. You're evading the goddamn question."

They both know full well that Chris (or Alex) will prescribe whatever is necessary, including the popular benzodiazephines, but Bryan isn't keen on it. "Gosh damn, why get her hooked on Valium, when she has no history of irrational phobia or neurotic anxiety? She's simply spooked about the surgery ... with good reason. And my counsel deals directly with her biggest dread—the *fear* of death? We're not talking about a dadgum cyst y'can suck out in two minutes. She's got a tumor the size of a barn mouse." Bryan snorts; he slaps, *ka-whap*, the side of the cart. "And it's deep and tangled. We're talking full-scale craniotomy ... hours of delicate excision. She could die on the f-ing table."

"Christ al*mighty*," Chris reacts, sweeping the clammy air. "I know all that. I've been looking at her goddamn scans since last year. Alex can get it if anybody can. But she *could* expire on the table, like any fucking patient." He snatches a Titleist from the rack; he rolls the dimpled ball between his flattened palms. "But I like her chances. Now Hershel ... he's got more risk, even though we just have to drill a hole with him. That aneurysm is like a time bomb in his head. Sarah's situation isn't rosy, but—"

"But *what*?" Bryan barks, gesturing pointedly with his gloved hand. "She's facing death, and I'm supposed to shut up and spout the damn party-line, the smiley-face Valium spin. 'Oh, it's gonna be *just* fine. You have the *best* doctors, and the *best* hospital, and we've done this procedure *hundreds* of times. And we're gonna keep you on a sedative to relax your emotions. You must focus on your recovery, on the *good* years ahead'—*SHIT*, she may not *have* any good years left. Or any time at all." His face heating, he rips off the golf glove. "And even if Alex *does* get it all, who knows the prognosis? It may've spread already? Hell, the stakes have been sky-high ever since y'all went up her nose last winter. You knew it wasn't benign then. I'm not an f-ing MD, but any jackass Joe Blow knows what happens when the chemo stops working. It could be in her blood, her liver, her lymph nodes."

"Come on, slugger, you're getting out of your league here. We're always concerned about metastasis, but it's not happening ... at least, according to her latest bloodwork. Besides, we have good success containing this type of malignancy. These tumors are slow—we're not talking about goddamn breast cancer."

"Well, hallelujah. She should jump for joy, and me too. I gotta be all cheery and bright, and tell her it's gonna be all right. Fuck that!" Bryan whips the glove into the recessed goodie-nook in front of him.

"Why limit our counseling to some *happy-face* routine, when I can *really* help her? I have knowledge and—"

"Knowledge?"

"Yeah, knowledge. I've *seen* the other side, and that's what people need to hear about. And I'm not the *only* one. Elmo McKinney saw it too, and Dudley O'Shea, and Mrs. Ledbetter."

Chris tosses the Titleist into the air. "*So* ... we all hear these isolated Dr. Moody-ish stories, like I've said all along? But we're talking two fucking percent, if that? It's not convincing."

"Well, it's rare to get a patient who actually flatlines and comes back. And even if they do, they may not have the same experience I did ... or remember it. It's a gosh-damn mystery."

The mustached resident tosses and catches the ball a few more times then jams it back into the rack. "It's a mystery all right. And it makes for great viewing on the goddamn Sci-Fi Channel. But it's not sound medicine. It's pseudoscience. It's religion. It's not real life. You don't have evidence." He blows out air; he folds his arms. "Goddammit, slugger, I feel for her too, and I hope there *is* life after death—but there's a fucking big gulf between wishing and knowing. You're a clinical psychologist, not a pastor. If she wants assurance about Heaven, she should go to her rabbi. Your NDE story is unprovable, and way out of bounds." He sighs. "Hell, we've talked about this a hundred times, all the way back to that day when we watched that plane in the backyard ... when you first came over—but we're *outta* school now."

"I know, I know ... but what do we have to lose? What I went through can help her more than any half-assed, happy-spin psychobabble, or chemo or valium ... or church for that matter." His face fevered, Bryan springs out of the cart. He downs a cup of water from the yellow fifteen-gallon cask. He paces like Pastor Ron back home. "For God's sake, Chris, we're *ALL* facing death! This's the biggest issue anywhere. And when we ponder the mystery and finality, it leaves us desperate and weak-kneed. We *all* come into this world with a death sentence on our head, me and you too, everyone, everywhere. We're all hurtling toward the grave, and we're desperate for hope, for Heaven, for something to grab onto." Bryan circles the squat vehicle; he chops the air. "There's no evading it. You doctors can *ex*tend life, but in the end you *lose*. You lose every goshdang patient to the reaper. But I have something unique to give, and by golly, I should be able to give it!" Returning to his side of the cart, he plunks down on the cushioned seat. He pops his fist into his open hand. "And I'm supposed to bow down to gosh-damn Barry Spigler ... while Sarah lies awake at night, wondering and trembling?"

"Okay, okay, I'm sorry. I didn't mean to set you off. I guess I overreacted, because of the heat on my own ass." He gives a chuckling snort, a good sign. "You're right about the desperate death-sentence thing. And in a perfect world, your NDE stuff would be accepted as alternative therapy. If it was up to me, I'd say share it all"—he gestures expansively—"and let the patient take what she wants. But in the real world we can't, because of egomaniac cocksuckers like Barry Spigler." He smirks amid more chuckling. Bryan laughs too, the tension defusing between them.

The rain has slackened to a muggy drizzle. The shower has cooled things a bit, but that's not saying much in Houston where the temp rarely drops below 75° from May to September. When summer storms blow in off the Gulf, they just condense the heat into a steamy, sticky, ground-hugging miasma thick enough to launch a boat on. Coursing through this saunalike humidity, a gray squirrel scampers onto the 17th tee. He snatches up a soggy something, a morsel of cracker or candy, then perches on one of the blue, cube-shaped tee-markers, the treat held gingerly in his little hands. His bushy tail quivering, he eats quickly. As he does, he keeps his eye on the golfers in the shed, lest they make a move, or perhaps he's looking for more human food. But he's quickly gone, disappearing up a large pine, amid a series of grunts and chattering shrieks. The sense of nature's presence calms Bryan all the more. He stretches then sits back. He steeples his hands under his chin. "So how'd Spigler find out?" he asks.

"Well, Sarah talks a lot, needless to say—don't ever let her get you on the phone." Chris titters. "But anyway, she must've confided to one of the nurses, and they passed it on to Spigler, or it could've been one of the techies at tomography ... or Edyth even—she gossips with the other girls at the waiting-room desk. Or someone down in hematology? In any event, Spigler heard somehow, and then he must've talked to her directly. I'm not sure if she already knew him ... but they're both Jewish, so I'm sure she didn't hold back once she got his ear." Chris grimaces, but the expression seems more good-natured than disturbed.

"Yeah," Bryan says, tucking his hands under his thighs. "I reckon she told Spigler *every*thing."

"But I'm sure she wasn't complaining ... about you."

"No ... she seemed quite relieved when I was counseling her."

"Sarah likes to gab, but she does it with a childlike innocence, which is more than I can say for Spigler. He's always got his ears tuned for suspicious gossip ... or any kind of incriminating info. He's into the whole law-and-order thing."

"But *I'm* the one who counseled her ... not you?"

"No shit, Sherlock," the surgical resident wisecracks, as he grips the small steering wheel from underneath. "That's a goddamn irrefutable fact. But Barry the Great trawls with a big fucking net." Chris pulls on the wheel, flexing his arm muscles, his leanish biceps going taut inside the blue sleeves of his Houston Shell Open golf shirt. (He was in the gallery when Tiger Woods and the rest of the pros played at the Woodlands back in April.)

"That sucks. If he has a problem, he should tell Laura, and let her handle it?"

"True, true—that's how it works on paper: you're a goddamn shavetail assigned to neurosurgery, but you answer to Dr. Sterling, and she answers to Dr. Bernie Gilman, if he was ever here, and he answers to Dr. Fogg himself." Chris playfully distorts his Midwest monotone, going nasal and older, and very British. "Dr. Archibald *Fogg*, the renowned head psychiatrist at *Harvey* Cushing Medical Center." He laughs, a sardonic pause. He gestures toward himself, dropping the false voice: "And on my side of the house, I answer to Alex who reports to Dr. Rishad. But I also report to Dr. Yau, my surgical residency director. You play on his softball team?"

"Yeah, but he's never at the games—he travels a lot."

"Ahah, that's a key fact that tells us how things really work. In theory, Dr. Yau is responsible for all the residents, all six of us." Chris opens his arms above the steering wheel. "But he also lectures all over ... Dallas, LA, New York, New Orleans ... so he has to trust Alex to shepherd me, while Kathy Cantrall shepherds Michael Samsung, and Dr. Kim monitors Maureen Thomas, and Dr. Reynolds watches over Tanya Nishi, and so forth. Let's face it, it's not practical, the book way of running things—God, it's like everybody reports to everybody." Chris snickers. "Especially since all the higher-ups also teach. So in reality, it's Alex and me, and you and Laura, and because they have common sense, they give us room. Shit, I'm only four years younger than Alex, so he treats me more like a peer than a resident." Chris snickers again, impishly. "At least, when I'm acting my age. And Laura never rides hard on anyone. Plus, you're licensed now. So that leaves you and me, a very workable set-up, until goddamn Spigler sticks his ugly, bug-eyed mug into things." He contorts his face then vents a comic gust of disdain. "Hell, he may be Jewish but he looks Palestinian, like goddamn Yasser Arafat ... like he was born in a tuna-fish can." They share a hearty guffaw, which cheers them farther, as does the weather: the clouds are breaking.

"I reckon I get the picture," Bryan replies, after sobering.

"Spigler's a great politician and fund-raiser, which's amazing considering his ugly mug, or maybe not. But that's how he moved up the ranks—he's nil as a doctor. And now that he has a title, he's hyper-jealous of his turf, even though it's not really his turf. Dr. Rishad is in charge, not Spigler, yet Barry imposes himself into everything, whether it's his business or not. And he doesn't delegate; he comes in person ... to find and punish the guilty."

"Like when Sonya Abnecki mislabeled Emily's PET scans?"

"Exactly. He raised hell for two weeks, even though we had it straightened out in thirty minutes. He's like a cop on the beat ... always looking for crime." Chris gives a smirky sigh. "I'm sure I'll survive this—and you too. Spigler should butt out, and let Alex and Laura handle it, but he won't—until he gets his rocks off. Yet I can't see anything worse than getting a letter in our files. Besides, we can't let that homely bastard bring us down."

"He *is* ugly. I reckon he *could* pass for Arafat if he covered his head with one of those—"

"What the fuck!" Chris exclaims. "Why're we sitting here? The goddamn sun is out." Hazy splotches of blue overhead give witness to the breaking clouds, as do the shadows, and the steamy vapors rising from the 17th fairway, now sunny and green. "In fact, we got the whole fucking course to ourselves. To hell with Barry Spigler. To hell with rules and regs." Chris guns out of the shed, halting on the muddy cart-path to the right of the tee-box. "Fuck ... let's go thirty-six today. It's only four-thirty. I don't mind finishing in the goddamn dark."

"Well, we gotta finish *this* eighteen first?"

"Let's face it, slugger," Chris wisecracks, as he hops out—he slides his Callaway Big Bertha out of the bag. "Golf is my drug of choice. There's only *one* thing better."

"What's that?" Bryan asks, giving a knowing grin, as he fetches his own driver, a $29 Knight Titanium from Wal-Mart.

"Hot pussy. Speaking of which, did you see that new student-nurse up in the trauma center? God, what an ass." Chris whistles. "And I'm officially on the prowl, since Angie and I broke up."

"Gosh damn ... you'll still be single when you're forty?"

Chris tees up between the blue cubes. "That gives me *five* years." He waggles the huge clubhead, then he backs off, grinning sassily. "A guy needs variety, you know ... and girls do too."

Bryan blushes. "Cut the damn shit."

"Oh, forgive me. You're not looking anymore. But I can't say as I can blame you. And Mandy's a good cook too ... better than before."

"Just hit the *gosh*dang ball!"

* * *

MAGNOLIA, TEXAS - 22 SHERWOOD
FRIDAY, AUGUST 6, 1999 — 8:24 AM

Dr. Howard works in his home office (downstairs opposite the rec room). Mandy just left: she's taking her books and stuff over to Hatfield Elementary. Amy went with her. Before shutting down, Bryan checks his hospital e-mail. If there's news on the Spigler front, he'd like to get a fair warning. He tried to phone Chris but just got his voice mail. *I'll be damned*, he reacts, after bringing up the only non-junk message:

> Bryan ... hope you get this. I'm still down here in Peru,
> but I know you work at Harvey Cushing, and I dug up
> the hcmc@earthlink.net info, but I don't have the suffix.
> I've wanted to share something, man-to-man, since 1995

when Mandy went back to you. I just want you to know that I consider her to be YOUR wife, though she's stubbornly refused to get divorced from me. She sees your Louisiana marriage as the REAL one. And I agree, as far as gut-level truth goes. What she and I had was sweet, and I'll always be fond of her, but I discerned early on that her heart belonged to you. Looking back on it, I made an unwise decision. But that's how we learn on the road of life. In any case, I'm glad she's happy ... and you, and little Amy. At some point, the legal paperwork must be fixed, and I'm sure it will be in God's due season. "Man looks on the outward appearance, but the Lord looks on the heart." I make no claim to her. She's my sister in the Lord, but not my wife. I've been meaning to send this for some time, and I'm glad I finally did. Prayers and best wishes to all of you—Russ Snyder

Russell's got more heart than I gave him credit for, Bryan remarks to himself five minutes later, as he folds his jockish frame into the Chevy Blazer. *I always lumped him in with the overzealous types, like Marvin Latrobe.* Fiddling with the keys, he gives a snuffle. *And he's right about getting the paperwork fixed. She may wear my wedding ring, but it's confusing when she still has "Snyder" on her driver's license, plus the whole tax thing.*

Pulling down the visor he checks his hair, which he wears a trifle longer, though it would still pass muster if he were in the Army. *No way is Russ like Marvin. Yet it makes sense, and I shoulda realized it before.* He fires up the engine, and the AC—it's already stifling out. *I mean, if Mandy lived with the guy, he has to have a good heart. He's more like Pastor Ron back home ... or like old Pastor Heupal here in Magnolia—at Morning Star Baptist.* Bryan notices a problem with the windshield. Despite his pre-entry wiping, a triangle of dew remains in the corner on his side. Cranking down the window (he has crank-windows because of Amy), he grabs the T-shirt from under the seat and dabs away the moisture. He *could* keep the dark-green SUV in the garage, if he moves the lawnmower and the trash cans and the old Mustang tires, not to mention his golf clubs and softball equipment—it's *way* more convenient to park out here.

We haven't been to church for three weeks, he thinks on, as he backs out. *I reckon we should go more often, now that Amy's in Sunday school. Heupal's quite articulate from the pulpit, and he's not into fire and brimstone. Mandy says he was an engineer at Lockheed before he became a minister.* Bryan chuckles, as he commences his twenty-five-minute commute. *Course, the old codger would freak if I told him about my OBEs—no way. But why am I thinking about him anyhow? I gotta deal with Dr. Spigler today, or maybe he'll let it pass, the whole Sarah thing?*

Sherwood Circle, Stuart Drive, Hargrove Street, Mosby Creek Road, Jackson Road. Houston lies south of him, but he has to go more north than south to get to the Eastex Freeway (U.S. 59). New houses, old houses, meadows, piney woods, a small shopping center, a school, more woods, a rusty railroad crossing, high-tech enclaves. The suburban scenery repeats itself, as he negotiates the back roads between the sleepy hamlet of Magnolia and the McDonaldized town of Meadowhurst. As he nears the freeway, he encounters a sprawling moonscape of stores and parking lots: Staples, Home Depot, McDonald's, Burger King, Waffle House, Taco Bell, Blockbuster, KFC, Jiffy Lube, Meadowhurst Mini-mall, Super 8, Denny's, Pizza Hut, Safeway, Wal-Mart, Wendy's.

Red light: he eases to a halt. He ups the AC a notch. Heat waves wiggle up from the vast Wal-Mart lot on his left. He sighs. *This town SURE has a deceiving name.* No meadows in sight, just scores of boxy, glitzy, ground-hugging buildings amid oceans of asphalt, plus a jillion signs and poles and wires and light posts. A few cumulus drift by overhead, barely visible in the smog. The weather sucks, but Bryan gives little heed. He's thinking about Spigler, concluding, almost, that the ugly bastard will let this go.

8:47 a.m. He proceeds then takes a left on Tidwell. He whips under the freeway then veers onto the on-ramp. Mandy shops in Meadowhurst, and he gets his Blazer serviced here. Ditto for the Mustang. And they come here to eat out. Yet the place bugs him, the sterile, money-sucking, mind-numbing, auto-based sameness, the frenzied, land-gobbling, Potemkin-village conformity. It's like all the Meadowhursts in America: you can find anything but a *familiar* face. There *is* a residential district west of the highway, with homes and grass, and trees and dogs, and kids on bikes and skateboards, and if you go farther west you get to Hatfield where Mandy teaches. But you can't see any of that from this side of Meadowhurst, which has long since lost its identity, its intimacy. It's *no*where, it's *every*where. It could be Waco, or Mesquite, or Sulphur Springs even, or Kansas, or Kentucky, or California, *any* commercialized chain-store sprawl along *any* super highway.

He much prefers Spindle, with its dying yet unique character where there's a *real* downtown with a *real* main street, and local businesses. Despite his upward move in life, Dr. Howard remains a farmboy at heart. He likes Magnolia okay, though it too has lost much of it's old-Texas character, as cookie-cutter developments have turned it into a woodsy dormitory for commuters, while a Rite Aid pharmacy and a Blockbuster video store occupy most of the town common, leaving just a corner swath for the Civil War cannons and the statue of Colonel Jacob Riley on his horse (the colonel was a local plantation owner who gained fame in the War Between the States, as they still call it down here). The town was named for the tree, though pines far outnumber magnolias.

As Bryan cruises south on 59, amid heavy but fast-moving traffic, he wishes he was back in Hollis County driving his old pickup. He finally had to put the old truck out to pasture, literally: it's back on the farm (it burns oil like crazy but his dad and Billy Ray still use it to haul hay up from the fields, plus brush and firewood and such). The '98 Chevy Blazer S-10 is loaded, and it's comfortable on trips, even with Elmo, but the boxy SUV lacks character: no rattles, no hiss of the wind, no oily, gassy, horse-feed aromas, no memories of Gramps behind the wheel. It may be a Chevy, but Wallace Howard would've never been at home in this $28,000 vehicle. A tugging commences in his gut, a yearning for Gramps, for Buster, then comes a big tug for Millie— the old brown mare finally died on June 15th, some two months ago. He even feels for Snowball the cat, who died *last* year, at the age of twenty, which is over a hundred in human years.

But the nostalgic interlude quickly passes, as he rejects the idea that his Spindle days were better. He's happier NOW. He has Mandy and Amy, a beautiful home life, plus a satisfying career (save for Barry Spigler?). He even has a dog again, his first since Buster, and he and Elmo do a lot of ball chasing in the backyard, though the young lab seems most attached to Mandy.

The silver-cord mystery is yet unsolved, but he continues to read and ponder. He hopes someday to resume full-scale research, with emphasis on the cardio-pulmonary angle he pursued with Dr. Richardson during his thesis work at Baylor—they investigated the relationship between blood oxygen and brain function, finally focusing on the physical vitality of brain-dead patients in an effort to pin down the point where the chance of retrieval goes to zero (which IAW the silver-cord theory means that the soul, though still tethered, can only depart. They low-keyed the soul-talk of course.) As for his own astral life, he's had two OBEs (since the Easter, post-sex episode at the farm in '95), both in Waco—one in July '95, the second night after Mandy came home for good, the other a year later for no apparent reason.

He switches lanes to get around a school bus. Grabbing his cellphone, he tries Chris again, to no avail. The haze-shrouded Houston skyline looms ahead, the office towers shimmering in the sunshine. Exxon, Enron, Chevron, Citibank, Texaco, Merrill Lynch, NationsBank, Mobil, Halliburton, Schlumberger. Big oil is king here: energy wealth, banking wealth, as in Dallas, as in Denver. The state-of-the-art, squared-off skyscrapers dwarf the old Houston, and the old way of doing things in this booming gateway city, gateway to the American Southwest, and gateway to the world through its ship channel, not to mention William P. Hobby Airport, and the mega-huge Houston Intercontinental twenty miles north. The central business district commands, like a spider in its web, an extensive highway system: spokes, arteries, loops, elevated downtown sections. 59, I-10, I-45, I-610, 290, 288, 90—but the locals call them freeways: Eastex Freeway, Katy Freeway, North Freeway, Gulf Freeway, South Freeway, North Loop Freeway. There are exceptions: Hardy Toll Road, Beaumont Highway (U.S. 90), Sam Houston Parkway. The weird naming also applies to streams and rivers; they call them bayous: White Oak Bayou, Buffalo Bayou, Hunting Bayou, Charlotte Bayou (which runs through the golf course in Dothan).

The Harvey Cushing complex occupies a sixteen-acre campus northwest of center city, not far from the dumpy Amtrak depot. Bryan exits at I-10, jogging west, then he goes south on I-45, getting off on Memorial Drive from which he takes Butler to Washington then backtracks to the hospital. He parks in the reserved lot behind the new Easley Wing, which sports the same mirrorlike facade as the downtown office towers, whereas the older academic side of HCMC could pass for a smaller version of Fountain Mall (at Baylor). There's a fountain even, and spiffy lawns, and Southern-style columns on the med-school buildings.

Entering Easley through a private, code-operated, punch-number door, he ascends the stairs. There's an elevator, but he prefers the stairwell. The wing is named for John Whitcomb Easley, the famous Houston surgeon (1877-1951), who served under Dr. Harvey Cushing himself, both doctors accomplishing much as pioneers in the field of neurosurgery. Reaching the third floor, Bryan pulls open the steel fire-door and strides around the corner to the staff-distribution center where he finds a memo in his box: "Dr. Howard: Please report to my office ASAP."

What the hell? the young psychologist reacts, with muted emotion. *Chris was right. Spigler DIDN'T let go of it.*

*   *   *

9:16 a.m. Dr. Howard waits in a straight-backed chair facing the large mahogany desk (looks like mahogany). A shellacked block of wood blares the bigshot name, two lines, military-style: "Barry Eugene Spigler, MD. Deputy Director HCNP."

Gosh, this guy really IS into authority, Bryan observes to himself. *Nobody displays their name on their desk anymore.* He feels debased, like he's back at SHS waiting to be disciplined by Mr. Altom, the vice-principal, and that only happened once—because of an incident in Ms. Sparger's fifth-period study hall which met in the library, not the old gray-haired Mrs. Sparger, but her daughter-in-law, a foxy, twenty-something brunette who taught American Lit and supervised the study halls. Anyway, Spanky Arnold was whispering to the other jocks at the table, speculating lustfully about the hang-shape of Ms. Sparger's boobs. He couldn't help but cackle and blush—and *pass gas*, a loud, spluttering, horse-snort fart. This set off titters and guffaws, including Bryan, and drew a be-quiet warning from the sexy young teacher. But Spanky had the stage, and he wasn't about to give it up. For an encore, he produced a series of hand-under-armpit false-farts, jerking his elbow again and again like a rooster trying to fly with one wing. Needless to say, the whole table ended up in the office where they each received two days of morning detention, a nothing punishment. Bryan hopes for a similar outcome today. And yet the very idea of a 26-year-old licensed psychologist having to report like this already feels worse than high-school detention—it's insulting and humiliating.

"Dr. Spigler will be with you shortly," said the stoutly built, peasant-faced secretary, as she escorted the Baylor Ph.D. into the modestly large office—it's across from the staff-meeting room adjacent to Dr. Rishad's suite. The 2nd floor is primarily administration, and the neurosurgery honchos have staked out this far end of the floor, while Dr. Eric Seifter (chief of HCGSP) and his staff occupy the offices down the carpeted hallway. The General Surgery Program is larger, and Dr. Rishad answers, in theory, to Dr. Seifter, but in actuality they function like equals, with considerable admin and operational overlap as the two programs share the five-floor Easley Wing. Spigler's secretary looks like an "Olga," like a Russian collective-farm comrade from the Stalin era, but her real name is Karen, Karen Delleo. Bryan knows her from the staff meetings. She's married to some Italian guy, has to be. No way is she a "Delleo" by blood.

Commotion behind him, voices in the hall, but it's not Barry Spigler—he speaks with a tubalike Texas drawl, like Steve Jordan though deeper with an abrasive edge, and the doctor, of course, uses a more refined vocabulary than Jordan—in public anyway. Bryan crosses his legs, ankle on knee. He fidgets with the laces of his wing-tipped dress shoe. *Gosh, it's so clean and orderly in here. There's nothing on his desk but a pencil and a folder and that goshdang name-thing, and they're all lined up perfectly, like he measured with a ruler.* No piles of paper, no books, no mags, and no dust—the glass desktop gleams, as if they wipe it twice a day. Ditto for the computer table. And the office smells clean too, not the regular hospital clean, but more like Pine-Sol.

I sure don't see much sign of a warm heart around here. But he can't defrock me, though I reckon he could ask Dr. Fogg to hold a hearing about me, but he'll need Laura to sign off on that. Fogg did hold a hearing two years ago, but that was a sex scandal thing, according to Chris, and the guy is still practicing ... over in Beaumont. This's small by comparison—least I hope. Bryan has never talked with Barry Spigler, though the deputy director did shake his hand and give him a bassy "welcome to the team" when Bryan arrived in Houston last year.

Gosh, where is he? he frets, checking his watch. *I've got a session with Hector Torres at—*

Spigler appears abruptly, startling the Baylor grad. The burly surgeon enters through a side door next to the wash room, a door Bryan didn't realize was there. Knee-jerk reaction: he hops to his feet. "Keep your seat, Dr. Howard," Spigler commands curtly, without making eye contact. The deputy director, in a blue suit and crimson tie under his white physician coat, closes the main (hallway) door then sits down behind the desk. Slipping on his thick-framed reading spectacles, he opens the manila folder and scans the contents. Rheumy eyes, buggy eyes, pouchy cheeks, wide-bridged snout, huge fishy mouth, scruffy mustache and beard, greasy complexion dotted with blackheads—his face, in contrast to his natty clothes, cries for redemption, but even a skilled scalpel could do little to improve this hideous mug.

He DOES look like Arafat, Bryan can't help but conclude to himself. *All he needs is that towel thing on his head. He's only 53 according to Chris, but he looks 75. And yet, he IS married. And his wife's not bad-looking for her age. She was at the annual dinner back in March. She must see something good in him. Maybe he does have a heart ... down deep?*

Picking up the yellow pencil, Spigler scribbles something on one of the loose pages inside the folder. A Gorbachev blemish tops off his ugliness—the port-wine stain extends beyond his forehead into his thin, colorless hair. He's chubby for a doctor, and his hammy-fingered mitts seem ill-suited for surgery. He looks up briefly then returns to the paperwork. His eyes are especially repulsive, dark, bleary, and protruding, with dirty snotlike whites—they could pass for something coughed up by a TB patient. "Now, Dr. Howard," he says, "you came here with top-notch academic credentials plus a glowing recommendation from Dr. Richardson at Baylor ... Fred Richardson, a good friend and former colleague here at Harvey Cushing. And I must say, he evidently pulled some strings with Dr. Fogg to get you hired last year, since our program has been fully staffed with shrinks since '96. In my opinion we had too many *then*. Nonetheless, you *were* hired, and your intern reports from Dr. Sterling are A-plus across the board, and Dr. Goodwin speaks most highly of you as well." Except for shifty-eyed glances, Spigler speaks toward the open folder. "But after conversing with one of our patients, a Sarah Weinstein, I have some serious concerns about your counseling techniques. You know what I'm talking about?"

"Yes sir," Bryan replies humbly.

"Good. I won't have to elaborate. Besides, it's all here in the paperwork. You've crossed the line, Dr. Howard, and I have no choice but to place a letter of reprimand in your file." Still no eye contact, but Bryan feels relieved. "You'll get a copy from Dr. Sterling." The surgeon fiddles with the yellow pencil, popping it against his beefy palm.

"I understand, sir."

THE SILVER CORD

Spigler shakes the pencil at Bryan. "But let me *warn* you," he blusters, his voice going extra deep. "If you *ever* bring up that near-death nonsense again ... or any other whacko bullshit, I'll hang your goddamn psycho ass." He's warning Bryan, yet he addresses the pencil. "Do you understand me?"

"Yes sir," Bryan affirms, his sense of relief tempered by the intensity of this admonition.

Spigler hauls himself out of the chair and departs through the same door he entered. As he does, he issues a final order over his shoulder: "You may return to your duties, Dr. Howard."

* * *

A while later, Dr. Howard sits in his own office. No morning therapy—Hector Torres canceled at the last minute (he's a post-surgery patient). Bryan doesn't feel like counseling anyway. Besides, Hector (a construction worker who suffered a TBI last March; a front loader backed over him) is well on his way to physical and emotional recovery. That's why he had to cancel in fact—he has a meeting with his boss about going back to work.

Spigler IS a bastard, Bryan repeats to himself, again. *Doc Richardson was SURE right about that. But I DID get off the hook. Yet it still seems unfair, the way Spigler butts into our side of things. I mean, this's actually Laura's business—I wonder what she thinks about all this, and I haven't talked to Chris. I wonder if he's still getting heat on his ass.* Bryan chuckles, as he recalls their golf match yesterday.

The phone buzzes—speaking of the devil. "Well, I just saw goddamn Arafat," Chris quips.

"Yeah, me too."

"It was no big deal, actually," Chris explains. "He just gave me that duty, honor, fight-the-good-battle bullshit ... all that blah-blah, blaty-blah about how I'm responsible for my patients, even their psychotherapy. Then he kicked me out of his office—it didn't take two minutes."

"Yeah, same for me."

"And Alex said not to worry ... that Dr. Rishad doesn't give a shit about the whole shrink side of things." They share a laugh. "And Alex also says that Dr. Yau would never pursue such a matter. Besides, he's in Denver. But just between you and me, it's probably a good idea to cool it on the astral bullshit."

"No kidding," Bryan chortles.

"So, slugger, you want to hit the links later?"

"Get outta here. I *am* married you know? And we have softball tomorrow. Maybe Sunday?"

"Sunday sucks. It takes forever."

"Okay, Monday late ... maybe? Too bad I don't live next door to the course like you—oh, gotta go. I have another line flashing." He pushes the lit-up button: "Dr. Howard."

"Oh, Bryan, I'd like to see you if I could," Dr. Laura Sterling tells him, her matronly voice cordial and undemanding, a no-accent California voice—she hails from San Jose.

"Sure thing, Laura," he replies. She insists they relate on a first-name basis. "Y'want me to come to your office?"

"No, why don't we have coffee down in the caf." She titters. "On second thought, let's meet over at Friedman South, in the faculty dining room." She laughs again. "They have better doughnuts over there—to heck with counting calories."

Dang, she has the same counseling instincts as me, Bryan laughs as he hangs up. *But I wonder what she's gonna say.*

* * *

"It *is* rather bizarre," Laura Sterling responds, forking a bite of her honey-glazed doughnut. She uses a fork, Bryan his fingers. "But I still maintain"—she pauses to eat the bite, chewing then swallowing. "I maintain that what goes on in a patient-session is privileged information." Dr. Sterling just heard his side of the Sarah Weinstein story, the three-minute version.

"And most folks treat it that way," Bryan says, his voice thick with pastry. He wipes his fingers on his napkin, a cloth napkin no less. He adjusts his tie. They have real napkins and tablecloths in this restaurant-style dining facility, not to mention waiters and waitresses, and plush carpets, and soft lighting, and a tropical garden in one corner. Yet you pay a price, like twice as much compared to the main cafeteria. He swigs some de-caf.

Laura sips her own coffee. "Yes, most rational folks ... but not Barry Spigler."

"Yeah, I've noticed."

A dainty, middle-aged, owl-faced divorcee with brownish, gray-frosted hair and a Martha Stewart personality, Laura Sterling never goes negative. At least, he's never seen her gloomy or angry or bothered, though she does express an upbeat form of skepticism, mainly about the patriarchal nature of the Harvey Cushing leadership on the MD side. And she never uses slang, or even approaches foul language. She's pleasantly attractive for a fifty-something gal, though she's never had Martha Stewart's looks, mainly because of the beaky nose, but she surely has the M.S. style. Her bobbed hair is always groomed to perfection. Ditto for her make-up, and her conservative attire—she has on a gray suit and beige blouse, accented with a blue neck-scarf. And she wears contacts; she does have regular glasses, but rarely dons them in public. She's highly regarded as a shrink, having published several articles and one book regarding the various therapies involved in maintaining the emotional well-being of brain- and spine-surgery patients. Dr. Howard realizes that he's not seeing all of her. There has to be a downside, her divorce for example: Chris says that her ex, a midlevel exec at Enron, left her for a younger woman, and the divorce got rather messy in financial terms. Her upbeat facade doesn't allow the discussion of such matters, but Bryan's not complaining. With her as mentor, his one-year internship was a breeze, and she's still his mentor, his superior anyway.

"Besides, there was no complaint," Laura elaborates, her no-accent voice rising a decibel. "This whole issue did not come up because of a disgruntled patient. I talked with Sarah, and she has nothing but admirable comments concerning you."

"Yeah, she seemed quite content, relieved actually, when we talked on Wednesday." He dimples then chuckles. "And it was hardly a formal session. We talked over coffee in the caf, while she had bagels and cream cheese."

"You're learning *all* my tricks," Dr. Sterling kids, gesturing with another bite of doughnut.

"I wish Dr. Spigler would learn a few things from you."

"Most unlikely," she replies, after swallowing. "He's a narcissist, neurotically so." She dabs her prim mouth with the napkin. "He's got a textbook ego-problem."

"That's what Chris says too ... Dr. Hansen."

"Yes, Chris Hansen. He's quite gifted; he'll make a fine neurosurgeon. Goodness, he already is, according to Alex. But back to Spigler." She gestures with the blue coffee mug. "I've learned to *ignore* him. The main thing to remember is that he has authority *only* over the medical side of the neurosurgery program. In fact, he should've never called you in, or written a letter of reprimand. He should've referred all of this to me, but like I say, it's better to disregard him than to fight him. Let him rant ... but only Dr. Fogg can bring genuine disciplinary action, and that requires a hearing. Besides, I know Archie very well, and he feels the same as I do about the communication between a licensed psychologist and his patients. And any such matter would have to pass Dr. Gilman's desk, at least in theory, and he's still on sabbatical to the Mayo Clinic ... for who knows how long." She gives a matronly giggle along with an upward roll of her eyes. "Bernie Gilman is another story altogether. The fact that his career is still intact should give us all assurance." More titters. "Besides, when it comes to medical matters, Archie Fogg responds to Dr. Rishad only. He'd never jump, just because that egomaniac deputy was demanding action. And especially when it comes to you, Bryan. Your record is impeccable. You're head and shoulders above your junior-staff peers. I've been shepherding Diane and Sidney for a few years now, and they're A-plus psychologists, but you've got sensitivity plus instinct, things that can't be taught." She sips from the mug. "So I can assure you that nothing will come of this. Spigler's just spouting off."

"I figured as much ... but it's good to hear you say it."

She laughs. "As long as you don't *mur*der your patients, you're free to do what you want—or seduce them." More titters. "But seriously, we should be at liberty to venture into any subject, if we do it to relieve anxiety, or whatever. That's the whole idea of cognitive therapy ... to give counsel that consoles directly and boldly, as opposed to Freud and other passive long-term regimes. Not that I'm a total modernist, yet we must use ingenious and proactive approaches when it comes to alleviating emotional pain. Of course, bold creativity requires mutual trust, but I believe you have that with Sarah Weinstein."

"Yes, we do," he agrees, as he downs the last of his doughnut.

Dr. Sterling turns sideways a bit, shifting her legs under the table. Ditto for the conversation: "But do tell me more, off the record, about this near-death incident." Her big, light-brown, owlish eyes widen with curiosity.

Bryan gives a quick synopsis, a guarded rendition.

"It's unverifiable of course," she responds, "but fascinating nonetheless. And I don't like to dismiss anything as impossible, especially when I've heard similar accounts, even from patients in *this* hospital." She nods her head. "Have you had any other episodes? Other metaphysical experiences?"

"Yes, about twenty in all ... ever since I was a kid."

"Do you keep a journal?"

Bryan, his face heating, kills the last of his coffee. He dimples. "Well uh ... well—"

"I'm sorry," she says, giving a grin of her own, a disarming smile. "I don't mean to pry ... but I'm curious about such things." She laughs. "I may be fifty-four and fat (she's short and hippish, but hardly fat), yet I'm still eager to learn."

"Well, I have sort of a journal," he says, answering her question. "It goes back to '91 anyway, back to my freshman year at Baylor. I also tried to reconstruct some of the earlier stuff, from when I was a kid, but that part is sketchy and imprecise. It's all in a class-notebook thing ... in my desk at home. I've typed some of it into my computer, but the raw version is in the notebook."

"Sounds very intriguing. Have you shown it to anyone?"

"Just my wife, and Dr. Richardson back at Baylor ... and Chris Hansen saw part of it, plus a girl named Tracy, who used to work for Dr. Richardson."

Laura smirks. "Can I read it ... the raw version? I'd love to—off the record of course?"

"Sure ... I'll bring it in next week."

* * *

Same Friday, 9:22 p.m. Bryan works at his home-Macintosh, the long day having come full circle. He normally does his due-Monday patient evaluations over the weekend, but his parents are coming tomorrow.

THE SILVER CORD

In fact, Helen Stevens and Gretchen are riding down with the Howards, an all-in-the-family gathering which once seemed impossible. Gretchen and her mom are in Spindle, staying with Marge and Billy, while Charlie attends a three-week deliverance retreat up in Fayetteville—he's battling the bottle again. Bryan and Helen get along okay these days. Now past forty, well past, she's mellowed in her views, having accepted Mandy's life decisions, in much the same fashion as Russ Snyder. Gretchen will be starting her junior year at Newbury Christian Academy, and yet she remains very much a free spirit, and she's a jock like her older sister, starring on the NCA soccer team, despite her stocky physique.

The clicking keyboard echoes eerily in this large, mostly empty downstairs office. It could be a den, or a big bedroom (fourth bedroom), but Bryan uses it as a work chamber. The lower floor of their split-level house consists of two large rooms, which sandwich the laundry room and utility room. The rec room is slightly larger, but his office echoes more, and smells danker, more like a basement, since this end of the house is deeper into the ground; the property slopes upward in this direction, having been landscaped so the garage is flush with the downstairs. This space is paneled like the rec room, and has the same white, blue-speckled linoleum floor, but there's no furniture to speak of, just the computer desk (the same workstation he used back at Annie O'Shea's garage apartment), plus two bookshelves and a bunch of cardboard boxes (silver-cord research material for the most part).

Mandy picked out new furniture for the upstairs when they moved in fourteen months ago, pine, early-American pieces primarily, some Ethan Allen, while she put her old stuff in the rec room, mostly garage-sale items she acquired in Arkansas and stored at her mother's while she and Bryan were living in Waco. They watch TV in the rec room (a big wide-screen set), plus they have Bryan's old Sony in their bedroom, but the upstairs living room has no television—it's mainly used when guests are over, like when Chris comes for supper, or Lindsey and Philip Harrison, or when their parents visit, or Dr. Richardson—he's been down twice. As for the Harrisons, Mandy met Lindsey at Hatfield Elementary—she's a teacher too. She comes over occasionally, with her son Matthew, who's a year older than Amy, and Phil has been here a couple of times. Bryan and Mandy also go to the Harrisons' house in Groveton, but Bryan doesn't care much for Phil, a nerdy software wonk who works for NASA.

The AC fan kicks on, the muted whir joining the *peck-peck* of the Mac keyboard. It stays relatively cool down here anyhow, so Bryan keeps the duct vents closed halfway (low flow). As he prints out the first report, the telephone rings, and a moment later Mandy yells down the stairs: "It's for you, Bryan! That Sarah lady!"

"Hello," he says, picking up.

"Oh, *Doc*tor," Sarah Weinstein declares, inflecting her smoke-roughened voice. "I'm sorry I caused such a ruckus for you. I should've kept my big mouth shut."

"It's okay, Sarah. I think everything has smoothed out now."

"I never realized that Dr. Spigler would condemn you for it."

"I know ... but it's okay now."

"And he's Jewish like me, though neither of us are religious—but still, what you shared about your soul ascending through a tunnel all the way to Heaven was so good to hear. I'm not a devout Jew, like I say ... but I *do* believe in God, and the afterlife, and your story certainly reinforced my beliefs...." Sarah goes on for some time about the Jewish faith and the existence of the soul, and how she learned such things back in Queens, and then she talks about her husband's Uncle Matthias, who was a rabbi, then about her sister Ruth who lost a son, and on and on.

Bryan listens, half listens. *Gosh,* he thinks, *it's no wonder my counseling got spread around.*

She stops finally, having run out of breath.

"Well, thanks for calling," he says, getting ready to hang up.

But she has more: "There's one other thing, Dr. Howard."

"What's that?"

"Will you be there with me in October ... for the operation?"

"I uh ... well uh?"

"I'm not talking about the waiting room. I want you in the OR, where you can hold my hand."

CHAPTER THIRTY-THREE

TWO MONTHS LATER:

HCMC - EASLEY WING, 5TH FLOOR
THURSDAY, OCTOBER 28, 1999 — 2:03 PM

Dr. Bryan Howard removes his green OR-duds, tosses them into the hamper, then grabs his suit pants from the recessed wall-locker. After quickly donning his street clothes, he adjusts his tie in the mirror then runs a comb through his hair. As he exits the small locker room, he runs into Chris Hansen coming in. "Hey, slugger ... hell of a long day, huh? And it's only two o'clock."

"Gosh, I was looking for you," Bryan declares, retreating into the dressing area.

"Oh, I was with Alex in the family room. We were talking with Sarah's folks, mainly her daughter. He's still in there—so how you holding up, you goddamn shrink? I bet you haven't seen saws and drills like that since shop class in high school?"

"It was rather *grue*some ... but you guys seemed to handle everything okay?"

Chris pulls off his surgical cap. "At least, it turned out okay. But there were a few ticklish maneuvers, like when her BP plummeted. In fact, she might've flatlined a few seconds, till we got the adrenaline into her." Chris shakes his head. "There's always something. But barring complications, she's out of danger. Alex is goddamn quick on his feet, and he's a maestro with a scalpel, and the drill, and the saw, and all that micro shit we used to get at the tangles and minute residue. But we got it all."

"Well, you didn't do too badly yourself," Bryan chatters, patting his Baylor buddy on the back. "I'd say you're one hell of a surgeon, even if it isn't official for three more years."

Chris gives one of his rare blushes. "Get off it, you fucking jock. I know locker-room hype when I hear it."

* * *

"Just checking on yuh," Dr. Howard says to Mrs. Weinstein some two hours later. She's in the ICU on the fourth floor.

"I'm feeling okay, Doctor," she replies faintly—she grips his hand. "Thanks for being there." Bandages shroud her head like a tight ski hat, but they've removed the ventilator—she's breathing on her own, though she's still on oxygen, as evidenced by the nasal-canula tubes entering her nose.

"Well, I'd say you're doing *great*, considering that you just got here from recovery. But y'should sleep now."

He turns to leave, but she stops him: "Oh, Dr. Howard, I need to talk with you, but not here." She gives a little moan. "Some place private where...." Her voice trails off.

"Don't try to talk, Mrs. Weinstein."

"Don't call me *that*," she reacts, summoning the last of her stamina. "I'm *Sarah* to you."

He can't help but chuckle. "Sorry, Sarah ... but really, you hafta rest now. It's important."

"That's right," Charlene Comisky affirms, having returned to the cubicle. "You *must* rest." The forty-something ICU nurse turns a valve on one of the hanging i.v. pouches, adding a sedative to the flow of fluids, or so he surmises. Charlene, a lanky, long-necked, androgynous woman with nutmeg hair pulled tightly back, could pass for Ichabod Crane, especially with her half-lens spectacles and hatchet nose (she has Billy Ray's nose). Chris Hansen wisecracks about her, dyke jokes etc., yet he rates her number one among the ICU nurses. Bryan concurs.

As he exits Sarah's cubicle, he spots Barry Spigler, clipboard in hand, talking at the nurse's station with Rennie Couture, the shift manager. The sight of his stumpy white-coated corpulence, topped by that awful Arafat head, sets off a clawing sense of unease. Bryan, head down, circles around the other side of the oval-shaped command post. Spigler has said nothing to him since the August scolding, but the deputy director has given him a few condescending frowns, like yesterday at staff meeting.

The Baylor grad exits the ICU, pushing through the double doors into the long, brightly lit, beige-walled corridor. His wing tips clack like tapshoes on the grayish, hard-waxed tiles. It smells just as waxy-brilliant as it looks, chemically pure, sweetly clean, even more so than the rest of the floor, as the aroma of linoleum polish joins the pervasive iodine, hospital-smell, not to mention the flowers. There's a recessed wall-nook filled with viney plants and garden flowers, perhaps to conjure up a cheery mood before encountering the darker realities inside the ICU itself. Daisies, lilies, bluebonnets, whatever, occasionally roses—they change the set-up fairly often. But Bryan scarcely notices the current floral roster as he strides by. He just wants to put more distance between himself and Barry Spigler—but to no avail.

"Dr. Howard, hold it!" a tubalike voice blares from behind, catching Bryan, just as he reaches the reception-lounge doors. "I want to have a *word* with you!" The polished hallway, like the brassy throat of a real sousaphone, adds resonance and oomph to Spigler's abrasive drawl, driving home the command.

"Yes sir?" Bryan responds, his pulse drumming—he retreats to meet the deputy director.

"I have something for you," Spigler growls, extending his clip— NO! NO! It's *not* a clipboard. It's a speckled Pen-Tab composition book: BRYAN'S JOURNAL, the one he loaned to Laura Sterling back in August. Shock, no breath: Dr. Howard recoils, retreating against the side wall, but Spigler's in his face, as much as he can be with his five-seven doughboy physique. His froggy eyes shift rapidly from side to side. He shoves the journal into Bryan's rib cage. "You take this bullshit home and NEVER bring it back!" His breath reeks like rancid milk.

Bryan slides the hardback notebook under his arm. "But this's *per*sonal stuff. It's a private journal. How'd you get—"

"Save your wind, Doctor. I'll do the talking, not *you*!" More words blast forth from the tuba, but the young psychologist hears them as distorted echoes, a record playing on the wrong speed. Arafat. Yasser Spigler. Fishy mouth, anvil snout, greasy skin, anemic beard. But Bryan fears most his eyes, those ghastly eyes: rheumy, putrid, full of black light, frenetic, protruding, quivering, left, right, up, down, dark revulsion—a pair of stink bugs crawling in pus. He could pass for Lucifer, or at least a maniac. "I don't like you, Howard. I don't like shrinks in general. But you're a special *f-ing* case. And you shouldn't even *have* this job. Your position was created out of thin air, all because you're Fred Richardson's pet from goddam Baylor. We already have three psychobabblers, counting Dr. Sterling, which makes you a damn waste of money. Besides, there are enough weirdoes loose as it is—with the whole goddam Y2K hysteria. So I don't need any kooky stories from you. I'll not have this institution corrupted!"

* * *

Bryan, having escaped Spigler's wrath, recovers in his cubbyhole office. He tries to calm his emotions, a hot-faced mixture of fear and embarrassment, anxiety and indignation. *Gosh damn!* he exclaims silently, as he thumbs through the handwritten journal. *Spigler got this from Laura—but how? The guy is ruthless, and I'm number one on his shit list. It's humiliating. I spend half the day with REAL brain surgeons, life-and-death stuff, and then I get cornered and chewed out by that phony bastard. But why would Laura give—no, she wouldn't? She wouldn't. No way.*

Confirmation comes quickly, as his phone warbles—it's Dr. Sterling: "I'm so sorry, Bryan. I just got off the phone with Dr. Spigler. It was all I could do to keep my bleeping cool. He's a real winner ... needless to say." She exhales, a bothered sigh. "But it's my fault. I owe you a big apology. I had your journal with me at staff meeting yesterday, intending to give it to you, but Maureen sidetracked me, Maureen Thomas, and I ended up leaving it on the conference table. Karen must've found it and given it to Barry; she's a snitch anyhow. But we can't allow this to get us down. He's on my case as well, yet he's all smoke and no fire, like I've told you all along. Archie Fogg will never entertain his ranting accusations ... much less act on them."

THE SILVER CORD

"I sure hope not," Bryan replies, feeling somewhat reassured.

"Well, I'm in your corner all the way. After all, this was a personal record you entrusted to me—gosh, Bryan, I'm sorry I kept it so long. But I found it most profound. I'm still skeptical of course, but it's important to consider all the possibilities."

* * *

MAGNOLIA, TEXAS - 22 SHERWOOD
TUESDAY, NOVEMBER 2, 1999 — 12:44 PM

"Aren't yuh goin' to work today, Daddy," Amy asks, as Bryan comes up from his home office. Mandy is helping the little blond put on her jacket, a cute little windbreaker. It's not that cold out, maybe 65°, but in Houston anything below 72° calls for jackets.

"I *am* at work," he teases his daughter.

"No, you're *not*," she insists, slapping her denim-clad leg for emphasis, like she does. Mandy snickers. They all laugh. "I mean goin' to work at the hospital." She gestures upward with both hands, like Shirley Temple, suggesting distance, a faraway place.

"Guess I can't fool *you*," he declares, sweeping his daughter up into his arms. She shrieks excitedly, as he nibbles her neck.

Elmo, awakened by the commotion, clicks up from the rec room, his tail wagging.

"Well, we better get going," Mandy says, nodding her head, her ponytail bouncing (she still wears a ponytail and bangs, but no more softball hat except in the summer). "I hafta teach at one, and Amy has pre-kindergarten." She gives her husband a peck on the cheek. "So, y'don't hafta go in at all?"

"Nope ... I just have paperwork downstairs ... plus some phone calls, and then I'll be mowing the lawn."

"Good ... it *needs* it."

After Amy works her dad for a few more kisses, she and her mommy exit the pantry-nook door. But Mandy sticks her head back in; she purses her lips, crinkles her nose—her rabbity thing. She's never outgrown that most-adorable routine (adorable to Bryan anyway). "Honey, we're going shopping after school ... groceries plus Wal-Mart, so I won't be home till five-thirty or so. I'll grab a pizza for supper, or maybe swing by Burger King."

"Whopper Junior!" Amy chimes from the stairway. "*That's* what I want."

The girls clomp noisily down the steps to the driveway. Young Dr. Howard watches until they drive off in the blue '93 Mustang, his heart overflowing with love and thanksgiving.

* * *

1:28 p.m. Bryan, back at the Macintosh, drafts a report, his mind half working, half wandering. He's recovered from Dr. Spigler's Thursday-afternoon tongue lashing, thanks to Laura, and Chris, and Dr. Goodwin even, they all voiced their support—and Mandy of course, again and again. She detests Spigler, as much as Bryan does. *It's a good thing I don't answer to him,* he remarks to himself with the wandering half of his mind. He titters. *It's like Chris says: Rishad is GOD, and Spigler's just a wannabe in the wings, and he commands no one, except for Comrade Karen.*

He laughs again, as he closes the file on Hector Torres, who's fully recovered and back at work:

> During my entire association with Mr. Torres, he never exhibited neurotic symptoms (IAW DSM-III) beyond the normal pre-surgery unease, along with sporadic posttraumatic-stress symptoms resulting from the construction accident itself (he remained conscious at the scene despite severe head injuries: March 1999, see above). I counseled him before and after his second craniotomy (see above).

He doesn't use all his fingers when he types, as Mandy does—she took typing from Ms. Salinas back at Spindle High, but he taught himself (a fast forefinger-pecking routine) when he got his first Macintosh in September 1990, the first month of his senior year (oh what a year!). When he gets promoted in a few years, he'll have a secretary, someone like Nattie Brescoe, the light-skinned black gal who works for Dr. Sterling. But promotion will also bring additional admin responsibilities. No way will he be able to spend a day or two each week working at home, much less find time for silver-cord research. Maybe he should change his career, and get into college-level teaching, like back at Baylor. But he can't make long-range plans now; he's barely started at Harvey Cushing, and he has big-time expenses.

> As of my last contact with Mr. Torres (10-22-99), there was no sign of lingering PSD from the TBI. And the fact he's been working productively since August (same construction job, Downer Corp., see above) corroborates his upbeat attitude. Although he was distraught enough (April 1999) to accede to Dr. Goodwin's psychotherapy suggestion, to calm his pre-surgery fears, Mr. Torres had no history of neurosis, and he would've likely recovered in like manner with no counseling at all.

1:40 p.m. Bryan, leaning back in his desk-chair, stretches and yawns. *Gosh, I reckon I have two hours of paperwork for every hour of face-*

to-face, and most of it gets filed in some mammoth EMC cyber-storage unit, once I've signed off on the insurance claims. It's mostly CYA , but it could be a lot worse, if Laura required me to do it all downtown. So I can't complain. After another yawn, he adjusts his glasses then returns to his typing:

> Mr. Billingsly's bipolar disorder aggravated his pre-op phobia (Dr. Goodwin operated Sept. 23, 1999 to clip a cerebral aneurysm; see above), so we upped his lithium carbonate dosage (see above) to dampen the episodes of depression. Ditto for his post-op swings, where manic episodes dominated, and....

Minutes later, he copies the finished Hershel Billingsly report to the Zip disk, then he pushes up from the Macintosh workstation.

After taking a leak and grabbing a mug of ice cream from the kitchen (darkish Breyer's chocolate, his favorite), he clops back down to his home office, to his square-eyed Power Macintosh. He hears Elmo barking in the backyard, not a growly, hostile bark but a muted, more plaintive utterance, a plea for attention. *That hound must've heard me moving around,* Bryan chuckles to himself, as he works on his ice cream. *He doesn't miss a thing, or maybe it was old Mrs. Felt next door going out to her garden? She talks to him at the fence, and gives him fig newtons, so he's always tuned in her direction, not to mention her cat, though Felix is usually sacked out in the daytime.* After a few more barks, the dog goes quiet. *Nawh, I reckon it was me he heard.*

After Mandy and Amy departed, he put Elmo outside, because the young lab wouldn't let him work. Ball-in-mouth, he followed Bryan down to the computer desk, where he gazed eagerly at his master amid fits of canine whining and serious tail-wagging. No way could the Baylor Ph.D. attend to the weighty issues of human psychology, without dealing first with Elmo's ball-chasing mania.

Clomping and clicking, they raced up the stairs and charged outside. Elmo, in an orgasm of delight, practically flew off the deck, then he raced berserkly around the yard, two laps, finally dropping the old tennis ball at Bryan's feet. Dr. Howard, picking up the stinky, saliva-coated ball, playfully tried to trick his four-legged friend, faking left, double-pumping to the right, then he hid it behind him—all to no effect. Elmo *never* loses track of that gray sphere. No more tricks: Bryan tossed the ball toward the back fence. Elmo, in a mad dash, caught up to it before it stopped rolling, as he *always* does. Seconds later, he deposited it on the grass between Bryan's sneakers. He threw it again, this time more to the left where it bounced into the shade under the pine trees. Elmo, skidding among the roots and needles, scooped it up cleanly, as the ball caromed off one of the knotty trunks. He never makes a error, this dog—he's better than A-Rod, Alex Rodriguez.

Throw, fetch, throw, fetch, throw, fetch—the game continued for twenty rounds or so, then Bryan leashed the panting pooch to his run-line, which allows him to move about the backyard, or to visit his doghouse. Then, and only then, was the HC psychologist able to get to work.

Bryan takes more ice cream from the gray, wide-mouthed cup. He finds it easier to eat from a mug. He digs out some more, a large heaping bite; he sucks it slowly off the spoon, savoring the cold, chocolaty goodness, as if it's a drug, and it is—the caffeine anyway. He may drink neutered coffee, but he likes his chocolate rich and potent, whether it's Breyer's or Hershey bars or Oreos or Ring Dings, or his mother's devil's-food cake. Ditto for Mandy's Jell-O pudding. She makes pudding for Amy, the kind that bubbles to a slow boil, *blup-blup*, in the saucepan, but Bryan likes it just as much as his daughter, especially when they eat it warm, before it gets that film on the top. Yet his dad ranks number one when it comes to the ultimate chocolate experience. Henry Howard seldom cooks in the kitchen, but he's a master at making fudge the old-fashioned way. Bryan recalls licking the pan as a boy, while the big platter of fudge cooled and solidified.

Leaving a few bites, he sets the mug to the side. Re-energized, he shuffles through the stack of handwritten material on his left, looking for Emily Gray's paperwork. Finding it, he attacks the keyboard, typing as fast as his hunt-and-peck style allows. Thank goodness for the Word 6.0 spell-checker (he still uses old software, despite the new Microsoft stuff on the market):

> Emily Gray, a learning-disabled adolescent (17), suffers from dysthymic disorder deriving from social-phobic syndrome, her episodes of depression arising in connection with low self-esteem, feelings of inferiority, and extreme anxiety when faced with social situations that call for conversation—all of which is related to her inability to process language, especially when spoken rapidly. In Emily's case (unlike most of my patients), the etiology of her depression is organic in nature (see Dr. Goodwin's Sept. '99 diagnosis—attached), arising because of a benign tumor, which exerts undue pressure upon Broca's area of the left hemisphere. The objective of her scheduled surgery (Jan 00) is to excise the tumor, thereby relieving said pressure.
>
> The fact that she was able to process speech in a normal manner until five years ago (the evident onset of the neural pathology), along with the fact (established during psychotherapy) that she can carry on a one-to-one conversation, if the pace of the exchange is slowed, corroborates Dr. Goodwin's diagnosis, and gives promise of a full recovery. And her depressive neurosis

has already improved, as she now understands the source of the....

I'll never get all this done this afternoon, Bryan surmises to himself, as he pauses to kill off the melting dregs of ice cream. *Not if I'm gonna mow the lawn. I still have ten reports to go.*

But the burdened feeling quickly evaporates, as he turns his attention to the pictures beside the computer: a recent shot of Amy, plus the old one of Mandy. He lovingly studies his cherub-faced daughter, her blue eyes beaming under blond bangs, her valentine lips canted into a smirk, a slightly shy, slightly coy, I-like-attention smirk, a very female expression which makes her seem much older than three and a half (she's definitely got her mommy's genes). Bryan can't help but laugh. *I think she's got the woman-thing down already. It's no wonder, she showed off for the photographer at Sears, while the other pre-schoolers were hyper, or screaming.*

Moving from daughter to wife, he devours the old but still cherished photo-portrait of his dear pretty lady, the one she gave him at Magruder State Forest the summer before he left for Baylor, a picture that has been with him through all the travails and triumphs. He gathers her, and gathers her, his sweetheart, his lover, his life, his joy, his dream partner, his reason for making each day count. A warm swell crests in his bosom then breaks, bathing his heart, making him weak. He can't get enough—of the blue dress, the white daisy, her legs on the grass, her angelic gaze, her honey-gold hair, which she's passed on to their daughter.

The awe, the wonder, it's still there, the ache to love *more*, give *more*, feel *more*, to know and be known. Love, lust, tender allure, sheer X-rated need, a beast of desire that must devour itself again and again, like last night on the rec-room sofa, a spontaneous storm of Eros, with Mandy the aggressor, Mandy on top. They've made love *so* many times, and yet each session leaves something indelible in his memory. When he harks back to last night, he sees the hot blush in her face, the marble flush on her cheeks as she rode toward climax. The pink then burgundy pulsing sticks in his mind, as does the smell of coffee and bananas and womanly sweat, her perspiry pits. She was drinking coffee and eating banana-cream pie when the tempest broke. They often save their dessert until Amy's upstairs asleep.

Though a seasoned woman of twenty-five, Mandy still acts like a teenage kid sometimes, getting all coltish and rambunctious and picking pillow fights, and sticking out her tongue, and giving that goofy grin. And Amy's picking up the same routines. Bryan laughs some more. *Damn, I'm really daydreaming—I better get back to work.* But before he can, the phone rings. He grabs it.

"Hello, slugger," comes a refined Yankee voice—it's Dr. Richardson. "I was hoping I'd catch you at home."

"Well, this *is* a surprise. We haven't talked since August."

"I know. I've been meaning to check in. But I saw Chris on Sunday, at the club. He was up for the Halloween scramble." The professor gives his unique chuckle, his throaty *yeck-yeck*. "He and I played as a team, and we finished sixth, mainly because of Chris; he was stiffing every wedge he hit. It was *best* ball, but my ball wasn't the best very damn often." They share a quick guffaw. "We would've finished higher, but we both found the trees on sixteen—you know the goddamn hole. You're *dead* if you lose it to the right. But anyhow, it was fun, the whole thing."

"Yeah, he told me about it."

More crowish clucking. "Hell, slugger, you should come up and be my partner sometime ... now that you can stay on the same card with Chris."

"Get outta here, Doc. He still beats me twenty strokes."

"But you out-drive him I bet? You sure hit some monster drives when I was down there in June. Hell, I could never jack the ball like that, even when I was your age."

"Most of 'em were foul though, like so far off the fairway I needed a machete just to get near my ball, much less find it. And the last time I played with Chris I lost so many balls, I had to borrow a sleeve from him just to get back to the clubhouse."

More mutual titters, then Richardson quips, "Well, like I always say: golf is a *true* sport. It's not a big-jock thing like football or baseball, though I must admit we could've used your bat in our softball lineup this past summer. We got creamed. I think we won two games total. But that's old news—I told you that when you phoned me in August."

"Yeah, you did."

"It was my last season anyway. I'm retiring next May. I might even move back to New England."

Bryan, removing his reading glasses, squeaks back in his desk chair. "So you're actually gonna step down?"

"I expect so. I'm getting on in years you know?"

"Come on, you're barely seventy?"

"Try seventy-five."

"But you're *young* for your age. And you're not *required* to retire, not at Baylor?"

"No, I'm tenured, so I can stay forever or until I'm clinically demented, and some do ... but I don't care to be led around like Senator Strom Thurmond." More chuckles. "Besides, this place is driving me mad. Politics, money, busy work. I'm always straight out, but it's frustrating admin stuff. You wouldn't *be*lieve the paperwork. Damn, we paid a million dollars to Dell for all these computers and storage devices, and yet we're still doing stuff by hand, more in fact, not to mention the down time. To hell with actual academics, and meaningful research."

"Tell me about it. I'm doing reports now, patient reports."

"But at least you're at home."

Bryan laughs. "Just a fringe benefit for us junior staffers, thanks to Chris Hansen."

"Yes, he said you were home most Tuesdays, and sometimes Thursday—and those are great *golf*ing days."

"Bingo," Bryan replies, after they share a laugh. "But that's something Chris and I don't let on about ... especially if Barry Spigler's within earshot. The only good thing about Spigler is the fact that he's gone a lot himself, like most of this month—he's got a series of conferences back East. I think he left today."

"Yes, he's a champion lobbyist and publicity hound," the professor mocks, "especially when it comes to research money, or *any* kind of money. He kisses up to all the bureaucrats and drug-company insiders, plus the insurance pimps; it's whoredom on a vast scale, a mammon-crazed con game where the patient gets screwed. Prescription drugs and insurance premiums—it's goddam obscene ... whether it's Merck or Pfizer or Immunex, or Cigna or Aetna, or Oxford Health. They just want their stock price to go up. To hell with healing people." He gives a resigned laugh. "Forgive me, slugger—I'm a cynical old-timer."

"No biggie, Doc. I know what you're talking about, now that I'm out here in the *real* world. I see the money bullshit every day." Bryan leans forward; he fiddles with a pen, a Paper Mate roller-point, removing then replacing the cap. "But getting back to Barry Spigler, I reckon you heard about the journal incident?"

"A*hah* ... I was *waiting* for you to bring it up. That's the main reason I called. Chris told me, but I wanted to get your version of what happened."

* * *

4:53 p.m. Bryan chuckles, as he cuts the ankle-deep grass with his walk-behind mower, Elmo looking on from the safety of his doghouse. *Doc Richardson is SOME character. I can't believe he actually screwed Adele Trotman, after all this time talking about it. He's a Baylor bigshot, yet once you get to know him, he's more like Chris, or Spanky even.* Bryan laughs louder, a boyish ha-ha lost in the throaty growl of the Briggs & Stratton engine. Adele left Duane, opening the door for the professor, but now she's decided to go to Albuquerque to live with two girl friends, who've also discovered mid-life freedom. Richardson described it with his usual flair: "She's turning into a goddamn hippie."

Bryan mows around the side of the house, where a pile of firewood occupies much of the narrow space, the pickup load he bought last week; it's destined for the garage, the cluttered side. Their fireplace is more for looks than utility, like on Christmas last year, when they had a fire going despite the mild weather. Yet it does get cold enough, on occasion, to use it for real.

THE SILVER CORD

Returning to the backyard, he works around the boxy AC unit. He has to mow all year, unlike Mrs. Felt next door. She has a professionally maintained Bermuda lawn that turns brown in winter (usually by December). He has some Bermuda, but years of inattention have allowed an alien invasion to gain control (rye, fescue, ripgut, crabgrass, Johnson grass, sandburrs, plus clover and dandelions), and much of it grows year round. He cuts as close as he can to the Trane compressor, but it'll take the weed-whacker to trim the weeds hugging the concrete base. Ditto for the doghouse and the baby magnolia, and the creosoted posts which support the deck, and the steps need the whacker as well—a set of wooden stairs ascend to the deck from the yard (temporary toddler-fencing secures the deck, the gaps under the railing, for Amy, though she's hardly a toddler now).

The Adele news came at the end of his conversation with the doctor, after they had addressed the Barry Spigler matter: "Now, slugger, don't let that ugly, ass-kissing bastard intimidate you. He doesn't give a damn about your journal, not really. It's just an excuse to rant and bluster, and play god. He's good for nothing except politics and fund-raising, and he *knows* it. He preys on the blue-haired Princess Line crowd, hustling big bucks with guilt trips and sob stories. And if he gives you any more grief, Bryan, I'll come down there and *shoot* the fucker myself."

Finishing the lush grass around the back door, Dr. Howard pushes up the landscaped slope, attacking the southeast quadrant of the half-acre lot, a patchy, rather anemic expanse of lawn, anemic because of the pine trees: needles, cones, embedded roots, the conifer-effect on the soil, plus the excessive shade. In addition to an oak, a red ash, and a sapling magnolia, they have eight loblolly pines on the property, five of which guard this corner of the backyard. He descends the opposite side, having gone around the trees once. The whole I-fucked-Adele report reassured Bryan regarding the professor, even more than the Spigler stance: *I reckon I could tell Doc Richardson ANYTHING. Gosh damn, the guy's seventy-five. and he's still got SEX on his mind. It was like I was talking to Spanker. Wow, that makes me believe in God. It's an f-ing GREAT thing. But seriously, it IS like proof of eternal life, the spirit I see in the professor, or in Spanky—I mean, how could hearts that beautiful just cease to exist? I've got my own evidence of course, but even if I didn't, I'd be very much convinced, just from knowing THEM.*

He laps the unmowed rectangle of lawn, returning to the upslope leg. He halts to adjust his baseball cap, to hike up his jeans. Throwing his weight behind the mower, he pushes up the gentle rise. It's gentle but the heavy mower is a bitch to get up any incline. He bought the 5 hp, 21-inch, self-propelled, Scotts TurfMaster at T. F. Rawlings, the Trustworthy Hardware outlet here in Magnolia, but the drive belt slips, so it's more "push" than "self-propelled." He needs to tighten it, but it's low on his list. He doesn't mind *push*ing; it's good exercise, especially on dry autumn days like today, when a half-sleeve underjersey (he still has a few) is perfect for working outside. The pine-scented air has just enough chill to make the sweatband perspiration feel pleasantly cool as it haloes his head. And five p.m. seems much later now, since the clocks were moved back over the weekend.

The sun sinks in the west, a pink-orange fireball among the trees next door. Mrs. Felt has pine trees too, plus a swimming pool. Most of the neighbors have pools, but Bryan and Mandy don't care to have one, not with Amy running around, not to speak of the cost, and the ongoing service required to keep them clean, especially with all the needles and cones. *Gosh, I'm getting hungry,* he declares to himself, as he completes another lap. *I reckon I could eat three Whoppers tonight. I should hurry, so I can take a shower before they get home.*

* * *

5:46 p.m. Bryan, after showering, slips into fresh jeans plus a flannel shirt. His stomach growls. He pads barefoot into the kitchen, sneakers in hand plus a pair of white socks, his green baseball cap propped on the back of his head—as it is anytime he's not wearing a coat and tie. He still has that Gramps-like trait of feeling naked without a hat, though he wears the Baylor cap more often than the Spindle Tiger one, which now hangs floppily on a hook in the garage, having lost its shape.

He looks out the pantry-nook door (side door above the driveway): no sign of the Mustang. *They're late: she must be shopping her head off, maybe for Christmas? But we're barely passed Halloween.* He gives a husbandly laugh. *No way can I think about Christmas until the week before, but it's like women have an instinct to shop ahead. Or maybe she's getting new clothes for Amy? I just hope she doesn't max out our Cap One card.* Going over to the kitchen table, he plops down in one of the cane-seated chairs and puts on his socks and shoes.

I'm too hungry to wait. I need an appetizer. Grabbing a bag of Fritos plus a Dr. Pepper, he thumps down to the rec room where Elmo has crashed in his doggie bed. Upon finishing the lawn, Bryan unhooked the playful lab, and they chased each other around the yard, lap after lap, then they dodged in and out of the trees, running, yelping, jumping, until they were both panting for air. Elmo looks up sleepily, a one-eyed, hound-dog glance, then he resumes his nap. Dr. Howard sinks into the easy chair, a grayish wicker thing with pea-green, tie-on cushions; it's tacky but comfortable. Same goes for the two sofas: a tannish, fake-leather monstrosity plus a cushiony, well-faded, floral-print piece (that's the one he and Mandy made love on last night). She did buy a new LA-Z-BOY recliner during the summer, but after trying it down here, they moved it up to the living room.

Zapping the TV, he checks CNN: "Lou Dobbs Moneyline." The

THE SILVER CORD

Dow fell 67, closing at 10581, but the tech rally continued, the NASDAQ gaining 16, to reach a new all-time high of 2982, just 18 points shy of 3000. He watches with moderate attention, while he munches on the corn chips. He pays more attention to Wall Street since he and Mandy started investing in a mutual fund last year (Mass. Investors Growth), maybe four grand now—no it's up to six, as of the last statement. *We're making money,* he remarks to himself, as he swigs his soda pop, *way more than a savings account. I mean, our fund's up forty percent in a year—it's weighted toward high-tech. It's too bad we don't have ten thou to put in. Those techs are hot. Look at that ... EMC is up another three bucks today, and it just split two-for-one. Chris was sure right, what he said last year: "The NASDAQ's at 1500, and I predict it'll double in eighteen months."* Bryan, his mouth stuffed with Fritos, gives a muted laugh. *We could borrow off our credit cards— no, no, let's not get greedy here.*

More laughter around a loud burp, then he toasts the TV with the purplish Dr. Pepper can. *The market's hot, but I can only take so much of this corporate-news jabber, and the whole Russian financial recovery thing, for the umpteenth time—see yuh later, Lou.* Bryan whips over to The Weather Channel, where he gets Kristina Abernathy, the bright-eyed, platinum blonde with the softly sumptuous bod: "This low in Colorado will intensify and move northeast to Wisconsin by tomorrow night." She points at the map, showing the forecast trajectory of the early-November storm. "The Dakotas should get their first big snow of the season, up to a foot possibly. Same goes for the Arrowhead of Minnesota, but the Twin Cities should escape with a cold rain. The trailing cold front will set off thunderstorms over the Southern Plains tomorrow, as it collides with warm, moisture-laden air surging northward from the Gulf. This'll put an end to the pleasant autumn conditions, which have prevailed over the lower Mississippi Valley the past few days, and...."

She's quite fuckable, the Baylor grad observes, as he focuses on her hips and thighs, which deliciously fill her weather-gal skirt—she wears a stylish, lemon-colored suit. He shakes his head, a Spanky-like waggle. *She's on every night—I reckon that's how they hold the male viewers. It doesn't take long for a guy to get the weather. But picturing her in her panties, or less, can go on and on—shit, what am I thinking? I'm acting like goshdang Chris Hansen, when I'm happily married, and I'm having the GREATEST sex imaginable.* He chuckles. *But I reckon God designed the male psyche to zoom in on sexy chicks ... even if we have no intent to stray. It's like—well, you can't help but notice.* Kristina disappears, replaced by "Local on the 8's," the Houston forecast plus conditions. It's 63° downtown.

Firing the remote like a gun, he switches to "Headline News," the top-of-the-hour rehash, with Butch Roberts at the anchor desk. Snacking and sipping, Bryan watches with little reaction (yawn), as he gets the latest on Campaign 2000—Gore deals with a controversial advisor, while Bill Bradley goes after his party's heart with big-spending ideas, and Senator McCain continues his pitch for campaign-finance reform, while fending off critics of his own fundraising tactics. Then some Senator from Utah, not Orrin Hatch but the other guy, gives a frumpy sound bite concerning the Y2K computer meltdown, which is only sixty days away (yawn). Some folks are building survival shelters, but it seems way overhyped to Bryan. Next the health news (they always showcase some life-and-death medical stuff in the first five minutes): a report by Dr. Ian Smith plays down the risk of cellphones causing brain cancer (a neurological story, though it's old news to Dr. Howard—yawn). Next the White House beat: Hillary Clinton's brother, Hugh Rodham, reflects on his connections with the first family (double yawn). Then religion (they usually get God in before the first break), something about Jerry Falwell reaching out to gays and lesbians.

This stuff's more like gossip than news—he mutes the TV. He listens for the Mustang, for the garage-door opener, but he hears nothing save for the distant bleating of a freight train. He puts the sound back on—in time to hear about Indonesia: a blind Muslim cleric and a political princess have just taken office. *I reckon Suharto's departure is more important than the Hugh Rodham bullshit, but I can't see how it affects us* (yawn). A Barron's ad comes on, the fat guy floating in ultra-blue water: "The market goes up, you make money, the market goes down—"

He zaps over to ESPN for "Sports Center" where they're doing a baseball feature on the Yankee World Series dominance, then he goes to the Golf Channel and Bobby Jones himself, who's giving sand-shot lessons in a grainy, black-and-white 1930s film. Bryan laughs. *Gosh damn, the game was just as impossible sixty years ago.* Back to "Moneyline" then to the Weather Channel again, where the winter-weather guru, Dr. Kocin, gives his assessment of the developing storm in the lee of the Rockies. Bryan goes off cable to check WHOU— more local weather: meteorologist Larry Pierce elaborates about the mid-week return of hot weather to the Houston area. Warm is the norm, but it can get pretty cold here, when a norther blows all the way to Mexico, yet such outbreaks are rare, and snow is even rarer.

Eating, drinking, surfing, Bryan kills off another five minutes plus *all* the Fritos; he wads the bag and tosses it into the waste basket. *Damn, it's past six-thirty. Where the hell are they?* He feels a bit perturbed at Mandy's tardiness. *She shoulda phoned me, if they're running late. I mean, that's why she has a cellphone. I could call her, but I shouldn't hafta.*

* * *

6:41 p.m. Bryan finally calls, getting nothing, just her voice-mail recording. *They must be in Wal-Mart or Safeway, and she's not getting a signal, or maybe she left her phone in the car, or the beeper might be off?* He calls again, same result, but this time he leaves a message: "It's me, honey. I was just wondering where y'all are? No biggie, but it's *way* past five-thirty?"

Elmo, hearing Bryan's voice, hauls himself out of his bed. After licking his master's hand, he clicks over to the door, which leads to the garage. Sitting alertly, he gazes at the closed door. How can he sleep when Mandy and Amy are late? It's doubtful he understands English, but the lab's no fool. He knows the girls are not home, and he evidently realizes they're well overdue, from the tone of Bryan's voice, or maybe it's canine intuition. In any case, he *does* know that they normally enter the house from the garage, though he's quick to react if they fake him out and come in through the kitchen, or the front entrance (seldom happens).

6:52 p.m. Bryan douses the TV and goes up to the kitchen, Elmo following. Flipping on the light over the sink, he calls her again: still nothing. *This's getting weird*, he reacts, as irritation gives way to concern. *O Jesus, what's going on?* Elmo, again sitting alertly, gazes wide-eyed at the door off the pantry nook, waiting, yearning—he gives a canine mewl.

Grabbing a handful of Oreos from the leftmost cabinet above the counter, Dr. Howard washes them down with the last of his Dr. Pepper. As he does, he joins his faithful friend at the pantry-nook door. Pushing the curtain aside (blue cottage curtains adorn the top half of the windowed door), he checks out the driveway below. The Blazer, on the far side, looks more black than green in the thickening gloom. Despite an anxious downdraft in his gut, he turns on the outside light to welcome the girls.

He crushes the soda can then retreats to the kitchen proper where he tosses the waded aluminum into the trash under the sink. *Don't overreact,* he counsels himself, as he steps over to the back entrance, the pair of sliding doors which lead out onto the deck. *They just got super-involved with shopping, or maybe the checkout lines are impossible, or maybe they had car trouble, and her phone's on the blink, or it needs to be charged.* He slides the door open. Murky backyard, twilight sky. *Damn, it's night out there. She's almost an hour and a half late.* Elmo whines behind him, as if concurring with this worrisome assessment.

7:04 p.m. He calls again: voice mail, nothing. After a visit to the bathroom, he strides up and down the hallway, laps the living room twice, then circles through the dining room back to the kitchen where Elmo remains as before, watching the door. Bryan searches the driveway—nada. *I should call Lindsey Harrison. She may—no, no, not yet. Get a grip on yourself. You're acting like a caged neurotic. You're assuming the worst, while ruling out the benign explanations.*

He grabs more Oreos, this time washing them down with milk, a few swigs right from the jug, a guzzling method he forgoes when the girls are home: "Hey, you big jock, use a glass. You're not a Baylor bachelor anymore, in case you haven't noticed." Amy too: "*Dad*-dy, you're not sup-*pose* to drink outta dah jug." He'd love a wifely chide right now, but he hears nothing except the drone of the refrigerator which kicked on when he got the milk.

7:10 p.m. He calls Mandy again—nada. *Dear God, why won't she answer?* Commanding Elmo to "STAY," Bryan exits the side door, hustles down the stairs, then trots out to the street, as if his presence will hasten their arrival. No cars, no dog-walkers, no joggers, no breeze even—and no sound save for the whispery hiss of a descending plane, a jet on final to Houston Intercontinental. He inhales the coolish, pine-scented calm plus the sweet aroma of just-mowed grass, but the evening also exudes a foreign spiciness (like fallen leaves back in Spindle) mixed with the sulfury stink of auto smog; the fallish air mass has gone stale, as it awaits the south wind destined to replace it. No cars: Sherwood Circle is just that, so there's no thru-traffic, just the neighbors, and *everyone* is home, except for Mandy and Amy. Or so it seems to Dr. Howard. A shiver courses up his spine; he hugs himself; it may be 63° in Houston, but it's more like 53° out here in suburbia, yet the shiver is way more than a temperature thing.

The weather, the heavens, the stars winking overhead: this profound evidence of God's handiwork usually inspires childlike trust and awe, such as he felt as a boy back on the farm when he sat outside with Gramps in the evening. But Gramps seems a universe away, God even farther. Bryan feels alone and helpless amid a cold, uncaring cosmos—he's a tiny shred of expendable nothing, no more significant than a sand flea. *If they're stuck somewhere with a dead phone, she woulda used a pay phone? This isn't right.* Another shiver snakes through him, this one accompanied by a premonition, a sense of foreboding.

"O Lord," he prays, whispering skyward. "I got a bad feeling about this." He gestures in the same direction as his words, futile words. He prays on anyhow: *But God, it wouldn't make sense if something terrible happened. Not now? You've made everything work for good, even the years Mandy and I were apart—and you gave us Amy. Our dream is— O God, this sucks. Forgive me, but I can't find any faith right now. It's like I got formaldehyde in my veins. It's weird and cold, and getting scary.*

Headlights: a rattling vehicle trundles by, a pickup coming from the left, the west, the wrong direction. Scant reaction: it's merely Red Wheelock in his capped Ford-150 (which he uses in his sign-painting business). Dr. Howard gives a reflexive wave in the near-darkness; he chatted with Red once, while he (Bryan) was jogging around the circle. The Wheelocks live three houses beyond Mrs. Felt. The rattling truck offers no consolation. In fact, it leaves a stronger sense of foreboding, much like Bryan experienced during the I-35 tornado eight years ago. His thoughts flash back to that fateful October afternoon when he waited in Waco after Mandy ran away from home to be with him. That roller-coaster saga ended happily, very happily. *O Jesus, please bring them home soon,* he implores. *Please, please.*

He imagines the joyful relief, as they pull in the driveway, as they go laughing into the house, as they eat their hamburgers, as he and Mandy lie cozily in bed later, reflecting on this day—but the burgeoning sense of dread eats away at this scenario until it's gone from the screen of his mind. *She didn't have a cellphone back in '91. This is worse. She woulda called by now?*

* * *

7:24 p.m. Bryan, back in the kitchen with Elmo, calls his dear pretty lady again: ditto, ditto, zilch. His heart drumming, he digs in the corner drawer, coming out with her address book. He slips on his glasses then flips to Harrison. He keys the number into the cordless phone: *beep-bap-boop-beep—*

"No, Bryan, I have no idea," Lindsey responds to his inquiry. "She and Amy left the school around three-forty five. I talked with her in the daycare room, when she was picking up Amy."

7:30 p.m. He checks the driveway one last time, stepping around Elmo, who's still at the door, though he now crouches Sphinx-like on the floor. *Oh, dear Mandy. Oh, dear Amy.* The weight of their absence grows heavier and all-pervasive, as if Bryan is drowning in a thousand fathoms of water, a crushing urgency. His eyes filling, he punches 9-1-1 into the phone—but quickly kills the call. *No way, not yet.* He bolts out the door again. *I gotta look for myself first.* He hurtles down the steps, his sneakers scarcely touching the planks. He hops into the Blazer.

* * *

7:36 p.m. Dr. Howard, more hopeful now that he's moving, zips north on Mosby Creek Road, but he doesn't turn off on Jackson. He's going all the way to FR 6137, a roundabout but faster way to Meadowhurst, to Wal-Mart, etc., except during rush-hour. Using his trusty Nokia, he attempts to raise Mandy again, to no avail. Reaching the east-west farm road, he whips left, lurching, skidding, then accelerating. Twice daily, commuters choke this straight stretch of asphalt—it barely moves—but at night he has clear sailing westbound, and even the eastbound traffic (from the freeway) has diminished to a moderate flow. Pushing the SUV up to seventy-five, he makes it to the highway in five minutes then races south, getting off at the Meadowhurst exchange.

He takes a left on Tidwell. *Gosh, they could be anywhere. But I'll try Wal-Mart first.* Zooming under the highway, he hangs a right onto Jackson, then another right into the Wal-Mart lot. Cars, cars, a sea of cars—it's not like Friday night, but it will take a while nonetheless, to search the many rows. He figures he'll look for the Mustang rather than going inside. The sporty little Ford should be easy to spot among the pickups and minivans and SUVs, and Hondas and Toyotas, and Geos and Subarus and Escorts. But before beginning the hunt, he tries her cellphone, same result, then he calls the house to see if she got home—she didn't.

Working from the outside in, he guns up the nearest row, then down the next, braking hard halfway to avoid an old lady pushing an overfull cart. Up, down, up, down: no sign of the blue Mustang. He does spot a red one, but nothing in blue. *There's no sign of them,* he sighs to himself five minutes later, as he checks the last few rows of the superstore lot. *It's eight o'clock. They hafta be home by now?* Pulling into a parking space, he calls home, getting nothing but the answering machine, then he retries her cellphone: voice mail, same old thing.

I gotta check Safeway now. But he doesn't back out. He simply sits there, the engine running, hope draining away. He gives a pained murmur; his eyes go blurry. *What's the use? This's crazy. She'd never leave me hanging for three hours. Never.* It was invigorating, the high-speed driving to get here, and the idea of having a plan of action, but it didn't change shit, not really.

Can't wait any longer. I hafta call 9-1-1. I didn't notice any sign of an accident anywhere, but if she was okay, she woulda contacted me. Maybe there was a shooting, like that maniac at Luby's. O Jesus. Or the black guy on the Long Island Railroad, or some mugger car-jacker in one of these lots. Bryan grabs his cellphone, but before he can key in 9-1-1, it rings, chirping in his hand. *MANDY! O GOD! GOTTA BE HER! Thank you, Lord.* His heart leaps, rebounding so violently he fumbles the phone onto the other seat, but like a barn cat nailing a shrew, he pounces on the singing Nokia: "Hello."

IT'S NOT HER—but Chris Hansen.

That which I greatly feared, Bryan quotes to himself, his mind going numb, time screeching to a halt. Chris wouldn't be calling his cellphone at this hour, unless it was something BIG.

"There's been an accident involving Mandy and Amy," Dr. Hansen confirms, as time resumes. "They crashed into the woods up your way, but they're now here at the hospital." His somber un-Chris-like tone says more than his words. "I was doing my late-shift rounds when I heard about it. Amy's injuries are not life-threatening, but Mandy has suffered a TBI, and it's touch and go. She's up with the trauma team, Kathy Cantrall's team. That's all I know. Cindy Burns was going to notify you—she's the FR coordinator on duty tonight. But I told her I'd take care of it."

CHAPTER THIRTY-FOUR

HCMC - MILDRED WADE PEDIATRIC WING
TUESDAY, NOVEMBER 2, 1999 — 9:43 PM

"I wanted to drink my Coke, Daddy," Amy Howard explains from her kid-size hospital bed, her blue eyes big and innocent. "But when Mommy pulled it out of the Burger King bag, it spilled, and then we went off the road." Amy sweeps the air with her right arm—her left, in a cast up to the elbow, is restrained by a sling harness. "I was in the back seat, and we went *ZOOM* down the hill, and then there was a big *BANG*, and the car got *all* bent up and broken, and my head got cut, and my arm got broken, and I started crying, and then a man came, a policeman, and he pulled me out through the back window ... but Mommy was under that bag thing in the front seat, and she didn't talk at all."

"I know, honey," Bryan consoles, as he kisses his daughter on the forehead, to the left of the flesh-colored bandage. "But you hafta sleep now. It's way past your bedtime."

"But I *dough*wanna stay here. I wanna go *home* ... with you and Mommy."

Her little-child naiveté cuts to the quick. He fights to hold back, a little longer, the hurricane of hurt bottled in his bosom. "But, honey, we're not going home either. I'm gonna be here *all* night ... with you." Taking her hand, he leans close. "Mommy's hurt very bad. The doctors are working on her now."

Amy's Mandy-like eyes fill. "Is she gonna die now and go up to Heaven? Is she Daddy?"

"No, honey," he equivocates. "With God's help, she's gonna be *all* better. We just hafta pray and be patient, and be glad that she has a *very* good doctor." Sitting down in the bedside chair, he continues to hold her wee hand in his.

* * *

10:31 p.m. Bryan, still sniffing and snuffling, recovers in his Easley Wing office, having escaped here to cry and ponder. *It's weird? The airbag deployed, but it didn't help her?*

The storm of emotion finally broke as he was leaving Amy's hospital room shortly after ten. He stayed with her until she nodded off, and the pediatrics desk knows how to reach him. But now comes another hard thing: *Dear Jesus, help me get through this call.* Slipping on his glasses, he clicks the computer mouse, opening the family-info file to get the number.

"So tell me what you *do* know," Helen Stevens says a few minutes later, having collected herself after the initial shock.

"Well, according to Chris, Dr. Hansen, she suffered a violent blow to the left side of her head which fractured her skull ... and there's intracranial bleeding and swelling. She also has a fractured clavicle ... collarbone ... plus two broken ribs, but the *brain* injury is the critical issue of course. She's in surgery now ... on the fifth floor. It could take a long time, like half the night."

"So where did it happen ... the accident?"

"On Jackson Road ... near Sturbridge Systems ... maybe ten minutes from our house. I haven't been to the scene, or talked to the police, but that was the location on the paramedic report."

"Was she conscious after the accident?"

"Not when she was admitted; she may have been at some point, but I don't know *that*. The details are sketchy at best."

"So is Dr. Hansen her doctor?"

"No, no," Bryan replies, clicking the mouse to shut down his computer. "Dr. Cantrall, Kathryn Cantrall. I know her, and she's *good* ... and it's not just her, but a whole team."

"So how does Dr. Hansen fit into this?"

"Oh, he's my friend from Baylor, Chris Hansen. He's a resident still ... on Dr. Goodwin's team, the team I work with; I do their psychotherapy. But Chris was here making his rounds. So he called my cellphone, when he found out it was my family. I was out looking, needless to say, since they never came home."

"Oh, oh ... *Chris* Hansen. Yes, I think you mentioned him when I was down in August, or maybe Mandy said something about him before—so he notified you right away?"

"Not *right* away. The accident occurred about five-thirty, but the EMT crew took them initially to Westview Regional, the closest hospital ... then they were transferred here. And it was confusing when they first got here, since Mandy was admitted as Amanda Fay Snyder. That's the name on her driver's lic—"

"Oh my, that's *right*."

"She's also Snyder in the Blue Cross file, yet it's *my* policy, so they shoulda figured it out. Plus the Mustang's in my name, but during the heat of battle things fall through the cracks. Chris just happened to *spot* Amy, thank God—she was being moved into the pediatric wing, after her arm was put into a cast. He was over there with Jesse Walner, one of Dr. Goodwin's patients, a ten-year-old dirt-biker who smashed his head on the base of a utility tower; he's a lucky kid." Bryan swivels toward the window, toward the nighttime traffic on nearby I-45, the elevated freeway which loops around the west side of downtown Houston. "Sorry to get off track, but that's why Chris was over there."

"And he briefed you ... when you arrived at the hospital?"

"Yeah, he has access to the radiologists ... plus he's privy to other info I can't get myself. But still, he couldn't say much about Mandy's condition. That'll be Dr. Cantrall's job, after she's completed all the surgical procedures."

Helen snuffles, fighting back tears. "But *Amy's* okay?"

"Right—she'll be fine. Her left arm is fractured above the wrist, and she has a checkmark gash on her forehead, fourteen stitches ... plus numerous contusions ... bruises. Dr. McNeese, the pediatrician, says she may have a mild concussion as well, but nothing worse. He's doing more X rays and such tomorrow, to make sure. And then she'll be coming home Thursday."

"Thank God for that. She's such a precious little tike, all blond and full of energy ... the way she scampers around your house chasing Elmo the dog. Gosh, she reminds me so much of Amanda at that age." Silence, then sobs—they both break.

* * *

11:22 p.m. Bryan, still red-eyed and flushed, departs his office, headed back to the Wade Wing. He's desperate for news, but it could be hours before he can talk with Dr. Cantrall. So in the meantime he plans to stay with Amy. As he rounds the corner at the end of the hallway, he runs into Chris Hansen.

"I'm going home now," the mustached surgeon reports, his brown eyes brimming; he caresses Bryan on the shoulder. "But I'll be back at eight a.m., and you've got my number. I wish I had something concrete for you, but nobody's going to say shit till she's out of surgery, and even then, Kathy will be very cautious about making any prognosis."

"I know ... I know—but still ... I appreciate all you've done."

The two Baylor grads make eye contact, a brief, tear-blurred encounter, then Chris wraps his arms around Bryan. "We've been through a lot, slugger, and I'm a big-time wise-ass ... but I do love you ... and I sure hope there's a God up there, a God who cares."

* * *

HOUSTON INTERCONTINENTAL AIRPORT
WEDNESDAY, NOVEMBER 3, 1999 — 11:26 AM

"Gretchen begged to come along," Helen Stevens tells her son-in-law, as they drive out of the fumy-sweet HIA complex, sweet from jet exhaust. (Though not an in-law on paper, Bryan surely is in actuality.) "And Charlie wants to drive down Friday, him *and* Gretch, but I told 'em both to cool it, till we know more." Ascending a long ramp, they circle up onto the Eastex Freeway.

"That makes sense," Bryan replies, squinting against the midday sun, which is lower in the sky now that it's November. Even with sunglasses it takes a moment for his eyes to adjust.

"Besides, *I'm* between jobs right now. I quit Kroger's in Ft. Smith. The new manager—well, she's impossible. But I may get an AM position in Van Buren, assistant manager ... at Safeway, in January. I interviewed for it anyway." As they accelerate south, the kerosene-like airport-smell gives way to the scent of pine trees, loblolly pine, shortleaf pine, longleaf pine: the default aroma of the countryside throughout this part of Texas—and today it has a hint of Galveston in it.

"I reckon you'll get it," he responds matter-of-factly, despite the churning in his stomach, a sinking nauseated sensation that calls on him to vomit up his anguish, to break, to sob again, but he continues to suppress this need, as he's done all morning.

She fingerfluffs her brownish hair; she still wears it short, like always. She also wears the same perfume; he can smell it faintly, a rather exotic scent, like foreign or something, a scent that signaled her motherly presence in the house when he used to come over to visit in the old days on Colby Drive. "There's no point in them coming down," Helen sighs, picking her thumbnail. "I'll keep 'em posted over the phone. In fact, I hafta call Charlie when we get to your house."

"No problem."

"He's doing good, since he attended Pastor Morrison's RCA retreat ... this summer... Recovering Christian Alcoholics. He even got promoted to assistant maintenance chief at the Bible college, with his own desk and all."

Bryan nods but doesn't reply; any response about Charlie's sobriety would likely be negative—or a lie. He notches the AC back a bit; it was hot in here when they first climbed into the Blazer, but it's more comfortable now. Fair-weather clouds dapple the dingy sky: cottonball cumulus. Summerlike conditions have indeed returned to the region, the wind bearing upon its breath the salty, fishy, humid smell of the Gulf.

"What uh? Didyuh? I mean—" Helen starts to ask a question but stops. She gazes instead at the highway ahead, a silvery, sun-reflecting double-ribbon slicing like a long scar through the vast piney woods. Despite the developers, the forest remains.

"There could be a shower later today," he observes. "But I reckon the front won't get here till tomorrow, if at all."

She fiddles with her stubby bangs. Pulling down the sun visor, she checks them in the backside mirror. "It *is* a big change from Newbury. In fact, we had frost this morning. Charlie had to scrap the windshield before he drove me to the airport. It's a long drive, so we had to leave the house at seven-thirty." Giving a remote ha-ha, she pats the green windbreaker on her lap. "Looks like I won't need this right away."

Bryan gives an affirmative murmur but that's all.

Since she arrived from Little Rock on American Flight #433, they've skirted the grim truth that brought her here, exchanging little more than pleasantries and mundane comments. During the long night, most of which he spent cat-napping beside Amy's bed, he slipped into a sense of detachment, the dragons retreating into caves of denial. Before leaving for the airport, he stopped at the house to shower and feed Elmo. Everything seemed weirdly serene, as if Mandy and Amy were at Hatfield Elementary. He's a clinical psychologist, yet he can't control his own psyche, which has obviously devised a defense mechanism, something to shield him from reality, which at the moment is totally unacceptable. And Helen seems much the same, as the Chevy SUV cruises along amid the tall, sunny-green conifers.

Silence, save for the purr of the engine and occasional traffic noise, like the muted fast-lane whoosh of a Houston-bound limo, or the rumbling roar of a Ryder truck as the Blazer swings around it. The churning in Bryan's gut subsides to a dull gnawing. No more small-talk, and yet the hush in the car speaks much louder than the shallow babble about Charlie or Kroger's, or cold fronts, or frost up in the Ozarks. The hurt does seep out, in slight but revealing ways, a knowing glance from Helen, her gray-hazel eyes making brief contact with his, a knowing touch, as he gives her a bit later a pat to the arm, not to mention the occasional telltale sighs from both. Little safety-valve signals to relieve the pressure, to temper the unspeakable.

But he also feels amid the hurt a new, profoundly kindred, affection for this forty-something woman beside him, for this pixie-faced Baptist who gave birth to his dear pretty lady twenty-five years ago. And he senses similar vibes coming from her. They've been on congenial terms for some time, having long since let go of the animosity that divided them in the old days, the whole run-away-and-elope thing, the mother-daughter-lover, God-in-Heaven conflict, but now fate has hurled them into a foxhole kinship, knitting them in that unique, no-choice way that only a joint calamity can accomplish, as when they cried together on the phone last night. They share the same horror, dread, and desperate hope, a gut-level connection that transcends family status, with its labels and roles and little white lies.

She's a generation ahead, a life-seasoned matron, a grandma no less, not to speak of her faith. Though less overbearing in recent years, she's still a devout, self-possessed Christian who normally has the answers—yet on this muggy autumn day, she comes across as meek and vulnerable and dependent, a wounded soul in need of compassion and assurance. Dressed in sneakers and jeans under a white polo, she seems more like a peer than a parent, as she fiddles with the zipper on her jacket, a far cry from the zealous matriarch who once threatened his dreams. Compassion he has, though it's bottled up at the moment, but assurance he *cannot* give. He's on empty himself, and he doubts he'll have any such thing for a good long while.

Helen fishes inside her handbag, a big pouchy item with a drawstring. As she does, a peppermint aroma escapes (gum? Life Savers?), but she's after sunglasses he quickly realizes as she slips them on, a wire-rimmed jazzy pair, like you might see on a Harley chick, but no *way* on Helen Stevens. She may have the same conservative hair, but he's never seen these quirky glasses. They take ten years off her face, reinforcing the sister, peer, foxhole-buddy bond between them. She's always been young for her age, but in these shades, she could pass for a student nurse, a pretty one at that—as the dark-green, oval-shaped lenses accent her elfish features, especially her nubbish nose and dollface lips.

Bryan adjusts his Baylor hat. *This's weird,* he says to himself, as they zip by a green freeway sign: Houston 19 miles. *She's always been a take-charge, kick-ass mother, but all of a sudden we're on the same slippery slope, and she has no more footing than I do. And she seems way younger, like she's my little sister or something, especially with those mod-squad glasses.* He gives a whispery snort. *Gosh, she normally has lots of advice, even when she was down in August, but right now I reckon she has more questions than answers. And the same goes for—*

"So tell me, Bryan," she asks, interrupting yet confirming his thoughts, "didyuh see Amanda ... after the surgery?" She speaks straight ahead, as if addressing the highway.

Grief gathers in his throat at the mention of Mandy's name, yet he remains composed. "Yeah, I did ... a few times in fact."

"Is she unconscious?"

"Yes ... I'm afraid so."

"So she's got all those tubes and wires and all?" Helen inquires, gesturing about her face to indicate such hook-ups.

"Well, she's on life support."

"What does that involve?"

"Basically ... a respirator, plus oxygen, plus the i.v. fluids." The ache in his gullet recedes a little—it consoles him to finally be talking about this nightmare. He gestures over the dashboard. "I'm not a MD or an ICU therapist, but that's the key stuff I think, plus the urinary catheter."

"Whaddabout those computers and things ... with all kinds of buttons and knobs and lights and wires ... like they have on TV, like on 'ER'? And they hiss and beep and all?"

"Like I say, she's on a respirator—and it does hiss, and the heart monitor beeps, and she's also wired to a EEG, but—"

"You mean those electrode things they put on yuh ... plus greasy stuff that looks like vaseline. They did that to me when *I* was in the hospital, to get a graph of my heartbeat. That was years ago, when I was going through my rough time."

Bryan laughs, his first since they left the airport. "No, you're talking about an EKG, an electrocardiogram—that's for cardiac function, like the heart monitor. I said E-E-G. It's confusing, but it stands for electroencephalograph—it's used to monitor brain waves." A shiver courses through him, as he mentions brain activity. "It's important for anyone who's comatose."

"So she's *officially* in a coma?"

"Well, I reckon it's a matter of semantics. The word coma is actually an old 17th century term which is rather imprecise, but it connotes a long period of profound unconsciousness. And we're only into this— well, it's not even twenty-four hours yet."

"So she's never been conscious ... at all?"

"No, she was unresponsive at the scene, and ever since."

"So they thought she was dead?"

"Not quite—the paramedics noted a weak pulse at the scene, and her blood pressure was dangerously low, but the trace became stronger and more regular, once they got her on the respirator. Her heart has never stopped... or so it appears."

"Canyuh have a pulse ... and still stay in a coma forever?"

"Well, not forever ... but for years anyhow ... as long they keep yuh on life-support."

Helen paddlewheels her hands above the windbreaker. "So uh ... does that brain monitor, EE whatever, give us any hope. Is she gonna wake up? I mean uh—what are the odds?"

"It's too early to say, but the early signs are mixed at best."

Helen hugs herself, blowing out a silent whistle. "Well, what does her *doctor* say? Dr. Cantrall ... the lady surgeon?"

Bryan's busy exiting the freeway. After turning left (east) on FR 6137 he replies, "I talked with her early this morning, and she says that Mandy's neural function is marginal, and sporadic ... based on her post-surgery EEG and the neuroimagery results. That's not good, but it's not the worst-case scenario either. Dr. Cantrall says things can still go either way ... that she'll have a better handle on things in a few days." Shaking his head, he blows out a silent whistle of his own. "I'm praying that things *will* go our way ... and yet to be honest: I have a bad feeling about it."

"Why is that?"

"Well, it's quite curious, this whole thing ... I mean the nature of Mandy's injury."

"How so?"

"Remember when I got hurt in high school, and they had to medevac me to Dallas?"

"Yes, of course. You got hit by a baseball. I wasn't there, but I know all about it."

A herd of grazing Herefords pans by on the left, the forest having given way to farms and pastures. "Well ironically, her TBI is very similar to mine, even originating on the same side of the head." He pats the scar above his cheekbone. "Except in her case the blow impacted the skull about two inches higher." He fingers the side of his baseball cap to indicate. "But the result was the same, a compound skull fracture leading to intracranial—"

"Wait a minute. How'd she hit her head so hard, if the car has seatbelts and airbags? I wondered about that on the plane."

"Me too—it struck me as weird ... but after looking at the EMT report, and talking with the police in Meadowhurst, I think I have a better idea of what happened. It seems likely that her head struck the left doorpost." He points to the post on his door. "The Mustang skidded sideways into the forest ... and it hit a large pine which crushed the driver's-side door. Amy escaped the worst, since she was restrained in the back seat, but the collision hurled Mandy laterally, and her head whipped violently into the post. The airbag did deploy, but her momentum was sideways. She needed a sidebag, an airbag in the door, but few cars have 'em. Same goes for the belts. They woulda helped if the tree had hit the right side, but not the driver's side. We can swing by the scene if you like. It's on Jackson Road."

"No, no ... that's all right. I've got enough on my plate."

"I figured as much. That's why I got off on this farm road. To get on Jackson, you hafta get off at Meadowhurst. Plus, I went by the scene on my way to the airport, and there wasn't much to see, except ruts in the grass and scrape marks on the tree they hit. The Mustang's at Reynold's Salvage in Groveton, but I had no desire to go look at it—no way."

"Me neither. In fact, I don't *ever* want to see it."

"The police said Mandy almost hit a UPS truck—they got a statement from the driver. He says she drifted into his lane, then swerved back and lost control."

"She spilled a Coke ... y'said on the phone?"

"She was trying to hand it to Amy, as best I can gather. It had to be something weird. I mean, she's a super-good driver? But that's what Amy says ... anyhow."

Helen sighs then grabs her purse from the floor. Digging out a blue roll of Life Savers, she extends it toward him, peppermint. He declines, so she pops one of the white candies into her mouth. Crossing her legs, ankle on knee, she shifts to face her son-in-law, obliquely. "What were you telling me before ... when I got you off track? About her injury? Cranial whatever?"

"Oh, how it's ironic that her TBI is so much like mine back in '91—skull fracture and ruptured vessel leading to intracranial hemorrhaging and herniation through the tentorial—"

"You *lost* me, Dr. Howard. Y'may not be an MD, but you're way over *my* head. I'm just a high-school grad remember, G.E.D. in fact." She gives a double snort, a near chuckle. "I did get a few college credits later, word-processing plus two business courses, but I'm a dunce in science. So you're losing me big-time."

"Sorry, Helen," he responds, calling her by name for the first time since she got off the plane (he started calling her "Helen" a few years ago, though he rarely addresses her at all).

THE SILVER CORD

She grins under her jazzy shades. "I reckon we're really breaking the ice, huh?" She titters, a henlike utterance.

He dimples. "I reckon so." More titters, from both. They face a life-and-death crisis, and yet their new-found camaraderie, because of this crisis, makes it tolerable, even light-hearted, not to mention the ongoing emotional detachment. It's peculiar yet very human, as when the passengers on the Titanic bantered and laughed more than weeping, as they waited for the ship to sink.

"I *pre*fer Helen actually. I've been called 'Mama' enough. I'm—" Stopping midsentence, she takes a slow shuddering breath. He likewise struggles, as he can't help but associate 'Mama' with Mandy, and it has to be torture for Helen, as she wonders if she'll ever hear 'Mama' from her eldest child again. She sniffles but doesn't break, yet the mood remains sober—no more dimpling or tittering. Uncrossing her leg, she faces forward. She wads her windbreaker into a ball.

He turns right on Mosby Creek Road. He needs to cry, but talks instead, to occupy his mouth, his mind: "Lemme explain what I said before about our injuries being similar. The problem is bleeding and swelling inside the skull, which causes the brain tissue to herniate, or push down through the tentorial opening; that's the hole between the upper brain and the lower brain." Letting go of the gear knob (the Blazer has a stick shift), he points down with his forefinger. "The most vital player in the lower brain is the brain stem. It regulates respiration and blood pressure plus other vital systems. And it's crucial for maintaining alertness. Now herniation, the tissue being forced down from above, will damage the brain stem, if the swelling isn't fixed. That's why surgery was super urgent in both our cases ... to halt the bleeding. Without a viable stem we have brain death, or coma dépassé, which can't be reversed. That's the *biggie*, the worst case ... and it might've happened already."

Helen unballs her jacket then twists it with both hands, as though trying to wring water from it. "But Dr. Cantrall said she had brain function?"

"She does ... sorta ... but it's low amplitude and unstable. It doesn't tell us much about the viability of the brain stem."

Willows on the left, a sluggish bayou. They bump across a bridge crossing the mossy creek. "But *you* recovered, Bryan? If Amanda has the *same* kind of injury, isn't that a hopeful sign?"

He tilts his Baylor cap back on his head. "It's not quite that simple. The injuries are almost identical, put the physiological consequences are different in a few key respects."

"How so?"

"Well for one thing, *her* heart never stopped ... but *mine* did. It was a quirky thing—the ball put me into cardiac arrest, like a bolt of lightning." He taps his chest. "I was clinically dead. The paramedics had to use those paddles on me to get my pulse back."

"And that's when you had your near-death vision?"

"So Mandy *did* tellyuh about that?"

"Not the details, but she mentioned it a few times. Y'can tell me more if yuh like. I'm not so uptight about such things now."

"That's good to hear ... but let's stay in the physical realm for now." A large, grayish home, a recently constructed colonial, looms amid the pines on the right, followed by a blue Dutch on the left. New mid-scale houses guard both sides of the winding road. "Anyhow ... if Doc Wilson hadn't given me CPR, I woulda suffered irreparable frontal lobe damage, because of anoxia."

"Anoxia?"

"Oxygen deprivation—if yuh go two minutes without blood to the brain, y'can end up mentally impaired, if not dead, and anoxia can also cause indefinite unconsciousness."

"But, Bryan, you said Mandy didn't have that?"

"No, she never suffered cardiac arrest; that's the good news ... but there could be other things just as bad as anoxia, or worse."

Dropping the windbreaker, Helen gestures palms up. "So let's have it."

"Well, in my case, I was breathing on my own, and my pupils were responsive to light, which made it clear, once the herniation was reversed, that my brain stem was functioning okay. They had me on a ventilator as a precaution, but I could breathe on my own. But she can't—she has *no* respiration without the lung machine. The herniation was evidently more severe in her case."

"What about her pupils?"

"Kathy—I mean Dr. Cantrall—says they're unresponsive so far. But y'can't monitor continuously, so it's less conclusive."

"But the hernalation, or whatever you call it, was corrected?"

"Herniation—yes, they halted the bleeding, so the pressure cone of herniated tissue should retreat into the supratentorial compartment, the upper part of the brain case where it belongs. Dr. Cantrall will take scans to confirm this. And the bruised cerebral lobe itself should heal okay. And they reshaped and wired the fractured areas of the skull ... and while Mandy was on the table, they also attended to her collarbone and ribs."

"So that's good, right?"

"Well, there should be no *additional* stem damage. But it could be non-viable already. The big question is whether it can regain its function, and the fact she can't breathe is a *real* downer. If God has a miracle reserved for us, we need it *now*."

Mosby Creek Road, Hargrove Street, Stuart Drive, Sherwood Circle—while they complete the final five minutes of the drive, Bryan pushes deeper into doctor jargon without altering the essential facts: apnea, capacity for consciousness, midbrain, the pons, the medulla, limbic system, memory, voluntary movement, speech, abstract thought, sensory perceptions, ascending reticular activating system, gray matter, white matter, X rays, PET scans, CT scans, permanent sleep, spontaneous recovery.

Although quickly losing Helen, he rants on, in a desperate effort to elude the awful knowing: he's on his way home to a Mandy-less house, to a life that's altered forever. Yesterday at this time, she and Amy were just getting ready to leave for school, but now, but now—*O God, please save her.* Pulling into the drive, he squeaks to a halt in front of the garage, parking to the right by habit, so Mandy can get the Mustang by him into the garage—*O Jesus, I'm cracking up.* His eyes going blurry, he hops out, but his mother-in-law remains in the Blazer, gazing straight ahead, as though in a trance. He gets back in.

"I uh ... I-I," she stammers, her voice trembling. Shedding the sunglasses, she wipes her tears, to no avail. They're coming too fast; they streak down her pixie cheeks.

Fighting his own tears, he caresses her shoulder. "I know ... believe me, I know."

"I don't wanna LOSE my daughter," she gasps, collapsing into his arms. He breaks as well, a storm of crying engulfing them. She pants between sobs, a wheezing hysterical, almost-animal sound, as though she's being asphyxiated. She smells of shampoo and peppermint.

"Why is God doing *this*?" she weeps a few minutes later, as the tempest abates. "Is he judging me, d'yuh think?"

"Nawh," he snuffles, patting her on the back—her childlike doubt draws him even closer to her. "I don't think so. I'm not sure *what* he's up to ... but I don't reckon he's judging us."

Like barfing during a bout of stomach flu, the crying spell makes him feel better, as the dragons escape their dens and run amok—not to speak of his new bond with his mom-in-law.

* * *

Same day, same driveway, but some nine hours later—9:41 p.m. Just back from the hospital, Dr. Howard grabs the (rarely used) Stanley remote from the glove compartment. He zaps the garage door; it cranks open; he eases the Chevy Blazer inside, into the left stall where the Mustang is usually stabled—he nudges a trash can on the way in. His SUV has only been in here a few times, and it feels strange, especially now. He's alone: Helen stayed at the hospital, to be with her daughter and granddaughter through the night. Amy's tests were A-OK; she'll be released tomorrow. But Mandy remains on life support—nothing has changed since this morning.

He sighs and gets out. Flipping on the light, he goes around to deal with the trash cans, the one he bumped plus the other two. He moves the bulky, green-plastic containers farther to the right, over with the lawn mower and golf cubs and softball bats, and everything else that clutters this side of the garage. As he does, he spies, in a corner box, Mandy's championship basketball, the one everyone signed back in March of '91, after the Tiger girls won the playoffs. He was there on that rainy night in Tyler, and he was with her afterward, as they drove back to Spindle in the old Chevy pickup, cuddling all the way. That was the first time they listened to the Stevie Nicks tape, and they got hooked on "Talk to Me." The song plays in Bryan's soul, as he picks up the autographed Wilson ball. He gropes for meaning, for something solid to hold onto, but he only finds that hellish sinking sensation, the same slippery torment, the same black void.

"Why *God*?" he asks, as he hand-wipes the ball, clearing the dust from the girlish, hastily scrawled signatures. "Why'd you let this *happen*?" He dribbles, once, then tosses the B-ball back into the box—it bounces crazily, rolling away; it disappears under the Blazer. "I don't see any reason or purpose. No way." He kicks his golf bag knocking it over; the irons rattle and ping. Giving a sorrowful whimper, he closes the garage door then heads for the rec room, but he never makes it inside the house.

"FUCK IT ALL!" he rages, as he rushes back to his golf bag. Pulling his Wal-Mart driver, he attacks the side wall, smashing holes in the Sheetrock. "I HATE YOU, GOD! I've tried to be good, and I've trusted in you! BUT YOU *SUCK*! I HATE YOU! I FUCKING *HATE* YOU FOR THIS!" After a few more blows, he flings the big-headed golf club toward the Blazer. It flies over the hood, nailing the rec-room door: *ka-WHAP!* Grabbing his putter, he snaps it over his knee, then he hurls both halves at the windshield, in hopes of shattering it. The first sails high and wide, clattering against the gray-metal box on the far wall, the circuit-breaker thing. The second caroms grip-first off the windshield—no damage—before it *ka-RINGS* into the steel pipe that feeds the circuit box. Shrieking and sobbing, he throws *all* his clubs, not at the car but against the closed garage door on his side: *BANG! BAMB! BAMB!* Next he pegs the golf balls, breaking two of the garage-door windows—he *gets* his shattered glass. He fires the baseballs and softballs too. Then he hurls the weed-whacker against the wall, followed by the hoe and the rake and the bicycles. Finally, he attacks the green trash containers. "I hate these fucking GODDAM CANS!" He kicks and stomps until two of them are destroyed beyond use.

* * *

10:17 p.m—Bryan collapses into the LA-Z-BOY in the living room, after bringing Elmo inside—the hound was leashed in the backyard all day. The lab licks his master's hand then lies down beside the maroon recliner. He whines twice then goes silent, sadly silent. Bryan stares blankly at the cold, dark fireplace, then at the log rack, half full, last year's wood, mostly oak—they've not had any fires this fall. His gaze retreats to the Ethan Allen sofa on his left (dark-pine arms and back, autumn-print cushions). The soft light from the lamp on the end table gives the brand-name couch a yellowish tint. Ditto for the matching armchair opposite. He recalls the tiff he had with Mandy over the furniture-shopping spree (the end table and coffee table are also matching Ethan Allen pieces). He gives a weak murmur. *Money, credit cards, budgets—it doesn't mean a damn thing now. How could it?* He seldom sits in this recliner, or in this room, but after his fight with God in the garage, he dares not venture into the more familiar rooms of the house; it tortures him too much: Mandy's clothes, her stuff in the bathroom, her kitchen set-up, her scent in the bedroom, her old furniture in the rec room, her angelic portrait by his computer.

Dear Lord, he prays, *I'm sorry for freaking. I don't hate you ... but WHY is this happening? I mean, you brought us back together after all our youthful craziness, and you gave us Amy, and then you brought us here. But now—ka-BOOM! Amy's okay, and I thank you for that, but how's she gonna cope without a mommy.* Tears well up, but his soul is dry and cold, too drained to sob. Pulling the lever, he reclines, the footrest coming up. It's still warm outside, but he's downright chilly. He hugs himself.

Closing his eyes, he lays his head back—back, back, back. He's falling. No, he's rising—above the recliner, through the ceiling, through the attic. He's suddenly above the house looking down. The outside lights are still on, illuminating the driveway and the deck. He feels wonderful, a profound sense of well being. No more exhaustion, no more sorrow—and no moon. But the stars glimmer above, their brightness muted by the Houston haze, the dome of smog that shrouds the region when the weather's warm, especially at night when the winds are light. He drifts toward the street then accelerates. He zooms over the suburban neighborhoods, over myriad houses lit from within like jack-o'-lanterns, plus trees and fences and shadowy yards, and swimming pools, and streets and lanes and circles and pole-mounted lamps. Leaving Magnolia, he takes a shortcut above the piney woods of Groveton. Reaching Meadowhurst, he swoops low over Jackson Road then hovers above the entrance to Sturbridge Systems.

This's where it happened, he reminds himself, still feeling nothing but peace and warm contentment. *She went off the road and crashed into the trees over there.* Bryan floats closer to the forest, but it's too dark to see what he saw this morning, the tire ruts and the naked scars on the tree.

Now he's moving again. Faster, faster—he's headed toward Reynold's Salvage. "No, no!" he cries, as he wakes up in his living room. "I don't *wanna* see the Mustang." Sitting up, he shakes his head. "Damn, I just had an OBE." Heavy anguish reengulfs his psyche, amid pangs of guilt for feeling so good up *there*, when things are so bad down *here*.

THE SILVER CORD

MAGNOLIA, TEXAS - 22 SHERWOOD
THURSDAY, NOVEMBER 11, 1999 — 4:42 PM

"I'm sorry, Elmo, but she's *not* coming home," Bryan tells his canine friend. Elmo whines but remains focused on the pantry-nook door, waiting for the knob to turn. The black lab looks for Mandy every evening, at this door or the rec-room door. Bryan sighs, the room going blurry. Wiping his tears, he grabs his denim jacket, from a hook above and to the right of Elmo's gaze.

That hound just won't let go, he remarks to himself, as he descends the rain-slicked steps into the backyard. *It's time to accept the inevitable, and we all have—except Elmo.* The chilly, daylong rain has diminished to a thick drizzle which has coated everything with a silvery film of tiny droplets. They glisten like ice on the grass and shrubs and pine trees, especially on the long loblolly needles. It *is* cold out but not freezing, maybe 45° or so. *O God, how d'yuh explain death to a dog?*

Bryan trudges across the yard, his sneakers getting wet in the grass. He adjusts his Baylor cap, pulling the bill down to keep the mist out of his face. He's adapted to his Mandy-less house, at least enough to live in it. Her absence still cries out, tearing at his insides, but he no longer breaks at the sight of her robe draped on the chair in the bedroom, or her blow-dryer in the bathroom, the cord still plugged into the wall, or the perfumy aromas atop her dresser—but he did change the bed linen. He couldn't deal with the Pantene sweetness on the pillowcases, or her fleshy, mink-oil scent on the sheets. Reaching the patchy, needle-strewn lawn under the trees, he executes an about-face, heading back toward the house. He shoves his hands into his jeans, the front pockets.

Slowly back and forth he paces, his outlook just as dismal as the weather. Kathy Cantrall confirmed his fears last Friday: "The lack of pupil response, along with Mandy's inability to breathe on her own, increases the likelihood of coma dépassé. But the EEG signal, though sporadic and diminishing, remains detectable. It's too early to pin down any prognosis, yet her brain-stem function is marginal at best. To be candid, I must rate her chances as one in ten ... and *de*creasing. Time is not on our side."

It's just him and Elmo at home now. His mother-in-law lives at the hospital, or almost so, and Amy's in Spindle, at the farm; she went home with his parents on Sunday—they were down for the weekend. Helen spends most of her time in Mandy's ICU cubicle, whereas Bryan can scarcely bear to sit in there at all. The sibilating respirator torments like Cantonese water torture, as it goes *on* and *on* and *on*, driving home the futility of it all. But he does relieve Helen most evenings, so she can freshen up in the family suites, or nap in his office (where they keep an airbed now). They continue to grow closer, as they talk in the car, the hospital cafeteria, and some here at the house, though she hasn't been here since Tuesday when she came home to shower and get fresh clothes. She's also resigned to losing Mandy, and admits it during candid moments, yet she presses dutifully on, staying near her daughter's side, holding her hand, stroking her bandaged brow, running out the clock—till it's time to let the Lord have her.

And that time *has* been chosen: 11:00 p.m., December 15. If there's no change by then, the life-support apparatus will be disconnected. They decided this at a family meeting in Bryan's living room on Saturday night. Helen, having received a power-of-attorney from Russ Snyder, has sole legal authority, but she of course gave Bryan equal say, and they both listened to Henry and Ginny—and Gretchen over the phone. They thoroughly discussed this dreadful matter, but in the end it was unanimous: we mustn't try to hold onto her, if Christ is calling her home. If she can only be kept alive with machines, it's better to let her die, to let her go with God into Heaven. In the deepest recesses of his gut, in his visceral core, Bryan continues to agonize over this agreed-upon course of action, but in his *head* he's convinced that it's right. There's no choice. It's best for Mandy, and *every*one, especially knowing what *he* knows about the afterlife, the glory of it.

Stopping between Elmo's doghouse and the AC compressor, he gazes up into the foggy murk—it's getting dark. The drizzle tickles his face, cold pinpricks. *O dear Jesus*, he implores, *please help me get over this selfishness. I hafta let her go, and I have. But I keep getting these awful tugs on my heart ... like just now with Elmo. It's better out here. I can think clearly.* Gesturing Godward, he groans resignedly. *It's a done deal; the decision is made—if she doesn't wake up. And she's NOT gonna ... NO WAY. But that's old news.* He shrugs then resumes walking. A drop of water dribbles from the visor of his cap. *Her trace is hardly more than noise. She's going on, with our help, and it's the best, most godly thing, not to mention the four grand a day it's costing Blue Cross. Shit, how could I think such a thought? Money is fucking meaningless. I'd pay a million to get her back, but there's no such offer on the table.* He circles the yard, now doing laps instead of pacing back and forth. The muted *shhhhh* of a descending jetliner echoes down through the gloom. *They got balls landing in this soup. But dying in a plane crash is better than lingering in limbo for forty-three days.*

Spanky and Wendy called this week, and Annie O'Shea, even Billy Ray Campbell—they offered encouragement, but it seemed more like condolence, as if Mandy's with the Lord already. Ditto for the Harrisons, and the other teachers at Hatfield Elementary. (The schoolkids sent—Lindsey brought it over—a huge art-class get-well card, with a hospital and ambulance on the front, and fifty names inside, printed in crayon.) Bryan has talked with Dr. Richardson of course, three times since the accident; the doc, though pessimistic, is reluctant to concede. He's more like Elmo the dog, and Yogi Berra, when it comes to finality: "It ain't over until it's over." Or maybe he's seen too many surprises in the realm of neurosurgery to ever accept any coma as irreversible.

Laura Sterling is taking some of Dr. Howard's therapy load, but not all. Working occupies his mind, temporary solace, and he's at the hospital most days anyhow. Plus, he doesn't have to deal with Barry Spigler, who's still away on his fall conference tour (due back 12-10). Bryan has seen Mrs. Weinstein once since the accident. She knows about it, as does the whole Easley Wing, and she's most empathetic, but she also reminded Dr. Howard that she needs to have a private chat with him at some point.

The drizzle has turned to rain again, the drops growing larger; they dapple his jacket, darkening the denim. Yet he continues to walk around his yard like an inmate getting exercise. Another airliner hisses overhead, bringing to mind his own recent flight—the astral journey to Meadowhurst a week ago: *It doesn't surprise me that I had an OBE, considering my emotions, but it was sorta weird that I returned to the accident scene, as if she might be there too. But OBEs are different from near-death experiences. It's a big mystery. It's the whole silver-cord question, like Doc Richardson and I were wrestling with back in Waco. What happens to the soul when someone's in a coma? Now many would chuckle and say, "What soul?" But I know different— I've been there. Either that or I'm totally deluded.*

He halts under the pines, which protect him from the rain but not the *drip-drip* from the boughs. The wetness enhances the pungent scent of the needles, clearing his nostrils, as though it's raining turpentine. *It's like the whole mystery of the silver cord is playing out in real life. I mean ... what is it? Where is it? And when does it sever? It's peculiar. I glimpsed the other side back in '91, and I've studied it since—and yet, the mystery remains. I wonder where Mandy is right now. Is her soul in her body still, or is she zooming back and forth through that tunnel, or is she up there in that beautiful realm ... where I spotted Gramps under the tree?* A warm glow floods his bosom. *Oh, dear pretty lady, where are you? Can you hear me? Can you see me? I know there's something up there—I saw it in '91. It was no illusion, yet I reckon I gotta go farther than Meadowhurst to find you. I reckon I gotta go ALL the way ... like through that tunnel again.*

Thunder rumbles amid this thought, or maybe it was his heart bucking. *Cool it, fellow,* he reacts. *Don't get sucked in by some wild Keifer Sutherland notion. That FLATLINERS flick was pure fiction. It's just a fancy way of committing suicide.* The Chicago med-student story has always fascinated him for obvious reasons, but now it beguiles him. He rented it Monday, watching it again by himself. *What God doeth, he doeth it forever. Nothing can be added to it, or taken from it. That's the official word, and you must heed that truth. Amy's already losing her mother. D'yuh want her to be FATHERLESS as well? Put it to rest. Y'gotta get on with you life, your goals, your service to humanity. You must raise your daughter ... and love her and teach her. That's what Mandy wants. And then someday you too will pass on, and then you'll be with your dear pretty lady forever.*

5:22 p.m. Back in the house, he heats milk in the microwave, for hot chocolate: *I commit her into your hands, O God ... and I thank you for giving me peace about it.*

*   *   *

Next day, Friday—10:19 a.m. Peering carefully to see ahead, Dr. Howard turns off Stuart Drive onto Sherwood. "I appreciate the ride," Helen remarks, as they wheel through the thick fog. "But I figured this was a good time to grab some clean clothes, and to hop into the shower."

"No problem," he replies, as he pulls into the driveway, the wide SUV treads grabbing the gritty, rain-soaked pavement. "You need a break anyhow." The rain has stopped, but the clouds have descended to the deck, shrouding the region in a chilly, ghostly, London-style gloom.

*   *   *

Elmo, snoozing in the rec room, hears the Blazer, but the garage door doesn't open, no grinding mechanical noise. Upstairs! He bounds up to the kitchen where he posts himself by the pantry-nook door, his eyes fixed on the brassy knob, his tale wagging, his canine heart pounding and hoping.

*   *   *

Down in the car, Helen gives a little murmur, dropping her eyes. She fiddles with the drawstring on her handbag. "Yes, I suppose I do need to get away for a few hours. Besides, they're bathing her and changing the sheets, and the technicians are coming in to check the equipment like they do most mornings. They don't mind me sitting in there, but it gets crowded sometimes. And Charlene will be in with fresh i.v. pouches. I think she's doing the day-shift today. The nurses rotate; it's hard to figure it."

Loosening his tie, Bryan starts to get out, but she clutches his arm. "Wait ... there's something I've been meaning to say to you, and I reckon now's a good time." She gives a cozy half-grin.

"What's that?"

"I just wanted to apologize, for being such a bitch back in the old days. It was *tot*ally unfair ... the way I tried to control and protect Amanda, especially when I cut you off, after we moved to Arkansas. I was so arrogant and pompous, like *over*protective in the extreme. And I was *over*zealous in my faith—to the point of being obnoxious." She titters. "I reckon it's all part of being a mother ... plus I was still recovering from my depression thing." She gestures toward the double garage, toward the two broken windows in the rightside door. "You'n I uh ... well, we've gotten along pretty good since Mandy got pregnant ... but I wanted to tellyuh anyway, especially now, considering all this." She places her hand upon his, as he grasps the shift knob.

He dimples, his cheeks heating—same for his heart. "Well, I reckon I'm sorry too ... for all the wild shenanigans I put *you* through ... like when I banged on your door in the middle of the night, and then I slung Mandy's stuff into your yard, and all over. I was halfway berserk, like *foam*ing at the mouth."

They share a spirited laugh, then Helen sobers: "This has been the most *horrible* ten days of my life, but I'd hafta chalk this moment up as positive, and good. The Lord giveth, and the Lord taketh away. It's a peculiar thing, Bryan, how God works. You've become the son I never had."

* * *

A minute later, Elmo hears footsteps ascending the wooden stairway. The yearling lab yearns and aches, his eyes growing large, his body shivering with anticipation, his nostrils searching desperately for the telltale scent—to no avail. Before the door opens, he knows the score: NO MANDY. It's just Bryan and Helen. Elmo greets them anyhow, licking hands, clicking about the linoleum floor, but sadness continues its long reign over the biggest part of his doggie heart.

"Hello, boy," Bryan announces, his voice rising a couple of octaves. "I reckon y'need to go outside. Just gimme a sec, then I'll get your leash."

CHAPTER THIRTY-FIVE

ONE MONTH LATER:

MAGNOLIA, TEXAS - 22 SHERWOOD
MONDAY, DECEMBER 13, 1999 — 11:07 AM

Dr. Howard works in his home office, doing paperwork. But he must report to the hospital this afternoon. He has a two p.m. with Emily Gray, the teenager with the tumor-induced speech-recognition problem, and he must see three of Chris's (Dr. Goodwin's) in-patients. Dr. Sterling is gone; she left Friday, for an extended Christmas vacation with her family in San Jose.

Elmo naps beside him, curled on an old blanket. He won't sleep in the rec room unless Bryan's in there. The dog, still neurotic over Mandy, mopes around all day then waits at the door all evening. But everyone else has come to terms with the inevitable. Bryan found peace during that rainy-evening walk in the backyard last month, and despite a number of "bad" days, he no longer wrestles with God, not zealously anyway—no more tantrums certainly. And he and Helen are making plans for the funeral, a quiet, close-family thing, with burial back in Spindle. They've likewise explained the situation to Amy, with Ginny Howard's help, and the precious little preschooler seems to have reconciled herself to the fact that her mommy's "goin' up to Heaven to be with Jesus." She remains at the farm. Bryan went up for Thanksgiving, and he and his mom decided it would be best if she stayed with the Howards until this whole ordeal is over.

Steve Jordan called yesterday, from Phoenix (he's a set-up reliever for the Diamondbacks). Bryan had e-mailed him about Mandy. The big guy, like all the rest, sounded resigned, as he reminded his old roomie about Coach McKinney's burial and the talk they had that day at Denny's. Jordan shared the latest about himself of course, going on about his off-season training regime, and about Susie and the kids, but he was downright considerate compared to his oblivious Baylor manners—perhaps because of Bryan's crisis, or maybe the real world has matured him. Tracy McCollum also called Sunday (actually Tracy Neustadt; she married a Jewish pediatrician in '97), and she and Bryan cried together on the phone. She said she found out three weeks ago, from Chris, but it took a while to get up the courage to call.

Bryan confers with Dr. Cantrall daily, or with Michael Samsung, a resident on her team, and the news has progressed from bleak to bleaker—Mandy's trace is noise-level at best. So in accordance with the legal papers, signed by Helen, the ICU life-support technicians will disconnect all systems on Wednesday night, the day after tomorrow.

THE SILVER CORD

Even Dr. Richardson has thrown in the towel: "I talked with Kathy Cantrall myself, and I must say, she's painting a *grim* picture. Our ability to diagnose coma dépassé remains fallible, even with our high-tech instruments, but I see no reason to change your plans."

Last night however, Nurse Comisky did notice weird activity on the monitor, the signal bouncing like a seismograph in an earthquake. It only lasted a few seconds, yet it got everyone excited—but Dr. Cantrall, after consulting with one of the EEG techies from the third-floor lab, dismissed it as an instrument-induced voltage surge, and there's been nothing since. "Spike aberrations are not uncommon," she explained. "These machines are fickle. We're trying to assess brain-stem viability by looking at electronic output on a cathode-ray tube, so even when the device behaves, it's not a cut-and-dried thing. But her trace has never been more than marginal, and it has deteriorated with time. I've seen patients revive with less EEG amplitude, but never after a six-week inability to respire, plus no pupil response."

Moving the Macintosh mouse, Bryan clicks on the Weinstein file, with the intention of finishing his summary report, but then he decides, on impulse, to call Sarah, since he didn't get a chance to see her Thanksgiving week, her last week in the hospital.

"Oh, Dr. Howard, it's *so* good to hear from you"—she goes on to express, again, her sadness concerning Mandy. Then she shifts to various subjects, Bryan interjecting a word here and there. He almost regrets calling her, but then she stops.

"So how are *you* doing?" he asks, taking opportunity. "Sorry I didn't get by to see you before y'were released." Squeaking back in the chair, Bryan removes his reading specs.

"Oh don't fret about that, Doctor. I didn't expect to see you much, considering your situation. Besides, we never had much privacy anyway, not enough for me to tell you my secret."

"Oh yeah, that's right—so what's your secret all about?"

"I saw Benny."

"Benny?"

"You know, Benny ... Benjamin, my husband."

"But I thought—"

"That's right," she declares. "He's dead ... but I *still* saw him, or at least I knew he was there."

"What uh? Whaa—"

"It happened to me too ... what you told me before."

"You had a near-death experience?"

"You betcha. It happened during my surgery back in October. I floated up over the operating table, and I saw all of you doctors, and the nurses, and I saw my own body, but I couldn't tell it was me, because I was all covered up with bluish sheets—and then the next thing I knew I was in this cave, like a mine shaft. I went faster, and faster, and then I was suddenly in this big rose garden, yellow roses—

THE SILVER CORD

and that's when I saw Benny."

After hanging up ten minutes later, Dr. Howard gives a silent whistle. *Damn, it happened to her too. It's like a handful now, the number of NDEs I know about. And she's Jewish. It's not a matter of religion, or being a Christian. And she saw Benny there. O Jesus ... whaddeyuh trying to tell me?*

* * *

HCMC - WADE WING CAFETERIA
MONDAY, DECEMBER 13, 1999 — 5:13 PM

Bryan sips his Dr. Pepper. "No, I didn't feel any pain at all," he explains, gesturing toward his mother-in-law with the styrofoam cup. "It was blissful in fact, a total sense of well-being. And—"

"Hold that thought," Helen cuts in, as she slides out of the booth. "I'm dying to hear the rest, but first I gotta run to the ladies' room." Her denim-clad legs striding briskly, she weaves through the mostly empty tables, the drawstring of her big purse slung over her shoulder— cowgirl style. Her western shirt adds to the effect. She may not have passed on her features to Mandy, save for the valentine mouth, but the pep in her step is *certainly* the same.

He chuckles. *It's still hard to believe she's a grandma, but Amy's the proof.* He toys with the cakey remnants in his ice cream dish—he had a brownie sundae to top off his cheeseburger and fries, while she had a turkey club with no dessert, just coffee. *And now she brings up my NDE again. Gosh, she's more feisty than I realized.* He starts to loosen his tie but adjusts it instead. He's still in his psychologist uniform: a grayish pin-striped suit.

Save for a two-day, post-Thanksgiving trip back to Newbury (Charlie and Gretch drove down finally, and she rode back with them, but only after Bryan had returned from Spindle), Helen has been doing the same day-to-day routine: holding Mandy's hand, reading by her bed, watching the little, wall-mounted TV, napping in Bryan's office— and they often eat supper together, usually here in the main caf. After sharing this forty-day ordeal, he knows Helen almost as much as he knows his own mom, more so in some respects. And as the days have passed, they've wept less and laughed more, growing more accustomed to the truth at hand: Mandy's going on to be with God; it's her appointed time. The day and hour approaches, and they share a similar (mostly unspoken) sense of anticipation, for closure, for an end to this limbo status—and for liberty, theirs and Amanda's.

They're suffering unspeakable loss together, and because of this, they will forever relate on an intimate basis, like shipmates at Pearl Harbor, or soldiers who survived Normandy. It's not a Chris bond, or like with Doc Richardson, or Spanky in the old days—Bryan doesn't share "guy" stuff with his mom-in-law—but things *are* getting deeper,

593

like right now. They've skirted the near-death subject a few times, even that first day in the car, but she seems more eager this evening, like hungry for details.

And when she returns, fresh coffee in hand, he does his best to describe everything that happened on that Saturday in May eight years ago. Her hazel eyes wide, she listens intently as she sips her coffee. He sighs and gestures; he finishes his pop; he crunches his ice. He expands the report to include Dudley O'Shea and Elmo McKinney, then he relates the most recent case: Sarah Weinstein. He explains how she saw her deceased husband Benny at the edge of Glory. As he talks about Benny, an anxious tugging commences in Bryan's gut, like the tugging he felt this morning when Sarah first told him on the phone. The vibes excite and frighten at the same time—tugging, urging, calling.

Helen shakes her head, rolling her eyes "This's *wild* stuff. I used to doubt near-death stories, or attribute them to Satan. But I've long since let go of the pat answers that come from Bible-study booklets. I reckon life has a way of *un*locking our brains."

"No kidding," he replies, dimpling. The tugging diminishes.

She smiles as well. "Besides, I trust you. I know you're not *josh*ing me." She titters, then sobers. "But I *do* have questions ... like how does our soul connect to our body?" She links her forefingers to illustrate. "I've heard a few preachers touch on this subject, and Bible-teachers, but they never get much beyond the vague Baptist notion of the body being an envelope, with the soul inside. But there *has* to be a coupling? And what does it take to break this coupling? Or what is it that makes death *final*?"

He squeezes the empty styrofoam cup until it snaps. "I reckon you've hit the nail on the head. That's the *big* mystery, the mystery of the silver cord." He drops the crushed styrofoam onto his plate.

"Silver cord?"

"You know, from Ecclesiastes, the cord that severs when we die. That's the coupling you're talking about. At least, that's what I call it." He laughs. "Not that I have the solution. I have a *name* for it ... but it's still beyond me to explain how it works, or where it resides in the brain. And I have a Ph.D. in neuroscience no less." More titters. "But I'm in dadgum renowned company when it comes to being baffled. Theologians and great thinkers have considered this issue for centuries ... from St. Augustine to Leonardo da Vinci ... all the way up to Einstein himself ... like a hundred great minds. They've all wondered and theorized about the link between the physical and the metaphysical, without pinning down the silver cord."

"It seems like there *has* to be a link, like I say ... but can we be sure? I mean, does it *really* exist ... this silver cord?"

"Ahah, that's the *other* big question. I reckon it's impossible to be sure. But I'm certainly *bank*ing on it ... for Mandy's sake ... for our sake ... for everyone's sake." He goes on a few minutes, citing the negative possibilities, the non-spiritual explanations for the near-death experience, the accepted views of reductive materialism—but he quickly balances by bringing up his OBEs, his astral journeys that do not involve a brush with death.

More questions, more give and take, more coffee, another shot of Dr. Pepper from the soda spigot opposite the cafeteria line—astral realm, physical realm, God, salvation, immortality, Christian, Muslim, Jew, Omega Point physics, pseudoscience, love, hate, death, despair. They pause finally to catch their breath. Bryan checks his watch: 6:15 p.m. They've been on this subject a good hour, but Helen's not done. "So tell me, Bryan," she says, leaning toward him, her elbows on the table, her eyes gazing directly into his. "What about Amanda Fay? Where d'yuh think *her* soul is right now?"

"I-I ... well uh, it's hard to say," he responds, as the tugging vibes recommence inside him.

"Well, that *Jewish* lady saw her husband in a garden?"

Bryan sucks a breath, his heart drumming amid the pangs of hope and fear. "But Benny was actually *dead* ... just like I toldjuh about my grandfather. Mandy's still here ... in a coma."

"I know she's in a coma ... but where *is* her soul?"

He gulps, as the tugging turns into words: "I don't know ... but there might be a *way* to find out."

"How?"

"Didyuh ever see the movie *Flatliners*?"

Helen recoils, her face going ashen. She grabs his hand; she frowns. "No way, Bryan. Don't even *consider* such a thing." Her eyes fill. "I love you. I don't wanna lose you *too*. And you have Amy. O Lord, *for*give me. I shoulda never brought it up."

* * *

Same night, 9:06 p.m. While Helen naps in his office, Bryan sits with his dear pretty lady in cubicle #7. High-tech gadgetry fills the small ICU room, but he focuses on the respirator: *swissssssh*, then silence, then *swisssssssh*. The bladder in the glass drum contracts, then rises, then falls—supplying air through one tube, disposing of carbon dioxide through the other, two channels of crimped tubular plastic converging into a valve near her mouth, where a smaller, more-rigid tube descends down her throat. Tape holds the mouthpiece in place. She's also getting oxygen, from the tiny nasal canula tubes; more tape secures the canula clip.

She *looks so peaceful and beautiful,* he sighs, *even with that butchy hair.* They've removed most of the bandages, and her blond locks have grown out an inch since the surgery. Pinkish-red scars adorn her head amid the electrode attachments from the EEG. *It's amazing how she heals without knowing it, and her hair grows, and her fingernails.*

And according to Michael Samsung, her ribs and clavicle are almost mended.

His heart lurches and shudders, desperate love—it grows so strong he almost falls out of the chair. He takes her hand in his, being careful about the i.v. *Oh, pretty lady, it's so hard to say good-bye. I thought I had peace about it, but now I've got this crazy idea, but maybe it's NOT crazy? I blurted it out in front of your mama, and she just about freaked. I shouldn't have told her.* He chuckles. *I think I saw that stern-mother face you always used to talk about. But I must say, she's an A-OK lady, once you get to know her. Course, you always said that too.*

Too much—he retreats, hoping to shunt his train of thought to a different track. Grabbing a magazine, last week's *Time*, from the shopping bag beside the cushiony armchair (Helen brought in a bunch of mags), he scans the different stories (most related to Y2K), but salvos of love and fear and hope keep taking him back to his *crazy* idea. He has much *bigger* things on his mind than whether his Macintosh is going to crash on January 1, 2000.

* * *

10:50 p.m. Bryan stretches to his feet. *Well, precious, I reckon it's time to wake your mama. She said to come get her at eleven.*

Swisssssssh, silence, *swisssssssh*, silence: the ventilator works on, and on, while he adores his dear Sleeping Beauty—butchy blond and tubed to the hilt but no less BEAUTIFUL. For a long moment, he gathers her into his senses, then he kisses her on the forehead. *If this was a fairy tale, I could wake you with a kiss. But I don't have that kind of magic. Yet it might be possible to find out where you are—no, no, your mama's right. I hafta let go of you, pretty lady, but you're gonna be in a glorious place forever, a realm of perfect love and joy and harmony. I reckon you've glimpsed it by now, if you're not already there for good.*

As he exits cubicle #7, a shiver shoots through him: Barry Spigler—he's talking with Dr. Samsung outside cubicle #15.

Looks like Arafat is back, Dr. Howard remarks to himself, as he pushes through the swinging doors into the long hallway. *But what's he doing here this time of night?*

The answer comes instantly, as a gruff drawl stops Bryan in his tracks: "What the hell's going on with you, Dr. Howard?"

"I-I ... whaddeyuh mean?"

Double déjà vu—the October scene plays out again, same hallway, same characters, except this time Spigler catches the Baylor Ph.D. at the ICU end of the brightly lit corridor. "I just saw you come out of cubicle #7."

"So?"

Spigler's eyes fidget fiendishly, disgustingly. "The patient in seven is comatose. She has no need for a psychologist. So you have no *god*dam business in there."

"Get off it. She's my wife."

"Yeah, right. She was admitted as Mrs. Snyder, not Howard. She's married to a Russell Snyder. I checked it out, asshole."

"I-I ... I uh—"

"Don't say another goddam word. Just listen, and listen well. I don't want you anywhere near cubicle #7. Mrs. Snyder is not receiving visitors, only her nearest kin, and that does not include *you!*" The rebuke rides a gust of sour breath. "Shit, you're more of a goddam twilight-zone loser than I thought."

Shock, shame, nefarious eyes—then rage, but before Bryan can react, the white-coated Spigler disappears into the ICU. But then he pokes his ugly mug back through the door: "You make me sick, Howard. And you have an illegitimate kid to boot. I checked the records. You're supposed to be an upstanding professional, but instead you've been shacking up like white trash. Now get *outta* my sight ... before I call goddam security."

* * *

11:40 p.m. Dr. Howard spurs the Chevy Blazer, merging into the light northbound traffic on the Eastex Freeway. *How can any doctor be so hostile and insensitive? Helen couldn't believe it when I told her ... but she's never met the bastard.* Bryan shivers; he feels a draft. It's about 35° out, frigid for downtown. He turns on the heat. He has a trench coat, but it's wadded on the seat beside him, and it's a hassle to put it on while driving. The tears in his eyes spin halos about the freeway lamps and headlights. He feels empty, defeated. *Spigler is like Lucifer himself. He's heinous and cold, and totally unjust ... yet his fucking spirit rules the earth.*

But by the time Bryan gets off on FR 6137, the fire in his belly has begun to rekindle. The moonlit forest speaks to him, as does the FM radio, which blares *ZZ Top* and "Sharp Dressed Man," a rough-talking redneck tune, but the song has always stirred his Mandy-heart, all the way back to Spindle High. Ditto for Roy Orbison, who fans the flames with "Pretty Woman." Bryan can't help but sing PRETTY LADY in place of pretty woman, as he does anytime he hears this classic hit.

He loosens his tie. *Fuck Spigler. Next time, I'm gonna break his ugly nose. He's just a blowhard bully looking for someone to pick on, and I'm high on his list. He has no real power. But even if he did, so what? Let him call security. Let him get me fired. It doesn't mean shit—not compared to what Mandy's dealing with.* He gives a cowboy yelp; he slaps the dash. *To hell with Spigler! I got a much bigger dragon to slay.* More yelps. *Maybe we CAN pull it off? If I was put under with sodium penathol, and then my heart was jolted into cardiac arrest ... I'd have one or two minutes to look for her, and that could expand to hours in the astral realm, as Einstein showed us ... when v approaches*

THE SILVER CORD

c. The tricky part is getting back, but Johnny Edwards and Mark Adams got my heart going again in '91, when I flatlined at home plate.

* * *

While Bryan exhorts himself, Elmo snoozes at the house—in the living room, curled cozily on the Ethan Allen sofa, normally a no-no, but there's a beach towel spread on it now. Helen put it there. A little while later, the sound of the Blazer awakens the black lab. His heart springs to attention. After a yawn and stretch he trots into the kitchen, but the cranking rumble of the garage door sends him scurrying the other way. He clicks down the stairs to the rec room, to the door off the garage. He gazes longingly at the knob. Maybe this time? No, not so—he smells Bryan only. It's not *her*, Elmo deduces, even before the knob turns. Yet he greets his master warmly, licking his hand, nuzzling his suit pants. They share the same loss—and the same yearning.

* * *

I gotta think this through, Bryan counsels himself a few minutes later, as he waits on the frosty deck for Elmo to do his thing. *Enthusiasm is one thing, but science is another.* He hooked the dog to the run-line, lest he take off after Felix. The big yellow tom from next door prowls both yards at night. *Plus, I sure can't do it by myself. And I have less than 48 hours. It's past midnight, so it's Tuesday on the calendar, the 14th of December. Jesus, it's too late already. C'mon ... y'gotta get real.*

Bryan, now wearing the trench coat, can see his breath in the moonlight. It's colder out here in suburbia, quite cold—upper 20s and calm. The ice crystals on the deck railing glisten artistically: white paisley. It's beautiful, the frost, the trees, the stars, the slate-colored heavens—and the moon, a huge, round, blue-white moon. He can't help but gaze up at it:

"*I wanna make a promise on the moon.*"

"*Whaa ... whaddeyuh talking about?*"

"*I wantcha to promise me that every time you look at the moon, you'll think of me with all your heart, no matter where you are, or what you're doing—and I'll do the same.*"

He bombs into the kitchen, almost breaking the door. *Beep-bap-bip-boop*—he dials as fast as he can. "Whaaa ... hello?" comes a sleepy monotone.

"Chris, it's Bryan. I gotta see you ASAP. This's big ... like the biggest thing ever ... and we don't have SHIT for time!"

* * *

"I'm *se*rious," Bryan insists an hour later—he gestures with his beer can, his second Budweiser.

Chris sips his own brew then gives his classic smirk. "God damn,

THE SILVER CORD

I believe you are."

"It's the only way to be sure. I mean ... if she's trying to wake up, and we cut her off, that would be the *worst*. And the procedure I've described *is* feasible ... risky but feasible."

"This's fucking bizarre, but you *have* done your homework."

They talk in the Howard kitchen, at the cherrywood breakfast table. Chris wears tattered corduroys plus a rumpled pullover, hastily grabbed items. Elmo, sitting at attention near his master, looks on, as if he realizes the crucial nature of the conversation.

"So you think it'll work?" Bryan asks.

"Death by lethal injection ... yeah, it works all the time—up the road in Huntsville."

Chris snickers puckishly, yet the pointed quip hits home, puncturing Bryan's boldness—his mood deflates, as gusts of doubt jet downward into his bowels. He persists nonetheless. "But we're not talking *that* kinda dose. I'm talking 20 cc's, after the nitrous, then you'll *shock* me into cardiac arrest."

"Sounds pretty goddamn lethal to me."

Bryan fingers his neck then fiddles with the collar of his dress shirt—he's ditched the coat and tie. "But you're gonna bring me *back*. That's the whole dadgum point?"

"No way in hell, slugger. It's too risky. Defibrillation is a ticklish fucking procedure. It doesn't always work for godsake. And we're talking about a capital offense here. Christ Almighty ... we could lose everything. Shit, you'll be dead, and I'll never practice again, and I'll spend the rest of my life in jail, if they don't inject me as well." After a quick laugh he sobers, knitting his brow above a darkly solemn gaze. His brown eyes have lost their impish sparkle. He stares beyond his Baylor buddy, as if he can see through the kitchen wall, as if he can discern the future in the frosty night outside.

Bryan, his eyes filling, gives a murmur but no reply.

The mustached surgeon sips some Bud then runs his hand through his curly locks. "I know you're desperate, Bryan, but we're talking about playing dice with death, and I don't see the odds in our favor. Plus, you have a beautiful daughter, remember? If we could ask Mandy, I'm sure she'd say the same things I'm saying." He shakes his head slowly—he gives a sigh. "Exploring the other side in a goddamn Hollywood flick is one thing, but this's no movie." He pauses, as if fighting to keep his Midwest monotone on the tracks. "I-I ... well, I'm not too keen on losing you, slugger ... and who knows if you'll find her, even if you do get to the other side, even if I do get you back?"

No reply from Bryan—his eyes brimming, he simply stares at his Baylor buddy, as when Elmo homes in on the door knob.

Looking down, Chris fidgets with the sleeve of his pullover. "Besides, I couldn't do it by myself anyway. We'd need a team, plus an operating room—it's too far out. People would know? And if Barry

Spigler found out, he'd hang us by our toes from the Enron office tower. And he'd have just cause, which is fucking *rare* for him." Chris forces a laugh. "You think he was pissed tonight about the ICU thing. That was his usual contrived bluster, and I doubt he'll press the issue if you defy him—he has no case—but if he catches wind of this scheme, God help us. Go directly to jail. Do not pass go. We'd be out of the game."

* * *

INTERSTATE 45 - SOUTH OF HUNTSVILLE, TX
TUESDAY, DECEMBER 14, 1999 — 3:40 AM

Dr. Howard, half-drunk but no less desperate, speeds through the frosty moonlight. *O Lord Jesus, I need you like never before,* he cries in his heart, as he gazes at the Big Dipper in the pewter sky ahead of him, dark pewter but not black, because of the moon. *Ever since the accident, you've seemed distant, like farther away than those stars. But Elmo is bringing you close again. That dog teaches me more about love than any sermon ever did.* Bryan gestures toward the Big Dipper, a warm upwelling in his bosom. *Not that Pastor Ron said bad things when we talked on the phone the other day. He was kind and compassionate, and he emphasized the mercy of God, and so did old Pastor Heupal when he came over to the house. But Elmo speaks directly to my soul— without using words. Gramps was right about animals—they DO have a heart, a heart that beats with TRUE devotion. There's no "but" or "maybe" or "what if" in Elmo's love for Mandy. He's gonna be at that door waiting for her, no matter the odds, no matter how crazy it looks, no matter if she's alive or dead, no matter if she's a Christian or an infidel ... or rich or poor, or old or young, or pretty or ugly ... no matter WHAT! So many religions, including my own, have a scary side—they exhort us to "fear God and live," to fear judgment and Hell. But I can't make it that way. None of us can. Elmo shows me a higher love, a love that doesn't use fear to gain its goals. "God is love"—PERIOD! That's what I need, a love that never ceases, that never turns away, that waits for me, and waits for me ... even if I'm trapped in a goshdang coma.*

Pushing ninety mph, the Blazer S-10 hums along the deserted interstate, deserted except for an occasional eighteen-wheeler—and the *moon* skirting the treetops on his left. *Oh, pretty lady, I'm NOT giving up yet. Doc Richardson—I gotta see him. I hafta try.* The piney woods give way to rolling pastures, a gray-bright stretch of open country that looks strangely surreal in the cold, argentine light, as if he's driving though a Dali dreamscape done in ashen tones, a bleached phantasma, an apt expression of the nightmare that devoured his world six weeks ago.

After Chris left at 2:45 a.m., Bryan moped about in a state of surrender, resigning himself to the status quo. But as he prepared to get into his cold Mandy-less bed, he heard a plaintive whine in the kitchen. Poking his head around the corner, he found Elmo staring at the door knob—against all odds. The dog's steadfast devotion blew him away, literally. Getting quickly dressed, this time in jeans and sneakers plus a flannel shirt, he hustled down to the garage, grabbing his green Baylor cap and Spindle jacket on the way (his old letter jacket).

Slowing to eighty-five, he whips past the old antebellum community of Huntsville: two exits, blip, blip, plus a town-sized cluster of lights straddling the raised highway. Huntsville has a rich history, not to mention a thriving university, Sam Houston State, but it's *famous* for its prison, the Texas State Penitentiary which holds the current U.S. record for most executions in a year. As the lights recede in the rearview mirror, a shiver wiggles up his spine. He can't help but hark back to Chris's sarcastic remark regarding lethal injection, a sobering recollection that tempers his zeal, turning the warm upwelling to no welling at all.

Huntsville, Madisonville, Leona, Centerville, Buffalo—covering the sixty-two miles in forty-four minutes, Bryan exits I-45 at Buffalo, heading west on Route 164. Battling waves of fatigue, he negotiates the narrow two-lane highway: side-road junctions, moonlit alfalfa, a railroad crossing, a desolate stretch, a wooded hollow, a silvery lake, a flashing amber light, a silver NASA rocket—no, it's a cone-roofed water tower. Bryan, shifting down, slows to 25 mph as Route 164 becomes Main Street. Covered sidewalks, boarded-up stores, a Texaco station buttoned-up tight—a squad car lurks in the shadows, Barney Fife asleep at the wheel. Couldn't be Barney? But Kilty could pass for Mayberry. Kilty, Texas: hickish and forgotten by time, save for the post office—there *is* a new post office; God knows why? He shifts up, then down, then up again, each move sapping him all the more. He's in the bowels of redneck land. No more fast lane up on the interstate. He's trapped in a Texas time-warp, as if he's gone back fifty years, as if he's somehow driven into that Larry McMurtry movie: *The Last Picture Show.*

Kilty, Donie, Dingham, Groesbeck, Punker, Mart, Halisburg: he goes through one podunk village after another, dingy, dinky, dead little towns, which is saying a lot for a guy who grew up in *Spindle*, but these places make his hometown look utterly prosperous, save for Groesbeck which could pass for Spindle.

O God, I'm losing it. Why can't I be steadfast like Elmo at the door? Down, leaking, draining away: his hope, his stamina. He rubs his bleary eyes then fingers the stubble on his chin. By the time he spots the lights of Waco, he considers turning back. *Gosh, this's crazy. Doc's gonna say the same thing as Chris, plus I can't just barge in on him at five in the morning. I got here sooner than I expected.* His ardor has forsaken him—like the moon, which now looms like a dirty, half-melted ice cube on the horizon, trapped in the hazy glow that blankets the city. *Plus, I'm not sure I remember how to get to his house. I was just there once. It's east of the river, over in Deer Creek, not far from the golf course. You take 340 and get off on Bailey, or is it Baxter?*

He sighs then shakes his head, trying to clear the cobwebs. *O Jesus God, what the heck am I doing here?* He flips on the radio, some dreadful rap tune. He punches around, getting a shredded weather forecast, shredded by static: something about increasing clouds, chance of rain. He punches some more but gets nothing worth keeping. He kills it—the clock says: 5:32 a.m.

* * *

146 DOUGLAS STREET
TUESDAY, DECEMBER 14, 1999 — 5:45 AM

Pulling into the familiar driveway, Dr. Howard gets out. He notes the house next door, a light in the kitchen plus old-man Lipski at the table, his wide-brimmed gardener's hat on his head. *That ole geezer's up early as usual,* Bryan observes, as he plods through the slatted gate into Annie's courtyard. *It's too cold to do much in his yard except to rake leaves, but he looks ready. Gosh, it's hard to believe he's still alive. He's gotta be ninety, or close. Talk about the unexpected. We had him buried years ago.*

The O'Shea house, by contrast, is dark and silent. *She's asleep. I shouldn't wake her.* He knocks anyway. *This's crazy—God, it's freezing out here.*

The seconds tick by, maybe twenty, then the outside light pops on. "Bryan Howard—what are *you* doing here!" Annie exclaims hoarsely, after opening the back door.

"I uh ... well, I was—"

"Come in, young man ... come in. Don't just stand there. Come on in. Lemme make you some breakfast. Something to warm yuh on this cold morning."

"Thanks," he says, following her inside. Her white sleep-mussed hair drapes the collar of her robe, a raggedy, pinkish, quilted garment. She smells like Ben-Gay ointment.

"I declare, Bryan ... you look like hell," she remarks over her shoulder. "Your eyes I mean ... like yuh haven't slept for a week, but I reckon it's to be expected ... considering what you're going through. It's such a shame ... *such* a shame."

* * *

6:13 a.m. Bryan finishes his fried eggs and bacon, sopping up the yolk with a piece of toast. As he does, Annie gives her take on the situation, "Y'should do what yuh came up here to do." He's filled her in as much as possible. "Go ahead ... give him a call. It sure as hell can't make things any worse."

"Well maybe," the Baylor grad replies, after drinking some coffee. The food has quickened him somewhat, not to speak of the coffee—it's the real, high-octane variety.

"I mean it," she persists, her tawny eyes sparkling—she gives an affirmative nod of her kerchiefed head; her snowy locks are now bound in a blue bandanna. "I don't reckon I can predict what Fred Richardson's gonna do." She gives a gruff, septuagenarian giggle (Annie's seventy-seven but looks the same as ever). "Even Martha couldn't do that—bless her soul. But he's very fond of you, young man, and I'm sure he'll hear yuh out."

Bryan gestures with his mug. "I know ... I know. I doubt he'll go along ... but I reckon he *will* listen to my proposal."

"Of course, he will. And don't jump to a negative conclusion. It's a way-out notion, and it goes well beyond my Catholic beliefs, but I have a hankering it just might work. And it *would* give yuh peace, if y'can talk to her somehow " As if preparing for action, Annie pushes up the sleeves of her robe, exposing her chubby arms, which are dimpled at the elbows. "I'm not a doctor mindyuh, or a preacher, but there's *something* on the other side I reckon, something real and beautiful—that *is* part of my Catholic faith, the good part, and I know it's big among you Baptists. I still have doubts, but what Dudley told me was mighty convincing. Maybe he was having near-death illusions, but I never saw him so serious about anything. And you've seen it as well, Bryan, so it's not like you're going into this as a blind fool."

"Yeah, but finding *her* over there—now that's a big if, and if I don't make it back, Amy will lose me, as well as her mother."

"Very true ... but I still say it's worth it, and it's not just for you and Mandy and your family—though that's the biggie right now. But this's the most crucial damn question facing all of mankind. We all hafta die, even Amy someday. It's the scariest, most crucial thing we hafta face. So we're all desperate for answers and assurance. That's why religion attracts everyone, even in this modern age ... but folks don't get the answers they need, no matter what church they worship in. But y'can bring back something bigger than faith. Yuh already have a good hunch about the soul and the afterlife, but this could *nail* it down." Annie nibbles her toast then sips her java (she didn't have eggs, just a piece of toast, with peanut butter on it). "I reckon there *is* a God up there who loves us, and a Heaven to live in. It may not fit with all our Christian notions, Catholic or Baptist, but we're still desperate for it. And yet, hope can be dashed. That's the scary part. But you can explore our fears head-on—at least, more than any church, or college. And if yuh do make contact, then maybe you'll find out how she feels about being on life-support, and about being disconnected and all."

Bryan sucks a slow breath. "That's what I'm hoping for."

Annie gives a husky snort that turns into a laugh. "Course, you *could* kill yourself. And most folks will freak over the idea, and urge yuh—"

"No kidding," he interrupts, giving a laugh of his own. "I sorta told Mandy's mom, and she made me promise I wouldn't do such a thing, and Chris—well, I already toldjuh about him."

"Yes, yes, but that's *most* understandable. They don't wanna lose you." Annie smirks, her cheeks dimpling—she has dimples from head to foot, like a huge Irish dumpling. She leans forward, creasing her cowlike bosom against the table. "It's instinctive, to protect yuh, and hold on. And Fred may do the same, now that you two have gotten close, and I uh—" Pausing to sip, she stares into her mug, as if looking for the right words.

God, this's weird, Bryan tells himself, *being in this kitchen again, with all the memories of Mandy, and Tracy, and Chris ... of everything that happened back in the old days when we lived upstairs. It's definitely weird.* He swigs the last of his own coffee.

"Not that *I'm* anxious to get rid of you," Annie laughs, having collected her thoughts. "Since I lost Dudley, I've had more good talks with you than anyone I reckon, and I got to know Mandy a hell of a lot too, after y'all got back together. And I almost feel like Amy's grandmother, as much as I was with that baby back then." More laughing and dimpling, but then she sobers. "We're talking about all the marbles, young man. The stakes are goddam high, but I say ... *go* for it. Everyone likes to play it safe, but I say go for it. The best things in life are often the *scariest* as well." She gestures heavenward with her plumpish arm. "Let's find out about that damn silver cord once and for all. That's what y'been looking for all these years. Well, now you have a chance to stare it right in the face, mindyuh. Y'should talk to the professor at least. Why drive all this way, if you're just gonna turn tail and go back?"

He starts to respond, but Annie's on the move, waddling out of the kitchen. She returns with a cordless phone. "Here, young man ... call him. It can't hurt for goodness sake."

Bryan, slipping on his reading glasses, fishes a slip of paper out of his wallet, Doc's number. He punches it into the phone. "Yes, whaa ... who uh?" Dr. Richardson stammers sleepily.

"It's Bryan."

"Oh *damn* ... so it's over already? I mean you lost her?"

"No, no, not yet. It's tomorrow, the fifteenth."

"So what gives, slugger? It's damn early for godsake?"

"I know ... but, *Doc,* I need yuh to help me, like *pronto.* Will yuh come back to Houston with me. I'm already in Waco ... at Annie O'Shea's. But I can swing by and pick yuh up?"

"What? Whaa? What the hell?"

THE SILVER CORD

"I needyuh down at Harvey Cushing, and it's *big*, this thing."

Silence, a few seconds, then the professor replies, "I don't uh ... I mean uh—what the hell's going on? Tell me more—no, on second thought, let's talk in person ... if it's *that* big. Meet me at the club in thirty minutes, the golf course ... Oakvale, the coffee shop. I eat breakfast there anyway, most days. They don't serve till eight, but it's a good place to chat."

* * *

HCMC - EASLEY WING ICU
TUESDAY, DECEMBER 14, 1999 — 11:58 AM

Amid the ever-present *swish* of the respirator, Bryan gazes at Mandy, as she lies unconscious in cubicle #7. He takes off his baseball cap; he fiddles with the snaps on his SHS jacket. He's alone with her, Helen having gone to the ladies' room, while Charlene Comisky, after closing the cubicle curtain, retreated to the nurse's station, to distract the on-duty team if necessary. Nonetheless, he dares not stay long, lest Spigler arrive. Bryan avoided the command post on his way in, with Nurse Comisky's help—he buzzed her from his office, and she informed him that he was indeed on the "no-visit" list regarding Mandy (Amanda Snyder); but then Charlene gave him the updated code for the patient elevator in the back corner of the ICU, and he was able to sneak into cubicle #7 unnoticed—like a janitor in jeans.

Mandy sleeps adorably, angelically—like last night. His eyes filling, Bryan moves closer. "I tried, pretty lady," he whispers. "I tried ... but I can't get anybody to help me. They all *love* me too much." Pecking his fingers, he places the kiss on her butchy new bangs, touching her tenderly, yearningly. "I'm not sure I'll be in tonight—I'm about to crash. And tomorrow's gonna be dadgum hectic in here; it's the last day. Plus, Spigler's gone mad." Bryan pauses, his words catching on the ache in his throat; a tear spills down his unshaven cheek. "In any case, this could be my *last* moment alone with you ... so I reckon I gotta let go and say good-bye. I love you forever, pretty lady ... forever, and ever."

* * *

MAGNOLIA, TEXAS - 22 SHERWOOD
TUESDAY, DECEMBER 14, 1999 — 12:33 PM

Elmo guards the pantry-nook door. It's no longer just an evening routine. He hears a hum then a gritty *rrrrrrp* in the driveway: the Blazer. His tail swishes—but it's only Bryan who comes trudging inside moments later. He pets the black lab. "I tried my best, Elmo boy. But it's no use. Plus, I'm beat outta my f-ing mind. As soon as I feed yuh and get yuh outside, I'm going to bed." He pats Elmo on the flank.

605

THE SILVER CORD

"It's getting sorta cloudy out, but I doubt it's gonna rain right away. Besides, you got your doghouse."

* * *

12:41 p.m. Shedding his sneakers, Bryan flops onto his bed, without pulling back the covers or taking off his clothes. He simply wraps up in the comforter and buries his head in the pillows. The house is chilly, and he has the shivers from lack of sleep, but the old blue-and-white quilt warms him quickly. As he drifts off, he hears Dr. Richardson again: "As a neuroscientist, I could say yes. Let's venture beyond all medical knowledge. Let's push through the outer limits. Let's 'break on through to the other side,' as Jim Morrison called us to do in his heyday. And as a romantic, I could say *yes* as well. Let's find out if love lives on amid the jaws of death. And the whole idea does excite my gambling instincts." A clucking snort, a shake of the head, then sighs, and tender eyes, pale-blue and tearful. "But as a friend, slugger, I must decline. I can't wager a life I love."

Only Doc and Annie know Bryan went to Waco, and Mandy, if she somehow heard him during his brief time with her at the ICU. But it's over now. No more hope, no more fight—they'll disconnect tomorrow night. And he'll be glad it's over.

* * *

6:06 p.m. A loud rapping wakes Bryan. He pads into the kitchen, his mind, and body, staggering for balance. "What the hell?" he reacts, finding Chris at the door; he's dressed in exercise duds, an olive-drab sweatsuit.

"It's like this, slugger," the mustached MD announces, as he comes in, "we need to discuss this whole goddamn thing some more. I been thinking about it all day. Where the hell have you been anyway? I rang you five times, even your cellphone. And your mother-in-law said you were home, that you came in briefly but left the ICU about noon. Chris plunks down at the breakfast table, in the same cane-seated chair as last night. He smirks reflexively.

Bryan yawns and stretches then clears his throat. "I didn't hear the phone. I was taking a nap."

"A nap? What the—but anyway, I'm glad I caught up with you. We need to brainstorm this whole goddamn mess."

"So there's no change in Kathy Cantrall's assessment?"

"No, none ... which is no fucking surprise. Kathy's in San Antonio, at that bigwig powwow, but Mike Samsung says that Mandy's prognosis remains as bleak as ever." Chris spreads his surgeon hands on the cherrywood table, graceful hands.

Bryan hugs himself; the house is still chilly. He gives a yawny chuckle. "So y'got some lightning-bolt urge to rush over here?"

"I was down in the workout room, and I couldn't get it out of my mind, our talk last night. So I tried to phone you again, then I ran like hell to the parking lot ... and I had my fucking Audi on the red line all the way here. This can't wait. It's eating at me."

Bryan's heart perks up, amid more stretching and yawning. "You mean uh ... the inducement procedure?"

"Yeah, yeah ... but mainly your face."

"My face?"

"That hurt look you gave me ... when I turned you down last night. I keep seeing it, and seeing it."

"So you're ready to—"

"Not exactly, but uh—we need to chew on it. Everyone has given up, including your mom-in-law. But after last night, I'm not sure what to think." A dog barks.

"Elmo's outside. I gotta get him. Dang, it's dark already. I been in the sack all afternoon." He flips on the deck light.

"All afternoon? No wonder I couldn't get your ass. What the hell? You don't take naps?"

Bryan slides open the glass door. "Not normally ... but after you left last night, I took off for Waco, like up and back."

"Waco?"

"I'll tellyuh all about it. But first, I gotta get Elmo."

A minute later, the lab's inside; he prances excitedly, licking Bryan, licking Chris, wagging his tail, clicking his claws on the linoleum. "Gosh, it's colder out than I thought," Bryan remarks, above the canine commotion. "And it's starting to rain. It may even be sleeting a little." He hangs the dog lease on a hook next to the deck doors. "Let's move into the living room. We'll make a fire in the fireplace, and we can whip up some ham sandwiches, and grab a couple of brews. Plus, I gotta call Helen at some point, and tell her I won't be in tonight."

As Bryan grabs the ham and stuff from the fridge, his pulse skitters, good vibes. The wintry air outside cleared the cobwebs, allowing the crucial significance of Chris's visit to hit home. Many obstacles remain, but the game's not quite over. They're still down fifteen runs, but they have a couple of outs left.

* * *

6:45 p.m. The aroma of burning wood sweetens the air in the large blue-carpeted room. While Dr. Howard pokes the fire, Dr. Hansen sits on the sofa under the night-black window, Elmo's beach towel wadded beside him. Priscilla curtains (sandy-pale) frame the double window, along with a tasseled shade (Mandy always pulled the shade at night, but Bryan pays no attention to it, so it's up).

"You couldn't persuade him, huh?" Chris says, toasting the air with his Budweiser. "Doc Richardson?" He leans over the coffee table, over his paper plate, which contains the remnants of his sandwich plus a few potato chips and a two-pack of Ring Dings. Bryan spread a

607

newspaper to protect the dark-pine table.

Moving the screen, he adds another log to the popping blaze. Sparks fly, jetting up the chimney: a red burst. The fire's going good—too hot to stand on the raised hearth. "That's about it," he affirms, picking up his own can of beer plus a Ring Ding. "The idea seemed to catch his fancy, but then he backed off, like I was asking him to assist me in suicide, like some Kevorkian thing." He munches on the Ring Ding, washing it down with a swig of Bud. "Yet I reckon it's a normal reaction, just like Annie said." Giving a cakey laugh, Bryan plops down in the recliner. "Too bad *she* isn't a doctor. She's the only person who endorses the idea."

"Not quite."

"I thought you said *maybe* ... that we had to dig deeper?"

Chris wags his head jauntily, like he does. "Well, it could be the beer, but if you're willing to put your life on the line, I guess I'm ready to do the same with my career, and my freedom." He snickers. "They might get me for manslaughter, but not murder one." More snickering, from both. "But it's all academic anyway ... unless we can find someone to help me, someone good. No way can I do it alone. I'd lose you for sure. I need four hands."

* * *

8:25 p.m. Bryan lounges in the LA-Z-BOY, Chris on the couch, while Elmo sleeps near the fire, which has settled into its mature stage: hot coals below, a few orange flames licking upward among the logs. "How'bout Alex?" the junior psychologist asks, as he nurses his third Bud—he already knows the answer.

"No way," Chris snorts emphatically. "He may give us lots of latitude, and he'd probably keep quiet if he found out, but he'd never get involved himself."

"And Jenny Sue?"

"She's topnotch, but she passes everything by Alex." Chris gives a smirky chortle. "Hell, she doesn't even go to the god-damn ladies' room unless he signs off on it."

"Whaddabout Maureen Thomas?"

"We already ruled her out."

"Oh, yeah."

Dr. Howard twirls his cap on his finger then returns it to his head. He's mellowed into a numb sense of capitulation, as the earlier optimism has run aground on the rocks of implausibility—there's no one to assist Dr. Hansen.

"So uh, how'bout Michael Samsung?" Bryan persists, despite the futile nature of the exercise—it's *way* too late for this list.

"He goes strictly by the book," the mustached MD replies, giving a dismissive gesture. "Plus, he's on Kathy's team ... which means no free time until this's over with, especially since she's in San Antone, though I expect she'll be in the ICU tomorrow night to oversee the disconnection process."

The "disconnection" remark causes a queasy downdraft in Bryan's gut. He swigs more Budweiser, which only reinforces the sensation. "Whaddabout Charlene? Nurse Comisky? I toldjuh what she did for me today. She's on my side regarding Spigler."

"Yeah, that didn't shock me ... and she just might be the one, if we had a chance to bring her up to speed—not fucking likely." Chris sips his beer. "She's a skinny goddamn dike, yet she has better instincts than a battlefield medic." He sucks more Bud from the can; some dribbles onto his sweat shirt; he wipes it with a wadded napkin. "Besides, Rennie Couture keeps a fucking tight leash on her ICU staff. But mainly ... there's no damn time. We barely have twenty-four hours, unless you get your mother-in-law to withdraw the legal permission?"

"On what grounds?"

"She doesn't need any ... not legally, not to postpone."

Bryan shakes his head. "I can't ask her to do that, not after I agreed to everything. She's come to terms with this nightmare, and she needs to resolve it, to get it *over* with. She's not gonna drag it out, unless there's a super-good reason, some big change or something."

Chris runs his finger around the top of the Budweiser can. "You could tell her the truth. I mean uh ... deal her in?"

"Not a *chance*. I sorta brought it up at the caf yesterday, and she got all over me. She's accepted the Mandy thing, but no way does she wanna lose me too. She's *super* concerned about Amy, not that I blame her; I'm concerned too. But Helen will never go along. And it's not a Baptist thing. She's more open now when it comes to death and the afterlife. But if I told her, she'd blow the whistle, and blow it *loud*. Just like my own mom would. And she doesn't know I went begging to Waco." He sips then burps amid a sigh. "If Doc Richardson says no for the same reason, and you too, at *first* ... then it makes sense that Helen would freak."

"So the deadline is firm?"

"I'm afraid so ... unless there's a dramatic change in Mandy's medical prognosis."

Chris doesn't reply. Bryan studies the lazy flames in the fireplace, till his left eye goes whacky, an ongoing reminder of his own brush with death back in '91. He drinks more brewski; he gives a weary murmur. It's a depressing situation, yet he's more trancy-numb than sorrowful, as the beer and fatigue sedate his psyche, not to mention the mesmerizing effect of the fire, the undulating flames, the rustic aroma. He's still physically fagged from lack of sleep, and his emotions are even more exhausted. Six weeks of torment and inner turmoil have wrung him to the limit. "There's always José?" he offers blankly, more to break the silence than to address the problem.

"José?"

"José Ramos ... the heavyset inhalation therapist?"

"Now I know you're fishing. He's a maestro ... when it comes to his equipment, but I've never heard him talk. Hell, I don't even know if he can speak English."

"How about Angie? She used to work in the OR?"

"Yeh right ... she'd make damn sure you didn't get back, then she'd report my ass. She's been shitface since we broke up."

"How'bout all those student nurses that work in the—"

"I know a few I'd like to bang," Dr. Hansen cuts in smirkily, "but that's a far cry from what we're talking about." Pursing his lips, he twitches his mustache. "We can't even think of anybody on staff, so it's most doubtful we can persuade some baby-faced, nurse-school chick to step forward and risk her career. Same for the med students. They're just trying to survive till Christmas break. Hell, slugger, it's taken me eight goddamn years to come around to your way of thinking, so we're not going to find a bunch of *Flatliners*, Julia Roberts, risk-taking cunts on the HC campus. That's Hollywood shit. Ditto for the guys. You have to be a twilight-zone renegade to even consider this."

Bryan sighs then chuckles. "Yeah, and Julia Roberts—she even went on a near-death trip herself, and so did Kevin Bacon, but Sutherland was the ringleader, and there were two other guys as well. I can't think of the actors."

"There were five in the group ... if I remember that movie. Med students, all from the same campus. Fat chance—I doubt we could find five in the whole goddamn country."

"It's too scary, that flick ... and it's full of spooky Catholic music. Some of it's okay, like similar to what I experienced, like zooming over sunny fields and going through that tunnel toward the light, but I never saw anything dark and hellish ... like how Keifer Sutherland kept seeing his crippled dog down in a subway. That was *super* creepy. But *my* NDE was beautiful and uplifting ... and wonderful and sublime, and full of love ... like better than anything. Y'know, I toldjuh?"

Chris smirks. "That you did ... by Annie's barbecue pit back in '91." His smirk grows into a grin then a chortle. "You rode an astral orgasm right into Heaven. How could I forget? That was fucking way out ... coming from some farmboy Baptist." More laughs. "I should've run like hell after hearing shit like that. But instead, I got caught up in it ... and *now,* it's come to this."

Bryan waits for the mood to sober; he sips then snuffles. "But seriously, Chris, that's how I deal with this. I mean ... if Mandy *has* to die, it's not hellish and terrifying. It's glorious—at least, what I saw was. It's still a mystery, but what I experienced sure gives me a measure of solace."

"I know, slugger. I didn't mean to laugh about it."

"That's okay. I reckon I *woulda* run ... if I'd been in your dadgum shoes." Bryan chuckles himself, plugging it with a swig. He gestures with the can. "But with Mandy, the mystery's even bigger. It's uh—well, we don't know where she *is* right now ... the whole coma thing. Maybe her soul is dormant and doing nothing, or maybe she's having a series of NDEs, or maybe the silver cord is severed, and she's already in Heaven. This all presupposes the existence of the soul of course. But that's a *fact* now, as far as I'm concerned—unless I'm a deluded neurotic. But anyway, if I could find out where she is, one way or the other, I'd have more peace about disconnecting the life support ... especially if we can communicate somehow."

"If we have to disconnect at all?"

"Oh ... to have her wake up—that would be the *ultimate* ... like a fairy-tale miracle. But I'm not gonna get my hopes up for that. It's not like inducing an NDE is gonna change her medical condition. Making contact and getting her *take* on the disconnect deadline—that's as far as I dare to hope. But right now, it looks like we won't even be trying. There's no one to help yuh."

Chris kills off his beer, then leans forward, placing the empty can on the coffee table, on the newspaper. "What if you had one of your OBEs?"

"Whaddeyuh mean?"

"Perhaps you can communicate with her during one of your out-of-body dreams? You know, the trips you take while you're asleep?" Chris smirks and waggles. "I can't fucking believe I'm actually here talking about this stuff."

Bryan sips then replies, "I have considered that possibility, but it's not like I can make an OBE happen. Plus, when I had my last episode in November, I had no sense of Mandy's presence. I toldjuh about it ... going to the accident scene and all."

"Yes, that was bizarre. But there was no sign of her?"

"No, I reckon I hafta go through the tunnel to find her ... *if* she's out there. Y'can't trick death ... or fool God." Bryan gives a snuffly titter. "The cord lets you go farther when the heart stops, and I reckon it severs, if the heartbeat is not restored ... or maybe it's the anoxia that sends you through the tunnel, the strangling of the brain. I've been studying this ever since high school, but it's still a goshdang enigma, and that's why I tend to doubt haunted-house ghost stories and such, and seances, and things like that. Let's face it, you gotta put me *down* to get me over there. It's not a carnival-trick thing."

"That's for sure. It's all fake, that razzle-dazzle necromancy bullshit, like on the Sci Fi Channel, that stand-up psychic guy who performs to please a crowd of relatives." Chris pops a leftover chip into his mouth. "But shocking you into CA and making your EEG go flat—that's another goddamn matter altogether." Stretching to his feet, he runs his hand through his curly locks. "Gotta take a leak." He disappears around the corner (there's no door, just a wide opening that marries the living room to the hallway and entry area at the top of the stairs).

A wind gust buffets the house; rain peppers the window over the sofa, sleet too, a few icy pings. *It's downright wintry out there,* Bryan notes, as he hauls himself out of the recliner. Grabbing a log from the rack, he feeds the fire. Elmo moves a few feet, giving a sleepy whine. While the rejuvenated flames crackle and pop, he replaces the screen then warms his backside. *Gosh, it's only nine o'clock. It seems like we've been talking for ten hours—without accomplishing a damn thing. O Lord, if it has to be, let's get it over with. So I can bring Amy home, and we can get on with our lives.* He tilts his Baylor cap back on his head. *This's so weird—Chris decides to go along, yet we have no place to GO. It's like a movie that ends in the middle. It's weird ... but it fits my trancy frame of mind. I'm out of it ... like overtired.*

Chris reappears. "Well, slugger, I wish we had a more heroic conclusion to this whole matter," he offers, as he returns to the sofa, plunking down amid a weary, drawn-out exhalation. He clasps his hands behind his head. "This's very anticlimactic, like kissing your goddamn sister."

"No *kid*ding. I was just thinking the same—"

Bang! Rap! Rap! Front door. Elmo barks then growls. Bryan hustles to answer the knock, the black lab at his side. "Who can that be at this hour? Maybe Helen decided to come home? But she doesn't have a car? And she wouldn't use this—Doc! What the hell are *you* doing here?"

"I'm here to get this damn show on the road," Richardson announces, as he bops into the house accompanied by an icy gust. Snow and sleet dapple the shoulders of his rumpled coat, a grayish overcoat. Elmo barks then wags. The doctor, dropping his overnight bag, bends down to pet the hound. "Hello, Elmo—my God, you're full grown now. You were just a pup back in June." The dog licks him, nuzzles him, the full canine welcome.

"So uh? What gives?" Bryan stammers. "I mean uh ... y'just came from—"

"Hell of a drive. It was snowing hard in Waco, and the rain down here is changing over as well. There's a norther blowing in, the second one since Saturday. It's damn cold for Houston. Hell, this weather reminds me of Connecticut." He brushes the melting ice from his coat then pushes by his Baylor disciple, bounding boldly up the stairs, Elmo in hot pursuit. "I hope you have some heat in this pl—ah-*hah*, you got a fire going. Perfect. And look who's here: Dr. Hansen *him*self. I figured as much. Just get me a beer, slugger, if you have any left, and we'll get started."

* * *

9:15 p.m. Dr. Richardson takes a lefthanded sip of Bud then replaces the can on the mantel. He removes his bow-tie and slips it into the side pocket of his suit coat—he wears his old blue-corduroy suit, the one with the leather elbow patches. He paces back and forth in front of the fireplace, his hands clasped behind him, as though he's back at Baylor getting ready to teach a class. Bryan sits eagerly forward in the now-upright recliner. Ditto for Chris on the edge of the sofa. "Now here's our battle plan," the shortish doctor declares, in his familiar Yankee accent. "T-hour will be seven p.m. tomorrow evening ... in Goethals South, up in the training OR, #404. We'll be cutting it a bit close, but that's the earliest we can safely proceed. I still have keys to the place, plus the pharmacy-vault codes. And I already notified Leroy Bannister, the security chief over there, that I'll be using that OR after hours tomorrow night—he's an old friend of mine, and I told him I'd be conducting a class, which is quite plausible, since I *do* conduct a visiting-professor seminar in Goethals South each summer. But needless to say, this entire mission remains *top* secret. All the students should be out of there by five, so we'll meet to set up and rehearse at five-thirty, the three of—"

"Hey wait a second, Doc?" Chris chimes in. "How do you know I'm aboard this train?"

"Why *else* would you be here for godsake?" Richardson fires back, his blue eyes dancing like the flames in the fireplace. He gives his wry chuckle, *yeck-yeck*, the crowlike clucking—then they *all* laugh, a much needed release. Even Elmo joins in, with a canine moan. The professor grabs his brew from the mantel. He swigs then steps toward Chris, toasting him. "I've already chosen you anyway ... from ten thousand goddamn applicants."

Hearty laughter all around, then the professor sobers—he retreats toward the fireplace. "But seriously, Chris, there's no one else I trust to assist me. This's cutting-edge science, perhaps the boldest of all endeavors, and yet most of our goddamn peers would scoff and call us kooky ... or criminal, especially Barry Spigler. That asshole would try to jail us if he knew. I doubt he'd get far, since I outrank him, but it would certainly torpedo the mission. I still can't believe that visitation technicality he pulled on you, slugger. It's all swagger-mouth bullshit. But I'm still going to *get* him for that, one way or another." He swigs some Bud then replaces the can on the mantel. Shedding his suit coat, he tosses it on the empty armchair. He rolls up the sleeves of his dress shirt. The mood has sobered, but with less tension than before—they're *ready* for action. The professor resumes his pacing, near the fire screen. He hand-combs the back of his head, running his fingers through the gray fringe of hair that spills over his collar. "Now, Bryan, I'm going to take you down with nitrous and sodium penathol ... along with a refrigerated blanket. Chris will hold the mask; I'll release 20 cc's into your i.v. fluid."

Bryan, agog with wonder, gives a nod. Same for Chris.

Dr. Richardson rubs his hands together, as if rolling a piece of chalk. "When your body temp has dropped to 86°—that'll take five minutes, perhaps more—Chris will hit you with 200 joules, 250 if necessary. That should put you into CA ... with your heart-trace going flat, which means you're clinically dead. We'll give you forty-five seconds at 86°, then Chris will warm the blanket to 93°. We can warm much faster than we cool. At 93° I'll release one cc of adrenaline into the i.v. plus the bicarb."

He chops the air, his patrician voice assuming a resolute quality, like that of a British brigadier briefing a commando squad. "At one minute and thirty seconds, Chris will defibrillate your heart again, 200 joules, or 300, or whatever it takes, and hopefully we'll get a good pulse. Then we'll put you on oxygen. I'll also have epinephrine just in case, plus a ventilator ready." Richardson is short and slightly built, but he seems suddenly large and Bunyanesque, bigger than life, especially with his shadow, upcast by the fire, playing on the ceiling. "Getting you back is the biggest challenge of course, but I feel confident we can do it, since you're strong and robust and young." He sweeps an open hand toward Bryan. "Normally, we can't tolerate much more than a minute of anoxia without causing damage, but with your BT reduced we can do a hundred seconds, at least. Still, to be safe we'll be initiating the resuscitation process at the 90-second mark." He does his crow cluck, a high-pitched version. "So you'll have a minute and a half to look for her ... Earth time. Who they hell knows how that translates in the twilight zone?"

THE SILVER CORD

CHAPTER THIRTY-SIX

MAGNOLIA, TEXAS - 22 SHERWOOD
WEDNESDAY, DECEMBER 15, 1999 — 7:08 AM

Elmo gazes yearningly at the pantry-nook door, the knob, the knob. He assumed his usual station after coming inside from the snow-covered backyard, a freezing, paw-deep blanket that made his morning routine less than pleasant. No leash, no games, no playful antics: Bryan simply opened the deck door and let him out, and he was back in three minutes.

His hound-dog stomach growls. He has dry food in his bowl, but he knows he'll get the canned stuff later (plus human food: usually toast and leftover cereal and milk), so he remains faithfully at his post.

* * *

10: 35 a.m. While Dr. Richardson showers in the bathroom at the end of the hall, Dr. Howard pads into the kitchen, wearing the same jeans and shirt he's had on for two days, not to speak of his BO and beard—he's going to shower shortly (in his own bathroom). "Goshdang, Elmo," he declares, as he swigs some orange juice. "You've been sitting by that door since I was up before." Going over, he pats the black lab fondly on the head. Elmo, wagging and mewing, licks his hand but stays put.

It's dadgum late, like going on eleven, Bryan remarks to himself as he finishes the OJ. *But Chris didn't leave until one-thirty and Doc and I sat up by the fire another hour after that. It all seems like a dream.* He yawns. *My head's still fogged, and I gotta do these dishes, and get rid of the beer cans, but I should eat something first.* He grabs bread from the fridge. After placing two slices in the toaster, he steps over to check out the backyard, a rare Christmas-card scene. The snowy lawn and trees glisten in the sunshine, a sea of shimmering sequins. The sight stirs boyish wonder, reinforcing the awe from last night, the awe of what's coming. The storm deposited an inch of white stuff, maybe two, sleet plus snow. But it's already melting on the south-facing deck, turning ugly, going to slush. *This's the first time it's covered the ground since we've lived here. In fact, it hasn't snowed like this since '95, according to Mrs. Felt next door.* She yelled over to Bryan earlier, while he was outside with Elmo.

The toast pops up; the phone sings out. Ignoring the toast, he grabs the phone; it's Helen. After exchanging a few comments about the snow—there's less downtown, and it's almost gone—he asks, "D'yuh need to come home today?"

"No," she replies. "I'm all set."

615

"Sorry I didn't make it back in last night. Chris was over, and we had a good talk."

"Yeah, y'said he was there ... when you called."

"Plus, it's tricky ... dodging Spigler."

"No kidding. He's a first-class bastard. Pardon my language, but I plan to tell him off good ... once this whole thing's over. I finally saw who he is yesterday—he *is* ugly as sin—and he gave me a curious look, like he knows I'm Mandy's mom, but he didn't introduce himself or speak to me." She exhales loudly. "And he better not say anything about you, the visitation thing, or he'll get his *eyes* clawed out."

"That *would* improve his looks," Bryan quips. They both laugh. "But there's no point in making a stink, not now. It's just a good thing that he's been gone for most of this ordeal."

"Yes, I suppose," she sighs.

"I *will* be in tonight of course ... but I'm gonna be late, like nine o'clock."

"That's fine. I won't be napping anyhow. This's the last...." Her voice trails off, then comes a sob.

Bryan, fighting to keep his own poise, aches to tell her about Dr. Richardson and the bold and desperate mission embarking from Goethals South this evening—but he dares not.

* * *

EASTEX FREEWAY - NORTH OF HOUSTON
WEDNESDAY, DECEMBER 15, 1999 — 5:05 PM

Rush-hour traffic clogs the northbound lanes, but the inbound Blazer cruises right along. Dr. Howard jockeys around a slow-moving dump truck then returns to the center lane. The Houston skyline looms ahead of them, red-tinted by the setting sun, the same sun that melted the snow. It's all gone, even the puddles, though it remains chilly out, fifty at best. Dr. Richardson stares steadfastly ahead under the visor of his Oakvale Country Club hat. Blue jeans for Bryan, khaki Dockers for the professor, plus sweaters for both. They're dressed casually, as if returning from a December round of golf. But their purpose is *hardly* casual, and they've spoken little since leaving the house. The affidavit in Dr. Richardson's pocket testifies to the nature of their venture. Bryan gave it to him as they left, a signed statement declaring that he's doing this of his own free will, lest he die or suffer severe brain damage.

Love versus death, triumph versus agony, horror versus glory. The excitement and wonder, the hope, the anxiety, the dread—it's still there inside Bryan, but he's calmed his emotions with quiet resolve, as Marines do before a landing, as airborne troops before hooking up to jump, as astronauts before a launch, as the Spindle jock did so often before a crucial game. Baseball hardly compares, but when it comes to the supreme journey, he has more experience than most, and he's intent on probing that mystery again—this time for Mandy's sake.

A mile or so later, he breaks the silence, "So, Doc, what made you change your mind? You sorta said last night, but I reckon I'm still wondering?" He chuckles, yet the mood remains solemn, decidedly so.

"I said no for your sake of course, and mine," Richardson replies, speaking straight ahead toward the city, "but then I got to thinking about love, about what makes it *real*, and I settled on the notion that it trumps *all* things, and risks *all* things, even safety and sanity." Gesturing toward the sunset, he gives a nod plus a snuffle. "It's like you said last night ... love *has* to try. Besides, I'm seventy-five. What's the point of laying up now? I'll soon be crossing over myself. In fact, the only time we really *live*, is when we're on the edge. It's like Einstein says: 'The most beautiful thing we can experience is the mysterial.' And this's the *big*gest damn mystery of all." He chuckles, his crowlike clucking. "I just pray that I can get you back, slugger. That's the *big* risk, and I hope you can somehow make contact with Mandy—that's the *big* reward." His blue eyes filling, he gives Bryan a pat on the shoulder. "It's most unlikely that she'll ever recover—we both know the prognosis—but to establish where she is would be an astounding breakthrough ... not to mention the peace of mind, if she's in a good place. Then we can let go with assurance. But who the hell knows? There's no map on this. You may encounter something miraculous ... or horrendous? I hope the former."

5:18 p.m. They negotiate a narrow alleyway on the old side of the HCMC campus, a shortcut to the parking lot behind Goethals South— it's only a five-minute walk from the Easley Wing, but walking may not be an option afterward.

"Using that alley keeps us out of the traffic," Richardson comments, as Bryan parks the green SUV. "No big d—ahah, looks like Chris is here already." He nods toward the light-tan Audi, Chris's car. He gives another *yeck-yeck*, but it comes out more dry than wry—pre-mission butterflies? Bryan starts to get out, but the professor stops him. "I have three kids you know, two sons and a daughter?"

"Yeah, y'told me. Your daughter lives in Dallas, but your sons left Texas ... one to Colorado, the other to Florida."

"Right on, and I also have eight grandkids and three great-grandkids. My grandson, Ricky, is about your age, slugger."

"I reckon y'told me that too. He's the one who became a golf pro, at least good enough to play a few times on the Lone Star mini-tour."

Richardson snorts. "You have a goddamn good memory. But what I'm getting at—" He pauses, as if thinking how to say it.

Bryan studies the rusty fire escape winding back and forth up the backside of the old, art-deco academic building. He feels like he's back at Baylor, in the rear of Peyton Hall.

"It's not like a family thing," the professor explains, having garnered his thoughts. "I mean, I could say I love you like a son, or like a grandson, or as a special student of mine, and that's how most people talk when relating to younger folks ... but that's not it, slugger ... not what I feel for you. It's peculiar, but I love you like a buddy, like a peer ... as if we grew up together ... or bunked together in Korea. That's why I drink beer with you, and share my deepest secrets with you. And that's why I'm going through with this. I'm not God, but I'm a *fucking* good doctor, and I plan to use *all* my knowledge and experience to pull this off. And I hope like hell you'll be able to make contact ... at least enough to ease your mind about Kathy Cantrall's 11:00 p.m. disconnection order over at the ICU." He grips Bryan's hand, a tear overflowing, spilling down his cheek. "I'm with you *all* the way. In fact, I'd go too ... if I didn't have to stay to get your ass back."

* * *

HCMC - GOETHALS SOUTH - RM 406
WEDNESDAY, DECEMBER 15, 1999 — 8:50 PM

While Dr. Hansen wraps Dr. Howard in the refrigerated blanket (it could pass for a pleated shower curtain), Dr. Richardson attaches the remaining electrodes to Bryan's forehead and temple, stick-on conductive patches. Fear shakes the young psychologist amid equally fierce pangs of hope. The white-coated professor, his tortoise-shell glasses propped on his nose, gazes warmly at his friend. "Well, slugger, I guess we're almost ready."

"Okay, let's roll," Bryan replies, his words breathy with emotion. "I trust yuh, Doc ... and you too, Chris."

They're running two hours late, because they couldn't open the pharmacy vault—new codes. Chris hurried over to the Easley Wing to get the drugs, but it took a while, since he had to write up a bullshit story for each one, especially the sodium penathol.

Richardson checks the suspended i.v. pouch that will deliver 20 cc's of the sleep juice. "Is the BT monitor all set?" he asks Dr. Hansen.

"Aye-aye, sir ... 98.6° ... and ready to go down."

Chris bends close to his Baylor buddy: "We're going to get you back, believe me."

"I sure *hope* so ... but give me as much time as you can."

Hiss—Dr. Hansen opens the valve on the tank of nitrous oxide. "See you soon," he quips smirkily. He places the mask over Dr. Howard's nose and mouth.

Bryan inhales. Giddy vibes subdue his senses delivering him into a carefree stupor, then comes the tidal wave, the sodium penathol, a tsunami of sleepiness: *I'm going. I'm going.*

* * *

"He's flatlining," Dr. Hansen announces six minutes later (OR time)—he still holds the defib paddles. "The 250 did the trick. BT remains steady, at 86°. The clock is ticking: three ... four."

"Very good," Dr. Richardson replies, his patrician voice calm and professional. "When we get to thirty-five seconds, bring that blanket up to 93°."

Bryan, oblivious to the passage of time, hovers blissfully above the brightly lit scene: wires, tubes, i.v. pouches, long-necked lamp, blinking monitors, defibrillator unit, nitrous cart, oxygen cart, stand-by ventilator, Doc's bald head, Chris's curly brown locks—and Bryan's *own* body wrapped in the blue-plastic blanket. Amid the boundless sense of well-being he hears a song, a country tune? No, it's *The Beatles*, a soulful rendition of "Hey Jude." He glides out into the empty corridor. Save for the music, it seems like a regular OBE—but not for long. He's suddenly above Goethals South, above the HCMC campus, above the traffic on I-45. As *The Beatles* sing louder, he ascends along the looping interstate, banking like a biplane around the glassy, blue-green Enron tower, around all the many-windowed skyscrapers.

Then a great *WHOOSH* drowns the music. No control: he skyrockets toward the stars, leaving Houston, leaving Earth, leaving this reality. Faster, faster—he hurtles into the tunnel, racing toward the light, the ultimate light. As before, his life pans by, a kaleidoscope of scenes, Mom, Dad, Buster, Gramps, Millie, baseball, Mandy, Mandy, oh dear Mandy. Time unwinds in this trans-dimensional wormhole, allowing him to digest it all without rushing, yet he *is* rushing, ripping along at warp speed. Good vibes, happy vibes—bliss, glory, utter contentment. Death does not destroy or damn. It delivers us rather to the LIGHT from whence we came, to heart and mercy and compassion, to GOD our shepherd, to our Father, Mother, Eternal Friend, to Christ, to Allah, to Jehovah Lord, to joy unspeakable and full of glory!

The LIGHT speaks inside Bryan, silently, but oh so clearly: "The Lord is my shepherd.... Yea, though I walk through the valley of the shadow of death, I will fear no evil; for thou art with me." And Bryan Howard *has* no fear. The brilliance ahead looms larger and brighter, as does the ecstasy, the ineffable sense of jubilation and acceptance. The LIGHT is calling him, GOD is calling him, LOVE is calling him, wondrous neverending LOVE. The same LOVE that created him, and sent him, now raptures him, ushering him into the halls of Heaven.

Blessed euphoria fills him, devours him, drowns him. The LIGHT swallows him, a pearly fog that grows brighter, brighter, becoming almost incandescent. He weeps with joy. He knew about this, from '91, but only in the throes of death itself can you really KNOW. He hears within himself more words from the LIGHT, and this time they're personal and specific: "Bryan Wallace Howard, your soul is precious and beautiful and childlike, *perfect* when it comes to trust and devotion. LOVE *is* the highest good, and LOVE has brought you here. You can see *clearly* now ... the purpose of your trials and tribulations. You have learned well, my son. What you've known in your heart of hearts is TRUE, now and forever. In quest of this highest good, you've laid down your *life*, the utmost gift a human can bestow ... and this undying LOVE *shall* bear fruit."

Voices resound, a heavenly chorus singing "Pretty Woman." *Oh, Mandy,* Bryan exults, *I've come to look for you. But, dear pretty lady, if you're here already, why would yuh want to leave such wonder and joy? I don't wanna leave myself. O Lord—thy will be done.* The celestial fog darkens a bit, turning softly violet yet remaining nacreous—then lightning flashes, red lightning, green lightning, then strobes of blue, and pink, and yellow. The cloud swirls into a vortex, which umbrellas outward, spewing wavy rainbows of Day-Glo color against a dazzling, ultra-blue sky. The psychedelic cyclone spins faster and faster, then *poof*—it dissolves like a genie returning to his lamp.

Bryan spins as well, but slowly like a falling leaf caught in an updraft. Then, *ka-WOOSH*, he finds himself sweeping low over the ocean. Spellbound, he rides the tropical wind, skimming at high speed above choppy turquoise waves. New music: George Thorogood and "Madison Blues." Sassy sax, rollicking guitar, kick-ass drums. The rip-roaring, roadhouse beat exhilarates him all the more, heightening his anticipation: *"This undying LOVE shall bear fruit."* Mandy, Oh Mandy ... I'm on the way.

No more water: he's over jungle, a thick rain forest, then a grassy savanna, then rose-tinted dunes, pink sand, lavender sand, aquamarine too, a painted desert, an endless empyreal Sahara. But it does *end*—at the mountains. Gaining altitude, he soars over majestic snow-capped peaks, lilac-tinted, purple *glory*—the music soars as well, "Amazing Grace" replacing Thorogood, a souped-up instrumental arrangement of the famous hymn, with piano riffs and splashing cymbals. Amid the brassy crescendos, Bryan descends into a milky-gray notch, milky with falling snow. He bursts through the clouds into a dreamy manifestation of the Great Plains, sunny plains, wheated plains, lush plains dotted with cattle and buffalo as far as the eye can see. He blitzes the grazing herds, then the scene shifts totally, as in a movie.

He zooms over a vast yellow field, yellow with milkwort and sunflowers and honeysuckle, a sublime mixture of warm color, deep primrose dappled with florescent orange, a billion blossoms. Inhaling the sweet nectars, he slows to a glide. The music fades, as the yellow flowers give way to wooded hills and rolling pastures. He spies a familiar hayfield and barn. *Dear God, that's my house! That's my horse!* A glorified rendering of the Howard farm sprawls below him, the meadows and trees richly verdant in the sunshine, a luminescent yellow-green beyond anything in the earthly realm. A flatbed truck trundles down the tractor trail, while Millie frolics like a filly in her romp-around lot, kicking up her hooves and tossing her head. Bryan focuses in her direction, but he has no control. The truck draws him like a magnet, and he soon realizes why. Descending to ten feet, he follows the slow-moving vehicle.

Elmo McKinney, clad in his coaching garb, sits on the back of the flatbed, his legs dangling, while a collie trots alongside—it's Buster, Bryan's boyhood dog. Coach McKinney removes his baseball cap and wipes his kinky hair. He grins and rolls his eyes, the whites sliding to the side. "Hey, Howard," he calls (in the silent supernatural fashion), "your grandpa's been lookin' for yuh all afternoon."

Whooosh—Bryan is instantly over Ruby Pond; he flits over the calm water like a soul-sized dragonfly. Atop the grassy knoll to the west, the giant oak, the glorified version, towers above him, its leafy backlit crown gleaming like an enormous emerald in the heavenly sunlight. *Gramps! Oh, Gramps!*

His joy overflowing, Bryan tries to get closer, to fly up the hill, but an ethereal force prevents him. Wallace Howard, clad in overalls plus his Texaco hat, leans against the massive trunk, the same lone silhouette. His heart speaks, and his grandson hears: "Buddy, I love yuh forever, and one day we'll be together. But for now, y'gotta finish the quest. And I hear tell she's on the far side of the sea. But there ain't no cause for worry. Just rise up a mite and let the world turn beneath yuh."

Bryan ascends, without effort, to a thousand feet. No wind, no movement—he floats in place, like a hot-air balloon. But not so below: the glorified landscape begins to advance beneath him, slowly at first, then swifter and swifter, as though he's rushing backward, yet it's the divine realm that's moving, not him. The farm recedes, then the previous hills and fields pass under him, then the yellow flowers, and the plains, and the mountain range, and the desert, and the jungle; *blip, blip, ka-ZOOM*—he's back over the ocean, but it's bluer than before, bluer than Wedgwood, as it reflects the sky. The sea surface is remarkably calm, more so than Ruby Pond. The glassy surface continues to advance until he can see nothing but water—no mountains, no forest, no fields, no shoreline even.

The sea halts finally. All is still. The sun dissolves—no more gold. He hears Gramps again: *I hear tell she's on the far side of the sea.* Bryan turns, looking the other way, yet he sees nothing but darkening ocean and sky. Everything turns gray then black. All is still. A choir sings "Silent Night," the same chorus that did "Pretty Woman" before, but now their voices are soft and tender and hallowed, full of godly wonder.

He discerns on the far horizon a silvery glow—it quickly grows into a rising moon, a huge celestial moon. It grows bigger and brighter, then she blushes and smirks—IT'S HER!

"OH, MANDY! DEAR MANDY!" he shouts heart-to-heart. Up here it's all heart-to-heart.

She hears him though, or seemingly so, her smirk warming into a smile. Blue eyes, cupid mouth, golden bangs, ruddy cheeks. The moon morphs all the way, fleshing out into a full-faced yet ethereal rendering of his precious pretty lady. She wrinkles her nose, purses her lips, then she gives her goofy little-girl grin.

Overwhelmed with affection, he races toward her, galactic speed, Star Trek speed—but she recedes even faster, her blushing grin going blurry and distant, fuzzy like a faraway nebula.

But as she fades, she calls to him, in the same heart-to-heart way of calling: "Don't let go of me. Don't let go. Oh, dear babe, hold me *tight* ... 'cause I'm coming home! I'm coming home!"

* * *

"We got *him*!" Dr. Richardson exclaims, as Dr. Howard regains consciousness amid a fit of gasping and wheezing. The OR comes into focus then fades again.

"Here, breathe this," Dr. Hansen directs, placing a mask over Bryan's face. The room stabilizes. Chris smirks. "Welcome back, slugger. You were dead for two minutes, clinically speaking." He removes the oxygen mask.

Bryan coughs, his thoughts tumbling. "Two minutes? It uh ... what? It uh ... how? Gosh uh ... seemed like a *whole* day?"

"We actually got you back at the 1:56 mark," Richardson adds, patting his disciple on the arm. "116 seconds."

"Mandy uh, Mandy ... O Jesus," Bryan stammers. "I uh, I uh ... can't think." He can't quite retrieve some wonderful knowing; it eludes him, as when you try to recall a dream.

"Don't try to talk just yet," the professor counsels.

Chris attaches the nasal canula, the little-tube apparatus. "Here, let me give you some more O-2 ... the steady variety."

"Okay," Dr. Richardson directs. "Let's get him out of this goddam shower curtain." Removing the refrigerated blanket, the two neurosurgeons cover Bryan with a regular blanket.

* * *

9:03 p.m. Dr. Howard, eyes closed but awake, recovers on the operating table. Chris and the professor continue to watch the monitors and readouts, checking his vital signs. Bryan sighs, his mind reviving— now it comes, the memory: *Oh, dear babe, hold me tight ... 'cause I'm coming home! I'm coming home!*

"I saw her!" he shouts, trying to sit up. "I hafta tell Helen!" Getting halfway up, he goes woozy, the room reeling. "Mandy, Mandy ... she's coming back. I hafta go to the ICU."

His cohorts restrain him. "No, Bryan," Richardson declares. "Don't try to get up. It'll just make you faint. You could even have a seizure." He caresses Bryan's head; the woozy feeling recedes. "That's *great* news ... but we have *plenty* of time." Your vitals look A-OK, so you should get your wits back quickly, and your strength ... but let's not press our good fortune."

"You tell her then—you guys go and tell Helen. Tell Dr. Cantrall. Mandy's coming *back*. I know it. I saw her. She spoke to me. They can't disconnect. She's coming *back*."

"It's okay," the professor consoles. "It's only nine o'clock. Besides, it's best if you tell her yourself. I'm an unrelated third party, same goes for Chris ... so Helen is unlikely to accept such news from us. But there's plenty of time. We'll *all* go up at ten."

"Nine forty-five," Bryan counters.

"Fine," Richardson agrees.

They all laugh, the mood rising triumphantly—they did it; they pulled it off; they got Bryan Howard to Heaven and back, and he didn't return empty-handed.

"I could call Helen on the phone," Bryan says, backtracking. "I'm plenty strong enough to do that. I can do it lying down. Lemme have your cellphone, Chris."

"Not a good idea," Richardson cautions. "She'll want to know *why*, which means you'll have to get into this *whole* thing over the phone. Plus, anyone near the nurse's station could overhear. She could even faint, or go into shock or something. It's much better to explain face to face." He pats the air with his left hand, a slow-down motion. "The cellphone is a good back-up, but only if we encounter some unexpected emergency."

"And I have another goddamn suggestion," Chris wisecracks. "When we do go over, slugger, I highly recommend that you divulge your evidence discreetly, like alone with your mom-in-law. Or they'll be getting straitjackets for all of us ... especially if fucking Spigler is anywhere around."

More laughter, then Richardson says, "Okay, that's enough. Let's cool it, so he can recover."

* * *

HCMC - GOETHALS SOUTH - REAR PARKING LOT
WEDNESDAY, DECEMBER 15, 1999 — 9:55 PM

Dr. Howard, walking under his own power, glances up at the stars before climbing into the back seat of the Blazer. The idea that he just journeyed beyond them seems incredible, to say the least. Dr. Richardson offered a wheelchair-ride for his patient, but Bryan put that to rest, declaring he was quite fit to walk. The professor closes Bryan's door then gets in up front. Chris, in the driver's seat, has been out here for five minutes, warming the SUV on this cold, calm, December night. They could've taken the Audi, but Doc chose the Blazer—more roomy. Bryan, a bit queasy yet fully alert, wraps his jacket more tightly around him (his old Spindle letter-jacket). The car's plenty warm, but he's chilly, from the ordeal. "You'll feel cold for a few hours," the professor explained, as his ace patient donned his clothes.

"This's the greatest night in human history," Chris exults, as they exit through the same narrow alley. "God damn ... this's fucking stupendous. I can hardly believe it."

"It ranks right up there no doubt," Richardson declares.

"Well, I reckon we're gonna find out," Bryan offers from the back seat, his triumphant sense of elation now tempered a bit by Murphy's Law anxiety—he *must* tell Helen before eleven p.m.

* * *

HCMC - EASLEY WING ICU
WEDNESDAY, DECEMBER 15, 1999 — 10:03 PM

Dr. Howard, still queasy and shivery, but inspired by the moment, marches triumphantly into the deserted ICU waiting room, Chris and Dr. Richardson by his side. "Damn, slugger," Chris quips, "you've got pretty good lung action, for a guy who was flatlining an hour ago." They share a muffled titter.

"We should wait here," the professor tells Chris. "Helen is expecting Bryan. If we all go bopping into the ICU, it will just create confusion."

"Good point," Bryan concurs. "Getting up here was the key ... and I'm doing *just* fine. I've got most of my strength back. I'm sure I can make it down *one* more hallway."

"We'll give you ten minutes," Richardson replies, "but no more. It's 10:04 now, so we'll expect you back with a report by 10:14. And remember the mission—your mother-in-law must declare her change of mind to Dr. Cantrall, or to the ICU shift manager. Only Helen has the authority, not you."

"Gotcha," Bryan replies, giving a jockish laugh. "Piece of cake ... considering."

Chris gives a snicker of his own along with an impish head-waggle. "Unless Arafat's around—then Doc and I will have to rescue your soul-traveling ass."

Bryan pushes through the swinging doors into the long corridor. He strides with purpose toward the ICU. *Dear Jesus. God Almighty. I don't believe it.* Triple déjà vu. Chris's wisecrack proves instantly prescient. Halfway down, Bryan runs smack dab into Dr. Barry Spigler, who has just exited the unit.

"Where the hell d'you think you're going, Dr. Howard?" Spigler growls, his rheumy eyes jumping around like they do. "You have *no* business whatsoever in the ICU at this hour."

"I'm going to see my wife," Bryan announces boldly.

THE SILVER CORD

"Not a chance," the deputy director tells him, exhaling reeky breath. "You're not authorized. Besides, Dr. Cantrall has *already* removed Mrs. Snyder from life support. I gave the order. There was *no* point in waiting until eleven ... *no* point in prolonging a hopeless condition. Now you get you psycho ass *outta* here."

Shock, dread, no time for discussion. *Ka-WHACK!* Bryan decks the ugly bastard with an upper cut to the jaw, using *all* of his revived strength, then he hurries around him. Spigler, cursing a purple torrent, scrambles to his feet, but before he can pursue, Dr. Richardson cuts him down from behind with a flying tackle. Dr. Hansen attacks as well. Spigler fights to get up, but Chris restrains him with a neck-lock. His comrades having gained the upper hand, Bryan bolts (as fast as his rubbery legs will carry him) toward the ICU. A new and terrible sense of loss rips at his gut—too late, too late. *No, it can't be.* He bursts into the unit. "Helen! Helen Stevens!" he shouts, as he notes a crowd of professionals in cubicle #7. "Helen! Helen! Stop the proceeding!"

A buxom redhead quickly blocks his way—Nurse Couture. Some Mexican fellow (a new technician? a therapist?) joins Nurse Couture, as does Harry Simmons, the pasty-faced security guard, who's pulling swing-shift duty tonight. Dr. Howard reins in his furor, as he spots Helen emerging from Mandy's room, a stunned look on her face. "Helen!" he cries. "She's *not* brain dead. She's gonna wake up—if I'm not too late."

Helen goes pale, her eyes wide with bewilderment. "Whaa—what? But uh ... but we—" Loud commotion cuts her off, as the hallway wrestling match spills into the ICU.

CHAPTER THIRTY-SEVEN

MAGNOLIA, TEXAS - 22 SHERWOOD
THURSDAY, DECEMBER 16, 1999 — 2:55 AM

Dr. Richardson is in the guestroom, Helen down in the rec room (the big tan sofa converts into a bed). The professor insisted she take the guestroom, her usual bedchamber, but she wouldn't hear of it. Elmo remains in the living room, getting the last bit of heat from the dying coals in the fireplace. Quietness rules the house, though Bryan wonders if anyone is actually sleeping. He surely isn't. He lies awake in his bed, his emotions still reeling from the awful drama. He listens to the lonely drone of the refrigerator and the occasional whir of the furnace fan. Covered with blankets plus the comforter, he's feels warm, finally. His door is ajar a few inches, so Elmo can come in; he wakes his master each morning, for the backyard routine.

Folding his pillow, Bryan shifts onto this side. As he does, he hears a rap on his door. "Yeah," he responds hushedly.

"Can I come in?" Helen asks.

"Sure ... yeah," he says, turning on the bedside lamp.

Tiptoeing in, she sits down on the side of the bed. He props himself up, with the pillows. She wears her old terrycloth robe, the bluish one, the same robe she had on back in '91 when he banged on her door at three a.m. A lot has happened since—to say the least. She caresses his arm. "So are you okay?"

"I think so. I'm just having trouble getting to sleep."

"Me too ... but how can anyone sleep, after *this* night?"

"That was *so* close," he sighs. "I was scared as hell—at least, I thought it was close."

"Yeh ... but that GD-asshole Spigler was lying—pardon my language, but I can't help but cuss." Helen gives a whispery titter. "He never told Dr. Cantrall to speed up the schedule. Besides, she couldn't have anyway. He's just a pompous troublemaker, with a major chip on his shoulder ... but I reckon you nailed him *good* ... along with Chris and the professor."

Bryan gives a hushed laugh. "Yeah, Doc Richardson really took him out ... like a leaping tackle. And he held on like a free safety, while Chris got the ugly bastard around the neck. Doc's one helluva fighter for his size ... and age. Gosh damn, he's *seventy*-five." More whispery laughing, both of them.

Helen halted the LS-disconnection process, no problem, but Bryan narrowly escaped arrest. A cadre of HCMC police escorted the four doctors (Spigler included) to the main security office. But no charges were filed, thanks to the direct intervention of Dr. Omar Rishad himself.

Dr. Richardson called his old pal, and the director came right down. The question of disciplinary action remains officially unresolved, but the professor's assessment was most assuring: "That homely goddamn bully is finished at Harvey Cushing. I should shoot him, like I said, but I have a feeling that Dr. Rishad will come up with a better idea."

Bryan and Helen came home in the Blazer, while Richardson, after his talk with Rishad, hitched a ride with Chris, arriving an hour later. The four of them talked for another hour, sitting around the fire in the living room. They shared-reshared their amazement over the heart-stopping (literally) roller-coaster ride they've been on together. Only four souls know that Bryan went over and back. He explained everything to Helen during the ride home. She was horrified—yet very *thankful* in retrospect.

Helen snuffles. Her bangs fall; she pushes them to the side. The soft lamplight gives her brunette hair a blondish sheen. She giggles, a happy but incredulous titter. "I still can't believe you *actually* went through with it. It hasn't sunk in, the reality of it."

Bryan dimples. "That's for sure."

Her gray-hazel eyes widen with wonder. "So you really saw her ... and she spoke to yuh?"

"Her face ... I saw her face."

"And she said she was gonna come out of it?"

"Well, she said she was *coming* home ... like I toldjuh in the car, and she also said don't let go ... but it's different from how we communicate down here. It's sorta like mental telepathy, like we hear each other's heart talking. Y'know ... I toldjuh. Yet the message was crystal clear."

"So uh ... d'yuh really think she's gonna wake up?"

He sighs, nodding his head slowly. "I'm about as sure as I *can* be ... but I reckon we're gonna find out."

"Yes, I reckon so." Dropping her eyes, Helen crinkles her brow. "So how long d'yuh think? How long do we hafta wait?"

"I dunno, but I'm betting on soon. 'Don't let go of me ... 'cause I'm coming home!' That sounds like soon, like hours or days ... not next year or something."

"O dear God, I sure hope so. I sure hope so. This could be more nerve-wracking than *any*thing."

"No kidding. It's like winning an extra-inning baseball game ... on the road. Getting that final out ... when y'know you're ahead. It can be a real nail-biter. But I feel *dad*gum sure—I do."

"I can *tell* ... and that's keeping me sane right now."

"Well, the stakes couldn't be higher—but I reckon we're gonna win. Either that ... or I'm totally deluded."

Getting up, she gives Bryan a motherly kiss on the head then heads for the door. But before exiting she says, "Y'know I woulda stopped yuh, if I knew what you guys were up to."

THE SILVER CORD

"That's why I didn't *tellyuh*," he laughs; they both laugh.

"Oh, Lordee, Lordee. I must say my views have certainly expanded since I met you, Bryan Howard ... the whole God and Heaven thing. It's enough to take my breath. But how can I argue with an eyewitness?" More hushed giggles.

After she departs, Bryan prays: *O God, thank you for getting me through all this. Thank you for Doc Richardson and Chris. They're amazing in the clutch. And Helen too, and Dr. Cantrall. And thank you for dealing with Spigler—he's got a big-time ego problem. This whole thing is wild and crazy and way out ... but so far so good. I just pray that Mandy DOES wake up. That's the clincher, and we can't truly celebrate until she does. We're close, really close ... like one out away from the greatest victory ever.* He sighs longingly. *I'll have what I been aching for my whole life: my dear sweet Mandy—plus proof that my astral trips are REAL. O God, forgive me for begging, but PLEASE finish this triumph ... and QUICKLY. Just bring her BACK.*

* * *

EASTEX FREEWAY - NORTH OF HOUSTON
FRIDAY, DECEMBER 17, 1999 — 10:45 AM

Dr. Howard, after conducting a morning psychotherapy session and picking up his mail and such, cruises northbound, on his way back to Magnolia. A Geo Tracker packed with teenagers *whooms* by him in the fast lane. It's the last day of school before Christmas break, and they're out early, making the most of this sunny, warm weather. The brief wintry spell ended yesterday, typical for Houston. Christmastime is the slow season for the HC psychologist staff, a good thing, since Bryan has virtually zero time for professional matters, and zilch room in his thoughts.

Helen has resumed her daily watch in cubicle #7, yet nothing has changed, save for the rampant scuttlebutt among the ICU staff concerning the abrupt postponement on Wednesday night, not to mention the wrestling match in the corridor, which has red-lined the gossip meter. But Mandy's condition remains the same: no pupil response, can't respire, marginal EEG. It's only been thirty-six hours, so Bryan isn't in a panic. Still, each passing hour grinds on him, giving rise to a spoonful of anxiety, a fretful gnawing in his belly.

Positive wish-fulfillment within a dream: that's how the reductionists would explain it. He knows different; he *did* visit her in the empyreal realm; he *did* see her face; she *did* communicate with him. He's sure—as *sure* as he's ever been about his OBEs, or about his first NDE back in '91, ninety-nine percent sure. Yet the one percent remains, and he can't be *ab*solutely certain, until Mandy backs up what she told him. *I'm coming home!* That's the news he brought back. When she does indeed come out of her coma, that will *seal* the deal, that will extinguish *all* doubt.

Dr. Richardson left yesterday, after giving Bryan a thorough physical, with Dr. Hansen's help, and everything seems okay. The professor also met again with Dr. Rishad, who later issued his verdict on the ICU ruckus: no disciplinary action, no reprimands, but Dr. Barry Spigler has been awarded a two-year sabbatical grant to the University of Alaska in Fairbanks—he departs the day after Christmas, and will be on vacation until then. Dr. Rishad also issued a terse statement declaring that Dr. Howard has full next-of-kin visiting rights regarding Mandy.

The Meadowhurst shopping district pans by on his right, but he gets off two minutes later, exiting onto FR 6137. As he shifts, accelerating eastbound, his Nokia begins to chirp. He answers—it's Helen: "Bryan, I have news."

"Whaa ... what?" he asks, his pulse taking off.

"She's breathing. Mandy's breathing without the respirator, and her pupils are suddenly responsive to light."

* * *

"YES! YES!" Bryan shouts, as he pulls into his driveway ten minutes later. "YES! YES! O JESUS, *YES!*" He pounds the seat. He high-fives the dash. He drums the steering wheel. He's been freaking and yelling ever since he hung up with Helen. "O God, thank you! We're gonna win this thing yet. She's breathing on her own. That's a goshdang miracle. YES! YES! O JESUS, *YES!*"

* * *

ONE WEEK LATER:

HCMC - WADE WING CAFETERIA
FRIDAY, DECEMBER 24, 1999 — 5:20 PM

Bryan works on his chicken-fried steak, while Helen nibbles on a grilled cheese sandwich. Last week's jubilation has long since faded. It's Christmas Eve, and the cafeteria is deserted, save for diehard visitors and low-ranking staff.

"So is it possible to breathe, yet never wake up?" she asks, between nibbles. "I think y'said, but I wanna get this straight."

He sighs, shaking his head. "Yeah, I'm afraid so. There are many comatose patients who can breathe and respond to light, yet they *never* come out of it."

Helen winces. "Dear Lord, that's *worse* than disconnecting."

"I know ... the stakes have grown, and we're looking at nine days. It's still possible. I mean, she could still wake up. I just don't—well, maybe we're just *too* close to it ... to be rational."

"I reckon so, but what else can we do, except stay close?"

THE SILVER CORD

Same night (Christmas Eve), 9:44 p.m. While Helen catches some shut-eye in Bryan's office, he sits in Mandy's cubicle—the usual routine. It's been a week, more than a week, so he no longer gets weird looks from the ICU staff, as he did the first couple of nights after the wild scene up here with Spigler. A *Time* magazine lies open on his lap, more Y2K mania. But he's lost in prayer, more resigned pleading: *O God, why bring us this far, just to leave her like this? But she TOLD me? And it was REAL. It had to be real? It had to be? But how can I know for sure, if she never wakes up?* No more hissing respirator—she's breathing on her own, though she's still getting oxygen through the tiny-tubed nasal canula. The room seems strangely quiet, despite the hypnotic beeping of the heart monitor, and even that is less loud; Nurse Comisky always turns it down a few notches when she's working the evening shift.

Mandy, on her left side, sleeps in the bed. She faces Bryan, a comatose angel. *She's so beautiful,* he yearns, *especially without that clunky mouthpiece. She has such pretty lips. I love her lips. O God, don't do this to us. I can't stand it.*

Losing her to Heaven is one thing—he had come to terms with that—but losing her to a lifelong coma is unbearable, a torture for all, including Mandy. *O Jesus, it's like I made things WORSE by going to look for her. What's the point of having her talk to me, if it doesn't mean anything? Or maybe she just meant she'd breathe again—no, that's bullshit. But maybe she DIDN'T talk to me? Maybe the reductionists are right ... and there IS no soul, no afterlife, no nothing? Maybe all my astral trips were bogus, just mind trips, and nothing more. O Jesus, this sucks. I hate these horrible thoughts. Yet I can't get 'em outta my head.*

"I'm rooting for you, Dr. Howard," comes a hushed voice from behind him; it's Charlene Comisky, her gaunt, androgynous face earnest with concern. "I could never say this openly," she adds, leaning close, "but I'm *glad* you punched Dr. Spigler. He's a first-class asshole, the worst I've known. Dr. Rishad is right on, for taking your side." She gives a chuckle. "I like your style, just like with Dr. Hansen. You guys give me hope." She pats Bryan on the back. "But I'm sorry about your wife. It seemed like a miracle was about to happen, but now things have fallen back into a dreary routine." Charlene's half-lens spectacles slip a little; she reprops them on her Billy Ray nose. "It's especially hard on Christmas, when most families are gathered around the tree, exchanging gifts. But y'never know. I've seen comatose patients revive after months even. And she *is* breathing now."

He gives a pained grin. "It *is* hard ... the uncertainty."

Charlene, nodding her hatchet-faced, Ichabod head, steps around to the far side of the bed. "How about giving me a hand? I need to turn

Mandy." (The ICU team changes her position a few times a day, to keep her from getting pressure-point sores.)

Together, they shift his precious pretty lady onto her back. Charlene firms the pillow, checks the nasal canula, then the i.v. receptor in Mandy's right hand. After making sure all is A-OK, she exits, giving Bryan another sisterly pat, as she departs. He returns to the chair, plunking down with a sigh. It's Christmas Eve on the calendar, yet he's barely noticed. No tree, no gifts, no cards, no holiday meals.

What's the point? Amy's in Spindle, and Helen's here day and night. It's just me and Elmo at the house, and the way that hound mopes around, and me too—it's hardly a festive thing.

His heart aching, he gazes at his unconscious wife. Her butchy hair has grown out more, enough to cover some of her surgery scars with a semblance of bangs, and the golden Mandy-sheen seems healthier than ever. Ditto for her face—her cheeks pulse with warm color. *God, how can she look so robust ... and yet be so distant?* Tears blur his vision; he fights them back. Her cupid lips, pinkly parted like a pair of rose petals in the morning, draw him, and draw him, casting a love-spell that pulls him up out of the chair. Moved with grief and affection, he can't help but kiss that wondrous dollface mouth—he gives her a tender little peck. Too much: his heart pangs; his tears spill. He *has* to turn away.

"Hey, mister," comes a hoarse voice, "you can kiss better than *that.*"

SHOCK, DISBELIEF. Crazy with joy, and *fear*, he turns around. "Whaa ... what uh? O Jesus God!" His face goes hot.

"C'mon, you big jock," Mandy quips sleepily, her blues eyes opening to meet his. "Whaddeyuh so surprised about? I *told*juh I was coming home." She gives her goofy grin.

Sobbing openly, Bryan embraces his wife.

* * *

SIX DAYS LATER:

HCMC - EASLEY WING PARKING LOT
THURSDAY, DECEMBER 30, 1999 — 10:30 AM

After pulling in, Dr. Howard has to sit for a bit in the Blazer, lest he come out of his body and soar up into the blue, blue sky. It's chilly out, but sunny, and beautiful. Everything is beautiful and wonderful, so much so, he has to stop like this all the time—to gather himself. The silver cord remains a scientific mystery; it's still beyond reach from a research perspective, but not the glory and happiness and triumph it bestows. Bryan has seen this, and tasted it, and heard it, and felt it—inside and out. He can even *smell* it, the glory of it all. Joy unspeakable—Mandy continues her remarkable recovery. She's no longer in the ICU. She moved on Tuesday to a regular room. Dr. Cantrall says the CTs and MRI scans show no lingering damage from the traumatic brain injury (TBI), though she wants to observe Mandy a few more days before releasing her.

Christmas has passed for this year, but not for Bryan Howard. Every day is Christmas for him, and for Mandy, and for Helen, and for Amy—the storms of joy just keep rolling in, and rolling in. As he sits here, it all comes back: Nurse Comisky's shrieks of delight on Christmas Eve, as she discovered the miracle in cubicle #7; Helen's jubilant reunion with her daughter, after Bryan raced down to wake her in his office; the quiet but fervent celebration among the ICU personnel; Chris's smirky look of astonishment on Christmas Day itself; Dr. Richardson's victory dance around Mandy's bed on Monday. Charlie arrived as well on Monday, and Gretchen, and Henry and Ginny, and Amy of course. She couldn't visit her mom until Tuesday however, when Mandy was moved to a regular room—but that glorious reunion will forever bless and inspire Bryan. "Mommy, Mommy," the little blonde exulted, as she crawled up onto the hospital bed to hug her mother. "I'm so *glad* yuh came back from Heaven."

Spanky and Wendy arrived Tuesday afternoon, joining the celebration. Bryan's parents even put up a Christmas tree, and they all ate a big late-Christmas feast at the house yesterday, the whole crowd of family and friends, yet only Helen and Chris and Doc and Bryan know the full unspeakable story, and Mandy of course. No, that's not quite all; there *is* one other: Annie O'Shea. Bryan called her, telling her everything, and he thanked her for the clutch encouragement that freezing morning in Waco. Annie wept on the phone. (Bryan may tell the others at some point, after the wonder of all this sinks in for him and Mandy.) He also phoned Tracy and Steve Jordan with the news, the short version.

Helen and Bryan took a heaping plate (turkey and the works) into Mandy last night. She ate it all, her appetite having returned as strong as ever. His parents left this morning. In fact, everyone has departed but Helen, who's back at the house, with Amy.

* * *

Same morning, 10:40 a.m. Easley Wing, room 337. Mandy gives Bryan a good-morning kiss, more tongue than lips. "Oh, babe, I think I'm ready to come home *today*," she quips, rolling her eyes and doing her rabbity routine. "I doubt I can wait till Monday."

"Yeh ... I reckon your systems are working okay."

"Y'got that right, mister ... if yuh know what I mean."

He gives her a playful punch on the shoulder. "I reckon I do, but y'better change the subject, pretty lady, or I'll hafta crawl under the covers with you."

She giggles. "That sounds like a *super* idea ... we just need a lock on that dadgum door. We've barely had ten minutes alone since I came outta my coma."

After a little more conjugal flirting, she comes up and hugs him tightly. "Oh, Bryan honey," she coos, her breath warm on his neck. "I miss you *so* much ... and I don't mean sex, even though I reckon we're gonna have one *heck* of a honeymoon when I get to the house." More girlish titters. "I mean ... I'm happy to be well again, and I thank God all the time. But it's like part of me is missing, until we're back in our home, back in our bed, back with Amy, back into our life."

Bryan caresses her back, her shoulder, her short crop of hair. "I know, I feel the same. This whole ordeal was so horrible, but God turned it around ... like the *greatest* miracle possible."

"It is rather miraculous, what happened to both of us. I had three near-death trips, as best I can remember, but I only sensed your presence during the last one. That's why I called out to yuh. I didn't see you exactly, not like now, but I knew you were close by. It was like liquid waves of love ... and warm ... the sensation."

"So, pretty lady, how'd you *know* you were gonna wake up?"

"My dad told me," she says, still speaking into his shoulder. "My real dad. I saw him beside his biplane in this big grassy field. He didn't yell out or anything, but I *knew* what he was telling me, as much as I ever knew anything."

"That *is* awesome. It's like Gramps, how he told me about you ... where you were."

"You risked your life to look for me."

"That's how love is. I had no choice."

"I love you too, babe—forever." She gives a blissful sigh. "We may not be able to explain it ... but we both *know* it now—the truth about life and hope and true love. It never stops ... no matter the fear, no matter the hurt, no matter the odds. It goes on forever ... and for*ever*."

* * *

MAGNOLIA, TEXAS - 22 SHERWOOD
MONDAY, JANUARY 3, 2000 — 2:22 PM

Y2K has arrived—no problem. The whole computer-crash thing turned out to be a colossal sham, but the foursome in the Chevy Blazer— well, they have *much* happier things to think about, as the SUV wheels through the fog and drizzle, Bryan and Mandy up front, Helen and Amy in the back.

"This place looks awesome, honey," Mandy remarks, as they pull into the driveway, "even the lawn."

"Thanks to a lot of frost," Bryan quips. "Half of it's gone dormant." They all share a laugh, as he squeaks to a halt by the wooden stairway.

"Grandma, are we *really* gonna have Christmas again?" Amy pipes, as everyone unbuckles.

"Yes, we are," Helen replies. "One more time ... now that your mommy has come home. And then on Wednesday, I'll be flying back to Arkansas ... if this fog ever clears."

* * *

Up in the kitchen Elmo, in his ever-faithful position, gazes at the door knob. His heart stirs, as he hears the Blazer pull in, followed a minute later by voices and footsteps on the stairs. Catching the scent, he vibrates with anticipation, his tail wagging berserkly. Yes, Yes. The knob turns, the door opens. "Oh, my dear *puppy*!" Mandy exclaims, as she comes down to Elmo, petting him, hugging him, patting him on the rump. "Oh, my baby boy ... I missed you. I missed you."

Licking and wagging, the yearling lab dances frantically about, his claws clicking, his collar jingling. He nuzzles Amy, then Bryan and Helen, but quickly returns to Mandy, dear Mandy. He gives an ecstatic whine, a canine hallelujah.

We *all* know it now—the truth about life and hope and true love. It *never* stops ... no matter the fear, no matter the hurt, no matter the odds. It goes on forever ... and for*ever*.